The Dark Virgin

The Dark Virgin

Book One of the Night of Songs Trilogy

OAKLAND ROSS

The Dark Virgin
Copyright © 2001 by Oakland Ross.
All rights reserved.

Published by Harper Weekend, an imprint of HarperCollins Publishers Ltd.

Originally published in Canada by
HarperCollins Publishers Ltd in a hardcover edition: 2001.
First mass market paperback edition: 2002
This digest paperback edition: 2013

HarperCollins books may be purchased for educational, business, or sales promo-
tional use through our Special Markets Department.

HarperCollins Publishers Ltd
2 Bloor Street East, 20th Floor
Toronto, Ontario, Canada
M4W 1A8

www.harpercollins.ca

Library and Archives Canada Cataloguing in Publication
information is available upon request

ISBN 978-1-44341-644-3

Printed and bound in the United States
RRD 9 8 7 6 5 4 3 2 1

For Cessie,
Kate, Nikki,
and Dori

Contents

The Principal Characters in This Book • VII

Prologue • 1

Mansions of the Gods • 3

The Spanish Castaway • 127

In the Land of Edom • 235

The House of Birds • 357

The Hummingbird Bride • 475

The Sorrowful Night • 643

Epilogue • 775
Author's Note • 783
Selected Bibliography • 787
Acknowledgements • 789

I say again that I stood looking at it, and thought that no land like it would ever be discovered in the whole world . . . But today all that I then saw is overthrown and destroyed; nothing is left standing.

—Bernal Díaz del Castillo

We eat of the earth,
Then the earth eats us.

—A Nahuatl song from the Sierra of Puebla

GULF of MEXICO

Tlatelolco

Tenochtitlán

Texcoco

Tlaxcala

Cholula

Cempoala

Veracruz

THE AZTEC EMPIRE
CIRCA 1520

PACIFIC
OCEAN

Helen Flook

The Principal Characters in This Book

Pitoque, a citizen of the vassal city of Cholula, is a traveling merchant who sometimes undertakes missions of espionage on behalf of the Aztecs.

Maxtla is the son of Pitoque and of Kalatzin, Pitoque's wife. Zaachila is his sister.

Toc is Pitoque's chief of porters.

Moctezuma II is the *huey tlatoani*—"He Who Speaks"—and the emperor of the Aztecs.

Cacama, a nephew of Moctezuma, is the king of Texcoco, one of the cities of the Aztec Triple Alliance.

Azotl is a powerful Aztec official who bears the title Keeper of the House of Darkness. He is often referred to in these pages as the master functionary.

Ometzin is the young ward of Azotl. She is passionate about many things, particularly frogs and birds.

Huitzilopochtli is the principal Aztec deity, the warrior god, represented by the likeness of a hummingbird.

Quetzalcoatl is another potent deity, the Feathered Serpent of Mexican legend, worshiped throughout the Aztec empire and beyond. To the Maya, he is known as Kukulcán. By either name, he is the god of knowledge, who combines the forces of earth and sky. His consort is Tonantzin, the earth goddess.

Quetzalcoatl is prophesied to return to the realm of men in the Aztec year 1-Reed, which coincides with the Roman year 1519.

Hernán Cortés is the Spanish captain-general who leads an illegal expedition of conquest westward from Cuba in the year 1519.

Pedro de Alvarado is Cortés's favorite lieutenant.

Alonso Puertocarrero is Alvarado's chief rival for Cortés's favor. He is related by marriage to the Count of Medellín.

La Virgen de los Remedios, the Virgin of Remedies, is the patron saint of the Spanish conquistadores.

Jerónimo de Aguilar is a Spanish castaway, marooned on the Maya coast eight years prior to the arrival of Cortés. He is fluent both in Spanish and in the tongue of the coastal Maya.

Doña Marina or Malantzin, as she was once known, is a Nahuatl-speaking princess sold into slavery to a Maya chieftain. She speaks both Nahuatl and the language of the coastal Maya.

The Dark Virgin, better known as the Virgin of Guadalupe, is the patron saint of Mexico.

The Pronunciation of
Some Names in This Book

Pitoque: Pe-tóh-kay

Moctezuma: Mohk-tay-zú-ma

Cacama: Ka-ká-ma

Azotl: Ah-zóh-tul

Quetzalcoatl: Ket-zal-koh-áh-tul

Tenochtitlán: Ten-och-tee-tlán

Huitzilopochtli: Weet-zee-lah-póch-tlee

Popocatépetl: Poh-poh-ka-téh-pet-ul

Iztaccíhuatl: Ee-sta-shée-wot-ul

Prologue

First, there were dreams, and they all promised ruin. Next came comets, streaking toward the earth. In the east, strange stars appeared, crazy with brilliance, where no such stars had been before.

Later, the voices of women could be heard, wailing in the night. "Flee," they cried. "Flee. Take only what you can carry. Run for your lives."

Ten years whirled past in this appalling manner, the world bristling with omens and signs. And then came the ships, except that no one knew they were ships. People thought they were mountains or towers floating upon the sea.

In the royal court at Tenochtitlán, capital of the empire of the Aztecs, the priests and elders shuffled about in circles, pulled at their hair, slashed at their chests with obsidian knives, and prayed to their gods. They offered up sacrifices. Before long, they received pictures, crude ones, hastily drawn on the rough paper they used then, made from sisal. The pictures were no help at all, for they depicted only what had already been described. Absurdities. Mountains or towers that rode upon the sea.

The next reports were even more alarming. These mountains or towers, or whatever they were, contained men or beings that looked like men—weird, scowling creatures, tall, pale of skin, with thick beards and stringy hair that hung down past their ears. Even from a great distance, they gave off a sour smell that could make a man choke. Pictures of these strange specters were received as well. They had the appearance of giant monkeys.

This was the year 12-House, the sixteenth year of the reign of Moctezuma II, emperor of the Aztecs—or 1517 A.D., as time would come to be calculated. In Tenochtitlán, all was consternation. What were these creatures? Were they demons, gods, or men? Did they come in peace or to make war? Fearful of the omens that had long haunted his rule, the great lord Moctezuma II and his advisers debated and conferred, ingested mushrooms, saw visions, made sacrifices to their gods. They were desperate to find out the meaning of these events, but they resolved not to panic. Instead, they decided to follow their normal course.

They dispatched spies.

BOOK ONE

Mansions of the Gods

The Merchant of Cholula

"I am worried about Maxtla." The woman named Kalatzin set down her drink of chocolate and smoothed the folds of her cotton robe. "He's becoming incorrigible. I can't manage him anymore. I'm afraid he'll do something they won't forgive."

"They?" The woman's husband, Pitoque, worried at his forehead with his right hand. These domestic discussions always tired him out. He was a traveling merchant by profession—a *pochteca*—and lived for the open road. "Who do you mean by they?"

She shrugged. "His teachers. The elders. The priests."

"The priests? Why would priests be concerned about Maxtla?"

She sipped her chocolate drink and began to explain. Her son—that is, *their* son—had fallen in with a rough crowd at the *telpochcalli*, the school where he was pursuing his studies. A gang of headstrong boys had taken to causing trouble there, and Maxtla had somehow got among them.

"They have no respect for anyone or anything," she said. "They roam about at all hours, getting into all sorts of mischief. They trouble innocent people. They spit and swear. I hear they sometimes get their hands on jugs of pulque—I don't know how. Goodness knows, they don't find pulque here. But they get it somewhere. They become intolerably drunk and stagger about and throw up in public."

Pitoque laughed and shook his head. "Throw up in public, do they? Whatever next? Is there no end to this delinquency?" He remembered being a youngster himself. Had he not thrown up once or twice after an unfortunate encounter with a little too much pulque? "They are boys," he advised his wife, "pretending to be men."

She bridled in irritation. "That may well be so. But listen to me. I am not talking about mere youthful pranks. There have been incidents. There—"

"Incidents?" said Pitoque. "What sort of incidents?"

Again, she set down her chocolate and proceeded to explain. She and her husband were seated in the interior courtyard of their house in the small highland city of Cholula, where the air was cool and fresh all the year around. Their house was nothing to boast about from the exterior—a deliberate subterfuge to avoid attracting unwanted attention—but inside it was a small palace, a network of dark passages and compact, sunny patios. Here, in the main courtyard, a fountain burbled amid rosebushes and blossoming trees. Cockatiels chattered in their bamboo cages. Like others in his trade, Pitoque was a man of considerable means, but he dressed simply and avoided outward shows of affluence. This was a fundamental article of the *pochteca* code, for there was nothing to be gained by arousing envy in others. Besides, a man who looked poor could drive a better bargain than one suspected of deriving riches from his trade. Pitoque had driven many successful bargains in his time. Thirty-five years old—with a beautiful wife, a handsome son, a lovely daughter, and a prosperous livelihood—he had much to be thankful for. The gods of his people had blessed him over and over again.

Or so they had done once.

Ten years earlier, during his twenty-sixth year, his good fortune had changed. The memory prickled in his mind, as it often did, and he briefly lost track of his wife's words. He felt a remembered agony in the back of his mouth, saw a slender forearm flail in a dim light against a backdrop of smoke, heard a muffled cry. He fought off the urge to shout in protest, to put up his hands, leap to his feet. *Stop it! Stop it now!*

"Pitoque?" Kalatzin eased forward in her chair. "Are you well, my husband?"

"Eh? Yes. Yes, of course. It was just . . . just a bee. A maddening little bee. Ah, there it is again." Pitoque swatted at the air, where no bee was. For ten years, he had been doing this—disguising his secrets by some such device, some equally idiotic gesture. "Please," he said to his wife. "Please, go on."

Kalatzin sat back, smoothed her skirt, and cleared her voice. Her husband had his eccentricities—swatting at imaginary winged insects, for example—but he was a good man. It was just that he was too often away from home, and his journeys seemed to have addled his brain. But what could be done? He was a *pochteca*. Traveling was the basis of his profession. She returned to the problem at hand, which was Maxtla, their son.

As he listened to his wife explain her worries about the boy, Pitoque's brow furrowed and his manner changed. This was not a frivolous subject after all. These "incidents" she spoke of—they were evidently cause for concern. They sometimes involved Aztec sentries or emissaries. Stones had been thrown. Blood had been spilled. Aztec blood.

Pitoque edged closer to his wife. "And you think Maxtla is involved in this business?"

Kalatzin shrugged. She didn't know, but she was worried all the same. His participation was certainly possible. "These boys," she said. "They are afraid of nothing. They go about the city, shouting the most outrageous insults."

"Such as?"

"'Death to the Aztec dogs.' 'Down with Moctezuma.'"

"Shhh!" Even here, inside his own home, Pitoque could not permit such words. They clashed against his ears like a collision of sharp obsidian blades. It wasn't that he disagreed with the sentiments, or not exactly. It was just that a man—or a woman—could be killed for uttering them aloud. "Be quiet, woman."

"I was just—"

"I said, be quiet."

"But you asked me to tell you."

So he had. "I'm sorry," he said.

Here was a phrase that he would never have spoken during the early years of their marriage, for it had been inconceivable to him that a man could be found wanting in his behavior toward a woman. But he had changed his thinking in this respect. Circumstances had intervened. Now he felt awkward in his wife's presence, at times even ashamed. For ten years, he had carried within him a terrible weight of guilt, a secret, like a sack of shameful memories. One day, the netting would rot, the contents would spill out, they would heave across the floor for all to see. Once exposed like this, they could not be disguised—and one day, he knew, they would be exposed. Now he shook his head, repeated his apologies to his wife. In fact, he *was* sorry.

Kalatzin gave a pinched smile. Apology accepted. She folded her hands in her lap and continued with her account. These boys wandered out at night, she said, chanting slogans against the Aztecs, and sometimes there were incidents with stones. So far, no one had been apprehended, no punishments had been inflicted—but still, it was worrisome.

Pitoque agreed. A small and prosperous place, Cholula was located at no great distance from the Aztec capital of Tenochtitlán, which loomed a two-day trek to the northwest, beyond the snow-clad volcanoes of Popocatépetl and Iztaccíhuatl. Cholula was a vassal city, one of countless such settlements dotted about the empire ruled by the Aztecs. Like the inhabitants of other such places, Cholulans were required to pay regular tribute to Tenochtitlán and their streets were patrolled by Aztec agents, but otherwise they were left to go their own way, cultivate their own fields, practice their own customs, worship their particular gods. Their freedom certainly had limits, however. Speaking out against these Aztec overlords? Or worse, stoning them in the night? No, no. This was going much too far.

"And that isn't all," said Kalatzin.

"There's more?"

"There is." She hesitated, for it seemed that what she now had to say was even more serious than what she had said already. "I'm worried that temples may be desecrated."

"What do you mean? What temples?"

She shrugged, fretted at a loose thread in her robe. She looked up. "Who knows? The temple of Quetzalcoatl perhaps? I don't know."

"By whom? These same boys?"

"So it seems. They have been heard shouting slogans at night—that we are shameful people for obeying the Aztecs, that our gods must be worthless if they cannot protect us from our oppressors. So far, it is just chanting, just talk. But it's sacrilege all the same. These boys are so impetuous, and they drink . . ." Her voice trailed off. Who knew where it all might lead?

Pitoque considered this information, which was deeply troubling. Defamation of the gods—that was unthinkable. But the dishonoring of Quetzalcoatl himself? Why, Quetzalcoatl was the patron god of Cholula, a king-turned-deity who would one day return from his journeys across the sea to bring order and harmony to the world. To show disrespect for Quetzalcoatl was not merely unthinkable. It was . . . it was . . . Pitoque flopped back in his seat, suddenly very tired. He couldn't think what such an act was, couldn't find the words. It was beyond him. In his own mind, he drew no distinction between the man-god Quetzalcoatl and all that was good and precious in this life. All these pleasures that Pitoque enjoyed—his home, his wife, his children, the treasure trove he kept secreted away in a sealed-off vault in his house—what were they but the blessings of the gods, Quetzalcoatl especially? What were they but proof that Quetzalcoatl, the feathered serpent, would one day return?

Oh, that would be a glorious day—or so it was said. Pitoque wasn't certain. He sometimes feared that he had earned the god's enmity. In truth, he owed all that was good in his life to the munificence of Quetzalcoatl. But at the same time, he worried that if the god did return—as was promised—it would be to punish and not to save.

He struggled to put these thoughts aside. He sat up and looked squarely at Kalatzin, at the dense pattern of purple tattoo lines upon her dark, oval face. "But there have been no such occurrences as yet?" he said. "No one has desecrated any temples as yet?"

"No," she said. "Not as yet."

They both understood the importance of this fact. The desecration of a temple would surely be punished by death.

"Good," he said. This detail at least was a relief. "Very good. Well then, I will talk to the boy."

But his wife would not let him off as easily as that. She shook her head. "I don't want you to talk to him. I want you to take him away."

"Away? But he's only twelve. He's just a boy."

"How old were you when you began to travel with your father?"

Pitoque hesitated, as if he needed to calculate the answer in his head, although he knew it perfectly well. "Thirteen," he said.

"There you are, then. Maxtla's practically the same age."

"Not quite. He has a year remaining before he completes his studies. I insist upon that."

Kalatzin threw up her hands and let out an exasperated sigh. "Have you heard nothing that I have said? I'm worried that if you don't take Maxtla away from here, he will do something terrible." Her shoulders began to shake, and she covered her face with her hands. She was crying now, her voice choking from the spasms. "My only boy. I'm afraid he will die."

Pitoque left his seat and went to her, tried to comfort her as best he could. The problem was that he traveled so much. He was so often away from home. Even now, after all these years of marriage, he wasn't confident that he truly knew his wife, that he understood what made her happy or that he could name the sources of her grief. Was she exaggerating her worry? He shushed her and put his arms around her, felt her shoulders shudder against his chest. He told her again that he would talk to the boy. All would be well. He was home now. Her husband was home.

In the end, she seemed to calm down. She used the sleeve of her robe to dry her eyes and cheeks. She reached for her chocolate drink, raised it to her lips, and swallowed once, then again. Finally, she looked up at him, her eyes still red and sore. "But that's just Maxtla," she said. "I haven't said a word yet about Zaachila."

She meant their daughter, now fourteen years of age.

Pitoque took a long, slow breath. He nodded and settled himself into his chair. These household upheavals—would they never end? "And what of Zaachila?" he said.

"Well . . ." Kalatzin pushed back a loose strand of her jet black hair. She launched into a chronicle of the woes besetting Zaachila, who was now of marriageable age but apparently had no hope of attracting a husband. She'd been targeted by some evil eye, it seemed. There was a curse upon her.

"An evil eye?" said Pitoque. "A curse?" He crossed his legs and folded his hands beneath his chin. He nodded again. "Tell me, dear wife. I'm all ears. Please. Go on."

And she did.

What Kind of Missions?

Pitoque led his son up onto the roof of their home, where there was a small terrace with a clear view of the Great Temple of Quetzalcoatl, glimmering against a backdrop of mountains. Here, he meant to speak to the boy—and severely.

Dressed in a loincloth of cotton and a short cloak, Maxtla kept his head low throughout the interview and, for the most part, did not speak unless his father instructed him to do so. He agreed with everything Pitoque said, that the Aztecs were to be respected, that the gods were to be worshiped and revered. He said he would attend to his studies and keep out of trouble and cease causing his mother these torments of worry. He gave his solemn word on all of these promises.

"And, a year from now, when you are finished with your studies, you may join me on my travels. Would you like that?"

Maxtla lowered his head, which was covered by a thatch of thick black hair cut in the shape of an inverted bowl. "Yes, Father," he said.

"You would like to be a *pochteca?*"

"Yes."

"Like your father and his father before him—and his father before that? You would welcome such a life?"

A nod. "Yes, Father."

"Good." Pitoque hesitated. He had it in mind to carry this conversation a step further, to reveal to the boy something he had never spoken of before—at least, not to his children. But it was important that Maxtla see clearly how matters stood, how closely his own life and that of his father were tied up with these Aztecs he professed to hate. "Maxtla," he said.

"Yes, Father."

"I have something to tell you, something important. I want you to listen closely, and I want you to understand. Can you do that?"

"Yes."

"Yes, what?"

"Yes, *Father.*"

"Good." Pitoque cleared his throat and explained to his son that a *pochteca*'s life was sometimes a complicated affair. In his own case, for example, and the same was true of many other traveling merchants, he was obliged on occasion to carry out certain, ah, missions on behalf of the Aztecs.

"Missions?" said Maxtla.

"Yes. On occasion."

"What kind of missions?"

"Missions that have to do with the gathering of information. In short, we gather information during the course of our travels."

"What kind of information?"

"Various kinds. It depends."

"And what do you do with this information?"

Pitoque frowned.

"*Father.* I meant to say Father. Father, what do you do with this information?"

"Well, like many other *pochtecas*, I supply it to the Aztecs. In Tenochtitlán. I have certain, ah, contacts."

"Spying, you mean. You mean that you serve the Aztecs as a spy?"

"Oh, that's one way of putting it, I suppose. I prefer to think of it as the science of communication. So much depends . . ."

Pitoque's voice trailed off. He had sensed some sudden, partly disguised reaction in his son, a stiffening, a drawing away. He was about to refer to it when, just as quickly, it disappeared. The boy seemed to relax. An expression of dutiful attention returned to his features.

"Please go on," said Maxtla. "I mean, please go on, Father."

"You do not find this discussion boring?"

"Not at all. The science of communication. I see how important that is. Besides, you have to travel, anyway—in your work. Of course. It all makes sense."

"It does?"

"Yes." The boy nodded eagerly. "Yes, Father."

This reaction was a surprise. In truth, the arrangement had never made complete sense to Pitoque. It was one of life's many contradictions that he labored as a spy in the service of the Aztecs—the very society that kept his own people in vassalage. It was something he had to do, something that couldn't be helped, even if the missions sometimes troubled him. Still, Maxtla had to understand that his father's prosperity—and his family's—depended precisely on close and cordial relations with the Aztecs. Pitoque had no other choice.

But—wonder of wonders—the boy seemed to accept the arrangement without protest, without explanation. This little talk had gone off without a hitch, far better than expected. Pitoque shrugged. Obviously, Kalatzin had been letting her worries get the better of her.

He beckoned to the boy. "Now you may kiss me."

Maxtla stepped forward, reached up, and planted a kiss upon his father's proffered cheek.

"There," said Pitoque. "That will be all. Now you may go."

"Thank you, Father."

The boy darted off. He turned and clambered down the ladder that led back into the house. His hair glinted in the late-day sunshine and then disappeared. Pitoque turned and folded his arms upon the wooden railing and gazed at the tall stone pyramid dedicated to Quetzalcoatl, towering above the slender pillars of several cypress trees. Well, he had averted one crisis. He reached into his robe and closed his hand around a small keepsake he kept there, a necklace of shells. As always, at the touch of it, he shuddered and felt a sudden coldness in his chest.

For several moments, he did not move. Then he flexed his jaw, turned, and climbed back down the ladder into the house.

Next on Pitoque's list of domestic chores was a discussion with his daughter. He had already agreed that the girl should be taken to a council of priests, who would determine how best to remove this curse that was apparently upon her. Twice already she had been rejected by possible suitors. A third such episode would be most unlucky. It would be best to consult with the priests beforehand.

However, such consultations were expensive—very expensive, in fact. He would need to make a dent in his cache of gold. But that couldn't be helped: such was the price of being a husband and a father. And it so happened that he was able to pay this price. No one seemed to understand this. Yes, he *did* happen to possess a supply of gold. And why was that? Because he *did* travel far from home and because he *did* work on behalf of the hated Aztecs. His life had two separate sides, and it was a struggle to keep them in balance. But he had no choice except to try—even though at any moment the gods might strike him dead. He took a deep breath and strolled along the main corridor, with its walls of smooth glazed mud.

"Zaachila!" he called out. "Zaachila!"

"Good," said Kalatzin, when Pitoque told her the outcome of his conversation with Maxtla. "That's very good."

He could tell she didn't really mean it. She still wished that he would take the boy away immediately, keep her only son far from harm. But Pitoque was unwilling to take that step so soon. There was an appointed time for everything in this life. The ancient rhythms still applied. But he had spoken to the boy, and Maxtla had given his word that he would stay out of trouble. He told Kalatzin not to worry. "All will be well," he said, although he was far from confident himself. "I am certain of it."

"Yes, my husband." After a pause, she sighed. "It's not that he's a bad child. He just has too much energy. This house is too small for him."

"You wish a larger house?" Pitoque approached his wife and turned her toward him. He ran his fingers over the indigo serpentine of tattoo lines upon her neck and shoulders. "For that, I will have to trade a great deal of cotton."

She smiled. "The house is fine. I just wish you were more often in it." She shrugged. "But it can't be helped."

Nor could it. Pitoque was a merchant, like his father before him, and his father's father before that. Such verities could not be changed even had he wanted to change them. They were ordained. Besides, they served a purpose. Everything did.

Two days later, it was time for Pitoque to depart his home and return to Tenochtitlán. He made his farewells to Kalatzin and their two children. He drew his cloak around him, a crude garment made of maguey fiber. It was a custom of long tradi-

tion that merchants eschewal cotton robes on their travels—
they must not appear rich, must not stand out in any way. He
turned to Toc, his chief of porters, a man who had served him
for many years and had traveled in former times with Pitoque's
father. Toc was an old man now, with his years etched upon
his face in deep furrows, but he was still as spry as someone
half his age. If there were a more honest man in the empire, or
a wiser one, then Pitoque could not have named him.

The old man motioned to the gang of porters who were
waiting patiently in the street in front of Pitoque's house.
Dressed in loincloths, some of them barefoot, some in makeshift sandals, they stood about, chatting in low voices, thirty
lean and wiry men. Now they gathered up their cargo—a
large supply of fine Cholula pottery—and with Pitoque striding in front, Toc at his side, they began their journey to the
northwest, toward the shimmering peaks of Popocatépetl and
Iztaccíhuatl. Beyond those great volcanoes, in the green Valley
of Anáhuac, lay the Aztec capital.

Maxtla watched his father depart. As soon as the procession
of porters was out of sight, he tossed his hoop and stick aside.
Children's toys. He played with them now only because his parents seemed to expect it—a boy amuses himself with games.
He straightened his shoulders. Well, he wasn't a boy anymore.
He was practically a man. He was as tall as boys a year older
than he was, boys of thirteen—boys who *were* men, or almost.

He loitered at the entrance to his father's house, even after his mother and sister drifted back inside. He was waiting for Nahuauc, his friend from the *telpochcalli*. While he waited, he mused about the extraordinary conversation he'd had with his father just two days earlier. Fortunately, he'd managed to keep his temper in check during the entire interview—and that had not been easy. Lately, he found his temper got away from him at the slightest provocation.

That conversation with his father, though, had challenged his resolve. It had been bad enough to nod dutifully and mouth his "yes, Fathers" and "no, Fathers" until he thought his tongue would fall out. But far worse was had been keeping his emotions in check when the old fool had imparted this grotesque news. The man was an Aztec spy! The fact was incredible, shocking. His own father—a traitor. Nahuauc and the others were right. Cholulans were a spineless lot, or at least the old ones were. The new generation, the young men like Nahuauc and the others—like Maxtla himself—would have to lead the way, show these Aztec dogs that they were not wanted here.

"Ah, Maxtla."

It was Nahuauc himself, sauntering up the dirt lane that ran in front of Maxtla's home.

"Nahuauc. I was hoping you would pass by." Maxtla hurried out to join his friend, felt the older boy's right arm settle over his shoulder like a warm cloak. "I haven't seen you in ages."

"Three days, I think. What news have you?"

"Shhh." Maxtla lowered his voice. "You'll never guess . . ."

"Guess what?"

"What my . . . my . . ."

"Your what?"

The two boys continued along the dirt lane, in the direction of the Great Temple of Quetzalcoatl.

"*What?*" said Nahuauc.

But some unnamed scruple stopped Maxtla's tongue. What his father had told him he could not divulge, not to Nahuauc, not to anyone. "Never mind," he said. "It's nothing." He darted ahead. "I'll race you Nahuauc. Race you to the temple."

And they were off.

The Master Functionary

Two days later, in the great city of Tenochtitlán, a hulking man named Azotl was slouching at his working table. The table stood in a large, stone-walled chamber deep in the House of Darkness, where Azotl—the master functionary—presided. Now it was mealtime, normally the most enjoyable of occasions, but he did little more than pick at his lunch, a plate of corn mold and warm, freshly grilled tortillas. The corn mold, known as *cuitlacoche*, was probably his favorite dish in the world. He could eat it all day long and, if the mood was upon him, through much of the night as well. Just now, however, the mold lacked its usual savory zest. Something was missing, and Azotl thought he knew what it was. Concentration—that was the key. He couldn't properly enjoy what he was eating unless he was able to devote his entire attention to the task, and that was hardly the case now.

The master functionary lifted his great jowled head with its one mournful eye—the other had been knocked out in a childhood game involving sticks. He peered out at the broad courtyard beyond his chambers, where countless men in long cotton cloaks hurried back and forth in the hazy afternoon light. Here was the organizational nerve center of the empire, where reams of chaotic information were turned into sound, methodical sense—how many prisoners were required for sacrifice today, how many tomorrow, how much tribute should be exacted from this tribe or that one, how many floating gardens were to be planted this season, what degree of Aztec authority was required where.

For the answers to all of these questions and countless more besides, this large stone palace was the source. All the scattered strands of information in the empire were gathered here, and it was here that they were subdued, forced to make sense, twisted and braided into submission. Priests were all very well for divining the will of the gods—Azotl would be the first to admit it, at least for the sake of appearances. But for the successful operation of so vast an enterprise as the Aztec empire, more was required than ceremonial bloodshed and mystical cant, vital as those commodities might be. At the end of the day, what one needed was a hard nose and a clear head—and Azotl prided himself on possessing both. His formal title was *tlillancalqui*. Keeper of the House of Darkness. It had an august and somewhat ominous sound that proved useful at times. But he liked to think of himself as the master functionary. A man who got things done.

And this was, at the moment, the essence of the problem. Frankly, he hadn't the ghost of an idea what to do. He used a torn-off bit of tortilla to mop up another dollop of *cuitlacoche.* He mashed it into his mouth and slumped at his desk, chewing. The wooden surface in front of him was strewn with more of these senseless sisal rolls riddled with drawings that were patently absurd. Mountains. Towers. Floating on the sea. Great hairy monkeys dangling from what looked like trellises in the sky. What on earth were these structures? The drawings were useless, worse than useless. He sent out spies—in the form of traveling merchants—and then he sent out more spies, and all they did was dispatch more runners back to Tenochtitlán, bearing more of these idiotic drawings. Drawings that made no sense at all.

What was he to do now? Was he to go before the imperial court, bow and scrape, and then declare in the presence of Emperor Moctezuma that "Yes, my Lord, it is just as we suspected—mountains or towers that float upon the sea. Crawling with great big monkeys." For such insolence and stupidity, he would likely be taken straight outside, marched to the top of the Great Temple, and sacrificed to Huitzilopochtli, the hummingbird god. And he would deserve no other fate! His job right now was not to repeat the same absurdities that had been reported before. His job was to make sense of these drawings. What *were* these mountains or towers? What *were* these monkeylike creatures? For what purpose had they come?

But to answer these questions, he required much better information than he possessed at present. Good, hard, reliable information. Not children's scrawls on sisal paper. He mopped some more *cuitlacoche* and pushed it in his mouth. These spies he used—they were incompetents, every last one. He should pass an ordinance: kill them all. Yet Azotl was a just man, a man of reason. There were measures that one might like to take, but one did not always do so. He ran a bit of tortilla through the mash of corn mold on his fine Cholula plate. He recognized that his current difficulties were not the *pochtecas'* fault entirely. Unfortunately, these traders were usually Aztecs themselves—traveling merchants from Tenochtitlán who dabbled in espionage. Wherever they went, they encountered hostility, for the Aztecs were hated in every corner of the empire, as Azotl knew. As a result, the poor *pochtecas* didn't like to intrude too much, didn't like to ask probing questions. They were afraid of having their throats slit under cover of darkness—and they were not wrong to be afraid. Such "accidents" had happened, more than once. Thus the merchants provided these idiotic drawings instead of information that made sense.

With an impatient sweep of his fleshy brown arm, Azotl pushed the scrolls off his desk and onto the floor. He was tired of looking at them. What he needed was a spy he could count on, a spy who could travel in regions far from Tenochtitlán without arousing enmity, a spy who could discover the truth about these bewildering apparitions, these mountains or towers that floated upon the sea. But Azotl had no such spy. He slumped at his desk, picked at his *cuitlacoche*, and brooded.

Just then, something odd happened, a circumstance that might almost have been willed by the gods—it had a strange, serendipitous quality. Distracted as he was, Azotl started to muse about matters of little consequence, whatever caught his attention. For example, it occurred to him what a handsome plate this was, this plate of Cholulan manufacture, the plate that bore his meal of *cuitlacoche.* Those Cholulans, he thought, certainly had a rare way with ceramics.

And just at that moment, he heard a commotion outside his chamber. It sounded like someone arriving. With the hem of his cloak, he wiped his lips and glanced up from his meal. Instantly, he was gladdened by what he saw. It was the merchant from Cholula, the one named Pitoque. With considerable difficulty, for he was extraordinarily fat, Azotl hauled himself up from his chair and waddled around to greet the trader. For a moment, he felt as if his mind were expanding in all directions at once, but then his thoughts settled— as eventually they always did—into one clear and simple direction.

"Ah, Pitoque," he said. He held out his arms to greet the visitor, to enfold him in a warm embrace. "Well met, old man. I was just thinking what wonderful plates you people make, and here you are. You're exactly the fellow I want to see. I have the perfect job for you."

Mountains or towers, adrift upon the sea?
  Great bearded monkeys?

Pitoque ambled through the streets of Tenochtitlán, his hands clasped behind his back, his brow furrowed. One moment, he was convinced that these reports must be nonsense. Mountains or towers afloat upon the water? It was impossible. Surely they would sink. And monkeys the size of men? He had traveled the length and breadth of the world. He had observed a great many strange sights, but he knew of no such creatures.

And yet. And yet. Something about these reports troubled him in a vague, unsettling way that he could not sort out. It was as if he had heard these rumours before, but not while awake. Perhaps they had come to him in a dream and, in the sometimes way of dreams, had left him with only the faintest of memories, just footprints on the water, and now those footprints lapped at the edges of his consciousness, where they raised dark misgivings, a recollection of omens.

He turned a corner and nearly collided with an old woman, almost black of complexion, a troll. She threw up her arms in fright, as if he had been about to inflict some harm, and a dozen sapota fruit scattered in the air. She began to shriek.

Pitoque scrambled about, trying to pick up the fruit, but each red orb had exploded as soon as it hit the ground, and now the cobbles ran with a mess of pulp and what looked alarmingly like blood. The fruit had been rotten. Now she was enraged, pointing at Pitoque and calling down the wrath of the gods upon him. At least, that was what her words sounded like. In fact, he could not understand them. It was as if she were speaking a language of her own invention, a dreadful, clattering tongue that clanged with sharp, staccato sounds, like a flint blade grating against a stone. Her voice stormed against his ears. Gibberish. Pure gibberish. But suddenly something changed. The words began to make sense, even though he could not quite place the language she was speaking.

Flee. Flee. Take only what you can carry. Run for your lives.

"What are you talking about?" he said. "What do you mean?"

But she paid no attention. She kept stamping amid the blood red pulp of fruit, waving her fists and shrieking out those same words, over and over, in that strange language.

Flee. Flee. Take only what you can carry. Run for your lives.

All around, passersby and workers stopped what they were doing and stared at this inexplicable scene, this alien fellow— a Cholulan, perhaps?—being berated in public by a hunchbacked woman, a dwarf, who was cackling in some lunatic tongue, while what looked like the blood of several corpses sloshed at their fret.

Pitoque tried to address the woman. "I am deeply sorry," he said. He reached into his robes for the small purse of gold dust and pellets he always kept there. "I would willingly repay you for the fruit. I—"

But it was no use. She did not listen. She seemed not to hear. She shouted and fumed, danced on one spot like the madwoman she obviously was.

Pitoque shook his head, drew up his cloak, and hurried away, feeling dozens of eyes burning into his back. He made for his lodgings, a small, unobtrusive house where he stayed whenever he found himself here in Tenochtitlán, the city of the Aztecs. He did not slow his pace until he reached the portal of his dwelling, and it was only now, when he had pounded on the door and been admitted by a servant, when he had called out for a jar of water and settled himself by a window so that he could peer out across the pale surface of the lake—it was only now that the disorder in his mind began to assume some sort of shape, like images floating up from the past.

Mountains or towers adrift upon the sea? Great bearded monkeys?

Could this be the fulfilment of the prophecy—the terrible return of an angry god? Immediately, his heart began to pound. He could not bring himself to pronounce the god's name. Not now. For ten years, he'd been waiting for a sign. He reached into his robes to finger once more the small necklace of shells he always kept there. In the voice of that cackling troll he'd just run into, he had heard the echo of some distant, dimly remembered dream.

Flee. Flee. Take only what you can carry. Run for your lives.

He'd heard that voice and those words before. But he hadn't understood them then, and he did not truly understand them now. Flee what? Flee why? Run where? What did the warning mean? Pitoque raised the jar of water to his lips and drank. He did not stop drinking until the jar was empty, and then he called out for more water. He wondered whether he had ever felt so thirsty before.

A Necklace of Shells

Pitoque had no choice. If the master functionary instructed him—a *pochteca* from a vassal state—to leave for the coast of the rising sun in order to make sense of these mysterious reports and drawings, then so it must be. The following morning, the merchant set about making preparations to depart. He instructed his gang of porters to be ready as soon as the gods willed, and he himself oversaw the careful repacking of his goods. They would travel on foot, of course.

While in his home city, Pitoque had made sure to acquire a large stock of pottery. The ceramics of Cholula were renowned far and wide for their quality—the best in the world. Why, the emperor himself, Moctezuma II, insisted upon the wares of Cholula both for his feasts of state and for his private banquets. Nothing was allowed to pass his lips that had not been served upon the plates of Cholula. Or so it was said. Pitoque, of course, had never dined with the emperor, had never even set eyes upon him. He was merely a merchant, after all—a man of substantial means but hardly the sort to mingle with high priests or nobility.

Even given the urgency of this mission, Pitoque was required by custom to await a propitious day for departure, and so he cut his hair, made an offering of turkey heads to his gods, and finally left the capital on the day 1-Serpent. He wore his usual merchant dress, a loincloth of henequen and a rough maguey cloak. Owing to the difficulty of the terrain, the trek would require many days. At first, the party marched across

29

high rolling plains, stippled by cactus and covered in places by quivering stands of pine. To the north soared Citlaltépetl, tallest mountain in all the empire, its summit swathed in glimmering snow. Beyond that great mountain, the central tablelands gave way to steep cliff walls and plunging ravines, and the cool, dry climate of the highlands turned suddenly wet, as the humid air of the coast rolled up the walls of the eastern mountains and smothered the tumbling earth with the shadows of sodden clouds.

With dense mists swirling all about, Pitoque could see only as far as the nearest trees. He and his porters clambered down through the fine rain they called the *chipi-chipi*, a drizzle that fell almost constantly on the eastern slopes. Down to the coast they trundled, down to the coast and its dense jungles, soggy marshes, slow rivers, and torrid, sticky air, rife with insects and sweat. The going was rough and the roads were poor. In fact, they were not really roads at all—just tracks.

Pitoque's assignment was to overlook nothing, to find out as much as he could about these intruders, and to relay his reports back to the capital in the hands of his most trustworthy porters. He had undertaken many missions of espionage before, but now his thoughts were troubled by strange fears and doubts. By night, they camped outdoors beneath the slow swirl of stars, but he slept only fitfully, and in the snatches of dreams he saw great armies advancing in the night. He heard the clash of swords, an anguished howling. Sparks exploded all around.

By day, he trudged eastward and wondered at the meaning of these visions. On the seventh day of the journey, after the party had marched out onto the coastal flatlands, one of the porters—a fellow named Kepantl—let out a terrified yelp, dropped his cargo of ceramics, and leapt away to cower beneath the large green awning of a ceiba tree. Pitoque and Toc hurried back to find out what was the matter, and discovered the answer. An owl lay dead upon the path.

Toc took a deep breath and prodded at the bird with his foot, turned it over. It bore no injury, no outward sign of disease, except that it was obviously lifeless. The old man looked up at Pitoque.

"It wasn't here when you and I passed."

Pitoque agreed. Surely they would have seen it, for they had walked over this very spot only instants earlier. There had been no dead owl then.

A voice behind them shouted: "It fell from the sky!"

Pitoque turned to see who had spoken. Still hiding beneath the ceiba tree, the terrified porter, Kepantl, was pointing up at the broken clouds above them.

"It landed on my head," he shouted. "An owl!" He fell to his knees and began to whimper.

Pitoque looked at Toc. "What do you think?"

The old man scratched his chin. "First, owls do not fly by day. Second, they do not fall out of the sky. Or not without a reason. It must mean something."

Pitoque felt his organs shifting inside him, had a sudden, urgent need to vent his intestines. An owl falling from the sky in the middle of the day—of course, it meant something. It could only mean something terrible. Even alive, an owl sighted by day was a dreadful omen. What of an owl dead? It had to foretell the grimmest news imaginable. But what could that news be?

He felt another bitter cramp in his gut and shuddered. "Please," he said. "Excuse me."

He hurried off into a copse of scrub trees, desperate to be alone. He found a little hollow bisected by a log. He bunched up his cloak, squatted down, and his bowels emptied. All at once, in the same sudden rush, the memories overwhelmed him, for this was not the first time he had seen a dead owl in the day. He had witnessed the same spectacle once before: ten years before.

Ten years ago, the feast day of Quetzalcoatl had found him far to the south, in the distant lands of the Maya, where the feathered serpent was known and worshiped, but by another name. There, the people knew him as Kukulcan.

At the time, Pitoque had been traveling in a large convoy of merchants, as was his practice in those days. But on this occasion, he had happened to fall in with a very rough crew. All were Aztecs, and they swaggered about those southern lands as though they owned them. They drove harsh bargains— swindles, really—and later slapped their knees and guffawed at the poor fools they had cheated. They drank a great deal, cursed without cease, and seemed to have no respect for anyone or anything apart from themselves. Many times, Pitoque had thought about abandoning their company and striking out on his own, but he was a young man then, not as well traveled as he would later become, and he lacked the courage or the will to test his luck alone against the world. Besides, he was plagued at the time by an appalling toothache—a fire that burned in the pit of his mouth, a pain beyond description.

Normally, he liked to be at home in Cholula in order to celebrate the feast day of Quetzalcoatl, the patron god of his city, but that was impossible on this occasion, and so he remained on those southern tracks in the midst of those Aztec ruffians. Their company pained him even more than the burning in his mouth. What did these men care of Quetzalcoatl? To them, the feathered serpent was an uncertain deity. They knew him, or of him, but he was not central to their lives or beliefs, the way he was for the people of Cholula.

Still, to honor Pitoque—or so they said—these Aztec merchants decided that they would celebrate the feast day of Quetzalcoatl and do so in a grand style. They gathered great quantities of food and arranged for musical players and urns of pulque. They also sent a party of their younger and stronger porters to a nearby village, with instructions to obtain a supply of women, for what was a celebration without women? Or girls, in truth. Virgins were required.

"Virgins?" said Pitoque. "For what purpose?"

But the other traders merely sniggered. As if the Cholulan didn't know.

In fact, Pitoque did not know. But he could imagine. He explained to his fellow traders that it was not the custom in Cholula to make human sacrifices to Quetzalcoatl. In fact, the practice was proscribed. There were other means of honoring the gods. Pitoque made these points as forcefully as he could, but no one paid him any attention. These men had been a long time on the road, with little in the way of amusement. Liturgical details did not much interest them.

Nor did it seem that they were much interested in doing honor to Quetzalcoatl. On the night of the feast, they ate and drank, and danced and drank, and then descended upon the girls that had been procured—a half-dozen, none of them much above the age of twelve. It turned out that the virginal condition of these captives was of more secular than spiritual significance. In any case, it was promptly ended. That nicety out of the way, the men continued to gorge themselves upon these children, passing them around one to another and becoming steadily more violent as the evening progressed.

Pitoque clutched his hands to his head, while an agony raged in his mouth, as if the horror of these deeds were somehow located inside his own skull. He tried to block out the screams of these youngsters, these girls. He did not participate in this carnage, refused to have anything to do with it, no matter how eagerly the other merchants urged him to give it a try. One after another, they sought to drag him into their orgy.

Here's a pair of fresh buttocks, or nearly fresh, not too much blood. Have a go. Come on, man. You don't get a chance like this every day. Pretty soon, it'll be back to your wife, and everyone knows what that can be like. Here, just feel how firm this bum is. Take a whack at it. Make the baby cry. Have a peek at this little tit, hardly bigger than a mouse. Goon, suck it. Come on, man. Don't spoil the fun.

They gave him a girl, one who could not have been more

than ten years old. She still wore a robe—a robe now fouled with her blood. She knelt at his feet, wordless, staring at the ground. He crouched down, reached out with one hand. He wiped away some grime that had worked itself into the skin on one side of her face, where she must have been pressed against the ground as one of the others went at her.

"Look at me, daughter," he said. "It's all right. I'm not going to hurt you."

And she did look up, her eyes swollen from pummeling or from her sobbing. Blood dribbled from her nose and she wiped it away with the back of her hand. At first, she said nothing, as if she could not believe that she had not been turned over, her robe pushed up about her shoulders, her body invaded again. She nodded at Pitoque, swallowed several times, and then did something extraordinary. She reached into some secret fold of her robe, a pocket hidden somewhere. From it, she removed a small object and held it up to Pitoque in a trembling hand.

A necklace. A little necklace of shells.

"Tacalpa is my name," she whispered. "Please, take this necklace to my mother." The blood began to drool again from her nose. "To remember me by."

She put the necklace in Pitoque's hand, and he was about to say something, to tell her not to worry, that all would be well, that no further harm would come to her. But he stopped himself. He knew it was a lie.

He should have done something, but he didn't. Soon another of these Aztec brutes happened by, noticed this girl kneeling at Pitoque's feet, and decided he could put her to better use.

Pitoque stood up, started to intervene. But the man drew a knife and bared his teeth.

"Stand back," he said. "Just because you are not hungry, that's no reason I can't eat." He let out a roar and carried the child away. "Some of us are men! With appetites!"

Pitoque thought he would scream out, and maybe he did. Who knew? Who could separate one shrieking voice from another? The horrors went on and on, and he endured them— he did not participate but neither did he do anything to end this circus of evil, this abomination that was done on the feast day of Quetzalcoatl, ten years ago. Before the morning sun rose on the following day, all six of those children were dead—sacrificed to some dark purpose, though not to any known god.

A day later, Pitoque struck out on his own. He left the other merchants with only a muttered farewell, and heard them cracking jokes at his expense as he led his gang of porters away, a fire still burning in his jaw, a necklace of shells tucked away in a pocket stitched into his cloak.

Tacalpa, she had said her name was. He did what he'd said he would do. He tried to find the girl's mother. For several days, he trekked from village to village in those distant parts. But no one would own up to being the mother of a girl named Tacalpa, or to knowing any child by that name, or to possessing any knowledge at all. No one wanted anything to do with these monsters that had come down from the north to rape and kill their daughters. As far as any of the villagers were concerned, Pitoque was just another alien brute. They shook their heads, looked the other way. Finally, he gave up. He gathered his porters for the return journey. He had a piercing heat in his jaw, a stench in his nostrils, a swill in his gut. He couldn't leave soon enough.

He headed north with what remained of his wares, and with a necklace of shells tucked away in his robes, a necklace of shells that felt like a chain of stones.

It was about this time that the plague of portents began, the strange comets, the lake waters surging in the absence of any wind, the sudden appearance of uncalculated stars, the voices of women—or were they children? girls?—wailing in the night, invading his dreams. For years after, he had thought they spoke a kind of gibberish or a language he did not know. But the memory had surfaced now, like footprints reassembling upon the water. *Flee*, they had cried. *Flee. Take only what you can carry. Run for your lives.*

But what did the words mean? All Pitoque knew was that terrible omens began to haunt the empire of the Aztecs in the wake of that hateful night in the far southern lands of the Maya. Someone was being warned. But who? Could these signs be aimed at one man, at himself? At times, he believed it might be so. He had thought so on his return to Cholula after that long-ago trek, a journey dark with the most dreadful omens— strange, cackling birds, flowers that withered at the touch of a man's hand, animals found dead along the way. An owl that toppled from the sky in broad daylight. It had landed at his feet, as if to say, *You, Pitoque of Cholula, you have been marked for a dreadful fate.*

In time, the pain in his jaw subsided. A tooth rotted away and fell from his mouth of its own accord. Soon after that,

Kalatzin gave birth to their third child, but the foetus was lifeless. She would not conceive again. And something else went out of her with the loss of that child, some freshness, some essence of her youth, some source of delight. She became wizened inside, fell prey to fits of temper, lost her former pliancy and generous nature. She devoted herself after that to her two living children, to Zaachila and Maxtla, but she did so with an angry passion and with little demonstration of joy.

Pitoque understood that he was the cause of this misfortune. On that terrible night, he had infuriated Quetzalcoatl. He had cast filth upon the god's good name. He was convinced of it. And now everything seemed out of balance, not only his own family. The firmament itself quaked with portents and warnings. Did this mean that some new horror would come, some further punishment? He consulted priests, but they were no help. They couldn't explain the strange events. They brooded and speculated, but they did not know. All that could be predicted—or hoped—was that the situation would come clear in the year 1-Reed, the beginning of a new cycle in the calendar of fifty-two years. According to the prophecies, in the year 1-Reed Quetzalcoatl would finally return to his former kingdom, to resume his reign. Only then would his judgment be known.

Whenever he had thought of that prophecy, during ten long years, Pitoque had closed his eyes and trembled, for the judgment of Quetzalcoatl could only be guessed at. Finally, he had decided that there was only one course he could take. He would return to his family for good, determined to serve their interests and theirs alone. He would abandon his life of travel, give up the profession of his father and forefathers. He would find some other livelihood and devote himself to those closest to him, to his family. He had fingered the necklace of shells that he carried in his cloak and had hoped he might expiate his sins by devotion to his wife and children. He would protect them and await the judgment of the gods.

But only a fool believes he controls the course of his destiny. Again and again, Pitoque had been summoned by Azotl and instructed to undertake yet another mission on behalf of the Aztecs, and how could he refuse? All men have their masters, and either they obey or they perish. Pitoque chose not to perish. Now, here he was again, ordered by the master functionary to carry out one more task, stranger than any before, and again he had complied.

He took a deep breath and adjusted his cloak. He clambered out from the copse of trees. He instructed several of his porters to build a small pyre of wood and there they burned the dead owl. Pitoque hoped that, by these means, some of its evil power might be directed in a more positive way, as an offering to the gods. He made everyone kneel down and prostrate themselves before the smoldering ashes.

When this was done, Pitoque clapped Toc on the shoulder, and the two men rose to their feet. The gang of porters followed, including poor Kepantl, the man upon whom the owl had fallen. He still whimpered, terrified by what had happened to him and what it might mean. They turned and resumed their journey to the coast, their stomachs grumbling and their intestines still groaning in protest, for the food in these poor lands left much to be desired. Crude stews of squash and chili peppers. The odd lumpy tortilla. Here and there, a bowl of moldy beans. No meat of any kind, of course—unless one counted an occasional slurp of toad. The water was rank.

Three days later, Kepantl was dead. Sometime in the night, it seemed, he had roused himself and staggered forward along the path, alone. He must have lost his way, wandered off onto a rocky outcropping that ended in a cliff, and gone over the edge. They found him in the morning, crumpled on the ground below amid some scrub brush and thorns. The blood was still damp where he'd smashed his head. His limbs were twisted at impossible angles, and his neck was broken. His face was contorted in an expression of horror.

"An accident," said Toc. He shook his head. "Poor fellow. He was a good man. Got lost in the darkness, I suppose."

Lost in the darkness? Pitoque doubted it. There'd been a gibbous moon and a clear sky all night long. He knew, because he'd stared at the heavens almost without cease. Kepantl hadn't lost his way in the darkness. Whatever he'd done, he'd done it on purpose. But Pitoque decided against expressing these thoughts aloud. He gazed down at the man, remembered him as a decent, honest soul—a good porter, and an excellent messenger when the need arose. He sighed.

"You are right," he said to Toc. "An accident. A terrible accident."

They buried Kapantl beneath a cairn of rocks, offered several sacrifices—some lizards, a large scorpion—and continued on their way.

The Height of the Gods

Around Xicalango—on the Bay of Campeche, as it would come to be known—Pitoque journeyed from village to village. He spoke to many people who said they had seen these strange towers floating past. The people of these lands were members of the coastal tribes, who spoke a dialect of the Maya language. As a native of the central highlands, Pitoque had Nahuatl as his first tongue, but his years of travel had made him fluent in many ways of speech.

He asked one group of villagers whether these structures they had seen—these floating spires—could have been some innocent reconnaissance by a neighboring tribe. But the people shook their heads. No, no, they insisted. It was a great deal more than that, whatever it was. They reported that these strangers had come ashore farther east, at Catoche and Champoton, where there had been encounters with the local people. Or so they had heard.

"Encounters?" Pitoque repeated, an edge to his voice. He was wary of euphemism.

"Maybe," one man said. "Why do you ask? Do you have some special interest in these matters?"

"Not at all. I am merely a humble trader from Cholula. See,

here are my wares." He waved at several of his porters. "It is just that I am plagued by a curious mind. My father was the same and his father before him. You spoke of encounters?"

"Not just encounters," someone said. "Fighting."

"To what end?"

A bad one. Despite a great advantage in numbers, the coastal people suffered considerable losses. These newcomers were formidable warriors, it seemed.

"Describe them," said Pitoque. "What did they look like?"

And the description he received fit what he had already been told. These beings were larger than men and hairier beyond anything ever imagined. Furthermore, they were white of skin.

"White of skin?" Pitoque broke in. This news caught his attention. "What do you mean?"

"White," replied an elderly man missing most of his teeth. His cheeks seemed to cave in, but his eyes were bright and had none of that dampness sometimes seen in the eyes of the aged. "You know what white means. Their skin was white, as white as cotton newly spun."

"You saw this for yourself."

"Yes. From a distance. Across the water. We all did."

The others nodded their agreement. Their stories matched. Large creatures. Hairy. White of skin.

With Toc at his side and his porters in tow, Pitoque traveled even farther east, to Catoche. Here, he learned that battles had been fought against these strangers, waged by the people in neighboring Champoton. The fighting had gone badly, it was said. Pitoque expressed his thanks and continued on his way. In Champoton, he learned that the stories were true—great contests of arms had been waged against these strange beings, these white-skinned creatures riddled with hair. The townspeople gathered around him now, all eager to speak, all bursting with news about the battles that had been won.

"The battles lost, you must mean," said Pitoque.

The people hung their heads. Oh. He already knew about that part.

Still, their descriptions of the intruders matched all the others and they had further details. "Those creatures stink."

"I beg your pardon?" Pitoque thought he had misheard.

"They stink," repeated a jolly fellow, who wore a constant grin and possessed more chins than a man could count at a glance. He rolled his eyes. "Ooh, they smelled. Enough to make you gag."

The others around him said it was true. They curled up their noses and mimed the act of choking. The stink was like nothing ever experienced, they said. Those interlopers—they smelled like rotting fish.

"I see." Pitoque could make nothing of this strange report. But he filed the information away with the rest.

The people of Champoton had more to tell him. These beings, whatever they were, had come in search of gold.

"Gold?" said Pitoque. "Are you certain?"

Indeed, yes. At every opportunity, they asked for gold. It was believed they had a disease that could be cured only by gold. This had been the main idea communicated between the two sides—there had been severe linguistic difficulties. In any case, the people had done what they were bid. They had offered up what little gold they could scrounge. In exchange, they had received what they thought were *chalchihuites*—beautiful green stones made of jadeite. Only later did the truth become known. The green stones were worthless. They broke if you dropped them. A child could crush them between his teeth. These townspeople of Champoton slumped their shoulders and shook their heads. Most of their soldiers were dead, and they'd traded all their gold for some bits of colored glass.

Following this encounter, Pitoque spent many more hot and stifling days reconnoitering the coast, but he discovered no further signs of these strange beings in their great floating mansions. It appeared that they had floated away.

The mission was complete. Pitoque decided that he had done what he could. Now, he reversed his course and began the long, slow trek back across the sweltering coastal flats and up the mountain walls, back to the central highlands, to the cool, blue skies and Tenochtitlán. Along the way, he sorted the information through in his mind, over and again, until gradually a theory began to take shape. One afternoon, as they climbed up the mountain slopes through the mist and the constant dampness of the *chipi-chipi*, he spoke of his theory to Toc. He repeated all they had learned of these creatures—their superhuman size, their thick beards, the whiteness of their skin.

Toc inclined his head. "Yes," he agreed. He grasped at the trunk of a small tree to pull himself up the mountain slope. "Just as you say."

"Don't you understand?"

"I'm not sure that I do."

Pitoque explained what he was thinking. The descriptions they had received could as easily have described Quetzalcoatl in his human guise—bearded, white of skin.

"And larger than a man?" said Toc.

"As a god, he would be—don't you think?" A flat stone shifted beneath Pitoque's foot, and he almost stumbled and fell. Toc reached out to help him. "Thanks. Thanks, old man. Where was I?"

"The height of the gods."

"Oh, yes. I've never heard this question addressed directly— Quetzalcoatl's stature, I mean. But one would expect a god to be taller than a man. So that fits, too."

"And to smell like rotting fish? Would one also expect that of a god?" Toc smiled. "I mean no disrespect. I'm merely quoting."

Pitoque nodded. "I've considered their odor. Perhaps it has something to do with this disease they speak of, the one that can only be cured by gold. Perhaps the two are connected somehow."

"Perhaps."

"You don't sound convinced."

"Well, if these beings represent the return of Quetzalcoatl, why have they gone away?"

"Ah." Pitoque frowned. He had no answer and so had to concede the point. He looked up. "What else?"

"The year 1-Reed."

"Yes?"

"It is still two years away."

"Hmm." Pitoque scrambled up a steep bit and stopped to rest upon a small plateau. He took a deep breath, felt his heart racing. Another good point. He put his hands on his hips and grimaced. He'd have to think about it—that was all. He'd have to give these ideas more thought. He swept a glaze of dampness from his brow, put back his shoulders, and resumed his climb.

"I see," said Azotl. He wiped his lips. Reluctantly, he withdrew his attention from his repast, a most delicious meal—meatballs of armadillo in a wonderful sesame-seed sauce. He reiterated the gist of Pitoque's report. "They are equipped to fight. They seek gold. And then they leave. Is this what you are telling me?"

Pitoque nodded.

Azotl removed a bit of meat that was caught between his teeth and swallowed it down. "That's something, at least. Something to report." He made a discreet belch, pushed his plate aside, and crossed his arms before him on the wooden surface of his working table. "But I don't understand their desire for gold. What's so special about gold?"

"A source of wealth, perhaps?"

"Perhaps." Azotl considered the idea. "But not as valuable as quetzal feathers. Why don't they seek quetzal feathers?"

Pitoque repeated what he had heard, that these beings were beset by some strange malady, curable only by the application of gold. He mentioned the smell they apparently gave off, which might suggest a degenerative condition, a wasting away of the flesh. The gold, it seemed, had a salubrious effect.

Azotl puckered his lips, as if testing this idea on his tongue. He frowned. "I have never heard of such an illness." He leaned forward. "Tell me, in your considered opinion, are these creatures by way of being men?"

Pitoque had to struggle to keep his eyes open. He was exhausted—ten straight days he'd been on the road, on that arduous trek up from the coast. "As I say, I didn't see them myself. They'd already gone."

"Yes. Yes. But based on your encounters with people who did see them, what would you say?"

Pitoque put a hand to his brow and shook his head. "I don't know."

Azotl scrunched up his face so that his one good eye disappeared and he looked like some great gourd. "Did I hear you correctly? You don't know?" The master functionary let his face relax. He shook his large, unruly head, and his chins waggled back and forth. He closed his one eye and then opened it again. "Not good enough, I'm afraid." He hauled himself forward in his seat. "Pitoque. I will be presenting your report before the royal court—Moctezuma and all the princes and all the chieftains. And this is the sort of question that they are going to ask me. Are these creatures men? What am I to say? That I don't know?" He flopped back in his seat and shook his head again. "They will not be greatly pleased."

Pitoque shifted his weight. Should he tell Azotl what he had told Toc? In truth, he did not feel ready to speak about his theory yet. It was too conjectural. He lacked the proper documentation. Still, it seemed he had little choice. The master functionary was clearly telling him that a bit of conjecture was better than nothing at all. He decided to say what he thought. He sat forward and cleared his throat. He began by pointing out that the calendar was approaching the year *Ce Acatl*, or 1-Reed—the very year in which the return of the man-god Quetzalcoatl was due. The prophecies were very clear on this point—at least, some of them were. Besides, these creatures had arrived over the eastern sea, the very sea on which Quetzalcoatl had departed, on a raft of serpents, hundreds of years ago. "As well," he said, "these creatures are white of skin. They—"

"What did you say?" said Azotl. His one eye stared straight at Pitoque. "White of skin? You didn't tell me that."

Pitoque realized that he hadn't. Consciously or unconsciously, he had been withholding certain pieces of information, trying to make sense of them on his own before trotting them out for others. He thought again of that tormented night ten years earlier and of all the portents since then, the wailing voices, the owls, a stillborn child. Dark omens. For him, the return of Quetzalcoatl was not an event to celebrate but to fear. He shook his head to clear his thoughts. He said, "It's true.

The people who saw these beings, they all say the same. White of skin. And, as you already know, with thick beards."

"Thick beards," repeated Azotl. "That fits the description of Quetzalcoatl, I take it?"

Pitoque said that it did.

"So what are you saying? The man-god returns? Is that it?"

He shrugged. "Not exactly. The time isn't right, as yet. *Ce Acatl* is still almost two years away." Since Toc had raised his objections to the theory, Pitoque had been thinking a good deal about the old man's questions. Now he sat forward. He might as well explain his thinking. "Perhaps these intruders are envoys of the gods," he said. "An advance party sent to prepare the way for Quetzalcoatl." His heart quaked at the thought.

"I see," said Azotl. He slapped his hands on the table, making the dishes rattle. "Well, your theory's a bit mystical for my taste, but I suppose it will have to do." He reached for another armadillo meatball and popped it into his mouth. He chortled, and sesame-seed sauce dribbled down his chin. "After all—I will have to say *something*."

On Pain of Death

Pitoque returned to Cholula just in time to discover what had happened. Maxtla was gone.

"What do you mean?" he said. "Where has he gone?"

Kalatzin was desperate with worry. Some time passed

before she calmed down sufficiently to explain. "They simply appeared," she said, "and they took him away."

"They? Who are they?"

"A group of elders."

"When did they come?"

"Just this morning."

"Why?"

"They said . . ." She started to sob again and had to will herself to be still. "They said he desecrated the temple of Quetzalcoatl. He and some others."

Pitoque decided it might be best if he sat down. Her news was worse than he could have imagined. "They told you that?"

"They said it was the first time the temple had ever been damaged."

"They were angry?" Stupid question. Of course they were. "How angry were they?"

"Not angry as much as afraid. They seemed to be afraid."

Pitoque rubbed his forehead. Of course. Their principal reaction would be fear. He felt it himself—his palms were watering already and a chill was forming in the small of his back.

Kalatzin stumbled toward her husband and fell to her knees. "They'll kill him, won't they? They'll put him to death." Again, she began to sob. "Oh, why didn't you take him away? When I asked you to, why didn't you? Why?"

She began to beat at him with her fists—limp, ineffectual blows. And yet they found their mark and caused him more pain than she knew. She was right—why hadn't he? It seemed he had failed again, failed in the first duty of any man, which was to protect his family from harm.

Tizot, an elder of Cholula, shook his long, sad head, which had the appearance of an old garment spread across a rock to dry. "Never has the temple been desecrated before," he said. "You realize that."

Pitoque swallowed. "I do."

Tizot shook his head again, as did the other assembled elders, the most prominent laymen in Cholula. Naturally, they were a somber group—but they were also fearful. Pitoque could see it in the tense set of their jaws, the way they clenched their hands. The patron god of their city had been subjected to the most abominable insults and defilements. Sacred vessels had been reduced to shards. Scrolls had been ripped apart and burned. Why, human excrement had been introduced to the inner confines of the temple itself. These were unspeakable acts. Who would not be afraid? At any time, the god might mete out his punishment, and it would surely be severe.

Tizot blinked his dark and melancholy eyes. "You, of course, understand the consequences of these actions."

"I'm not sure that I follow," said Pitoque. "By consequences, do you mean—?"

"That *all* will pay. For the abuses committed by these boys, including your son, all Cholula will pay." The elder narrowed his eyes. "Perhaps there will be a drought. Or a flood. A plague of locusts. A terrible massacre. Who can say? The crime has been done, and there will be consequences. The priests tell us so. There is only one hope. Just one."

Pitoque waited for the man to go on, but Tizot merely gazed back at him in silence, blinking those grieving eyes. Pitoque realized they had at last reached the heart of this encounter— the moment he had come to prevent. He started to speak, but just as quickly his voice faded. He found he could not go on, could not say the word.

Tizot grimaced. "Precisely."

It was clear what he meant. The boys—there were six of them in all—would have to be put to death. Perhaps in that way, the feathered serpent might be placated and would not seek revenge. Pitoque understood this. It was well known among his people that a god—especially a god of Quetzalcoatl's stature—could not be insulted so directly, except on pain of death. He knew it better than most. For ten years, he had lived under what he feared was a sentence of death. But now it was his son who would die.

Pitoque worried at the folds of his robe and juggled a hundred words in his head. In fact, he had an idea how to proceed. A plan had been taking shape in his mind from the moment he had first learned of this blasphemy. But the strategy would have to be executed with prudence, with the utmost delicacy and tact. One wrong word, one inadvertent comment or misplaced sentiment—and any hope of saving Maxtla, or any of the other boys, would immediately be lost. The elders were not evil men, but they feared their gods.

"I am very sorry," said Tizot. "I know how this must pain you. I speak as a father myself."

Pitoque looked up. He squared his shoulders and began. He explained to these elders of Cholula about the strange beings that had been sighted off the eastern coast.

Tizot inclined his head. He himself had heard rumors to this effect. "But what do these reports have to do with us?"

"I take it," said Pitoque, "that you are not aware of who these visitors are or what they represent?"

"Represent? What do you mean, represent? As I understand it, these questions are little understood by anyone. I gather their appearance is a mystery."

"What would you think," asked Pitoque, "if I were to tell you that I myself had set eyes upon these creatures?"

"That you . . . that you had seen them *yourself*?"

Pitoque promptly realized his misstep, his straying from the truth. "Or, I mean to say, that I have spoken at length to many who have."

"People who have seen these beings?"

"Yes. What would you say to that?"

"I don't know. I would be surprised, I suppose. However, it is well known that you travel widely. Who can say what you have or have not encountered?"

Pitoque proceeded to divulge what he knew—secrets known only to a few on the eastern coast and transmitted thence to the highest levels of the Aztec state. He understood that he was betraying a solemn trust, a vow he had taken to Azotl himself. The master functionary had told him not to speak about any of these matters. But what else could he do? His son's life was at stake. He had to choose between one responsibility and the other. He could not serve both the empire and his family. Something had to be sacrificed.

The elders listened to his presentation. When it was done, Tizot spoke up.

"Fascinating," he said. "You have obviously conducted a most thorough investigation, although I confess I do not understand why such a task was entrusted to you. Still, your reputation as a man of formidable knowledge and intellect has certainly been enhanced by this report. I have just one question." He tilted his head. "Why are you telling us this?"

Pitoque took a deep breath and began to stride back and forth across the hard day floor of the gloomy meeting chamber. He turned to face the assembly of elders. "I am telling you this because the appearance of these beings presages the return of Quetzalcoatl himself."

"*What?*" The elders spoke in unison and then took a deep, collective breath. Utter quiet followed.

Again, it was Tizot who broke the silence. "Pitoque," he said, "this is an extremely provocative claim. Not even our priests have yet declared themselves with such certainty on the subject. How can you be so sure?"

Pitoque explained his reasoning. He put the case, not as an exercise in personal conjecture, but as a declaration of established truth. The prophecies. The physical appearance of these visitors. Their beards. The whiteness of their skin. Their very height. He stepped forward. "I mean to say, one would not expect a god to be of the same height as a man, would one?"

"Are you asking my opinion?" said Tizot.

Pitoque said yes.

The elder shook his head. "I suppose not," he said, and the others nodded.

"Good." Pitoque resumed his pacing back and forth across the floor. "Now," he said, "my belief is this. These gods can only be an advance party for Quetzalcoatl himself, who is, as you know, ordained to return in the year 1-Reed—just two years away. All the prophecies tell us so."

"*Some of them*," said another of the elders, a stocky, angular fellow named Bactal. "*Some* of the prophecies. Not all. There is a lack of unanimity on this point."

"You are right," said Pitoque. "*Some* of the prophecies." He cleared his throat. He decided to take a dangerous leap. "But the prophecies, combined with these reports that have lately been received from the coast, have been enough to persuade the Aztecs. They are convinced that the way is being prepared for the return of Quetzalcoatl."

"You know this," said Tizot, "for a fact?"

Pitoque chose not to reply. Let them wonder how and what he knew. He waited for a time, and he could see that the strategy was working. People in Cholula knew, of course, that he was a *pochteca*. They knew further that he traveled regularly to Tenochtitlán and that he seemed to have some special relationship with the Aztecs. They did not know, however, what that relationship might be or how it worked in practice. Instead,

Pitoque and his mysterious journeys were the subject of rumor and speculation, and the merchant hoped to use the elders' curiosity to his advantage now. When he judged the time was right, he spoke up again.

"I have it on excellent authority," he said, "that the Aztecs regard the prospect of Quetzalcoatl's return with keen anticipation. Already, in Tenochtitlán, the preparations are being made, at the highest levels. I know this for certain." He paused to let his words sink in. "I wonder," he continued, "if it would be viewed in an entirely positive light in Tenochtitlán, were it known that some blot had been cast on Quetzalcoatl's promised return, or that such a blot had been cast here in Cholula, where Quetzalcoatl is revered above all other gods." He turned to Tizot. "You spoke earlier of consequences, that we must think of consequences. I agree. I think that we must think very clearly what the consequences of this information might be." Pitoque waited, but no one responded. Good. They were all thinking. That was what he wished.

Finally, Tizot spoke up. "What do you suggest?"

"What I suggest," said Pitoque, "is that this is not the time to be punishing wayward boys, no matter how badly they have behaved. This is a time for celebration, to sing the praises of the gods, to prepare for the feathered serpent's return."

Regarding the damage done to the temple, Pitoque said he was extremely sorry and offered to underwrite whatever repairs were required. In addition, he was willing to pay a generous sum as further restitution, to compensate the elders and the priests for any practical inconvenience and mental discomfort they had suffered as a result of this impetuous behavior on the part of these extremely reprehensible boys. He gave his own word that no such outrages would ever happen again.

Pitoque did not expect that his case would be accepted soon or easily. First, the priests were summoned. They tossed shells, consulted the ancient texts, conferred with the elders. The following day, the elders conferred among themselves. They called for Pitoque again and requested that he set out his main arguments once more. When he had finished, they traded uncertain glances with each other. He was permitted to withdraw. For hours, then days, the elders debated the matter in private.

Pitoque paced the perimeter of the plaza outside. He returned home late at night, caught brief intervals of sleep, was up early each morning to return to the palace of the elders' council, determined to be on hand when they emerged. During all this time, Maxtla and the other boys were kept under strict detention. Pitoque tried but was unable to communicate with his son.

At last, after four days and nights, the elders rose from their deliberations and paraded out into the morning sun. They had reached a decision at last.

"Yes?" said Pitoque. "What have you decided?"

Tizot raised his arms. "We have agreed," he said, "to accept your proposal." He emphasized that it was only because Pitoque was so well respected in the community that they were willing to make this exception, and only in this one instance. "There can be no repetition of this blasphemous behavior."

"There won't be," said Pitoque. "I promise you." He felt a great weight remove itself, as if well-gorged serpents were sliding out through holes at the ends of his arms. He had succeeded. He had plunged these good men into a turmoil of their own fears. He had pitted their terror of the gods against their fear of the Aztecs. In the end, it was the Aztecs who had won out. "When may I see Maxtla?" he said. "When may I see my—"

"Not so quickly." Tizot strode forward. "There is one condition."

"Yes? What is it?"

"That, should there be any repetition of this evil, you will be held responsible, for it will be you, Pitoque, who is at fault. The gods have demanded that you be put under this obligation. On pain of death."

On pain of death. Pitoque heard the words, but he did not truly sense their import. He was too preoccupied by thoughts of his son. He gazed at the elders, then bowed. "Very well," he said. "I accept this condition."

Tizot narrowed his eyes, red and puffy from his long exertions. "In that case, the youths may go." He said that prayers and offerings would now have to be made, not only to Quetzalcoatl, but also to the goddess Tlazolteotl, She Who Devours Filth. On behalf of the other elders of Cholula, he accepted Pitoque's payment of gold and quetzal feathers, of jadeite and puma hides. They agreed that the temple would be restored at Pitoque's expense. Tizot reminded him a last time of the obligation he was now under, and the affair was deemed to be at an end.

A Sprinkling of Gnat Dust

When they were at last brought out into the light of day, most of the boys were pale and shaking. They squinted in the sudden sunshine and stepped gingerly, as if just learning to walk or terrified that they might fall. Maxtla had lost weight, and much of his customary bravado seemed to have seeped away. Beneath his left eye, a muscle quivered involuntarily, a nervous spasm that would continue off and on for several days.

In fact, all the boys seemed badly shaken by their brush with death—all except Nahuauc, the leader of the group. He expressed neither regret at his behavior nor gratitude for Pitoque's intervention. He simply sneered and laughed and walked away with his doting mother, who thought the world of him and of everything he did.

Pitoque watched them go and shook his head. He had a bad feeling he'd be hearing about that boy again. He clutched Maxtla by the arm. "Come," he said. "Let's get you home. Your mother has been worried half to death."

The youngster started to say something, but Pitoque didn't want to hear.

"You, keep quiet. Just put one foot in front of the other. Let's see if you can do that."

Pitoque confronted his son one morning in the boy's bedroom. A week had passed since Maxtla's release, and the boy seemed to have recovered somewhat. The muscle had stopped twitching beneath his left eye, and he no longer brooded in silence, alone in his room. Indeed, he seemed to have got back some of his old defiant air, judging by the set of his shoulders this morning and by the scowl on his face. Pitoque felt a twinge of foreboding but decided to bear on with this meeting anyway. The boy had to understand the gravity of his offence. Pitoque bid his son good morning and started straight in.

"I don't know what is to be done with you," he said. "You seem to have no understanding whatever of the power of the gods." He reached up and plucked at the air with his fingers, as if catching a flying insect, then snapped his thumb and forefinger together to make the imaginary insect disappear. "To the gods, you are nothing mare than a troublesome gnat. If they chose, they could turn you into a sprinkling of gnat dust, right now, this very instant."

"Why don't they?" Maxtla looked at his father, and his mouth curled down in an ugly pout. "Why don't they turn me into a sprinkling of gnat dust then, if that is their will?"

"Did I give you my permission to speak?"

"No."

"No, what?"

"No, *Father*."

Pitoque began to stride back and forth across the room, his hands clasped behind his back. "You could have been killed, you know. The elders had decided to put you and your foolish companions to death. They would have, too, if they'd had their way."

The boy muttered something under his breath.

"What did you say?"

"Nothing."

"I asked you a question. What did you say?"

Maxtla looked up, his chin trembling now and his eyes shining. "I said, maybe they should have killed us. We are willing to die, you know. All of us are. At least we have the courage to act on our beliefs. Not like the rest of you."

"The rest of who?"

"Of you. All of you. Everyone in this cowardly place. You let the Aztecs run our lives. You act like their servants. You cower and cringe. It's despicable. You're too afraid to stand up to them. At least we tried."

"How? By desecrating the temple of Quetzalcoatl—the patron god of Cholula? This is how you stand up to the Aztecs?" Pitoque had not intended to engage his son in a debate. He had intended to lay down the law and be done with it, but his tongue seemed to have got the better of him, as it so often did. "You're speaking nonsense, boy. How do you hurt the Aztecs by defiling your own gods?"

"Our gods are dead."

"What!" Pitoque took several steps toward the child. He raised his right hand and almost cuffed the wretched ingrate across his miserable little chin. Somehow, he managed to stop himself. "That is blasphemy and a lie. I myself have seen the gods. With my own eyes."

Maxtla looked away. He made a bored face. "Yes. I'm sure you have."

"I have."

It wasn't true, of course. He'd merely spoken to others who

had seen these floating mountains, inhabited by these great monkeylike beings. But once again, it almost seemed as if he had seen them himself—the images were burned that deeply into his mind. Now, like some ancient prophet, Pitoque began to wave his hands in the air. When he spoke, his voice trembled with a combination of awe and terror, for he revered the gods, but he also knew how gravely he had sinned against them.

"I have seen the gods myself, afloat upon the eastern sea." His voice rose to a crescendo. "They are the envoys of Quetzalcoatl himself. They herald his return. How dare you say the gods are dead? Your father has seen them, and they live."

Maxtla peered up at his father and narrowed his eyes, as if he found himself in the presence of a lunatic. He said nothing, but Pitoque realized from the look on the boy's face that the interview had accomplished little. He had intended to chastise the child, but all he had managed to do was convince Maxtla that his father was deranged. He let out a tired breath, told his son to tidy his belongings and to be quick about it. He flung his cloak over his shoulder with what he hoped was a magisterial air, then turned and strode from the room.

"So," said Kalatzin. She looked up from her half of the iguana, bathed in a pumpkin-seed sauce. She and her husband were sharing a late dinner, dining apart from their children. Normally, lunch was the main meal of the day, but lately all of their usual patterns had been knocked awry. "Did you settle everything?"

Pitoque laughed and shook his head. "I've made my feelings clear, at least. I've told him what I think."

"And what does *he* think?"

Pitoque stared down at his plate. After a time, he looked up. "It does not seem as if his thoughts have altered. I do not believe that this episode has changed his mind about anything."

"He was always a stubborn child."

"He is lucky to be alive."

Kalatzin grimaced and worried her upper lip between her teeth. She finally said that she was aware of this. Had it not been she who had warned that some disaster might happen if the boy were not taken away from Cholula? "I don't want to blame you, Pitoque, but I predicted that something terrible would take place. If we aren't careful, it will happen again." She looked her husband squarely in the eyes. "*Now* will you take the boy away?"

Pitoque let out a long breath. It pained him to admit it, but his wife had been right all along. He should have listened. Take the boy away? Yes. What else could he do? He crossed his arms on the table. "I will do as you say. I will take Maxtla with me when I leave."

Kalatzin tore off another piece of iguana. She dabbed it around in the thick, brown sauce and raised it toward her mouth. "I'm glad we have just the one boy—that's all I can say." She slid the meat between her lips, swallowed it at once, and shook her head. "Incorrigible creatures."

Pitoque knew she wasn't being serious. It had always been

clear that she was besotted with the child. Maxtla was her favorite. How hard it must be for her to see him leave home before the normal time. But there was no choice. He told her that boys were indeed incorrigible. Always had been. Always would be. He turned back to his meal. For a time, they both ate in silence, until Kalatzin reached for her jar of chocolate.

"Now, about Zaachila . . ." she said.

Zaachila. Here was another headache. That night, lying awake in his bed, Pitoque reflected on the girl's situation. It did indeed seem that his daughter had a curse upon her. In any case, the priests had decreed that it was so. Her condition was revealed, they said, by the strange appearance of her eyes. They did not move in their sockets the way the eyes of others did. Up and down—yes. But not from side to side. She had to turn her entire head to take in that which lay on the edge of her vision, a trait that gave her an aloof and even otherworldly air.

Pitoque rather liked this oddity in his daughter. Her eyes had been this way since birth, and it had never been a problem. In all other respects, she was a normal girl and extraordinarily beautiful as well. Pitoque and Kalatzin were both in complete agreement about that. Or they always had been.

"They say it is a curse," Kalatzin had said at dinner that night. She'd swallowed a morsel of tortilla, shaken her head. "They say that no one will marry her in this condition."

"Nonsense," Pitoque had replied. "You have only to look at the girl. What man could possibly wish a better wife?"

"You are forgetting about Raulac?"

"The man was a fool."

"Or Xamtl?"

"A drunk. You said so yourself. We are well rid of him. I can't believe we ever considered him as a potential suitor. We ought to be consulting with the priests on our own account, not on Zaachila's. What kind of parents would marry their daughter off to a doddering old drunk?"

Kalatzin shrugged. Old, he may be. Drunk, certainly. But doddering? He took one look at Zaachila's eyes, and he was on his way. He knew what he saw. "I tell you, the priests are right. The girl is cursed."

Pitoque had let his half-eaten leg of iguana plop back onto his plate, sending up a small spray of pumpkin-seed sauce. He knew—his wife knew—that it was only a matter of time before he gave in. "Fine, then," he had said. "What do you propose?"

"It is not what I propose that matters," she had told him. "This is an affair of the priests."

What the priests had in mind was a series of curing ceremonies aimed at withdrawing from the girl whatever evil spirits had entered her. It looked to be a serious case, however, so the treatment would be arduous and long.

"And expensive, I presume," Pitoque said. He knew the cost might be taken for granted. Where the priests were concerned, all ceremonies were expensive. "I presume I shall be expected to pay for this."

"You are her father," Kalatzin had said. "She is your daughter."

He had picked up his leg of iguana and bitten off a piece. An important business, fatherhood—none more so. Just not very lucrative. "Very well," he had said at last. "Let the cure proceed."

Now, in bed, with his hands clasped behind his head—sleepless again—Pitoque reflected on his daughter's plight and on the belligerence of his son. He decided that the emperor Moctezuma himself could not face greater challenges or dilemmas than he did—he, a mere merchant of Cholula, a father and husband. But he had to muddle through. He shifted onto his side, felt the warmth of his wife's body rise against him, and closed his eyes.

Now if only he could sleep.

The God of Travelers

A year spun by, and all was as it had ever been—except for one change. Now on his travels, Pitoque was accompanied by his son. Maxtla was nearly thirteen now and wore a maguey cloak of his own and walked by his father's side as they roamed the far reaches of the empire—the northern deserts, the jungles of the south, the sweltering coastal plains.

In every village or town they came to, they put their goods on display. Whatever they had, they would exchange for something else. The profits poured in, for always it was possible to find people who craved something they did not have and who were more than willing to part with something that they did.

And so, on their return journeys, Pitoque's porters were always burdened by exotic fare—scallops or snails or tortoises from the sea, or fine woven cotton pieces from the eastern coast, or quetzal feathers from the southern lands of the Maya, or polished turtle shells, or pearls, or amber.

Each time they prepared to set out on another journey, Pitoque practiced his customary rituals, but now he did so in company with Maxtla. Together, they knelt before small images of the fire god and the earth lord and their own patron—Yacateuctli, the god of travelers—and made an offering of turkey heads. They washed and cut their hair, as did Kalatzin and Zaachila, and none of them would cut their hair again until the men returned. When Pitoque and his son departed, they did so quickly, without tears or any show of emotion or even a backward glance. Long years of the wandering life had taught the merchant it was better this way. Just to go and be gone. Besides, it was the custom.

Trudging behind them, the porters carried all manner of valuable goods for trade—lovely dove feathers, pieces of lapis lazuli or jadeite, fine eiderdown blankets, many-colored ribbons, goldwork rings called *matzataztli*, animal pelts, cacao beans, and the most excellent Cholula pottery.

Later, on their return to the central lands, they always stopped in Cholula, for Pitoque preferred to leave the boy there so that he could travel on to Tenochtitlán alone. He still worried that his son might behave rashly in the capital of the Aztecs, that he might say something intemperate or cause some offence. Besides, it was only right that the boy be reunited with his mother and sister.

At the sound of their arrival, Kalatzin and Zaachila leapt up from whatever they were doing, spinning cotton or weaving blankets or grinding corn or shaping tortillas on a metate stone. They gathered their robes and raced outside to greet the returning men.

Almost a year after first setting off with Maxtla at his side, Pitoque and son returned to Cholula once again. As usual, their arrival was met with a great flurry of excitement, with sudden embraces, calls for drinks of chocolate to be served. Tales of the road were begun but left unfinished, to be completed later. The latest gossip of Cholula received a similar treatment—snatches and tidbits of news. Pitoque stretched out his legs. As always, he found it a little strange but also gratifying to be once again at home. Zaachila, he noticed, seemed a little thinner than before, but no less lovely. His wife, by contrast, seemed to have become more voluptuous in his absence. He sensed a stirring of his blood.

Soon, Zaachila and Maxtla went off on their own to exchange stories and whatnot of interest only to themselves. Before long, Pitoque found himself alone with his wife in their sleeping room. They stood apart, both ill at ease after being so long separated from each other. Pitoque shifted his weight from side to side, crossed his arms at his chest, unsure how to proceed. He had always been this way, awkward in matters of the flesh. So, instead he spoke.

"I owe you an apology," he said.

"An apology?" She raised her eyebrows. "What do you mean?"

He meant, he said, how right she had been—how apt this desire of hers to begin their son's apprenticeship before its time, and not only because of that incident involving the temple of Quetzalcoatl. He found the boy good company.

"He's no trouble then?"

Pitoque waggled his head. "I wouldn't say that." Maxtla still harbored a rebellious streak, worrisome in many ways. His hatred of the Aztecs had not diminished at all. There was nothing unusual in the boy's sentiment—hatred of the Aztecs was almost universal. The problem was his son's lack of discretion. At times, Pitoque feared that Maxtla's outbursts might place them both in jeopardy.

"But he's only thirteen," he assured his wife. "It's not so surprising that he is somewhat rash. I'm sure it will work itself out. In fact . . ."

His voice trailed off, for Kalatzin was approaching him, and he could sense the heat rising from her body, a mixture of perfume and a faint, exciting musk.

"In fact?" she repeated.

"Yes," he said. "In fact, I . . ."

"Yes. You?" Kalatzin ran a hand beneath his cloak and began to massage his chest—an uncustomary boldness on her part.

"Yes. I . . ." He meant to say that he had decided to take Maxtla with him this time, in a few days, when he continued on to Tenochtitlán. It had to be done sooner or later, and he was ready to take the risk. He felt there was sufficient understanding between him and his son to avert any untoward consequences. He felt . . . he felt . . .

"Shhhh," whispered his wife. Her hands descended.

"Ah . . ." Pitoque gathered her luxuriant black hair into his hands, breathed in the scent of ocher and copal that drifted from her body, mixed with other, earthier odors, a hint of salt, a trace of loam. He slipped her huipil up over her head, baring her tattooed shoulders, and eased her down onto her knees, where he joined her, the heat rising at his groin. "All," he whispered, "will be well."

Her hands closed around his penis, and she sighed. "I see," she murmured. "I see you have brought proof."

Later, they lay on their backs beside each other, basking in the glow of their lovemaking, each sighing once in a while or reaching over to stroke the other's arm or leg. For a long while, neither spoke. But, eventually, they began to exchange gossip and news. Soon, Kalatzin was describing the progress of their daughter's curing ceremonies. So far, there were no positive consequences to report. Her eyesight was unchanged, and no other suitors had presented themselves. Still, the priests were optimistic. It was simply a question of time.

"And more ceremonies?" said Pitoque.

"And more ceremonies," said his wife.

"Expensive ceremonies."

"She is your daughter. What does it matter if they are

expensive? Would you prefer her to be an old maid, to live out her days alone? Who would pay for that? *You.*"

In the semi-darkness of the evening, Pitoque settled back. He sighed and scratched his chest. In truth, now that he thought of it, the idea of having Zaachila about the place long into his own dotage wasn't such a terrible idea. But he knew it would never please Kalatzin. Besides, there was the matter of grandchildren to consider.

Two days later, Pitoque and Maxtla gathered their porters once again and set out on foot toward the great volcanoes, Popocatépetl and Iztaccíhuatl. Their real destination lay beyond those snow-bound crests. As he had decided earlier, Pitoque meant to take his son to visit the capital of the empire, the principal city of the Aztecs—Tenochtitlán, the greatest city in the world.

He knew how keenly the boy hated the Aztecs and everything associated with them, but Maxtla's attitude was simply too extreme. He failed to consider both sides. Yes, the Aztecs had their faults—huge faults—but they had their virtues, too. It was time for Maxtla to understand the need for a certain balance in his judgment. Pitoque only hoped that he wasn't forcing the issue too soon. The boy was impetuous—there was no denying it. What if he did something foolish in Tenochtitlán?

That was the danger. But Pitoque felt he had taken sufficient precautions. He had gone to the temple of Quetzalcoatl in Cholula. He had made an offering of turkeys and had waited for a sign. On his way home that day, a rainbow had formed over the horizon to the northwest, shimmering against the floating outline of Popocatépetl, pointing in the direction of Tenochtitlán. Perhaps the gods had not abandoned him, after all. They spoke in rainbows—even to him, who had gravely sinned.

Now, as he and Maxtla tramped across the grasslands that led to the high volcanoes, Pitoque tried to prepare his son for what would confront them on the other side, when they descended into the Valley of Anáhuac toward Tenochtitlán. Before them, they would see a city of unbelievable splendor, constructed upon islands and surrounded by the sprawling and briny waters of Lake Texcoco, glimmering under a faultless sky. In reality, there were two cities—Tenochtitlán itself and its sister city, Tlatelolco, built upon the northern portion of the same island. They were linked to the mainland by a network of broad causeways built across the water. All the year around, these cities were decorated by the iridescent blossoms of flowering trees, the green pillars of cypresses, and the proud stone towers of sacred pyramids.

As the pair walked northward, and as old Toc attended to the porters behind them, Pitoque declaimed to his son upon the subject of Tenochtitlán and the people who dwelled there.

First, what sort of lives did these people live? Enviable lives, on the whole—at least, those who were nobles or freemen. They visited their temples to conduct their religious observances. They attended to their domestic affairs. When not otherwise occupied, they amused themselves by drinking pulque or consuming hallucinogenic mushrooms. They gathered in the many stadiums of the city to watch ball games that were notorious for their speed and drama. Later, they might pay visits to one or another of the city's innumerable houses of joy, where pleasure girls from vassal tribes were waiting to entertain them. They—

"Pleasure girls?" said Maxtla. "Entertain them? How?"

Pitoque halted. He realized he had got a bit carried away with his theme. He cleared his throat and waved his hand. "I mean to say, the women dance. They are very adept at this . . . *dancing*. It is remarkable to see."

"May we visit such a place?"

"Well, perhaps. But I expect our schedule will prove too hectic. Maybe another time. Now, where was I?"

"The nobles. How they live."

"Yes. Of course." Pitoque continued with his account. He described how the rich of Tenochtitlán swanned about in finely embroidered cotton cloaks knotted at the shoulder. They wore sandals encrusted with precious stones. Some carried flowers in their free hands, which they periodically pressed to their nostrils.

"Why?" said Maxtla; "To block out the stench of the place? I Imagine the city must stink to an intolerable degree."

"Not really," said Pitoque. "In truth, quite the opposite. Tenochtitlán is actually very clean."

It was true. From the earliest hours of the morning, laborers were hard at work sweeping the streets and the grounds of the plazas. Other workers were charged with collecting human waste, which they carried by boat out onto the lake to be recycled as fertilizer for the *chinampas*. On these large float-ing gardens, anchored in the shallows of the lake, all manner of vegetables and fruits were grown. They were like huge, liv-ing emeralds adrift upon the water. Indeed, the entire city was bejeweled, a sort of paradise. It had a spacious air, a feeling of order and decorum. It was dissected by canals, festooned with flowers. Food was varied and plentiful. Sweet water tumbled down in distant mountain streams, to be scooped up and car-ried to Tenochtitlán by great stone aqueducts. True, the people suffered diseases. But the Aztecs had become adept at find-ing cures. Their scientists devoted themselves to the study of plants and their medicinal properties. They maintained elabo-rate botanical gardens, containing every species of flora that grew in the empire.

The people of Tenochtitlán, Pitoque said, did indeed lead remarkable lives. The wealthier neighborhoods were filled with grand two-story houses that contained rambling inte-rior courtyards and verdant gardens. Aztecs of more modest means dwelled in smaller structures built of adobe brick. The poorest residents of the city had small huts constructed of mud slapped onto shafts of bamboo.

"Ugh," said Maxtla. "Like animals."

"It is not so different in Cholula. Not everyone is as fortu-nate as you."

Pitoque continued to sing the praises of the city—a per-formance aimed more at impressing Maxtla with the capital's benign aspects than with expressing his own sentiments, which were ambivalent. Yes, he labored in the service of the Aztecs, but he did not love them. Eventually, Maxtla asked the question that called out to be asked, for the boy was no fool.

"How," he said, "do the Aztecs pay for this wonderful existence?"

Here, of course, was a ticklish problem. Pitoque conceded that their main source of wealth was the tribute the Aztecs received from hundreds of vassal cities, such as Cholula. The tribute took countless different forms. All sorts of commodities were supplied to the Aztecs, whose armies were by far the most powerful in the empire. In honor of their authority, they received food to eat, clothes to wear, furniture to sit upon, riches to store in hidden vaults.

"And people to kill?" said Maxtla, who knew the answer already, as well as anyone.

Pitoque took a deep breath. It was impossible to deny. To nourish their gods, the Aztecs also demanded that human beings be paid as tribute. Each year, along with other vassal cities, Cholula was required to supply its share. To acquire still more sacrificial victims, the Aztecs waged periodic military campaigns, which they referred to as their Flowery Wars. All prisoners captured were marched back to Tenochtitlán, where they were kept in wooden cages near to the temples.

The temples, it had to be admitted, were factories of blood. For the Aztecs, human sacrifice was a serious and almost unrelenting business—the engine that kept the cosmos in motion. Day after day, the temple floors ran with blood and viscera. Bodies tumbled one after another down the precipitous steps of the pyramids, to be bundled away by old men whose occupation it was to chop the cadavers up and distribute the flesh—some to the families of the warriors, some to the royal aviaries and menageries, perhaps a morsel or two for the old men themselves. Whatever remained of the sacrificial victims, once all these obligations had been met, would usually be burned—although the skulls and other bones were often preserved as souvenirs. Pitoque had seen all these horrors himself. They were all true.

"I see," said Maxtla, who entertained no illusions on this matter. "How utterly delightful. Your Aztecs are butchers on top of everything else."

Pitoque remained silent. What could he say? More than anything else, it was this system of tribute, payable in human lives, that tormented him when he sought to justify in his own mind the pact he had made with the Aztecs. And yet, what would be gained if he were to do otherwise, if he were to refuse these commissions he received from the master functionary? He would lose his livelihood, possibly his life, and to no purpose. Nothing would change. Just as many victims would be put to death.

He let out a sigh and shook his head, more for his own benefit than for Maxtla's. In silence, they both continued to climb. Soon they reached the summit of the col between Popocatépetl and Iztaccíhuatl, where the cold air blew and hawks swerved on the wind. Now they would climb down into the green Valley of Anáhuac, down toward the capital of the Aztecs, the greatest city in the world.

Maxtla drew his maguey robe more tightly around him, on account of the chill. "I can hardly wait," he said.

Climb and You Will See

Azotl had an odd way of showing his affection for youngsters. "Ah, what a plump little fellow," he said when he was first introduced to Pitoque's son. He tugged at the flesh of Maxtla's cheek and smacked his lips. "A little pumpkin sauce, a few chili peppers, and what do you know—hot, stewed fricassée of Cholulan! The perfect repast. Mmm. Mmm."

Maxtla shook himself free and took a large step backwards. He didn't say a word, but simply glared up at this great hummock of a man, who smirked back at him with large, moist lips and a single eye. He knew who Azotl was. The tlillancalqui. Keeper of the House of Darkness. As evil a man as existed.

Pitoque noticed his son's smoldering expression and wondered what bothered the boy—being treated as a child or being inspected by an Aztec, with a view to digestion. Perhaps both.

Azotl seemed to realize his attempt at a joke had gone badly. He didn't risk compounding the offence, but instead summoned an aide and instructed him to take Maxtla off and find him something to eat. "I imagine you must be hungry. To the best of my recollection, young boys always are."

Once Maxtla had departed, Azotl settled himself at his working table and indicated that Pitoque might be seated as well.

"Your arrival is well timed," he said. "In fact, extremely so." He reached up to rub his several chins. "To make a long story short, we have received additional reports from the eastern coast."

Pitoque closed his eyes briefly, uncertain what he felt. "Yes?" he said.

"It seems that these floating mountains have made a return appearance."

"Indeed?" The year 1-Reed was still months away—and now these creatures had come back? For what purpose? Only now did Pitoque realize to what extent he had persuaded himself that his dread of Quetzalcoatl's return was over, that these floating towers, these phantasms, would never come back. He gazed at Azotl.

The master functionary reached for a bowl filled with various kinds of fruit. He withdrew a sweet sapota and tossed it to Pitoque.

The *pochteca* caught the fruit and held it at a distance, as though it were something poisonous.

"It won't harm you. Eat." Azotl chose a large apple for himself. He took a large bite and smiled at Pitoque. Through a crunching of apple flesh, he said, "Indeed. It is all quite worrying. I shouldn't tell you this, but Moctezuma is greatly troubled by it all. I have never seen him so agitated. He had hoped that this business with floating mountains was over. But now he seems to think you may be right, after all."

Pitoque lifted his head. "I?"

"That's right. You. Pitoque, merchant of Cholula." Azotl

gulped down whole what remained of his apple—core, seeds, and all. He hauled himself to his feet and trudged to the window overlooking an interior courtyard, where underlings hurried back and forth against a backdrop of stone walls and green shrubs. Parrots bickered in their cages. He turned and looked at Pitoque with his one good eye. "I must say, this theory of yours about Quetzalcoatl's return—it didn't win much favor when I broached it the first time around. Indeed, I felt obliged to disown the idea. I was forced to attribute it entirely to you. So now I can hardly reclaim it. I'm afraid it is yours for eternity." The master functionary grimaced. "In any case, Moctezuma now believes your theory. He has consulted his own gods. He has read the stars. And now these new reports—they have practically convinced him that it must be as you say." Azotl returned to his working table and slumped into his chair. He crossed his flabby arms and leaned across the wooden surface toward Pitoque. "What do you think these latest reports mean?"

Pitoque could only shake his head and make a blank expression. What did he think? Just now, he was having trouble thinking anything at all. Imagine—his own name being mentioned in the presence of the lord Moctezuma. The idea was astonishing to contemplate. He found it impossible to say a word.

"I asked you a question," said Azotl. "What do you make of these reports? Speak up."

Pitoque swallowed. He decided to say what he now thought—that the reappearance of these creatures must be another preparation for the eventual return of Quetzalcoatl, another confirmation of the ancient prophecies. It confirmed the theory he had advanced a year earlier. It proved what he believed. And yet the mere thought made him tremble with foreboding. He ran the back of one hand across his brow, and it came away damp with sweat.

But Azotl seemed pleased. He pressed the palms of both hands against the surface of his table and smiled. "Good," he said. "That will do very well. At least I shall have something to contribute when I go before Moctezuma. Let us see what the emperor says."

The following morning, Pitoque was summoned to appear before the master functionary once again. At the merchant's entrance, Azotl looked up and pushed aside a scroll he had been studying. He said, "You will return to the coast."

The master functionary had gone before Moctezuma and gathered elders of the imperial state. The emperor had issued specific instructions that Pitoque, this merchant of Cholula, be dispatched to the eastern coast to investigate these latest reports. "He wants you to leave at once, without delay."

To Pitoque's dismay, the order made sense. After all, Quetzalcoatl was his city's patron deity. Cholula was the center of a cult devoted to the feathered serpent, a cult that found adherents throughout the empire and beyond. In Cholula, the god's glory shone most brightly.

Therefore, send a Cholulan.

Now Pitoque could only nod and defer and mutter his agreement. "Yes," he said. "I will return to the coast."

"And bring back concrete information."

"Yes. Concrete information."

"Not secondhand reports. Get a look at these beings yourself."

"Yes. I will look at them myself."

"Talk to them, if you can."

Pitoque said that he would.

"Find out what they want, who they are, where they come from. Find out what they are doing here."

"Yes. I will." But all the time, he was thinking, *Why me? Why me?* He felt as though some invisible force were propelling him into a confrontation with these creatures—he, Pitoque of Cholula. He had a sudden, dreadful image of the sea swelling up, turning into a great, vicious maw and swallowing him whole. He felt his past rise around him like a wall of angry water, crashing down, drawing him under, drowning him.

"Good," said Azotl. "You are agreed, then?"

If he could have, Pitoque would have renounced this mission and walked away. He would have abandoned this building, this city, and never returned. But the emperor Moctezuma, the most powerful man in the world, had declared that he must go. He now found himself in the same position as the elders of Cholula, caught between his fear of the Aztecs and his terror of the gods. He swallowed down a salty trickle of bile, like a trace of sea water in his throat, and inclined his head.

"I hear," he said, "and I obey."

✝

Before his departure, Pitoque was summoned once more to appear before the master functionary. This time, they met in a garden overlooking the silver waters of Lake Texcoco. Azotl arrived aboard a simple-looking palanquin made of wood with curtains of plain cotton, borne by six slaves. With some difficulty, the carriers set the litter down, and Azotl struggled out. He waddled over to Pitoque, who was waiting on the grass near some flowering shrubs.

"I would have walked," Azotl said, "except I find that walking is unsuited to my character. But I will make an exception now." He motioned to Pitoque and led him down a gentle slope toward the lake. "Come. Let us speak."

Pitoque walked alongside the master functionary and waited to hear what the man would say. He had left Maxtla behind at their small lodging.

Azotl clasped his hands behind his back. "About this affair of the temple . . ."

Pitoque paled. "The temple?" he said. Sweat began to prickle at his brow.

Azotl nodded. "The damage to the temple in Cholula. I understand your son got himself into some trouble a while back. Desecrated the temple of Quetzalcoatl, unless I'm mistaken."

Pitoque couldn't believe what he was hearing.

"I understand it took some quick work on your part—and not a little expense—to set the matter right."

Pitoque conceded that this was so. He was astonished at the quality and extent of Azotl's information. Evidently, the master functionary had spies practicing espionage on his spies.

The Aztec chuckled. "Nothing to be alarmed about," he said. "I like to keep myself informed, that's all. These are dangerous times, as you know. A man can't be too careful." He explained that he had kept the matter quiet. The story had not gone beyond his own chambers. Pitoque did not need to be alarmed on that account. "And I commend you. You handled the situation very well, from what I hear. Spilled a few state secrets, of course, but—"

"I know. I admit it. I'm sorry. But I—"

"But you had no choice. Of course you didn't. Your son's life, after all. You did what you had to do. I understand."

Pitoque frowned, unsure what Azotl was implying. "Thank you," he said.

"There's nothing to thank me for. I bring the matter up now only because there has been a complication."

They had reached the lake's edge, and the master functionary reached out to balance himself against a wooden railing that ran along a clutter of rocks. The waters lapped and swam below. Azotl was breathing heavily from the exertion of walking, but he continued to speak, pausing now and then to fill and empty his lungs.

It would be best, he told Pitoque, if Maxtla did not make this trek to the coast with his father. If these alien creatures were indeed emissaries of Quetzalcoatl, they might well take a dim view of being reconnoitered by someone who had defiled their lord's temple, even if the culprit was only a boy.

"Do you see my reasoning?" he said. "As I say, we have to be careful. I suggest you leave the boy here, under my protection.

Alternatively, you may drop him off in Cholula on your way. It's your decision. For my part, I would be delighted to watch over the child in your absence. I wish I could give you my word not to eat him, but as you know, I have made such promises before, with mediocre results." He patted his belly. "Where my stomach is concerned, I fear my word is capricious."

In fact, Pitoque didn't like to leave the boy alone among the Aztecs. There was no telling what mischief he might get up to. He declined the invitation on his son's behalf.

"Very well," Azotl said. "But you mustn't take him with you to the coast. Other arrangements must be made."

Pitoque assured him they would. He said he would leave Maxtla in Cholula with the boy's mother and would proceed to the coast alone.

Azotl agreed. He turned, and began to trudge back up through the grass. But already his litter-bearers were hurrying down to meet him. It seemed that his distaste for walking was fairly well known.

Pitoque's decision had the additional benefit of improving his relations with Maxtla, who repeated his gratitude at least half a dozen times during the trek south to Cholula. The boy promised that he would take good care of Kalatzin and Zaachila, and avoid any contact with Nahuauc or his other dubious friends. Pitoque felt reasonably sure he could trust his son, who was deeply grateful not to have been left behind in Tenochtitlán as a ward of the master functionary.

Pitoque spent one night in Cholula and was ready to leave the following morning, which fortunately was a propitious day for travel. Yacateuctli, the merchants' god, had appeared to him in a dream and told him so. Sure enough, as the morning light crept across the pale earth, the smoke of cooking fires rose straight into the sky—a good sign. It was bad luck to begin a journey on a windy day.

As always, Pitoque and his family said their goodbyes quickly, and then he departed without looking back. Soon he was well on his way, with Toc at his side, both of them trailed by the usual company of porters. Now, unexpectedly, a cool wind kicked up and swept across the high grasslands, whistling through the occasional oak thickets and the scattered silhouettes of cacti.

Pitoque felt the wind beat against him and gave thanks that he was not accompanied by his son. Yet his own crime against Quetzalcoatl weighed on him. These emissaries of the gods, if that was what they were—surely they would require him to answer for his sins. He felt a tremor in his chest. What punishment would they inflict? Was it for this reason they had come?

He would soon find out.

"Come Toc," he said. "We must make better time."

Followed by his porters—all of them laden with Cholulan pottery and other fine goods—he and the old man increased their pace.

They hiked across the lofty plains in the shadows of the great volcanoes. They wound through narrow mountain passes and picked their way down the eastern wall of the central highlands. They slouched through the misty drizzle called the chipi-chipi, down toward the coastal plain and the lowland heat, down toward the end of the world, where strange and sacred towers roamed upon the sea.

Pitoque caught his first glimpse of these exotic creatures from a considerable distance. Near a settlement called Cempoala, several Totonac people guided him to a densely forested hillside that overlooked a half-moon bay. They stopped at the base of a cottonwood tree, a gnarled but sturdy-looking growth. One of his companions pointed up.

"Climb," he said. "Climb and you will see."

Pitoque did so at once and soon found himself peering out through emerald leaves and dark branches. His gaze fell upon a scene so perplexing and miraculous that at once his heartbeat quickened, and he had to tighten his grip or fall from his perch.

Out on the bay stood one of the floating towers. To his mind, the structure looked more like a great wooden palace, but a palace that undoubtedly had the ability to ride upon the water. It was inhabited by creatures who milled about, gathered and parted, engaged in some business with ropes. Even from a distance, he could tell that they were indeed light of skin and thickly bearded. They didn't look like monkeys to him. They looked like men, but coarse and ungainly men, with chests that seemed too large for the rest of their bodies. He thought of large, hairy beetles.

Soon he saw a group of these beings depart their floating house by means of a small boat. They paddled about for a time, casting lines and nets over the sides of their craft, and it was apparent to Pitoque that they were fishing. Some had on jackets of red; others wore gray or green. On their heads, they sported red kerchiefs or scarlet bonnets. They betrayed no hint of knowing that they were watched. Silent, Pitoque climbed down from the tree. He could hardly speak, and his knees shook. With his own eyes he had seen the *teules*. The gods.

What else could these creatures be?

The Mansion of the Gods

Pitoque resolved to observe these gods at closer quarters, and he proceeded by surreptitious means. As a first step, he arranged to have a gift of figs laid out on the shore near the floating palace. He made sure it was conspicuously placed. Next, he retreated with Toc and several of his porters and a few local men, so that they could observe the results without fear of detection. The bearded ones soon came ashore aboard their small boat and just as quickly withdrew, taking the figs.

On the following day, he put out a more elaborate offering, an entire meal—roast fowl and slabs of boar, a stew of salamander and eel, sapota fruit, and even drinks of chocolate, all obtained from local residents at no small expense. With his companions, Pitoque settled down once again to wait. They huddled a short distance away, hidden by bushes and a sandy hillock. Soon enough, a few of the gods clambered up onto the shore again and promptly settled down to eat, making a great deal of noise and gesticulating wildly. They cast bones into the air, some of which landed not far from Pitoque's feet where he hunched with the others behind a sea grape bush. He was in a turmoil. The master functionary had been explicit in his instructions. *Bring back concrete information. Not second-hand reports. Get a look at these beings yourself. Talk to them, if you can. Find out what they want, who they are, where they come from. Find out what they are doing here.*

At the time, Pitoque had merely nodded, to show he understood. If knowledge was required, then knowledge he would obtain. But now, while these strangely undignified deities were having target practice with the sapota fruit just a few feet away, it was difficult for him to be businesslike or self-assured. His heart pounded in his chest, and beads of sweat sprouted upon his brow and dribbled down his cheeks. What should he do? Simply climb to his feet and walk over there and introduce himself? What would the response be? They might very well kill him. Who could possibly say what these creatures might do?

Still, there was no choice. Either he risked a calamity out here on the eastern coast or he faced certain disaster on his return to Tenochtitlán. Pitoque leaned to one side. "Toc," he whispered. "I'm going out there."

"Shall I come with you, master?" The question was not forcefully expressed. "On the other hand, I might be more use-ful here."

"Yes. You stay here. If anything goes wrong, you . . . Well, I'm not sure what you—"

"I'll inform the family, sir. I'll carry the news to Tenochtitlán."

Pitoque frowned. He'd been hoping for more active intervention on the old fellow's part, but he could see that such an offer was probably too much to expect. No sense in both of them being carried off and killed. "Agreed," he said. "Wish me well."

He raised himself to his feet, slapped the sand from his cloak, and made his way through the waxy-leaved sea grape trees and then over a sandy hummock. With each step, he thought his head would explode. It is one thing to see the gods. It is another to pay them a visit. He felt the blood thudding at his temples like the feet of a hundred warriors.

As soon as they saw him—stepping into their midst without any warning at all—the strangers reeled back. They crawled about on all fours like gigantic insects and looked ready to run away. But soon they recovered a little of their composure. They didn't try to escape. Instead, they climbed to their feet and started to brush away the remains of food from their beards and clothing.

Pitoque raised his arms. "Welcome, honored friends," he said. "I am sorry to interrupt your meal, which I hope has been to your taste, poor fare though it may be. Please be assured that I come in peace." Here he gave a low bow. "In all humility, I wish to ask a question or two. What manner of beings are you? From where have you come? What is your purpose here?" He stood back and crossed his arms, an indication that they might now speak.

They said nothing, not a word. They just stared at him, wiping their hands on their clothing. One turned sideways, coughed, and spat.

Pitoque tried again. "Your names," he said. "Let us begin with that. Mine is Pitoque, a merchant of Cholula."

Still nothing.

"Cholula," he repeated. "Where stands the great temple of Quetzalcoatl, honored deity. Soon may he return."

The strangers traded more glances, more shrugs.

Pitoque decided he had better own up to his failings, just in case. "Concerning that unfortunate incident at the temple, involving my son—I am most heartily sorry. I have, you may be interested to know, made complete restitution. All has been repaired. You have my word. Now, may I be granted the honor of knowing your names?"

Nothing. Nothing at all. Just an awkward silence.

While he waited for a reply, Pitoque took stock of the visitors. At first, it was their height that most impressed him. Next, the quantity of their facial hair. Surely no mortal could be at once so tall and so well supplied with whiskers. Now one of them reached down and scratched at his groin. At this point, Pitoque became aware of something he had not noticed at first. But he did so now and found that it was almost overpowering. A stench. An appalling stench that emanated from these creatures and now seemed to fill the air, all but stopping up his nose. Ugh, it was a terrible reek. His eyes began to water, and he found it difficult to breathe. He remembered that he had been warned about their odor, but no warning was quite equal to the reality.

Oh, they stank.

"Forgive me," he said. He dabbed at his eyes with the hem of his cloak and began to cough. "Very sorry. I seem to have got something in my eyes. Some sand, I think. Please, excuse me."

Still, they said nothing.

Pitoque hardened himself against the smell—which was unlike anything he had ever experienced, impossible to describe—and squared his shoulders. "About that night," he said. He meant the episode far to the south, in the lands of the Maya, the butchering of those girls. "I can offer no excuse for my behavior. I failed to honor my duty as a man and as a servant of the great lord Quetzalcoatl, king among gods. May his name flourish forever. I can only offer my most profound apologies and throw myself upon your mercy." He fell to his knees, hung his head, and waited for the judgment that surely now would come.

But it didn't. These creatures or gods or whatever they were—they simply stood their ground, shifting their weight from one foot to the other, occasionally turning aside to spit. They responded to nothing he said. Slowly, the truth dawned on him. They didn't understand. He decided to try a different language, just in case. He spoke to them in several different tongues—he had mastered seven—but the results were the same. Nothing. Soon the newcomers seemed to grow bored with his efforts. They began to chatter to one another in a language that had the sound of *cacahuate* shells being crunched between their teeth. Utterly incomprehensible.

Despite these linguistic problems, Pitoque felt himself growing bolder. They hadn't killed him yet, so maybe there was hope. He decided to try communicating with the visitors by means of signs. He took a deep breath, rose to his feet, and proceeded to indicate that he wished to accompany them onto their floating palace. He further sought to convey the idea that he had a fine stock of dishes to trade. Surely even gods might be in want of dishes, especially such fine pieces as these, for the handiwork of Cholula was renowned throughout the empire. He let his hands drop to his sides and waited, a little unsure about how clearly he had managed to express himself, particularly concerning the exceptional value of his plates.

But it seemed that the gist of his message had been more or less understood. The visitors nodded, gathered up what remained of the food, and began to march down to their little wooden landing craft. When at first Pitoque did not follow them, they turned back and motioned for him to come. By this time, old Toc and a few of the locals had wandered out into the open to stand by Pitoque's side.

The merchant turned to his companions. "Shall we go together to join them on their floating palace?" he asked. "Shall we all visit the mansion of the gods?"

It seemed the answer was yes. Curiosity had replaced fear, now that Pitoque had shown that one could approach these strangers without running an immediate risk of death. Now everyone was willing to be as bold as he. The entire party— Pitoque, Toc, and four local men—marched together across the gray sand to join the emissaries of the feathered serpent, if that was what they were. For his part, Pitoque was a little disappointed by his first encounter with these creatures, by their shoddy manners, their disreputable appearance, and their alarming stench. Nonetheless, he was inclined to believe that they were gods—diseased gods, perhaps, gods a little down on their luck, but gods all the same.

If not gods, what on earth could they be?

Pitoque soon found himself being rowed along with the others across the glassy bay. Overhead, the sun smoldered through a dark canopy of clouds, and gulls circled, swooped, swerved away. Before long, the landing craft nosed against the wall of this great floating palace, and by means of a netting of ropes Pitoque and his companions climbed up onto what seemed to be the palace's roof. Like huge trees, wooden pillars swayed above them, interspersed by horizontal branches and connected by a tracery of cords. Some of these creatures, even now scrambling about upon the high reaches of these pillars, did indeed look like monkeys, although considerably larger.

Dozens more of the beings gathered atop the mansion's root; chattering among themselves in their indecipherable tongue and pointing at Pitoque and the others. Several of them stepped forward, those who seemed to be the senior members of this group. They were dressed in an elaborate fashion—colored tunics and short skirts, with leggings that clung to their lower limbs. All of them were thickly bearded and white of skin. Assembled like this, in so large a number, they gave off a stink that was practically overpowering, hardly to be endured. But out of duty to the royal court of Tenochtitlán, Pitoque forced himself to bear it. Toc and the others must also have discovered internal resources of their own—beliefs or principles that permitted them to withstand this unimaginable reek.

As before, it was impossible to converse by normal means. Pitoque had already exhausted all the languages at his command without arousing a single sign of comprehension among these creatures, and nothing they said made the slightest sense to him. They settled upon the use of physical gestures, assisted by whatever props came to hand. These included some very impressive pictures that the visitors brought out and passed around. Many depicted an emaciated individual dangling from some sort of wooden device, with blood dribbling from his hands and feet. He seemed to be in a very poor state. Pitoque gazed long and hard at these images, and slowly the truth revealed itself.

Quetzalcoatl. These must be likenesses of Quetzalcoatl. It all fit. The beard. The whiteness of skin. Besides, the fellow wore some sort of crown upon his head, denoting a king.

Pitoque looked up and spoke to the leaders of these beings. "Quetzalcoatl?" he asked. He pointed at the figure on the wooden frame. "This is Quetzalcoatl?"

They exchanged glances and said something that sounded like Haysoos Creestoh. Haysoos Creestoh. Pitoque chewed his lip for a while and then sighed. Maybe that was close enough. In part, he felt excited by his discovery, but he was also troubled. Look at the poor fellow, hanging on this wooden cross, bleeding from his hands and feet as well as from his head, where the crown seemed to be far too tight. Clearly, Quetzalcoatl was in a bad condition. Perhaps this was why these beings had come—to alert the people hereabouts that their god was in difficult straits. Pray for him. Pray. Pray.

Pitoque made a solemn bow and indicated that he wished to take possession of one of these pictures, which the visitors permitted him to do. First, however, they required him to hand over the one gold bracelet he wore on his right wrist, as a form of exchange.

Now the strangers seemed to lose all interest in the figure on the cross. Instead, they showed Pitoque some small artifacts of gold that were in their possession. By means of signs, they communicated the idea that they wished to acquire more. Did he happen to know of places where gold might be obtained? Would he guide them there?

Pitoque made a show of great sadness, for he was in no position to oblige these emissaries of Quetzalcoatl. He cursed himself for not having brought along a supply of gold. It seemed to him now that his suspicions had been right, that the stuff must indeed have some medicinal property for these beings. No doubt they wished to obtain a quantity of it in order to minister to the distress that so evidently afflicted their lord Quetzalcoatl, where he bled upon his wooden resting place. But Pitoque carried no supplies of gold—apart from that one bracelet, of course, and the few pellets he kept in his purse. Moreover, he doubted whether many sources of gold remained. It was not common in these parts. The Aztecs had stolen it all.

Instead of gold, he produced some samples of the finest Cholulan pottery, which Toc had carried with him in a maguey sack. Pitoque indicated by hand gestures that he was willing to trade the plates. He would surrender them, if something were given him in return. A bargain was soon struck, and Pitoque acquired a half-dozen bright red stones that shimmered in the light. Rubies, he took them to be.

After this barter, the two sides seemed to exhaust the topics of conversation that they could easily conduct by hand signs and pictures. Pitoque indicated that he and his companions were ready to depart. He had worried about how this news might be received, but his hosts made no objection—with one proviso. They let it be known that they wished at least one of the men to remain. For his own part, Pitoque felt compelled to demur, as did Toc and all but one of their Totonac companions.

The man willing to stay was named Melchior—a gallant fellow, evidently possessed of an unusually adventurous spirit, although perhaps not the keenest of minds. He seemed delighted to accept the proposal. He explained to Pitoque that he was burdened at home by a shrewish wife, who had lately begun to wear on him intolerably. He believed that an extended stay aboard this floating palace might be a means of achieving two purposes at once—a relief from his travails at home, combined with a chance for new experiences. To think that he would bask in the company of the gods!

"I shall happily remain here," he said. "Who knows? I may even learn to communicate in their language."

Pitoque had his doubts. Still, as it seemed the man genuinely wanted to stay, and as there was no choice but to leave *someone*, he reluctantly agreed. He took Melchior by the shoulders and embraced him warmly. "Farewell, my friend," he said. "You are a brave man, and you shall be rewarded either in this life or in another."

It was time to leave. Pitoque, Toc, and the three others climbed down the webbing of ropes and settled themselves again in the little landing craft. They were rowed ashore and deposited on the beach, none the worse for having spent the most remarkable afternoon that any of them had ever known.

They waved goodbye to the gods and trudged back up the strip of sand toward the long bank of tatty grass and sea grapes. Pitoque weighed the day's events in his mind. He felt that he had done a respectable job under difficult circumstances. True, he hadn't managed to elicit a great deal of information from these creatures—neither their names nor their intentions. But he could blame that failure on the difficulty of tongues. What he had confirmed was that they came on behalf of Quetzalcoatl, and he had the picture to prove it. This would certainly please Azotl. It would also impress Maxtla. What his account would mean to the great lord Moctezuma . . . well, who could say? For his own part, he felt enormous relief. He had survived.

They reached the bank and turned to make their way back along the shore in the direction of Cempoala. Pitoque let out a sigh and felt another flood of relief wash over him, like a shower of cool water.

"There we are, Toc," he said. He patted the old fellow on the back. "We have consorted with gods today. We will have much to tell our grandchildren, eh?"

Toc looked up and smiled. Unlike his master, he was a grandfather many times over.

The Emperor of the World

Azotl set the picture down on his desk. He pressed his lips together and grunted in approval. "Excellent craftsmanship," he said. He evidently meant the artwork. He lit a long-stemmed pipe, and an aroma of tobacco and ambergris swirled through the room. "More realistic than our images."

"Well, they are gods," said Pitoque. He was by now all but certain of it. "Superior beings, superior art. One would expect it."

"I suppose that's so." Azotl squinted through a cloud of smoke. He tilted his great head. "You're sure about this Quetzalcoatl theory of yours? You've no doubts at all?"

Pitoque bridled. He pointed at the picture of the man on the cross. "You can see for yourself," he said.

"The drawing is certainly persuasive," he said. "Still, I'm simply trying to sort this matter out. Frankly, I wouldn't know Quetzalcoatl if he marched up and tapped me on the shoulder, unlikely as that might be. He's *your* god."

"He's *everybody's* god. This entire empire used to be his."

"Yes. Yes. I've heard the legend."

"It's not a legend. It's historical truth."

"Yes. Well. Be that as it may . . ." Azotl set down his pipe and picked up the picture, scrutinized it for a time with his one good eye. He hauled himself to his feet. "Here is what I will do. I'll consult with some of my colleagues, maybe even find out what the priests think. Then we'll have a better idea how Moctezuma might react to this news."

Pitoque thought he understood what Azotl meant to do. The master functionary had not been appointed to his post by accident or a trick of fate. He had reached his position by intrigue and cunning. Now, with the fate of the empire in the balance, he wanted to avoid a costly blunder—one costly to himself. If Pitoque's interpretation of events turned out to be well received, he wanted to share in the credit. If badly received, he wanted to shirk the blame.

"Wait for me here," said Azotl. "I won't be too long. Make yourself comfortable. Do you smoke?"

Pitoque shook his head. "No, thank you."

"A drink of chocolate then?"

"That would be most welcome. I've had nothing but water to drink for days, and most of that fetid."

"You had only to ask." The master functionary clapped his hands and called for an aide, who quickly appeared. "Ah, Xintal," said Azotl. "There you are. Please fetch our guest a drink of chocolate, would you? And maybe something to eat. Some of those ants' larvae dumplings?" He glanced at Pitoque, raised his eyebrows. "You are partial to ants' larvae?"

"Yes. Of course."

"Good, good. Enjoy your refreshments, then. Wait for me here." The master functionary lumbered out of the room with the picture of the suffering god clutched against his robe.

Azotl returned an hour later with dramatic news. It had been decided that Pitoque should present his report directly to the emperor himself. Already, Moctezuma's afternoon schedule had been completely revised to accommodate the meeting.

Pitoque felt his blood begin to race. "When?"

"Just as I said. Today. Immediately."

Pitoque protested that he was hardly dressed for such an occasion. He was still decked out as a simple trader. Azotl agreed that he should change his clothes. Robes of cotton would be more suitable, certainly. He should probably bathe and perfume himself as well.

Pitoque attended to these matters and before long found himself being hurried to the House of the Eagle Knights, a great assembly hall used for meetings of the tlatoacan, the supreme council that gathered only for affairs of the highest importance. Azotl told him that all the leading statesmen and ministers of the Triple Alliance—the Aztecs and their allies in the nearby cities of Tacuba and Texcoco—had assembled and were waiting inside.

The master functionary led Pitoque to the entrance. "Remember," he said, "make your obeisances as you approach the emperor—and don't look him in the eyes." To do so would be a sign of disrespect.

"Where should I look, then?" The problem had never occurred to Pitoque before.

Azotl smiled. "His feet? That's what I do. Try that."

Pitoque nodded, but in fact he could hardly listen to what was being said. To think that he, a mere merchant of Cholula, would soon find himself in the company of the emperor of the Aztecs.

Dazed, he followed a pace or two behind as the master functionary waddled through several antechambers, all paneled in sweet-smelling cedar and dotted with terra-cotta figurines. They proceeded out through a courtyard covered by an awning of woven cotton, and thence along a corridor giving onto a great hall. The emperor and his courtiers had just finished eating their luncheon, judging by the procession of servants parading past, bearing wonderful dishes of every description. Pitoque saw frogs with green chilies, baked pigeons with toasted corn, succulent stewed duck, gophers in tomato sauce, prickly-pear cactus with fish eggs, tadpoles, and newts in a corn porridge, and much more besides. It had obviously been an enormous feast.

His mouth watered at the sight, and still the servants filed past. He saw slabs of roasted turkey garnished with coriander, and whole sides of wild boar, boiled heads of deer, and singed flanks of dog slathered in onions and peppers, not to mention many platters of fruits and vegetables—yucca and okra, apples and sapota fruit—and beeswax and honey and rich chocolate cakes. The odors seemed to twist and spiral through the room, like the undulating breasts and loins of a dozen imagined pleasure girls. Little of the food had been touched.

"You may go in now," Azotl said, and Pitoque felt a large, meaty hand on his shoulder, prodding him forward.

In those brief instants, as he stepped into the inner sanctum of the Aztec empire, Pitoque felt his mind spinning beyond his control. Overwhelmed by the import of this moment, his brain seemed suddenly to shatter, to overflow with a flood of facts and memories—all he knew or remembered about these people, these Aztecs, who now governed most of the world. The knowledge welled up in him, from his days in school, the instruction of his father, the studies he had undertaken on his own. To understand the Aztecs was to understand the world.

True, they were not the first people to have established a great empire in these parts. Legends told of other powerful dynasties in neighboring lands—the Mayas, the Olmecs. Both had fallen into decline, but not before their people made extraordinary advances in astronomy, mathematics, the arts. Pitoque had studied these subjects in his youth and knew that it was the Maya who had developed an annual calendar based on a cycle of three hundred and sixty-five days in a year. They had also discovered the zero and explored its uses. With the hieroglyphic system of writing they had devised they recorded their ideas and beliefs in picture books. They had excelled in the arts—in painting, architecture, music, and pottery—but had somehow lost their way. Their temples had fallen into ruins and were now completely overgrown.

Later, around the city-state of Tula—birthplace of Quetzalcoatl—a new empire took shape under a people called the Toltecs. They developed a system of military control, exercised over a large network of vassal peoples—a system the Aztecs now imitated. But they, too, fell into decline. Their greatest legacy was Quetzalcoatl, a human emperor who became a god. He was known as the plumed serpent, for he was generally represented as half-bird, half-snake. He possessed the powers of both creatures, and thus was able to unite the conflicting forces of the earth and the sky. He was master of the wind, god of human intellect and education. He had gone away over the eastern sea, but his return was promised.

Following the collapse of the Toltecs, the world entered a dark and terrible time. A welter of competing tribes and rough, unsophisticated city-states competed for power. Bands of ragged, barbarian nomads swarmed in from outlying territories to roam the Valley of Anáhuac, attracted by the green and fertile lands. Although they would never admit to such humble beginnings, the Aztecs were among these invaders. They called themselves the Mexica—the People—but that was an arrogant name, not one that other tribes would use to describe them. According to the Aztecs' own history, they came originally from a lake island far to the north, an island they called Aztlan. For years, they had traveled south, wandering down across the northern steppes, over an arid domain of dirt and rocks, stippled by tuna cactus and mesquite scrub. Their great deity was Huitzilopochtli—the hummingbird god.

Over time, Huitzilopochtli would transform himself into

a god of war. But for many years, the Aztecs were too weak for much in the way of fighting. When they could, they raided other tribes in order to steal wives, but this was about as much glory as they could manage. For many decades, they shunted about the Valley of Anáhuac, trying without success to found a permanent settlement and devoting much of their energy to running away from other, more powerful tribes. In time, they found themselves wandering along the marshy shores of Lake Texcoco, a shallow body of briny water that sprawled across the basin of the central valley. There, they remembered an ancient prophecy. It had long ago been foretold that they would recognize their promised land when they came upon an eagle devouring a snake while perched atop a nopal cactus.

On an island in Lake Texcoco, a party of Aztecs witnessed just such a vision, and so they and their people decided to settle in this place. They began to build a city that came to be called Tenochtitlán. On the northern reach of the same island, they established a second city, Tlatelolco.

They prided themselves now on their refinement and learning, but at first, the Aztecs did not amount to much—dirty, bellowing newcomers of no political or cultural distinction, a rude people who had long hunted and gathered for their keep. They wore simple loincloths and flimsy sandals made of rough fiber. They carried basic tools and weapons such as stone knives and small wooden bows. Ill-fed and unschooled, they hardly seemed to be the children of the sun or the favorites of the gods. But that was what they believed themselves to be. They settled in their promised land and started to build.

Whatever their shortcomings, they were an industrious and ambitious people. Over time, they perfected an ingenious system of agriculture—a network of floating gardens called *chinampas* that yielded huge crops of fruits and vegetables without requiring vast tracts of land. To construct these gardens, the Aztecs dug canals through their two cities, and then used the displaced mud, roots, and reeds to form solid clumps of reeking, fecund soil that floated out into the shallows of the lake and anchored with willow trees and stakes. They dredged up more mud and slapped it on. These floating gardens, extraordinarily fertile, played a central role in the Aztecs' steadily increasing prosperity.

They were blessed in another way. As an island people, they were forced to become skilled shipwrights and boatsmen, for how else could they get about? Eventually, their prowess on the water brought them advantages over people from neighboring tribes, who moved about on land. Wherever these other tribes went, they traveled by foot. Whatever they carried, they loaded on human backs. With their boats, however, the Aztecs were eventually able to develop trading routes, systems of transport, and communications networks far superior to those of their neighbors.

With their growing strength, they managed to resist the dominant tribe of the region, the Tepanecs, centered in the city-state of Azcapotzalco, located on the western shore of the lake. Over time, they ingratiated themselves into the power structures of the Tepanecs, through marriage alliances and by choosing a Tepanec lord to govern Tlatelolco, one of their two settlements. They also hired themselves out as mercenaries to fight in the Tepanec wars of conquest.

At about this time, another city was emerging on the lake. Called Texcoco, it was built by a separate group of nomads come to settle in the fertile basin of the Valley of Anáhuac. The Aztecs and the Texcocans formed an alliance, later joined by a third city, known as Tacuba. Together, they made war on the Tepanecs. After a conflict of more than one hundred days, the Tepanec city of Azcapotzalco was forced to surrender, and the Triple Alliance of the Aztecs, the Texcocans, and the Tacubans became the most formidable force in all creation— or at least in the world familiar to Pitoque, merchant of Cholula, who now ventured into the presence of Moctezuma II, the emperor of the world.

He Strikes at Kings

Pitoque had to blink several times to accustom himself to the sudden light. He looked up and saw that he was in an open courtyard. A mere canopy of cotton fluttered overhead. The air around him seemed unnaturally luminous. An abundance of blossoms burst on all sides. And he understood that he was in the presence of the emperor.

Almost at once, he heard a man's voice—rather high in register, perhaps, but authoritative nonetheless.

"Approach and identify yourself."

Pitoque bowed and kept his eyes low as he advanced across

a deep carpet, dyed in cochineal red. "Lord, my lord, my great lord," he intoned, just the way Azotl had instructed him to do. The merchant of Cholula came to a stop several paces from the emperor, who was seated upon a throne made of polished wood, worked with gems. Above the throne hung a canopy of shimmering cotton, decorated at its four corners with the bright green feathers of quetzals. Pitoque kept his gaze firmly trained upon the emperor's feet, which were clad in golden slippers, richly bejeweled.

"We bid you again," the emperor said, "to identify yourself."

Pitoque found his voice. "Pitoque, may it please your lordship. An agent in espionage, may it—"

"Say what you mean," Moctezuma broke in. "A spy. It is an honorable profession."

"Yes," he said, "may it please—"

"Whether it pleases me or not is of no account. I merely wish to hear what you have to tell us."

The emperor identified some of the other nobles in attendance. They included his allies Cacama, who was king of Texcoco, and Totoquihuatzin, who was king of Tacuba and a renowned poet as well. Also present were princes of other neighboring cities, along with various advisers and priests— two dozen men in all. Everyone was clad in opulent robes, embroidered at the hems and dyed in vivid colors, and all looked down at Pitoque from thrones that were very grand, but not as elaborate as that of the *tlatoani*, as Moctezuma was known. He Who Speaks.

The emperor clapped his hands and commanded Pitoque

to provide an account of what he had seen and heard among these visitors who had come to the eastern coast. Pitoque made a second bow, cleared his throat, and did as requested, trying to remain calm throughout.

Moctezuma listened in silence. When Pitoque had finished, the emperor waited for a time before responding. "You speak," he said at last, "with the accent of Cholula. I understand that you are from there."

The trader conceded that he was. He knew that Moctezuma would understand what this meant. Cholula was a vassal state and harbored no great love for Tenochtitlán, its people, or their lord emperor.

"And yet you serve me and my people. Why is that?"

At first, Pitoque was tempted to heap unctuous praise upon the Aztecs, lauding their great accomplishments in arts and sciences, as he usually did when such matters were raised. This time, some instinct told him to simply speak the truth.

"In this short life," he said, "a man does not always choose his masters. He chooses to survive."

"A sincere answer," remarked Moctezuma. "It isn't often we get one of those. Now look me in the eyes."

Pitoque demurred.

"Look me in the eyes."

And so he did. He raised his head and gazed upon a pleasant-looking man of about forty, with a complexion that was more light than dark, and with only a few stray whiskers for a beard, most of which were clustered at his chin. The emperor wore his hair quite short, barely touching the tops of his ears.

His face was adorned by a lip plug of lapis lazuli in the likeness of a hummingbird. He wore a carmine-colored cloak with a mantle of coyote fur. What surprised Pitoque, however, was that Moctezuma was quite identifiably a man. Somehow, he hadn't expected a human. He'd expected something else, although he'd have been hard-pressed to say exactly what— something more alarming, more glorious. He'd expected to be terrified.

"That's better," Moctezuma said. "Now tell us—what do you think these omens presage? Who are these creatures in floating palaces? Why are they here?"

Pitoque gave the only reply he could, the one he had given before. These creatures were gods of some sort, an advance party of the great lord Quetzalcoatl, whose return had been foretold by ancient prophecy. "I have no other explanation," he said. "Nothing else makes sense."

Moctezuma seemed to roll this answer around in his mouth. Addressing no one in particular, he said, "We have all heard the prophecies, have we not?"

No one replied. They waited to hear what Moctezuma would say.

The emperor closed his eyes and put the fingers of one hand to his forehead. He recited the words of one prophet, who had spoken of the return of the feathered serpent, of Quetzalcoatl. "If he comes in the year 1-Reed, he strikes at kings."

Pitoque swallowed. He, too, had heard this prophecy. There were others, less harsh. But it was understandable that the emperor would remember this one.

Still, no one spoke. The emperor reached into his robes and withdrew the picture of the emaciated god bleeding upon the wooden cross. He looked at Pitoque. "They gave you this?"

"Yes, my lord. They did."

"And you say it is a likeness of Quetzalcoatl?"

"I do." Pitoque felt his confidence begin to grow. "My lord can see for himself. The depicted figure is white of skin and bearded. Who else can it be?"

The emperor gazed at the picture, slowly shaking his head. "He doesn't look happy, does he?"

"No," said Pitoque.

"What do you think is the meaning of this blood and these bars through his hands and his feet?"

"Ah. That I cannot say. But he . . . he does not seem well."

"Perhaps your Quetzalcoatl is dying."

"Perhaps. But I don't think so. The prophecies . . ."

"Just so." The emperor inclined his head. "The prophecies."

Moctezuma II made a fist and rested his chin upon it. For a time, he merely gazed off into the middle distance with an air of great sadness, for he had evidently been contemplating these matters for quite some time. Finally, he began to cry—a truly shocking sight. Pitoque shifted his weight from foot to foot. He withdrew his gaze from Moctezuma and stared at the floor. What is a man to do when an emperor weeps?

His voice still choked with sobs, Moctezuma asked the others present what they thought of the situation. A long discussion ensued, in which there was much disagreement—and a great many vague generalizations and platitudes. Some of these august nobles concurred with Pitoque that the creatures in question might well be gods. Others shook their heads—they wanted proof. As to what ought to be done, that was even less clear.

"If these beings stay away and do not return, perhaps the whole affair might safely be forgotten," suggested one of the lords. This was Totoquihuatzin, the king of Tacuba.

"But if they return?" asked Moctezuma. He dabbed at his eyes with the fabric of his cloak. He seemed to have recovered his composure. "What if they return?"

"Ah. If they return, then that is a different matter altogether."

The discussion continued in this meandering vein. Only Cacama, the king of Texcoco, declared himself firmly. He thought it very unlikely that these beings were gods.

Moctezuma turned to him. "Why do you say that?"

"For one thing, they do not seem to speak any language that men can understand. Surely gods would be able to converse with their own creatures."

Pitoque scratched his head. The same thought had occurred to him. He didn't know what to say.

"Furthermore," said Cacama, "they do not declare themselves. They do not divulge who they are or why they are here—apart from their desire for gold. If they are gods, why must they seek gold? Why not simply have it?"

Another wise observation. Pitoque could not deny it.

Cacama turned his gaze upon the merchant of Cholula. The king was a tall and slender man with a stern, rectangular face.

He seemed a humorless fellow, intelligent, straightforward, and intolerant of equivocation or cant. "I do not think much of your theory," he said. "If these strangers are gods, let them prove it."

Moctezuma frowned and fell silent. After a time, he looked up and asked the question that perhaps weighed most heavily upon him. "What if these strangers seek to make their way to Tenochtitlán? What then should be done? Should we welcome them? Should the city be turned over to the gods, if gods they are? Should the empire itself be surrendered?" Quetzalcoatl would surely wish to reclaim his domain.

But, once again, there was little agreement on the question, just long speeches that went off in various directions. Cuitláhuac, who was the brother of Moctezuma and lord of Iztapalapa, said such a dilemma must be prevented at all costs. These beings must never be admitted to Tenochtitlán, whether they were gods or demons. But Totoquihuatzin took a different view. He felt it would be wise to welcome these envoys into the city, honor them with goodwill and comfort, and hear what they had to say.

The discussion rambled on and on, and Moctezuma slumped on his throne, shaking his head and sighing to himself. He appeared overcome by what he had heard, and Pitoque could understand why. On the emperor's shoulders rested the weight of the world. Who would not groan beneath that burden? At last, Moctezuma raised his hand and announced that the matter would be put off for now, pending further developments or signs. Having made this decision, he seemed to recover. He drew himself upright on his throne and peered down at Pitoque. "Can I trust you completely?"

At once Pitoque said that yes, His Lordship certainly could.

"Good," the emperor replied, "for I may have some future need of you. May I expect your help?"

"Of course," said Pitoque. "My lord has only to ask. Whatever my lord pleases, I will do."

Moctezuma seemed satisfied with this reply. He clapped his hands. "Refreshments," he declared. "Refreshments for our guest."

Almost instantly a pair of servants entered the chamber, bearing ceramic jugs and small jars, which they filled and passed around. Then they withdrew, treading backwards and bowing all the way. Pitoque waited for the emperor and the others to sip from their cups first. Then he did the same from his own. At once, he spluttered and almost gagged. What was this? The drink was extremely cold, and something within it was clinking, something sharp and hard. He looked up, and Moctezuma was laughing, his head cocked to one side.

"Ah, I see you have not ventured to enjoy ice in your drink of chocolate before. I detect it from the expression on your face."

Ice? How strange, and yet how very pleasant. How soothing and cool. He took another sip and then another. But how was this done? Pitoque knew of ice. He had encountered it once while climbing almost to the summit of the great mountain Popocatépetl. There, he had held a piece of ice in his hand, had felt its unbearable sleekness as it burned his skin. He had pried some of it loose and brought it back with him from his climb.

But soon it began to cry and in the end was reduced to nothing but tears. He wondered, how did it come to be here?

"Runners," said Moctezuma, anticipating the question. "Every night they are dispatched to climb the slopes of Popocatépetl, and they return with a supply. We wrap it in blankets of agave fiber to prevent it from melting."

"Melting?" It was not a word that Pitoque had heard before.

"Yes. Turning to water." The emperor raised his cup. "I prefer my drinks this way. What is your view?"

Pitoque took another long sip and nodded. "The taste is greatly improved. Quite delicious."

"Good. I am glad that you agree."

Moctezuma set his cup down and looked at Pitoque again. He asked for the Cholulan's thoughts on what course the Aztecs might sensibly take.

Pitoque said that he agreed with the emperor himself. For the moment, there was little they could do but be vigilant, keep a close watch on the eastern shore. According to the prophecies, the lord Quetzalcoatl would return in the year 1-Reed, just a year away. In the meantime, all they could do was pray, make offerings, and wait.

Without thinking, Pitoque took a step forward and then stopped, horrified by his boldness—but Moctezuma didn't seem to mind. In fact, he called upon a servant to bring a chair so that their guest from Cholula might make himself comfortable.

"Now," said the emperor, shifting forward on his throne, "tell me. What is it like to find oneself in the presence of the gods?"

And Pitoque did his best to recount the experience, in all its unexpected detail. The only points he omitted were his own private concerns—that long-ago night in the lands of the Maya and the offences committed by his son. But he told the emperor everything else, even divulging the matter of the deities' appalling smell. It was enough to make a man gag.

"Gag?" Moctezuma crinkled up his nose and shook his head. "You can't be serious."

"But I am."

The emperor rolled his eyes and laughed, as if nothing would please him more than to choke on the reek of the gods. He told Pitoque that he was enormously grateful for this remarkable intelligence. He trusted that he and the Cholulan would have occasion to discuss these matters again at some point in the future, after circumstances had become more clear.

Pitoque struggled to slow his heartbeat. He made a shallow bow. "I will be only too glad to oblige you, my lord."

"Good." Now Moctezuma's gaze darkened. He inclined his head forward, lowered his voice to a whisper, and spoke to Pitoque in an urgent tone. "Do you think they come in peace? You don't think they come to make war?"

"Ah . . ." said Pitoque, and he let out a sigh. "That is the same question I ask myself. For the moment, I do not know."

"I see." The emperor sighed as well. "I see."

Pitoque waited.

Finally, Moctezuma gave himself a shake, as though arousing himself from some private reverie. "Well, we shall hope for happy tidings in the coming seasons. In the meantime, I am glad to have made a new confederate—and a friend."

The House of Joy

"How was your meeting?" Azotl was waiting outside the royal pavilion. "Did it go well?"

Pitoque's head was spinning. He had no words to describe what he felt. He raced ahead of the master functionary, his arms flailing before him, as if he were swimming. He rushed out of the House of the Eagle Knights and along the clean-swept streets of the city. His heart seemed to leap inside him, in time with the emotions that were roiling in his chest. He, Pitoque of Cholula! Welcomed into the innermost conferences of the lords of the Triple Alliance! The most powerful men in all the empire! He—addressed by the emperor of the Aztecs! He could not wait to tell Kalatzin, to tell Maxtla.

He stopped, wrapped his arms about his chest, and waited for Azotl to catch up. At last, the master functionary drew alongside him, puffing from the exertion.

"I asked, how was your meeting? What did the emperor say? What has been decided?"

Eventually, Pitoque calmed down enough to reply. Nothing yet had been decided—but what did it matter? He himself had gazed into the face of Moctezuma and exchanged words with the emperor. It was simply unbelievable. And yet it was true.

In the end, Azotl gave up. He saw that the trader was in

no state to give an intelligible response. He'd have to obtain a report on the proceedings by other means. He patted Pitoque on the shoulder and told him to visit the following morning. They'd have much to discuss then, when the dust had settled, so to speak.

"Yes," said Pitoque. "Tomorrow. Good."

"And try to relax, man. You're trembling." Azotl shook his enormous head. Like everyone else in the empire of the Aztecs, he would just have to wait.

Pitoque had no idea what he ought to do now. What does a mere trader in merchandise do after conferring with the emperor of the world? But he could not simply stand here, in the middle of the street, with his jaw hanging down around his waist. He turned and began to amble through the city. Some instinct directed him to the ball court that was located not far from the Great Temple of Huitzilopochtli. The game of tlachtli was his passion, and offered him a means of purging the agitation that trembled through his body. It was true, what Azotl had said. He was shaking all over.

He arrived at the ball court just in time to lay down a wager— a quantity of cacao beans, in this case—and to find a good place in the stands from which to watch. For the next several hours, he was lost in the intricacies and sudden violence of the game. Clad in padded trunks, knee-guards, and large gauntlets, the front players hurled themselves about the walled court, trying to direct the small black ball past their opponents. Often, there were astonishing collisions, which brought the spectators to their feet, roaring their approval. Sometimes, players hit the stone walls with such impact they were knocked unconscious and had to be carried off the court. On this afternoon, the ball struck one excellent player square in the face and put out his eye—and yet he continued to play! Pitoque stood and cheered the fellow on, for the man's bravery meant that the Cholulan's wager had been saved.

In the end, he made a handsome profit on the game and went away exhilarated and restored to something approaching sanity. Still, he had not forgotten the events of the day. What a day it had been! His skin still tingled. But soon Pitoque felt his mood begin to drift downward, as it so often did. He, a simple merchant, alone in this massive city. Far from his home. Far from his family.

Without quite meaning to, he found himself wandering in the direction of a certain house of joy. It was strange how he still sometimes ended up following this route, without any sense that he had willed himself to do so. Now here he was once again, standing outside a square-faced building of white-washed stone, tucked along a narrow street beside a little-used canal. He knew from ancient experience what would happen now, if he called out to be admitted. The matron would acknowledge him with a vague nod, nothing more, and let him pass inside, and soon she would bring to him a young daughter of joy.

She would be clad in feathers, this one. Her hair would fall long and loose, blackened with indigo or mud, and she would move her mouth around and around as she chewed a piece of chicle. She would kneel in greeting and smile at him, eyes lowered. Her teeth would be dyed orange with cochineal. Already, he would feel himself growing stiff. Her face would be painted yellow, her arms and belly tattooed in ways that would make the perspiration begin to trickle beneath his robes. The girl would stand again and begin to dance for him. He would watch in silence, sipping from a bowl of pulque. Soon, she would approach, lifting up her robe. He would lie back, and she would kneel above him, grinding down. She would fan him with her feathers, murmur into his ears in the accent of some distant tribe, and put an end to all thoughts of trouble, if only for a time.

The whole scene played out in Pitoque's mind as he stood alone outside the house of joy. A pair of men, strangers to him, pushed past. They guffawed and belched and called out for admission and soon made their way inside. The matron waited, peering from the doorway at Pitoque. She raised her eyebrows. Did he wish to come inside?

But Pitoque reached into his robes for the necklace he always kept there. He closed his hand around it and shook his head. He turned and walked away. Some strange scruple had eased the heat in his groin and changed his mind.

A Barge of Snakes

A year passed. Pitoque and his son roamed the cool highlands in their maguey robes, followed by a gang of porters who operated under the instructions of Toc. For weeks at a time, Pitoque found himself free of the terrible dreams and visions that had haunted him for so long. But just as he thought that perhaps he was quit of them forever, they returned. And there were troubling signs. On the high northern steppes, he would catch sight of seabirds, creatures that had no place there, that normally dwelt on the coastlands, hovering on the humid breeze. Early in the morning, he might wander off from his camp, meaning to relieve himself in private, and he would suddenly stumble over the carcass of some strange beast, freshly slaughtered. By whom? And why left here, in his path?

All at once, the fears erupted again. Again, evil dreams invaded his sleep. At night, he heard women's voices crying through the darkness, but they were too distant to understand, or too weak to make out. What were they saying? And to whom? More than once, he roused Maxtla, so that he might hear as well. But the boy professed to be mystified. He heard nothing. These were dreams, nothing more.

Once, Pitoque suddenly awoke with a single word roaring in his mind. *Confess. Confess.*

"Confess?" whispered Maxtla, groggy from sleep. "What are you talking about? Confess what?"

Pitoque realized he'd been speaking the word out loud. His shoulders sagged. "A dream," he said. "I must have been dreaming. It's nothing. Go back to sleep."

Wordless, Maxtla pulled his blankets around his shoulders and laid down his head. Meanwhile, Pitoque drifted alone through the high northern night. Unable to sleep, or afraid of dreams, he listened to the desert wind that keened among the tabletop hills and sang through the deep ravines that knifed across these remote and barren lands, like scars inflicted by the gods. The wind sang in the voices of invisible women. He heard them now. Now he understood the words that rode upon the wind.

Flee, the voices moaned. *Flee. Take only what you can carry. Run for your lives.*

The following night, and for three nights after that, Pitoque dreamed of Quetzalcoatl, of the feathered serpent's return. The god would reappear in the year 1-Reed. He would come in the guise of a man. He would strike at kings.

On the afternoon that followed the fourth such night, as he and Maxtla journeyed across a sweeping terrain of wind-blown grasslands and piñon cactus, Pitoque decided to raise the matter with his son. He did not speak of his fears or his dreams. He spoke instead as a schoolmaster might address a pupil. He wished to discover what Maxtla knew about this god, the patron deity of Cholula.

As he discovered, Maxtla knew almost nothing. To each of his father's questions, the boy replied with a shrug and the mumbled admission that he did not know. Pitoque became increasingly agitated. What on earth were they teaching in the *telpochcallis* these days? In reply, Maxtla grew steadily more taciturn and finally refused to say anything at all. They strode in silence across the vast unfolding plain, bristling here and there with prickly-pear cactus and broken by the dark purple smudges of flat-top hills. Somewhere in the distance, an owl hooted. An owl hooting by day.

Pitoque grimaced but said nothing.

That evening, one of the porters brought them dinner— grilled rattlesnake in sesame sauce—which they consumed by a low wood fire, near the edge of a precipice that overlooked a yawning view of the mauve hills and valleys, slow waves shifting against the rose horizon. The rest of the porters were making preparations for the night ahead, searching for likely spots on the ground, spreading out their maguey bedsheets, wrapping themselves in their cloaks. They shifted from side to side until they found comfortable positions, and soon drifted off to sleep.

The cooks lounged on rock benches and chatted as they watched the skullery slaves attend to the scrubbing of the pots. Occasionally, the cooks called out for greater care to be taken. Water was scarce and should not be wasted on overanxious cleaning. They chuckled and shook their heads and smoked their pipes and amused themselves by telling stories of their families and of home. Darkness fell.

Not far from the main fire, beds of shoveled sand and dried leaves had been prepared for Pitoque and Maxtla. As they usually did, they would sleep in the open air beneath a canopy of stars. Toc was making his final rounds, ensuring that all was secure for the night. Later, he might join them—or not, depending on his mood. The light faded, and the two travelers found their spirits rise. How could it be otherwise, with their stomachs full, and surrounded as they were by such splendor?

It was winter now and cold, but they huddled by the fire, whose embers glowed like a small red star dangling beneath a great tapestry of somersaulting constellations—a thousand jewels scattered upon the vast black fabric of the night. Pitoque asked if he might return to the subject of Quetzalcoatl, not to provoke or chasten his son, but simply because the subject was such an important part of their people's past and future. Maxtla didn't say no. He merely pulled his blanket more closely around him and grunted in what his father took to be assent.

Pitoque cleared his throat and began his tale—the story of the feathered serpent. "The god known to the world nowadays as Quetzalcoatl was born many eras ago," he began, "the son of an ancient king named Mixcoatl. He was conceived after his mother Chimalma swallowed a jadeite bead that formed itself into the shape of a child. She—"

"A jadeite bead?" Maxtla sat up. "The form of a child? Is this some nursery tale?"

"Hush. Listen. These are the teachings of the past."

"Ah."

Pitoque shifted onto his side so that his face and chest would be warmed by the fire. He proceeded with the story. As a young man, Quetzalcoatl quickly proved himself to be of heroic mettle. He was tested many times. On one occasion, he set out to do battle with a great dragon that plagued the land of the Toltecs, demanding human sacrifices. During that terrible struggle, Quetzalcoatl allowed himself to be swallowed whole by the beast, but this was merely a ruse. Once inside the creature's belly, he cut his way to freedom with a flint-bladed knife he carried in his robe. And so his people were freed from the dragon's torment.

Later, as lord and high priest of the kingdom, Quetzalcoatl presided over a time of peace and prosperity. Commerce flourished, and merchants traveled vast distances to trade with other tribes. Indeed, the trading profession was honored above all others in those days, save that of poets.

"I can see why you like this tale," said Maxtla, "or are you making that part up?"

"A storyteller's licence." Pitoque peered into the smoldering coals of the fire. "We pick and choose."

"And invent?"

Pitoque smiled. "Sometimes. Now let me continue."

Metals of all kinds were discovered. There was a flowering of crafts and the arts. In the trees of the forests and the plants of the earth, holy men found the cures for many varieties of illnesses.

But darker forces were also at work. During his rule, Quetzalcoatl waged a long struggle against a powerful sorcerer named Tezcatlipoca, or Smoking Mirror, so called because his right foot took the form of an obsidian glass. Over the years, Smoking Mirror tried by every means possible to corrupt Quetzalcoatl and bring him low, but without success. Finally, Tezcatlipoca sent a band of demons in the guise of blathering old men, who preyed upon the emperor without cease, urging him to drink pulque, sweet nectar of the maguey cactus.

Finally, simply to stop their constant pestering, Quetzalcoatl obliged these old men. He intended to drink a very little, merely dip his fingers into the bowl and then lick them dry, but in time he became thoroughly drunk. He called for a woman to be brought to him—his own sister it was, Quetzalpetlatl—and he lay with her. Thus were two taboos broken, those against drunkenness and incest.

Disgraced, his blood curdling with self-hatred, Quetzalcoatl ordered that all his palaces be burned to the ground and that his vast treasures of art be buried beneath a range of mountains. He waved his hands, and all the cacao of his kingdom turned immediately to cactus. All birds were banished from the land. Quetzalcoatl determined to set off in the direction of the rising sun, to begin his long wanderings.

Before leaving, he vowed that he would one day return to rule his people again. He promised that all wickedness in the world would at last be rooted out. With those words, he departed. He was accompanied by a band of dwarfs and cripples, his only remaining allies, all of whom died from the cold during the harsh climb over the mountains. At last and now entirely alone, Quetzalcoatl reached the eastern coast, where he fashioned for himself a barge of entangled snakes, climbed aboard, and floated away.

"A barge of *snakes*?" said Maxtla. "How ingenious."

Pitoque raised his hand as if to smack the child. This was supposed to be the most moving part of the story—the lord's departure. It should be met with awed silence, not clever gibes. Besides, it hardly suited someone so young to make sarcastic remarks to his parent. Instead of striking the boy, however, Pitoque lowered his hand. Oh, well. Where was the harm? When he thought about it, Maxtla's comment had some truth. Given the other choices available—wood, for one—snakes were indeed an unlikely construction material for a boat.

"Perhaps," he said, "these were merely logs carved in the likeness of snakes."

"Oh, I see," said Maxtla. "Now the story makes sense."

Pitoque narrowed his eyes and gazed at the burning embers not far from his feet. What made sense, and what didn't? All was as the gods determined—what other sense was there? He yawned and shook his head. He had told his tale, and now his son understood at least something of the feathered serpent. Another day, or another night, Pitoque could continue with these lessons. He would speak of the prophecies that heralded the god's return. But it was too late tonight for a man to torment his head with the mysteries of the universe. The fire flickered against a backdrop of stars, and the pair of travelers—father and son—pulled their blankets around them, laid down their heads, and fell asleep.

In the darkness behind them, Toc made a last slow turn around the perimeter of the camp, just to be certain that all was in order, everything safe. Persuaded that it was, the old man settled down by his own fire and closed his eyes.

Overhead, silent and invisible, eleven owls streaked through the night.

BOOK TWO

The Spanish Castaway

Strange Waters and Golden Lands

"Don't tell me that you plan on wearing that." Catalina Suárez de Cortés snorted and set down her needlework. "You look like a peacock."

Her husband, Hernán Cortés, smiled to himself. In fact, he felt like a peacock. The likeness of a peacock was precisely the effect he had been at considerable pains to achieve. To judge by the reaction of his wife, he had succeeded. He'd have been happier, however, if she had selected a different tone of voice in which to say so, something gentler and more respectful. But he'd despaired long ago of that ever happening. Now he strutted into the drawing room, decked out in cream-colored leggings, a burgundy skirt and tunic, and an elaborate breastplate worked with gold. His sword dangled from his hip in a polished leather scabbard. To complete the ensemble, he wore a purple cloak and several gold chains around his neck. He'd had the outfit made up according to his own personal specifications, a uniform befitting a Spanish captain-general, his new rank.

"I designed it myself," he said. He strolled over to the bay window and peered outside at the gardens of his Cuban hacienda, an hour's ride west of the capital, Santiago. Outside, several natives were toiling amid the greenery of the grape vines. As always, the sun glared down. "I'm glad you like it."

"I don't like it. I think it's absurd. You look idiotic."

"Appearances, you know, can be deceiving."

"I do know it. They can also be ridiculous."

"Ah, well." Cortés shrugged. He was determined not to be drawn into another argument with the woman. Such disputes were beneath his dignity now. He had, after all, been selected by Diego Velázquez, the governor of Cuba, to lead an important reconnaissance expedition. He was to chart the mysterious and apparently vast lands that lay to the west of Cuba itself. Nameless and unknown, those territories lurked beyond the western sea, promising gold and riches to the man who dared to grasp them. The thrill of his mission swelled yet again in Cortés's chest, until he wondered whether he ought to loosen his breastplate by a notch or two. But such a maneuver would undoubtedly trigger some unfortunate comment from his wife, something about his weight. He decided against it.

"What am I to do for money while you are gone?" The woman tugged at an obstinate thread. She glanced up. "I don't suppose you have thought of that."

In fact, he had. It was just that it didn't matter to him. He raised his right hand, fingers bent at the knuckles so that he might inspect his manicure, freshly attended to that morning. He frowned. "Not to worry, my dear. All has been arranged. You will be amply provided for."

It wasn't true. To finance this expedition, he had been forced to take out a mortgage on his Cuban estate and to liquidate quite a few of his other holdings. God knew what would happen in his absence, and God was welcome to that knowledge. To tell the truth, Cortés was content to leave the matter in divine hands. He cared very little. If worst came to worst, his wife could always fall back on the magnanimity of her own blood. Let them support her.

By then, he would be far away—and he did not plan on soon returning. That dolt Velázquez expected him to conduct no more than a mere charting expedition, the third such mission to these unknown western lands, but Cortés had other, grander ideas. He didn't mean to waste his time with logs and dreary reports and mere reconnaissance tasks. Far from it. He meant to do as Julius Caesar had done—to go, to see. To conquer.

Of course, Velázquez had no inkling of this plan, the imbecile. If he found out, there was no question what the governor would do. He'd put a stop to the expedition and likely bring Cortés up on charges, too—anything to prevent someone else from winning even a share of the glory.

In order to keep his patron in the dark, Cortés had been required to finance most of the operation on his own. He had commissioned eleven ships. He had assembled five hundred and eight men, not including those required to navigate the vessels, as well as sixteen horses. He had ten brass cannons, a good supply of powder and shot, and four falconets. Thirteen of his men were musketeers equipped with well-made harquebuses. In addition, he had acquired thirty-two skilled crossbowmen. For more diplomatic purposes, he had put in a generous supply of the colored glass beads that seemed to be as great a success in the unknown territories as they had been here in Cuba. Cortés had learned this on the authority of Juan de Grivalva, who'd led a second expedition the year before. Grivalva, good soul, had helped a great deal. Not so that popinjay Francisco Hernández de Córdoba, who'd commanded the first mission, the one in 1517. Pompous oaf.

But he would gain nothing by dwelling on the past. Now it was the middle of February in the year 1519, and it was time to be off. He planned to weigh anchor the following day, at eventide, to set sail at dusk. From Santiago, he would bear west along Cuba's southern coast, gathering his fleet along the way and taking on supplies at various points. At Havana, they would all assemble—and then away! *¡Buenos días, aventura!* Ha. He could barely wait.

"You know," said Doña Catalina, "on account of your fecklessness, we will miss the governor's ball. I had particularly wanted to go—but I shall be here all alone."

"Eh?" Cortés turned and gazed at his wife, at her pale and bloated face, at her dark eyes rendered barely discernible now by an accumulation of flesh, at her bunched and disgruntled expression. Some pool of bile shifted in his stomach. Had he ever even liked the woman? "What's that you say?"

But she merely shook her head and went back to her embroidery. As far as she was concerned, her husband never listened to anything she said.

"*What?*" Cortés dropped his breastplate onto the floor of his dressing room. "What do you mean?"

"Just as I say. We have been found out." Pedro de

Alvarado—a blustery, golden-haired man, and Cortés's chief aide—smacked a fist into his palm and stamped about the room in his heavy riding boots. He had raced here on horseback directly from the governor's palace in Santiago the instant he'd heard the news. The entire palace had been buzzing with it. "Velázquez knows about our plans. Someone must have told him—how many ships we've lined up, the cannons and harquebuses. Everything. He knows this is no reconnaissance mission. He has already rescinded your commission. The voyage is off."

At first, Cortés could not get his mind to work clearly. The only thing he could think of was that now he'd have to go to the bloody governor's ball, after all. "What do you mean, the voyage is off?"

"Exactly that," said Alvarado. "Someone must have betrayed us. Some sniveling little traitor. If I find out who it is, I'll slit his throat. I'll flay him. I'll stomp on his nether regions until his viscera fly out through every orifice. I'll . . . I'll . . ."

"Calm down. Calm down." Cortés slumped into a strategically located chair and stretched out his legs. He was more than a little agitated himself, but he resolved to project an air of quiet resolve. *Someone* had to. As usual, the younger man approached the execution of his duties with a degree of enthusiasm that was perhaps a little *de trop*. In truth, Alvarado's vigor was among the characteristics that Cortés most valued in his lieutenant, but it was a trait that bore watching. In any case, now was not the time for threats and fulmination. Now was the time for sober reflection.

Cortés sought to reflect, soberly. He frowned at his breast-plate, which now squatted on the floor like some strange, unidentifiable beast. He looked up at Alvarado who, for the moment at least, had stopped his pacing about.

Cortés stroked his beard. "As likely as not," he said, "Velázquez put two and two together for himself. He might be dull, but his head is not constructed entirely of wood. A fool can see that our preparations are beyond what one would expect for a reconnaissance mission. I'm surprised it took him this long to figure out our plans."

"Well, now he has." Alvarado resumed his pacing but at a more measured speed. Occasionally, he reached up and ran the fingers of both hands through his long blond locks. He was an extraordinarily handsome fellow, but almost laughably vain. Even now, he couldn't keep his hands from himself. He stopped and planted both boots squarely on the black-checkered rug spread across the middle of the room. He heaved a long sigh and shook his head. "So, our fine hopes are dashed. Everything is lost."

"Lost?" Cortés began to laugh. Already, he'd had an idea. "What do you mean, lost?"

"You don't seem to understand," Alvarado said. He grit his teeth in irritation. "The governor has specifically revoked your commission. Everybody is talking about it. At the governor's palace, no one speaks of anything else. I've just come from there."

Cortés crossed his legs at the ankles. "Alvarado, you disap-point me. I thought you possessed more pluck than this."

"But I'm telling you. The order has been issued."

Cortés shrugged. "I have yet to see it."

"See it? But I've told you what it contains. You don't need to—" Alvarado broke off. Slowly, his eyebrows began to rise as the light of recognition began to seep in. "That's right," he said. "That's absolutely right. You haven't *seen* the damn thing."

Cortés smiled. "I haven't heard about it, either." He gave a dismissive wave. "I mean, apart from some vague rumors transmitted by, by . . . I don't remember who brought them to my attention."

Alvarado grinned, delighted now. "And that individual, whoever he was, might very well have been mistaken."

"Wouldn't be the first time."

Alvarado nodded. "That's right. It wouldn't be the . . . hey. I resent that."

"The truth often hurts. But never mind. You see my point. The governor may issue all the edicts he pleases, but if I don't know about them, I can hardly be held to account. And, so far, I know nothing about this particular decision. Nothing official."

"So," said Alvarado. "What do we do?"

Cortés reached down and picked up his breastplate. With the sleeve of his doublet he began to wipe away some scrape or smudge on the gilding. He looked up. "We will do the only thing we can do."

"What is that?"

Cortés stood up and began to buckle the apparatus on. "We

set sail for strange waters and golden lands. We weigh anchor tonight."

The halyards creaked, a passel of canvas sails suddenly bloated in the evening breeze, the wooden hulls groaned against the forces of ocean and air, and three vessels of Hernán Cortés's fleet sailed out from Santiago de Cuba, plowing through the purple sea and fading into a faint bronze mist of salt spray and ebbing sunlight. Cumulus clouds swarmed across the horizon like huge balls of cotton.

They would gather the fleet along the way, for Cortés had taken the precaution of scattering the rest of his eleven vessels at various points on the southern coast in order to avoid attracting attention. Now, aboard the flagship, he felt the thrum and arch of the deck beneath his feet and braced himself against the heeling of the vessel. He clapped Alvarado on the back. Praise the *Virgen de los Remedios*—they had done it! They had bloody well done it! They had beaten Velázquez. Now nothing remained but a journey along the south coast of Cuba, provisioning themselves at small ports here and there. Finally, they would spend a last day at Havana in order to take on various military items not readily available elsewhere. Then—open waters, adventure, and untold wealth.

"¡El Dorado!" cried Cortés. He gripped a halyard and leaned over the railing to watch the foaming water wash and churn in the darkening light. "¡El Dorado!"

The Golden Land!

Alvarado ran his hands through his hair, then steadied himself against the wheelhouse. He would have laughed out loud or said something appropriately bold, but in fact he felt a trifle green. It couldn't be the sea, for he was an excellent sailor. He was expert in everything he did. No, it couldn't be the sea. It must have been something he'd eaten.

Cortés recognized the discomfort on his comrade's face and shook his head, chuckled. "Never mind," he said. "We'll be no more than a month at sea."

"A month!" At least, this was what Alvarado meant to say, but it came out more like a wail of agony. He staggered to the deck railing and bent over it, emptied his stomach into the drink.

Cortés felt the night wind whirl through his hair and chortled at the misery of his friend and aide. "I'm joking," he called out. "Not a month. Hardly a month. A matter of days. A pair of weeks, at most."

This reassurance did not seem to provide much comfort to poor Alvarado, who now was overcome with a bout of the dry heaves—and they, as any unhappy sailor knows, are the worst of all.

In the ensuing days, they traced the south coast of Cuba, anchoring several times along the way in order to take on provisions and assemble the fleet, which sailed into Havana harbor on February the eighteenth in the year of our Lord 1519. That day was spent in procuring additional ordnance and firearms from the armory at the Spanish *fortaleza*. Unaware that Cortés had lost the governor's trust, the officers were willing to oblige him in any way they could. They also supplied him with several sets of wheelbase for the cannons. A good deal of the cassava cake that the fleet had taken on at Trinidad turned out to be moldy and rife with insects, and had to be replaced. Then the preparations were complete.

Cortés stretched out his arms and yawned, reveling in his victory. By now, of course, Governor Velázquez would be fully aware that he had been played for a fool. He would be raging about the palace in Santiago, kicking at clay urns, abusing the servants, roaring at the walls. That miscreant devil! That Cortés! He had ignored—more likely deliberately disobeyed— a direct order revoking his commission! He'd shown utter contempt for viceregal authority. Such humiliation. All of eastern Cuba would know it by now. Everyone with eyes and ears would realize that Velázquez's authority had been flouted, that Cortés's vessels were gone from the port at Santiago.

Meanwhile, near the far western reach of the island, the glow of the setting moon slowly ebbed from the sea, and now a faint sliver of reddish light peeked above the horizon of morning. Eleven anchor chains groaned and rattled, splashing water back into the sea. Acres of canvas slapped down from dozens of yards and gaffs. Seamen grappled with sheets and halyards. And their captain-general, Hernán Cortés, felt his heart thrill at the alarm and sudden chaos of it, the wild slap of the sails overhead, followed by a shuddering silence as the pilots brought their vessels into the wind and the canvas suddenly stiffened. Already, he was picking up the strange, intriguing names, the square sails and lugsails, the lateens and spankers. They puffed out their chests in the spreading light. The fleet bent to the wind.

Cortés laughed out loud. In another life, he might have made a fine sailor. But this was not another life. It was his life, a life he had created out of thin air—and a little luck. A little luck never hurt. For example, he had below decks a fellow who was a native of these strange lands to which they were bound, a walking skeleton by the name of Melchior or some such. Grivalva had brought the creature back with him, meaning to teach him Spanish. According to Grivalva, the main difficulty in these new parts was the barrier to communication caused by the absence of a common tongue. In typically generous fashion, Grivalva had turned this Melchior character over to Cortés, proclaiming him to be the solution. But Cortés had conversed with the man and had not been greatly impressed. A sickly little imp, he'd turned out to be. And thick. Still, he spoke more in the way of Spanish than anybody else who was native to the Golden Land, Grivalva swore. There was something to be said for that. A lucky stroke, all in all.

On the rear deck of his flagship, Cortés straightened his shoulders and watched the daggers of morning spill their golden blood across the sea. He laughed again, for suddenly he'd had a vision—a party of royal dragoons even now racing overland from Santiago, on the desperate orders of that lump of earwax, that Velázquez, hoping to intercept him at Havana.

Ha. Good luck to them!

‡

In fact, Cortés was exactly right.

The governor's dragoons nearly caught up to him, too. Had their quarry delayed his departure by even an hour, they would have been in time.

But on the morning of February the nineteenth, the tropical sun exploded over Havana harbor, and the fleet of eleven ships under the self-styled captain-general Hernán Cortés was nowhere to be seen. It had weighed anchor at the very break of day, and the peacock was gone.

In the rising light of dawn, after riding straight through the night, the dragoons cantered their horses to the summit of El Moro high above Havana, but all they could see were a few sticks and bits of cloth disappearing over the western horizon. Disappointed at having so little to show after so arduous a journey, they dismounted, raised their skirts, and pissed toward the west. What else could they do?

"Drink," said one. "And maybe find something to fuck."

The others liked the sound of that. They remounted their horses and plodded down toward Havana, which still lay at a distance on the far side of the bay.

A Man Must Answer to His God

They had an easy crossing. The western tip of Cuba was separated from the first landfall by only fifty leagues or so, and the February waters were calm. The fleet surged west upon a moderate swell, although Pedro de Alvarado did not find it moderate. To judge by the way he suffered, these slow, rolling waves might have been some ungodly tempest. By day, he roamed the poop deck, looking lost and ghostly, and he could not be prevailed upon to venture below decks even at night. The stuffiness down there was beyond enduring. He tried to eat but could keep nothing down. Cortés joked that he had never seen a prouder man brought so low by so little. Alvarado merely grit his teeth and moaned. He didn't care what anybody said—he just wanted this misery over. He got his wish. After only a week at sea, the flotilla of eleven vessels anchored off the coast of these strange new lands, near a place that was marked on Grivalva's charts as Cape Catoche.

It was here that Cortés decided to put this native fellow, this Melchior, to the test. God knew, the man had straw for brains and could barely articulate a coherent phrase. Still, he was their only ambassador, and so Cortés sent him ashore under the care of Alonso Puertocarrero, a scrawny, awkward man who claimed to be related to the Count of Medellín. It was on this account that Cortés chose him—it never hurt to court nobility or, failing that, the relatives of nobility.

A few hours later, the landing party returned—with the most astonishing information. They had made contact with a party of natives and had learned that other men of light complexion inhabited these lands, having arrived by some unknown means a good many years before. They were thought to dwell now some distance inland.

What was this? Cortés scrunched up his forehead and settled

his weight against the deck railing. Overhead, a canvas canopy flapped in a desultory breeze. "How many?"

At the question, Puertocarrero started, as if someone had pricked him with a sword. He rubbed his bony, narrow jaw with its sparse beard, whose whiskers did not disguise a pronounced overbite. Across his shiny dome, scattered filaments of brown hair fluttered in the wind, as if mocking his baldness. He did not speak.

"I said, how many?"

Puertocarrero finally found his voice. "Two, apparently."

"Are you sure?"

He gestured at the native, Melchior. "I think that's what he said. You can never be quite sure."

Cortés agreed. This could easily be a misunderstanding. Still, if true, it was extraordinary news. He made up his mind at once. "We have to find them."

"What on earth for?" This was Alvarado, evidently feeling a bit of his old mustard back, now that the fleet lay at anchor. He slapped the palm of one hand against the canopy.

"Because," said Cortés, "it's the Christian thing to do."

"They may not even exist."

"On the other hand, they may."

"It will cost us time, and that is a commodity we do not possess in unlimited supply. For all we know, Velázquez is already raising a fleet to pursue us. We should carry on."

"So we shall." Cortés smiled. "So we shall. But first we have to make an effort to locate these fellow Christians, if that is what they are. A man must answer to his God."

Alvarado shook his head. Cortés cared as much about God as he did himself, which was to say a judicious amount and no more. God was all very well, as long as He didn't get in the way of accumulating gold. Still, the captain-general seemed to have made up his mind, and Alvarado knew from experience that it was better to go along. Once made up, the mind of Cortés was not readily subject to change. "All right then," he said. "What do you propose?"

The captain-general rubbed the back of his neck and smiled. "We'll see if we can't arrange through our native friend to send some of these local people off in search of our Christian brothers. I'll write out some letters, which the messengers can carry. We'll leave a single ship here for, let us say, a week. I'll put Puertocarrero in charge of it." He turned to Puertocarrero. "Is that all right with you?"

Once again, the poor man stiffened with surprise, as if astonished that anyone should so much as speak to him, let alone single him out for an important commission. He gazed at Cortés, open-mouthed, then finally nodded. "Sí. Sí, *mi capitán*."

"Good." Cortés wondered whether Puertocarrero's claim to noble blood could conceivably be true. The fellow seemed more likely to be related to a family of rabbits. He turned back to Alvarado. "Meanwhile, you and land the rest of us will bear south to have a look at these interesting islands." He meant, in particular, the rather large island marked on Grivalva's charts as Cozumel. "In a week, we'll return and see what Puertocarrero has discovered. At least we'll have made an attempt to save these poor souls. Assuming they exist. Agreed?"

Alvarado pursed his lips and nodded. Another godforsaken week at sea—that was his chief concern. He also wondered why Cortés was singling out this homely nitwit Puertocarrero. But the captain-general had reached his decision. Might as well accept it. "Agreed," he said.

Cortés went off to write his letters. Alvarado remained on the deck, gazing at the tangle of greenery and palm fronds that straggled above the ivory strand and the low wash of breakers. It didn't look like the sort of place that harbored an immensity of gold. But on the other hand, who could really tell?

The Spanish Castaway

When Jerónimo de Aguilar first heard these incredible tales—that floating mountains had been sighted off the coast nearby—he let out a shriek of joy, got down on his knees, and gave thanks right then and there to God in heaven and to the Blessed Virgin of Seville, for he believed that these visions described as floating mountains must be sailing vessels manned by Europeans. What else could they possibly be?

Unfortunately, he did not know what to do, for the stories had lacked specifics. Where were these floating mountains now? News traveled slowly hereabouts, and by this time the Europeans had most likely sailed on. Damn. Damn. Damn. He was lucky, though. Rumors of his presence here—and of Gonzalo Guerrero's as well—had been passed along to these Europeans.

He knew this for a fact. On a fine March morning in the year of our Lord 1519—he'd kept careful track—a pair of native messengers had arrived in the village where Aguilar was living and where he labored as a field slave in the employ of a local chieftain, Ezaak by name. They bore a letter from the captain of the Europeans, who was called Hernán Cortés and who—like Aguilar himself—was a Spaniard. This captain explained that he had sailed to these shores from the island of Cuba, on a mission to celebrate the glory of the one true God, and to win new territories and honors for Charles I, King of Spain.

"I have heard that a pair of Christians are already dwelling in these parts, and I beg you to join my company. I am sending a small ship to a place called Catoche, where it will stand for seven days. Enclosed with this letter you will find a quantity of green beads, which may be used as currency to pay the cost of transit overland.

"Wishing you Godspeed and good luck, I sign myself Hernán Cortés, captain-general."

God in heaven! This was unbelievable. Aguilar tucked the beads away in his robes and read the letter through a second time and then a third. Eight years after being shipwrecked here, his Spanish had suffered, and he didn't trust his ability to make sense of what he read. Apart from poring over a tattered and musty prayer book that he always kept with him on a string tied around his neck, he hadn't had the opportunity to absorb a word of printed text in all this time. Eight long years. Eight years of drawing water, chopping wood, and hoeing in his chieftain's cornfields. But he seemed to have understood this letter right. He questioned the native couriers, and they confirmed it was true. Two days' journey from here, by the Island of Women, there were mysterious beings who dwelled upon mountains or towers that drifted upon the sea. The couriers said they had been dispatched with orders to hand this letter over to one or the other of the two Castilians who dwelt here already.

"Good work," said Aguilar. "I thank you. I thank you a thousand times."

He gave the pair a green bead each and then, sensing that this was not an occasion for parsimony, he gave them each one more. They seemed delighted. They trotted away, arms in the air, cackling with pleasure. Aguilar watched them go. He frowned. What now? What must he do? In fact, he realized exactly what came next. He had to seek out his chieftain, Ezaak, and beg permission to leave.

Fortunately, Ezaak was a companionable sort and, at least when he was sober, possessed of a benevolent streak. Aguilar found him in his hut with his latest wife, a child of twelve. The man was grunting like a wild boar and was slapping the girl about the breasts, such as they were. She seemed to be giving as good as she got, though. Even pinned on her side on the palm mat on the floor, she had somehow got her shoulders twisted around so that she could pummel her husband in the chest with her small brown fists.

"Ha!" he roared between groans. "Ha! I am the victor! I am the victor in the war of love!"

Aguilar didn't like to interrupt, but his news was important.

"Excuse me," he said. "Excuse me, please." He explained about the two messengers and the letter. He said that a ship awaited him at Catoche even now. He wanted permission to go.

"Wait," said Ezaak. "Wait. Wait. Wait."

He was wild now, the moment of greatest ecstasy almost upon him. He flopped and wriggled about on the palm mat, as if transformed into a fish dancing on the shore. With a huge groan—the longest and loudest yet—he arched his back, quivered for several seconds, and then was still. The girl slid herself out from beneath him, climbed to her feet, and padded away, naked as a baby. Ezaak hauled himself upright and adjusted his loincloth. "Sweet little girl," he said. "The perfect wife."

Aguilar inclined his head. A priest himself, he had initially been somewhat discomfited by the native complacency regarding coitus. Later, at various times, he had been tempted to treat the matter as the people did themselves, as a gift from the gods, to be shared freely, and in no way a source of shame. But certain scruples had intervened—his vow of celibacy, for one. During eight years of being marooned on these shores, he had not lost his faith in God. His belief had sometimes wavered, but it had not disappeared. He had even drifted toward despair, but he had always recovered, trusting that he would be saved. Many years since, he had resolved to ensure the purity of his soul, in order to promote the likelihood of his rescue. And now, at last, it seemed that his prayers and his fortitude had been rewarded.

"So," said Ezaak, "what is your news?"

Aguilar explained the situation again, and the chieftain listened intently, as if rapt. He seemed to be in an expansive mood. He insisted that Aguilar share some palm wine with him, and before long, he grew maudlin, which was the effect that drink generally had on him. Aguilar had been counting on exactly this result. When he judged the time to be right, he informed Ezaak that he wished to be released from bondage so that he might rejoin his own people—the only chance in eternity for him to do so.

Ezaak drained his mug and reached for the flagon of palm wine. "The only chance," he repeated, apparently awed by the words. "In eternity." He shook his head, refilled his mug.

"Yes," said Aguilar. "That is why I wish to leave. Soon."

Ezaak sighed, and Aguilar could tell from his lolling gaze that the chieftain would soon be embarking upon the next stage of his drunkenness, in which he tended to be surly. It was time to act.

Aguilar stood up. "Good-bye."

"Eh?" Ezaak reached for his mug of palm wine and drank deeply. He rubbed the back of his hand across his mouth. "What do you mean, good-bye? Where are you going?" He seemed to have forgotten already.

"Away," said Aguilar. "To rejoin my own."

Ezaak tilted his head so that it wobbled at an odd angle. "To rejoin?"

"My own. As I just told you."

The man frowned for a time but finally nodded, as if Aguilar's words were all coming back to him now. "Well, be quick about it, then."

"Yes, I will. Farewell." Aguilar turned and hurried away at

once, before Ezaak could realize what was happening. There was no time to pack his belongings, but he did not care. After eight years in this place, he had accumulated little in the way of material encumbrance and nothing that he could not easily abandon.

But first he had a duty to perform. Rather than make straight for Catoche and the Spanish ship, Christian honor obliged Aguilar to trek through the coastal forest a good deal farther inland—in the opposite direction. He must seek out Gonzalo Guerrero, who had been a mate of his at the time of the shipwreck eight years earlier. They had been making passage across the Caribbean Sea from a place called Darien to Santo Domingo on the island of Hispaniola—not a destination that Aguilar had greatly relished at the time, considering that he was under some financial obligation to a powerful merchant there, by the name of Enrique Enciso y Valdivia, a man of harsh ways and limited patience. Perhaps the shipwreck had been for the best—for Aguilar at least, if not for the others. In all, seventeen of the ship's passengers had survived that mishap at sea—fifteen men and two women—and of those only Aguilar and Guerrero still drew breath eight years later. Aguilar had chanced to find a liberal-minded chieftain, and Guerrero was a man of unusual grit. The natives had killed all the rest, more out of curiosity than anything else. They'd wanted to see what was inside.

Aguilar and Guerrero were no longer in frequent contact, owing to the distance that separated them and to the disparity in their social standing. Guerrero had taken up residence in a village several leagues away, and there he had greatly prospered, certainly more than Aguilar himself had managed to do. Married to a native woman and with three children by her, Guerrero was a figure of some authority in his adopted clan. He was treated as an elder and granted the rank of captain in time of war.

After a sticky and rather unpleasant trek, Aguilar finally marched out of the forest and into Guerrero's village. He found his compatriot lounging in a clearing in front of his house, a round hut of woven palm branches, surrounded by cashew trees. Guerrero was sharpening a flint blade on a stone and now glanced up from his labors.

"Ah, Aguilar," he said. "What a surprise. Welcome. Welcome."

"Guerrero. It's good to see you looking so fat."

With his arms outstretched, Aguilar approached his former shipmate. It was odd, and yet seemed quite natural, that the two men addressed each other in Maya rather than Castilian, which neither had occasion to use any longer. Aguilar showed Guerrero the letter he had received from this man Cortés, and while the other man read, Aguilar took stock of his fellow Spaniard, who huddled on the swept earth, surrounded by animal bones, a couple of little dogs, and three trundling children. The results of this inspection were disconcerting. The other man's hair was long and untidily cut. Moreover, his face was a riddle of tattoos, his ears were pierced, and long copper coils dangled from the distended lobes. He had an ornament of jadeite pinned through his lower lip, and his skin was as dark as a native's. How would the Spaniards respond to him? With a start, Aguilar realized that he himself probably looked almost as exotic. The tattoos and the flesh piercing, he had eschewed. But in all other respects, he must have resembled a native himself. He sighed. He could not help his appearance.

Now he explained to Guerrero what he had resolved to do. Aguilar had made his decision. He was heading for Catoche to join these Spaniards and to let the course of his life unfold from there. He had no hesitation at all.

He looked at his old shipmate. "What do you propose to do?"

"Why, I propose to do nothing," said Guerrero. "I mean, nothing out of the ordinary. I propose to remain where I am. I propose to continue with the sharpening of this damn blade."

"You can't be serious. Think, old friend. An opportunity like this may not come around again for years. You could die in this place."

"I could indeed. No doubt one day I shall. Until then, I am content to remain. Look at me. My face is covered with tattoos. I wear coils in my ears. I have a wife. And look at my children, how plump they are. In truth, if the Spaniards were to see me now, I don't know what they would make of me. You, of course, must do as you please, and may God bless you. But I am happy here."

Aguilar tried to change the man's mind, but Guerrero was quite decided. He had taken to the native life, and it to him.

Here he would stay. Even so, Aguilar might have continued with his arguments, but he was stopped by Guerrero's wife, who had been listening from inside the hut. Now she stormed out into the clearing, her hands on her hips, her eyes like stones of amber glinting in the sun.

"Enough!" she shouted at Aguilar. "You, who are dressed no better than a slave, why have you come to tempt my husband away? Go away yourself, and take your nonsense with you."

Aguilar glanced over at Guerrero, who smiled, as if to say, "You see? The decision is out of my hands."

That being the case, Aguilar took his leave of his old shipmate, turned, and headed back into the forest. He lost his way twice on the journey to Catoche, proving the old adage lamentably true—more haste, less speed. Finally, after three days and nights, he emerged onto an open beach and hurried along it until he came to the small native settlement at Catoche. The people told him that, yes, there had been a strange apparition off the coast, one that looked very much like a floating mountain, and it had indeed been populated by great monkeylike creatures. But it had gone away.

"*It has left?*" Aguilar was trembling with frustration and fear. Had he been forsaken, after all? Had he been abandoned by God? "When? When did it go away?"

Several villagers traded uncertain glances, apparently unwilling to answer a question that was evidently of such import to this agitated stranger. What if they answered wrong?

"Yesterday?" suggested one.

"This morning?" offered another.

"Tomorrow?" speculated a third, who promptly shook his head, confused.

Yesterday? This morning? *Tomorrow?* God in heaven, what were these people talking about? Furious, Aguilar stomped around the beach for a time until he stubbed his right foot against a driftwood log and collapsed on the sand, rubbing his injury and sobbing in disappointment. With his usual luck, he would be obliged to spend the rest of his miserable life among these dimwitted folk, none of whom could give a straight-forward answer to even the simplest of questions. Then he remembered the glass beads he had secreted away in a stitched compartment of his cloak. They gave him an idea.

He looked up at the villagers. "All right," he said. "Never mind when. *Where?* Which way did the floating mountain go?"

As one, the villagers raised their hands and pointed off to the south, toward a low islet of sand and greenery that crouched offshore, visible through a haze of sea spray—the little Island of Women. "That way," they said.

The green beads worked like magic. Aguilar divvied up most of them among the villagers and said more would be payable if this journey proved fruitful. A half-dozen natives pushed one of their big dugout canoes into the shallow turquoise glaze of the sea. They leapt aboard with their rough-hewn paddles, and Aguilar climbed in after them. At once, they were racing across the ocean waters, which turned steadily darker—now sky blue, now navy—as they ventured farther out. A steady swell rose and fell around them, so that at times Aguilar could make out the island ahead to the south, and at times he saw just a sloping wall of water.

"Faster!" he cried. "Faster!"

The villagers of Catoche promptly put even more blood into the effort, and the canoe sluiced with still greater speed through the slow surge of the ocean. Frantic, Jerónimo de Aguilar craned his neck and peered ahead, desperate to lay his eyes on anything that bore even the remotest likeness to a floating mountain.

Soon, the boatmen from Catoche ran the canoe up against the shore at the Island of Women, leapt into the shallows, and splashed onto the beach. They dragged their canoe with them, and Aguilar hopped out. Here, he and the others had no choice except to wait, and so they did.

Within an hour, they were rewarded. A sailing dinghy hove into sight around the point, manned by several Spaniards. It immediately put ashore, and the sailors clambered out. They wore doublets and breeches and gave off a phenomenal stench that thrilled Aguilar to the core. It reminded him of things he had almost forgotten—garlic, rancid butter, old socks.

"By Mary of Seville!" he shouted. "I am saved!" He ran toward the Spaniards and fell to his knees. He clasped his hands together. "May God bless you."

The leader of the small group—none other than Alonso

Puertocarrero—seemed at first not to believe that Aguilar was what he claimed to be, a fellow Spaniard.

Dressed like an Indian slave, in a wretched maguey cloak and a soiled loincloth, Aguilar understood that he looked more native than Spanish. During his journey he had lost a sandal so that now one of his feet was bare. His entire body was bruised and cut from encounters with rocks and brambles. Moreover, he could barely express himself in the Castilian tongue, so long had it been since he had last used it. The language was still there, rattling around in his head, but the words wouldn't assemble themselves in a coherent way. Luckily, he remembered his ancient prayer book. He produced it from under his cloak and held it out to the Spanish officer, nodding his head in encouragement and smiling like a lunatic. Desperately, he began to mouth the Lord's Prayer, for these words he did recall.

It was enough. The Spaniards immediately began clapping each other on the back and broke into a cheer. As the first men to make contact with one of the mysterious lost Castilians, they were bound to reap a huge reward from their commander, Hernán Cortés. Wonderful. Excellent. Splendid news. They laughed and clowned about, congratulating each other.

Aguilar remained where he was, kneeling on the beach, riffling frantically through the crumbling pages of his prayer book and mumbling to himself in a gibberish that was neither Spanish nor Maya but a sort of glossolalia, a speaking in tongues. Finally, several of the Spaniards marched over to retrieve him.

"Come," said the one called Puertocarrero. "Come with us."

To the boatmen from Catoche, Aguilar paid out what remained of his green beads, and he went off with his saviors in their sailing dinghy. Now that he was rescued, he couldn't contain his euphoria. He giggled like a madman, thinking that laughter might also help him to block out the infernal reek. What an ungodly stench. He'd damned near forgotten. The dinghy rocked and swerved on the ocean swell, and Aguilar found he was close to nausea. God in heaven, you could cut the Spaniards' stink with a sword.

An Army of Ghosts

Hernán Cortés was delighted with this latest sign of God's munificence. Just think—a Castilian who spoke the local tongue! True, the swarthy aspect of the castaway and his rather haunted gaze made the captain-general uncomfortable at first. But, on reflection, he realized the man's strange appearance was not surprising. Eight years in slavery to savages—that was bound to have an effect. Some of the fellow's more obvious deficiencies were soon corrected. He was promptly outfitted with a new doublet, a lace shirt, black breeches, and a pair of leather sandals. It was amazing how much difference Spanish clothes made. Next, Cortés appointed Aguilar to serve as chief translator. In this capacity, the man truly was a godsend. That slow-witted native, the one named Melchior, had hardly been better than a toad. Getting a word out of him was practically impossible, and you could barely understand what he said, even when you did. Besides, he looked sickly. They put him in irons below deck and promptly forgot about him. Good riddance.

Meanwhile, there was Puertocarrero to attend to. He deserved some sort of reward for his good work in finding the Spanish castaway. And Cortés also wanted to chasten that firebrand, Alvarado. On Cozumel, the fool had taken it upon himself to organize a raiding party and had gone off to pillage a couple of villages, stealing various artifacts of copper and obsidian—disappointing stuff, really—and knocking a native head or two in the process.

When he had found out about the incident, Cortés had flown into a rage. The attack had been stupid—completely unprovoked. One didn't conquer a strange territory by making enemies for no good reason. Such a rampage was bloody foolishness, offering no advantage and exacting an unnecessary cost. He made Alvarado go back to the two villages and return every last article he'd stolen. Naturally, the strutting blond hero had found this penance to be a blow to his pride. But he'd done as he'd been told. He did not seem greatly humbled.

Cortés decided that further punishment was required, something ingenious, and he had just the thing in mind.

Puertocarrero.

As a reward for rescuing the marooned Spaniard, Cortés furnished Puertocarrero and his men with promissory notes against the treasure they would reap in these strange new lands. Next, with Alvarado squarely in mind, he resolved to promote Puertocarrero to the rank of lieutenant, for there was nothing like one man's good fortune to make another man blanch. For the occasion, he organized a brief ceremony on the poop deck of the flagship.

"Excellent work," he said. Although not much taken with Puertocarrero as a person—a rickety bundle of bones and nerves—he had to admit the fellow had done well. Cortés stepped forward and pinned a rosette to the breast of the man's doublet. "You have performed a great service to your king and your God."

Puertocarrero beamed, his teeth almost leaping from his head.

Alvarado, of course, said nothing. He merely glowered. Later, Cortés found him wandering the decks, seasick as usual and now aghast that another man had eclipsed him.

Cortés gave an inward grin. The punishment wouldn't last much longer. He planned to let Alvarado stew in his own soup for a few days yet, and then he'd arrange something to cheer the man up. Give him some grand and reckless job to do.

The fleet weighed anchor and set sail. The eleven vessels rounded Cape Catoche and bore west along the low, green coast. They were following the course charted by Grivalva the previous year and by Hernández de Córdoba before him. The territory that they sailed past was marshy for the most part, tangled with mangrove bushes and small swampy scrub. Occasionally, Cortés saw parties of natives gathered on sandy headlands beneath spreading silkwood trees. For the most part, the people seemed peaceable enough, clad in loincloths and not much else. The women went about bare-breasted. Sometimes, the men raised wooden hatchets or spears tipped with what looked like obsidian or flint, but they didn't appear to be brandishing the weapons. Waving, he thought.

Cortés waved back, and so did many of his men. He had Aguilar, his new translator, call out some greeting in the local tongue, but what came back was largely absurd—mainly shouted inquiries as to lineage and preferences in the culinary arts.

"They are confused," said Aguilar. "They are trying to work out what we are."

"*What* we are?" said Cortés. "Don't you mean who we are?"

The translator shook his head. "They are not convinced that we are men."

Cortés put back his head and laughed. "What else could we be, dear God?"

Aguilar shrugged. "Oh," he said, "all sorts of things." He turned and leaned his elbows on the railing. He watched the green and undulating land drift past, punctuated by the pinwheel bursts of royal palms. "The native imagination is a rich device. As you will see."

After a while, Cortés sauntered off to inspect the condition of his flagship. This tour was mostly an empty show, for he understood little of navigation. Still, he was the captain-general. He was supposed to be in command. It looked well to take an interest in knots and sheets and so forth. He liked to act as if he knew what he was talking about, even if he didn't.

Aguilar remained where he was, hunched over the railing

and surveying the coast, a sequence of lagoons and islets and low sandy spits, fringed by sea grapes and mangrove—a lovely, unobtrusive terrain, utterly familiar to him now. With a start, he realized how much he would miss it. Strange to think that a man could long for his prison. He let out a sigh and peered up at the blue dome sprawling overhead. It was another fine morning. No sooner had this thought occurred to him—*¡Qué bella la mañana!*—than he realized that it had formed itself in Spanish. He was thinking in Spanish! It was amazing how quickly the language was coming back.

Yet in almost every other respect, the years of his abandonment had left their mark. He felt nearly as isolated among the Spaniards as he had as a slave among the Maya. The only subjects the sailors ever spoke about were women or gold. Aguilar, of course, had put aside his carnal appetites, the better to serve the Lord, and he had never had much interest in gold. These deficiencies made him poor company. At first, he'd thought that his new shipmates might want to hear about his hardships, and some of them did ask. A couple of times, he'd made the mistake of answering them, and he'd learned soon enough that the questions had been mere formalities, asked out of a crude courtesy. Now he gave it about three breaths before the eyes of his comrades began to glaze over as he tried to describe the long, desolate years spent as a slave in these unknown parts. Three breaths, and he was gasping at the air.

Well, never mind. Their indifference didn't really bother him. He had more important matters to consider. He understood, for example, that his rescue had been no mere stroke of good fortune. It was clearly part of a Plan. Eight years had he prayed for his release from captivity—prayed without cease—and at last God had answered. He'd been plucked from the edge of despair and clutched to the bosom of the Lord. Why? It could only be for some divine purpose. Otherwise, why not leave him to labor in the fields? Why not let him die, the way so many others had died? Aguilar watched the low coastline slip past, watched kestrels and egrets sway and dart on the morning breeze—like angels, they were—and he believed more strongly than ever that God had acted with a purpose, as He always did.

Almost everywhere he looked, Aguilar found proof. Earlier this morning, shortly after rising, he had glanced up, and in the creases of a canvas topsail, he had seen a hieroglyphic likeness of the *Virgen de los Remedios.* The vision lasted only a few moments, until a shift in the wind sent the Virgin drifting away upon the blue arc of the morning light. But Aguilar had seen her, a pulse of the Holy Spirit. Undoubtedly, he had seen her. There had been other signs as well. Why, only yesterday, he had fallen and cut his hand while climbing down a companionway. He had looked at his hand and watched as the blood in his palm formed the exact likeness of a cross. He had kept his hand still and let the blood coagulate in that very shape. Even now, he could make out a faint discoloration, a pattern of the cross etched upon the skin of his right hand. He heard voices, too. They spoke in the groan of the rigging, in the foaming of the sea. They spoke in his head.

All the time, he heard them. He couldn't make out what

they were saying, or in what language they spoke. But soon he would understand. He knew this on faith—the faith he held in the very God who had saved him at last.

The fleet traced the southward arch of the coast, past the native settlements marked on the charts as Campeche and Champoton, past Xicalango. Then, after two weeks of shadowing the landscape, they came to a more substantial settlement, identified in Grivalva's log as Tabasco—several dozen clusters of mud-walled hovels covered with thatch and poking through a blind of coconut palms and cashew and silkwood trees. All but naked, dark as blackamoors, the inhabitants peered out at the Spanish vessels and seemed to confer among themselves. Pot-bellied children romped amid the sea grapes and the clusters of bamboo.

Cortés gave the order to drop anchor here. He'd had a brilliant idea. In part, he wanted to restore Alvarado's spirits. Still moaning at the surge and wallow of the sea, the poor fellow had suffered enough since his humiliation at the Island of Women. Here was an opportunity to cheer him up. Besides, it was time for the Spaniards to make their presence felt upon these shores. Cortés announced that they would mount a spectacle here, one the natives would never forget. He put Alvarado in charge of the entertainment.

The blond one was delighted with his commission and threw himself into it with his usual gusto. The performance went off extraordinarily well. The entire population of the town assembled for the show, with their *cacique*—a word the Spaniards had brought with them from Cuba, where it meant "chieftain"—seated with his entourage in a place of honor, beneath a canopy of palm fronds. All morning long, the Spaniards paraded and swaggered about, dressed in their military raiment. The harquebusiers tamped the powder into the matchlocks of their weapons and sent balls of lead flying into the trees, where they astonished quite a number of birds. With Alvarado in the lead, the small cavalry of sixteen pranced in formation, with their banners of the Virgin flapping in the air and their scarlet plumes catching the sun. Later, they staged several mock charges that sent the villagers scrambling for cover. It had been clear already that the horses had utterly bewildered them. Now they were terrified, too.

The dogs were even better—great mastiffs trained to kill. They wore breastplates and additional armor to protect their flanks, and they bounded about, yelping and drooling, like four-legged demons of hell. As soon as the dogs were loosed, the natives began to scream and tried to bury themselves in the ground, as if all their worst nightmares had materialized before their eyes. Yet there was more, and better, to come.

The cannons achieved the most potent effect. The Spaniards lugged one ashore aboard a landing boat, set it up on its wheelbase, and hauled it up into a clearing bordered by a stand of ceiba trees. They took several shots at a low hummock across the way. The roar of the blasts terrified the villagers, but the spectacle of the hummock being pulverized into a pit, as if by some divine and invisible force—ah, that was a most memorable sight. The poor natives must have thought they were witnessing an attack of lightning and thunder, unleashed by an army of ghosts.

It was a most commendable performance. Alvarado got the strut back into his gait. Puertocarrero, while not overly pleased that his rival had been restored in the captain-general's esteem, nonetheless recognized that the display had been a worthy project and therefore held his tongue. Perhaps he would have done so anyway. He was a meek and tremulous soul.

All in all, Cortés was entirely satisfied.

In fact, among the Spaniards, the only man unhappy with the affair was Aguilar, the translator. He considered it unchristian to intimidate the natives in this manner, and declined to participate. He spent the entire morning alone below decks, and thereby came upon his unfortunate predecessor, Melchior. The poor man had been clamped in irons and was now half dead, having received almost nothing to eat or drink for days. His face was riddled with sores that oozed a particularly noxious sort of pus. It looked to Aguilar like a case of the pox.

Without hesitating for more than a moment or two, Aguilar took an iron bar and broke Melchior loose, then got him some water. That done, he half-dragged the man up onto the deck. All the other Spaniards had gone ashore, so there was no one to interfere.

"Can you swim?" said Aguilar.

The poor fellow mumbled out a vague and tentative reply, but it was more a yes than a no, and that was all that Aguilar wanted to hear.

"Then you must swim," he said. "Otherwise, you will surely die."

He helped the man over the railing and gave him a push. Melchior hit the water with a splash and went straight under. Aguilar thought for certain that he had committed a mortal sin—sent a man to his death by drowning—but soon Melchior reappeared in a flurry of flailing arms and sputtering gasps. He floundered toward the shore, and despite some difficulty in the pounding breakers, managed to drag himself up onto the sand. At first, he simply lay where he was, and again Aguilar feared the man was dead. Eventually, however, the dark, naked figure staggered to its feet and stumbled away.

Cortés's main purpose in mounting this spectacle of war at Tabasco—apart from putting Pedro de Alvarado back in a better temper—was to serve notice that he commanded a formidable military force. He calculated that this news would be relayed far into the interior parts of these territories, and thereby communicated to the great *cacique* whose existence he'd heard about from Grivalva—the *cacique* who was said to rule all these lands.

As it happened, the performance had another consequence which, though unexpected, was very nearly as welcome. As an act of propitiation to these terrifying visitors, the *cacique* at Tabasco made a gift to them of twenty slave girls. On behalf of his men, Cortés accepted the honor most graciously. In return, he ensured that the *cacique* was rewarded with a particularly generous quantity of colored beads. He then instructed the chaplain, Father Pedro de Olmedo, to conduct a baptismal ceremony so that the girls might all be converted to the true faith, for it was a sin to lie with infidels. That done, he divided them into two groups, based on their comeliness. The prettiest of the girls, he presented individually to his most trusted officers, to be kept as chattels.

He took special care that Puertocarrero was given the first choice, in consideration of his services at Catoche and the Island of Women. Whatever his other faults, the man now proved himself to be a fine judge of the feminine sex. He chose the best-looking of the lot. Her name—Malantzin or some such—had been changed during the baptism to Marina. She was young and pretty and had a regal sort of bearing, almost like a princess. Cortés felt a stab of regret when Puertocarrero made his selection. He'd half-wanted her for himself. Ah, well. It was better to look ahead. There would be greater prizes to come. Meanwhile, he sent the remainder of the girls out among the rest of the men, where they were put to good use as a general resource.

The arrival of the slave girls produced a palpable improvement in morale. The canvas itself seemed to protrude farther than usual in the wind as the fleet probed west along the low green shores, past Cintla and Ayagualulco, past Tonala and Coatzacoalcos, all of which were marked on Grivalva's charts. Now the coast veered north, and the shoreline swelled with an impressive range of verdant mountains.

As before, it was only Aguilar who seemed unhappy. He watched the mountains, where they towered beyond a blue shard of the sea, and he sank a little lower into this unexpected melancholy. For so many years he had longed for his liberation, and now that it had come, he found he had been released into the clutches of animals. Consider the horrible treatment of these native women. In his view, the Spaniards comported themselves as dogs. Another torment was the reek of these men. Reassuring at first, it was beginning to wear upon him now, almost past bearing. Granted, he understood the reason for the stink—the Spaniards were loathe to bathe—and he knew the explanation for that, too. Only lately had Castile raised itself against the Moorish occupation and driven the invaders back across the sea, at Gibraltar. But spies were everywhere and suspicions remained rife, not least at the Holy Roman Office of the Inquisition. A wise Spaniard eschewed any practice, custom, or trait that had a Moorish taint about it—including frequent bathing.

Aguilar gritted his teeth and took to breathing through his mouth. As for the women, there was little he could do to prevent their mistreatment. At least there had been one useful aspect to that demeaning affair. In the excitement over the gift of the slave girls, no one had noticed that the native named Melchior had somehow been released. By the time someone did notice, the Spaniards were all too sated to care.

Aguilar grimaced and began to stroll along the leeward railing of the vessel. Off to port, the blue sea snapped and beat with a spreading froth of whitecap waves. Like angels' wings, they were. Everywhere he looked, he saw angels. The wind rose, the sheets groaned, and now he heard them, too. Angels. They sang in his head, in a language he did not know.

What a Princess Does

The slave girl named Marina slumped in the hold, along with most of the other women, and contemplated her fate. It was intolerably stuffy down here. At first, they'd been permitted to walk about upstairs on the roof of this strange floating house, and that had been frightening, but also exhilarating. Now she could barely breathe, and the constant motion threatened to make her ill. Some of the other girls already *were* ill. She ran her hands through her hair, dug her fingers deep into her scalp.

What a mystery this was. First, these bewildering brutes— españoles, as they called themselves—had chanted something in a slow, clanking tongue and later splashed water on her face. Then they had changed her name, to Marina or something of the sort. Finally, they had turned her over to one of them, to be as a wife, which was all right in principle. It was certainly better than being held in slavery by the chieftain of Tabasco, which until lately had been her fate.

So, why wasn't she happy? Well, for one thing, there was the smell. It was beyond belief. But in time, she supposed, one got used to it. One got used to most trials in this strange business called life. The smell she could endure. What concerned her more was the unpleasant way this mysterious affair had arranged itself in her particular case. She was not at all happy about that. Even though she could not understand a word he said—nor he a word of hers—she saw plainly that the man who had selected her was a groveling sort, not apt to go far. She'd have preferred the taller one, the one with the golden hair, but his turn to choose had come too late. Even better would have been that stocky one, the one with the thick beard that did not quite cover a rather nasty-looking facial scar. He was obviously the chieftain around here. He would have suited her quite well.

Instead, she'd got stuck with . . . with . . . oh, she couldn't remember, let alone pronounce, the man's name. Puerto-something. He was thin, bony, and his teeth stuck out. Among his other deficiencies, he was impotent.

At the moment, he was off somewhere, and she had been put back with the other girls. As usual, she kept herself apart from them, for they were a common lot. She, on the other hand, had been born to nobility. Her father had been chieftain of the town of Olutla, near Coatzacoalcos. He had also held sway over several vassal towns. Accordingly, she had been raised amid wealth and comfort and had known most of life's privileges, certainly all that were due a princess, which was what she was. It wasn't her fault that her father had died while still a young man, or that her mother had then married another nobleman, the chieftain of a different town, to whom she bore a son. Life had deteriorated from there. To avoid any difficulty with the half-brother's inheritance, the chieftain had decided to hand Marina—or Malantzin, as she was then called—over to some villagers from Xicalango. In turn, those people had presented her as a gift to the chieftain of Tabasco.

She shook her head and adjusted the lie of her cotton skirt. She shouldn't complain. By being handed over to these huge, hairy men—these Spaniards—at least she'd got herself out of Tabasco. That was something. But she wanted more, as she always had. She was the daughter of nobility, not a common slave. Didn't people understand that?

Apparently not. But they would. Standing by herself in the hold of this huge floating house, the princess called Marina took another deep breath of the damp and fetid air. Soon she would have something better than this. She was determined. And already she had an idea about how to accomplish such an end. She was no fool. She'd spent only days in their company, but she thought she understood what these Spaniards wanted. They had not come to these shores by accident. They were intent on conquest. Conquest and plunder. Any dullard could see that. And she had an idea, an emerging idea, of a way in which she might be able to help them. How truly it had been said—a knack for languages is always useful. It so happened that she had such a knack.

She glanced across at the other slave girls, the ones who had been selected for their prettiness, just as she had been herself. They *were* pretty, too, if rather green in complexion at the moment. But that was all they had, their looks. They didn't have what she had—a knack for languages—and this made her special. Marina resolved to keep her plan to herself until an opportunity presented itself. Then she would know what to do. She smiled at the other girls.

"Cheer up," she said. "No one likes a pouty face. Cheer up for the sake of your handsome new husbands." She smiled again.

Some of the other girls smiled back, several groaned and rolled their eyes, the rest gazed stonily ahead. No one said a word.

"Oh, very well," said Marina. She arched her back. "Be miserable, then. For my part, I prefer to be perfectly, perfectly fine—happy and at ease. And I am."

This assertion was slightly short of the truth, but Marina always behaved as though everything were turning out exactly as she would wish. She was a princess, and that is what a princess does.

Melchior peered up at the morning sky and thought he saw something monstrous, a jaguar larger than the sun. Its maw gaped above the horizon, dripping blood. Earthquakes rattled the ground underfoot, and stars glared down even now in the blue morning light. He picked himself up from the place where, sometime the night before, he had collapsed. He began to run, staggering along the track that wound inland from Tabasco toward the mountains. He felt great dogs snapping at his heels.

He had been running for days. Ever since that morning when he had been freed from the Spaniards' ship, when saltwater had forced its way down his throat so that he choked and could barely breathe—ever since then, he'd been on the run. He'd survived on berries and swamp water. Once he'd happened upon a snake sunning itself on a narrow footpath that wound through the scrub. The snake's body had been distended at the midpoint by what turned out to be a large frog. Melchior had smashed the snake's head with a rock and eaten most of the flesh raw, savoring the frog in particular. What he hadn't eaten then, he had stuffed into the pocket of his doublet.

The snake meat helped to clear his head, remind him why he was running. He was trying to reach Tenochtitlán, with a string of ominous words spiraling in his mind. He had heard them, as if in a dream, and at first he'd had no idea what they meant. *Flee. Flee. Take only what you can carry. Run for your lives.* But in that place called Cuba, he had learned the meaning of those words, divined it in the hollow gaze of dead men's eyes. He had to keep from crying out as he ran. Giants tottered all around him, clutching their heads—heads that sometimes burst apart like volcanoes. Bolts of lightning exploded from their mouths. In their wake, the cornfields shot arches of blood into the darkening sky. The clouds crashed from the heavens, huge as boulders. The raindrops stung like beads of molten copper. They hissed upon his skin, opened rashes, drew blood.

For three more days, Melchior stumbled forward. He thought he was running as fast as a puma, but in fact he made very poor time. So often did he stagger and lose his way and fall down. At night, he collapsed and was beset by nightmares even worse than the visions that tormented him by day. On the fourth morning, he awakened, struggled to his feet, and started to run. He was still running several hours later, or thought he was, when he rounded a switchback on the steep mountain wall with the *chipi-chipi* aflame upon his skin. Without warning, he stumbled straight into a *pochteca* and a convoy of porters, striding down from the high hinterlands. He fell to his knees, sobbing from exhaustion and fear. He managed to force the words out in a metallic rasp that tore at his throat.

"Flee. Flee. Take only what you can carry. Run for your lives."

"What's this?" said a male voice. "What on earth is this? Why, I believe I know this man."

A Portent of War

"In fact, I'm sure I know him."

Pitoque hunched down to take a closer look at this strangely familiar man. He felt Toc's hand grip his shoulder, a kind of warning or caution. And at once he saw why. The poor fellow kneeling before him was in a truly alarming condition. Certainly, he was haggard and scarred from what must have been a punishing journey. He was emaciated. And his clothing—unusual apparel, quite unlike anything that normal men wore—was soiled and tattered. But there was something else, something worse, something very wrong with the man. Everywhere, blisters and pustules had risen upon his skin. Some had opened, and from them dribbled a dreadful, foul-smelling pus.

173

Pitoque grit his teeth against the reek and helped to ease the man over onto his side. He was sweating like wet moss and shivering as well. Pitoque ran a hand over the fellow's hair.

"There you go," he said. "Perhaps you would like something to eat?"

The man nodded so violently, it seemed his head might fall off. Pitoque arranged for a meal to be provided—cooked toad in green chilis was the best that could be produced on such short notice—as well as water to drink. While the man slurped at his food and slurped at his water, spilling more than he drank, Pitoque watched him carefully. Slowly, the memory returned. This was the very individual who had been taken away by the gods a year earlier, on that day when Pitoque himself had walked upon the roof of one of their floating palaces. Now here was the same man again, a good deal the worse for wear. That wasn't all. What were the first words he had uttered? The sounds had been muffled, hard to make out, but Pitoque was fairly certain the phrases had been the same as those he'd heard from the lips of invisible women crying out in the night, the voices of the omen.

Flee. Flee. Take only what you can carry. Run for your lives.

A cold sensation welled in the pit of his stomach. What on earth did the words mean? What was this man running from? What had happened to him? And what had caused this terrible blight upon his body?

During the course of that morning, Pitoque asked all these questions, and more. But the answers he got were more bewildering than enlightening. The poor man seemed to be suffering from some sort of madness. He started at the slightest movement, hunched his shoulders, closed his eyes. He seemed beset by a thousand terrors, none of them visible to anyone else. When he wasn't mumbling that dark omen—*flee, flee*—he ranted on about furies that made no sense whatever, strange visions he had witnessed. He described great two-headed dragons, creatures that were not of this earth, with the face of a man and the head of a deer. They galloped about, snorting and waving great horns or spears. He spoke of beings that wore impregnable armor, that carried huge two-handed swords. He said they looked like giant ants swollen to the size of men.

And dogs. He spoke of dogs—but not the little dogs that Pitoque knew, the ones that civilized people liked to cook over a wood fire and consume with squash flowers and chili peppers. No, these dogs were enormous, with great ears that flapped in the breeze and blazing yellow eyes and tongues that dangled from their jaws, dripping foam. These dogs were wrapped in a kind of armor, too, and they raced around, panting and barking and leaping. When they raised themselves upon their hind legs, they were at least the height of a man, only vastly stronger. They could tear a man apart, limb from limb.

He spoke as well of diabolical machines. One of these was a huge pipe into which balls of stone might be fed. With a furious roar, the machine emitted a profusion of fire and smoke and flying sparks, and at once, as if by magic, an explosion roared in another place, a great distance away. A tree might be reduced to splinters, or a patch of earth to a gaping pit. There were smoking spears as well, spears that gave a burst of fire—

and at once, somewhere else, a man would clutch at his chest and fall to the ground, dead. That was magic, too.

Melchior—Pitoque remembered his name now—rambled on and on. None of his fantastic tales held together. Just when he seemed about to say something approaching sense, he suddenly threw up his hands and screamed and began moaning about giants, their heads splitting like the sides of mountains. Or he pointed away toward nothing—a copse of trees—and swore there was a huge jaguar there, a flaming jaguar. He'd shriek and grasp his skull.

"It seems the poor fellow is mad," said old Toc. This was later that day, when he and Pitoque stepped aside to speak about the man privately. "Quite out of his head, in my view."

Pitoque frowned. "I fear it's so. You can tell he has a fire inside. He's burning up. You know who he is, I gather?"

"Yes. The one on the floating palace. Last year. They took him with them."

"And now it seems they've brought him back."

Pitoque took in a long, slow breath. So, the reports were true, after all. The gods had indeed returned, if gods they were. A year had passed since he had encountered them, that time with Toc. Now he had been summoned once again by the master functionary and dispatched to the coast, for there had been reports of further sightings of these strange structures adrift upon the sea. It was the year *Ce Acatl* now, 1-Reed—the year in which it was prophesied that Quetzalcoatl would return. Azotl had instructed Pitoque to make for the eastern coast immediately. He was not to wait for a propitious day or make a preparatory offering to the gods. There was no time. *Just go.* On this occasion, Pitoque had even brought Maxtla with him, partly because speed was paramount, but also because Azotl had changed his mind. He had decided that the merchant should take his son, after all.

Pitoque had been against the decision. But in the end, he'd been unequal to the combined arguments of Azotl *and* Maxtla, who desperately wanted to make the trip. Traveling with the boy was a risk, Azotl said, but maybe the risk was inevitable. Besides, if Maxtla were in any danger, would it not be better if he had his father at his side, to protect him? Only then would Pitoque have any chance of saving his son.

Finally, Pitoque had been forced to acquiesce.

"Go, then," Azotl had said. "I need to know what is happening. Hurry. Find out. Send word back."

This was the mission that Pitoque was trying to carry out now, as he and his company descended the switchback tracks that led down the eastern mountain wall on their way to the torrid coast. And look what he had found—a man half-crazed and near death, a man who spoke of horrifying visions.

"Father," said Maxtla. He hurried over to where his father and the head porter were standing by a clump of moss-covered rocks. "I thought you said these visitors were gods. I thought you said they came in peace."

"What do you mean?" said Pitoque. "Why do you ask?"

Maxtla had heard Melchior speak a few more words, sensible ones this time. Apparently, the poor man had insisted that it was those creatures on the floating palaces who possessed the terrible machines, the smoking spears, the two-headed dragons, the man-eating dogs.

"He told you that?" said Pitoque. "When?"

"Just now. He said they have come to conquer the Aztecs, to murder everyone. He said they aren't gods."

"Let me hear this for myself." Pitoque started to push past the boy. "I'll see what the fellow has to say."

"I don't think you will."

Pitoque stopped, turned toward Maxtla, angry at this impertinence. "What do you mean?"

The boy slumped down upon a rock and shook his head. He stared at the ground and then looked back up, clenched his jaw. "The poor man's dead. He died just now."

Pitoque went at once to see for himself, but he needn't have bothered. It was true.

There wasn't much to be done after that, except to give up an offering to the gods—it consisted of various toads and salamanders, all they had—and then to bury the poor wretch in soft ground near the base of their descent. That done, they hurried on.

Night fell, another day passed, and darkness returned once more.

Again, Pitoque could not sleep. Or, rather, he was afraid to sleep. His dreams—horrifying, monstrous dreams—had returned. He spent his nights now suspended in a foul state, midway between wakefulness and oblivion. This night, he was jerked from an unpleasant torpor by a terrifying sound. He sat upright and waited, somehow sure that he would hear it again. And he did. Soon it wailed through the invisible trees like laughter, the most alarming laughter. He recognized it at once—the wild, keening song of a white-headed hawk.

It was an omen, a dreadful omen—a portent of war. He clutched his hands to his head as the mad shrieks rose again, flinging themselves against the walls of the night. He fumbled at his breast, felt the necklace of shells. He closed his eyes and moaned. Why was he here, in this prison of darkness? Why had he received this commission? Why he, of all men? Why had he crossed paths with a dying madman along the way? Why should he be tormented by these portents and omens? Why could he not escape them, whether awake or asleep?

He could think of only one answer. The gods were angry, and they were angry at him.

A hot wind muttered through the branches of the ceiba trees, the night seemed to bristle with danger, and Pitoque imagined owls swooping through the darkness overhead. He shivered at the thought of their eyes shining down like embers of burning wood. He fell back, pulled his blanket close to his chin, and lay awake until morning, when a blood red sun climbed above the scribble of scrub growth on the eastern horizon. It was time to be on the move again. He blinked and swallowed, fought his terror down, while the others roused themselves, exchanged idle chatter, shook off the stiffness of their limbs.

After a breakfast of watercress and tortillas, they struck camp and continued their eastward march. They had a good idea of their destination. It was at Cempoala that Pitoque had encountered the gods a year earlier. They headed there.

Unless They Meant to Swim

The fleet commanded by Hernán Cortés continued up the coast until it reached a bay not far south of the place marked on Grivalva's charts as Cempoala. Here, the captain-general ordered his pilots to come about and tack back south a distance until the flotilla reached a better anchorage, a spit of land protected from the open sea by several islets and two good reefs. Here, he gave the order to drop anchor.

"We'll establish our base here," he said. "You." He turned to Puertocarrero. "You may take the first party ashore."

Puertocarrero grinned, thrilled to be singled out in this way. He hadn't really expected such attention, and it awed him more than a little. Why, he'd even been given first pick of the slave girls they'd obtained in Tabasco. He'd chosen the best one of all, the prettiest of the lot—and hadn't she given him a night or two already? And now, he would lead the first men ashore. He suddenly frowned. In truth, he was not entirely comfortable with having other men do his bidding. He reached up and pulled some stray shanks of hair across the top of his head, where they belonged. He took a deep breath, not quite sure what to make of this latest honor. But he knew it was an honor, and that imparted a pleasant feeling. He set off at once to organize the landing.

For his part, Alvarado was only briefly vexed by his rival's good fortune. As soon as the first landing party rowed out in a dinghy, Cortés turned to him and declared that he might have the even more signal honor of naming the new settlement that was to be established at this place. Alvarado replied without hesitation, for he knew just the sort of name that might please Cortés most.

"*La Villa Rica*," he said. "*La Villa Rica de la Vera Cruz.*" The Rich City of the True Cross.

Cortés furrowed his brow. "A little long, don't you think?"

Alvarado grinned. He'd thought of that, too. He said, "We can call it Veracruz for short."

Cortés tilted his head and tested the name on his tongue, as if he were sampling an unfamiliar vintage of wine. "Veracruz?" he repeated. Finally, he smiled. "Veracruz, it shall be."

Two days later, Cortés summoned Alvarado. He greeted his lieutenant outside his tent and invited him for a stroll, so that they might speak in private. The two sauntered along the gray, pebbly beach. The breakers pounded in, crashed and hissed, swirled around the two men's feet. An onshore breeze worried the fronds of the coconut palms.

"I am concerned," said Cortés, "about mutiny."

"What?" Alvarado lifted his head. "Do you mean a mutiny now? Why?"

"Not now. Eventually. We have many adventures ahead of us, as you can well imagine, and they may not all end in our favor. Some of our men might lose their desire to carry on."

"And?"

"And they might prefer to return to Cuba."

"I see."

"Well," said Cortés, "what do you think we should do?"

"Do?"

"To prevent any such occurrence."

"Ah." Alvarado put a sage expression on his handsome face and squinted out to sea, like a philosopher contemplating the deepest mysteries of the firmament. Finally, he shook his head, and his features reverted to their usual, rather vacant cast. He said, "I don't see what we can do, except exhort the men onward, inspire them with our courage and our will."

"I wonder if that will be enough." Cortés frowned and clasped his hands behind his back. He let out a long sigh. Secretly, he was wondering how long this discussion was going to take. With Alvarado, one never knew. He sighed again. "I wish I could think of another plan."

Alvarado was silent for a time, and the two men continued shambling through the shifting pebbles, occasionally wading through a sudden surge of warm seawater.

"Well," Alvarado said at last, "I suppose we could always sink the ships." He let out a bellow of laughter. "That would keep the men in line. They could hardly think of Cuba then."

Cortés closed his eyes. Finally. He opened them again, and he gripped his lieutenant by the shoulder. "Are you serious?"

"Serious? About what?"

"About sinking the ships."

"No. Of course not. I was making a—"

"It is an utterly brilliant plan."

"It is? What do you mean?"

"I mean that it is a stroke of genius. You're a genius, Alvarado. Your idea solves all my worries. It is just as you say—with the ships under the water, the men can hardly have second thoughts about settling in this new land." Cortés turned and began to march back along the beach in the opposite direction. "Very well," he called over his shoulder. "I'll leave this matter with you. Summon the men tomorrow. Carry out your excellent plan."

Alvarado stood knee-deep in a wash of seawater that had suddenly rushed in, drenching his breeches. He watched his commander recede, and he wondered what had just happened. Had he come up with a brilliant idea? Or had he just been duped? It was difficult to tell. He shook out his soggy pant legs and hurried to catch up with Cortés.

The following morning, Alvarado called for all the men to assemble at the base of a low bluff overlooking the bay of Veracruz. By now, all the Spanish supplies, equipment, and arms had been ferried ashore. With Cortés standing only a few feet away and gazing at him sideways, Alvarado stepped forward and cleared his throat. At first, no words would come out.

Cortés shifted his weight and slapped one hand against the handle of his sword. He let out an impatient sigh.

Alvarado tried again to speak. How could he make this

announcement without sounding ridiculous? In the end, he blurted the order out in the most abrupt way possible.

"We are going to sink the ships," he said.

At first, dead silence. The men exchanged glances. What on earth was the blond lieutenant talking about?

Alvarado frowned. "The ships . . . we are going to sink them. All of them."

Someone began to laugh—one voice in the entire assembly, more than five hundred strong. The laughter rose for a few moments, quavered uncertainly, and then faded. Alvarado recognized the voice at once, the thin, high-pitched sound of Puertocarrero. He bridled immediately and tried to think of something to say to the scrawny lapin, but he was not quick enough.

It was Cortés who marched over to Puertocarrero and stared him in the face. The man's hair flew about in the breeze, leaving his pate denuded and absurd.

"Why do you laugh?" Cortés's tone was sharp. "Do you think Alvarado is funny?"

"No, no. I was laughing at what he said about sinking the ships. For a moment, I thought he was serious."

"He *was* serious."

"Ah, yes. Of course. Of course, he was." Puertocarrero tried to laugh again, but it came out sounding more like a whimper, owing to some constriction in his throat. By now, he realized that something was very wrong. Why wasn't anyone else laughing? Why wasn't Cortés? He drew himself up straight and cleared his throat. "Very sorry, sir," he said. "I got a bit carried away."

"So it seems. Somehow, you find a source of hilarity in simple orders. Would you care to explain why?"

"Yes, sir. I mean, no, sir. That is, I appear to have misunderstood Alvarado's meaning."

"His meaning seemed clear enough to me."

"Yes, sir."

"You don't agree that we should sink the ships?"

"I suppose, if you wish, we could sink *some*."

"Not all?"

Puertocarrero considered the question. He was in a deep swamp now and could not see a clear way out. Still, he had no choice but to answer in the best way he could. "Not if we mean to return to Cuba."

"But that's just it." Cortés wore his severest expression. "That's exactly it." He turned to address all the men. "We do not mean to return to Cuba. It is here that we shall seek our fortune, and here that we shall win fabulous wealth and great honor and bring glory upon our own names and upon the names of the King and the *Virgen de los Remedios* and the one true God. In token of our earnest, Alvarado has proposed that we sink our ships. It was entirely his idea, and you should commend him for it." Cortés gestured at his blond lieutenant. "Carry on, Alvarado," he said. "You may proceed with our plan."

"Sir." Alvarado puffed out his chest and put back his shoulders, although he wondered once again why he was being given all the credit. He'd made a half-hearted jest about sinking the ships, and look where it had got him. But he had his orders now. He narrowed his eyes, cast a haughty glance at

Puertocarrero—who had done little to improve his fortunes today—and then set about organizing a party of workmen to see to the sinking of the fleet.

The rest of the Spaniards stood about in small groups, muttering to each other and shaking their heads, more bewildered than anything else. If they had any clear sentiment at all, it was relief that they'd kept their mouths shut, unlike that stuttering beanpole, Puertocarrero. God in heaven, hadn't he taken it on the chin?

Before long, Cortés emerged from his tent and ordered the men to return to their duties. Did they not have a garrison to construct? Let them set to it.

Meanwhile, some of the Spaniards rowed themselves out onto the bay in their wooden dinghies. They proceeded to attack the hulls of the eleven seagoing vessels with axes, swing after swing. A brilliant sun burned down, and the blows rang out across the growling water.

The reports of the axe blows split the morning air. From atop a wooded bluff overlooking the bay, Pitoque watched this bewildering operation. Two days earlier, he had arrived at this place from Cempoala, where he had left his gang of porters in the care of Toc. Since then, he had been observing the newcomers from a distance. Up to this point, he had seen little to alarm him. Now he shook his head in disbelief. Had these *teules*, these gods, gone mad? Were they all lunatics?

Maxtla came over and stood by his father's side. "How will they ever leave?"

The question struck at Pitoque in an unexpected way. Suddenly, the answer was obvious, staring him right in the face. He peered out at the endless waters, over which these gods had come.

"They are sinking the palaces," he said, "because they do not mean to leave. They mean to stay."

Before long, nothing could be seen of the floating structures but a few stray poles and struts of timber that poked above the blue waters of the bay not far south of Cempoala. Battered shafts of wood drifted out to sea. Pitoque patted his son on the shoulder, heaved a long, slow sigh, and turned away. Almost at once, he dispatched his swiftest runner to Tenochtitlán with a message for the master functionary. Whether they were gods or men, whether benevolent or evil, one thing was certain. Now they would never depart these shores.

Unless they meant to swim.

There was one happy occurrence. Pitoque sold some plates.

He had approached several of the newcomers with his hands raised high, palms forward—a gesture meant to signify that he came in peace. By this time, he had summoned a half-dozen of his porters from Cempoala, along with a cargo of dishes. He proposed to present himself as a trader, for a trader he was. The porters followed him, stepping gingerly forward on trembling feet. They did not think much of this idea, but they were bound to obey. Maxtla remained behind, on a hillock hidden by trees, in case anything went wrong.

When he had caught the attention of the strange beings, Pitoque immediately made a deep bow, straightened up, and stretched out his hands again. He stood aside and motioned to his porters, all of whom held up their wares, just as he had instructed them to do.

The newcomers approached him, evidently curious. They chattered among themselves in that strange, clacking language of theirs. Already, however, Pitoque found that he recognized the repetition of certain sounds, certain constructions. He had a gift for tongues, having learned so many over the years, and he mastered new ones now almost without knowing how he did it. Even now, he could make a good guess as to the meaning of certain words, the ones they repeated most often.

Platos. That word meant "plates."

Bárbaros. That meant "savages" or "strangers" or something of the sort, used in reference to Pitoque and his porters.

Coño. That was an oath of some kind, a foul-seeming word.

Trocar. Ah, here was a term close to his heart. It meant "to trade."

And so on. He loved this feeling. A new language, a tongue that began as a river of gibberish, was gradually diverting itself, flowing into familiar territory, into channels that made sense. But he did not let on about his growing comprehension. Better to appear ignorant. Better to comport himself as what they thought he was, a *bárbaro* come for the purposes of *trueque.*

The *teules* inched forward, frowning and muttering. Several carried long wooden spears with metal ends that were strangely blunt—hardly a great threat. Besides, they were pointed toward the sky. Pitoque ignored them. He turned and pulled out a plate, held it up, and stepped forward. Immediately, he was almost overpowered by the awful stench. He batted his eyes and clenched his jaw. He had almost forgotten about this terrible reek. He swallowed the bile in his throat and indicated by means of signs that, indeed, he wished to trade.

In the end, he made what he thought was a passable bargain—a selection of plates and other dishes in exchange for a handful of green jewels flecked with what he took to be gold.

As he and the porters returned to Maxtla's hiding place, Pitoque puzzled over the dreadful stink. It was evident that the *teules* rarely bathed. This was perplexing. At his home in Cholula, Pitoque had a bathhouse with heated water, which he was at pains to visit at least twice a day. It was a source of dismay to him when, during his travels, a lack of water barred him from daily ablutions. Here on the coast, he and Maxtla went down to the sea to bathe every morning. And yet, with all the water in the world stretching out before them, the *teules* were loathe to touch it.

Pitoque had an idea. If there were to be any direct encounters between the newcomers and representatives of the Aztecs—an event that seemed inevitable to him, now that the *teules* had destroyed their floating palaces—he would advise the emperor's servants to furnish burning braziers, and fragrant oils with which the newcomers might be liberally anointed, particularly their lower extremities.

He promptly selected a trustworthy runner to bear this advice to Tenochtitlán.

Whores by Night, Prisoners by Day

Burning braziers.

Fragrant oils.

Special attention to feet.

In his chambers in the capital, Azotl checked the recommendations off and resolved to ensure that they would be followed precisely. Perhaps owing to the limitations of his sight, he found himself especially sensitive to unpleasant aromas.

That morning, Moctezuma and his courtiers and priests had decided to follow the advice they'd received from the merchant Pitoque. They planned to send a party of envoys out to the coast in order to meet these *teules*, if that was what they were. They had been deeply shaken by the merchant's recent dispatches concerning the sinking of the sea-bound palaces. Destroy their modes of conveyance? What on earth did this mean? Did the creatures plan to remain? Worse, did they propose to travel inland? Before any such developments took place, some peaceful encounter was definitely in order.

After considerable debate, Moctezuma decided that gifts should be carried to the coast, and that they should be presented with considerable ceremony. The court agreed, furthermore, that a meal should be provided, as elaborate as local conditions might permit. As usual, Azotl was left to take care of the practical arrangements. He wondered now how many of these strangers there were. He peered down at his hieroglyphic notes, etched upon sisal paper. Close to five hundred, according to the merchant's estimate. That would take some degree of organizing. Well, it would simply have to be done. Once the meal was over, the visitors would be encouraged, as politely as possible, to leave—if not by floating away upon the sea, then by some other means. This request was deliberately left vague as no one had the least idea what these "other means" might be.

And there were other problems. According to the information received from the merchant, language was still an impediment. These *teules* did not speak Nahuatl. In fact, just as Pitoque had observed a year earlier, they seemed unable to converse in any of the languages spoken in these parts, with one exception. They had in their company an individual—rather darker in complexion than the rest of them—who seemed adept at conversing in the language of the coastal people, a version of the Mayan tongue. He served as an interpreter for the rest, a sort of intermediary between the realm of the gods and the world of men. It had been Pitoque's suggestion that a translator be appointed, someone capable of conveying meaning in both Nahuatl and Maya. He even volunteered to fulfill this duty himself.

When he first received Pitoque's recommendation, Azotl had been all in favor. Why arrange a parlay if none of the participants could understand one another? But in the House of the Eagle Knights, the idea had been rejected out of hand by Cacama, the king of Texcoco, who was a nephew of Moctezuma's. As before, Cacama had heaped scorn upon the notion that these foreigners should be unable to speak Nahuatl. What kind of god could not converse in the language of his people? And if these interlopers were not gods—as he suspected—then what mattered words? The Aztecs were the rulers of these territories. They did not require translators to impose their will—they imposed their will by divine right and by natural superiority. Cacama would hear nothing more about the need for interpreters. Let these so-called *teules* supply interpreters of their own. The grim-faced king resumed his seat and folded his arms. He stuck out his jaw. In the end, Cacama's view had carried the day.

Well, so be it. Azotl realized it was probably wise for Pitoque to keep a certain distance, disguise himself in a cloak of anonymity, the better to observe and report. The master functionary noted all these matters in his response to the merchant, a response he planned to dispatch via the same runner who had lately arrived from the coast. A delegation would be sent, complete with braziers and scented oils. It would be led by Cacama. The Aztecs would arrive without a translator, and Pitoque was to make no attempt to take on that role for himself. The Aztec delegates would simply have to muddle through as best they could.

"Finished," said Azotl. He rolled up a scroll of sisal parchment and handed it to the runner, who had been summoned by one of his aides. "Take this to your master. Go quickly. Like the wind."

The man nodded, stuffed the scroll into the little sack he

carried at his hip, and left the room. Already he was running. Azotl rubbed his chin, impressed. He wondered how he could obtain such energetic messengers for himself.

Cacama, the king of Texcoco, waved at his face and chest with a fan. Utterly useless. How was a civilized man to keep his composure with such a flimsy device as this? Despite his best efforts, sweat still ran from every pore, tickled his skin, and sopped his robes. He might as well have been taking a bath fully dressed. Truly, he had never known such heat. But he had never left the cool highland climate of the Valley of Anáhuac before. Judging by his experience so far, he understood perfectly why the Aztecs were the rulers of the world, for no one but a savage could survive in this infernal lowland steam. He threw down his ridiculous fan.

"Water!" he called out. "Bring me water!"

The bearers who carried his litter came to a stop and waited silently while a servant hurried up with a clay pot filled with water garnished with chrysanthemum blossoms. Another servant carried a handsome ceramic drinking cup.

Cacama gulped down two glasses and then half of another. He tossed the cup away, content to let it smash upon the ground. There. He'd drunk water, and he'd broken something. Now he felt better.

"Tepehuatl!" he called out. "Tepehuatl!"

Soon his senior adviser came bouncing into view aboard his own private litter. "My lord?"

Cacama shifted around and drew a hand across his brow, sending a shower of perspiration onto his robes. "Tepehuatl," he said, "how much longer will this unbearable journey continue? When do we reach our destination?"

The adviser stroked his chin while he considered the question, taking his time. He never liked to make a hasty response. "At this rate," he said at last, "another two days. Maybe a trifle more. Three?"

"Three days!" Cacama fell back in his litter. "That's absurd."

"We have to bear in mind the condition of the litter-bearers, my lord. They can only move so fast. Besides—"

"Besides *nothing*. If the litter bearers are the problem, they are a problem easily resolved."

"My lord?" Tepehuatl's voice, usually measured and calm, now rose toward what, in another man, might have been taken as surprise. "What are you doing? Why—?"

"Doing? What am I doing? I am proposing to walk on my own two feet. That is what I am doing." Already the king of Texcoco had climbed out of his litter and was striding forward under his own power. "If you don't wish to fall behind, I suggest you do the same."

What was this? Walk? Venture forth upon the earth like a common slave? "My lord," said Tepehuatl, "please wait." He'd never seen a monarch walk any distance before. Still, if Cacama could do it, so could he. He climbed out of his litter and gave chase, stumbling at nearly every step, so unaccustomed was he to walking upon the uneven ground. "Wait, my lord. Wait for me!"

Cacama did slow down but only by a little. He was determined to reach the coast as quickly as possible. If that meant walking on his own, so be it. He would walk. He had no time to waste, especially not in this horrendous climate. The time had come for quick, decisive action. All this uncertainty had to be resolved once and for all time. For how many years had the Aztecs been plagued by doubt and riven by dark omens? Far too many. He was determined to find out who or what these interlopers were, and to determine how they might be made to depart—whether by swords or by bribes. One certainty—they would have to leave. They might be gods, they might be men—Cacama didn't know or particularly care. He knew only that he wanted them gone.

But there was no time to waste. He peered about at these strange lands, etched with scrub growth and interrupted here and there by the round green fountains of ceiba or cashew trees, and he realized it was a good deal pleasanter to walk than to ride. Cooler, on the whole. And invigorating. He felt a refreshing tingle in the muscles of his legs, a new experience. He made a note to himself. When he returned to Texcoco, he would issue an edict. From now on, and whenever possible, all the nobles of that city would walk. Not on ceremonial occasions, of course. But with some frequency. At least once a day.

"Walking," he mused aloud. "A very pleasant activity. Why was I not informed of this before?"

The princess, now known as Marina, pressed her back against the gnarled trunk of a silkcotton tree. She crossed her arms at her breast and scowled. Being a wife unto a Spaniard was not working out to her taste at all. This fellow Puerto . . . Puerto . . . Puerto-*something*—he was a poor sort of a husband. She'd known at first glance that he was a weak and indecisive man, a man unlikely to go far, and she had quite different intentions for herself. She was determined to change her circumstances— and she even had a plan—but she was uncertain when, or if, she'd have the chance to put it into practice. For now, the only compensation was that they were back on dry land, which was certainly a blessing. All the girls agreed on that.

Marina glanced around at her companions—the nine other young women who had been selected, like her, to serve as wives to various individual Spaniards. The beautiful ones. At the moment, they were all gathered in the shade of several ceiba trees, required to spend the long, hot midday hours in a kind of confinement. It was only at night that they were split up and taken off to their several beds. While the sun shone, they were treated as prisoners.

Why? She could only speculate. The Spaniards were jealous of their personal belongings and worried that some might go missing. Maybe their concerns were not entirely misplaced, for included among their possessions were many remarkable objects. Whenever she had the chance, Marina immediately found herself rooting through her new master's goods and chattels—not to steal any of them, of course, but simply to touch and to wonder. Half the time, she hadn't the remotest idea what the articles were or what they were for, and yet her fascination only increased.

Every once in a while, she came upon something extraordinary, something she understood. For example, a mirror. Oh, she had thought she would faint! She had held a mirror in her hands before, but it had been a poor thing, made of obsidian. But this! It was extraordinary. Her own face had been reflected back to her with a brilliance that she could never have imagined. *Her own face.* Even now, the thought of it danced in her mind. She had known that she was lovely, but she had not imagined the full extent of the truth. Her own beauty made her feel weak. She could not wait until she had the chance to hold the mirror again. She thought that she would never grow tired of gazing at herself.

She imagined that the other girls must have found items of similar interest. Granted, she hadn't asked them. It wouldn't do to be too familiar, to set herself on their level. She had to maintain a certain distance and reserve. But she didn't see why any of them would be less curious than she was herself. And, to be blunt, one or two of them might not be above slipping some coveted item into the folds of a robe, to spirit it away for her own private perusal and amusement. Most of these girls were low born, without breeding of any kind, so theft was a legitimate concern. But she sensed that the Spaniards were worried about something else. Perhaps they feared that some of the slave girls might actually gather their wits and run away.

Marina shook her head and smiled to herself at the thought. Run? Run where? Where could an escaped slave girl go? She had no wherewithal, no means. She was entirely dependent upon whoever happened to be her master. Not that the rest of these girls seemed especially unhappy. On the contrary, they had the air of people quite content with their situations. Here in the shade of the ceiba trees, they were doing as they did every day. They chattered and gossiped, shared lurid tales of their nightly adventures, and drew comparisons of various kinds, salacious and otherwise. They tittered and laughed.

Well, this was what the girls had now become—whores by night, prisoners by day. This life seemed to suit the others. It did not suit her.

Although her secret plan had come to nothing so far, she still had hopes. Sooner or later, there was bound to be an encounter between these Spaniards and the Aztecs. She prayed that it would be peaceful, at least at the outset, for that meeting would be her chance. Luck would be required, as well as daring. So she prayed for luck, and she waited, even as she had been waiting for days now, forced to squat like a pumpkin beneath these ceiba trees and listen to the other girls carry on among themselves about the most trifling and idiotic affairs.

Thank goodness, for their sake, that they were pretty—or passably so. They'd never get by on their brains.

Marina spent two more days in this dreary manner before something finally occurred to break the monotony. It was just what she had been waiting for—a party of Aztecs arriving from the hinterlands that lurked beyond the wall of mountains to the west. She recognized at once that they were Aztecs. The grandeur of their robes gave them away, and they bore themselves with a stiffness and reserve that were immediately noticeable, so different from the swinging gait and casual ways of the coastal folk. She leapt to her feet and would have run out to greet them if a native guard had not stepped forward and stopped her. Ah, well, such an impetuous gesture would have been a mistake anyway. Somehow she had to reach the commander of the Spaniards, the one named Cortés. She had to win his confidence first.

Instead of dashing out into the open, she remained where she was and watched the Aztec delegation parade past. But something seemed to be wrong. The dozen members of the honor guard marched by with all the usual Aztec arrogance, but they were followed by a pair of men who, despite the elegance of their dress, were now the very antithesis of Aztec hauteur. One of them—their leader, to judge by his robes—hobbled into view, as though he had suffered some terrible injury along the way. He groaned at every step. The same was true of his companion, who was clearly a royal aide. Finally, both men let their attendants help them into a pair of empty litters, which were raised onto the shoulders of slaves.

The procession continued, followed by a variety of servants, more slaves, and various porters. Marina glanced off to her left and noticed that several Spaniards had already assembled and were walking out to greet their mysterious visitors. They advanced cautiously, with their smoking spears lifted high.

She prayed there would be no bloodshed—or none just yet—and she ransacked her mind for some way to put her plan into effect. All she had to do was gain the attention of Cortés—but how was she to manage that?

A Certain Slave Girl

"Yes, Aguilar. What do they say? What do they want?" Hernán Cortés tugged at the purple tunic beneath his breastplate. He had pulled the armor on in a great hurry, and his clothing was uncomfortably bunched beneath it. "Who are they? Where are they from?"

Aguilar would have liked to know as well. He squinted through the glaring sunlight at these two men, both nobles, apparently—that much seemed clear. They stood several feet in front of him in the shade of a cashew tree, flanked by several of their guards. Both had bronze complexions riddled with tattoo lines and wore large lip plugs of precious stones that glinted in the morning light. They were grandly dressed in long robes dyed in lurid colors and geometric designs. One had a rigid, stony demeanor and seemed to hold some authority over the other, who was shorter and whose features seemed slightly more pliant and agreeable.

Cortés had a complement of guards on hand as well, and they had taken up positions behind and to the sides of their commander. The cashew branches shifted overhead in a desultory breeze, and Aguilar began to translate the questions put by Cortés. *Who are you? Where do you come from? What do you want?* But before he could utter more than a mouthful of words, the larger of these two—a dark, regal fellow, evidently the leader— put up a hand and cut him off. He made it clear that it was he, and no one else, who would ask the questions.

He began to speak.

Aguilar tried to pry some sense from the sounds he made. As an aid to comprehension, he nodded at intervals as if he were taking some of the words in. Unfortunately, he was not. To him, the language was gibberish. He waited while this impenetrable monologue continued, and then he broke in, as delicately as possible, to explain that his commander had some queries of his own.

Once again, he began to articulate his questions. He wished to know who these two were, whence they had traveled, and for what purpose. Did they come in peace or to discuss terms of war? Were they by any chance acquainted with the great *cacique* who dwelled inland at some considerable distance from the coast?

He posed all of these questions in Maya, which took a little time. Maya was a formal and elaborate tongue, one that required many honorifics and salutations and assurances of respect, coupled with a rather serpentine phraseology. When he at last expressed all he had to say, he stopped and nodded encouragingly. He waited for a response. "You may reply at your convenience," he added. "Honored sirs."

But they did not reply. They only looked at each other, eyebrows raised in surprise, evidently bewildered by Aguilar's words. Meanwhile, they had begun to bob and weave a little, as if hard-pressed to remain on their feet. Apparently, they were feeling the rigors of their journey. They seemed to be in some discomfort, perhaps even pain.

With evident difficulty, the taller one started to speak again. But it was no use. Aguilar was as baffled as ever. He turned to Cortés.

"Mi capitán, it saddens me to inform you that I do not understand what these men are saying." To clarify, he added, "I don't understand their form of speech."

"Not a word?"

Aguilar shook his head. "Not a word."

"I see." Cortés slapped the handle of his sword. "You are the translator here, I believe?"

"Yes, but—"

"Then surely it is incumbent upon you to understand what is being said. And yet you tell me you do not."

"That is so. They are speaking some different language. They are Aztecs, I believe."

"Aztecs?" Cortés peered at these two individuals more closely, at their strange costumes and the ghastly contraptions they had affixed to their mouths. He knew a little about Aztecs, having read about them in Grivalva's log. They were reported to live in a grand city located in a high, cool valley, beyond the mountains and above the clouds. They were the wealthiest and most power-ful people who dwelled in this new world. He shifted his weight. Aztecs, were they? Odd-looking beasts. He inclined his head toward Aguilar. "What's wrong with their feet?"

Aguilar shrugged. He'd noticed it, too. Both of the men who now stood before him were badly blistered and abraded about the feet. They seemed almost lame, an unexpected condition considering they were apparently noblemen. "I don't know," he said. "I would ask them, but they don't seem to understand me any better than I do them. They don't speak Maya."

"This is delightful," said Cortés. "I travel all this way, and what do I find? A tower of Babel. Savages that I cannot comprehend." He slapped the hilt of his sword again, turned and wandered away. He needed some time, to compose himself, to think. He'd been under the distinct impression that his language woes had been solved.

The two Aztecs—if that was what they were—took the Spaniard's departure as a signal that they might sit down, which they promptly did, but in a hurried, clumsy way. God, they looked sore.

After the morning encounter had disintegrated into a shambles, Cacama elected to do as the purple-frocked interloper had done—withdraw and rethink. He and Tepehuatl limped across a swath of cleared land and gathered near a grove of cashew trees, along with their entourage. Cacama was deeply distressed by the way the meeting had turned out. He was also a little humbled. After all, he was the one who had insisted that communication with these beings would not be a problem, and it was proving a disaster. As well, he had in no way been prepared for the newcomers' unearthly appearance, even though it was exactly as the merchant of Cholula had described. And the smell! He remembered, rather late, that braziers had been carried down from Tenochtitlán, along with quantities of scented oil. He gave instructions now that they be brought out and made ready, just in case. He also took the precaution of dispatching a party of his guards to round up whatever food they could acquire locally, to be paid for in the usual manner—which meant not paid for at all, but simply taken.

Now both he and Tepehuatl were at rest, reclining on the wooden-framed cots that had been set up for their convenience. They'd also had a series of cotton canopies erected overhead, so that they might consider in greater comfort the challenges they faced. In fact, lying down was a welcome relief, for both men were in a badly depleted state. Although a fine and bracing activity to begin with, the act of walking had taken its toll. Cacama's feet were so badly blistered and swollen that he could no longer fit them into a pair of sandals. Meanwhile, the muscles of his legs burned like all the chilis of Xalapa. Tepehuatl appeared no better off.

"Damn," said Cacama, who was not one to shirk the truth for long. "Damn. Damn. Damn. This is all my fault."

Tepehuatl did not reply. In fact, he tended to agree.

Cacama moaned and lay back on his cot. What could he do to remedy the situation? He called for water. Water and a fan. "And start preparing the banquet!"

Tepehuatl sat up. "Prepare the banquet *now?*"

Cacama shrugged. Why not? "If we cannot talk, we may as well eat."

For days now, Pitoque had watched the slave girl as she lounged on her own in the shadows of a grove of silkcotton trees. She kept herself apart from the other girls and seemed to do nothing all day long except comb out her long black hair, apparently lost in her thoughts. She was quite possibly the loveliest creature he had ever seen.

Still, he wondered what she was doing here. From her bearing, he could tell at once that she was an entirely different manner of person from those around her. A noble, surely. Possibly a princess. It aroused his curiosity. Finally, he could put it off no longer. What harm could it do? Since the first encounter between the *teules* and the emissaries of Moctezuma had proven to be a fiasco—much as he had predicted—there were no other demands on his time just now. He'd warned them about the language problem. But had they listened?

Now he stood up and prodded with his foot at his son, who had fallen asleep in the intensity of the midday heat.

The boy yawned, struck out with his fists, and frowned, unwilling to wake up amid this weight of steaming air. "What is it, Father?"

"Come."

"Come where? Where are we going?"

"For a stroll," said Pitoque. "A nice, refreshing stroll." Now that he had made up his mind to take a closer look at the girl, he was keen to begin. "Come along."

Pitoque had intended merely to walk by the girl, simply to watch her for a while. Nothing more. He hadn't expected that they would speak. But she called out as they strolled near a dark pool of shadows cast across the open grass by several silkcotton trees. A man could have drowned in that pool, it looked so dark and deep.

"You!" she called out. "You there. Yes, you. You and your grandfather."

"He's not my grandfather." Maxtla laughed, as if he'd heard a fine joke. "He's my father."

"Ah, yes. So I see. I'm very sorry. A trick of the light." The girl quickly recovered her composure. She gave Pitoque the sweetest smile imaginable. "What an absurd mistake. Now that I see you more clearly, you better resemble brothers. You could almost be twins."

"Do you think so?" He straightened his shoulders, ran a hand through his hair. "That's very kind of you to say."

"Oh, but I speak the truth." She frowned. "Forgive me, but which of you is the father?"

"Really," said Pitoque. "This is too much."

"You can't be serious," Maxtla said. "He's twice my age. More than that. He's old."

"Now, now. The girl is merely stating her opinion. She has as much a right to her impressions as you do to yours."

Maxtla rolled his eyes and looked away.

Pitoque turned to the girl and was about to ask her name when the realization hit him—she'd been speaking Nahuatl. He tilted his head. "Where did you learn to speak my language?"

"Your language?" She laughed. "You Aztecs. You believe that you own even the language that you speak."

"We are not Aztecs. We are from Cholula. We are *pochtecas* by trade."

"Are you indeed?" She raised her eyebrows. "So much the better."

She took another step forward, then stopped, considering how to proceed. In fact, it was precisely on account of their speech that she had called out to them. As soon as she had heard them speaking to one another in Nahuatl, she had decided to attract their attention. Language—that was her advantage. It was language that would save her. She was certain of it. And now she saw her chance.

"My name," she informed them, "is Malantzin. Nahuatl is my mother tongue." She smiled again, knowing that her smile was among her more striking assets. "How I envy you. I can think of no more fascinating profession than that of a *pochteca*. Such exciting and dangerous travels. So much bravery required. You must have countless stories to tell."

Pitoque smiled. "As a matter of fact—"

"Father." Maxtla released a long, low breath.

Pitoque hesitated, then chuckled in what he hoped was a bemused, indulgent manner, as if to say, *Boys will be boys.* He smiled at the girl. "Perhaps another time."

"I would look forward to it."

Pitoque could not take his eyes from her. She was so lovely—slender of build, with an oval face, sloe-eyed, with a luxuriance of long black hair dyed with indigo, hair that she had just now been knotting into a single braid. Everything about her—her looks, her bearing, her evident self-confidence—proclaimed that she was nobly born, and yet here she was, treated as a slave.

She tilted her head and smiled, apparently amused by the intensity of Pitoque's gaze. "You find something wrong with me?"

"No, no. Nothing at all." Pitoque looked away, fixed his eye on a dab of blue beyond a screen of branches and leaves. The sea. "I mean to say . . . no, nothing."

"I am relieved to hear it."

He did not reply.

She held out her hand. "My name," she repeated, "is Malantzin, but they have taken to calling me Marina. I do not know why. They splashed water on my face and deprived me of my former self." She laughed, as if the loss of former selves were a daily event.

Pitoque nodded. "My name is Pitoque, and this is my son, known to the world as Maxtla."

The girl took Pitoque's hand and then Maxtla's. "I am honored to meet you." She could not have been more than fifteen years old. "If you will permit me, I will briefly recount my story."

She did so, speaking in a kind of melody and punctuating her remarks with long, graceful movements of her arms, as though she were an actress upon a stage. First, she explained how she came to speak the language of the highlands. "I was born a princess," she said. "I am the daughter of the chieftain of Olutla, a town near Coatzacoalcos. In that place, a form of Nahuatl is spoken, and it is my first tongue."

Pitoque listened, fascinated as much by the girl's composure and her elegance of speech as by her beauty. He asked her to go on, and she did, recounting simply and clearly the chronicle of her young existence.

She spoke without any melodrama or pleas for sympathy. This had been her life. Although her station in the world had been reduced to that of a slave, her noble origins shimmered through. The girl carried herself with all the dignity and poise of a princess, for a princess she was.

"Father?"

"Yes, my son?"

"Does it not seem fortunate that this young woman speaks Nahuatl?" Maxtla turned back to her. "I assume that you speak Maya as well."

"Of course." Here was the talent that set her apart—a knack for languages. It was upon this ability that her future now depended. "I speak both Nahuatl and Maya."

Several seconds passed before Pitoque recognized the significance of this statement. Of course. Here was the solution. This native princess could serve as interpreter between the Aztecs and the gods. He saw it now, and he realized at once what he should do. "Wait," he told her. "I want you to stay here. I'll be right back. Don't go anywhere."

She arched her eyebrows, gestured toward a cluster of native guards assigned to keep watch over the women. "I do not seem to have a great deal of choice in the matter."

Pitoque looked around and saw the guards. "Ah, yes. So I see." He turned to Maxtla. "Come."

The two set off across the broad grassy clearing, their shapes disappearing and re-forming in the waves of leaden heat.

†

To tell the truth, Aguilar had never heard anyone speak in Nahuatl before, and he had been surprised by how utterly unintelligible the language was. On the instructions of Cortés, he had asked the natives to determine whether any of them could speak even a few words of the highland tongue. But none of them could. Now he walked back across the broad clearing, intending to provide an account of his failure to his commander. He wondered how he would phrase it, some sequence of words that would not throw Cortés into a rage.

Just then, he saw a pair of men striding out to intercept him—not a pair of men, actually, but a man and a boy. Both were dressed in dowdy robes of maguey fiber and seemed eager to have a word with him. A pair of *pochtecas*, by the look of them. He stopped and waited.

It turned out that they had the most extraordinary news.

Gifts of the Moon and Sun

Hernán Cortés was delighted.

"Her name is Marina, you say? Pretty thing." The Spanish captain-general turned to the girl, evidently very taken with her. He vaguely remembered having seen her before. Wasn't she the one chosen by Puertocarrero? "A pleasure to meet you," he said. He bowed and then addressed her as *doña*. Doña Marina, he called her.

Aguilar translated these words for the girl, explaining what an honor it was to be addressed as *doña*, especially by someone of the stature and authority of Hernán Cortés. She replied that she was, after all, a princess by birth—why should she not be accorded a degree of respect? She briefly recounted the story of how she had come to be in her present circumstances, a slave girl handed about as a sort of currency. Aguilar translated her words for Cortés, who seemed strangely moved. He approached Marina, took one of her hands, and raised it to his lips—something no Spaniard had ever done before to one of these native creatures. He smiled at her, then turned back to Aguilar.

"And you say she also speaks the language of the Aztecs?"

Aguilar inclined his head. "It is her mother tongue."

Cortés shook his head, amazed. "I've never been able to pick up a second language myself. You must have a head for it, I'm told."

"Not necessarily." Aguilar remembered his eight years of enslavement. "These things depend to a large degree on circumstance."

"I suppose. Still, she seems a bright young girl, don't you think?"

"Oh, yes. Very bright. Very young."

"How old is she, would you say?"

He asked Marina and looked back at Cortés. "Fifteen, she says."

"Indeed? A good age, fifteen. The age at which a girl becomes a woman." Cortés frowned, remembering something else—Puertocarrero. Although he already knew the answer, he decided to ask. "This one, has she been given to one of my officers?"

Again, Aguilar turned and spoke to the girl. She experienced some difficulty pronouncing the name, but he understood. "I think," he reported, "that she was given to Alonso Puertocarrero."

"*Was* she?" Cortés gritted his teeth. He'd known it was so, but the fact was still unpleasant to hear. Already he was letting his mind rum freely about this girl. Unfortunately, that damn Puertocarrero was notoriously sensitive to slights. He would be severely distressed, and he had a tendency to sulk. Despite the man's displeasure, however, Cortés was determined to have the girl—one way or another. Now, however, it was time to deal with other affairs. He turned to Aguilar and announced that he wished to conduct another parley with the two Aztecs. "The pair of you will serve as my interpreters," he said. "Please go now and inform our visitors that I will receive them at once."

Aguilar bowed his head. Soon he and Marina were walking in the direction of the Aztec encampment, located across a grassy expanse in the shade of several portly cashew trees. He decided that he would have to alter the wording of Cortés's message. Surely, it was the Spaniards who were the visitors here. The Aztecs should more properly be addressed as hosts. He sensed that the Aztecs might be sensitive about this point.

The distance was short, but Cacama and Tepehuatl opted to ride in litters on the way to their second meeting with the interlopers, as it was now beyond their power to walk. They both were dressed in brilliant cotton robes dyed red with cochineal, and they tottered across the broad clearing in the piercing afternoon sun. Cacama wore a beribboned hat. This time, he had ensured that the slaves carried the braziers with them. He ordered that they be set up and filled with burning coals, and that quantities of sweet-smelling oil be heated therein. He directed that the oil be used to anoint the visitors.

"An Aztec custom," explained Marina, although in fact the ceremony was new to her. She could understand the significance of it, however.

Off to the side, Pitoque observed those preliminary rituals, pleased to see that his advice had been followed.

Cacama made a deep bow and announced that it would be his honor to offer a banquet prior to the more substantive portion of the afternoon's proceedings. Would this be suitable to his guests?

The invitation was translated. First, Marina put the words into Maya. Then Aguilar rendered them into Spanish, careful to juggle the concepts of "host" and "visitor" to suit the conceits of both sides. Cortés nodded. The invitation was accepted.

The banquet turned out to be a sumptuous affair, for the Aztec dignitaries had brought cooks with them and great quantities of food, supplemented by local produce acquired just that morning. The feast was soon ready, for work on its preparation had begun some time earlier. Now the dishes were carried forth, all freshly cooked and elaborately presented— great slabs of roasted boar and venison; cooked fish with chili peppers and tomato, turkey served with maguey grubs and honey-gorged ants. All were accompanied by cooked beans and locusts and sage. There were platters of tamales stuffed with savory mushrooms, minced rabbit, and turkey eggs. When all these dishes had been laid out on portable tables erected by the Aztec slaves, still more food arrived. Great quantities of steaming onions were brought out, along with sweet potatoes, yucca, and avocados. For those with a sweet tooth, there was guava, beeswax, and succulent sapota fruit. In order to wash the feast down, clay urns were supplied, filled with an aromatic chocolate drink.

The quantity of food was staggering to see—enough to satisfy more than five hundred men. It had been a long time since the Spaniards had eaten nearly this well, and they all fell to it.

When the banquet was finally over, Hernán Cortés drew himself up straight. In his plumed helmet and purple sash, he led Doña Marina by the hand, as though she were his queen. In fact, she looked every inch the part. On Cortés's orders, several new sets of clothing had been acquired for her, obtained in the village of Cempoala in exchange for a quantity of beads. She was dressed now in a fine embroidered blouse above a long henequen skirt, both of which billowed in the breeze. Aguilar followed a pace or so behind. The trio approached the Aztec nobles, and Cortés made a deep bow and gave a salute. He said a few words in his own language, and these were translated by Aguilar into Maya. Marina turned at once toward the Aztec lord.

"We represent a great king," she declared in Nahuatl, sounding for all the world as though she spoke for herself as well as for Cortés, "and we bring greetings from him, from Charles I of Spain, who lives across the sea."

Cortés grinned to hear his thoughts expressed so winningly and by such a slender and captivating woman, even though he understood nothing of what she said. It was her voice, her tone, the set of her shoulders. After a few moments, he spoke again, and his words were duly translated by Aguilar and then by the native princess, who strolled about with her back arched and proud, like a fine antelope metamorphosed into human form. From time to time, she flung back her hair and stared directly at the Aztecs.

"We assure you," she told Cacama, "that we have long known of your great lord and his magnificent accomplishments, and we should like nothing better than to travel to Tenochtitlán to meet your emperor in his great city, which is built, we understand, upon an island surrounded by a beautiful lake, in a region where the air is always cool, in a land of eternal spring."

On hearing these words, Cacama frowned. He took a step forward and put up his hands. In fact, a visit to Tenochtitlán was precisely what he was determined to prevent. Bad enough that a mere woman—a girl—dared to address him as an equal. That impertinence, combined with the pain in his feet and legs, had already managed to put him out of temper. But he could endure such annoyances. What he could not brook was the presumption of these creatures, thinking that they might travel through these lands as though they owned them. He didn't care if they were gods or men. He wanted them to go away. But how could he bring that about?

He swept a fold of his cotton robe over one shoulder, cleared his throat, and replied directly to Cortés. He avoided casting as much as a glance toward the native girl, even though it was she who would interpret his words. He declared that his people had learned of the newcomers' armed exploits on these shores and had been most highly impressed. He glanced around at Tepehuatl, who nodded vehemently and even made a show of clapping his hands. Cacama waited while the translation was done. Then he turned back to Cortés.

"But as to a meeting with Lord Moctezuma," he said, "regrettably such an encounter is impossible to contemplate. The journey is long and uncomfortable, with little opportunity for refreshment along the way. These are poor lands, populated by crude people with nothing to recommend them, and this miserable situation only worsens as one proceeds inland. What interest can so desolate a region possibly hold for beings of such evident refinement and culture as yourselves?" Cacama stared at Cortés. It was time to drive the point home. "It would likely be better for you and your assembly if you left these shores. You might wish to return when conditions are more propitious—perhaps in twenty or thirty years." He looked directly at Cortés. "It is for your own good that I am suggesting this."

Marina listened to these words without betraying any hint of disapproval. So far, her plan had been working very well, even better than she had hoped. But now she saw a chance to secure her fortunes, to make herself indispensable to the commander of the Spaniards, which had been her purpose all along. Calmly, she translated Cacama's speech, and maintained a cool demeanor while Aguilar interpreted her words for the benefit of Cortés. But then she struck. She informed the great, bearded man that the Aztec was speaking complete nonsense and should not be believed.

"There is, you should know, stupendous wealth to be found in Tenochtitlán," she said, "riches beyond anyone's dreams, for the Aztecs have been stealing from everyone else for hundreds of years." She said that Cacama was speaking out of pure self-interest. "He has no concern for your well-being. None at all. He is lying to protect himself. I tell you this because I wish your interests to be served, my lord." She dared to look Cortés squarely in the face. Then she lowered her eyes.

Cortés raised his head, struck by these extraordinary words and sentiments. What an excellent young girl! Really, she surpassed anything he had ever imagined. And so pretty too, albeit dark of skin. He reckoned that there were long hours of amusement to be found beneath that blouse and skirt. He mode up his mind. The hell with Puertocarrero. The fellow would just have to accept his loss. He, Cortés, would lie with the native princess tonight. But first, he had to deal with the Aztecs. Through Aguilar, he thanked Doña Marina for her intervention, and then instructed her to inform the Aztec nobleman that his cautionary remarks, while much appreciated, would have to be taken under advisement. Cortés smiled to himself. He might have known that the severe-looking one was a double-talking hypocrite. He could see it in the man's eyes. And all those tattoos.

Cacama listened to this response, blinking his eyes and clicking his teeth. He hadn't really expected these creatures to give in immediately. It was time to take a different approach. He motioned to his aides. Soon, a group of porters appeared, weighed down by two great disks, one of silver for the moon, the other of gold to represent the sun. These were massive pieces, both splendidly worked with elaborate details and glyphs, both so large that six men were required to carry them, three to each.

These magnificent disks were set down at the feet of Cortés, who gazed upon them in silence, rapt. A light first flickered and then began to burn in his eyes. He hadn't dreamt of receiving any gifts as grand as these.

"Honored guests," said Cacama. "Please accept these offerings as proof of our high esteem."

Off to the side, Pitoque shook his head and let out a long, sour breath. He'd heard what Doña Marina had said, and now he saw the greed in the eyes of Hernán Cortés. He could imagine what the *teule* was thinking. If the territory of the Aztecs was as impoverished as these envoys claimed, how could they so easily part with such extraordinary riches?

Pitoque turned away. He'd seen enough. He walked alone toward the headland overlooking the sea, and he suddenly felt a terrible sadness, a need to be alone. He stopped and leaned against the trunk of a cottonwood tree. He stared out at the breakers pounding inland and shook his head. The idea that Marina would be taken as a consort by the commander of the *teules*—an arrangement obvious to anyone with eyes—left a hollow feeling in the pit of his stomach. But that wasn't his only source of sadness. There was something else, something worse. If before he had hoped that they could persuade these interlopers to depart, that hope was shattered now. Idiots. Did the Aztecs think they could purchase the compliance of these *teules* with gifts? Did they understand nothing? This was the year 1-Reed, and what the prophecies had foretold had come to pass. The old ways would no longer work. Those disks were a terrible blunder, a deadly mistake. Just how deadly, who could say?

He feared that he would soon find out.

The following morning, Cortés put Alvarado in charge of mounting another spectacle of war, specifically for the benefit of the Aztec ambassadors. First, he sent out his small cavalry, the horses tossing their heads, while the riders waved long swords that flashed in the sun. The Aztec nobles and all the local people watched from a distance, their mouths agape. They could not believe what they saw. Great two-headed beasts that pranced about on four stonelike feet. Flashes of thunder and lightning that burst from the mouths of spears. And even greater explosions that roared from great stone pipes. Rocks and showers of dirt flew from the earth. Branches snapped from the trees. Overhead, birds shrieked in terror, wheeled in the air, spun away.

Pitoque stood silent, unable to believe what he saw. A short distance off, Cacama held his ground, did not cringe or take shelter as the others did. Tepehuatl fell to his knees and began to moan. Each man reacted in his own way. At his father's side, Maxtla threw back his head and began to laugh. He announced that he had never witnessed anything so wonderful. He didn't care who or what these beings were. They were glorious. They were impossibly, unbelievably glorious.

"And you favor glory?" said Pitoque, who understood the workings of his son's mind—here was a military force that might be a match even for the Aztecs themselves. "You found this display impressive, then?"

"Yes," said Maxtla. He glared at his father. "Didn't you?"

"Oh, without question. Most impressive indeed." Pitoque left the matter there. He clasped his hands behind his back, turned, and walked away.

The two Aztec ambassadors decamped. They tottered off in their twin litters, with their honor guard leading the way, with their porters and their cooks in tow, on the long return march to their capital hidden beyond the western horizon. They receded along the narrow trail that led through a maze of tangled green scrub, across the marshes and coastal lowlands, toward the distant mountains, invisible from the coast.

Pitoque and his son remained behind, close to the *teules*, waiting to see what would unfold. These were the orders Pitoque had received from Azotl, and he had no choice except to obey.

A Cousin of the Count

Cortés turned his attention to domestic affairs.

First order of business—the girl called Doña Marina. She was to be brought to his quarters that evening. He summoned Alvarado to the shelter of logs caulked with lime that had replaced his temporary canvas tent. He told the man to arrange it.

"Sí, mi capitán." Alvarado hesitated. "Just one question."

"Yes?"

"What about Puertocarrero?"

Cortés scowled. "I understand. Leave Puertocarrero to me. You see to the girl."

Alvarado said that he would, then bared his teeth in a knowing grin.

"Why do you smile?"

"You have made a good choice. A pretty girl."

Cortés relaxed his shoulders and smiled. "Thank you, Alvarado. As always, your opinion is most welcome. Sinking ships and native women—these are your twin strengths."

That night, as Cortés had instructed, Marina was brought to his quarters. The girl lowered her eyes and then fell to her knees before him in an attitude of complete submission. Cortés eyed her hungrily and felt the blood throbbing through his veins. Ah, this was a welcome treat. Where, oh where, to begin?

Later, amid an entangling of limbs, he briefly recollected that he would have to make amends to poor Puertocarrero.

That was an annoying thought, but one that he would consider later. Now he groaned with pleasure and turned back to the job at hand.

"I beg your pardon, my friend." Cortés put on a smile that was part charm, part chagrin. He had summoned Puertocarrero before him, and the two men now stood in the well of shade cast by a large cashew tree, not far from the captain-general's shelter.

In truth, Cortés felt little remorse, and almost loathed the man standing before him, with his rabbit grin and his nervous ways, forever pulling stray locks of hair across his glistening dome, as if anyone could be fooled for a moment—the fellow was bald, bald, bald. Cortés smiled once again, trying to suggest by his manner that this whole episode had taken place by accident, not by intent. One moment, the girl was Puertocarrero's, to do with as he pleased. The next moment— gone. A trick of fate had carried her away. "You don't bear any grudge, I hope. But the girl has a gift for languages that makes her services indispensable to me. Our cause depends upon it. I trust that you understand. You'll forget all about her when you're rich. In the meantime, I'll get you another girl."

Puertocarrero stared straight ahead, stony-faced. He wondered what he ought to do. He tried to imagine what Alvarado might do if he were to find himself in such a position. No doubt, Alvarado would draw his sword and challenge Cortés to a duel on the spot. That was the sort of behavior that most befitted a man who had just been ill-used in an affair of love. It was a question of honor. Still, it was no use. His shoulders slumped. Puertocarrero knew he wasn't going to draw his sword or challenge Cortés to a duel. Such histrionics would seem ridiculous and would accomplish nothing. They would only make matters worse. Finally, in desperation, he resorted to the only real weapon he possessed.

He reached up, patted down his hair, and forced himself to look Cortés straight in the eyes. "You realize," he said, "that I am a cousin of the Count of Medellín."

As soon as the words were out, he realized that they were a terrible mistake. He felt a shudder run up his back.

The captain-general bridled at once, put a hand to the hilt of his sword. Was this some sort of threat? The blood prickled at the base of his neck, and he took a step closer. He brought his face to within inches of the other man's, this cousin of the Count of Medellín. "I do realize it," he said. "And I beg you to convey to the Count my warmest regards when next you are in his presence although, considering the recent demise of our fleet, that happy event is unlikely to be soon."

Puertocarrero felt the hot breath against his skin. There was a roaring in his head. He wondered whether his legs would long support him. First, he had lost his little brown-skinned princess, and now he had infuriated his commander. He prayed that he would manage to avoid crumpling to the ground in a whimpering heap. He felt a stab of self-loathing. Had ever a more miserable creature been born? He struggled to stammer out a reply. "Yes," he said. "I will . . . I will do as you say."

It was all he could manage.

"Good." Cortés stepped back. He made a mental note to punish Puertocarrero for his impudence. The Count of Medellín, indeed. For now, he clapped the miserable bag of bones on the back. "There's a good man. Everything will work out in the end. You'll see."

Puertocarrero nodded, thrust his hands into his pockets, and turned away. In a sudden tumult, he had been reduced to what he truly was—the second cousin, by marriage, of the Count of Medellín. That, and nothing more. He felt as if one of his limbs had been ripped from his body. Cortés dismissed him, and he trudged away across the brittle grass through the leaden heat.

The rest of that afternoon and long into the night, he wandered alone down by the sea, kicking at shells and cursing his rotten luck—his rotten luck and his stupidity. He, a cousin of the Count of Medellín.

The Fat Chieftain

The chieftain of the native settlement at Cempoala let it be known by messenger that he wished to speak to the leader of these gods, the illustrious Hernán Cortés. He hoped that the honored gentleman might come to visit him, rather than the other way around, because he was too fat to move. The chieftain's name was Tlacochcalcatl, and he was monumentally obese.

Cortés accepted the invitation, and with a small party accompanying him, he ventured up the coast a distance. The Spaniards forded the river Cachalacas at its mouth and traced an old native track toward Cempoala.

Pitoque followed, with Maxtla at his side. Along the way, they fell into another of their discussions about the Aztecs. By now, they had both heard repeated tales of the military prowess demonstrated by the *teules* at Tabasco. News had traveled quickly through the native communities dotted along the coast, and they had seen their own eyes what these beings were capable of—the creation of lightning and thunder, the destruction of hills and trees. Maxtla thought he knew exactly what should now be done. The *teules*—if they were *teules*—should march on Tenochtitlán and destroy the Aztecs in one glorious assault.

"You would consider such an attack to be desirable?" Pitoque had made up his mind to remain calm during his son's outbursts. He climbed over the trunk of a fallen ceiba tree. "You would think the world a better place if this were to happen?"

"I would." Maxtla leapt to the top of the moss-covered trunk and jumped down. "Then the rest of us would be free."

Pitoque rolled his eyes. He found it difficult to navigate a logical course through the maze of recent events. Why had these beings come? Was it to punish him? Would they bring down an entire empire on account of one man's sins? More to the point, *could* they? He had counted only five hundred individuals in their ranks. What threat could five hundred pose to the massed army of the Aztecs, even if the strangers were gods? He decided to raise this concern with his son. "You do not think," he said, "that your heroes might be somewhat out-numbered?"

Maxtla shook his head. "They have bigger swords. They have smoking spears. They have huge magic pipes. They have two-headed dragons. They—"

"Yes. Yes. I understand." Pitoque hopped across several stepping stones that provided passage over a boggy stream. "Still, I find it astonishing that you would wish all the Aztecs dead."

"Not *all*." Maxtla darted across the stream, lighting on every other stone. He wobbled on the last one and then jumped onto the bank. "Just the men."

"I see. Merely all of the Aztec men. A delightful circum-stance, I'm sure, for the women and children." Pitoque stopped and rubbed his forehead, for he felt a headache coming on. What was the use? These discussions never accomplished any-thing. He peered ahead over the low green scrub that hugged the shoreline. He could just discern the party of *teules* advanc-ing in front of them. "Come," he said. "We should catch up."

Tlacochcalcatl was waiting outdoors, reclining beneath a broad cotton awning in a grassy plaza near his small palace. Like many of his clansmen, the chieftain wore an elaborate and bejewelled facial ornament that pulled his lower lip down beneath his chin, a display that seemed to excite a degree of unease among the *teules*. Several of them kept reaching up and worrying at their jaws, as if trying to imagine what such a device might feel like.

Once his guests had settled themselves, and after the two sides had exchanged formal greetings, Tlacochcalcatl began to speak, and once he had begun speaking, there seemed to be no stopping him. On this occasion, only Aguilar was in attendance as translator, for the chieftain spoke in Maya. Still, it was no easy matter to keep up with the torrent of words that tumbled from Tlacochcalcatl's bejewelled lips. He was as loquacious as he was fat. Before long, he was pouring out all the anguish that roiled in his heart. He was practically in tears.

Oh, how he cursed the day that he and his people had fallen under the sway of Lord Moctezuma and his abominable Aztecs. He spat out the names and turned almost purple with anger. His rolls of flesh rippled and shook with each word, as though he were some sort of dumpling. He clutched his head and moaned. There was no end to the injuries his people had suffered at the hands of these wicked, wicked fiends.

"Why, I myself have lost all of my jewelry," he said, apparently forgetting the ornament in his mouth. "And my people are forced to pay the most onerous tribute to these monsters, simply to avoid worse abuse." He wiped his eyes and cleared his throat with an astonishing honk. "All," he declared, "has been recorded."

He called for the pertinent documents. Great folded sheets of sisal paper were produced at once, and he proceeded to read from a list that represented a single year of tribute. During that period, his people had supplied the Aztecs with

65 warriors' suits
23 battle standards
72 practice targets
280 bunches of bird feathers, various species
32 dried parrots
2 live eagles
400 cotton blankets
28 loads of corn
21 loads of beans
16 loads of red cacao
160 bales of chilis
87 jugs of maguey syrup
220 jugs of bee honey

On and on, the catalogue went. The chieftain unfolded and refolded the pages, his voice quavering at each additional outrage. So many bales of cotton. So many sacks of copal or gum of liquidambar. Cords of wood. Tables. Chairs. Reams of paper. Quantities of lime. Loaves of refined salt. Turquoise ornaments. Jade collars. Deer skins. Jaguar pelts. Seashells. On and on and on.

Even Pitoque, who was familiar with the onerous burden of Aztec tribute, began to think the recitation would never end. But finally, the chieftain laid down the documents and shook his head.

"There is nothing we can do," he said, "for Moctezuma is a mighty lord with vast armies that he may unleash at the slightest provocation." He heaved a long sigh. "They treat us like husks of corn."

His shoulders slumped, he shook his bejowled head, and it seemed for several moments as if he had finished speaking. Just then, however, he looked up. He'd suddenly had another thought. He began to describe the Aztec stewards who came to oversee the collection of all this tribute.

"Oh, they are haughty men, those ones. They swagger about in gold and finery. They slick back their hair with fragrant oils. They carry walking sticks and hold flowers to their nostrils." He rolled his eyes. "Why, they act as if even the air that we breathe offends them. They have servants about at all times, who must carry whisks to swat away any mosquitoes or flies that dare to irritate them. Then these Aztecs order us about as if we were dogs, and they will hear no objections from any quarter. First, they insult us, then they rob from us, and then they order us to bow down before them and pretend to be grateful for this abuse."

None of the chieftain's words came as a surprise to Pitoque, who understood how the Aztecs treated others. Resentments festered everywhere, and in most cases they were not without justice. The Aztecs were arrogant, aloof, and often greedy, not to mention cruel. Would another governing race have been more benevolent? That was a question best left to the philosophers. For Pitoque's part, he had seen enough of the world to suspect that those with power would always be a little careless of those without.

The chieftain's complaints may have been familiar to

Pitoque, but they were evidently a revelation to the newcomers. The *teule* named Aguilar translated the obese man's rant, and a gradual transformation came over Cortés. He concentrated more intently, word by word, stroking his beard. The light in his eyes reappeared, the gleam that Pitoque had seen when the disks of the sun and the moon had been presented. He could almost see the outline of the ideas now taking shape in the commander's mind. A great empire might be a formidable adversary, but an empire riven by discontent was another proposition altogether. Such an empire was not beyond being conquered, even by a force of only five hundred.

Finally, the fat chieftain rounded to his point. He stifled a belch, lowered his voice, and made a proposal. He wanted his honored visitors to make an alliance with his own people, as well as with the people of Tlaxcala, which was a city in the highlands not so distant from Tenochtitlán. The Tlaxcalans, he said, were sworn enemies of the Aztecs.

Cortés gave a slow nod of his head, as if he did not quite understand. "An alliance?" he said. "To what purpose?"

The chieftain emitted a deep rumbling laugh. "I think you take my meaning. I know that you have not come unprepared. I have heard of what took place at Tabasco. My agents witnessed the more recent events nearby, which I was prevented from seeing for myself on account of my girth." He laughed. "It seems you have come prepared for war."

Cortés smiled and pulled himself to his feet.

"I will give thought to your proposal," he said, but his tone suggested he had already made up his mind.

-|-

On their return trek southward from Cempoala, Pitoque and Maxtla rounded a bend in the track and found themselves suddenly face to face with a party of travelers—Aztecs, from their appearance.

One of the Aztecs shouted in surprise and gave the order to halt. He was surrounded by a guard of perhaps two dozen warriors. A square-built man with a bemused expression, he stared at Pitoque and Maxtla and made a dramatic sigh of relief. "Do we not know one another?"

Pitoque considered the question for a few moments, gazing at this man, evidently an official of some kind. Yes, the fellow was right. They did know each other. This was Qualpopoca, the Aztec agent for this corner of the empire, responsible for the collection of tribute and other sundry duties. They had crossed paths before.

Now they greeted each other warmly, and Qualpopoca admitted that he'd been more than a little fearful at the moment of their encounter. "We just narrowly missed running into the most terrifying band of creatures I have ever set eyes on." The beings he described were obviously Cortés and his party. Qualpopoca had been particularly struck by the great two-headed beasts that led the procession. "Fortunately, we had the wit and the time to get off the track and hide among the trees," he said. He wiped his brow. "Do you have any idea who those monsters were?"

Pitoque replied that he was not sure. He'd heard there were strangers about, but he had received no other information.

"Be careful," said Qualpopoca. "They look dangerous to me."

Pitoque thanked the man for his kindness and wished him well. "Come, Maxtla," he said. They continued their southward journey.

Qualpopoca and his guard hastened off in the opposite direction, no doubt toward Cempoala, presumably to address some administrative matter there to do with the collection of tribute. Pitoque wondered how the man would be greeted now that the *teules* had preceded him. He didn't envy Qualpopoca his job. No one likes a collector of tribute.

"I propose," said Pedro de Alvarado, "that we march at once on this city, this whatever-it's-called—"

"Tenochtitlán," said Aguilar. "The Aztec capital."

"Yes, yes." Alvarado still could not get his tongue around a native name. "I propose that we strike straightaway, take them by surprise. Why wait?"

"I am not so certain. Let us consider the question." Cortés turned to his native consort, Doña Marina. With Aguilar's help, he asked her opinion.

She replied without hesitation. "It is very large, Tenochtitlán," she said. "And the Aztecs are many. I do not think you could win. Not that way."

"I cannot agree," said Alvarado. "We are five hundred strong. And we are Spaniards. Besides, we have these native reinforcements."

That was so. As proof of his good faith, the fat chieftain

of Cempoala had loaned four hundred of his finest warriors to support the Spaniards' cause. In addition, he had also provided a substantial number of porters.

"Our timing is important," continued Alvarado. "For all we know, those two Aztecs—those ambassadors, whatever they were—have already returned to their city and have raised their people against us. We—"

"All the more reason," said Cortés, "to proceed with some measure of caution. I agree with Marina. Quite likely, given our present number of men, we are not strong enough to win a pitched battle."

Alvarado let out a groan. "Then what are we doing in this country? Why did we even come?"

"Calm yourself, my friend. Listen to me. It may be that we can win this campaign without a head-on fight. You have heard for yourself how unpopular these Aztecs are. That, in my view, is our greatest weapon. You know the old saying—Who is not my enemy, is my friend?"

Alvarado nodded.

"I am beginning to suspect that we will find a great many friends in these parts. We have only to be patient. We have only to look."

Alvarado ran his tongue over his upper teeth. He shrugged, a kind of assent. "Where should we begin?"

Cortés turned to Marina. "Where do you think we should begin?"

Aguilar translated the question. He turned to Cortés with the girl's reply. "Tlaxcala, she says. Definitely Tlaxcala. They are the sworn enemies of the Aztecs. They will surely be our friends."

Cortés smiled. Our friends. Ours. He ran the palm of one hand over the handle of his sword, delighted to have so lovely a girl in his care, especially one of such evident intelligence, such certainty of her own mind—and such loyalty to him. "It's settled then," he said. "Tlaxcala it will be."

Even Alvarado seemed satisfied with this decision. In fact, the only discontented party to the discussion was Aguilar, but he didn't say so. He knew better than to do that. Still, he left the others' company that afternoon with a grim feeling in his heart. He did not think the good Lord had saved him from enslavement so that he might serve as an instrument of greed and war. He returned to his small hut, pulled out his tattered prayer book, knelt down, and started to pray. On a little patch of cleared earth, by a cluster of sea grape trees, he beseeched the Lord for a sign, a vision. A dusky light was splayed across the green lands of the coast, and a low growl of breakers grumbled against the shore, but the heavens were silent. That night, when the sky turned dark, a raft of clouds sailed overhead, obscuring the stars.

BOOK THREE

In the Land of Edom

How Then Should You Be Judged?

Pitoque spent his time lurking around the perimeter of the *teules'* camp, hoping to pick up some useful information, but it was frustrating work. Anyone with eyes could see that the newcomers were preparing to depart. But depart when? Depart for where? Even if he did manage to overhear some snatch of conversation or some brief barked instruction, he couldn't understand it. Nonetheless, he was lucky. On the second day, he made two discoveries.

First, he found out what these terrifying, two-headed dragons were, the ones that galloped about with a thundering stride. In fact, they were a hornless species of deer. The *teules* climbed atop them and were carried about, thus giving the appearance of one creature with two heads. Pitoque found it thrilling to imagine being transported hither and yon upon the back of an animal, and resolved to make a report on the matter to Azotl as soon as possible. Here, at least, was one mystery solved.

His second discovery was even more remarkable. He had been lingering about at the edge of the camp, making a show of trying to barter some more of his Cholula pottery, when the *teule* named Aguilar wandered over, the swarthy one.

"Greetings," he said. "A fine day, don't you think?"

Pitoque agreed that it was. He held up a ceramic bowl. "You are not, by any chance, in need of dishes?"

Aguilar dipped his head. "Not just now. We have a journey ahead of us, as you can see."

"So I have observed. Still, it is never an encumbrance to possess an extra plate."

"I am sure you are right. Perhaps another time."

"Perhaps." Pitoque handed the bowl to one of his porters who stood behind him. "So, you plan a journey. I wonder—just out of curiosity, you understand—where is it that you are bound?"

"Inland."

"You will find the climate much improved."

"So I have heard."

"Still—inland. It is a very large place."

Aguilar realized that he was being tweaked for information, and he thought he knew why. He was aware that itinerant traders often served as agents of espionage on behalf of the Aztecs. He wondered what, or how much, he should say. Just then, something caught his eye. He gazed up and started—an angel drifted overhead. It was the most glorious being imaginable. His chest swelled, and he nearly fell to his knees, nearly clasped his hands in prayer. An angel. An angel in flight.

In a part of his mind, he understood that what he had glimpsed was a cloud, and yet for a moment it had assumed the shape of an angel—the very angel, perhaps, who had guided him to this clearing, so that he might find himself in the company of this trader from the highlands. Why? To what end? He turned back to the man, frowned. "You are a long way from your home."

"That is so."

"You find yourself often in these parts?"

"From time to time. My journeys are unpredictable."

"I'm not surprised. These are unpredictable times."

The *pochteca* shrugged. "Sadly, it is so."

Aguilar wondered what to do. He had a powerful feeling that something was required of him. An angel had directed him to this place. There had to be a purpose. Why else had he survived eight years of bondage in these strange lands? He felt a sourness in his gut, the same sourness that had been stirring there for many days, since the Spaniards' show of military prowess at Tabasco, if not before. And now Cortés proposed to march inland. Already, Aguilar dreaded the consequences—a river of blood, the skewering of human flesh. What else could result? Suddenly, a terrible disquiet trembled inside him, and he knew what he had to do. He turned to the trader.

"My friend," he said. "If it is of any use to you, I will tell you exactly where we are going."

Pitoque could not believe this stroke of luck. "Where?"

"Tlaxcala."

Pitoque raised his eyebrows. He had suspected as much, but being told was another matter. "Tlaxcala?"

"Yes. And from Tlaxcala, we propose to proceed to Tenochtitlán. We leave on the morning after tomorrow, at first light. Tlaxcala, then Tenochtitlán. I should inform you that we mean to possess these lands in the name of our king."

"Your king?"

"Yes. Charles I, who dwells across this great water." Aguilar waved at the sea. "It is why we have come. You should be forewarned."

"What do you mean?"

Aguilar grimaced. "Great troubles will come. I wish to warn you."

Pitoque felt his palms grow damp. This encounter was beyond all expectations. He felt a question thudding in his mind. These creatures—who were they? *What* were they? He swallowed, clenched his fists, and managed to get the words out. "Are the prophecies true?" he said. "Is one of you called Quetzalcoatl? Are you *teules*?"

"Are we *what*?"

"Gods. Are you gods?"

For a time, Aguilar said nothing. He simply stared back at Pitoque, his eyes enlarged. Finally, he put back his head and began to laugh. He laughed harder and harder until he bellowed. He howled. His eyes began to water, and he had to stagger over to a tree, press his hands against the trunk to support himself. "Gods!" he repeated, speaking in a high, thin tremor. "Gods, he asks." He looked back at Pitoque. He recovered something like his normal voice. "I beg you," he said, "to judge us not by these prophecies you speak of."

"How then should you be judged?"

"By our deeds. I ask of you only this—that you judge us by our deeds."

Pitoque waited, hoping that Aguilar would reveal more, but

the translator had fallen silent. "Very well," he said. "By your deeds shall you be judged."

"Good. You are a *pochteca*, I take it?"

"I am."

"I assume you will know what to do with what I have told you."

Pitoque frowned and tried to feign an ingenuous air. "What *can* I do? I am a mere trader. I travel here and there, with my porters and my cargo of plates."

Aguilar straightened up. He took a step forward, reached out, clasped Pitoque on the shoulder. "Farewell," he said. He suddenly seemed overcome by some great sadness. "Farewell, my friend. May we meet in happier times."

Pitoque watched as Aguilar bowed his head and turned and strode away. The *teule*, if that was what he was, disappeared in the shadows of a ceiba tree like a play of light, an illusion.

Later that day, Pitoque debated what he should do. What would Azotl wish? In his heart, he already realized what the master functionary would ask. Go to Tlaxcala. Find out how these beings are received there. Report back at once.

But if he waited out here on the sweltering coast until he received Azotl's instructions, it would be too late. The teules would long ago have decamped, and he would be hard-pressed to catch them before they reached Tlaxcala. How much intelligence would he have lost by then? He decided not to run that risk. He would depart for Tlaxcala at once, the following morning—a day ahead of the teules themselves. He informed Toc of his decision, and the old man suggested they dispatch a runner to Tenochtitlán, to inform Azotl of their plans.

Pitoque agreed. "See to it," he said.

They slept that night in the brooding heat of the coastal darkness and rose at first light to begin the westward trek. Their journey took them across an expanse of sprawling, green flats toward the steep flanks of the eastern mountains, where the damp, slanting woodlands climbed to the interior highlands through the cooling air and the rolling mist.

A day later, at break of dawn, the Spaniards departed the coast. With their supplies and their weapons, they withdrew from the sea, pushed across the low, sweltering plain, and headed inland. Their numbers were reinforced by the four hundred Totonac warriors they had received on loan from the fat chieftain of Cempoala, as well as a multitude of porters. To man a rear-guard garrison at Veracruz, they left behind only a small detachment of Spanish soldiers, for they believed they had nothing to fear from the people of the coast.

Pedro de Alvarado was especially pleased to be on the move. For him, everything was working out splendidly. He now rode side by side with Cortés, while his chief rival, Puertocarrero, had been ordered to remain behind on the steaming coast, to keep company with mosquitoes. This had been Cortés's decision, but Alvarado had done little to discourage it. The captain-general had decided to punish Puertocarrero for his insubordination a few days earlier—that foolish boast about being related to the Count of Medellín. The remark, with its hint of a threat, had been very poorly received. Cortés had stripped the man of his lieutenant's rank and ordered that he be left behind.

That wasn't all. As further punishment, Puertocarrero would serve only as second-in-command of the rump rear-guard garrison. This demotion had been proposed by Alvarado. He told Cortés he didn't much like the way the fellow had taken to skulking about, stalking the deserted beaches at all hours. He looked as if he might get into serious mischief. Better to keep him under someone else's thumb.

"Very well," said Cortés.

In fact—and Alvarado understood this perfectly—Cortés cared little how severely Puertocarrero was dealt with now. To hell with the malnourished little beggar. The harsh truth was that Puertocarrero had committed the one unpardonable sin in this or any life—he had lain with a woman before another man had. That was his real crime, and it was one that few men were likely either to forgive or to forget.

Cacao Have I

From years of travel, Pitoque knew the shortest and quickest routes, and was sure he could make better time than the *teules*. After two days' journey, he, Maxtla, and the porters reached the lower steps of the mountainous wall and began their ascent. The air cooled steadily as they climbed, and soon they were trudging up through the relentless drizzle called the *chipi-chipi*. They traveled first to Xalapa and then to Xico, the moisture working its way through their robes and slithering down their skin.

Even so, Pitoque did not begrudge one step of the climb. He had spent too long already in the leaden heat of the lowlands, where mosquitoes shrieked around them like the crazed tips of arrows and where, during the middle hours of the day, it was a struggle just to remain awake. Now, as he found his mind clearing in the cool air, the questions began to crowd in more urgently.

Who were these great, bearded creatures? Was he himself responsible for their presence? If so, why hadn't he been identified and punished before now? And why didn't the gods speak in the languages of men? If the commander named Cortés really was an embodiment of Quetzalcoatl, why did he not go by that name? Why did he not transform himself into a serpent with a great plumed pelt, spread his pinions, and fill the sky? And, if not gods, then what could these creatures be? Aguilar's admonition on the subject—*Judge us by our deeds*—had only confused Pitoque further. What deeds were those?

He reached a switchback in the trail, called a halt, and settled himself on a moss-covered boulder. The porters were strung out along the path below, and he told Toc to announce that they might rest, attend to their toilet, refresh themselves. There was a stream nearby—he knew this from memory—where the men might drink. He stretched out his arms, ran his hands through his hair, and yawned.

"Tired, sir?"

He nodded. "And you?"

"Always a little tired nowadays, sir. Age, you know. It catches up."

Pitoque knew for a fact that Toc was still as spry as a man of half his years, but he let the remark pass. He turned to Maxtla.

"How about you, my son? How are your legs holding up? A bit sore?"

"A little." Maxtla squatted on his haunches.

Pitoque smiled. Probably the boy was just being polite. In fact, he could climb all day without a break and not feel the effort in the least. No, if anyone was feeling the strain, it was Pitoque himself. Well, so be it. He was simply glad to be able to rest. He yawned again and looked up at the wisps of mist drifting through the black branches and green needles of the pines. He recalled the questions that had occupied him during the climb so far, and he reached over and slapped Toc on the shoulder. "So, old man. What say you? These creatures that have come—are they men or gods?"

Toc hawked his phlegm and spat discreetly off to the side. "Men," he said slowly. "They spit. They piss. They shit. You have seen it for yourself. How could they be gods?"

Pitoque considered this argument. In some ways, the *teules* did not seem especially godlike. And yet, who could say? He looked at his son. "Maxtla?" he said.

"Yes, Father?"

"What's your view? The great bearded ones. Men or gods? What do you think?"

The boy let out a breath and looked away, as if he'd rather have been anywhere on earth at this moment than in a damp, precipitous forest debating metaphysical questions with his father. Finally, he shrugged. "I do not think it matters," he said.

"What do you mean?"

Another sigh. "I mean that I do not think it matters what these beings *are*. I think it matters what they *do*."

Pitoque lifted his head. Was this what Aguilar had meant—that it didn't *matter* whether they were men or gods? He gazed back at Maxtla. "And what do you think they will do?"

"Isn't it obvious?"

"Not to me."

The boy gripped a branch near his head and pulled himself up onto his feet. "I would say they mean to make war."

"Against the Aztecs?"

"Who else?"

Pitoque turned to Toc. He raised his eyebrows. "What do you think?"

Toc said he was inclined to agree with Maxtla.

"And the outcome?" Pitoque affected a light-hearted tone, but the talk of war was like a great stone weight, pulling him down. "Who do you think will prevail?"

Toc curled up his nose and tested the air, as if the fusty scent of these mossy, rain-damp trees might determine the fortunes of the world. "The Aztecs," he said. "One great battle would do it."

"Are you certain?" Pitoque listed the terrors possessed by

these creatures—the massive dogs, the great deer upon which they could ride, the smoking spears.

"True," Toc said. "But their warriors are few in number."

It was so. Even reinforced by their Totonac allies, they amounted to a small force. If the armies of Moctezuma were to march down from the highlands at once, led by the Jaguar Knights and the Eagle Knights, decked out in the full panoply of war—their feather headdresses and animal hides and cotton armor—then these *teules* might very well be dealt with in short order, captured in one mighty assault and carried away to Tenochtitlán for the pleasure of the hummingbird god.

But Pitoque did not expect that to happen. Instead, at the royal court at Tenochtitlán, Moctezuma and his advisers would prevaricate. There would be more sacrifices, more aimless talk, more consulting of ancient scrolls, more watching for messages from the constellations. The Aztecs would do what Pitoque was inclined to do himself. They would wait for signs from the stars.

Not Maxtla. The boy had begun to stroll about, to get the blood moving in his legs again. He said he was all in favor of war. If the Aztecs failed to begin the hostilities themselves, that was so much the worse for them. The newcomers would launch the attack instead, and they would win. The Aztecs would be reduced to morsels of flesh that one might feed to little dogs to fatten them up. He was certain. "It would serve them right, too," he said. "The Aztecs are cowards and thieves. They do nothing but rob."

Pitoque frowned. "Nothing but rob? Who says this?"

"Everybody. Everyone hates them." He hesitated. "Everyone but you."

Pitoque held his tongue. Maxtla's outbursts were worrisome, but he knew better than to argue. The boy was besotted with these creatures. They were far grander than any beings he had ever encountered—larger, more exotic, more powerful. All else seemed to grow dim and dreary beside them. How their eyes blazed. How their outbursts of laughter reverberated on the air. Their weaponry sent thrills of exhilaration coursing up and down his spine. Maxtla had already said that he wanted to be just like them, to wash away the tattoo lines on his face and grow a beard—and carry a smoking spear! And go to sea upon a floating palace! He would hear no criticism of anything the *teules* said or did.

Ah, well—the boy was young. Pitoque slapped his knees and hauled himself upright. Enough dallying. He told Toc to instruct the porters to reshoulder their cargo. It was time to be off.

The temperature fell with each upward stride, the clouds turned slow somersaults against the earth, and soon Pitoque and his party were climbing above the mists, over the high ridge, and onto the lofty tablelands of the central plateau. They were above the clouds now. A cobalt sky yawned overhead, the light dazzled, and the air was cool as morning all day long. They stopped that night in Ixhuacan. The following day, they proceeded to Xocotlan. After that, their journey took them through a succession of small towns, Ixtacmaxtitlan and Atalaya and Tzompantzinco. Soon, in the distance, they could see the great snow-covered peaks of Popocatépetl and Iztaccíhuatl. The volcanoes floated above a faint morning haze, glistening in the sun, and Pitoque knew that they were almost at Tlaxcala.

So far, they had made good time, and he was sure their party would reach the walled city in advance of the *teules*. That was the easy part. The difficulty lay in gaining entry to the place. He knew that Tlaxcala was heavily fortified by a great stone wall that was more than two leagues long, taller than a man and many times as thick. Parapets, manned by sentries and archers, crowned the wall at frequent intervals, and no one could come within shouting distance of the fortress without being challenged or, more likely, punctured by arrows. Those who did get close risked being stoned to death.

The reason for the city's defences was simple. Almost alone among the peoples of these lands, the Tlaxcalans had managed to resist Aztec rule. They flatly refused to pay tribute. They would not bow down to the Aztecs in any way. They did exactly what Maxtla would have had Cholula do—with miserable results. The two peoples were almost constantly at war, but their encounters never yielded a clear outcome. The Tlaxcalans were never absolutely defeated, but neither could they end the attacks and privation they suffered.

And so they dwelt in miserable poverty, regularly subjected to sorties by Aztec raiding parties. The Aztecs seized male prisoners for sacrifice. They captured women and carried them off, as well—to serve as slaves or concubines. They blocked the trade routes of the Tlaxcalans and impounded goods bound for the walled city. Even so, the Tlaxcalans would not submit. They were as proud and warlike as the Aztecs themselves, but fewer in number, and so they remained behind their high stone barricades, ragged, embittered, and ill-fed. They hated the Aztecs with all the venom in the world, and would pay any price, even be destroyed entirely, rather than give in.

Clearly, they would make ideal allies for the *teules*.

To ensure safe passage on the final leg of the journey, Pitoque decided on a little-known route, one he judged likely to keep them free from interference by Aztec patrols. Trailed by Toc and the other porters, he and Maxtla made their way safely through a series of dry highland ravines and soon matched unmolested across the lofty central plain toward Tlaxcala. As they strode through waves of long blond grass beneath a startling sun, Maxtla returned to the subject that obsessed him.

"I do not understand how you can work for the Aztecs." The boy threw up his arms. "You are on their side. How can you not hate them yourself?"

"Hate them? What use would that serve?" Pitoque decided that now might be a good time to explain to his son the outlines of his philosophy of life, at least as it touched upon his relations with the Aztecs. Lift was a balance, he said, a matter of trading off one force against another. Not every conflict pitted an absolute good against an eternal evil. Sometimes, a man had to choose a lesser evil if only to avoid one that was greater.

Sometimes, it was necessary to befriend one's own enemies. A man had to compromise. He—

"*Compromise!*" Maxtla shook his head, and his dark locks swished across his forehead. "Why? What good can be accomplished by compromise?"

"Look at me," said Pitoque. He stopped and patted his chest, his arms, his hips. "I have legs to walk on. My heart beats. My blood flows." He turned and gestured toward the long file of porters that marched behind them. "I have these men in my employ. They bear all this wealth on our behalf. They themselves have food to eat. At the end of each journey, they have roofs over their heads. Your mother is never hungry, nor your sister, nor you. Yes, I trade with the Aztecs. Yes, I undertake missions on their behalf. But I have made a safe, prosperous life for my family. Are these not accomplishments? Is this existence of ours not a reasonable bargain?"

Maxtla closed his eyes, as if against some excruciating pain. He obviously was not persuaded. He believed that if an action was right, it was right in every way. If wrong, it was wrong for all time. Pitoque stood and listened to the boy's attempt to put these thoughts into words. When Maxtla fell silent, the merchant merely sighed. In a way, he envied his son. He sometimes longed for the sweet clarity of youth, when all that was not day was night, when all that was not chili was sweet. But Pitoque had come to believe what the Aztecs believed themselves—that all is duality, that everything exists with its opposite, that light and darkness are two aspects of the same reality, that life is death and death is life.

Does not the smiling face of a beautiful young woman contain a grinning skull?

They walked through a long, rambling thicket of oak trees, through criss-cross patterns of sunlight and shade, and Pitoque kept speaking, trying to explain these ideas to his son. It was foolish, he said, to speak of good and evil as separate entities. They were connected—indeed, they were the same. They were parts of a whole. They fed upon each other.

"Without the Aztecs," he said, "without their hunger for commerce, what use would there be for traveling merchants? Is not my profession good? Are you saying that I, too, am evil?"

Maxtla looked away, unwilling to challenge his father so directly, but the boy's meaning was clear from his silence.

Pitoque decided to let the matter rest. No doubt the debate would be raised between them again. There was no need to belabor it now.

"Come," he said. "We must keep up our pace."

Soon they emerged from the highland woods and marched with their porters out onto an open plain. Directly ahead, the vast stone wall of Tlaxcala swelled before them, reaching farther away than the eye could see. They stood now in the clear view of the sentinels mounted on the wall's high parapets. Pitoque felt his heart pounding in his chest, and he stepped ahead by one stride to put Maxtla behind him. He did not know whether the Tlaxcalans would now try to repel him with a tirade of curses and spittle. What would be far worse, and what he feared, was that they might mount an even angrier reception—a volley of arrows, darts, and stones. But he was

determined not to wait for their decision. Instea
a plan that had been taking shape in his mind d
trek from the coast.

"Cacao have I!" he shouted. He raised his ar... and waved
at his gang of porters so that they would spread out across the
grass and reveal his wares. "The richest dark cacao from the
coastal flats of Cempoala! And loaves of salt from the salt beds
of Qulahuitzlan! Finest cotton have I from Ayagualulco in the
green shadow of the mountains of Tabasco! Let me enter, and
let us trade! Cacao have I!"

Pitoque needn't have feared that the Tlaxcalans would turn
him away. So great was their need for these commodities that
they sent out a party to meet him, to shower him with blessings, and to welcome him into their city.

The Ramparts of Tlaxcala

Soon, Pitoque and his son, along with Toc and the rest, were
being conducted into Tlaxcala itself, a place of low stone buildings with flat roofs, where men walked about in loincloths and
cloaks made of rough maguey fiber. Many of the buildings
were crumbling because the city lacked lime or other caulk-
ing. Everything seemed to be in a state of disrepair. Pitoque
had come to this rude place as a *pochteca*, but he really wanted
to know whether these Tlaxcalans had heard of the *teules* who
were bound this way. He wanted to find out what reception the
teules might be granted here, whether they would be greeted as

enemies or friends. These were the questions that Azotl would want answered.

But the Tlaxcalans had other ideas. They were desperate to trade. A group of elders ushered Pitoque and his son into a large stone house. It was clearly a palace of some kind, but a crude and depressing affair. Its beams gave off no sweet aromas, for they were old and near to rotting. No gracefully embroidered canopies swayed overhead. There were no thrones, not even a chair. Instead, the Tlaxcalans swatted their way through a musty drapery of cobwebs and arranged themselves in a circle upon the floor, on mats of coarsely woven maguey. They began negotiations at once.

As it turned out, there was little room for dealing. These were a poor people, isolated from other cities, and they had few goods to trade. But they did their best. They unbundled a supply of old and tattered feathers, raising a small cloud of dust that sent Pitoque into a fit of sneezes.

"Quetzal feathers," an old man assured him, speaking in a whisper apparently meant to convey a sense of awe. "Finest quetzal feathers, transported all the way from Yucatán."

Pitoque had his doubts. These moth-eaten plumes seemed to be for the most part common parrot feathers—very old parrot feathers, from the look of them, plucked from the corpses of birds long dead. Still, he deliberately made a generous bargain because he desired the goodwill of these people. Several of the Tlaxcalans exchanged nods and even vaguely triumphant smirks. Because of the Aztecs and their blockades, it was a rare trader who passed this way, and the few who did were invariably cheats. This fellow with his son seemed to be an easier mark.

To celebrate the conclusion of business, a crude meal was arranged—plain tamales with a mash of beans and a gluey porridge made from pumpkins. Pitoque gazed at his meal and sighed—no meat in sight. The Tlaxcalan nobles gathered around a small fire that gave off a putrid smoke, and they began to gorge themselves. They had an inferior way of eating, plunging their entire hands into common bowls. This was sickening to behold, but Pitoque had traveled widely enough to know that different peoples had different ways. He pretended it was nothing. He himself preferred the Aztec custom—separate bowls, and the use of just the first two fingers and the thumb. That was the civilized way to deal with food.

Pitoque nodded at Maxtla to encourage him to eat and make no fuss. He himself tried his best to swallow some of the gruel down. For a time, the only sounds were those of mastication, for Tlaxcalans seemed not to converse while they dined—another low trait. Pitoque waited until they had finished stuffing their gullets, and then in a casual voice, as if the subject had occurred to him only now, he inquired whether they had received any news of the exotic creatures who had come on floating palaces from the direction of the sun.

He might as well have asked whether the Tlaxcalans enjoyed a drop or two of fermented cactus juice on a cold winter's night. The answer was obvious. At once, their eyes glinted in the firelight, and they sat up straight. Their hands trembled in mid-air, still dripping with the glutinous residue of dinner.

Now that the subject had come up, they could talk of little else. They entirely forgot to eat.

Had they heard of these mysterious bearded ones? Indeed, they had. It would be rather strange if they had not. Yes, they had received reports of the military exploits attributed to these beings. Yes, they knew very well that the aliens were even now approaching from the coast. Their own spies had told them so.

Pitoque swallowed another mouthful of the porridge and wondered how it was possible for food to be at once so disagreeable and so bland. He asked whether the Tlaxcalans had considered in what manner they would greet these interlopers. "I mean, taking into account the possibility that they might be gods."

"Gods?" This was one of the elders, a man named Ixcatzin. He was a gaunt fellow whose yellowy skin hung upon him like a rumpled cloak. He and several others exchanged puzzled glances. This idea had dearly not occurred to them. "What do you mean?"

Pitoque looked surprised. "Surely you recall the prophecies that concern Quetzalcoatl." In case they had forgotten, he reminded them, ticking the details off on his fingers—that Quetzalcoatl would return in the Aztec year 1-Reed, that he would reclaim his kingdom, that he would be fair of skin and wear a beard, that he would arrive from the direction of the rising sun.

The Tlaxcalan elders frowned and pursed their mouths in thought. One of them spat on the floor. They discussed this

new idea among themselves for a time—might these strangers, in fact, be gods?—but it soon became apparent that
another theory carried greater weight, particularly with their
warrior chieftain, a bull-chested man known as Xicotencatl the
Younger. He had a fierce-looking face, deeply pocked about
the cheeks and chin, and was clearly a man who liked to leap
into action first and engage in polite discussion later. If at all.

He climbed to his feet and roamed through the dance of
shadows cast by the fire. He strutted and waved and shouted
out his opinions. "Gods?" he said. "What nonsense. It is much
more likely that these, these . . ."

"Aliens?" suggested Pitoque.

"As you say. It is far more likely that these *aliens* are part
of some new trickery dreamt up by that dog Moctezuma."
Xicotencatl halted, threw back his head, and began to roar.
"This is exactly the kind of treachery the Aztec cowards would
try—send someone else to fight on their behalf. They're worse
than women." He set his hands on his hips, flexed his shoulders. "I say we follow the nobler course and meet these interlopers with sharpened flint. I say we put them to death."

"War?" said Ixcatzin, the sallow-skinned elder. He wiped
his hands on his robe and grimaced. "You propose war?"

"I do. Let these so-called aliens come. If they are gods, let them
prove it. If they are men, let them choke on their own blood."

The discussion bore on for nearly an hour. Xicotencatl
pushed his arguments relentlessly, driving them home like
spears through flesh, and finally the elders assented to his
view. War it would be.

✝

War was not what Pitoque had expected. But he had been wrong before, and no doubt he would be wrong again. In the aftermath of his meeting with the Tlaxcalan elders, he dispatched a runner to Tenochtitlán with news of the impending battle. Pitoque and his men would remain at the fortress city to witness the contest between the Tlaxcalans and the gods.

If they were gods.

The Tlaxcalans hastily assembled a force of several thousand warriors and readied themselves to meet the advancing party of Hernán Cortés. Their own spies had informed them that the aliens were approaching at a good pace, less than three days' travel away.

Pitoque wandered about the town with Maxtla at his side. Both of them observed the frenzy of preparations, the prayers and dances, the sharpening of spears, the gathering up of stones. Pitoque pulled his coarse robe tight to protect himself from the highland chill, and shook his head.

"Do you see?" he said to Maxtla.

"See what, Father?"

Pitoque tried to explain the absurdity of the situation. These Tlaxcalans—the Aztecs' own worst enemies—would now do Moctezuma an accidental kindness and put the *teules* to death. Like so many of the world's affairs, this battle would be conducted in the shadows, where all was contradiction, all a swirl of opposites, where it was difficult to determine who was foe, who was friend. All of life takes the form of a circle, he said. Nothing is ever quite what it seems.

But Maxtla did not agree. "The Aztecs are the enemy," he said. "Whoever is against them is a friend."

Pitoque was about to explain the situation a second time, but decided against it. What was the use? Maxtla was just a boy. It would be awhile yet before he understood the affairs of men. He closed his eyes and shook his head. In truth, he did not always understand them himself.

Two days passed, and scouts darted into the city, breathless and flushed. The aliens were just over the horizon, they reported. Five hundred or so. Accompanied by as many natives.

"Good," said Xicotencatl. He gave the order for his troops to assemble.

Soon the soldiers of Tlaxcala had formed themselves in orderly ranks. Those at the front blew upon their conch shells, raised their standards, and marched out of the city through a gap in the great rampart walls.

Pitoque and Maxtla watched the mustering for battle from a high parapet built atop the wall. They saw the *teules* advance across the broad plain, disappear into a forest, and then emerge again. It was clear by now that the newcomers realized they were in for a fight. Pitoque could see them in the distance, deploying themselves to meet the Tlaxcalans head on.

Pitoque had observed the clash of armies before, but never had he seen an enterprise so monstrously bloody as what erupted on the plain of Tlaxcala that day. The battle was entirely unlike the usual conduct of war, with its rules and norms and fastidious attention to the ancient rituals of conflict. When the Aztecs engaged the Tlaxcalans in battle, their purpose was not to inflict death but to capture prisoners for later sacrifice. Before taking up their arms—their obsidian-tipped spears called *atl-atl*, their swords called *macuahuitl*, their wood-and-cotton shields called *chimalli*—the Aztecs first prayed and made offerings to their gods. When they did enter the fray, their weapons and tactics were designed to terrify and perhaps to cripple, but not to kill. When they fought, they did not plunge swiftly into a pitched battle. Instead, they squared off, one against one, in a series of contests between matched fighters.

The soldiers sent out by Tlaxcala to meet the Aztecs were the best and bravest of the city's young men, heroes justly proud of their past exploits and eager for combat. And why not? To be taken prisoner by the Aztecs—as inevitably happened to many—was among the highest honors a man could achieve. Indeed, war was a gallant enterprise. Battles along these ritual lines were waged at Tlaxcala, at Huejotzingo, even at Cholula itself. They were terrible conflicts, and yet they possessed a certain familiarity, a kind of logic, a shape and form.

What Pitoque saw now was bedlam.

The *teules* attacked almost at once. They waded into battle, clubbing and slashing at anyone who came in their way, tearing human bodies to bits. Their heavy, flashing blades made short work of the Tlaxcalan warriors, who carried only wooden swords with obsidian tips. The defenders seemed bewildered as they fell. They had not dreamt they would be broken so easily or that they would actually die. Like monsters, like giants, these aliens swung their massive swords, lopping heads from shoulders, slicing arms and legs. They seemed to take an actual pleasure in causing death.

"Ha," muttered Maxtla, who couldn't contain himself. The battle was proceeding exactly as he had expected it would. If the Tlaxcalans would fight the *teules*, then he would happily see them fall. "Look, Father. Look at that."

Pitoque followed his son's gaze and saw another section of the Tlaxcalan front suddenly crumple, like men caught in a rushing tide. Down they went. Yet the Tlaxcalan army continued to fight. It had a huge advantage in numbers, and the soldiers gradually adjusted to this new form of combat. They altered their tactics. They massed their forces now against a single point in the alien lines and tried to penetrate there. They charged, thrashed, thrust. They pitted dozens of their warriors against a single alien, sacrificed ten of their own, or more, for each man they killed. Clad in loincloths and wearing skirts and tunics of sisal armor—useless against the heavy alien swords—they raced in, scuttling over the prone forms of their fallen comrades. They threw themselves at these new enemies, jabbed with their swords and spears. From the rear, their marksmen sent volley upon volley of arrows and stones and javelins into the enemy's midst. They killed several and injured more, but again and again the Tlaxcalan fighters were turned back, despite their greater numbers.

"Their swords are too flimsy," said Maxtla. "Their arrows don't fly straight."

It was true. Pitoque could see for himself that the *teules* were vastly better equipped for this sort of war, a war that was measured in blood and death. Their marksmen shot with greater range and accuracy than the Tlaxcalan archers could hope to achieve. And those strange beasts—the ones he'd once thought were two-headed dragons—were worse than dragons. They plowed into the Tlaxcalan ranks and did terrible damage. The men mounted upon them wielded long, death-dealing lances. They aimed straight at their opponents' faces or chests, tore off their heads, or thrust them through the heart. At closer range, the *teules* used their heavy double-handed swords to brutal effect, and now the giant, slobbering dogs bounded into the hurly-burly, howling like demons. They bowled over the Tlaxcalan warriors, ripped open their necks, and sucked out their blood, barking and yowling all the while.

Then the *teules* used their smoking spears—magical devices that did unspeakable harm at spectacular range. Still worse, they had several of the great pipes that Pitoque had already observed—long, exploding tubes that caused even worse carnage from still farther afield. Emboldened by the *teules'* success, their Totonac allies danced and hollered, rolled about in the blood of the dead, leapt to their feet and darted into the combat. They attacked the wounded who lay about the field, slashed open their chests, tore out their hearts, and threw them into the air.

And yet the Tlaxcalans did not surrender. Their drummers

and conch-blowers set up a glorious sound, and they attacked in wave upon wave, squadron after squadron. As one group was struck down, another stormed into battle.

The struggle raged on a full day and then the next.

A Man Who Values His Life

It was night. Pitoque and Maxtla were eating their dinner, both huddled beneath some scraggly oak trees. They had decent fare this time—scrambled turkey eggs spiced with chilis, prepared by one of Pitoque's own cooks and seasoned with salt. Neither spoke, for each was caught up in his thoughts in the wake of all they had witnessed that day.

For a moment, Pitoque managed to wrest his mind from the horrors of war. He was thinking what a difference a liberal sprinkling of salt made to a dish. Suddenly, he heard a commotion nearby and glanced up. Several of the Tlaxcalan elders were approaching. Among them was Ixcatzin, the yellow-skinned one. He stepped forward, made a shallow bow, and begged Pitoque's pardon for intruding at mealtime. He blamed the interruption on the city's somewhat disordered condition, a result of the lamentably adverse fortunes of war. "Otherwise we would not think of bothering you."

"I understand," said Pitoque. He hesitated. "Do you wish to share our meal?"

"No, no." The man waved his hands dismissively. "We have dined already."

Pitoque did not believe him. In their current state of distress, he doubted whether the Tlaxcalans had the time or the will to do anything as mundane as eat. He looked up at Ixcatzin and asked whether he could be of any service.

The old man squatted down. "I have come," he said, "concerning a question of metaphysics."

Pitoque frowned. "Metaphysics?"

"Yes." Ixcatzin tilted his head. "Today, we have witnessed the prowess of these aliens at war. A most unnerving experience."

"I agree."

"But Xicotencatl"—he meant Xicotencatl the Younger, their warrior chieftain—"is of the view that the powers of the aliens subside at night, in the absence of the sun. He has had a vision to this effect. He believes this is why they have withdrawn from battle for the moment. He thinks we should attack them now."

"I see," said Pitoque. "I take it that you do not agree?"

"I do not know. Nor do any of my colleagues. We wonder if you have any information on this subject."

Pitoque shook his head. "I'm afraid I do not."

The old man held Pitoque's gaze for a time, then looked back down at the barren ground. When he spoke again, it was in a low, hesitant voice. "We were wondering, then, if you would be willing to assist us."

"Assist you? How?"

The man looked up. "By acting as our agent. You could visit the aliens in their encampment. We know where it is. You could present yourself as a merchant, come to trade. That is what you are, is it not? You could make inquiries, observations. Then you could return to us with your report."

"I'm sorry," said Pitoque. "But—"

"We would pay you, of course." The old man waved to one of his underlings, who stepped forward with a tattered sisal packet, which Ixcatzin unwrapped. Inside were more of the musty, moth-eaten parrot feathers. "Quetzal feathers," said Ixcatzin. "As many as you wish. Name your price."

"It is not a question of price," said Pitoque. No price on earth would have induced him to accept this mission. A man who values his life does not travel between two sides in time of war, and especially not at night. "I am, as you say, a trader. I am not a spy."

"I did not say *spy*." Ixcatzin gave a nervous laugh. "A *collaborator* is the way I would describe it."

"Either way, I am afraid I must refuse."

"I see."

"But I think," said Pitoque, "that you are right to acquire more intelligence before launching a nighttime attack. I would ask you to be careful."

Ixcatzin nodded. "Of course. Of course. Xicotencatl wants us to carry out the attack tonight, but he is apt to be impetuous at these times." He stood up. "In any case, I thank you for your counsel. I am sorry to have interrupted your meal. I bid you good night."

He and the other elders turned and shambled away through the darkness.

"You did well," said Maxtla. "It would have been wrong to help them."

Pitoque said nothing. Right and wrong had nothing to with his decision—helping them might have been fatal. He felt a pang of regret, wondering whether he had been right to suggest that the Tlaxcalans send out spies of their own. Yet what other choice did they have? He returned his attention to his meal, but the eggs had grown cold, mucilaginous, impossible to eat. There was nothing to do but shiver in the chill night air and think.

Cortés heard footsteps and looked up. A figure appeared in the light of the campfire—Alvarado. Cortés could always recognize the man by his swaggering gait. He patted Doña Marina on the shoulder and rose to his feet. "Yes?" he said.

"*Mi capitán.*" Alvarado announced that three emissaries had arrived from the enemy side on a mission of peace. At least, he believed that was who they were and why they had come. "We cannot understand their language."

Cortés looked around. "Where are they now?"

"Down by those trees."

"All right." The captain stretched out his arms and yawned. He gestured to Marina. "Come, my dear."

She may not have understood his words, but she understood his meaning. The three of them walked down through the darkness to meet the Tlaxcalans.

Aguilar and several others were waiting for them, with the three strangers under guard. A fire burned nearby.

Aguilar looked up. "I'm sorry, *mi capitán*. It's Nahuatl again, I think. In any case, I cannot understand what they say."

Doña Marina peered through the shifting firelight. Already, something about the scene troubled her. She could tell from the rough cut of their dress and the poor fabric that these three were likely Tlaxcalans. But what were they doing here at night? She stepped forward. Without waiting for instructions, she asked these men who they were. She spoke in Nahuatl.

One coughed and rubbed his chin. He was an older man with a long scar on the side of his face, probably a former warrior. On hearing his own language spoken to him at last, he visibly relaxed. He said his name was Nebac, and he declared that he and his two companions were ambassadors sent by Xicotencatl the Younger in order to negotiate the terms of peace, for the Tlaxcalans were prepared to fight no longer. He looked straight at her as he spoke, and now he bowed.

Marina narrowed her eyes. Already, she was suspicious. She said, "And what position do you hold among your people?"

The man hesitated before replying. He said, "It is too complicated to explain. My people have many positions of honor, all very elaborate. I have won much glory in battle. See, I have quetzal feathers in my hair."

To Marina, they didn't look like quetzal feathers. They looked like turkey quills. She turned to Aguilar and explained in Maya what she had just learned. Aguilar translated her words for Cortés, who smiled and crossed his arms. So. A victory won already. He told Aguilar that he was prepared to dictate his terms.

But when Aguilar began to recite these details to Marina, she cut him off. "I do not believe what they are saying," she said.

"Why not?"

She explained. First, why would the Tlaxcalans sue for peace at night? Would it not have been safer to wait until the return of the sun? Second, these men were of no consequence or authority. The old one couldn't even name his office. If the Tlaxcalans truly desired peace, they would have sent someone of higher standing than this ragged fellow whose hair was entangled with the feathers of common fowl. Finally—and here she took a deep breath—she could not help noticing that the man had looked at her as he spoke and had even bowed in her direction.

"What is the significance of that?" asked Aguilar.

"He is absolutely terrified of giving offence, so terrified that he would even show respect to a woman. Look." She waved at the three Tlaxcalans. "You can see for yourself. They are trembling."

Aguilar turned to look at the three men, and he realized now that it was true. They *were* trembling. Their shoulders were hunched, and their eyes had a haunted look. But why wouldn't they be afraid? Even if they came in good faith, would they not be fearful of traveling by darkness to their enemies' camp?

"What is she saying?" said Cortés.

Aguilar explained the girl's suspicions. He said that he himself was not convinced the girl was right.

Cortés pondered for a moment. He said, "What does Marina believe is the true purpose of this delegation?"

When she understood the question, Marina marched over

to her commander. She clutched his forearm as she spoke. She told Aguilar that these men were undoubtedly spies— although, in fact, she was no more than half-certain this was so—and that they had come to determine the state of the Spaniards' defences by night, possibly in preparation for a surprise attack.

Aguilar translated these words, and Cortés smiled.

"Spies, are they? We know what to do with spies. Spies, we condemn to death."

And he would have given the order for the three men to be executed immediately. But Marina said she believed another course might be preferable—not executions. No, she had a better plan. She explained it to Aguilar.

"What is she saying?" interjected Cortés, frustrated because he could not immediately understand. "Tell me."

Aguilar clenched his jaw. Dear God. Dear God.

"Speak up," said Cortés. "I order you to tell me."

Finally, Aguilar explained to his commander what the girl had advised. As he did so, Marina let her mind wander. She was feeling content now. She had voiced her opinion. Whether or not she was right was of secondary importance. What mattered was that she had found a way to ingratiate herself even more deeply into her master's confidence. He must believe her to be indispensable—and now he would. She turned back to this trio of Tlaxcalans and their leader, the old fellow with the scar, the one named Nebac.

"Those aren't quetzal feathers, you know." She grinned at him. "You have turkey feathers in your hair."

The man didn't reply. He seemed too shocked, or fearful, to speak.

In the dull light of dawn, the three spies stumbled back into Tlaxcala, bleeding and half-dead. They had suffered terrible harm. One man's hands had been cut off. Two others had had their ears and noses severed. All three wore their dismembered parts like miserable trophies strung around their necks on leather thongs. They moaned and fell to their knees, blood streaming from their wounds. Nebac, the one whose face remained intact, explained that he had been instructed by the alien chieftain, Hernán Cortés, to inform his masters that the Tlaxcalans might launch an attack whenever they pleased, for the soldiers of a place called Spain were mighty gods who feared nothing and never slept.

He started to say it again, as if by rote, but was unable to finish. He toppled onto his chest, his face collided with the dirt, and it was clear that he was dead.

Pitoque felt the bile rise in his throat. He struggled to swallow it down. He reached up and felt his ears, reassured to find them in the same places they had always been. Still, he groaned, almost as if it was he who had been gashed and wounded, as if it was he who had died.

"Do you see?" he whispered to Maxtla. "Do you see what would have been our fate?"

But the boy refused to agree. "We are not Tlaxcalans," he said.

Pitoque closed his eyes, with the grotesque images of the mutilated spies still pulsing through his mind. He shook his head. "As always, I defer to your superior judgment."

Maxtla snorted and walked away. Soon, he began to run. In truth, he was horrified by what he had seen. But he didn't want his father to know.

The fighting ground on for another day and another night. But the Tlaxcalans had no more success than before. Pitoque paced back and forth upon the ramparts of the city, running his hands through his hair and wondering when the surrender would come. It was clear the Tlaxcalans had no hope of victory. Even Maxtla agreed it would be better if the war came to an end.

The chiefs and elders of Tlaxcala gathered by a cypress tree in the shadow of the great stone wall that surrounded their city. One after another, they urged peace, for there was no choice. But first they had to persuade Xicotencatl the Younger, who stormed about beating his fists against the air and extolling the feats of his soldiers.

"We've killed three of these dragon-beasts," he roared. "And a good many of these devils or gods or men or whatever they are—and many more wounded. Ah, they must be men, for they surely bleed when a sword is driven through them."

But the man's boasting meant nothing. The Tlaxcalans' successes had been puny in comparison to what they had lost, and they all knew it was so. For every *teule* they had managed to wound, dozens of their own had been killed. Meanwhile,

Cortés had sent squadrons of soldiers into surrounding villages, looting and murdering, in order to dissuade the people from coming to the Tlaxcalans' aid. In the end, Xicotencatl deferred to the elders. They would sue for peace and make an alliance with these creatures. What else could they do? Never had they encountered such warriors as these.

The following morning, the Tlaxcalan nobles marched out onto the battlefield to make their formal offer of surrender. When they had finished their statement, it was translated in the usual way by Doña Marina and Jerónimo de Aguilar. The Tlaxcalans were astonished to find a woman in such close association with the commander of the aliens, especially a woman of these lands, but they made no mention of it. They merely stood and gazed straight ahead and waited for the translation to be done.

Cortés listened and nodded to show that he understood. When the offer of surrender was completed, he rubbed his beard and strode back and forth in front of the Tlaxcalans. He proceeded to dictate his terms. These, it turned out, were astonishing in their generosity. Doña Marina presented them to the Tlaxcalans in the language they understood. But she considerably embellished the captain's words, adding warnings or comments of her own invention.

"A simple apology," she said. "That is all we ask." She stepped forward and waggled a finger at the elders, like a mother admonishing her charges. "Consider yourselves fortunate that my master is in a forgiving mood. On another day, it might have gone very hard for you."

The Tlaxcalan elders knelt upon the ground and bowed their heads. The one named Ixcatzin looked up and explained that the Tlaxcalans had attacked Cortés and his forces only because they thought he had come on behalf of the Aztecs, whom they hated beyond description.

"For any suffering or inconvenience our actions have caused, we are most sincerely sorry." Again, he lowered his head.

On hearing Aguilar's interpretation, Cortés frowned and glanced at his lieutenants, eyebrows raised. The battle had been caused by a misunderstanding? Three days of fighting and blood? He shook his head. Well, it couldn't be helped now. He turned back to the Tlaxcalans and assured them that nothing could have been farther from his mind than to do them harm. His forces were not in league with the Aztecs and never had been.

"Indeed," he said, "I have come for no other purpose than to make an alliance with you. This has been my intention all along."

Once translated by Aguilar and Doña Marina, these words greatly cheered the Tlaxcalan chiefs. They rose to their feet, smiles all around. They patted one another's arms. The decision to surrender had turned out unbelievably well. They soon arranged for food to be brought, and women to prepare it, and some two dozen slaves to chop wood for the fires.

Cortés and his men seemed content despite the poor quality of the Tlaxcalan fare. Soon, they were sprawled on the ground, stuffing their mouths, laughing, belching, and bellowing for more.

When the meal was over, Cortés rose to his feet and called to Marina. On her master's behalf, she thanked the Tlaxcalans for their hospitality and congratulated them on this happy new alliance they had formed. Cortés handed around a supply of what everyone believed to be beautiful green jewels. Pitoque had by now discovered for himself the dismal quality of these stones. He observed this pitiful offering and felt a sourness in his throat. What sort of gods were these, who fought like devils, slavered after gold, and cheated on their gifts?

He Wears Slippers of Gold

Within a matter of days, a party of Aztec envoys traveled down from Tenochtitlán. They desired an audience with Hernán Cortés.

Cortés put down a leg of turkey and waved to an aide. "Bring them here," he said. He and his forces were still encamped on the plain outside the walled city of Tlaxcala. "Where is Marina?" he called. "Find Aguilar."

Pitoque watched the envoys as they strode into the Spaniards' presence. They brought with them more gifts, and he swore at himself for having neglected to advise the Aztecs against exactly this. Gifts, especially gifts of gold, would only make matters worse. To Pitoque's dismay, the Aztec porters shuffled in carrying great quantities of hand-worked gold, not to mention handsome jewelled ornaments and twenty large bales of fine woven cotton, all of which they offered in honor of the great victory won by the *teules* over the Tlaxcalans.

A splendid victory, they proclaimed. Indeed, yes. Truly magnificent.

They were haughty men. They spoke disdainfully, as if their presence here were some great chore that had been imposed on them. Their leader this time was Huaxocitl, a cousin of Moctezuma's and a thin, austere man with dark shadows beneath his eyes. He made a shallow, perfunctory bow and announced that he brought a message from the emperor. Like others before him, he was careful not to look at Doña Marina as he spoke or to acknowledge her presence in any way. Her role was unthinkable but also unavoidable, and therefore best ignored.

"In view of all that we have learned," he said, "we would be most honored to pay tribute to the great king you have described, the one who lives beyond the sea and is known by the name of Charles I. Merely specify an appropriate sum, and we will see to the arrangements. We can deliver the tribute in any form you wish, be it gold or silver or *chalchihuites*."

Pitoque closed his eyes. The fools. Did the Aztecs really suppose that they could buy these creatures off? Did they not understand that the opposite was true, that each new gift— and each promise of further gifts to come—only increased the newcomers' hunger for gold? Yet here they were, making offers of treasure as though they were trying to propitiate their own more familiar gods. Had they learned nothing? The old ways would not work now.

At least one matter remained unchanged. As regarded the prospect of a visit to Tenochtitlán, the Aztecs were adamant. Huaxocitl shook his head and said he was very sorry, but such a project continued to be out of the question. He put his hands together in a gesture of deep regret. The route from Tlaxcala was legendary for its discomfort, he explained, and for the poverty of food and drink along the way.

"You will reach Tenochtitlán in a much depleted state, if at all," he said, "and it will be beyond our emperor's means to do much to alleviate your condition, as his own resources are somewhat over-extended at this time. Still, we congratulate you on a brilliant victory and offer our best wishes. May you encounter good fortune and great happiness on your homeward journey."

Doña Marina translated these words in a mocking tone, as if she were amused rather than offended by the Aztecs' lofty manner and their studied neglect of her presence. She informed Cortés that she had never encountered such transparent deceit. These promises of tribute were a delaying tactic, and this excuse—that Moctezuma found himself in strapped circumstances!—was merely absurd.

"He is the richest man in the world," she said. "Each day, he throws away more food than all of Tlaxcala consumes in a week. He wears slippers of gold."

"Does he?" said Cortés. "I've never encountered the like. His actual shoes are made of gold?"

"Yes." Marina nodded so that her hair danced about her shoulders like an ebony waterfall. "I have it on excellent authority."

Cortés nodded and drew the girl to his side, clearly smitten with her audacity and her slim loveliness.

"Tell them," he said, speaking through Aguilar, "that I accept their offer of tribute, payable in gold. And tell them that we will proceed to their city in spite of whatever privations we might face. Give them my thanks. Offer my most sincere regards to their emperor, which I extend on my own behalf and on behalf of Charles I of Spain. May God go with them."

After these sentiments were translated, and after some more colored beads had changed hands, the Spaniard turned and led his young princess away to the canvas shelter in which they were living at the time. Before long, the girl's giggles and laughter, and Cortés's enraptured groans, were audible to everyone.

The Aztec nobles glanced at each other in some confusion. They pressed their palms together, bowed three times, and announced that it was time for them to depart for Tenochtitlán. But there was no one now to translate this declaration, or to respond with any show of ceremony, so the men simply gathered up their belongings, climbed into their litters, and left.

From a low hillock, Pitoque watched the Aztecs weave their way across the grassy plain, their palanquins tottering on the shoulders of slaves, with banners of quetzal feathers quivering in the breeze. He turned to Maxtla. "They understand nothing," he said. "They rule the world, and yet they understand nothing."

"I hate them," said Maxtla.

Pitoque clicked his tongue, alert to the possibility that some Aztec spy might yet be about, unbeknownst even to him. "Don't say that. It's fine not to like them; that's up to you. But don't speak of it out loud."

"But I—"

"Did you hear what I said?"

At first, just silence. Then, "Yes, Father."

"Good."

The two walked back to the *teules*' camp.

Jerónimo de Aguilar was resting after his midday meal when he heard his name called out by Hernán Cortés. He climbed to his feet and hurried over to find out what service was required of him now. More translating, no doubt. The young girl, Doña Marina, was standing by her master's side.

"Ah, Aguilar," said Cortés. "I trust you are well."

Aguilar allowed that he was passably so.

"Good. Good. I'm glad to hear it." Cortés said that he had another commission for Aguilar to undertake. He gestured toward Marina. "On my behalf, I want you two to request a meeting with the chieftains of this place. Tell them they may present themselves at their earliest convenience."

Aguilar and the native girl set off to comply with this request, and in short order a party of Tlaxcalan elders arrived before Cortés in their rough maguey cloaks with an attitude of the greatest respect. Cortés proceeded to tell them about the conference he had just conducted with the party of Aztec nobles. The Tlaxcalans nodded politely, and Ixcatzin said it had pained his people to see their new friends dealing on such intimate terms with those scoundrels.

"We were in some doubt whether to permit the Aztecs to approach so close to our city. We decided to allow it only out of deference to you and your followers, honored sir."

Cortés smiled. "I am most grateful for your consideration." He brushed a smudge of dust from his doublet. "You may wish to know that the Aztecs do not seem very eager for us to visit them in their city."

Ixcatzin replied that he was in no way surprised by this news, for it was well known that the Aztecs lacked the social graces of a dog. He clucked his tongue and shook his head. He informed Cortés that, unlike the ambassadors of Moctezuma, his people would be more than delighted to receive the *teules* in their city. "Nothing would please us more. In fact, we are curious as to why you have not already requested such a visit. Could it be that you still do not trust us?"

In truth, Cortés was most wary of attack, but he did not like to say so. He frowned in concentration, then looked at Aguilar. "Tell them that our only concern has been for our cannons, which we do not like to leave unattended."

Aguilar translated these words into Maya and waited while Doña Marina put them into Nahuatl. The *teules*, she explained, were worried about the welfare of their great exploding pipes.

Ixcatzin and the other Tlaxcalan chiefs smiled at this answer, for they were much relieved. Ah, if this was the only impediment, why had he not mentioned it long ago? Here was a problem easily resolved. Ixcatzin declared that he would dispatch porters at once to see to the task of carrying the machines into the city, where they would be watched at all times. "How else may we be of service? Whatever it is, our new friends have only to ask."

Pitoque decided to make another report to Tenochtitlán. He summoned a runner, a trusted one, a muscular young man who could make excellent time but who also had the wit to convey a message of some complexity.

"Go to Tenochtitlán," he said. "Tell the master functionary that I strongly recommend against the practice of bestowing gifts upon these *teules*, especially gifts that consist of gold. You understand?"

"Yes, sir."

"Tell him, as well, that it is certain, beyond the slightest doubt, that the *teules* intend to travel to the capital, and that they will now be supported by the armies of Tlaxcala. Do you follow what I say?"

"Yes, sir."

"It is time for the emperor to formulate a policy of some kind, be it a plan of war or one of diplomacy. I myself recommend a plan of diplomacy. The Aztecs should invite the *teules* to Tenochtitlán and treat them as welcome guests. They should pray to the gods for a favorable outcome." He knew his approach sounded weak, but it was better than nothing. It was certainly better than simply asking these beings to go away.

Clearly, they had no wish to leave. He glanced back at the runner who stood before him, his eyes slowly blinking, waiting for further instructions. "Do you understand all that I have said?"

"Yes, sir."

"Then repeat it, please."

The man did so, without a misstep, and Pitoque sent him off.

He Who Lies, Wins

The runner took two days to make the journey to the capital. Once there, he promptly delivered his message to the master functionary. Azotl brought the matter before Moctezuma's court immediately, and another tortured debate ensued.

Huaxocitl, for one, was furious.

"Is my judgment to be disputed by a . . . a what? A merchant from some fetid provincial backwater?"

"Cholula," said Azotl, "is one of the empire's handsomer cities. And the man's name is Pitoque."

"His name is irrelevant. I am saying that I made a forceful case to these *teules*, these creatures—whatever they are. And I feel that we should wait, let some time go by, allow my arguments to achieve their effect. I think these beings will leave."

"Leave?" Here Cacama, king of Texcoco, spoke. "How can they leave? They sank all their floating palaces. Do you expect them to swim?" He stood up. "As you all know, I, too, asked them to depart. They didn't listen then, either." Cacama turned to Moctezuma. "My lord, I propose we put an end to these discussions. It is clear now that these creatures are in league with Tlaxcala, our worst enemy. How, therefore, can they be friends to us? If they are gods, they are not our gods. If we fight them, we shall be doing our own gods an honor."

Moctezuma shook his head, sighed several times, and seemed on the verge of tears, as he often did these days. "You are proposing war, Cacama?"

"I am, my lord. I fear that, if we delay, our position will only become more difficult."

At first, no one spoke, too stunned by this argument to know what to say. Finally, Huaxocitl climbed back to his feet. He launched into a description of the carnage he had observed on the open field outside Tlaxcala—bodies scattered everywhere, mutilated almost beyond recognition. One could barely breathe because of the stench. Perhaps this was why, he added parenthetically, he had not noticed the unpleasant odor that others had associated with these *teules*. Around Tlaxcala, everything stank.

Cacama scrunched up his face. "I can assure you, they smell intolerable. It was all I could do to remain upright in their presence."

Huaxocitl waved his arm. "My point is that these *teules* are horrific warriors. I have seen the evidence myself." He turned to address Moctezuma, whose face had turned very pale and whose lip plug of lapis lazuli now trembled on his chin. "My lord, you would not sleep if you had witnessed what I have seen. You would not like to think that so many dismembered bodies might as easily belong to Aztecs. We have learned what war has accomplished for our enemies. Shall we repeat their mistakes?"

Moctezuma closed his eyes and held up his hands, as if to keep all these terrible possibilities at bay. He begged his courtiers to give him time to reflect on all they had said. He agreed— a decision was required. At the moment, however, he could not say what form that decision might take.

Late that evening, the emperor summoned his advisers to return to the House of the Eagle Knights. There, he announced that he had consulted the oracles, conferred with priests, made sacrifices, and prayed—but he had not been vouchsafed a sign. He had been compelled to look into his own soul in order to arrive at a conclusion. Pale and hollow-eyed now, the emperor raised his shoulders, as if he were about to say something momentous, but he then let them slump. He looked beaten down by the burden of these terrible questions. He let out a long breath and remained silent for a time.

Finally, he spoke. He said he had appealed especially to the hummingbird god. Although his prayer had been met with silence, he had decided to interpret this silence in the following way. He took a deep breath and continued. "If Huitzilopochtli wished us to make war on these beings, then surely our god would have made his intentions clear. But he has not, which I take as a sign that war is not desired." Instead, Moctezuma told them, the Aztecs would take the course of peace. An invitation would be extended to these beings. They would be urged to visit Tenochtitlán, where they would be received as honored guests. "Perhaps, when I see them with my own eyes, I will know who and what they are."

Cacama and Huaxocitl both wanted to interrupt the emperor, to remind him that each of them had seen these creatures, and that they still hadn't the slightest idea who or what they were. But each held his tongue. Once Moctezuma made a decision, there could be no dissent. His word was law.

Cacama spoke up only to request that he be appointed to deliver the invitation. "I would like to see for myself how matters stand at Tlaxcala."

"In other words, you doubt my abilities." Huaxocitl climbed to his feet. "You think me incapable of delivering a simple message. I'll have you know that—"

"Peace, lords." Axotl decided it was time to step in. "Who carries the message is less important than what the message contains. May I suggest that the content of the invitation be formulated now? It may be determined later who is to carry it. Perhaps these matters might be discussed over dinner which, I understand, is almost ready to be served. Would that be suitable?"

This was the master functionary's secret weapon—a timely appeal to the digestive tract. Few disputes could not be resolved in this way or, at least, postponed. The present case proved to be no exception. Over dinner that night, the courtiers agreed that the message should be carried by Cacama. His mood now softened by several jars of pulque, even Huaxocitl consented to this decision.

‡

"Shall we walk, my lord, or shall we ride?" Tepehuatl stood in the plaza that sprawled in front of Cacama's palace in the city of Texcoco, located across the lake from Tenochtitlán.

"Ride, I think," said Cacama. He had learned his lesson during that abysmal journey to the eastern coast. Walking was all very well, but one shouldn't overdo it. "Perhaps, along the way, we shall take the occasional opportunity to test our legs."

"An admirable proposal."

The two men climbed into their litters. A dozen slaves—six to each—raised them aloft, and the mission began. The procession included an Aztec guard and a gang of porters, who carried victuals and other supplies, including canopies and temporary shelters that could be erected at night.

The journey to Tlaxcala required two days to complete, and during the trek Cacama brooded almost constantly. A haughty man, given to snap decisions and quick action, he was deeply unhappy with the course that Moctezuma had chosen. In his view, war with these interlopers was inevitable. On earth, he believed, there existed only two species of beings—the victors and the vanquished. Those who were not the first inevitably became the second. Sooner or later, all disputes came to blows, and so it would be in this case. He was certain of it.

Cacama expressed these thoughts to Tepehuatl. "Unfortunately," he said, fidgeting with the curtain of his palanquin, "it is not for me to question, much less override, the judgment of Moctezuma. But I think he is wrong. I think the man weak."

Tepehuatl gasped in astonishment. Such words were akin to blasphemy.

"He sobs in public."

"Ah!"

"He wrings his hands. He mopes about. He goes back and forth in his mind."

"Stop, my lord. I beg you. The slaves have ears. The guards as well."

"He is like a girl. A mincing, weeping girl. His manner makes me ill."

"Enough. Enough. Look. I have stopped my ears."

"He searches after signs and cannot find them and then confesses as much."

Tepehuatl uncovered his ears. "What would you have him do?"

"Lie. Put on a show. Make a grand spectacle. Claim divine powers. Manipulate the gods to serve his own ends. How else is a leader to act?"

"I see. You follow this course yourself, I take it?"

"Ah, well. An impertinent question. If I did, I would never admit it. A leader has not the luxury of being honest. Honesty in a man is a fatal weakness."

"He who lies, wins?"

Cacama laughed to hear his ideas put so succinctly. "Perhaps. I also recommend a large army."

"But," Tepehuatl reminded him, "we are currently on a mission of peace."

Cacama frowned. "Just so, my friend." He heaved a long, unhappy sigh. "Just so."

Cortés received the latest ambassadors of Moctezuma outside the city of Tlaxcala on a clearing of grass in front of his canvas shelter. As usual, Aguilar had been summoned so that he and Doña Marina might serve as the commander's interpreters. By now, the carnage of the war with the Tlaxcalans had mostly been cleared away. Some weaponry lay scattered about, along with the odd remnant of clothing and bits of flesh or bone not yet scavenged by the Spanish fighting dogs.

As before, Cacama greeted the *teules* with a ceremony involving smoking braziers and the administration of hot, sweet-smelling oil, a ritual that the visitors submitted to quite willingly.

With the preliminaries completed, Cacama drew himself up and made an announcement that seemed to have been rehearsed. He invited the newcomers to proceed to Tenochtitlán, where the great emperor Moctezuma would be pleased to receive them as his guests and to make whatever arrangements he could to ensure their comfort. He spoke as if this matter had never been raised before, as if the Aztecs had never suggested any other course.

Cortés, who was seated in a rough wooden chair, now stood up and made a salute. He turned to Aguilar and spoke.

"In the name of our king, Charles I of Spain, and on behalf of our men, we are pleased to accept."

Cacama nodded at Cortés, to show that all was in good order. Then he cleared his throat and assumed a more conspiratorial air. He wished, he said, to express an opinion of a confidential nature—some advice, as it were. He drew a step closer. "It would suit us," he said in a low voice, "if you saw fit to begin your journey at once, for you have lingered a long while in this wicked place." He gestured about him and rolled his eyes. "We are surprised that you have found it convenient to remain in the Tlaxcalan territory for so many days. You should understand that it would be foolhardy to enter into any treaties with these savages. It is well known that they are a pack of lying vermin who are unfit to wash the feet of slaves and who cannot be trusted in anything they say or do. Their very presence is an affront to civilized men, sufficient to befoul both water and air." Cacama took another step closer, and lowered his voice still more. "I bid you, sir, to look frequently to your purse, for it is apt to be looted at any moment, day or night."

Doña Marina repeated these sentiments while struggling to contain her laughter. She told Cortés that here was yet another example of the Aztecs' overbearing ways. They considered everyone but themselves to be animals—and yet they were the ones who raped and murdered and stole. Cortés nodded. Speaking through Aguilar, he asked Doña Marina to thank his visitors for their advice and to repeat that he would be pleased to accept their lord's gracious invitation. As was usual by now, he was content to leave the exact wording up to her.

"God willing," he said, "we shall indeed travel to Tenochtitlán."

On hearing these words, Cacama bowed, but there seemed to be something bitter on his tongue. He had a disgruntled look. "We shall depart. Thank you and good day."

The Aztec party picked up its belongings and withdrew. It seemed there would be no banquet served this time and no exchange of gifts.

A Section of Flesh

"Come." Ixcatzin tugged at Pitoque's robe. "You will be interested in this."

Pitoque was alone. Three days had passed since the end of the war between the *teules* and the Tlaxcalans, and he'd just had another of his maddening disagreements with Maxtla, again concerning the nature of these great, bearded strangers, these creatures from a place called Spain. Unable to endure the argument any longer, he'd demanded silence, turned on his heels, and walked away. Better to be alone for a time. Better to cool his temper.

And now he'd encountered Ixcatzin, who evidently had something to show him. The sallow old man guided him down a series of narrow alleys that zig-zagged through Tlaxcala until they reached a small plaza completely enclosed by stone buildings. Pitoque looked around. It was almost dusk, but there was enough light to make out his surroundings well enough. Several priests and elders had already gathered here, as well as their attendants. A wood fire burned off to the side, not far from a large pile of rounded shapes hidden beneath tarps of rough maguey fiber.

"Look," said Ixcatzin.

He lifted the flap of one of the tarps. The stink was abominable, and Pitoque reeled back and swore out loud. It seemed these beings smelled even worse when they were dead. Before him lay the bodies of five *teules* who had been killed in battle, plus two of the great deerlike creatures on which they rode.

"What are you doing?" said Pitoque, once he had steadied himself from the shock. "What is taking place here?"

"An experiment," said Ixcatzin. From beneath his robes, he produced a large obsidian blade. He tested its edge against his fingers. "All very curious. It was you—was it not?—who first raised the possibility that these creatures might be gods. Now we shall see."

The elder instructed several workers to haul one of the deer-like animals out, a job that required eight men. Immediately, he set to work with the knife. For an old man, and a wizened one at that, he was surprisingly dexterous and strong. The others in the square all gathered around. As Ixcatzin worked, he explained exactly what he was doing.

"Transportion of the gods?" he asked. "Or merely an animal, albeit a large one? That is the question. Ah! Look." By now, he had hacked through the beast's rib cage, and the guts started to tumble out and spill across the flat stones. Ixcatzin spread them out and then unwound the long intestine, which snaked back and forth across the ground, forming a long loop around the other organs. He gazed at them for a time, then shook his head. "Nothing unusual here, apart from the question of size."

Ixcatzin returned to the animal's cadaver and hunched down. He started to dissect one of the forelegs, which proved to be an unremarkable limb, much like a deer's, only bigger. The only strange feature was the foot—like a large stone. Finally, he set to work upon the creature's head, making an incision and then peeling back the skin lightly covered with brown fur. Beneath it lay only a thin layer of flesh and a large skull. He used a rock to smash a hole in the casing of bone, and some gobs of brain dribbled out. Teeth, tongue, eyes, nostrils, ears—all the other parts were quite standard.

Ixcatzin cut up some of the viscera and had a pair of workers cook the parts on the fire, while he sliced out a section of the creature's haunch to be cooked as well. When the meat was done, several of the Tlaxcalans nibbled upon it, with some trepidation at first, but then quite heartily. They declared the flesh to be somewhat stringy in texture, but otherwise agreeable. The organs were certainly ripe, but that was to be expected. By now, the creature had been dead for awhile.

Ixcatzin turned to Pitoque. "You have traveled widely, sir. What do you make of this demonstration?"

"I do not understand. What do you mean, exactly?"

"I mean, on the evidence we have just seen, are these four-legged beasts gods or animals?"

"Animals, I would guess. But this has been my assumption for some time. These creatures merely carry the *teules* about and do their bidding. They are exciting to watch and are very dangerous in war, but they are not, I think, divine. I believe we may conclude they are less than gods. I'm more uncertain about the *teules* themselves."

"Ah, well. Why didn't you say so?"

Ixcatzin released an exasperated sigh and shook his head, as if all his labors so far had been for nothing and it was all Pitoque's fault. He cleaned his obsidian blade on the folds of his robe and called for several torches to be lit and brought close, for it was now nearly dark. He motioned to several workers to haul out a corpse belonging to one of the manlike beings, and they started to carry out his wishes. Suddenly, Ixcatzin stepped forward, shook his head.

"No," he said out loud. "No, wait. I have a better idea."

He called the workers over and whispered something to them. They nodded and hurried away. When they returned some minutes later, they were half-carrying, half-dragging, another of these creatures. This one, however, was alive.

"We captured him on the second day of the battle," said Ixcatzin. "Still breathing, which is a miracle. Might be a god, after all. We shall see."

He approached the prisoner, who was sprawled on the dirt, unable to move on account of the maguey fibers that bound him by the feet and arms. A leather gag prevented him from shouting. His eyes practically bulged from his head, and he wriggled and squirmed. Blood had clotted around his midsection and over much of his legs. He made desperate grunting sounds, and his breathing was uneven and labored.

"Notice," said Ixcatzin. He pointed at the clotted blood. "The creatures bleed. We've established that much. Now watch this."

Before Pitoque could cry out, much less intervene, the Tlaxcalan squatted down and, using both hands in an abrupt, violent motion, jerked the blade of his knife across the being's neck. Blood poured out in a sudden, arching plume, and the fellow flopped onto his side. Ixcatzin waited until the flow subsided. Then he pushed at the creature's shoulders, slapped its cheeks, closed its gaping mouth, and opened it again. "This is another truth we've observed." He glanced up at Pitoque. "We can kill them."

He pointed to the other corpses, hidden beneath the rough tarps. "If you look closely at those ones, you'll notice they've begun to rot. You'll see as well that maggots are attacking them. Would you expect that of the gods?"

One of Ixcatzin's aides raised a corner of the tarp, and Pitoque could not keep himself from looking. It was true. By the dozen, maggots were crawling in and out of the creatures' mouths or scuttling up into their nostrils. The attendant reached down and tried to brush the maggots away.

"Leave them," said Ixcatzin. "They'll only come back."

Once again, he bent down to the corpse at his feet and devoted himself to carving an opening in the chest cavity. Pitoque kept the sleeve of his robe over his mouth and nose, for the stink was almost unbearable now.

"Large fellow," said Ixcatzin. "Like the rest. Also extremely hairy." He glanced up at Pitoque. "Significant? Or not?"

Pitoque shrugged. He wondered why Ixcatzin wanted him here. He decided that it must be on account of his far-flung travels, his many different experiences. He was apt to have learned more about the world than the Tlaxcalans had. A trait they considered rare might appear common to him. His knowledge might help them to draw the appropriate conclusions.

Ixcatzin proceeded with his surgery, which yielded no evidence of major differences between one of these corpses and a human one. The usual complement of viscera. Standard musculature. Bones like those of any man. Once again, the final test was culinary. Ixcatzin had a worker grill a section of flesh—the rump was selected—and several of the priests volunteered to try it. They judged it to be rather tastier than, but not entirely dissimilar to, Aztec rump. There was a higher fat content, which made for a richer flavor overall. But what did this prove? Nothing. As far as anyone could recall, none of the prophecies or holy texts made specific reference to the edibility of the gods.

Pitoque was feeling queasy by now—as a Cholulan, he forswore such reckless practices and found them disgusting. He thought, on the whole, that it would be wiser not to mention the episode to Maxtla, who was unlikely to approve of his father's playing a role, however minor, in the dissection and consumption of a *teule*. Pitoque was not certain that he approved himself. At least he would be able to report upon the experiment to Azotl. But what did it mean?

When Ixcatzin finished his investigation, he had the workers shove the cadavers and entrails back beneath the tarp and ordered the entire area to be sprinkled with floral water.

"What a foul stink." He shook his head and scowled. "We had better do something with these corpses, but I do not know what."

"Should you not bury them?" said Pitoque.

Ixcatzin shrugged. "I suppose so. But our new friends say they want them back. I cannot think why, but I believe we had better do as they ask—with the exception of this one body, of course."

He evidently meant the one he'd put to the knife.

"I agree," said Pitoque. "I don't think it would be wise to return that one."

The Little King of Plates

Who and what were these creatures?

As he crept back along the serpentine route of alleys that led to the center of the city, Pitoque found he was unable to stop worrying at the question. Even after seeing one of the *teules* dissected, he had no clearer idea than before of whether they were divine or not. Perhaps their bodies were merely vessels. Once the bodies were killed, perhaps the gods went elsewhere. Deeds—that was what Aguilar had said. *Judge us by our deeds.* How, then, was he to discover the truth? In so many ways, they acted like men. They ate like men, slept like men, fornicated like men. He had seen all this, or most of it, with his own eyes. True, they did seem blessed with magical powers—their terrible smoking spears, for example. But none of the evidence was conclusive. He had always assumed that he would recognize a god if one appeared before him. But maybe the truth did not reveal itself so easily. He wracked his brains for an answer—how did one distinguish a man from a god? If deeds were the test, what deeds were those?

It was then, in the moment between one footfall and the next, that he saw what he had to do. Of course. There *was* a test he could conduct. The sudden knowledge ran up and down his spine like a thrilling of heat or cold. He could not understand why the idea had not occurred to him before.

Cholula.

That was it. The newcomers would proceed to Tenochtitlán, but they should travel byway of Cholula.

The answer was so simple, the simplest way to discern the truth. Surely, if this Hernán Cortés was the god Quetzalcoatl, or if he was associated with Quetzalcoatl in some way, then his divinity would manifest itself in Cholula, where the feathered serpent was worshiped with greater fervor than anywhere else in the world. There would be a sign. The trees themselves would speak. Birds of the air would sprout scales and writhe in the dirt. The constellations would change their shape. Something momentous would take place, some signal appear. The truth would be revealed.

Pitoque was certain of it. He must persuade the strangers to visit Cholula. But how? Almost as soon as he had posed this question to himself, a solution darted into his mind. Gold, of course. These creatures would venture anywhere for gold.

The following morning, he summoned two of his runners. He instructed one to make for Tenochtitlán at top speed. There, he should seek out Azotl, the master functionary, and tell him to arrange the transfer of some Aztec gold to Cholula, to the temple of Quetzalcoatl. It did not need to be a huge amount—almost any quantity would do. He knew that this request lay within Azotl's power, for the Aztecs possessed a considerable treasure of gold, carefully hidden in vaults and caches all over the city. Only Azotl knew the location of every one. Pitoque repeated his instructions, to ensure that they were clear. He tilted his head. "Do you understand?"

The man nodded.

"Very good." Pitoque turned to the second runner and told him to make for Cholula and inform the elders there that a large party of visitors was to be expected soon.

Both men darted away, vanishing amid a network of broken-down stone and mud-brick buildings. Pitoque watched them disappear and then decided on his next step. He would seek out the swarthy *teule*, the one who spoke Maya—Jerónimo de Aguilar. He clenched his hands into a single fist and raised them to his lips. His plan was proving much simpler than he had imagined. Surely the gods were guiding him now.

As he hurried toward the quarters now occupied by the *teules*, it occurred to him again that his own role in these affairs must surely have some special significance. Why was he, a mere merchant of Cholula, bound up in these extraordinary events? Once again, he remembered that night long ago in the lands of the Maya, the unspeakable sins committed there. He recalled the transgressions of his son—the desecration of the temple in Cholula. Suddenly, he stopped, felt his knees go weak. In his mind, he saw a vision of maggots—armies of maggots swarming over his rotting corpse. He stood still, as if his bones were locked. What awaited in Cholula? Glory or horror? His thoughts careened between these two opposites until at last he realized that the worst affliction of all was not knowing. Better to find out, no matter the consequences.

He willed himself to move forward. He had to act. It was better for a man to seek out his fate, once and for all, than to live his life in darkness. He felt the blood return to his legs. He began to walk. He leaned ahead, as if straining into the future. He broke into a run.

Pitoque found Aguilar lounging alone in the scruffy central plaza of Tlaxcala, where several boys were scampering about with sticks, chasing a small wooden disk.

"Ah," said Aguilar. He stood up. "*El Reyecito de los Platos.*" It was the name they had coined for Pitoque. The Little King of Plates. Aguilar pointed toward the boys bounding about in the dirt. "You know, it astounds me—all these boys everywhere, playing with *ruedas.*"

"Roo-ay-das?" said Pitoque. He did not understand the word.

"Yes. Objects that go around." He made a circulating motion with his hands. "It has always amazed me that you people have devised children's toys involving *ruedas*, but not used these devices for other purposes."

"What other purposes?"

Aguilar spun off a series of words in his own language, none of which Pitoque could make out. "Methods of transport," the Spaniard said. "You can move people and goods a lot more easily on *ruedas*, you know. But you folks walk everywhere. You carry everything on your backs. Damned primitive, don't you think? During my time as a slave, I tried to explain the use of *ruedas* till I was gasping for breath, but no one would listen to me."

Pitoque tried to look as if he sympathized with Aguilar's predicament, but he could make no sense of it at all.

"Ah, well," said Aguilar. "I take it you have not wandered over here in order to engage in a discussion of modern technology."

"No," said Pitoque, "although it has been most illuminating." He explained his real reason for seeking Aguilar. As a native of Cholula, he said, he would be most honored to have the *teules* visit the city of his birth on their way to Tenochtitlán. "It is not far out of the way, and a visit will make your journey more pleasant. It is a fine city."

"Cholula?" Aguilar shook his head. "I have never heard of it."

"It is small," admitted Pitoque. "But it has much to recommend it. Many temples and much beauty. Not at all like this place." He waved around him at the miserable decrepitude of Tlaxcala. "You would like it there."

"I have no doubt." Aguilar shifted from one foot to the other. "But I'm not certain my opinion will carry much weight with Cortés. I do appreciate your generous invitation, but I'm afraid—"

"There is gold in Cholula."

"What did you say?" Aguilar straightened up at once.

"Gold." Pitoque explained that the city of Cholula was blessed with a quantity of gold, which the people would be pleased to turn over to the *teules* as a form of tribute. "It is our custom."

"It is?"

In fact, it was not. But Pitoque had decided to part company with the strict truth. "By nature and inclination," he said, "we are a generous people."

"So it would seem."

Pitoque assumed a confidential tone. "Your commander and your colleagues—they will certainly appreciate this generosity. They will no doubt remember that it was you who brought this invitation to their attention."

Aguilar frowned. In truth, his relations with the other Spaniards were strained. They all regarded him as an oddity, as something foreign to themselves. Information such as this would certainly enhance his standing among them. It could do him no harm. "Well, I agree with you, the gold's an incentive—not for me, but for the rest." He spread out his arms to show his helplessness. "It is all they talk about, you know. Gold."

"Alvarado," said Cortés. He turned to his golden-haired lieutenant. "What say you? Is it worth a detour? Shall it be Cholula then?"

Aguilar had just finished transmitting Pitoque's invitation.

"Of course." Alvarado stretched out his long legs, crossed his boots at the ankles. Had there not been talk of gold? What more was there to say? He clasped his hands behind his head and stifled a yawn. Ever since Puertocarrero had suffered his disgrace, Alvarado had been feeling pleasantly cocky. "Cholula is a pleasant-sounding name. Pronounceable, at least."

"Good." Cortés smiled. "I'm glad you agree. But it is not just a matter of the gold."

Alvarado raised his eyebrows. "It isn't?"

"No. I think we would be wise to take a more roundabout approach to our destination in any case. If it should happen that the Aztecs are planning anything suspicious, then a detour on our part might well keep us out of harm's way." He turned and addressed Aguilar. "Thank you, Aguilar. A most fortuitous intervention."

"You are most welcome, *mi capitán*."

Alvarado raised his hand in a kind of wave. "I second the sentiment. Well done."

Aguilar smiled to himself. This was the first time that Alvarado had even acknowledged him, never mind offered him praise. It was astounding what the prospect of a little gold could do.

Two days later, Hernán Cortés set out for Cholula, located a day's march to the southwest of Tlaxcala. He was accompanied by Doña Marina, his soldiers, his Totonac porters, and his cannons. Meanwhile, the Tlaxcalans supplied a force of one thousand warriors to march behind the great exploding pipes. They would have sent a far greater number, but Cortés had prevented it. To Pitoque, it seemed they would have sent ten thousand soldiers for they were certainly bent on war.

The procession of *teules* and their porters and allies dwindled toward the horizon, past the dark green domes of several madrecacao trees, all but disappearing beneath the slate gray surface of the sky.

Pitoque pulled his robe about him, his mind haunted by doubts. "Come," he said to Maxtla. "We must hurry. We must catch up."

By nightfall, the *teules* stood along the banks of the river Atoyac, a short distance from Cholula itself. A party of Cholulan emissaries ventured out through the dusky light to meet them, bearing cornmeal cakes and many roasted turkeys and repeated assurances of goodwill. They had musicians with them, who played on flutes and conch shells, to serenade the visitors while they ate.

That night, the *teules* slept on the open ground outside the city, and the following morning they were welcomed into Cholula itself. Meanwhile, the Tlaxcalans and Totonacs made their camp across the Atoyac, except for a small number who were required to carry the great smoking pipes.

The *teules* provided an unearthly spectacle as they marched into Cholula, or so it seemed to Pitoque, who hurried behind with Maxtla. His spirits rose with every stride. Now all would be determined. The doubts and fears that had haunted him for so many years would all be cast aside.

As he walked, he found himself gawking like a stranger, his neck twisting this way, then that. He was struck as never before by the wealth and order and refinement of his city, especially as compared to Tlaxcala, a rough and dirty place. Instead of forbidding walls and battlements, Cholula was surrounded by rich fields planted in corn, chilis, and maguey cactus. The houses were handsome structures, built of stone, glazed with a silvery whitewash, surrounded by flowering trees. A hundred temples towered above the surrounding plains, and the highest of all was the temple devoted to Quetzalcoatl himself.

Could it be that the ancient lord had returned at last?

A Dead Aztec

"Do not tell me," said Pitoque. "Not again."

Kalatzin nodded. "Again. That's three times, you know. An unlucky number."

The merchant turned toward his daughter Zaachila. The girl sat straight-backed with her hands folded upon her lap. Her long black hair streamed down over her shoulders, her skin was the color of polished cacao beans, and her proud, aquiline nose gave her the air of a princess. Pitoque was baffled. Why would any man not leap at the chance to have this girl for his bride? And yet three men had now rejected her. The latest was

a young man by the name of Huecantl, the son of a prosperous vendor and an excellent prospect, according to Kalatzin.
She herself had met the man's mother and father, and all had
been arranged—subject only to Pitoque's approval and to the
agreement of the young man himself. But after a single afternoon in Zaachila's presence, this idiot named Huecantl had let
it be known that he did not favor the union. Yes, the girl was
gracious, slender, full of life, and lovely to look upon. But—
those eyes. They weren't natural. Regretfully, he would have
to decline.

"And that was the end of that." Kalatzin made a washing
motion with her hands. "Just like the other two."

Pitoque said nothing at first, slightly irked at his wife for
having attempted these arrangements in his absence. Was not
the marriage of a daughter within the purview of her father?
He let out a breath. He glanced over at Maxtla, who was also
attending this family conference, at his father's insistence. As
the son and heir, he had a role to play in these matters, if only
to observe, to be informed. He had said little so far, merely listened patiently, now and again nodding or shaking his head
as the occasion dictated. For Pitoque, it was enough to see his
son assume his filial duties and take them seriously. Now he
turned and gazed again at his daughter. How anyone could
reject her was beyond his comprehension. He looked back at
his wife and shook his head.

"I told you," said Kalatzin. "I told you a hundred times. It's
a curse. Look."

She instructed Zaachila to move her head from side to

side, and the girl responded without protest, although Pitoque detected a slight impatience in her manner. Obviously, she had been put through this drill a time or two before. He watched his daughter shift her head back and forth and saw what he already knew he would see. The direction of her gaze changed along with the movement of her head.

"Now," said Kalatzin. "Do the same thing—but keep looking at me."

"Mother . . ." The girl put up her hands. "You know I can't."

"Don't contradict me. Just do as I say."

Zaachila shrugged and then tried to do as she was told. It was true. She could look only straight in front. If she turned her head, her eyes remained fixed. It was an odd trait but hardly a cause for so much alarm. What were they accomplishing by forcing her to demonstrate what they already knew? Pitoque reached over and patted his daughter on the shoulder. Enough.

"It's a curse," insisted Kalatzin. "Plain as plain can be. You can see it."

"I see only a trifling oddity. Nothing more. You know, my father had the same feature—all his life. It didn't prevent him from traveling the length and breadth of the empire. Or from marrying. Or from fathering children. He—"

"Well, I'm glad we have settled that at least." Kalatzin brushed some imaginary trace of lint from her robe. "I'm glad we have established something."

"What have we established?"

"That it comes from your side of the family. This curse." Kalatzin announced that she had been in touch with several priests, who had impressed upon her the gravity of the case. Curing the girl would be an arduous and lengthy undertaking, but they were optimistic that it could be accomplished—providing, of course, that the gods gave their blessing to the project. There were also certain financial issues to consider, which the priests had outlined in some detail. Kalatzin was about to summarize this side of the matter when Pitoque heard a commotion near the entrance to the house. A domestic slave hurried onto the patio, where the family congress was underway. Begging his master's pardon, he announced that Toc was waiting in the house's foyer, wishing to speak to his master.

Pitoque rose, excused himself, and hurried away across the small arcade that bordered the patio. Near the main entrance to the house, he spotted Toc and went straight over to him. "Good day, old friend," he said. "What news do you bring?"

Shocking news. Just that morning, at the foot of the pyramid dedicated to the god Quetzalcoatl, the body of an Aztec sentry had been discovered. The man was dead, his blood still freshly pooled about him. Meanwhile, the supply of gold, recently delivered to the temple on an order from Tenochtitlán, had gone missing. Stolen, it seemed.

Pitoque stepped back, suddenly unsure of his balance. He had been so caught up in the affairs of his family that he had almost forgotten his other purpose in Cholula. He now found it difficult to breathe. "Dead, you say? You're quite sure?"

"Yes. His throat was slit."

"And the gold is gone. All of it?"

"Yes."

Pitoque rubbed at his brow with the heel of his right hand. What was he to make of this catastrophe? Was this the sign he had been waiting for—a dead Aztec sentry and a cache of gold stolen from the temple of Quetzalcoatl? He felt a turmoil in his stomach. He had a sense of events suddenly spinning out of his control. What had he been thinking—that he could manipulate the gods? Had he imagined that divine forces might submit to his will? What sort of arrogance was that? His knees began to buckle beneath him, and he thought of his family. How could he have coaxed the *teules* here, of all places? What terrible dangers had he lured into such close proximity to his family? These and other questions darted through his mind, but he tried to blot them out, sought to calm himself. He asked Toc the only question that didn't need asking—who was thought to be responsible for the death of this Aztec, the theft of the gold?

Toc grimaced, as if the answer should be obvious. "The *teules*," he said. "That's what everyone is saying."

Maxtla stormed back and forth across the floor of his room. He was furious. He had overheard the conversation between his father and Toc, and he'd been enraged. Now he stalked about the place he'd used to sleep, a place he had not seen for so long that it was almost unknown to him, its stucco walls and cedar beams, his old wooden bow perched in the corner with its string of deer gut, the collection of ocelot ears that he had won at games, the wood-frame bed with its cover of eiderdown. From the table he picked up a rubber ball—a gift from his father after some long-ago trip to the eastern coast, where such objects were fashioned for the playing of *tlachtli*. He tossed it idly from hand to hand as he paced about the floor.

The blood throbbed through his veins. Naturally, everyone would rush to accuse the *teules*. People always seemed to think the worst of them, just because they were different. If something went wrong, of course the outsiders were to blame. And all this fuss over one dead Aztec! It made him furious to think of it. If a Cholulan had been killed, no one would have cared. But a dead Aztec—oh, a panic was raised at once. It was disgraceful. To think that the Cholulans could mourn their oppressors more than they mourned their own. Maxtla wouldn't have minded all that much if the newcomers had killed an Aztec sentry. Good riddance. Granted, the theft of gold would still have been troubling.

But he was almost sure the *teules* had had nothing to do with either of these crimes, and he had a good idea how he might confirm his suspicions. True, he was no longer on speaking terms with Nahuauc, the ringleader of the gang he'd once belonged to. But he had kept up contact over the past year with another friend and a better one, whose name was Teontin. The family congress this morning had brought the boy back to mind. It so happened that Teontin was the younger brother of Huecantl, the prospective suitor who had rejected Zaachila. Teontin had once been a confederate of Nahuauc and would almost certainly know what had happened to that Aztec and the gold. If Maxtla was right, he would be able to exonerate the *teules* and show how misguided the Cholulans were. If he was mistaken—well, that would be another story. But he didn't think he was mistaken.

Maxtla found his mother seated in the central patio, mending some garment of her husband's. He told her he had some errands to attend to. She nodded, and he withdrew. Once he was outside the house, he turned right and ambled along the narrow, hardpacked street. For a hundred yards or so, he acted as if he were in no hurry at all, and then he took off at a run for the house where Teontin lived.

I Propose We Kill Them All

"So," said Pedro de Alvarado. "What do we do now?"

Cortés shrugged. He did have a plan—but it would require some preparation and care. He was hoping that Doña Marina would soon appear so that together they might put the plan into effect. Meanwhile, he believed he had done everything he could do. As soon as Aguilar had told him about the dead Aztec, he had put his troops on alert. He did not know who was responsible for the killing, but it did not matter. The Spaniards would be suspected, and there would be trouble. Cortés knew what he himself would do if even one of his men were killed in this manner—in cold blood, alone. He would exact the bloodiest revenge possible, and at once. Put the fear of God into the hearts of whoever had done it. Any soldier would respond that way. Why expect the Aztecs to be any different? The Spaniards had to be prepared. Beyond that? His plan would oblige him to resort to a degree of duplicity. He did not want his own hands stained by undue bloodshed. He glanced at Alvarado.

"What do we do now?" he repeated. He paused. "We wait."

Alvarado was not accustomed to waiting. His natural inclination was for action. "Wait for what?"

"We will wait to see what happens next." Cortés was counting on his lieutenant's aggressive instincts to surface now. "I do not see what else we can do."

"We are dangerously vulnerable, you know." Alvarado began to pace across the stone floor of the small palace where he and the other Spanish officers were billeted. He pounded the fist of one hand into the palm of the other. "It could be a trick. Lure us here with the promise of gold. Kill one of their own. Blame us. If you ask me, it's a trick. And we're easy targets in this miserable town."

"That's putting it a bit strongly, I think." Cortés stroked his chin. In fact, Alvarado was right. An army could easily surround them here. "But," he said, "departing the city now would send the wrong message. It would suggest we were afraid."

"Afraid? Ha! We could soon persuade them otherwise. Show them the business end of Spanish iron."

"Calm yourself," said Cortés. Of all his lieutenants, Alvarado was his favorite. But the man did require some reining in—until the moment when one decided to set him loose. "For the moment, I think we should just keep calm and wait. If someone threatens us, we shall know how to behave. We—"

A noise outside the hall interrupted him. Cortés looked up.

He smiled as Marina hurried in, precisely on time. The girl was a little felon, the first person he'd met who was as crooked as he was himself. Earlier that morning—with the assistance of Aguilar as translator—he and Marina had mapped out the ingenious stratagem that was about to unfold. A necessary stratagem. After all, sometime in the future, he might be held accountable for what was to take place this day. The Governor of Cuba, the King of Spain, legions of courtiers in Santiago and Madrid—he might have need of their good opinion. If something controversial were to be undertaken now, he needed to have a pretext, provide himself with a means of shifting the blame. In that way, he might accomplish his ends and yet pay no cost. Was there a diplomat or courtier anywhere in existence who desired less?

He turned his attention to Doña Marina. Just as planned, the girl presented herself as out of breath and in a state of great agitation. She immediately began speaking, a flurry of incomprehensible words and phrases. Also as planned, Aguilar was on hand to put her tirade into Spanish.

Aguilar himself seemed severely out of sorts—his eyes shot with blood, his hair disheveled, his normally swarthy complexion now alarmingly flushed. This wasn't part of the plan—in fact, Aguilar had no role to play in this drama apart from translating what was said. What was wrong with the man? He looked miserable. He hemmed and hawed, stuttered as he spoke. Still, he got the words out. He managed to translate what the girl said.

Apparently—he informed Cortés, swallowing and trembling as he spoke—just a little earlier that day, the native princess had been walking alone through the streets of Cholula.

Suddenly, without warning, a woman of the city had called to her from a doorway, and so Marina had strolled over to speak to her. The woman introduced herself as the wife of a local noble and made light talk for a short while, complimenting Marina on her looks, her carriage, her dress. Then the woman's manner changed. In a low voice, she warned that there was great danger ahead. The Cholulans were planning a surprise attack on the Spaniards.

"Good God in Heaven!" roared Alvarado. "I told you. I told you there was trouble afoot."

"A surprise attack?" said Cortés, who was content to let Alvarado do most of the raging now. "What do you mean?"

Doña Marina described what had happened. She had inched closer to this nameless woman. "Why are you telling me this?" she had asked.

"Because," the woman had told her, "I see that you are one of our own kind of people and that you, too, are of noble blood. I hope that you will not come to harm."

"What would you have me do?"

The woman had glanced about, to make sure that they would not be overheard. "Come with me," she had said. "Come back to my house. Stay with us."

"Why?"

"I have a son, a fine man, well built and strong. He is in need of a wife. When the fighting is over, I would have him choose you."

Cortés let out a yell for show. "I'll have that fellow's skull. Where is he now? I'll throttle him myself."

Marina told her master not to upset himself over nothing. There was no chance of her going off with this nameless suitor. Grave danger was the issue here, not infidelity. It was the Cholulans themselves who had killed the Aztec sentry, the woman had told her. They had done it deliberately as part of their plot.

"Plot?" Cortés pretended to be surprised. "They have a plot?"

"Aha!" said Alvarado. "You see? I told you. I told you it was a trap." He looked around at the other officers gathered in the hall. "You heard me. All of you did."

"Yes, yes," said Cortés. "Your acuity has not gone unremarked, my friend." He turned to Marina. "Please, carry on."

She cleared her throat and resumed her tale. She had taken the woman's hands in her own and thanked her for the warning and for her generous offer of matrimony. She would be happy to accept.

"You *accepted* the offer?" Cortés grasped the handle of his sword as if he were going to attack someone. Anyone watching would have believed he was serious.

Marina smiled and shook her head. She placed her hands on the Spanish commander's shoulders, in order to calm him. To Aguilar, she spoke some words in Maya, and he translated them into Spanish—not without difficulty, for he looked as if he were about to be ill. He stuttered as he spoke. "She says to control yourself, *mi comandante*. She merely told the woman that she accepted the offer in order to humor her. There is no place in her heart for any but you. She begs you to believe this."

313

"I will try to do so," said Cortés. He smiled down at the girl. "Just as long as she was not serious."

The girl smiled as well and let her arms slide away from Cortés's shoulders. She began to pace the floor, like an actress. She recounted what she had said to the woman next—that she was obliged to go back to the palace where she was staying in order to collect her belongings. Then she would return.

"Hurry, then," the woman told her. "I will wait for you here. Remember, there will be great danger and much bloodshed. You must be quick."

Marina stopped, swallowed, and made a little bow. This, it seemed, was the end of her story. She waited while Aguilar translated her final phrases into Spanish.

Alvarado, as ever, was the first to react. "By the Virgin of Seville," he said, "I have never in my—"

Cortés raised a hand to silence his officer. He turned to Marina. "And when do you say this happened?"

"Just now. Just moments ago. I hurried straight here."

Alvarado could barely control his fury. He slapped his forehead with one hand and went back to pacing across the polished stone floor. "I told you this was a trap."

Cortés clasped the handle of his sword. "That you did, my friend. Indeed, you did. Do not think that I won't remember." He smiled to himself. His plan was working out perfectly. Almost as soon as he had heard about the dead Aztec, this scheme had unfolded in his mind like a kind of poetry. Here was an excellent way of sending a sobering message to the Aztecs in their great city of Tenochtitlán—a warning that they had better not trifle with the Spanish Crown. All he needed now was someone who, if worst came to worst, could be made to shoulder the blame. As he had often done before, he turned to his blond lieutenant. "Alvarado," he said. "What do you propose we do?"

"But isn't it obvious?" Alvarado continued to strut back and forth across the floor, clearly delighted to be asked his opinion on a subject of such urgency. "I propose we strike first. I propose we kill them all."

"All of them?" said Cortés. "What do you mean, all of them?"

Alvarado swept his right arm around the hall, a gesture that included his surroundings, entire. "The whole city," he said. "I say, we kill the whole town."

Cortés smiled again. His plan was in place. Now, if his enemies in Cuba ever brought charges against him, he would be able to say the decision had not been his. Some hot-tempered officers had got out of control. "Not the whole town," he said. "I think we should temper our ambition a little. Don't you?"

He took a poll of his officers, who had all been galvanized by Alvarado's rage. To a man, they agreed with their blond-haired comrade. Kill the Cholulans. However, in deference to their commander, they agreed to limit the extent of the carnage. Cortés nodded slowly, gravely. He announced that he was opposed to such an action, but given his men's unanimous support for it, he had no choice but to withdraw his objections. Let the majority rule.

"Done," he said. He placed Alvarado in charge of the operation.

‡

Jerónimo de Aguilar staggered about the streets of Cholula, unable to believe what had happened. That morning, he'd acted as translator between Cortés and Doña Marina—as he often did—and he had heard them cook up this scheme of theirs, after Cortés first swore him to secrecy. Marina would pretend she had encountered some woman of Cholula, who had told her of some dreaded plot. That other twist, the proposal of marriage—that was something the girl had come up with on her own. To tweak Cortés. Whatever else she was, the girl was a tease. But did she realize the purpose of this play-acting? Had she known that Cortés planned a massacre? A bloody massacre of the entire city.

A cool wind kicked up and skittered through the dusty streets under an overcast sky. Aguilar clutched at his head and moaned. He must do something, anything, to prevent this horror from unfolding. But what? How could he do anything? He couldn't speak the language of these highland people. He couldn't warn them even if he tried. He cursed himself for the role he had played in engineering this horror. He should have clamped his mouth shut, refused to translate another word. A weakling, that was what he was. Why else had he wound up as a slave in the Mayan lands, while Gonzalo Guerrero had been granted the title of captain in time of war? That was the reason. He was weak where others were strong.

He felt his skull straining against his hands as though it would burst. His vision wobbled and blurred. Had God preserved him during eight years of slavery and then plucked him to safety—for this? So that he might act as the instrument of a Spanish bloodbath? He fell to his knees, then dug through his pockets until he found his prayer book. He riffled through the pages, searching for an answer, but he could not hold the words clear before his eyes. They swam and faded, turned to insects, swarmed away. He climbed to his feet again, not knowing where he was bound, but sensing that some force was now propelling him forward, as if he were being guided. The blood roared in his head, and he heard the voices of women, singing to him in a language he did not speak. He saw before him a flock of dark creatures, the words of the Holy Testament in flight. They assumed the shape of angels, and he stumbled on in pursuit of those.

Maxtla tore down a narrow street at top speed, desperate to find his father. As soon as he'd found out what had really happened—that the *teules* had not killed the Aztec—he'd gone in search of his father. Now he could prove how wrong Pitoque's theory had been. He darted to the side to avoid colliding with an old man tottering up the street with a load of amaranth on his back. He flung himself around a corner and increased his pace.

He threw back his head, tempted to laugh. Persuading Teontin to open up had taken him quite some effort, but his friend had finally obliged. He'd recounted what had actually happened to the Aztec, and it was exactly as Maxtla had suspected. Nahuauc was behind it. Nahuauc and his gang. Not that Maxtla minded the death of an Aztec. If he had had his way, more than one would have wound up dead. But he did mind that many innocent people were likely to pay the penalty for this one corpse. Whoever had killed the Aztec would be responsible for the impending bloodshed. And it hadn't been the *teules.*

Maxtla raced up the street toward home as fast as his legs would bear him. He rounded a blind corner, saw a shock of black, took a blow to his chest, and felt the wind burst from his lungs. The world suddenly turned somersaults. A moment later, he was squatting on the dirt with a pain stabbing through his shoulder and a burning sensation on one side of his face. He shifted around to see who or what he'd run into. The man—a *teule!*—was slumped over, clutching one of those little black boxes that they sometimes carried, that they opened up and perused, moving their lips as they flipped through their leaves of paper. The fellow pulled himself onto his knees, and Maxtla saw who it was. The translator. The one called Aguilar. The one who spoke Maya.

Maxtla called out to him. "Are you all right? Are you hurt?"

Aguilar shook his head, trying to recover his wits. He felt a burning soreness in his neck, and it seemed he'd turned an ankle. God in heaven, that had been an awful collision. "I beg your pardon?" he said.

"I asked if you were all right."

Aguilar said he wasn't sure. Maybe. It was too soon to tell. He decided there was something familiar about the boy, and after a few moments he realized what it was. He was the son of that trader, Pitoque. As Aguilar's mind began to recover, an idea finally worked its way to the surface. This horror that was about to take place—perhaps he could not prevent it, but he might be able to save at least a few souls from death.

"Where is your father?" he said. "I need to speak to your father."

"Come," said the boy, as he pulled himself to his feet and began to wipe away several streaks of grime from his cloak. "It seems we share the same purpose."

For Every Crime

The cockatiels chattered in their bamboo cages, and the waters of the fountain in the central patio burbled and plashed upon the garden rocks. But Pitoque was aware of no sound except that of Aguilar's voice. This news was beyond all comprehension.

Aguilar said he could barely believe it himself, and yet he knew it to be true. He had been present when the order had been given. There was no time to waste. Preparations were already well underway. "You must take your family and leave. You must do it now. There is very little time."

"But why is this happening?" Pitoque could not help trying to find some sense in this terrible story, some logic, some design.

Aguilar tried to explain. In part, this act of bloodshed was meant to be a warning to the Aztecs, to sow alarm about who these Spaniards were and what they were capable of doing.

"Spaniards?" said Pitoque. It was not the first time he had heard the term, but he was still uncertain of its meaning.

"It is what we call ourselves. It is what we are."

"Ah. I see." He asked Aguilar why the Spaniards, as they called themselves, should wish to sow alarm. "The Aztecs are agitated enough as it is. All they wish to know is who you are and what you want. They think of nothing else. Nor do I. Nor does anyone."

Aguilar shrugged. He said that some of the Spaniards—the blond one, Pedro de Alvarado, in particular—seemed to fear that the Cholulans might mount some attack against them.

"But we have little in the way of weapons," said Pitoque. "We have no army to speak of. We are vassals of the Aztecs. We have no means of attacking anyone at all, much less your kind, with your giant deer and your dogs and your great exploding pipes. It's nonsense."

"I agree. I agree." Aguilar fell silent, not knowing what else to say.

The two men stood in the central patio of Pitoque's house. Maxtla had left by now. Breathless, he had told his father what he had learned—that it was Nahuauc who had been responsible for the dead Aztec, Nahuauc and his gang. If he had thought this revelation would prove a kind of triumph, he had been mistaken. Pitoque had behaved as though the information made no difference at all, as though it were a mere detail, a matter of passing importance. Maxtla had turned and stamped away, incensed that nothing he did seemed to mean anything to anyone. He'd rushed to his room, ignored his sister when he passed her in the corridor, and thrown himself upon his bed. Furious. Nobody ever listened to anything he said.

Back on the patio, Pitoque felt as if some great boulder were tumbling down a mountainside, crushing everything in its path, aiming straight for him—but not for him alone. It was a force that would not stop until it had destroyed everything. For the first time, he felt the weight of that force like a physical presence, a pressure that would flatten this city in no time at all, the city where he'd been born and grown up, where he'd married, raised children—the finest place in the world. He massaged his forehead, wondering what on earth he could do now. Suddenly, he remembered something that Aguilar himself had said. He looked up, spoke the words aloud.

"*By our deeds* . . ." he said.

"What?" Aguilar frowned. "What did you say?"

"*Judge us by our deeds.* You said so yourself. Is this—what is happening now—is this what you meant?"

Aguilar remained silent for a time. Finally, he shook his head. "I don't know. I don't what I meant. I don't understand what is happening here any more than you do. Be careful— that is all I can say. Take steps to save your lives. You know better than I do how to accomplish that." He placed a hand on Pitoque's shoulder, left it there for a moment, then turned and hurried away.

Pitoque stood at the portal of his house and watched the *teule*, the Spaniard, rush down the narrow street. A wind spout of dust and debris spiraled up and surrounded the man like a diaphanous robe. It seemed to lift him up and carry him away.

Pitoque sought out his son and found him sulking in his room, flopped on his bed like a landed fish; He had an urge to take the boy by the shoulders and shake him until he screamed. Enough of this miserable, infantile self-pity. Instead, he took several deep breaths.

"Maxtla," he said. "That was good work of yours, your finding out who killed the Aztec." He refrained from pointing out that the discovery was perhaps of little significance now that the Spaniards, as they called themselves, were bent on killing everybody else. He took a step forward. "You did well. You were right."

Maxtla said nothing, his face thrust toward the wall, buried in his eiderdown. The only movement was the slow rise and fall of his chest as he breathed.

Pitoque settled himself on the edge of the bed. He told Maxtla that he must forget everything else for the moment, however angry he was feeling. He must rouse himself right away, this instant. He must gather his mother and his sister and the servants. He must seek out Toc and all of the porters. They must leave Cholula at once, all of them except Toc. He must tell Toc that his master wanted him. But the rest must flee.

"Where?" Maxtla's voice was heavy, slurred, as if the act of speech were itself a burden imposed unfairly upon him. "Flee where?"

As soon as his son spoke, Pitoque heard in his mind the refrain that had haunted him for years, the women's voices howling in the night. *Flee. Flee. Take only what you can carry. Run for your lives.* He gazed about the room, at the faint shadows cast by the half-light of dusk, and he imagined these walls caved in, these cedar beams shattered, his whole life destroyed by a great, crushing force. Were the terrible prophecies coming true now? He shook his head to clear his thoughts. Flee? *Where* could they flee? Almost as soon as the question formed itself in his mind, he knew the answer. There was a small lake to the east, at a place called Amozoc, where he kept a cottage for his family. They sometimes spent time there in summer. It was a quiet spot, remote and secluded. Pitoque put out his hand and placed it on his son's shoulder, and was relieved when the boy did not recoil at the touch.

"Maxtla," he said. "I want you to take everyone to Amozoc, straight away. There is great danger here. I am putting you in charge of your mother's safety, and your sister's. When it is safe to return, I will send word. Now go."

For a time, there was no response. But finally Maxtla rolled over on the bed, looked up at his father, and nodded. He rose and took a cloak down from the wall. He said he would do as he had been instructed—simply that, nothing more. But at the door of his bedroom, he stopped, turned back. "What about you?" he said. "What will you do, you and Toc?"

"Never mind about us," said Pitoque. "You take care of your sister and your mother. We old men, we will look out for ourselves."

✝

Pitoque hurried out onto the street and set off at a brisk pace, half-walking, half-running, toward the palace that housed Hernán Cortés and his officers. Was there some way to put a stop to the attack? He did not know. But if it was he who had brought this punishment down, then it was he who must try to avert it.

When he reached the palace where the *teules* were staying, he marched straight inside, amazed that no one stopped him. Everyone was rushing this way and that, obviously preparing for some great activity. He decided to seek out Doña Marina, the only one who spoke his language. But he had picked up enough of the *teules'* own tongue by now that he was able to ask simple directions.

"Doña Marina," he declared again and again to the succession of Spaniards that he encountered. "I am seeking Doña Marina."

They pointed the way, then went back about their business, oblivious to him. The Little King of Plates. It was as if he didn't exist.

He finally found the woman alone in a dining chamber, feasting upon a sapota fruit sprinkled with grated chili pepper. His felt a tremor in his chest when he saw her. Even now, her loveliness almost overwhelmed him. Perspiration itched upon his forehead, burned his skin. But he was not here to admire the girl. He was here for answers. Abruptly, he asked her, "What on earth is going on?"

She put the fruit aside and wiped her lips in a delicate, unhurried way. It was as if she had all the time in the world, or perhaps she was merely plotting out her words with care.

"You must look to your safety and that of your son," she said at last. "Trouble is coming."

"I know that," he said. "I want to stop it."

She arched her eyebrows. "How did you know?"

Pitoque ignored the question. "What you are planning is . . . I cannot describe it. There are no words for what you are planning. Listen." He explained what Maxtla had told him, that the Aztec had been killed by some local ruffians. His death was not part of an elaborate trap.

"What about the stolen gold?" she said. "The gold you promised would be paid to the Spaniards as tribute? Where is it?"

Pitoque slumped into a chair opposite the girl. He'd forgotten about the gold. "I don't know. It was probably stolen by the same gang."

"Cholulans?"

"Yes, of course."

"Stealing my master's gold?"

"I suppose so."

She shook her head and heaved a slow, sad sigh. "Ah, well," she said. "Crime and punishment." She sat back, adjusting the sleeves of her blouse, taking care that they aligned themselves perfectly. "For every crime, there is a punishment. Is it not so?"

Pitoque saw that this discussion was no use. Even if he were able to provide the Aztec gold, it would not make the slightest difference. Again, he felt the weight of some terrible force, like a great boulder aimed at his back, barreling down. He rubbed at his neck, but the feeling would not go away. He stood up. "What now?" he said. "What exactly do the *teules* mean to do?"

"That is an affair of men," said Doña Marina. "I am but a woman. I know little of such matters." She reached for the fruit again, then paused and looked up at him. "But as I have said, I think that there is trouble to come."

"I understand that." Something twigged in his mind. "Just now, you called the Spaniards men. These strangers, you said they were men."

"Yes?"

"Are they men?"

"What are you asking?"

"Are they gods or are they men?"

She bit off a mouthful of sapota, chewed, swallowed, and started to laugh. She covered her face with one hand and shook her head. "Ah," she said, "that is the question, isn't it? Are they gods or are they men?" She frowned and gravely shook her head. "That, my friend, is for you to decide."

He realized she was playing with him. He could plead with her all day if he chose, and she would never answer him directly. Toying with his confusion was far more amusing. There was a streak of cruelty in her. He could see that, and yet it seemed to make her beauty shine out all the more. "Thank you for your counsel," he said. He turned to go.

"Wait," she called after him. "You must promise to protect your son, who is a particularly handsome boy. You must leave this city, both of you. At once. If, for whatever reason, you find yourself here during the time of punishment, you must weave a flower into your hair."

"A what?"

"A flower. Weave it into your hair. It has been agreed upon as a sign. These Spaniards, you see, cannot tell one native from another. Their allies will weave flowers into their hair to keep them safe during the punishment. Promise me that you will do the same."

But Pitoque was not obliged to make promises to young women who betrayed their own kind. He pulled his cloak around him and left without another word.

The Old Gods in Flight

Pitoque stood stock-still in the middle of the street, gripped by panic and indecision. What should he do now? Should he run through the streets of Cholula, crying out at the top of his lungs, exhorting everyone to flee, to take only what they could carry, to run for their lives? How much time would that require, to warn the entire city? Would anyone believe him? For precious moments, he remained where he was, as if he had been transformed into a rock. Questions pelted him from every direction. What if there was some problem at home? What if his family had not yet got away?

The panic heaved in his chest like an animal struggling to escape. He lurched forward, hurried through the narrow streets, stopping now and again to clutch at the arms of strangers. He begged them to flee. A great danger was approaching. They must go. They must take only what they could carry. They must run for their lives. They pulled away from him, as if he were mad. He scurried ahead, stopped someone else. He repeated his warning a dozen times or more. Who knew whether anyone believed him? Finally, he reached his house and found that everyone there had left. Only Toc waited for him, crouched near the entrance. He was using an old flint blade to carve the end of a straight length of wood.

"Walking stick," said Toc. He climbed to his feet, a little shaky. "I'm getting old. I need a walking stick now."

Pitoque explained what was about to take place, at least as he understood it himself. He told Toc he was free to leave, to head for Amozoc with the rest. He still had time. "There is great danger here."

"I understand." The man reached up, rubbed his brow. "But you'll be staying here, I take it."

"Yes."

"To protect the old place?" He glanced toward the door of his master's house.

"To try."

"Well, you'll be wanting company then." He gestured with the walking stick. "Besides, this handle isn't quite ready yet."

"Thank you," said Pitoque, who had been hoping for this, hoping he would not be left alone. He turned and led his servant inside. Both men made sure the door was securely barred, and then Pitoque picked a pair of roses from the bushes in the central patio. He told Toc to weave the blossom into his hair, and he did the same himself.

Later, alone, he slumped against the wall near the house's main entrance and listened to the blood throbbing at his temples, like the drumbeat of war. At least his family was safe. At least he had managed that. Despite all the sins he had committed, all the errors he had made, at least his family had got away.

The punishment began at nightfall, and continued all that evening, all night long, and into the following morning. Beyond the walls of his house, Pitoque heard voices bellow, heard weapons slice through wood and clang against stone. Women shrieked, children howled, men roared. Now and again, a silence fell, only to be broken within instants by a terrible cacophony only a short distance away.

Pitoque and Toc huddled on the floor just inside the front door. Both cringed and winced at this invisible spectacle. They heard the crash of tumbling walls, the whoosh and growl of flames, a bedlam of screaming voices that soared impossibly high, impossibly loud—and then stopped. Somewhere else, the clamor and din started up again.

Toward dawn, a party of *teules* armed with a battering ram broke through the door of Pitoque's house and lumbered inside. Pitoque and Toc scrambled to their feet.

"Goodbye, old friend," Pitoque said to his servant and stiffened, waiting to feel the swords shear through him—but the blades were still.

It was just as Doña Marina had told him. The Spaniards saw the sign—the flowers woven into his hair and into Toc's—and they stopped.

"Ah," one said, "it's the Little King of Plates. Leave him alone. Come on, men. No doubt there will be better hunting next door."

And so they left.

When the carnage was over, Pitoque and Toc ventured outside. Like the others who had survived, they gawked at their surroundings. Slump-shouldered, slack-jawed, like a pair of beasts suddenly aroused from some long torpor, they peered out stupidly, unable to believe what they saw. The old familiar world was changed, broken, gone. Where once had been a handsome city, Pitoque saw spirals of smoke, the scattered tongues of flames, the rubble of temples, the crumpled forms of the dead. He heard the chuckling of the *teules*, who poked through the debris or lounged among the corpses, cleaning their swords. He found he could make out the essence of what they said. They chatted about women or about the weather or about food, as if nothing had happened at all—as if the world were not coming to its end. The punishment was over now, and their tempers had cooled. The Spaniards hardly spared a glance for Pitoque or the others. What did they care? What was done was done.

With Toc at his side, Pitoque picked his way through the wreckage of the city. His head felt as if it had been battered by rocks. His eyes stung. It was he—he alone—who had lured these beings here, hoping that their presence in Cholula might yield a sign, a message in the wind or in the stars. He had his message now, and his mind reeled at the cost—his city half-destroyed and thousands of his clansmen dead. But what did the massacre mean? Did it mean anything at all? Surely, every circumstance meant something. Surely, the will of the gods was worked into the fabric of all events on earth, of everything, everywhere.

He had lived his life believing this was so.

But now a new idea began to worm its way into his mind, a possibility he had never contemplated before. Perhaps these horrors had no meaning at all. Some great boulder had plummeted from the sky, tumbled down the slopes of Popocatépetl, and crushed a small city, for no purpose whatever. Gods? What gods? Where were the gods? These Spaniards, as they called themselves, were stronger than the gods. The known gods, the old gods, had turned their heads, gathered their belongings, and moved away. That keening he now heard, like the keening of women—it was the sound of the old gods in flight.

"Toc." Pitoque took a deep breath. "You must travel to Tenochtitlán now. You must find Azotl and tell him what has happened here."

The old man assented. "And your family?"

"I will attend to them. But you must go. Hurry."

Toc fingered his new walking stick. "I will be off. Goodbye."

The old man trudged away through the ruins. For a time, Pitoque watched him go. Then he turned his attention to the horrors around him. For the next two days, he searched through the scorched and mutilated city for people who had survived the punishment of the *teules*. He did what little he could to comfort them as they died, or to remove them to some sort of shelter, or to find food for them, or water, or word of the family they had lost.

Even as he worked, Pitoque was awed by the thoroughness of the slaughter. Not even the Aztecs killed in this way, by falling upon their victims without warning, murdering them as they ran. They certainly did not go to war to attack children, and they did not fight without some reason. But there was no explaining this brutality. He soon lost count of those who lay dead, many of them known to him—friends, the wives of friends, their children. All around him, houses were reduced to rubble and fires burned.

The priests of Cholula were helpless to ease the suffering of their city, just as they had failed to ward off the evil before it had descended upon them. Now they brought out obsidian knives and cut off their ears and staggered through the debris, moaning out their torment. Blood drooled from their heads. Oh, these mighty priests—it was all they could think of to do. Pitoque could do little more. After two days and nights, he returned to his house, which was still standing and where, in the garden, the cockatiels sang. He staggered inside, collapsed on the floor, and remained there, weeping, wracked by a pair of torments, two monsters wrestling in his mind. One of them howled that he, Pitoque of Cholula, was responsible for this catastrophe. He had brought down the wrath of the gods. A judgment had descended upon his own people, his neighbors and friends—and look what had been done. But now the other monster roared out, bellowing in a language of demons, a language without words but crackling with horror. Pitoque could not imagine that Quetzalcoatl or any known god would speak in such a voice or impose a punishment as awful as this. These were new gods that had come, unknown gods, murderous gods. His mind reeled back and forth between these two grappling ideas, between guilt and terror.

For three days, he did not move.

A Man's First Duty

Pitoque stalked the rooms and corridors of his house, running his hands over old familiar objects—a grinding stone in the kitchen, his wife's robes where they lay folded in the cool darkness of their bedroom, a trumpet seashell that stood upon the dining room table, a hoop of wood that Maxtla had played with as a child, a quetzal feather he had once given Zaachila as a gift. In her hurry to leave, she had forgotten to carry it with her.

He remembered something else and hurried to the interior patio where the cockatiels perched in their bamboo cages. He unlatched the cage doors and let the birds out, five of them in all, all desperate from hunger and thirst, for he had neglected to feed them. They sprang from the cages. They sailed through the patio in short bursts of flight or hopped about upon the moss-covered rocks. Above them, the house was open to the sky—they could escape at anytime. He wondered whether they would. One way or another, they'd have to survive by their own wits now.

He had thought at first that he would send a messenger to his family at Amozoc to tell them the city was safe for their return. But he decided now that it would be better if they all remained there, on the shores of that distant and peaceful lake. It would be better if they stayed there the rest of their lives. He was finished with being a spy. He would travel no more. Something inside him, something previously soft and pliant, had hardened itself into a knot of decision. A man belonged with his family. His family was everything. Family was all.

It was time to leave. He turned and marched out to the main entrance. He had few qualms about abandoning the house. He soon found a pair of local men who were willing, for a fee, to stand guard. He was no longer concerned that the *teules* or the Tlaxcalans might ransack the place, for they were not interested in Cholula now. They were preparing to advance toward Tenochtitlán instead.

The oaken door was smashed apart, and its remnants lay scattered about. He told the two guards to see that the doorway was boarded up after him. He clenched his jaw, his mind still reeling. He slung a sack of maguey fiber over his shoulders and began to walk. He set out for Amozoc. He did not look back.

✝

A morning's journey brought Pitoque to the summit of a hill overlooking the lake, and below him he saw Zaachila wandering alone through a sloping field of gorse that tumbled down almost to the shore. Some sixth sense made her look up, and she waved. At once, she rushed toward him.

"Father!" she cried and soon threw herself into his arms.

For a time, neither spoke. They simply embraced and felt the warm midday breeze shift around them. A flock of butterflies fluttered past, like puffs of cotton tossed upon the air. The squawking of ducks drifted up from the shallows of the lake, amid a redolence of flowers.

Zaachila eased her grip. She took a step back. "We were afraid that you were dead."

"For a while, I thought that I was."

It was all he would say for now. All he wanted was to bask in the quiet and pleasure of this place, to be with his family, where a man belonged. He was certain now—he would abandon his travels. He would make some excuse to Azotl, something to do with his health, perhaps. A bad back. An ailment of the chest. He could no longer serve the Aztecs. He could no longer spend time in Tenochtitlán. He would devote himself to a man's first duty—his wife, his children, his home.

Why had he been permitted to survive? Why had his family? These were mysteries to him. Yet here they all were. Together, arm and arm, he and Zaachila walked down through the waving gorse toward the stone cottage at Amozoc. It perched amid rosebushes upon a small promontory overlooking the broad blue mirror of the lake, where the reflections of clouds floated upon the surface like imaginary boats. Kalatzin was at work in the yard, rolling tortillas on a metate. She looked up and let out a cry.

"My husband!"

"My wife . . ."

She climbed to her feet, and he hurried toward her. Four words spun in his mind. Husband. Wife. Daughter. Son. These were the only words that mattered to him now.

Maxtla crossed his arms on the table and glared at the wall. "I say that I am going."

"I say that you are not."

Pitoque stretched out his hand, but Maxtla shrank from his touch. The boy had announced that he intended to journey on his own to Tenochtitlán, to join the *teules* there and to fight on their side to bring the Aztec capital down. Nothing that Pitoque said seemed to have any effect on his son. Maxtla flatly refused to believe his father's account of what had taken place in Cholula—his beloved heroes going mad and leveling the city, killing thousands of people. He simply denied that the *teules* could commit such crimes. The entire story was just another attempt by Pitoque to discredit these creatures Maxtla so loved. Or it was part of some Aztec plot. Maxtla said that the Aztecs themselves must have committed the slaughter and destruction, only to blame these crimes on the *teules*.

"But I was there," said Pitoque. "I tell you, I saw."

"No, you didn't. You told me you didn't. You were hiding in our house. That's what you said."

"Yes, but I was still in the city. I spoke to Aguilar. I . . ." He shook his head. Perhaps it was no use. "I tell you, it was not the Aztecs."

"But how do you know?"

Pitoque felt a sudden pressure in his chest as words welled up inside him, sharp as obsidian blades. How did he know? He knew because it had been he, Pitoque of Cholula—an utter idiot, a fool—who had coaxed the *teules* to visit his city on their way to Tenochtitlán. Why? So that he, a mere merchant, might judge the conduct of the gods. He reached into his robes to finger the necklace of shells. Here were reasons. What other explanation did anyone need?

But Pitoque did not tell his son what he was thinking. These were affairs a man could not speak of, especially before his family. What mattered now was that Maxtla—however much he glowered and pouted and fulminated—was not going to travel to Tenochtitlán. He was not going to join the *teules* or the Spaniards or whatever they were called. He was not going to participate in any war against the Aztecs.

"Yes, I am."

"No, you are not. You will—"

"Please. Please, stop it." Kalatzin had endured all this bickering in silence, but could bear it no longer. She turned to Maxtla. "You will listen to your father. You will do as he says."

Maxtla gritted his teeth, evidently struggling to contain another outburst. Finally, his shoulders slumped. "Yes, Mother," he said.

Pitoque shook his head. He had spent an hour trying to get

the boy to submit, but without success. And here his wife managed to accomplish the feat with only a few short words. It was a gift, he supposed. What else could it be? He drew himself up in his seat. "It's late," he announced. "It's time for bed."

And immediately, Maxtla pushed back his chair and climbed to his feet. Without a word, he inclined his head toward his father, planted a kiss on his mother's cheek, and withdrew. Zaachila waited several moments and then did the same, except that she kissed both parents.

"Goodnight, Mother. Goodnight, Father."

She drifted away, graceful as a dream.

In the dim glow cast by a lamp of burning oil, Pitoque turned to his wife. He started to say something, something about the frustrations of fatherhood, but she shushed him with a finger to her lips.

"Please," she said. "Let us not speak of it now. Let us just be silent for a while."

"You are right," he said.

And no doubt she was. Still, when they awoke the next morning, Maxtla was gone.

The Valley of Anáhuac

Aguilar stumbled upward, some distance behind Cortés and the Spanish expedition. The silver light burned his eyes. Great clouds lumbered overhead, and in the distance he heard the low rumble of thunder. The rocks upon the path were crooked nails, driving into the soles of his feet, drawing blood, etching the patterns of stigmata. He clutched his prayer book to his chest. Without being summoned, words tumbled from his lips. *You shalt conceive chaff, you shall bring forth stubble; your breath, as fire, shall devour you.*

The highland wind whipped his clothes. *For the indignation of the Lord is against all nations, and His fury against all their armies; He has utterly destroyed them, He has given them over to the slaughter.*

His foot caught against a stone and he felt himself go down. Ah! He collapsed to his knees and remained there, alone on this great sloping plain, in an attitude of prayer. He gazed up at the clouds that scudded overhead. *For My sword shalt be bathed in heaven; indeed it shall come down on Edom, and on the people of My curse, for judgment.* Aguilar raised his prayer book, held it to the sky. *The sword of the Lord is filled with blood; it is made overflowing with fatness, and with the blood of lambs and goats, with the fat of the kidneys of rams. For the Lord has a sacrifice in Bozrah, and a great slaughter in the land of Edom.* He tried to swallow. His throat was parched, so painfully dry that he thought his very flesh might turn to chalk and then crumble away. "I have seen it," he said, his voice now reduced to a croaking, a pestilence of frogs. *A great slaughter in the land of Edom. Its streams shalt be turned to pitch, and its dust to brimstone; its land shalt become burning pitch. A great slaughter in the land of Edom.*

Without meaning to, but without being able to stop himself, Aguilar began to sob. Who could endure the horrors he had seen?

Alvarado felt his mount skitter sideways beneath him. He sank more deeply into the saddle, tried to settle the horse with his calves. Soon she arched her neck and strutted forward again. Alvarado thrust back his shoulders and stuck out his jaw, pleased with himself, pleased with the world. Here he was, first among all the Spanish lieutenants, riding side by side with Hernán Cortés. He hauled another draught of the cool highland air into his great lungs and blew out. Even now, several days after that business in Cholula, he felt a swelling in his chest, a tingling in his skin.

Dear God in Heaven, thousands had died. He had watched his men wade about with their harquebuses and their swords, meting out death as though they were fishmongers distributing the provenance of the sea. After you had punctured a chest or two, severed a head from its shoulders, you were past the initial discomfort, the impediment in the viscera, the reluctance that you always felt at first. A couple of corpses, and you were at ease again with killing. You started to enjoy it for the crude, sweet pleasure that it was. You remembered that it was a source of happiness to kill.

Alvarado put back his head and let out a roar. God, it was good to feel like a soldier again.

Three paces back, Cortés eyed his brash young officer and debated yet again whether he ought to upbraid the man, rein him in. The destruction in Cholula had gone too far. A show, a spectacle—that was what he'd planned. Some blood would flow, of course. He took that for granted. But the slaughter was to have been kept within reasonable limits. He himself followed a firm maxim, one he'd forged in his mind during the long campaigns in Cuba and in Hispaniola before that—never strike a harsher blow than you need to win the battle. Alvarado clearly adhered to a different ethic. But on this occasion, he had certainly gone too far.

Cortés had meant to demonstrate only that the Spaniards were implacable warriors, not that they were monsters. But monsters they had been. And their native allies had behaved even worse. The atrocities those infidels had committed! Cortés would never have believed it had he not seen it with his own eyes. Once the Tlaxcalans and the Totonacs had begun, the operation had become a madness, an inferno. Not content to kill, they mutilated. Not satisfied with mutilation, they arranged themselves in a circle and feasted on their eviscerated kill. ¡Ay, Diós! The bile rose in Cortés's throat, and he struggled to swallow it down.

His stomach heaved, and he thought he might be ill. But no. He settled himself in the saddle again and shrugged. The carnage was over now. No one could change what had happened. Might as well accept it and move ahead. He'd have to watch Alvarado more carefully in future. That was all. He pressed his heels into his horse's flanks, and the beast skittered in a sideways canter. He pulled up beside Alvarado and gave the man a sly glance instead of a rebuke. Dear God in heaven, the fellow was a hell-hound.

Maxtla caught up with the Spaniards just as they began their ascent of the high col that stretched between the lofty, snow-covered peaks of Popocatépetl and Iztaccíhuatl. From the Tlaxcalans, he borrowed a quantity of the thick pitch they customarily smeared over their limbs to ward off the cold—a sound precaution, for the cold worsened steadily as they ascended. But the native warriors didn't seem to mind. They were all in high spirits now, as befitted fighters after a great contest. They stalked up the steep mountain slopes with an effortless gait, oblivious to the weather.

At first, they seemed delighted to have Maxtla in their midst. They clapped him on the back as though he were a warrior himself. One man held up Maxtla's right arm, slathered with pitch. He tested the muscles and made a show of how impressed he was. The others nodded and flexed their own arms and let out whoops and roars. Warriors and champions! They were warriors and champions! After a while, though, they seemed to forget about Maxtla and merely spoke among themselves, and what they spoke about was Cholula and the killing that had been done.

Maxtla would have stopped his ears if he could have done so without appearing ridiculous. He did not want to hear. Instead, he pushed ahead of the Tlaxcalans and the Totonacs until he found himself at the fringes of the *teule* themselves. Few of them paid any attention to him at all, except now and then to elbow him out of the way. They were in a miserable temper because none of them was in the least prepared for this sort of weather. They had no pitch to slather themselves with and no heavy robes. Instead, they slapped their arms at their sides, knocked their feet together, and danced on the spot.

Each time one of the great deerlike creatures defecated in front of them, a dozen of the foot soldiers fought like madmen in order to be the first to plant his sandals in the fresh, steaming dung. Warmth! They were desperate for warmth! Meanwhile, the others spit and cursed and stared at their hands and feet, now worn red from the cold. Maxtla could tell they were cursing, even though he understood little of what they said. It was the tone of their voices, their gestures. He found it a little strange that gods would complain about the climate or be ill-prepared for its effects. He reached up and touched his jaw, where the *teules* had pushed or elbowed him, not wanting a boy in the way.

But it was a mere bruise, nothing more. He thought about other things, as well, like his being here. As long as he'd been at Amozoc with only his mother and sister, he had felt obliged to stay—as the man responsible for their safety. But once his father had arrived, that obligation came to an end. The prospect of remaining by a dreary little lake at the edge of the universe while the gods were advancing on Tenochtitlán—it was unthinkable, beyond imagining. He realized that it was a son's first duty to obey his father, but there were limits to filial obedience. Surely, there were.

Something stung his cheeks, and he looked up. Snow. It had begun to snow, and the wind raced all around him now, slapping at his cloak and through his hair. Some of the *teules* howled with outrage at this misery while others lowered their heads and groped ahead, grim as stones. Again and again, they slipped on the icy footing and fell down, barking their knees and knuckles against rocks. They roared out their anger and struggled to regain their footing. They behaved as children would, grousing and falling down, climbing back up only to topple again. They wept at the slightest misstep or stumble.

They did not act like gods.

At first, Doña Marina walked. But finally she could stand it no longer. Why should she not ride? She stalked after Cortés where he soared upon the back of his miraculous giant deer.

"Master!" she shouted. She spoke partly in Spanish, using the few words she had picked up so far, and partly in Nahuatl. "Stop! Stop now!"

Cortés reined his beast around, and the creature shied at the sight of Marina advancing at a run. The giant deer danced to the side. "Quiet now. Quiet." He peered down at the girl. "What is it?"

She made him understand by gestures and words that she wished to be raised aloft, so that she, too, might feel her forehead caress the sky while she was carried effortlessly over mountains on the back of this miraculous animal. "Why is it that you never let me ride?"

Cortés laughed, squeezed his calves into his mount's flanks, and drew near to Marina, until she was within arm's reach. Although she was suddenly terrified, she did not flinch at the creature's approach, at its great stone feet or tossing mane. Cortés reached down, and she gripped his arm with both of hers, felt herself being lifted into the air. Soon, she was settled before her master high upon the beast's shoulders in front of the leather seat. Both of her legs dangled to one side.

"There now," said Cortés. "Hold on."

She reached down and gripped the creature's mane. Suddenly, they were off. Marina felt the beast's pounding rhythm like a succession of physical shocks. But soon it began to flow through her—the striking cadence and its power. She felt her hair spreading in the cold wind. Cortés kept one arm wrapped around her waist, and she leaned back into his chest. Her heart was thumping inside her, and she felt an urge to scream, partly from fear, partly excitement. But she fought that temptation down. She was determined to mask all signs of weakness, now and forever. She was a princess, after all.

And that is what a princess does.

The blasts of frigid air numbed Aguilar's feet and hands, made his lips shiver, but he barely noticed. He squinted through the tumult of snow that swirled and scattered around him and felt as though he were being borne aloft by some power not his own. Voices sang all around him, but they were not the voices of his countrymen. They were the voices of women, voices that sailed on the wind, that careened over mountains. All he knew, beyond those voices, was that he was ascending, step by step, hour upon hour, into the heavens, a territory of blizzards and songs.

But in time, the Spanish expeditionary force under Hernán Cortés finally began its descent, down the far northern wall of the high col. The weather slowly cleared, and the world began to warm. In time, the men found themselves striding through a vast pine forest that sprawled across a conference of hills and hummed in a soft breeze, redolent with resin and a danker scent, that of the rich, dark earth. Butterflies darted about, and the air turned mild.

This was the Valley of Anáhuac. It yawned ahead, yielding a view of such splendor that the Spaniards halted, rubbed their eyes, and began to chatter to each other in voices that were like children's. They used words they rarely felt inclined to speak. *Beautiful. Wondrous. Divine.*

They saw before them a vast highland valley planted on all sides with green dagger-blade clusters of maguey cactus. The hillsides tumbled down to the valley's base, where a network of lakes shimmered in the morning sunshine, their shores smudged here and there by small stone-house villages. In the distance, the island-city of Tenochtitlán swelled above the lake waters and glinted like quartz in the sun. Even from here, they could tell that the city was a place of rare loveliness—a maze of streets and canals, cypress trees and swarming flowers, towering pyramids and endless rows of stone houses, all bathed in silvery lime. In the far distance, a range of blue mountains rode against the sky, straddled by long streaks of cloud, blushing mauve in the dusky light.

Aguilar, who wandered alone a fair distance behind the Spanish party, was so struck by the view that his legs suddenly locked in place, refused to move. He gazed out at what seemed to be a work of magic, almost numbing in its beauty. He had seen nothing in Europe to compare, not Córdoba or Sevilla, not Barcelona or Madrid. But now a veil of clouds swept overhead, and shadows spread across the valley below. The fire in his brain flared again, and everything was suddenly transformed. All lay in ruins. All lay dead. Words jostled in his chest, then gathered in his throat like slithery, reptilian creatures, salamanders, lizards, toads. They sprang from his lips, clutched at the air, tumbled to the ground.

But the pelican and the porcupine shall possess it, also the owl and the raven shall dwell in it. And He shall stretch out over it the line of confusion and the stones of emptiness. All its princes shall be nothing. And thorns shall come up in its palaces, nettles and brambles in its fortresses; it shall be a habitation of jackals, a courtyard for ostriches.

Up ahead, Hernán Cortés kicked his heels into the flanks of his horse, and the army of Spaniards and natives resumed its march, down into the Valley of Anáhuac, toward Tenochtitlán.

Aguilar stumbled after them, his mind still aflame with omens and portents, with images he had never encountered before. He tripped again and nearly fell, then staggered on, his arms outstretched. He saw a great darkness descend. Disgusting animals gathered around him. He shouted out loud: "The wild beasts of the desert shall meet with the jackals! The wild goat shall bleat to its companion! The night creature shall descend there, and find for herself a place of rest!"

He stumbled to the ground, picked himself up, and lurched ahead.

Enter Your Lands, My Lords

The travelers made their way past the pretty stone towns of Amecameca and Ayotzingo. They skirted the banks of Lake Chalco, where long green rushes clustered in the shallows. They continued over causeways and small islands and along the sedge of Lake Zochimilco. The lands that rose above the lakes were divided into orderly sections and planted with corn and other crops, worked by dark-skinned men in maguey hats. The men raised their arms and waved. Stone houses paraded along the shore. Out upon the lakes, the Spaniards saw strange visions—fine gardens floating upon the surface of the water, gardens that seemed like great emerald brooches set with clusters of precious stones cut in the shapes of fruit.

The Spaniards marched through Iztapalapa, where the earth burst with iridescent fountains of bougainvillea, with orchards of apple and sapota fruit. The houses here were even grander structures than they had seen before, built of stone, sealed with lime, and surrounded by lilacs and the violet haze of jacaranda trees.

At Iztapalapa, a lord named Cuitláhuac—brother of Moctezuma himself—traveled out to greet the visitors. Evidently, the Aztec elders had determined to treat the *teules* as honored guests rather than as enemies. Cuitláhuac rode into their midst upon a palanquin richly worked in silver and decorated with the long green feathers of quetzals. The lord was carried, not by slaves, but by several lesser chieftains, who set the litter down and proceeded to sweep the ground for their king. When they were done, he stepped forth wearing slippers of gold.

Cuitláhuac bade the Spaniards welcome, and that evening, he played host at a great banquet in honor of their leader, Hernán Cortés. Lodging was arranged for everyone in palaces constructed of huge cut stones with ceiling beams of sweet-smelling cedar. The palaces contained vast courts and long outdoor corridors, all festooned with canopies of woven cotton. The Spaniards wandered about, pointing and marveling at everything they saw, like buyers at a market.

Doña Marina announced in the smattering of Spanish she had acquired that her companions must save their exclamations and their praise. "You will have greater need of them," she said, "in Tenochtitlán."

Later, upon a bed of eiderdown, Cortés slipped a hand between the thighs of his native paramour and cupped her little mound in his hand. "This is mine," he whispered.

She laughed, for she had learned enough of his language now that she could make out much of what he said and could even reply in kind. It always made her laugh, the way he spoke.

He clutched one of her breasts. "And this," he said. "I claim title to this."

Again, she laughed. "Not in the name of your king?"

"No. In my own name."

She arched her eyebrows. "In *your* name?" She giggled. "All the better. My lord, I grant you title to my . . . to my . . . how do you say—?"

"Breast."

"Ah, yes. Breast. I grant you title to my breast."

"To them both."

"They are yours."

And so he took them, and much more besides.

When their lovemaking was over, Cortés lay upon his back, hands clasped behind his head. He gazed up through the semi-darkness at the ceiling of cedar beams, dimly visible overhead.

"I think," he said, "that our friend Aguilar is going mad. Have you noticed?"

"Mad? What does it mean?"

"Crazy. A sickness in the head." He explained the concept as well as he could. It was evident that something was wrong with the poor fellow. All during the banquet that night, he had interspersed his translations with snatches from the Old Testament. Lurid stuff. Fire and brimstone. Cortés sighed. "An, well. He has endured much. Perhaps his condition will pass."

"Yes," said Marina. "Perhaps his condition will pass." She slid her hand down between his legs and closed her fingers around him there, where the blood was beginning to pulse again. "And your condition, my master?"

Early on the morning of November the eighth, in the year 1519, Hernán Cortés prepared to enter the capital city of the Aztecs.

He assembled his small cavalry in the main plaza of Iztapalapa and ordered his men to mount. The horses tossed their heads, shied sideways, bolted, and reared, as if the excitement of the day throbbed in their veins, too.

Cortés raised his right hand. "*¡Vámonos!*" he barked, and the riders surged ahead.

Immediately, the Spanish foot soldiers fell in behind the cavalry, and the Tlaxcalans marched last, as a rear guard. Banners slapped in the highland air and trumpets sounded, while the helmet plumes of Cortés and his senior officers rippled, shocks of purple, in the blue morning light.

All along the way to Tenochtitlán, chieftains and holy men strode out to greet these *teules*, these champions of the kingdom called Spain. The nobles wore their finest robes and walked stiffly, erect. They raised their wooden staffs and bowed to the approaching gods, reached down and touched the earth with their open palms, then knelt to kiss the soil. Long dugout canoes plied the lake waters, and as they drifted past, their passengers waved palm branches that glittered in the sun. It was as if a carnival were in progress, as though something new and wonderful were about to unfold—a rebirth, an awakening. It was all as it had been ordained. On this fine day, it truly seemed that the Lord Quetzalcoatl had at last come home to reclaim what was his. No curse was uttered, no rock thrown, no arrow let fly.

Maxtla hurried along behind the Spaniards. He had been unsure what to expect. He had half-expected war. But this celebration was far better than blood. The wonder of it swelled in his chest. To his surprise, the thought that ran through his mind now, more potent than any other, was that he wished his father were here. He wished his father could observe these glorious beings now, these otherworldly Spaniards, as they marched in triumph into the capital city, to be welcomed as heroes, honored as gods, as if a new world were beginning, as if nothing would ever be the same again. He clambered up onto a great boulder and from there into the branches of an oak tree. He climbed until the trunk began to bend. From here, he could see everything. He began to cheer.

He wasn't alone. All around him, everyone was cheering. It seemed the happiest of days. All was music, all was joy, all amazement. The very ground seemed to tremble, not with fear but with hope.

Soon, the Spaniards approached a broad causeway that ran across Lake Texcoco to the great city of Tenochtitlán. The passage was some eight paces wide, built of stones and earth. The Spaniards stopped near the point where it reached the land. They drew their swords, held them high and ready, just in case. They still did not know what to expect.

In the distance, beyond a drawbridge, a party could be seen approaching, the city rising behind it, the towers and palaces shining against a backdrop of purple mountains. This, it soon became clear, was Lord Moctezuma himself, accompanied by his leading advisers, his princes, holy men, and scribes. The emperor rode upon a palanquin finer than any yet seen.

It swayed from side to side, thickly encrusted with jade and other jewels, and decorated with the plumes of quetzals, with flowers, with wreaths and garlands, with hoops of gold. The royal party advanced along the causeway, surrounded by glimmering lake waters and floating gardens and drifting dugout canoes, until it reached the mainland shore.

Here, the litter was set down, and the princes of Tenochtitlán and the cities of the Triple Alliance gathered around their emperor to support him with their arms as a sign of respect. These nobles were dressed in the finery of Jaguar Knights, with jaguar pelts thrown over their shoulders. The masks of jaguars bobbed above their foreheads, fangs bared. Moctezuma stepped from their midst. He himself wore a magnificent cloak of white duck feathers, richly embroidered with threads dyed in cochineal, its collar trimmed with coyote fur. He was crowned by a tall headdress of green quetzal plumes. To shield the emperor from the sun, his princes raised a canopy above him, fashioned of more quetzal feathers. Others hurried ahead, sweeping the earth and laying down carpets of fine cotton, upon which Moctezuma walked wearing sandals of gold, set with precious stones. In his lower lip, he wore an ornament of lapis lazuli, in the likeness of a hummingbird. Spools of turquoise shone from his earlobes, and a jewel shimmered at the bridge of his nose.

"Behold," a voice cried out. "Behold Moctezuma II, *tlatoani,* emperor of the Aztecs."

Cortés dismounted his horse, handed the reins to Pedro de Alvarado, and swaggered forward. At first, he made to embrace the emperor, but this gesture was evidently not permitted, not even by the gods. Princes and chieftains immediately intervened and pushed the Spaniard back, this strange bearded creature, stinking in his armor and his plumed helmet.

Yet Cortés seemed unperturbed. He merely stood his ground and waited. It was Moctezuma who first raised his voice to speak. He greeted Cortés as though he were addressing a god, and he spoke as if from memory, as if he had been rehearsing this speech for many days. If the stench of the Spaniards bothered him, he did not show it.

"Welcome to your home," the emperor told his visitors. "You have come to your land, your city, Tenochtitlán. You have come to take possession of your royal palaces, to walk beneath your canopies, to lie upon your beds. For many months, I have been in anguish. I have consulted the oracles. I have probed the sacred mysteries. And now you have come, from over the seas, from the direction of the jaguar sun. All has unfolded in the manner foretold. This is the fulfillment. Come, give comfort to your bodies. Enter your lands, my lords."

As the emperor spoke, Doña Marina stood near Cortés and interpreted the words to Aguilar. She, too, made a regal sight. Resplendent in new robes and finery, she seemed entirely at her ease, as if she had been preparing all her life precisely for this role, to mediate between captains and kings, to stand between two worlds. She translated the emperor's greeting with the elegance of a poet. Her voice seemed to dance upon the air like a sparkling song, and her hands swayed before her. She made a low, gracious bow to Moctezuma and then expressed her delight, and Cortés's delight, and the delight of his Royal Highness, Charles I of Spain. On their behalf, she accepted the invitation from the Aztec king of kings to enter the grandest city on the earth.

The Spaniards were ushered into Tenochtitlán amid the cheers and amazement of all. The people gathered upon the rooftops or paddled alongside in boats, all craning their necks to see. Musicians gamboled in the streets or performed in the rambling gardens. They played flutes, shook rattles, beat drums.

That night and for many nights after, the Spaniards and even the hated Tlaxcalans were lodged in the vast palace of Axayácatl. The building was an endless maze of private rooms and antechambers, of cool stone courtyards, cotton canopies, and shimmering halls, of sumptuous beds spread with the finest eiderdowns. The strange beasts known as horses were stabled in makeshift shelters, and watered and given plentiful supplies of dried field grass, specially acquired for this purpose, as requested by the *teules*.

Each night, a great banquet was celebrated in honor of these exotic visitors. They were served every imaginable delicacy—venison and dog, partridge, duck, iguana. Salads of thistles and cactus flowers were placed before them, and ingenious stews combining the most exquisite flavors—newts and tadpoles, waterfly eggs, salamanders and eels, agave worms, and lake scum, all blended in a purée of tomatoes with just a hint of chili spice. Drinks of steaming chocolate and honey were provided and continually replenished. Great ceramic jugs brimmed with pulque. Musicians played the most haunting music in their repertoire, and poets recited verses they had specially composed. When the meals were finished, tobacco was brought out, mixed with resin of liquidambar and presented in the finest reed pipes. Dwarfs and tumblers performed.

Cortés and his soldiers were shown every comfort and courtesy. Women were sent to bear them chrysanthemum water for their baths. Walking in procession, their feet anointed with incense of copal and dyed a heavenly blue, these Aztec women carried the sweet water in painted gourds. They swished across the cool stone floors. They sang across the night. In this way—with flutes, soft beds, and languorous voices—the world nudged up against its end.

BOOK FOUR

The House of Birds

The Existence of the Night

"I'll try the leg of puma in sesame sauce," said Azotl. "And a jug, I think, of your finest pulque." He glanced at Pitoque. "Have you two made up your minds?"

Pitoque could not decide. He finally settled on the armadillo meatballs with chilis. "That will do me well," he said. "I haven't tasted armadillo in a long time. Maxtla?"

Maxtla slumped lower into his chair. He wasn't hungry. He didn't want to be here, among Aztecs. He especially did not want to be in the presence of this obese character known as the master functionary. It was only because his father had ordered him to do so that he had come out at all to this eating place at the edge of the market at Tlatelolco. If he had had his way, he'd still have been dwelling among the Spaniards at their palace. Not that his time with the *teules* had been a success. They had proved to be not greatly interested in him. In truth, they seemed only interested in gold. He'd had no more luck with the Tlaxcalans, young men of the warrior class. They had little time to spare for a mere boy, the son of a *pochteca*. Worse, Maxtla spoke with the accent of Cholula, the city they had so lately defeated in a glorious and heroic battle. They had scoffed at him and ordered him to go away. They'd said he was lucky they did not kill him, too.

Now Maxtla looked up at his father. "No, thank you," he said. "Nothing for me. I'm not hungry."

"Not *hungry?*" said Pitoque. "How can you not be hungry? You're fourteen. When I was fourteen, I was always hungry."

"I said, I'm not hungry . . . *Father.*"

Azotl watched these proceedings with some amusement. He was fascinated by these youthful creatures, particularly those who found themselves at this awkward, perplexing age, suspended at the edge of adulthood. He glanced up at the servant. "Deer-salad tacos for the boy," he said. When Maxtla started to protest, the master functionary put up a hand. "Silence. I insist. You will find them utterly delicious. Dear boy, you will swoon."

But Maxtla was not to be cowed. "I'm sorry, but I am not hungry." He cleared his throat. "Thank you."

Azotl looked up at the waiter with a what-can-you-do? expression. "Just one deer-salad taco then. For me."

The servant nodded and glided away.

While awaiting their lunch, Pitoque and Azotl made light conversation and sipped from jars of pulque. It had been five days now since the Spaniards had entered Tenochtitlán. Pitoque had arrived a day afterward in search of his son, who had already been discovered by Toc. At the time, the boy had been wandering alone outside the palace of Axayácatl, in a dismal mood.

"I thought he might show up there, sir," Toc had said when he and Pitoque first spoke. "I thought he might come in search of the *teules.*"

Pitoque shook his head. "You know him better than I do myself then. I thought he would do as I told him."

Toc chuckled. "At his age, sir, one can never know for certain."

Maxtla hadn't wished to talk about his experience, and Pitoque had decided not to push the boy or to punish him. Better to let him brood a while. Maybe he would work the whole affair out of his system on his own.

The table servant arrived to refill their jars of pulque.

Azotl looked up. "Ah, good." He took a long draft and frowned. "Terrible news about Cholula," he said. "Devastating. I don't know what to say."

Pitoque sighed. He didn't know what to say, either.

Azotl set down his drink. "What do you make of it? Your report was very thorough, very graphic, but a little short on explanations. How do you explain it?"

"I can't." Pitoque did not wish to discuss this subject—too painful, too bewildering. He hunched his shoulders. "How does one explain anything? For instance, how does one explain the existence of night?"

"There are various theories, as you know."

"I thought you believed there was just one—that, without you Aztecs and your incessant sacrifices, the night would be permanent. Our natural condition."

Azotl tilted his head to acknowledge the point. "It is certainly the explanation that finds the greatest favor around here."

"But there are others?"

"Of course. You know it yourself."

Pitoque agreed. It was true. Every tribe had an explanation of its own. Those from Cholula believed that day and night related to Quetzalcoatl, that his absence brought the night, while each morning the heavens glowed once more with the promise of his return. According to that theory, and assuming that the feathered serpent had at last come back, the sun should now be burning all the time. But it wasn't.

He reached for his jar of pulque and raised it toward his lips. He hesitated partway. "The truth is, I cannot explain what took place at Cholula any more than you can." He glanced up at Azotl. "Or can you?"

It was a while before the master functionary replied and, when he did so, his answer was a kind of riddle. "When I look at a spear," he said, "I see a spear."

"I don't understand."

"One must judge on the basis of appearances, on the basis of what one sees."

"And what do you see now?"

"In truth?"

"Of course."

"In truth, I see a great evil. A great evil has come."

After this, the two men fell silent. Pitoque was thinking, *Judge us by our deeds.* Azotl's words sounded like just another way of saying the same thing. If one judged them by their deeds, these Spaniards were anything but gods. He looked over at Maxtla.

The boy did not react to his father's gaze. For days, he had been brooding, and he was brooding now. Nothing had gone as he had hoped. Could it be true, after all, what his father had told him—that there had been a great massacre in Cholula, committed by the Spaniards and their allies? He wondered what had become of Teontin and Nahuauc and a dozen others. Were they even alive? The questions rattled in his mind like a clash of swords, but he had no answers. And so he brooded, not wishing to speak, not wishing to do much of anything.

The food arrived.

"Ah, good. I had all but abandoned hope!" Azotl gloated as the steaming plates were carried to the table. Never content to sit back and observe, the master functionary now insisted on instructing the servants in their duties. "The puma's mine," he announced. "This haggard chap on my left has had the good sense to choose the armadillo. And if you would just put that deer-salad taco right here, in front of me, I'll see whether I cannot provide it with a worthy fate. Now then . . ."

The servants set the plates down, bowed, and withdrew. Pitoque waited for Azotl to begin, and then he did so himself. He realized he was hungrier than he had thought, and as soon as his mouth closed upon the first piece of armadillo, he knew he had made an excellent choice. It was delicious—tender and just a little rank. And the sauce was superb. He closed his eyes, reveled in a rich combination of flavors. He felt he had earned this meal, a welcome relief from the bouts of regret and worry he had suffered in recent days. This business with Maxtla, for instance—it had forced him to leave Amozoc, abandon his wife and daughter again. Now here he was, at a private table perched on a small sheltered pavilion overlooking the lake at Tlatelolco. The midday sunshine sparkled down through a faint haze of clouds and shattered against the broken waters.

He dipped his hands in the water bowl and looked at Azotl. "Delightful," he said. "I congratulate you on your choice of eating place."

The master functionary lowered his great head to acknowledge the compliment. "High praise," he said, "coming from a man as widely traveled as yourself."

Maxtla watched as the two men enjoyed themselves. He gradually realized that he was indeed quite hungry. Famished, in fact. It took him a while, but he finally worked up the courage to ask if he might sample the deer-salad taco, after all.

"Of course," said Azotl. "By all means. I was hoping you would ask." He slid the plate across the table. "You won't regret it, my boy."

Maxtla raised the taco and bit off a large mouthful. The flavors seemed to explode in his mouth. Within seconds, he had devoured the entire thing, and the master functionary promptly ordered that more be brought.

"Hurry now," he told the servant. "Can't you see the boy's perishing?" Azotl chuckled and took another gulp of pulque. His manner became serious. He turned to Pitoque. "You know, I have had some more unsettling news. About these Spaniards, as you call them."

"Yes?"

"You know that they are being housed in the palace of Axayácatl?"

Pitoque said that he did. Axayácatl was an uncle of Moctezuma's, and his palace was among the grandest in all Tenochtitlán.

Azotl narrowed his one good eye. "I probably shouldn't say it aloud, but this decision lacks a certain quality of—what shall I say? A certain quality of forethought. I—"

"I beg your pardon," said Pitoque. He leaned forward, spoke in a whisper. "But don't you think these matters should be discussed in a more private setting?"

"We are quite private here."

"I mean . . ." Pitoque nodded toward Maxtla.

"Eh? What's the matter with the boy?"

"Nothing. I just meant—"

"If there's nothing the matter with him, then what are you nodding at him for? You've interrupted my train of thought. Where was I?"

"The palace of Axayácatl," said Maxtla, whose mood seemed to have brightened considerably. "You were saying it was not the wisest of decisions to house the Spaniards there."

"Ah, yes. Now I remember. Thank you, young man. I'm glad someone was listening." Azotl turned back to Pitoque and peered at him with his single, blinking eye. "I myself had nothing to do with this decision. We recommended a half-dozen other possibilities, but the choice was made by the emperor himself. He selected the palace of Axayácatl precisely because of its grandeur."

"Surely the emperor simply wishes to make the Spaniards feel welcome," said Pitoque.

"No doubt he does." Azotl placed his great forearms on the table and leaned forward, lowered his voice. "But it so happens that the palace in question is one of the storehouses of Moctezuma's treasure. There are several other locations dotted about the city—discretion prevents me from being more specific—but the palace of Axayácatl houses a considerable cache of the imperial wealth. It is not one of the largest collections, but it is by no means insignificant."

"Surely the treasure is not on open display. I imagine it is hidden."

"Yes, of course. It lies in a secret vault sealed away beyond a false wall. Naturally." Azotl leaned back and fanned himself with his hand. The strain of the conversation had already caused bubbles of perspiration to sprout upon his brow. He shifted forward again. "In the normal run of affairs, I would not be concerned. We have entertained ambassadors in this very palace on many occasions before now. But we are not dealing now with the normal run of visitor. I take it you would agree?"

"Yes." Pitoque drained his jug of pulque. "I would, indeed."

"Good. You know, it is all very frustrating. While these Spaniards were outside Tenochtitlán, I was supplied with reliable and regular reports concerning their activities, thanks to you. Now they are here, right under my nose, and I know almost nothing of what they are doing." Azotl shook his head, apparently both amused and dismayed at the situation's irony. "Moctezuma, I will tell you, is in the habit of visiting them at least once a day. He lingers in their presence for an hour or so at a time, seems to be besotted with the fellows. But am I to summon the emperor into my presence, for the purposes of interrogation?" He shook his head. "Besides, I may as well admit it—I do not have unlimited confidence in the emperor's judgment."

"You lack confidence in the emperor?" The words were out before Pitoque could stop them. Distrust the emperor? The idea seemed heretical, especially coming from Azotl. "I meant to say—"

"I know exactly what you meant to say." Azotl raised a hand to the servant—more pulque. He glanced at Pitoque. "You wish more to drink?"

Pitoque shook his head.

Azotl crossed his arms on the table. "You find it unsettling that I would presume to question the *tlatoani*. Am I right?"

Pitoque nodded. As he understood it, the emperor's word was law. He had a sinking feeling he knew where this conversation was leading.

"Ah, thank you, my good man." Azotl leaned back while the table servant refilled his jar. He drank a little, smacked his lips, and resumed his presentation. "But I believe that I owe my loyalty not to the emperor but to the state of Tenochtitlán. Concerning these two concepts, I make a distinction in my mind. Do you understand me?"

"Yes."

"Good. I'm glad to hear it. You're sure you don't wish more pulque?"

"No, thank you."

Azotl turned to Maxtla "Dear boy, a drink of chocolate for you?"

"No . . . or, I mean, yes. Yes, please."

Azotl called for a serving of chocolate. He took another gulp from his jug, wiped his mouth with the hem of his cloak, and picked up the train of his thought. "As regards the emperor," he said, "I cannot deny that he possesses a—a what would you say? A sentimental character? He is inclined, I have noted, to let his feelings run a little too freely at times. I think that the weight of his office and the difficulty of these circumstances—all these omens and so forth—are proving to be more than his match. You have observed yourself that he is given to bouts of weeping."

Pitoque inclined his head. He remembered the occasion a year earlier, in the House of the Eagle Knights, when Moctezuma had broken down in tears. It had seemed remarkable at the time—and even more so now, in retrospect.

"In sum," said Azotl, "there is much to be alarmed about—and it is now, of all times, that I find myself deprived of information." He swallowed the last of his pulque and set the jug down. "Which brings me to my point . . ."

A Weakness for Frogs

By the time the master functionary had finished speaking, Pitoque's circumstances had radically changed. He would disband his gang of porters and report almost at once to the court of Moctezuma, where he would become an aide to the emperor. All had been arranged and approved. This was not a request. It was an instruction. Moctezuma was said to be highly pleased at the appointment, for he well remembered his encounter with the merchant of Cholula a year previously and had been most favorably impressed with the man's candor and intelligence. In reality, however, Pitoque's position would be more complex. He would function as an aide to the emperor— yes. But his true role would be to provide information to Azotl. He would be a spy in the royal court.

"Why have you chosen me?" Pitoque asked, and the master functionary replied at once.

"Because I trust you, and because you can understand what these creatures are saying."

It was true. Pitoque spoke the language of the Maya and even had a bit of Spanish now. No one else in the empire of the Aztecs—save the Spaniard Jerónimo de Aguilar—could claim as much. Even so, Pitoque tried to find a way to refuse the commission. He had made a pact with himself—to devote his life from now on to his family. Let the state take care of the state. A man's first duty lay with those closest to him. But Azotl had anticipated these arguments.

"I will send a guard to Cholula to protect your family," he said. "They will come to no harm."

"They are in Amozoc, a place we have, by a lake. I thought it better for them to remain there. It is—"

"I know where it is." Azotl smiled, evidently amused that anyone might think there was a corner of the empire he did not know. "I will take care of it. I will send the guard to Amozoc."

"What about Maxtla?"

Azotl had an answer for that, too. "I'll take care of the boy myself." He looked at Maxtla. "You may learn to think less badly of us Aztecs, unlikely as that may seem to you now. We are not monsters, you know, despite what you may have been raised to believe."

In the end, it was the killings in Cholula that changed Pitoque's mind. How could he do nothing after so many had died? He told Azotl that he would do as requested. The boy would stay with the master functionary, at least for now. He turned to Maxtla and raised his eyebrows. But the boy merely scowled and said nothing. Pitoque shrugged. With luck, Maxtla would sort himself out in time.

He gazed back at Azotl. "So. When do I begin?"

"Immediately." The master functionary said the arrangement could not get underway too quickly. He had a desperate need for good, accurate intelligence about these Spaniards. He worried especially about the possibility that Moctezuma would fall under their sway. "He is a highly impressionable man, given to sudden impulses and strange obsessions. I fear the worst."

Pitoque took a deep breath and climbed to his feet. He had the habits of a lifetime to guide him now, and so he decided to adhere to his usual code—leave-takings are best conducted at once and quickly. He bid goodbye to his son and to Azotl, stepped away from the table, and left the eating place. Out on the bustling street, he turned to his right and set out for the Aztec capital. As gulls swerved and hovered on the sparkling air, and swans patrolled by the reed banks near the shore, he hurried along the road that led to Tenochtitlán.

Azotl stretched out his arms and yawned. He smiled at Maxtla. "What would you say to a walk before we return to the city? I think we might both benefit from the exercise, me in particular. Walking is not among my preferred activities, but perhaps it would be wise to make an occasional exception. As you can see, I'm carrying some additional cargo."

Maxtla glared straight ahead, astonished by the turn that events had taken and yet unable to say how he felt. Finally, he agreed to a stroll outdoors in advance of their return to Tenochtitlán. He followed the master functionary out of the restaurant and walked behind him as they proceeded along the stone walkway that ran by the shore of the lake. The sun was nicely past its height now and shone down at an oblique angle from a sky of hazy blue. The light popped against the shifting surface of the water as though glancing against a thousand crystals of quartz. Various townspeople bustled past them, many followed by servants laden down with their purchases.

"Come," said Azotl. "Let us make an inspection of the market. It is quite famous, you know—the biggest market in the world."

"Yes, I know."

"You do?"

"We learned it at school."

"Ah. I'm pleased to discover that the Cholulan education system does not entirely ignore the accomplishments of Aztecs. Come."

The vast Tlatelolco market soon burgeoned all around them—a carnival of brilliant colors, ripe smells, and raucous sounds. Surrounded by so much life, Maxtla found that his mood was lightening again. In fact, it was a relief to be separated from his father. He was fourteen years old, after all—very nearly a man. He could fend for himself, even if that meant fending off this massive character, who now waddled in front of him, pointing at this and that and boasting about everything he saw—not, perhaps, without reason. In fact, the market was turning out to be almost as impressive as Azotl claimed. Even Maxtla had to admit it. It was larger than he had ever imagined.

"Look," said Azotl, "there is a section for everything. I hope you are feeling carnivorous, my boy. Here we are in meats. Meats and fowl. Just look at this display."

They wandered past an endless array of stalls, each devoted to selling the flesh of a certain animal or bird. There was ocelot, coyote, deer, badger, hare, wild boar, duck, turkey. They passed a stall strung with the carcasses of little dogs called xoloitzcuintli.

"Mmm," said Azotl. "I'm feeling peckish once again."

For more than an hour, they strolled through the market, with the master functionary pointing out and describing each commodity they passed. Cornmeal. Honey. Chocolate. An endless variety of nuts. Here, pinto beans. In the next stall, amaranth seed, or salt, or tiny hearts of quail, or jugs of maguey syrup. They skirted the area of the market where human slaves were bought and sold.

"I think we had better leave that subject for another day," said Azotl. "Look, my boy. Over here."

He led Maxtla to a section where fruits and vegetables were piled high in stall after stall—endless quantities of guavas, sweet potatoes, water chestnuts, slabs of prickly pear cactus. Next, they ambled through areas of the market where knives were on display, then cotton, then sisal, then pottery.

"Aha!" Azotl held up a plate and winked at Maxtla. "Unmistakably from Cholula. Such fine workmanship. I commend you."

The market stretched on and on. Even now, in the late afternoon, it teemed with vendors, traders, shoppers. Here and there, musicians performed on flutes and drums for the entertainment of the thousands of customers. Dwarfs put on displays of tumbling for the amusement of children. To Maxtla, it seemed that the entire population of Tenochtitlán was crammed into the place. Never had he seen so many people all at once. He knew that the master functionary was trying to impress upon him the wealth and sophistication of any society that could afford so ample and luxurious a market. And what could Maxtla say? The market *was* spectacular. It was practically overwhelming.

Azotl waddled ahead, smiling to himself. He could see that his little outing was having its effect—and in good time, too, because he did not think he could walk much farther. He announced that he felt compelled to bring the ambulatory portion of the afternoon's activities to an end for reasons of health or, as he put it, "on account of the excessive downward pressure on my poor feet." He waved toward a gang of ragged, barefoot litter-bearers lounging at the edge of the market.

"Two," cried Azotl. "We'll be needing two."

Maxtla climbed into the second of the litters and hunched there with his legs drawn up, crossed at the ankles, in an attitude that suggested his uneasiness.

There were a dozen litter-bearers in all, six men to each palanquin. They heaved their burdens up onto their shoulders and set off from Tlatelolco at a practiced stride. It was soon apparent that Azotl had instructed them to take a roundabout route, a tour of Tenochtitlán. They wound along narrow streets and bounced up broad avenues, past canals lined by flowering trees. The houses were mostly one- or two-story dwellings, mainly constructed of stone and then plastered with adobe or lime. Maxtla was familiar with the sight of multitudinous pyramids, temples, and shrines—what Cholulan was not?—but this city was fairly overflowing with monuments to the gods. It was also an extraordinarily verdant place, bursting with gardens, tree-rows, and small, carefully tended arboreta. Everywhere he looked, there were flowering trees—bougainvillea, jacaranda, poinsettia, and the starburst blossoms of tulip trees. Why had he noticed none of this before? On his previous visits to the Aztec capital, he had always kept his head lowered and his eyes half-closed, hating the idea of being here. But now—owing perhaps to his father's absence or to the master functionary's enthusiasm—he opened his eyes and began to see.

Orderly and green, Tenochtitlán was also extremely busy. There were no idlers anywhere. Almost everyone seemed to be striding about urgently. Only the priests seemed slow and melancholic. Theirs was a sometimes grisly trade, conducted in the currency of human sacrifice, and they shuffled in the shadows of the great pyramids—dour, slump-shouldered figures, with their blood-matted hair, their dark, blood-caked robes.

"A sad business, theirs," remarked Azotl. "Especially in these difficult days."

"Difficult?" said Maxtla. He wrapped his arms around his knees. What did the Aztecs know about difficulties? They ruled the world. It was everyone else who suffered difficulties. "What do you mean?"

Azotl heard the hard note of challenge in the boy's tone and decided to let it pass. He was not given to unnecessary confrontation. "What do I mean?" He chuckled and shook his head. "Sometimes I do not know myself."

Eventually, the pair of litters lurched to a halt in front of a small cut-stone mansion near a narrow canal bordered by jacaranda trees. Although modest in size, it was as pretty a place as Maxtla had seen that afternoon. Still, prettiness was of no great interest to him now. He had already decided that, when the first opportunity arose, he would simply leave the care of the master functionary. He would make his way back to the palace of Axayácatl and rejoin the Spaniards. This time, it would be different. He would present himself as a warrior. He would slay Aztecs. He would prove his worth.

"Here we are," announced Azotl. He hauled himself from his litter, paid the bearers with a smattering of cacao beans, and sent them away. He stifled a belch. "Well, my boy, what did you think of your grand tour? In all the world, can any city compare with this one?"

Maxtla suspected not, but he was disinclined to let the beauty of Tenochtitlán affect him. The Aztecs were still a cruel and despotic people—that was the truth. He decided not to be a hypocrite. The truth should be spoken. He gritted his teeth and then opened his mouth. Out flew the words. "I dislike your city," he said. "I hate your people." Now he paused but then went ahead. "I have no reason to feel otherwise about you."

Azotl raised his great eyebrows, which looked like a pair of furry caterpillars. "I must have wax in my ears. I could not make out a word of what you just said."

Maxtla was about to repeat himself, but the master functionary began to laugh and lumbered ahead. "Fat. Hard of hearing. And blind in one eye. Oh, you will find me a poor sort of host. But come. Let me show you my humble abode."

Maxtla hesitated for several moments, but saw no way to avoid the invitation. He turned and followed the master functionary inside.

Despite its modest appearance from outside, the house had an extraordinary interior, if interior was the word. In fact, the building was largely exposed to the open air. Its terraces commanded a splendid view over the shining lake, and the afternoon sunshine poured in. Azotl led his young guest through a network of rooms, most of them filled with thriving greenery and some dominated by great stone fireplaces, for the winters in Tenochtitlán were even cooler than those in Cholula. The floors were made of some sort of volcanic ash—that was Maxtla's guess—pounded to a rock-hard sheen, and each room was decorated by marvelous terra-cotta sculptures and wooden carvings. Thanks to his travels, Maxtla recognized some of the styles. Great Olmec heads burst from the floor, glorious Toltec weavings covered the walls, and stone friezes of dancing men were displayed here and there. Smaller statuettes and ceramic vessels cluttered every available space. It was wonderful work—even he could see that—and the effect was little short of dazzling. If he hadn't known better, Maxtla would have thought himself in a magnificent gallery of art, surrounded by all the finest works of the empire.

He let out a low whistle. He might have been in a gloomy, bitter mood, but he could not pretend he was not struck by what he saw.

Azotl smiled. "I have a low resistance to beautiful objects, as you can see. But it is not only objects that enchant me." He led Maxtla up a flight of wooden stairs and out onto a high terrace. "Wait here," he said, and trudged away.

Maxtla stepped out to the edge of the terrace and gazed at the brilliant blue waters of the lake, ornamented by white-cap waves. A dozen dugout canoes crept across the water like wooden dragonflies piloted by miniature fishermen, who cast out their great shimmering nets in a motion that resembled the beating of dragonfly wings. Bird hunters probed through the emerald rushes that grew by the marshy shore, and salt farmers raked the sandy flats. In the distance, beyond the lake, a range of mountains glimmered mauve in the late afternoon sunshine and pressed their backs against the cloud-flecked sky. Maxtla had encountered many lovely prospects in his life, but he had to admit that few were much finer than this. He heard steps behind him and turned around.

"Ah, there you are. You haven't run away yet. I see." Azotl waddled back out onto the terrace.

This time, he was not alone. He held the hand of a slender young girl dressed in a long white robe fringed with a blue pattern of copal dye. Her long hair, black and iridescent, was tied back and piled above her oval face. She had charcoal eyes, a wide smile, and nut-brown skin. Copper bracelets jangled at both her wrists.

"Allow me," said Azotl, "to introduce my niece, the most beautiful occupant of this rather cluttered house."

The girl strode toward Maxtla, her smile broadening with each step. She held out her hands in welcome. "My name is Ometzin," she said. "I am fourteen years old."

Maxtla took her hand. "My name is Maxtla," he said.

"I know. My uncle has told me much about you." She tilted her head. "Do you care for frogs?"

Maxtla frowned. "Frogs?" he said. "You mean, to eat?"

"No. I mean as a subject of inquiry. Their breeding habits. Their habitat. I warn you, I have a weakness for frogs." She rested a hand on each of his shoulders and kissed him lightly on both cheeks. "Have you ever dissected one?"

"A frog? No."

"Ah, well. In that case, you have great adventures in store. Now, let me show you to your room." She took him by the hand and practically dragged him behind her. "And birds," she said. "I am passionately interested in birds."

Is That Not Godlike?

"Mortal?" said Moctezuma. "Or divine? What do you say?"

Pitoque gestured helplessly. This was perhaps the twentieth time the emperor had asked him the question. He still did not know the answer. "Mortal, I suspect," he said, "but I'm not sure. In fact, I do not know."

"Mortal?" Moctezuma raised his eyebrows. He and Pitoque were seated in a quiet green courtyard in the emperor's palace. Several royal aides hovered nearby. "Why do you suspect that? On what evidence?"

Pitoque cast about for some sort of proof. Finally, he settled on that galling experiment conducted by the Tlaxcalan elder, Ixcatzin, on the corpse of the captured Spaniard. It had been a disgusting exercise, but it had established several facts. One, Spaniards bled. Two, they could be killed. Three, they possessed the standard allotment of human viscera. Four, their bodies, once dead, became infested with maggots and began to rot. All these were characteristics of mortals, not gods.

Moctezuma frowned. "Where did you come by this information?"

"In Tlaxcala, my lord."

"And it was the Tlaxcalans themselves, I take it, who supplied it to you?"

"Begging your pardon, my lord, but I myself was present."

"Really, Pitoque." The emperor began to laugh. "Tlaxcalans!" He shook his head, and his lip ornament glinted in the afternoon sunshine that filtered through the cotton canopy suspended above him. "Compulsive liars, the lot of them. I don't think much of your evidence on this occasion."

Pitoque bowed. "As you say." He hesitated. "There is also, as I have previously suggested, the case of Cholula to consider."

"Ah, yes. Cholula." Moctezuma propped his chin on his fist. "Yes. We have spoken of this before." He agreed that here was a troubling matter. "Such ruthless destruction hardly seems worthy of so esteemed a god as Quetzalcoatl. It is the sort of atrocity those abominable Tlaxcalans might commit."

"They did," said Pitoque. "The Tlaxcalans were guilty, too."

Moctezuma nodded. "So you have said before now. In fact, I wonder if that isn't the answer to this riddle." The emperor presented a theory he had devised—that perhaps the Tlaxcalans alone were responsible for the carnage at Cholula. He wouldn't be surprised. Perhaps the only crime of the gods had been to cast their lot in with those reptilian infidels who dwelt beyond the great wall of Tlaxcala. Perhaps the Spaniards were as shocked as Pitoque was by what had happened in the merchant's city. The emperor sat back. "What do you think of that?"

"Perhaps, my lord. It is possible. But I—"

"But you do not know. Am I right? You cannot say for certain?"

Reluctantly, Pitoque agreed.

"Well, then. It seems that we are right back at the beginning. None of your so-called evidence has established anything. Gods or men? You do not know."

Pitoque conceded the point. In fact, he remained almost as perplexed as ever concerning the nature of these Spaniards, although he had lately started to suspect that they were human, after all. It was neither their cruelty nor the sight of their blood that brought him to this way of thinking. It was the sheer intensity of their greed. The first time he had entered the palace of Axayácatl in the company of Moctezuma, he had seen immediately that the Spaniards had already begun. All the furniture had been overturned, the tapestries torn down. Mounds of rubble were scattered about the place because the Spaniards had taken to digging up the floors.

On that first occasion, Azotl had told him what he should do, and Pitoque had followed the master functionary's directions. He had pleaded a temporary shortness of breath, a need for fresh air. He'd told Moctezuma that he would just step outside and shortly return. He had then left the canopied reception hall and hurried down a narrow passageway, turned left at a small interior courtyard, and at once began to run his hand along the left-hand wall, a section of false stone panels that Azotl had described to him. He could tell instantly that they had been breached. The Spaniards had made a crude effort to patch the stonework back into place, but they were poor masons compared to the expert workers employed by the Aztecs—men who had no doubt been sacrificed in order to preserve the secrecy of the vault's location.

Well, it was secret no longer.

Pitoque had peered about to ensure he was not being observed, and then made his way back to rejoin the emperor and the royal entourage. He had let out a long breath and tried to appear nonchalant, as if he had learned nothing out of the ordinary. But, in truth, he was astonished at how quickly the Spaniards had discovered the cache.

It was as if they could smell treasure. Now, several days later and seated near the emperor in this sun-filled patio, Pitoque shook his head, cleared his throat, and said as much. These Spaniards or *teules*—one might be forgiven for thinking they could locate gold purely on the evidence of their noses.

"Aha!" Moctezuma clapped his hands. "You are right. You are absolutely right." He laughed in triumph. "And is that not godlike? I think I have caught you out, my friend. What attribute could possibly be more divine?"

Twice a day, the emperor was carried in his royal palanquin across the temple precinct to pay a visit on the *teules* in the palace of Axayácatl. He told Pitoque that the dictates of etiquette required him to show his respect to the Spaniards and most particularly to their commander, this Hernán Cortés.

Pitoque was not so certain. It seemed to him that something other than imperial courtesy was the guiding principle here.

Moctezuma was clearly obsessed. He could not get enough of these booming, barrel-chested creatures. He was convinced they were immortal, and this conviction thrilled him beyond words. What other emperor before him had been so graced? To dally in the company of the gods—what could be more rare and wondrous?

Moctezuma informed Pitoque that the Spaniards truly did suffer from a terrible disease, a malady unknown to the Aztecs. It was an affliction that could be cured only by gold. Cortés had told him so. Without gold, the Spaniards would die, as more ordinary creatures might perish from a lack of air or food. To the emperor, this strange illness seemed magnificent. He saw it as further evidence of the visitors' divinity. Who else but gods would sup upon gold?

"I do not think they sup upon it." By now, Pitoque had become sufficiently familiar with the emperor that he dared to contradict him, albeit gently and obliquely. They strolled side by side along a second-floor gallery near Moctezuma's private chambers. "I think the Spaniards used the expression as a figure of speech."

Moctezuma frowned. "Not at all. They were quite explicit on the point. They chew it with their teeth. They swallow it down."

As a *pochteca*, a trader, a man who dealt daily in the perceived worth of goods, Pitoque thought he understood the Spaniards' desire for gold. He tried to explain to the emperor that they were attracted to treasure because it would make them rich. It would give them power. It offered a life of ease. He himself understood gold's allure. But Moctezuma did not. To the emperor, gold was glorious because it could be worked into beautiful ornaments that he might keep or give away, depending on the needs of the moment. Such ornaments could be used to seal treaties or to mark high occasions of state. This was the luster of gold.

"You may wish to know," said Pitoque, "that they melt it down."

Moctezuma stopped and looked at him. "What do they do?"

"The gold that you give them—they melt it down. They make it into bars."

"They do?"

"I have seen it myself." More than once, Pitoque had watched them at work, sweating over great wood fires with improvised bellows and copper pots, turning ornaments into ingots.

"Ingots?" said the emperor. He frowned and then proceeded with his walk along the floor of sweet-smelling cedar, through a dappled pattern of shadows and light cast by vines that tumbled down the gallery's edge. Now he smiled. "Ah, ingots. Perhaps the gold is more readily digestible that way."

Kalatzin and her daughter hurried through the main plaza of Cholula, both of them down at heart. They were supposed to have remained out at Amozoc, of course. A group of Aztec guards had appeared one morning, supposedly to keep them safe. But Kalatzin was less concerned about safety—hers or anyone's—than she was about providing her daughter with a decent husband. She was not inclined to stay out by that lake for all eternity. What hope did she have of finding a husband there? So she had brought Zaachila back to Cholula, although now she was beginning to wonder why.

On every side, workers shuttled about, methodically repairing the damage the Spaniards had done during their passage through the city. The dead had all been hauled away and buried by now, but still a faint stench of putrefaction pervaded the place, along with an air of sadness, the ache of loss. It was said that the dead numbered in the thousands.

A goodly number of them—Kalatzin could not stop herself from reflecting—were bound to have been men.

She pressed ahead, lost in her thoughts. Many of those men would have been of marriageable age and not a few of them single. Husbands, they might have become. Husbands and fathers. Now the lot of them moldered beneath the earth, a feast for grubs and worms. Before long, their souls would inhabit the breasts of winged insects. They would skitter about on the highland breeze, their wings thrumming against the air, shimmering in the morning sunlight. Ah, what ecstasy it must be to zigzag through the afterlife in the guise of a flying creature. But no flying creature could wed Kalatzin's only daughter and undertake the conjugal duty that husbands are required to perform so that, several months hence, Zaachila might bring forth the mewling and babbling wonder of progeny.

Babies. When Kalatzin looked out at the silent ruins of Cholula, it was babies that she wanted most profoundly to see. Husbands and babies.

Ah, what was the use of it? To think of all the expense that they had already paid out to those grasping priests—and to what purpose? They had accomplished nothing, and yet still they promised results. First, however, there would have to be more ceremonies. That was their inevitable refrain. More rites and prayers. More cacao beans and gold dust. More bolts of cotton. A husband would be found! It was only a matter of time—of time and incantation and prayer. Do not abandon hope, dear mother. Simply pray and pay. Pray and pay without cease.

"Come, daughter," she said. She released Zaachila's hand in order to draw up the hem of her robe, to keep it free of dirt as she hopped over a dried streambed. She quickened her pace. "We mustn't loiter."

"Yes, Mother," said Zaachila, who hurried to catch up.

The wife and daughter of Pitoque marched in the direction of their home, one of the few buildings that had not been damaged or, worse, destroyed by the Spaniards. Kalatzin took her daughter's hand again. She frowned. Here was another strange business. Several thousand dead and an omnipresent mood of sadness—and yet no one seemed to hold the Spaniards to account for what had been done. More often, they blamed the Aztecs. After all, the Aztecs were at the root of every terrible event. They had to be behind this disaster somehow. Down with the Aztecs!

If you could make sense of that deranged logic, you could make sense of anything.

‡

"You know that this cannot go on." Doña Marina clasped her hands in front of her. She and Cortés were strolling through the temple precinct of Tenochtitlán. The mid-morning sun hung in the sky above the temples and pyramids. The tiles beneath their feet glowed, clean as glazed pottery. Aguilar walked nearby, in order to aid in translation. "It is just a matter of time."

"Do you mean, before our welcome wears thin?" asked Cortés.

"Yes. And, as you know, we are greatly outnumbered."

Cortés agreed with her. Outnumbered, they undoubtedly were. Indeed, there was a huge disparity in numbers. Out on an open plain, where they could use their archers and harque-busiers and cannon to full effect, it might not matter so much. It hadn't mattered against the Tlaxcalans. But within the confines of this city? That was a different proposition. They were certainly vulnerable. He was aware of it. He just wasn't entirely sure what to do about it.

Marina gazed around her as she walked. She was choosing her words carefully. Aztec noblewomen paraded past in long skirts and voluminous blouses, with their hair cut short and dyed black with indigo, their faces rubbed yellow with a cream they made from crushed insects. They shadowed their menfolk, who wore brightly colored cloaks over their loincloths, knotted at the right shoulder. Their faces were adorned by lip plugs or ear coils. These Aztec nobles all made a show of nonchalance, pretending that they were no longer curious about her or these two Spaniards, but she knew better. In fact, they were fascinated. When they thought she wasn't looking, they craned their necks and stared at her and her two otherworldly companions as they passed through the temple precinct.

Marina felt a flush of pleasure at being so conspicuous. She liked to be noticed, liked to stand out. She turned and gazed up at Cortés, at his beard, dense as a bed of moss, at his fist-like nose and broad brow. She realized that she was half in love with the man already—no, not half. She *was* in love with him. Why? Because he was strong. He was the strongest man she had ever known, stronger than any chieftain or prince. He intended to rule all these lands, and at his side, she would be empress. She would be queen. There was nothing she desired more. She took several steps ahead and then turned around and stopped in front of the Spanish captain. She announced to him that she had a plan.

He smiled at her, evidently amused at the notion. "Yes?" he said. "And of what does it consist, this plan of yours?"

She cleared her throat. She had been contemplating this idea ever since they had arrived in Tenochtitlán, or even before that—ever since Tlaxcala, when they'd first been invited to the Aztec capital. She put her hands on her hips and narrowed her gaze. "You must make the emperor your prisoner," she said.

Cortés's eyebrows rose. Aguilar stood at his side, with his usual glum expression, translating as quickly as he could. "Make the emperor my prisoner?"

"That's right," she said. "But first you must win his trust.

In truth, you have it already. He thinks of you as a god."

Cortés nodded. He was aware of Moctezuma's belief and found it most intriguing.

She placed her hands on the Spaniard's chest. "You must make him your prisoner—but your *willing* prisoner. With the emperor on your side, you can rule all these lands without war."

"You are averse to war, I take it?"

She shook her head. "Not at all. I am averse to the *losing* of wars."

Cortés put back his head and laughed. Delighted, he cupped her chin with one of his hands. "So am I," he told her. "So, most assuredly, am I."

She thrilled at his touch. "Then you agree to my plan?"

"Perhaps," said Cortés. Her idea was interesting— extremely interesting. But he had to be careful in everything he did. He had no authority from Cuba or from Madrid, and he would no doubt be called to account one day for all his actions here. Take the emperor prisoner? Perhaps. But he would require a pretext. It could not be done on a whim. He tucked Marina's hand beneath his arm and resumed his passage through this remarkable plaza. "I will take your idea under advisement," he said.

Aguilar translated the concept, and Marina smiled to herself. In her experience, a good idea—once planted in fertile soil—almost always grew.

Empress. Queen.

She gazed around at the Aztecs in the plaza, and her smile broadened. They were making no attempt to hide the fact now—without exception, they all were looking at Cortés and at her.

As well they might.

Of Stuffed Chrysanthemums and Gold

The idea of gold as a food quickly came to fascinate Moctezuma. He wanted to see this remarkable phenomenon for himself. If the Spaniards indeed dined upon gold, he thought, then this would provide further proof of their divinity. Naturally, one would expect the gods to require something very special in the way of nourishment. What was more special than gold?

He announced to Pitoque that he wished to host yet another banquet in honor of his guests. This time, he would instruct the royal cooks to sow one of the dishes—stuffed chrysan-themums—with pellets of gold. It would be a rare pleasure to observe with his own eyes a custom as exalted as the digestion of precious metal.

Two nights later, a great banquet was held in the great hall of the palace of Axayácatl, amid shallow trenches, mounds of refuse and debris, and a clutter of shattered timbers—for the Spaniards were digging everywhere in their hunt for gold. All day long, the Aztec *macehualtin*—the laborers—were hard at work. They set up dozens of trestle tables and put out wooden stools, sufficient seating for several hundred Spaniards. As darkness fell, a parade of servants filed into the hall bearing steaming dishes of every variety, including many platters of stuffed chrysanthemums. Others bore ceramic urns of pulque, great jugs of flower water, and vats of chocolate. Tumblers and dwarfs performed in the aisles between the tables, and musicians beat great vertical *huehuetl* drums or played wooden flutes. Torches mounted by the walls provided a dim, flickering light.

Moctezuma and his imperial entourage presided at the royal table, with Cortés and several of the Spanish officers at his side. Aguilar and Marina were seated between Cortés and Moctezuma, in order to do the work of translating. To make room, Pitoque had been relegated to a separate table for the evening.

He kept his eyes on the emperor, who said little and barely touched his meal. He seemed almost overcome at the prospect of watching the Spaniards feast upon gold.

Moctezuma felt a trembling in his nether regions, an almost uncontainable excitement. He merely picked at his food. In part, he was afraid of finding pellets of gold among the stuffed chrysanthemums on his plate—he had no intention of consuming gold himself. Who knew what effect it might have upon a mortal? He also did not want to miss the joy of seeing others as they feasted upon this shiny, pliant metal. He kept looking up, peering around the room, watching these Spaniards eat.

Another thrill of anticipation ran up his back. To witness the ingestion of gold! In fact, now that the moment had come, he somewhat regretted hiding the metal away in the stuffed chrysanthemums. It would have been more dramatic to watch the Spaniards consume the gold without elaboration. Did it not crack their teeth? Surely they must simply swallow it down. Perhaps it was this diet of gold that made them so hairy, so large.

"Agh!" Somewhere down the way, one of the Spaniards cried out and leapt to his feet. His hands went straight to his mouth. He spat something into his cupped palms and roared out a long stream of invective in his own tongue.

"What does he say? What does he say?" Moctezuma turned to Doña Marina, who turned to Aguilar.

It seemed that the Spaniard had broken a tooth on something in his dinner. He had then called down a torrent of abuse upon his own god, which raised an interesting metaphysical question—did the gods have gods? Moctezuma looked back out at the room. The Spaniard's mood had changed. He suddenly let out a howl of excitement, despite his shattered tooth. He had evidently discovered that the foreign object in his stuffed chrysanthemums was nothing other than a pellet of gold. He raised the object to his lips and tested it with another bite. Yes. Real gold! He performed a little dance, thrust the pellet into the pocket of his doublet, and promptly began to burrow with both hands into the contents of his plate.

Moctezuma sat back, suffused with a glow of expectation. Now he would see. Now the gods would reveal themselves.

But they didn't. Or, if they did, it was not in the way that the emperor had expected or hoped. Once the other Spaniards understood what had happened—a pellet of gold embedded in one of the dishes—they all promptly forgot about eating and embarked instead on a treasure hunt through the plates. Some of them climbed right up onto the tables in their efforts to find more gold. They dug through the food with their hands, groveling for any morsel that felt remotely like a bit of metal. Whenever one of them did find something, he immediately let out a whoop of joy and turned the platter upside down so that he could spread its contents out upon the floor and improve his chances of finding more gold. The Spaniards soon realized that the stuffed chrysanthemums were the surest bet. Before long, they fell to grappling and wrestling with one another until Cortés was obliged to order a halt to this nonsense.

"Enough!" he cried. "Enough!"

He requisitioned all of the food in the great hall, giving orders that it be searched on behalf of Charles I of Spain, who would receive the royal fifth of whatever gold or treasure might be discovered in the evening's meal. The rest would be divided according to a formula yet to be announced, but Cortés promised it would be fair.

"Now sit down, everyone," he shouted. "You have the table manners of dogs." He turned to Aguilar and requested that he convey the Spaniards' gratitude to Moctezuma. "Gold in the stuffed chrysanthemums," he said. He shook his head in a kind of wonderment. "A most novel repast."

When he understood what Cortés had said, Moctezuma waved a hand in acknowledgment. In truth, he was deeply disappointed with the way the banquet had turned out. Still, he did his best to play the part of the gracious host. He rose to his feet and praised his visitors, effusively and at length. Next, he invited Cortés to join him the following day for an outing to the great temple of Tenochtitlán. He sincerely wished to acquaint his guests with the deities of his people, particularly Huitzilopochtli, the hummingbird god.

Once the speech was translated, Cortés took to his feet once again to thank his host and accept his invitation. He concluded with a request that these delicious stuffed chrysanthemums be included as a fixed item on the menu for all meals from now on, without exception.

Moctezuma smiled at this excellent joke and said he would endeavor to comply. Later, he whispered to his nephew Cacama, the king of Texcoco, who was sitting on his left, that he believed the evening had gone passably well, but he confessed to considerable disillusionment that the Spaniards had not actually eaten the gold. Perhaps they would do this later, in privacy—a shame, as he'd wanted to witness this feat with his own eyes. As to making gold a standard item in all future banquets—quite frankly, he was a bit worried about the expense.

It was at this moment that Doña Marina suddenly cut the emperor off. She leaned over and asked him if he did not think it rather rude to be whispering. Did he wish to offend his guests?

Moctezuma gasped. He started to choke on his phlegm and found he could not speak. Even if he'd been able to find his voice, what would he have said? Never in his life had any woman—any *human being*—dared to address him in this way.

And yet he made no protest, not wanting to offend Cortés.

Cacama cast a long, dark look at this reckless woman and shook his head. She should be whipped and have her throat slit, he thought. A traitor, that was what she was. If he could have his way, he would whip all these Spaniards, one by one, then slit all their throats. But he was merely the king of Texcoco, not the emperor of the Aztecs. The emperor of the Aztecs was his uncle, this slender man on his right, choking on his own spit.

Cacama reached in front of him for another stuffed chrysanthemum. He took a bite and slowly chewed the sweet minced meat inside—armadillo, he thought. When his teeth closed on something small and very hard, he did not spit it out. Instead, he allowed himself to salivate a little, and then he swallowed the object down. He took another bite of meat and chewed it with conspicuous deliberation. He continued to do this—very, very slowly—until his meal was done.

The Temple of the Hummingbird God

The following morning, Cortés was in a foul mood owing to poor digestion and lack of sleep.

"Too many stuffed chrysanthemums, no doubt," joked Alvarado. "I'm not surprised."

Cortés merely grunted. He was in no mood for jests. Besides, the amount of gold recovered from the previous evening's meal had been disappointingly small. He had definitely been hoping for more. But it was the state of his inner workings that was causing him concern at the moment. He told Aguilar that he had decided not to make this infernal journey out to some godforsaken Aztec temple. What was it called?

"The temple of Huitzilopochtli," said Aguilar. "He is the patron god of Tenochtitlán. I think the emperor might be offended if you fail to attend. It might be wise to humor him."

Cortés stifled a belch and turned to Alvarado. "What do you think, Pedrito?"

Alvarado patted his belly. He said he craved another meal of stuffed chrysanthemums. He began to laugh.

Cortés turned and asked Marina for her opinion. Aguilar fully expected her to tell the commander that Moctezuma could stew in his own juices as far as she was concerned. Who cared about a ridiculous outing to some rat-infested Aztec temple? But this was not what she said. She said that she took the same view as Aguilar.

"You agree with me?" Aguilar was astonished. Rarely did he and the native princess agree on anything.

"Yes," she told him. "I think Cortés should see for himself what monsters these Aztecs are. At the temple of Huitzilopochtli, he will certainly see."

Aguilar clenched his jaw. He had lived eight years in these lands and was well aware of the Aztecs' infamy. She meant human sacrifices. All day long, they performed them—dozens, hundreds a day.

"You know what I mean," she said. "That's why everybody in the world hates the Aztecs. They capture prisoners from other nations and bring them here and sacrifice them to their gods. If you want to know these murderers you should go to the temple. You will see."

Aguilar rubbed his hand against his brow. It was not unknown for other peoples, including those on the eastern coast, to engage in human sacrifice, but the practice was rare, by no means a daily occurrence. The Aztecs were different. They had raised the sacrifice of human beings into a cult. In the past, he had imagined them to be a warlike breed—rough, grunting savages who spent all their time swaggering about, marauding lesser tribes. In fact, since his arrival in Tenochtitlán, he'd been astonished by the sophistication of these people, by the grace of their architecture, the loveliness of the music they played, the elegance of their dress, the rich variety of their cuisine. And yet they were inveterate killers. He had heard the lurid tales but had never come face to face with the reality. Now it seemed he would.

"Tell him," said Doña Marina. "Tell him what I said."

Aguilar turned to his commander. For an instant, he forgot what he was supposed to say, a common occurrence now. Although many days had passed since the bloodshed in Cholula, the massacre haunted him still. The truth was, he was surrounded by villains. Their depravity sometimes got the better of him, left him confused and miserable. Now he rubbed his eyes, shook his head.

"So?" said Cortés. He stuck out his chin with its thick beard and scarcely concealed scar. "What does the woman say?"

Aguilar remembered now. "She feels as I do," he said. "She feels that you should humor the emperor."

Cortés let out a sigh and stifled another belch. He turned to Alvarado. "Pedrito, it appears that you have been outvoted today." He shook his head. "I have become quite the little puppet, it seems—required to attend ceremonies for no other purpose than to be deemed polite. Lead on, Doña Marina."

Aguilar considered warning the commander about what he was likely to see at the temple, but he decided to let matters take their own course. In truth, he wasn't exactly sure what he would see himself.

When the Spanish party arrived at the temple precinct, the emperor was already waiting. Flanked by several attendants, he stood upon the plaza's gleaming, whitewashed flagstones, shifting from one bejeweled sandal to the other. He wore an indigo cloak trimmed with ocelot ears and he fidgeted with his hands, evidently in a state of high excitement.

Aguilar noticed that Moctezuma was accompanied by Pitoque, the merchant. The Little King of Plates. How very odd to see him at the emperor's side. Not where one would expect to find a mere vendor of ceramics. Still, it was good to see that the man had survived the atrocities committed in his city. That much was a blessing.

Aguilar felt a hand grip his arm. Cortés.

"Aguilar. Come." The captain-general strode ahead to greet Moctezuma. He bowed and began an impromptu address. "We have made the trip here as we promised," he said. "Once again, my thanks for the dinner last night. Those stuffed chrysanthemums—I can't praise them highly enough."

Moctezuma made a dismissive gesture. He said the banquet was nothing at all. His cooks had thrown the repast together at the last minute from leftovers. It would please him to entertain the Spaniards again very soon, and this time he would ensure that the menu were truly something to remember. Stuffed chrysanthemums—it was a simple dish. Little better than peasant fare. Wait until Cortés had sampled *tepexcuintle* in pumpkin-seed sauce. Now, that was food.

"*Tepexcuintle?*" said Aguilar. The term was unfamiliar to him.

"Prairie dog," said Marina.

"Ah." He informed Cortés.

The captain-general put a hand to his gut and groaned. Prairie dog! His stomach was still a little queasy. Besides, he was in no mood for chat.

Moctezuma waited for several moments before speaking again. When he did, it was to change the subject. He switched from matters culinary to the affairs of the gods. "We are here," he said, "at the pyramid of Huitzilopochtli." The emperor turned around and motioned at the immense structure behind him—a symmetrical conglomeration of cut stones that narrowed as it ascended to a lofty summit. Moctezuma pointed up to a small, distant platform at the top. "Up there is the temple itself," he said. "There are one hundred and fourteen steps. I have taken the liberty of supplying transportation." He indicated a small fleet of litters, each with its clutch of *mayeque*, as Aztec slaves were known. "Please. Let us ascend."

But Cortés insisted his men would rather walk than be carried. This seemed to catch Moctezuma unawares. He looked astonished but then shook his head and smiled broadly. He clapped one of his royal attendants on the back—the king of Texcoco, it was.

"You are all just like Cacama!" he exclaimed. "Advocates of the foot!"

He started to laugh, as did all those around him. Then Moctezuma settled himself into a grand litter decorated with hoops of gold and quetzal feathers and began his journey to the summit. Several chieftains and aides followed in a procession of litters.

The Spanish commander began his ascent of the pyramid, followed by a half-dozen lieutenants. Aguilar hurried to keep up. The climb was a steep and taxing enterprise, or at least it was for the Spaniards, who were not in the very peak of physical condition. But Doña Marina found little challenge in the ascent. Nor did Aguilar. They had both lived the hard life of native slaves. Soon they had pulled ahead of the Spanish party.

As they climbed side by side, Marina inveighed against the Aztecs' practice of human sacrifice. She was remarkably well informed, and it occurred to Aguilar that she was indeed a precocious young woman. She told him that these steps had been constructed at a severe angle precisely so that the bodies of the dead would more readily topple to the base, there to be collected and borne away. Aguilar looked carefully down at his feet and noticed that the surface of the rocks did indeed seem blotched and discolored. The spaces between the stones were jammed with some sort of blackened muck. There was a stink in the air, too—a rancid stench, like decomposing flesh. He felt a sour lump rising toward his gullet, higher with each step he climbed. He was tempted to turn around, make some excuse, flee this place. He thought he would be ill. Finally, he could stand it no more. He stopped, turned, began to descend.

"Aguilar. You look wretched. Are you afraid of heights?" This was Cortés, huffing up the stone stairs with his officers. "Do you need some help?"

"No. I am well. It is simply that . . ."

"Yes, yes. Speak up."

"*Mi capitán*," he said. "I should warn you that some of these Aztec practices are likely to offend a Christian sensibility. It is best to be prepared."

"I come in the name of my king and my Savior, Jesus Christ." Cortés straightened his shoulders, but his voice sounded strained, owing to the ascent. "I shall govern myself accordingly. Come. Let us finish this infernal business."

Aguilar gritted his teeth. Some part of him still wished to flee, but he decided to obey his captain's command. He trudged up the remaining stone steps along with the others.

The slaves who bore the emperor made better time than the Spaniards, and Moctezuma was already waiting for them when they reached the summit. He was keenly solicitous of their welfare.

"I hope you are not exhausted from your climb," he said. "I hope you have suffered no ill effects from the ordeal."

Cortés bridled at this idea. Although panting and red-faced from the exertion, he replied that he and his men were glorious warriors who never became tired in the least, no matter what the circumstances, and certainly not on account of so trifling an effort as this. "But I thank you for your concern." He made a crisp little bow.

Moctezuma seemed very impressed. "Never tired?" he repeated. "Never in the least?" Here was even more proof that his guests were divine. The plain fact was that they *had* made the climb on foot, which he regarded as a spectacular accomplishment in itself, something beyond human strength. He did not count women or slaves as human.

In fact, the Spaniards were badly winded from their ascent, and so Moctezuma allowed them a few minutes to recover. Most of them were doubled over, their hands clamped on their knees, while they struggled to bring their breathing back to normal. Up here, the air was perishingly thin.

While the others battled to recover their breath, Aguilar concentrated on his surroundings. Whatever else went on up here, the view was truly splendid. Far below, the city tumbled outward in all directions, with its canals and causeways and countless gardens bursting with shimmering blossoms of every color imaginable. For Aguilar's benefit, and with the help of Doña Marina, the emperor pointed out various sites of particular interest. Over there was the royal menagerie, with its vast collection of animals, every species known to man, including several jaguars and a gallery of dwarfs and albinos and deformed humans. Just beyond it stood the royal aviary, which he called the House of Birds. It was a most luxuriant place, he said, where every known variety of bird was kept in a natural setting of woodlands.

And over to the left was the royal laboratory of medicines, where the finest healers in the empire conducted experiments with all manner of herbs and plants, seeking cures for the myriad illnesses to which men were unfortunately prey. He identified several of the pyramids that surrounded the Great Temple and stood back to let his guests marvel in silence at the glistening blue carpet of the lakes, the proud array of mountains that scaled the heavens on almost all sides, and the shining summits of Popocatépetl and Iztaccíhuatl where they thrust above the rafting clouds.

Aguilar lost himself in the contemplation of this panorama for a time, but then realized that the emperor had begun speaking again. This time, he was addressing Cortés. Moctezuma explained once more that he wished to reveal something of the Aztec gods so that the Spaniards might understand a little of their grandeur. He pointed toward two thatch-covered structures. One he identified as the temple dedicated to Huitzilopochtli, god of the sun, and the other as the shrine to Tlaloc, god of rain. Perched here and there between the two shrines were small stone carvings that Moctezuma said were related to lesser gods, guardians of the main structures.

"And here," he said. He strode over to a great greenish boulder splotched with dark stains. "Here is the *techcatl.*"

Doña Marina worked out the translation in her mind. "The sacrificing stone," she told Aguilar.

"Ah." Aguilar turned to Cortés. "Here, on this stone, is where they sacrifice their victims."

Cortés clenched his jaw. "I see."

Moctezuma then led the party of Spaniards over to the shrine of Huitzilopochtli. As many of them as could fit ducked beneath the edge of the thatch cover and crowded together in the dim interior light. Here, they found an altar surrounded by several hooded priests, who stood in the shadows, wordless, like ghosts. Almost everything seemed to be encrusted with blood. The stench was as sharp as a blow to the head and brought a pool of bile to Aguilar's throat. He had to fight off an impulse to hold shut his nose. This was truly unspeakable.

Moctezuma was in his element now, his voice raised. He was like an actor delivering his lines alone on a stage. He explained that it was here, atop this altar, that the high priests of Huitzilopochtli placed the bodies of their human victims after their hearts had been plucked out. He pointed to several buckets that stood nearby. "We put the hearts in these, before salting them down and burning them in braziers, with scented oil." He turned and led his guests back out into the open air, to show them the sacrificing stone again. "Why, only this morning I . . ."

He rambled on. Cortés listened to the translation in silence, rubbing his beard, shaking his head. He wore a dark scowl on his face.

"It is here," Aguilar told him, "atop this pyramid, that Moctezuma himself, with his own hands, cuts out the hearts of his victims. He has sacrificed hundreds. Thousands."

The emperor carried on speaking, fervid with enthusiasm now, but soon Doña Marina stopped listening. She turned to Aguilar. "You see," she said. "These Aztecs are monsters. This is how they amuse themselves. The killing never stops."

"What does she say?" Cortés grasped Aguilar by the shoulder. "What is she saying?"

Aguilar began to tell him, but managed to speak only a few words before Cortés waved at him to stop. It seemed the Spanish commander had reached the limits of his tolerance. Now quite red in the face and trembling from the head down, Cortés threw up his arms. He marched toward Moctezuma, halted just a pace or two away.

"Stop!" he said. "Stop! Be silent! I will hear no more of this. These are unspeakable acts. May God forgive you."

He began to expound upon the Holy Catholic faith, with Aguilar hastily translating. Speaking for Cortés, Doña Marina described for the emperor the deity that these Spaniards so revered, the one who was *Jesus Cristo*, Savior of mankind, who died for men's sins and was their Lord and the one true God.

When she finished speaking, Cortés drew himself to his full height, which was only a little greater than that of Moctezuma, for he was not a large man. He stepped forward so that he stood with his nose no more than a handsbreadth away from the emperor's own. "I beseech you," he said, "to grant me permission to construct a cross in this place and to put here an image of the Virgin Mother. Such holy relics will surely bring far greater fortune to you than any number of these wicked shrines."

When he understood all that had been said to him, Moctezuma turned quite pale. What was this? A direct insult to his gods? Sensing his alarm, a few of his chieftains reached for their daggers and looked ready to make a fight of it. The Spaniards stepped forward, rattling their swords. For a few moments, it seemed as if the two sides would fling themselves at each other's throats.

Finally, it was Moctezuma who prevented the shedding of blood. He ordered his men to stand down. He turned to Cortés and declared that he wished to hear no more on this subject. "We request that you leave this place," he said. "Go now, at once, while we remain behind to attend to our prayers and our sacrifices. Amends must be made to Huitzilopochtli for the injuries that have been done to him today."

Cortés agreed to withdraw, but he did so angrily, without any hint of backing down. "Come, men. Let us depart this sickening place." He turned and began to climb down the long, steep steps that tumbled to the base of the pyramid.

Before following his commander, Aguilar looked around a last time and caught the eye of Pitoque.

"Greetings," he said, speaking in the Maya tongue. He found it an effort to keep his voice steady, to control his breathing. "I see that you have come up in the world. I see that you now consort with kings."

The merchant gave a thin smile. "I consort with whomever destiny places in my path. And you?"

Aguilar nodded. "The same."

"It seems we have something in common then."

"It seems we do."

The two men held each other's gaze a few moments, and then Aguilar turned and hastened down the steps of the pyramid, taking pains not to slip on the stains of clotted blood. The city sprawled beneath him out to the shores of Lake Texcoco, unaccountably beautiful, like a purse of jewels upturned upon a bolt of blue.

The Legend of Popocatépetl

"Listen. Just listen to this." Ometzin closed her eyes, and her shoulders began to sway in time with the melody. She said, "He's returning now, to find that she is dead."

In a small square by the edge of a moonlit lagoon, a dozen flautists were performing a work by one of the city's finest composers—Balpantl was his name. Ometzin said the piece was among her favorites. In the language of music, it recounted the legend of Popocatépetl, a great warrior who hundreds of years earlier had married a young princess named Iztaccíhuatl. Soon after their wedding, he went off to fight in wars of conquest far away, and for many years, he did not come back. Alone and stricken with grief; Iztaccíhuatl pined away until at last she gave up hope of her husband's return. She lost her desire to live and, in a tumult of sorrow, she died. Some time later, Popocatépetl came home from his battles. When he discovered what had happened during his absence, he flew into a rage of self-hatred and remorse, but there was nothing he could do to restore his bride to life. Instead, he laid her body atop the mountain that now bears her name. He took up a position at the summit of an adjoining peak, armed only with a flaming torch, and determined to serve forever as the sentinel of his fallen queen.

The final notes of the piece were played with a deep, quaking resonance that truly seemed to suggest the slow fire of a distant volcano. Ometzin sighed and shook her head.

"Beautiful," she said. "Have you ever heard anything more beautiful?"

Maxtla had indeed found the music strangely moving, but he did not like to admit it. He did not like to admit anything that reflected well upon the Aztecs. Earlier that evening, he had scoffed when Ometzin had explained the ancient legend of the two mountains. He had said that he didn't understand why the warrior, on learning his wife was dead, hadn't simply gone back to what he obviously loved best—the fighting of battles. That was what he, Maxtla, would have done. Fighting would have been much more exciting than clutching a torch on a mountaintop for the rest of a man's life.

"Not for the rest of his life," Ometzin had said. "Forever. For all eternity. Don't you understand? That's what the story is about—that wars are fleeting but love is eternal."

"Eternal, perhaps. But tedious, from the sound of it."

"Believe that if you wish," she had said. "But come to the concert with me. I have a feeling it will change your mind."

And, in a way, it had. But he was too stubborn to say so. As they filed out of the darkened plaza along with the rest of the audience, he would admit only that the experience had not been as miserable as he had feared.

"Ha!" She flung out her hands in a show of frustration. "I know what that means. That means you actually loved it, but your pride will not let you say so. Instead, you pucker up your nose"—here she scrunched up her own—"and you mumble, '*Oh, well, at least I didn't hate it.*'" She shook her head, and her long black hair glimmered in the moonlight "Why don't you simply admit the truth? You loved the music, did you not?"

He smiled, amazed at how easily she could see through him. It was a talent possessed by no one else he'd ever encountered—except perhaps Azotl. The master functionary had a similar ability to know what he was thinking or feeling even better than Maxtla did himself. Perhaps she had acquired the talent from Azotl. Still, he was reluctant to say anything good about Aztecs.

Instead, he laughed. He said, "I will admit this much. The Aztecs may be able to play fine music. But that doesn't mean they aren't a bunch of—"

"Shhh." She put a hand to her mouth and gave him a look that he had seen once or twice before—the look of a person one would not be inclined to cross. "Do not speak in that way. Not here. Not in public."

They walked back to Azotl's house in silence. A cool breeze blew off the lake, and Maxtla allowed himself a smirk of satisfaction, knowing she would not be able to see it. He'd proved one thing—no one could speak his mind in this place. That demonstrated what tyrants the Aztecs were. He felt he had won this round.

Not that it was a contest exactly. For several days now, Azotl's niece had set herself the challenge of proving to Maxtla that the Aztecs were not the unredeemed monsters he believed them to be. She had coaxed him to musical concerts, much like the one they had just attended. She took him to plays staged by companies of dramatic players, to readings given by the greatest poets of Tenochtitlán, to performances of dance. She dragged him out to galleries where fine stone sculptures were on display in handsome, airy settings. She ate with him at some of the city's best dining establishments. She led him through topiary gardens and menageries, laboratories and observatories, and tomorrow she was to accompany him to the House of Birds, the great royal aviary, where almost every species of bird in the empire was represented, all in the most natural settings imaginable. She had warned him that if; after all this, he did not recognize that there was more to the Aztecs than wars of conquest, then something was wrong with him—not with the Aztecs.

They turned a corner and began to walk along a darkened lane that led to the entrance of Azotl's house. The way ahead was empty now, and Maxtla felt he could speak openly.

"You know, I never said that all the Aztecs do is fight wars of conquest. I am quite aware that they have other talents."

"At last." Ometzin took his arm. "At last, the Cholulan hero admits it. He—"

"For example, they're superior at human sacrifice. They

are experts at cutting people open and tearing out their hearts. That skill must be worth something, don't you think? How would you feel about your beloved Aztecs if they had sacrificed someone you knew, if they had torn open someone you loved . . . ?"

Maxtla let his voice trail off, realizing he had gone too far. He was not certain why, but he sensed it was so. While he'd been speaking, Ometzin's manner had changed completely. Her shoulders had slumped, and she had let go of his arm. Now she stalked ahead, soon leaving him several paces behind. She did not say another word.

Neither did he. He followed her back to Azotl's house, where a fire was burning against the evening chill. What had he said that was so wrong? Everyone knew about the Aztecs and their human sacrifices. It was horrible, but it was true.

Run Like the Wind

The Aztecs' imperial agent on the far eastern coast was a laconic man by the name of Qualpopoca. On this particular afternoon, he was lounging on a large boulder beneath the broad shade of a cashew tree, smoking his pipe and nodding patiently as a hugely obese individual held court. The other gentleman's name was Tlacochcalcatl—known hereabouts as "the fat chieftain"—and he was leader of the people in this place called Cempoala.

Normally, Tlacochcalcatl was a reasonable man, someone

Qualpopoca could do business with—but not today. Not, in truth, for quite a while. This was the third time in recent days that Qualpopoca had stopped by Cempoala in order to speak with the chieftain. So far, the agent had been rebuffed on each occasion. Now it was happening again. Presumably, the refusal to pay tribute had to do with these strange beings that had come and were now bustling about to the south—a huge and perplexing mystery. But Qualpopoca had received no instructions from Tenochtitlán that anything was to change as a result. As far as he knew, he was to continue on as before. Here in Cempoala, however, that was not proving easy.

Qualpopoca took another puff of his pipe and shook his head. Tlacochcalcatl was in an especially prickly mood today, and worse, he would not shut up. He droned on and on as though he were trying to set some sort of record for verbosity, but finally he rounded to his point.

"In conclusion," he said, "the payment of all tribute is suspended immediately."

Hmm. Qualpopoca tapped his pipe on the rock and shifted sideways so that he could reach his pouch of tobacco. "All tribute?" he said. "You know, that decision seems somewhat excessive to me."

"Excessive or not, it is my decision." Tlacochcalcatl thrust out his many chins. He wore a loincloth of cotton and a leather chest halter, neither of which, despite their best efforts, had much hope of containing his immense girth. He sprawled in every direction, bearing a greater resemblance to some odd feature of geography—a reclining mountain, say—than to a mortal man. "It is my decision to make, and I have made it."

"Your decision?" Qualpopoca relit his pipe with a burning branch from the small fire at his side. He tossed the branch back onto the flames. "I was not aware that you could impose your decisions upon me."

"I am doing so now."

"Ah. I see." Qualpopoca pondered this response. He prided himself on being a cautious man and a just one. In the region around Cempoala, here on the eastern coast, he was the chief Aztec agent, and his duties included the collection and tabulation of tribute payable to his emperor, Moctezuma II. Now this fellow Tlacochcalcatl seemed to have other ideas. "Perhaps," said Qualpopoca, "I could work out a deal with you. These are unusual times. These strangers, for example—they have introduced a new and unpredictable element. For the time being, the future does seem uncertain. I appreciate that. But a complete suspension of tribute?" He shook his head. "I'm afraid my masters in Tenochtitlán would have difficulty accepting such a decision. They would consider me derelict, and they would not be pleased. Nor would I. What I suggest instead is that you pay out some portion of your normal tribute. It needn't be a great deal. It could be a token. Some salt cakes. A few dozen tortoise shells. But I must have something to show—to demonstrate your good faith and my own attention to my duties. Be reasonable, man."

But Tlacochcalcatl would not be moved. He knew that these gods were constructing a settlement of their own, not far to the south, at a place they called Veracruz, and he had heard of their victories at Tlaxcala and Cholula. He felt sure that he could stand up to this officious Aztec minion who now stood before him, this Qualpopoca. If the Aztecs tried to do him any harm, the gods would come to his aid. They were his allies, after all—and, beyond that, they were divine. He had loaned them his finest warriors, which made him doubly certain that they would stand by him. He understood that they could kill without making any sort of physical contact with their victims. A puff of smoke—and, just like that, a man was dead. A smoking machine. That would be something to see.

Qualpopoca drew on his pipe and frowned in concentration. If only he had received clear instructions from Tenochtitlán, these negotiations would be so much easier. But he hadn't. At the first sign of these troubles, he'd dispatched a runner to the capital with a request for guidance. He wanted instructions from Azotl, the master functionary, and from no one else. But so far he'd heard nothing back. That wasn't surprising—Tenochtitlán was a long way away—but it was disturbing nonetheless. Qualpopoca found himself operating in complete darkness. He tried to think what he ought to do and finally decided that, instructions or no instructions, he simply could not abide Tlacochcalcatl's intransigence. The man had spurned every attempt at compromise. If this sort of behavior were allowed to spread, the empire would collapse like a chair without legs.

Qualpopoca withdrew his pipe and waved to his captain, who stood nearby with a staff of six Aztec guards. He waved toward the fat chieftain. "Put this man under arrest," he said.

"Do not hurt him, but make sure he doesn't get away."

The order was carried out at once. In fact, the last instruction was laughable. The chieftain was far too fat to move, much less flee. He swore and huffed, made a token resistance, but that was all. He called to his own guards, but they had already been disabled—a precaution Qualpopoca had taken before even initiating this discussion. Tlacochcalcatl had no choice but to submit, which he did, albeit with a scowl that wobbled down through his half-dozen chins.

So far, so good. Qualpopoca promptly dispatched another runner to Tenochtitlán, with orders to seek out the master functionary, tell him what had happened, and obtain instructions concerning what ought to be done now. He made a special effort to impress upon the messenger the need to travel as quickly as possible. Speed was of the greatest importance, considering that word of the chieftain's arrest and capture would spread quickly. It would soon come to the attention of the gods at Veracruz. Who knew what would happen then? Qualpopoca started to wonder if perhaps he had acted rather precipitately by ordering this arrest. But it was too late to change his mind now. He took the runner by both shoulders and gave him a shake.

"*As fast as you can,*" he repeated. "Understand? Run like the wind. Now go."

The messenger's name was Salchan, and he nodded several times to show that he understood his mission perfectly. He turned and set off at once at a brisk pace. He kept up this speed for a while, at least until he was out of sight of

Cempoala. But then he slowed to a leisurely trot, and finally to a walk, and not a brisk walk, either—more a shambling gait. He stretched out his arms and yawned. In truth, he was not inclined to run all the way to Tenochtitlán, no matter what Qualpopoca had said.

A few minutes later, he glanced up at the sky and saw that the sun was almost directly overhead. No wonder he was so tired. It was noon, the hottest time of the day. He looked about and saw some bushes that seemed reasonably inviting. He crawled under them, made himself comfortable, and yawned again. A man had his entitlements, and a midday nap was near the top of Salchan's list. He would get to Tenochtitlán. He had orders, and he would obey them. But all in good time. What was the rush? A fellow needed his rest. He bunched up some leaves to serve as a pillow, put down his head, and soon fell fast asleep.

The House of Birds

It was the sky blue start of a gorgeous day, and Ometzin led Maxtla out to the royal aviary, known as the House of Birds.

"Prepare to be overwhelmed," she told him. "If you are not impressed by this, I shall abandon all hope."

"I've seen birds before."

"Have you *indeed?*" She shook her head in a mockery of amazement. "My boy, is there *nothing* you haven't done?"

Maxtla decided not to take the bait. He had offended Ometzin enough the evening before with his remarks about human sacrifice, and now he was wary of what he said. Girls. They were so sensitive.

He followed Ometzin through a succession of streets, most of them dotted with people going about their daily business. Here and there, they had to pick their way through a series of freshly dug pits and trenches. The Spaniards—with gangs of Aztec laborers—were out at all hours now, searching for treasure. They seemed to believe that if they dug, they would find gold.

Ometzin rolled her eyes and hurried past another site of excavation. She had a poor opinion of these Spaniards and had resolved, for the time being, simply to ignore them.

"Come," she said. "It's not much farther."

"Why rush?" said Maxtla. "We have the day."

As it turned out, they would need it. The House of Birds was every bit as impressive as Ometzin had promised. Of all the attractions of Tenochtitlán that he had seen thus far, it was the aviary that Maxtla loved best. He and Ometzin spent hours that day wandering through the lush grounds. The place sweltered with dampness, teemed with orchids and ferns, vines and creepers. Small streams meandered through the trees. Rushes gathered in emerald bunches by the banks, which were carpeted in long, feathery grass. Maxtla felt as if they were lost in a jungle somewhere, at the very edges of the empire. And yet flagstone walkways wandered through the foliage, and the entire aviary was enclosed by high stone walls. Overhead dangled a woven canopy of maguey fiber, suspended upon the crests of royal palms, to keep the birds within. In truth, the House of Birds was a kind of gigantic cage.

Ometzin proved to be an expert on birds. She said the aviary contained more than a thousand different varieties, and Maxtla found it easy to believe her. The place was bursting with the creatures. It echoed with the squawking calls of toucans and macaws. Parrots and cockatoos flashed through the leaves. Buzzards thrashed in the highest branches. Eagles perched themselves at the height of a rocky fastness. Each turn of every path brought Maxtla almost within arm's reach of another species of bird. Ducks and geese drifted in circles upon the small eddies of the streams. Herons and cranes strutted along the edges of glassy ponds. Hawks and jacamars swerved overhead. In a slow blur of rose streaks and splashing water, a flock of flamingos raced forward, then flattened themselves out and strained into flight. Once, Maxtla thought he caught sight of a quetzal, the most sacred of birds. Brighter than any emerald, carrying a long shimmering train of plumage, it drifted through a clearing just ahead and quickly vanished.

"Sly ones, those," said Ometzin. "One moment, you see them. The next, they are gone."

She had a genius for spotting different birds, many of which wore camouflage plumage and were nearly invisible against the forested backdrop. But Ometzin could make them out, and she guided Maxtla's gaze until he, too, could see. She rattled off their names, along with detailed information about their songs, their habitat, their ways. It was if she carried them all inside her head.

In the past, Maxtla had seen wildlife in a kind of haze, thought of animals as little more than so many extensions of his surroundings, creatures that served the purposes of men, or failed to, and had little importance beyond this. Unlike his father, he had no faith in the idea that birds embodied omens, one foretelling this, another presaging that. But under Ometzin's guidance, he began to see the birds through her eyes, as beings that were whole and entire in themselves. If men had never appeared upon the surface of the earth, these birds would still be here, arching overhead or tiptoeing through the shallows of ponds, rippling the surface of watery mirrors. They existed for themselves.

"Come," said Ometzin. "There is much more to see."

The girl was tireless. For hours, she led Maxtla through the aviary. Finally, the light began to grow dim, and she said it was time to think about leaving. Neither of them had eaten anything since that morning, and a day of tramping had left them both feeling hungry. Maxtla did not mind admitting that his legs were sore.

He looked at her. "And yours?"

She smiled. "Of course. My legs feel dead. I cannot remember when I have walked this long without a rest."

"Why did you not speak?"

"What? And admit that I could not keep up with you? Never."

He was about to say that this was absurd, but he realized that, in her place, he would have behaved exactly the same way. He said, "I see you are cursed with a competitive spirit."

She laughed. "That is one word for it. I have subjected myself to regular torments in order to purge this defect from my character. All in vain, so far."

"It's not entirely a defect, I would say."

She looked at him. "You are not a woman."

He pondered her words. "No. But then, neither are you."

"I am fourteen years old. Most of my friends are married already."

"You wish to get married?"

Her eyes grew large and round. "Absolutely not."

"What then?"

She shrugged. "That is the problem. If not marriage, then what?"

Maxtla had an inspiration. "I have an idea. I'd guess you are a virgin. Am I right?"

She seemed genuinely shocked. "What sort of question is that?"

Maxtla frowned. "I just thought that since you are from the highlands . . ."

"Oh, you mean rather than from the coast? The hedonists by the sea?"

He looked at his feet. It was exactly what he'd been thinking. The distinction was well known—the propriety of the cool highlands versus the casual ways of the sultry coast. "I simply meant—"

"Oh, it doesn't matter." She waved at the air. "A virgin? Of course, I am. My uncle has seen to that."

Maxtla smiled, a little bolder now. "Then my idea is perfect."

"What is this magnificent idea?"

"You have the essential qualification to offer yourself up as a candidate for sacrifice. You would be ideal. Young. Unmarried. They'd wrap you in flowers. They'd rub copal all over you. They'd lay you out on the sacrificing stone, plunge a knife into you . . ." His voice faded.

Something was wrong. Once again, he'd raised the subject of human sacrifice, and it was having the same effect as it had done the night before. Some perversity had overcome him, to speak of this again, and now, already, Ometzin had turned around and was storming away. She rounded a stand of rushes and vanished beyond a wall of high ferns and dangling vines. He started to follow her, his anger beginning to rise as it always did when he thought of the Aztecs and their gory ways, their sacrifices. What was wrong with the girl?

Maxtla hurried after her, wondering what had possessed him and angered her. He lowered his head and ducked through a dark tunnel of greenery. Beyond it, the path turned sharply to the left around a thicket of squat palm trees, and in a small clearing he came upon a garden of flowers, bathed in the afternoon light, where dozens of hummingbirds darted from blossom to blossom. Ometzin was nowhere to be seen. Just hummingbirds. They were enchanting creatures, but he loathed what they reminded him of—Huitzilopochtli, the hummingbird god of the Aztecs. Suddenly, the plume of anger in his chest surged up and exploded. He waded in among the flowers, batting at the birds and kicking at the flowering plants. He waved his arms and shouted a string of curses.

In the end, it took three Aztec guards to subdue him. In Tenochtitlán, it was a sacrilege to cause deliberate harm to a hummingbird. Maxtla spent that night in a dirty, unlit cell buried beneath a building he could not name.

All Spears Draw Blood

Azotl pushed aside his meal—fried gecko with peanuts, sprinkled with ants' eggs, normally among his favorite dishes. Strange and unsettling though it was, he seldom felt very hungry nowadays. Food, usually among his greatest pleasures, had lost its appeal. He ate but could not seem to taste. Now he wiped his lips. He eyed this latest messenger who had come from Cempoala on the eastern coast, with news from Qualpopoca, the Aztec agent.

Qualpopoca was an excellent official, but Azotl did not think much of his choice in runners. Salchan, he said his name was, but he sounded as if he was lying about even that. He had a shifty look and an evasive manner. Still, he seemed intelligent, and the situation he described was evidently very delicate. Azotl crossed his arms.

"Tell your master," he said, "that under no circumstances is he to engage in any armed hostilities with the Spaniards. None whatsoever. To ensure that peace is maintained, he must release the chieftain at once and retreat. I cannot stress this order too strongly. Under no circumstances is there to be bloodshed. Do you understand?"

Salchan said that he did.

"Good," said Azotl. "Now, go."

When the messenger had left him, the master functionary slumped at his desk. He realized that he'd just entrusted a matter of the greatest importance to a runner he did not know, one whose reliability might well be subject to question. He hauled himself to his feet. Was he losing his mind? He waddled across the stone floor, meaning to call out after the man, tell him to stop, wait. And then what? Azotl slowed to a halt. What could he do? Submit the fellow to some sort of test? A series of questions, perhaps? What questions?

He frowned, unaccustomed to this pestering tremor of indecision. The presence of these Spaniards upset him—that was it. Everywhere he turned, there they were. It looked as if they had conquered the city without even striking a blow. Their presence had rattled his nerves. He was fearful now of everything, of phantoms and shadows—he, the Keeper of the House of Darkness. And now this. He decided he was working himself into a panic over nothing, a trifle. Let the runner go. He turned, made his way back to his working table and settled himself there. He had plenty of other matters to worry about.

For one, he'd learned only the night before that Maxtla—the little fool—had got himself into trouble again. Ometzin had rushed into the house, all out of breath, to tell him the story. The idiot had flown into a tantrum and had plowed his way into the garden of the hummingbirds at the royal aviary. He had offered insults to the Aztecs' most sacred god. Apparently, it had taken three guards several minutes to wrestle him to the ground.

Azotl had determined the boy's whereabouts almost immediately. Beneath the palace of Moctezuma I—great-grandfather of the current ruler—an underground prison was maintained for just this purpose. He sent an aide there to confirm Maxtla's presence and to make certain the imp was safe and hadn't been harmed. Then he concluded that one night in detention might not hurt the boy. There the matter had rested, until now. Today, he decided he would wait a while longer. Later, he would arrange for Maxtla's release. Curse the child! What was he so angry at?

In fact, Azotl knew. Injustice. The boy was angry at injustice. And there was something about Maxtla's fervor that impressed the master functionary, that reminded Azotl of his own youth. He, too, had been passionate in his convictions but reckless in his behavior—because he had been unsure of his own worth. It wasn't until someone else—an older, wiser man—had entrusted him with an astonishing confidence, a secret of almost unimaginable power, that Azotl had come to believe in himself. He had kept that secret ever since, and now he was the master functionary, the tlillancalqui, the Keeper of the House of Darkness.

When he looked at Maxtla, he saw himself—a storming mass of possibilities requiring only the ballast of confidence in order to realize great things. Azotl decided what he would do. One day, the secret would have to be shared, or it would perish altogether, and now was the time. He would tell Maxtla. He shifted in his seat and nodded to himself. Now was certainly the time.

This very afternoon, he would see that the boy was released from detention. Then he would accompany him to the royal aviary. He would pass the secret on there, for it was not in the

House of Darkness that the secret resided. It resided in the House of Birds.

Now that he had made his decision, Azotl felt calmer than he had in days. He reached for the leg of gecko on his plate. It was cold now, but that did not matter. He had got a bit of his old appetite back. He began to eat.

The garrison commander at Veracruz was Juan de Escalante, an old man now, but once a hero of the *Reconquista* and the war against the damned Saracens. He was in his makeshift office, prying grit from beneath his fingernails, when an orderly rushed in to report an outrage that had taken place a little to the north, at Cempoala. The bloody Aztecs had seized a local potentate—the fat chieftain, no less. Immediately, Escalante leapt to his feet. This was intolerable. The fat chieftain was a Spanish ally!

Escalante decided that here was a good chance to serve up a little taste of Castilian iron, a diversion that he and his men had so far found little opportunity to enjoy. Why did everyone else get all the sport? He'd heard about the fighting at Tlaxcala. He'd heard about the great victory at Cholula. Damn, that sounded like fun. Escalante was pleased to know that some of his compatriots were amusing themselves, but what about him? What about his men?

Now, here was news of an injury to the honor of the Spanish crown. Cempoala was not far away, just a short ride to the north. The entire affair could be settled in a day, two at the outside. He was fairly confident he had the situation straight in his mind, allowing for a certain margin of error owing to this confounded difficulty with languages. Typically, translating a single sentence took about an hour of verbal wrangling. But if the Aztecs were throwing their weight around, Escalante was not going to sit still for it—not he, who had fought hand-to-hand against the Moorish infidels at Melilla and still bore the scars.

He quickly put together a small force of a dozen stout-hearted Spaniards, backed by a hundred of the Totonac scrappers. He debated leaving his second-in-command, Alonso Puertocarrero, in charge of the garrison at Veracruz. On second thought, he decided to bring the man along. God in heaven, he deserved a little recreation as much as the next man. Besides, Escalante rather hoped that Puertocarrero might put in a good word for him one day with his cousin by marriage, the Count of Medellín. A little favor now could do no harm.

The Spaniards under Escalante saddled their horses, mustered their infantry, and set off. The muggy coastal breeze ruffled the plume on Escalante's helmet, and he felt better than he had since the grand old days of separating Saracen heads from Saracen bodies on the north coast of Africa. He might almost have been Cortés himself as he rode at the head of his troops. At every village they passed, all eyes were on him, a distinctly invigorating sensation—and a well-deserved one. He had seen his duty, after all, and now he would perform it. He would show these meddling Aztecs who was who and what was what. They would either release the fat chieftain or they'd have an encounter with Spanish swordplay to remember. By God, they would.

Escalante shouted to Puertocarrero to give way. The man had an annoying habit of pushing his own mount into the lead. The garrison commander jabbed his spurs into his horse's flanks, and the beast leapt to the side and did a merry dance, sending up cries of panic from all the natives who had gathered to watch the procession. They began to scatter and run.

"¡Váyanse! ¡Váyanse!" Escalante shouted. He drew his sword and halved, then quartered, the leaden tropical air. "*Váyanse, todos!*"

Ah, this was excellent sport.

"Perhaps—and I offer this merely as a hypothesis—perhaps you should have considered the consequences of your actions before you went wading into that flower garden." The master functionary fumbled for the stoppered jug of chrysanthemum water he had brought with him. "Would you not agree?"

Maxtla clenched his teeth. "Yes, sir," he said.

"I mean to say, you must have known that the hummingbird is sacred to Tenochtitlán. You did know that, I take it?"

Maxtla nodded.

"And do you think, when their sacred emblems are desecrated, that people will not take it as an injury?" He poured a portion of the sweet water into a small gourd and drank. "Do you?"

"No, sir."

"And do you think it unjust that people, once offended, might demand that a punishment be meted out to those who have done them harm? Some chrysanthemum water?"

"Yes, please, sir." Maxtla accepted the gourd. In fact, his throat was painfully dry. "No, sir."

"Then it seems we are making progress."

Maxtla and Azotl were seated amid the long grass by the shores of the artificial lagoon, near the heart of the House of Birds. Across the water, a lone heron poked through a clump of rushes on the opposite shore. A macaw sang in the trees.

"What I detest," said Maxtla, "are the human sacrifices. It would be different if you Aztecs just sacrificed each other, but you don't. You capture people from other tribes. Or you demand more victims as tribute." Maxtla shook his head. "I trampled on some flowers, I swatted at some hummingbirds— I admit it. But I did not kill anyone."

Azotl unstoppered the jug again and drank more chrysanthemum water. He nodded his great, bejowled head.

Maxtla wound his arms around his knees. "There's something I don't understand."

"What is that?"

"Every time I so much as mention the words 'human sacrifice' to Ometzin, she behaves as though I have just committed the worst crime in the history of the world. But I am not the one tearing people open and ripping out their hearts. Why does she feel so angry at me?"

"Maxtla," said Azotl, "you should not be so quick to judge

the behavior of others. These human sacrifices—I agree, they are troubling. But they are not without a certain logic. It takes time and thought to understand them, but it is not impossible. And with regard to Ometzin, you do not know her history."

"Her history?"

"To begin with, she is not Aztec."

"What is she?"

"She is from Cholula, in fact. Just like yourself."

"But her accent. It's—"

"I agree. She speaks with only the faintest traces of Cholula, a certain sing-song quality in her voice. She was brought to Tenochtitlán at a very young age. Her parents were from Cholula as well."

"I thought she was your niece."

"I will explain. Her parents were both victims of the very system you decry."

"They were sacrificed?"

Azotl inclined his head. "They were."

"She knows this?"

"She does now. For a long time, I kept it from her. But I am a believer in the efficacy of the truth."

"How did you tell her?"

"As gently as possible. It is not a pretty tale."

"And yet she remains here? If I were in her place, I'd run away. I'd take up arms. I'd—"

"But you are not in her place." Azotl gave the boy a stern look. "For many years, she has thought of herself as an Aztec. She has believed that I am her uncle."

"Why did you tell her that? Why pretend that you were related to her?"

"It was a necessary lie."

Maxtla frowned. A necessary lie? Here was a new idea, or at least an old idea newly formulated. Now that he thought about it, he realized that he was already familiar with the concept, although he had never heard it expressed in these words. It was true—some lies had to be told. He rubbed his jaw, which had lately sprouted several sparse whiskers. "How did she come to be in your care?"

Azotl gazed across the water. "She'd been abandoned. A certain merchant found her and would have kept her himself rather than let her die. But I happened to see her and I took a liking. I wanted to care for her myself, provide myself with a companion, a daughter, a niece. I had led a lonely life. Of course, she was only an infant then."

The master functionary took another sip of chrysanthemum water. When offered some, Maxtla drank as well.

Now Azotl returned to the subject of human sacrifice. He confessed that he himself did not agree with the practice. At one time, it had seemed necessary. Many years ago, a drought and then a famine had ravaged the Aztec world, and the time of hunger had finally been brought to an end by a vigorous campaign of human sacrifices, or so the people had believed. Since then, the Aztecs had operated on the conviction that these deaths were essential, the engine of the cosmos.

"But more recent history belies this belief," Azotl said. "We have suffered droughts and other hardship, and the sacrifices seem to have done no good at all. There are two schools of thought as to why. According to one, we have somehow displeased the gods and must therefore redouble our sacrifices in order to placate them."

"And the other?"

He massaged his several chins. "The opposing view holds that these sacrifices are worthless now and always have been. The gods do not demand them. I suppose they serve a practical purpose as an instrument of authority. It is no easy matter to maintain control over so vast a region. Terror plays a useful role, at least in the short term. But, over time, I wonder if we are not sowing the seeds of our demise. I wish we were better supplied with friends—now more than ever."

"You are worried about the Spaniards?"

"Of course."

"Do you think they are evil?"

Azotl shrugged. "I am not a priest. Good and evil are not my domain. I think that they are dangerous. Extremely dangerous."

"Are they gods?"

"I doubt it. I'm not sure whether that makes much difference. No matter what we call them, they can do us great harm. Out on the eastern coast, there are troubles already. These Spaniards are already establishing a garrison and some kind of settlement not far from Cempoala. They have sunk all of their floating palaces, as you know. And now they are interfering with my agents, preventing them from collecting tribute. I have issued strict instructions to my people—they must be cautious. They must avoid armed conflict at whatever cost. But it is just a matter of time. Soldiers do not carry weapons in jest. Sooner or later, all spears draw blood."

"Do you predict war?"

"I predict trouble, whatever you call it." The master functionary suddenly straightened up. He pointed directly ahead. "Look. Look now. Do you see?"

Maxtla peered across the lagoon, and he did see—a splendid quetzal sailing above the water like a green emperor in flight. An instant later, it was swallowed by the dense froth of foliage and shadow.

"This is the sad truth about quetzals," said Azotl. "All glimpses of them are fleeting—unless the creatures are dead."

He heaved a sigh and began to fidget with the jug of chrysanthemum water, now empty. Maxtla stole a glance at the man and was surprised to see that his eye was glistening, as if at any moment the master functionary might lapse into tears.

"I have many fears," said Azotl, his voice laboring under some clash of emotions. "I am afraid that very dark times lie ahead. I have wracked my brains about what we might do. It was my opinion that we should never have allowed these Spaniards to enter Tenochtitlán, but on this I was overruled." He shook his head. "But they are here now, and whether they are gods or men, I believe we will soon regret their presence. I regret it already."

For a time, Azotl was silent, and the two of them simply gazed at the opposite shore of the lagoon, where the lone heron had been joined by a second. Now both creatures paraded through the shallows like the most delicate of characters in calligraphy, dancing across a green scroll. Maxtla said nothing, simply waited for the older man to speak, wondering what the master functionary was leading to. All sorts of possibilities darted through his mind, but none of them came close to the truth on that afternoon by the water's edge in the House of Birds.

Azotl turned to Maxtla and fixed him with a cold, hard gaze. "Can I trust you to keep a secret?"

At first, Maxtla did not reply. In truth, he was not sure.

"Can I?"

"Ye-es."

"Are you certain? What I am going to tell you may be the salvation of us both. The salvation of many. Can I trust you?"

"Yes."

"Good."

During the next several minutes, the master functionary divulged to Maxtla something known to no one else in the empire ruled by the Aztecs, a secret hidden here in the royal aviary. When he had finished speaking, the two of them contemplated the patterns of shadow and light that played across the smooth surface of the water.

Finally, it was the master functionary who found his voice again. "They say that knowledge is power," he said. "Let this be ours."

"Our knowledge?"

"Our power. To use when the time comes."

The Future of the Empire

Salchan slouched through the scrub growth scattered across the steamy coastal flats. He made no particular effort to go any faster. Instead, he proceeded at a comfortable, deliberate pace, one that suited his temperament.

Some said he was lazy, but Salchan preferred to think of himself as realistic. "Run like the wind," they told him. But why? What difference did it make? He could run like the wind or slither like the mud, and the results were the same, as far as he was concerned. A few cacao beans and something miserable to eat. Besides, the high-and-mighties were always in such a hurry. Everything had to be done at once. Everything was so desperately important—the Future of the Empire and so on. And maybe it was important. To them.

Salchan let his mind wander over these and other grievances as he ambled along the narrow trail in the sweltering heat. Every few steps, to amuse himself further, he kicked at a small, rounded stone. The vegetation in these parts was monotonously low and boggy. It never varied. The sun beat down with withering intensity. Salchan soon felt himself growing drowsy, and as he grew drowsy, his head began to ache, as if the rays of the sun were penetrating his skull and singeing whatever lay within. Before long, he wanted only to find some shaded spot where a sane man might curl up and fall asleep. He began to lurch as he walked, as if he might simply collapse in the middle of the track.

He forgot to kick the stone and left it behind him. In fact, he forgot about practically everything and so was taken entirely by surprise when a trio of Totonac warriors leapt out of the scrub growth with their spears raised. If he had been more alert, he might have turned and tried to escape. But then, they likely would have taken him down with their spears. As it was, he was too sleepy to run. So they captured him alive.

They promptly bound his thumbs behind his back with a length of maguey fiber, and were soon hustling him along the path, letting out idiotic war whoops and prodding at him every three steps with the tips of their spears. Salchan found that his brain had cleared remarkably. It was evident that these cackling, bloodthirsty dolts were taking him somewhere specific, presumably for some concrete purpose. If that purpose included interrogation, he decided, he would not resist. Not for an instant. He would speak, and he would speak in a fashion likely to produce the result he most keenly desired—his personal salvation. He would tell his interrogators whatever they wished to hear. To determine what that might be, he would have to keep his mind sharply focused and supremely alert. This was not easy, not with these three lunatic warriors leaping and twirling around him, shrieking and brandishing their spears. Nonetheless, as Salchan stumbled east, his brain whirred like the wind. Among his worries, the future of the Aztec empire ranked extremely low, if it registered at all.

Maxtla tramped along the shore of Lake Texcoco not far from Azotl's house. Every few feet, he crouched down and hunted about for a good skipping stone—flat, with slightly rounded edges, and of a size that would nestle comfortably between his thumb and first finger. When he found one, he straightened up, assumed a throwing stance—knees bent, body twisted, right arm well back—and then whipped the stone out across the lake shallows. So far, his best throw had taken ten separate skips before sinking. He was trying to improve on that score—or he had been.

Now he found he no longer cared whether the stones skipped, sank, or sprouted wings and flew to the summit of Popocatépetl. What he was thinking about now, as he pottered along the pebbly edge of the lake, was this secret that the master functionary had told him. His feelings alternated between pride that Azotl had chosen to tell him, of all people, and amazement that the master functionary could have been so rash. On the one hand, he felt an unfamiliar glow of warmth to think that Azotl had such confidence in him. It made him think that he might be worthy of the man's faith. On the other hand, maybe he was not. Maybe Azotl was mistaken. After all, what sort of man trusts a mere boy with one of the greatest secrets of an empire? Perhaps the master functionary had gone mad.

All Maxtla had to do now was take this information over to the palace of Axayácatl, seek out Doña Marina and inform her of what he now knew, and he would instantly become the toast of the Spaniards. They would sing his praises and reward him with one of their great shining swords and a helmet with a purple plume. They would teach him to ride about on one of their giant deer. They would tutor him in their language and instruct him in Spanish customs of personal hygiene so that one day he, too, might smell as richly as they did. In time, he would become a Spaniard himself. And all he had to do, in exchange for this unimaginable glory, was present himself at the palace of Axayácatl and say a few words. It was as simple as that.

So, why didn't he do it?

To Maxtla's surprise, some strange scruple kept getting in the way, like a physical barrier in his path. He had given his word to Azotl that he would share the information with no one, unless it were a matter of life or death. He walked on for a minute or so, troubled by this thought. No doubt about it, he had given his word. He hopped over a narrow stream and scrambled up a cut-stone embankment. That was undeniable. He had pledged an oath. But what of it? If the master functionary was foolish enough to entrust his secrets so carelessly, then he deserved to be betrayed. Did he not? Besides, who was to say what was a matter of life or death and what was not?

He walked a little farther, rolling these ideas around in his mind, until he caught sight of a promising stone, nicely sculpted for skipping. He reached down to pick it up. It fit into his palm as though it had been created there. He turned it over in his hand a few times, then took a step back and flung it out across the shore and over the lake. It curved, arched to the right, and then descended, skittering along the surface of the water—five, six, seven times. Then it sank. At that moment, Maxtla had an inspired idea. This dilemma he had been presented with was too great a responsibility for him alone.

Whether he should divulge it to the Spaniards or not—how could he know? He was only a boy. He decided to let the gods choose. He would set them a test. If the gods permitted him to skip a stone an even dozen times—or more—then he would take that as a sign. He would be absolved of any responsibility for his decision. He would go to the palace of Axayácatl. He would tell the Spaniards what he knew.

He looked down and scanned the jumble of rocks and pebbles that littered the shore at his feet. All he had to do was find a stone capable of skipping a dozen times. A perfect stone.

"*What* did you tell him?" Ometzin pushed herself back from her loom and stared at this man she called her uncle. Why, not even she knew this secret of his. She knew only that there *was* a secret and that it involved the House of Birds. "You told him that?"

Azotl acknowledged that he had.

"But why?" She shook her head. "He'll tell, you know. He'll go straight to the Spaniards and tell them. I'm sure of it."

The master functionary lumbered across the room and settled himself on a large bench. It creaked beneath his weight "I'm not so certain," he said. "In fact, I feel strongly that he won't. He gave his word."

"His word? Ha. He's only a boy. He has temper tantrums. He destroys sacred gardens. He has punching bouts with hummingbirds. He gets thrown into dungeons. He told me he once desecrated a temple in Cholula. He was proud of it."

Azotl sighed. "All true," he said. "But at heart, he is a good young man. He merely has to discover this for himself."

"How? By betraying the greatest secrets of the empire? Uncle—I love you and admire you. But would you not consider this a rather high price to pay for one spoilt boy's journey of self-discovery?"

Azotl closed his eyes and chuckled. He shook his head.

But Ometzin had warmed to her subject and carried on. "You would not believe what I have gone through the past several days. I've taken him everywhere, to concerts and plays, to galleries and gardens, and his reaction was invariably the same."

"And what was that reaction?"

"Boredom? Contempt? A complete inability to take pleasure in beauty. I thought Cholula was a city of some refinement. You would not know it from the example set by this boorish ingrate." Ometzin looked down and adjusted several of the fibers in her loom. "Oh, I am probably being unfair. It was that scene in the House of Birds. It has turned me against him."

"Not without reason."

"And the way he goes on and on about human sacrifice. It's so self-righteous."

"As no one would know better than you would."

Ometzin lowered her head again. She had agonized over the subject for years and would likely wrestle with it forever. How could she go on dwelling with the very people who had put her own mother and father to death? So far, she had no answer. She could not say what she owed to the memory of her parents, or how she could balance that debt against what she owed to herself. She straightened the strands in the loom and pulled a wooden comb down through them. Her shoulders slumped. She looked up at Azotl. "How can you be so sure?" she said.

"That Maxtla will keep this secret?"

"Yes."

He shifted his weight, and again the bench groaned beneath his bulk. "I know his father, who is a man who suffers greatly, but also a man of honor and integrity—a man who is honest with himself. And I see these same qualities in his son. What the boy lacks is confidence in his own being. Now that I have shown I trust him, he will come to understand that he ought to trust himself."

"Can you know this for a fact?"

"For a fact? No. We are dealing with a human being here, not with so many bales of cotton. There is an element of risk."

"An *element* of risk? That is putting it mildly."

"Yes. But I think the boy will surprise you." Azotl reached up to scratch his jowls. "This secret will weigh heavily upon him. It will burn in his throat and dance upon his tongue. He will be sorely tempted to divulge it. But in the end, he will resist. To do otherwise would be to betray himself, and he will not do that."

Ometzin seemed satisfied with this answer as far as it went. She smoothed the network of cotton strands as if to resume work, but then something else occurred to her and she frowned. "What I don't understand is why you told Maxtla at all. For what purpose? Surely, you did not do it to give him some means of learning that he is a better person than he thinks. There are other, safer ways of doing that."

"Are there?" Azotl hauled himself to his feet "Perhaps you are right. But there are not as many as you may suppose." He turned and gazed out across the terrace toward the waters of Lake Texcoco, shining in the sun. "But you are right. This is not the only reason I told him. In truth, lives may depend upon this knowledge, on its being shared among us."

Ometzin raised her eyebrows. "Lives? Whose?"

He turned back and looked at her. "Yours," he said. "Mine. His." The master functionary started to say something else, but then seemed to change his mind. He turned and peered out again at the mountains across the lake.

A Pot of Pig Fat

Juan de Escalante paced about, kicking at odd bits of wood that lay in his path. "What does he say?"

"This, *mi teniente*, is exactly what we are trying to determine." Alonso Puertocarrero let out a long sigh. "It is slow work, I'm afraid."

He wiped a gloss of sweat from his brow. Sweet Mother Mary, he hated this business. As second-in-command, he had been put in charge of the interrogation. The captive was an Aztec, from the look of him. Three Totonac warriors had brought him to the Spanish camp with his thumbs bound behind his back. Puertocarrero had promptly been ordered to find out what the prisoner might be able to tell them, and to that end the Totonacs now had the fellow down on the marshy ground by the side of a rotting log. But the project was not proceeding well. They had three different languages going at once, and no one man seemed capable of comprehending any two of them. A word here. A word there. It made for damnably slow work.

He looked at Escalante apologetically. "We are just trying to squeak the information out, bit by bit."

Escalante nodded. "Carry on then."

"Sí, mi teniente."

Puertocarrero bent over the prisoner once more, along with two other Spaniards and a pair of these Totonac ruffians. God, this was miserable—having to interrogate this Aztec and grovel before Escalante. Ah, well. He would be rid of the Spaniard soon. One way or another, Puertocarrero would be on his way to Tenochtitlán, to restore himself again into Cortés's good graces. Behind his back, the other men made fun of him—he knew it. The Cuckold, they called him, because of what had happened with Marina. They laughed at his bony frame and his shortage of hair. They thought he'd got what he deserved. But he'd show them. He was going to be a lieutenant once more, and he was going to have a woman of his own. Doña Marina again, with any luck. After all, he was a man. He'd even started to swear like one, which was awkward at first. But he was getting used to it.

Just now, however, he had a job to do. Dear sweet Mary's ass, this was confusing work. Everyone spoke at once, all hurling questions at the captive. Whenever the interrogators paused to catch their breath, the prisoner immediately began to babble as though his life depended on it. Unfortunately, no one understood a word.

The time wore on, and Escalante wandered back over for another update.

"What have you got?" he said.

"A few things, *mi teniente*. A little progress."

Puertocarrero had managed to establish two facts. The man's name was Salchan, and he was an Aztec messenger. Unfortunately, everything else he said might as well have been Arabic.

"There must be an easier way," said Escalante.

Puertocarrero quailed. "Easier, yes, but . . ." He let his voice trail off. He knew what the captain was suggesting, and he was desperate to avoid it. If the interrogation came down to torture, he was not sure he could manage. He was not sure he had the mettle for that—and he definitely didn't want the other Spaniards to find out.

Escalante crossed his arms. "I say we dip the prisoner in a pot of pig fat, one limb at a time. That'll loosen his tongue."

"Or kill him."

Escalante's eyebrows shot up like a pair of trained rodents. What was this he was hearing? "You have some objection to pig fat?"

"Not to pig fat, as such." Puertocarrero rubbed his hands

down the front of his breeches. "It's just that a dead man is unlikely to provide much in the way of useful information."

"Nor a live one, either, if you can't understand him."

That was certainly true. Still, Puertocarrero preferred to keep the man alive. He shuddered. Damn it to hell, but he had to face the truth—the thought of torture made him physically ill. He simply wouldn't be able to go through with it. Besides, he was desperate for intelligence—good intelligence. He had personally issued the order to intercept any messengers who passed this way, hoping that some precious nugget of information might fall into his lap, something that would help him escape this place. But he wasn't willing to dip a man in boiling pig fat to obtain it. Instead, he bore on with his questions.

Flat on his back, with his legs pinned down by his captors, Salchan had a poignant sense of his predicament. Lazy he may have been, and duplicitous, but he was no fool. He knew that these Spaniards wanted information from him, and that his life depended on his making that information as useful to them as possible. Potent material—that was what they were after. He knew that tensions were mounting between the Aztecs and the Spaniards. He also knew perfectly well that the master functionary had ordered the Aztecs not to launch hostilities of any kind in Cempoala. Unfortunately, this information was unlikely to interest his captors. But news of a planned attack—ah, they would have reason to be grateful for that. By telling them such a story, he would seem to be performing a vital service. He would be saving their lives. He hoped they would be sufficiently grateful to spare his life.

Over and over, he explained that he was operating on instructions from the master functionary in Tenochtitlán, a powerful man by the name of Azotl. He had been ordered to proceed to Cempoala, where he was to seek out the Aztec agent—Qualpopoca by name. He was to inform Qualpopoca of Azotl's wishes, which were as follows. First, Qualpopoca must execute his prisoner, the fat chieftain of Cempoala, forthwith. After that, he was to launch a lethal assault on the Spaniards at Veracruz. Attack and kill. Then eat. Salchan repeated these instructions over and over and over, until he thought the Spaniards were the most thick-headed beings in creation. Attack and kill. Then eat.

"Eat?" said Puertocarrero. His men had finally managed to piece together the rest of the messenger's meaning. "You don't mean *eat*. Surely not."

He did a pantomime of ripping off his own arm and chewing it raw. The Totonac natives then pretended to rip off their own arms and chew them raw as well. *That's right. Eat. Eat you. Ha-ha-ha.* They clapped each other on the back and wiggled their jaws, like children pretending to be monsters.

Flat on his back on the soggy earth, Salchan started to laugh as well. Wonderful! At last, the Spaniards understood. He was saved!

Puertocarrero was appalled. He had never heard any plot so diabolical in his life. War was one thing. But cannibalism? That was downright savage. He thought he might be ill. Still, he had obtained some excellent information—a warning of an imminent attack! Even better, he had the name of the fiendish kingpin in Tenochtitlán who had ordered the treachery. He had an idea that this fact might be particularly useful to him. Ah-zaw-tul was the man's name. Something like that. He committed the sounds to memory. Ah-zaw-tul.

Now that the interrogation was over, Puertocarrero made a report to Escalante. Not only had the Aztecs made a prisoner of the fat chieftain of Cempoala, he said, but they now planned to execute him. Later, they intended to organize an attack on the Spanish garrison at Veracruz. He made no mention of anyone named Ah-zaw-tul. That was a detail he'd keep to himself.

"Good work, young fellow," said Escalante. "You have performed a great service on behalf of your king. It will not go unmentioned in my report to Cortés." He slapped his thigh, thinking that, as a gesture of gratitude, Puertocarrero might one day mention Escalante's name to his cousin by marriage, the Count of Medellín. "Well done. A hard job but an excellent result. My heartiest congratulations."

Puertocarrero bowed. "*Gracias, mi teniente.*" He waited.

Escalante inclined his craggy face, lined and weathered by the harsh north African sun. "Is there something else?"

Puertocarrero nodded. "The prisoner, *mi teniente*. Should we let him go?"

"Go?" Escalante looked startled. He was surprised to hear the prisoner was still alive, let alone in a condition to be released. "What about the pig fat?"

"Sir?"

"Is there any left?"

Puertocarrero swallowed. "*Sí, mi teniente.*"

"Well, finish it up then." Escalante began to laugh. "For a moment, I thought you were serious. Let the prisoner go, indeed. What an idea."

Puertocarrero didn't move. "But the prisoner has already told us all we need to know, sir. I don't see—"

"Then he is of no further use to us. Don't you agree?"

"Yes, but—"

"I believe I have made my wishes clear. Finish up the pig fat."

Puertocarrero realized that the old captain would be satisfied with nothing short of a slow and complicated death for the poor messenger, a fate that could be avoided in one way only. He took a deep breath. "Sí, *mi teniente*," he said, and withdrew.

He stepped outside Escalante's tent into the blistering sunlight. His eyes winced at the sudden brightness, and he felt an aching in his jaw. Damn it to hell. For a moment, he considered getting someone else to do the job. But then he decided that he had got himself into this mess—he'd have to get himself out. Better to do it quickly and be done. He strode over to the spot by the rotting log where those Totonac louts still had the prisoner stretched out on the ground. Puertocarrero got down on his knees. He bit on his tongue so as not to scream. He drew the knife from his belt, placed the blade against the poor fellow's throat. He ignored the creature's bulging eyes, his imploring gaze. He shut his ears against a sudden cry. With both hands on the grip, he drew up with the blade in a sudden, sharp flick. The blood plumed into his face and ran down his chest He stood up, turned around. He took one look at the pot of pig fat and kicked it over. He motioned to the group of Totonacs, who were staring at him with puzzled expressions.

"Bury him," he said. He mimed the act of digging. "Bury him over there."

The natives nodded happily and at once began plunging sticks into the soft, marshy ground.

Puertocarrero spent the rest of the day alone, huddled by the banks of a stream a short way up the coast, with his freshly cleaned knife at his side and his chin cupped in his hands. He kept telling himself that it had only been a native, a low, witless creature without a soul, and yet he had the damnedest feeling he'd just killed a man.

The Hero of Cempoala

Maxtla felt as if his arm would fall off, but he had finally done it. Twelve separate skips. He thought it was twelve. To be honest, the stone's final ricochets had followed so closely one on another that it was difficult to say for certain how many there had been. But he was fairly sure it was twelve.

The gods had spoken.

Why waste any time? He decided to set out at once for the palace of Axayácatl. Soon, he was picking his way around the countless pits and trenches that disrupted the streets of the city. The Spaniards were making an infernal mess in their ceaseless search for gold. But they would stop turning the place upside down once he had told them what he had learned from Azotl.

He reached an intersection and had to sidestep a particularly wide and deep trench that was being clawed into the ground by slaves. Even now, at the darker side of dusk, they were still hard at it, about twenty of them, digging their way into the earth. They did not look up as Maxtla shimmied past along a narrow ledge against a cool stone wall. A pair of Spaniards stood nearby, chatting to each other and occasionally barking out commands to the workers—no doubt urging them to dig even faster, even deeper. One of the Spaniards glanced at Maxtla and made some remark, and he and his companion laughed. The first one called out some harsh-sounding words. Both of them straightened up and started toward him, looking as if they meant to take hold of him right then and there and put him to work.

Maxtla did not wait to find out what it was they wanted. He leapt from the ledge and broke into a run. He did not ease his pace until he was a good distance away and was certain he was not being chased. He slowed to a trot and finally to a walk. Trembling, he stopped to catch his breath. His chest heaved, and the blood pounded in his head. It was practically dark now, and the streets were deserted. People no longer liked to venture out at night, had not felt safe since the Spaniards' arrival. Maxtla had noticed this change before, but he hadn't given it much thought until now.

He realized that he himself did not feel entirely comfortable alone in the darkness. He began to walk once again. After a while, he saw that he was no longer making his way in the direction of the palace. He was tending more toward the house of Azotl. Well, it was late. Most of the Spaniards would be at dinner, or doing whatever it was they did during the first hours of darkness. Maybe now was not the ideal time to trouble them.

Something moved in the shadows to his left, something that moaned and made a scraping sound. He did not know what it was, and he did not wait to find out. He exploded into a run, and raced through the darkness as fast as he could go. It was not until he was within a block of Azotl's house that he slowed again to a walk. Ah, that was better. He felt calm and collected now. Maybe tomorrow would be a better time to visit the Spaniards—tomorrow, when it was light.

Backed by their Totonac allies, the Spanish troops under Juan de Escalante marched on Cempoala, where Qualpopoca remained with the fat chieftain as his prisoner. He was still waiting for a reply to the message he had sent to Azotl in Tenochtitlán. Once he realized what was happening—that a force of these *teules* was approaching, with arms at the ready, as if prepared for war—Qualpopoca threw his pipe to the ground. It promptly shattered, scattering tobacco and ashes across the grass.

He ordered his small force of warriors—thirty men in total—to take up positions at the entrances to the town and to put up what resistance they could. Within an hour, the battle began. Even outnumbered five-to-one, the Aztecs managed to hold their attackers off for the better part of that day. One of them, a crack archer, climbed onto the roof of an adobe storehouse with two quivers of arrows. He pulled out the first of them and set its tail against the string of his bow.

What was that? At first, Juan de Escalante had no idea. Some sudden crick in his neck. When he realized what it was, a shock of panic shuddered through him, combined with disbelief. How on earth could this have happened? He dismounted and tottered about for a time, badly disoriented. Goddamnit. He cupped his hands at his neck and tried to remove the arrow by hand, but that only made matters worse. He closed his eyes and started to gag on his blood. Goddamnit to hell. What an unholy mess—that he, the hero of Melilla and a hundred other battles, should be reduced to this. He had imagined a better death. Eventually, he settled down on his knees in an attitude of prayer, then eased over onto his haunches, and died.

When he saw the arrow strike the lieutenant, Puertocarrero turned on his heels and ran away from the battle, not stopping until he had reached a grove of dense, green trees. He hid himself among them. But he did not stay long. He whacked his fist against a tree trunk. No, no, no. This was clearly intolerable. He was the senior officer now. He decided he would rather die than hide. He had no idea what to do. He'd never fought a war. But he knew that his duties included being seen on the battlefield by the men who were now under his command. He took a deep breath, stepped out of the thicket, and advanced closer to the din of battle. Dazed by the hubbub, he forgot to protect himself. Instead, he walked erect, shoulders back, making an inviting target. When they saw him—striding out in the open, exposed yet seemingly unafraid—the rest of the Spaniards let out a cheer. If that quivering stick-figure Puertocarrero could be as bold as this, then what could they not do?

The Spaniards redoubled their offensive and before long—by force of superior weaponry and numbers—they claimed a resounding victory. Puertocarrero did little more than pace back and forth with his sword drawn, but that had apparently been enough. He had led his men to triumph!

Qualpopoca was taken alive, along with fourteen of his warriors. The other Aztecs lay dead. Tlacochcalcatl, the fat chieftain, also died in the battle, although it did not appear he had been wounded. Fear, perhaps, had sufficed. In addition to Escalante, two more Spanish soldiers had lost their lives. Others had suffered injuries of greater or lesser severity, but most could walk.

Now the remaining Spaniards collected several of the Aztec corpses and cut them up right where they lay. Then they boiled down the natives' fat to use as a dressing for their wounds. Several of them cursed bitterly that their supply of pig fat had unaccountably vanished. Now they had to use the fat of savages. That night, two more of the Spaniards died from their injuries.

Despite these losses, Puertocarrero was delighted at the outcome. This was his first real taste of combat, and look what had happened. First of all, the Spaniards had won another fine victory, mostly under his command. Second, he had taken prisoners, who might prove to be of some value. Third, he still retained in his memory the name of that Aztec higher-up in Tenochtitlán, the one called Ah-zaw-tul. He decided that he had better write the name down. He did so and tucked the leaf of parchment into the folds of his doublet. Then, as the sun crept across the coastal bog, he ordered his men to dig graves for the dead, including Escalante. On a shoal of dry land, they gave each of their fallen comrades a Christian burial and erected over each grave a small wooden cross.

That was a sad business, but even so Puertocarrero could not help feeling pleased with himself. He had won! He was the hero of Cempoala now! But there was still more to be done. He selected two of the Totonac warriors who had distinguished themselves in the fighting. After a good deal of verbal seesawing, he managed to make his orders clear. They were to run flat out to Tenochtitlán, there to seek out the Spanish captain-general Hernán Cortés. They were to present him with a written message. Puertocarrero wrote the missive out in his somewhat clumsy hand. A party of Spaniards had been set upon in a heinous and cowardly attack, at Cempoala—thoroughly unprovoked. In the end, they had prevailed, thanks to God Almighty and to their courage and to daring leadership. Alas, Juan de Escalante had perished in the fighting, along with four other Spaniards. Their Totonac ally, the fat chieftain, was also dead—murdered by the Aztecs, in all likelihood.

There. He handed the message to one of the two warriors, both of whom seemed passably bright for natives. With
rapid hand gestures, he ordered them to be off. *Away. Run to
Tenochtitlán. Seek out Cortés. Go.*

A Habitation of Jackals

Jerónimo de Aguilar slumped on a stone block outside the
palace of Axayácatl. All around him, crews of native slaves
were gouging at the ground or dismantling stone buildings.
They were searching for gold, of course, convinced that the
Aztecs were the wealthiest people on earth. Those two great
disks Cortés had received on the eastern coast—one of gold,
the other of silver—had persuaded them of this. If the great
emperor Moctezuma could part with such wondrous items so
easily, then God knew what riches he must possess.

Aguilar rubbed his forehead, closed his eyes. It disgusted
him, the whole ungodly business. If his countrymen had traveled to these shores for no other purpose than to rape and
murder, to steal and plunder, then he believed that they should
never have left Cuba. Better yet, they should never have left
Spain.

He thought: *And thorns shall come up in its palaces, nettles and
brambles in its fortresses; it shall be a habitation of jackals, a courtyard
for ostriches.*

He opened his eyes again and peered around at this festival of destruction. Was he to consider it a blessing that he had

lived to see this? During his eight years of servitude on the torrid coast, he might have perished at any moment, as the others had done. But he had survived. It had been God's desire that he should live. And now the hand of God had guided him here. To what end? He looked up at the streaks of clouds that stretched across the sky overhead, silver rents in a fabric of blue. He was searching for shapes, patterns, signs. Just then, a shadow passed nearby, and he lowered his gaze—a young native lad stood before him. Ah, he knew the youth. He was the son of Pitoque, the merchant of Cholula. What was the boy's name? Maxtla? Yes, that was it. Aguilar nodded in recognition. They had crossed paths before. In Cholula—he remembered it now—before the horrors there.

"Good morning," he said. He remembered that the boy spoke Maya.

"Good morning." Maxtla folded and unfolded his arms at his chest, evidently a nervous habit. "I hope that you are well."

"I find myself in reasonable health. Thank you. And you?"

"I am well also."

"Then we are doubly blessed." It seemed the boy had something on his mind, to judge by his agitated air. "What do you wish?"

Maxtla shifted his weight, evidently wanting to say something but at the same time reluctant to speak. "I wish to be presented to Cortés. I have something to tell him."

"You do?" Aguilar raised his eyebrows. "May I ask what it is?"

"I prefer to tell Cortés directly."

"No doubt. But as you know, it will be necessary to inform

me in any case. I will have to interpret your words for my captain. You might as well tell me now."

Maxtla realized it was so. He might as well speak up now. It would come to the same thing. "Well . . ." he said. "What I want to say is . . ."

"Yes?"

"It is difficult to explain."

"All the more reason to practice. Go on."

Maxtla dug with the toe of one foot in the dirt, trying to formulate the words. But he was having trouble organizing his thoughts in a coherent fashion. How should he go about telling what he knew? How could he explain by what means he, of all people, had come to possess this information? Would anyone believe him? Strange—these concerns had not occurred to him before. He continued gouging into the soil with his foot.

"You are at liberty to speak at any time," said Aguilar. "At your earliest convenience. Meanwhile, you might desist from digging that trough. As you can see, we are well supplied with holes in the ground hereabouts. We do not need any additional hazards."

Maxtla stopped poking at the earth with his foot. He remembered that episode several nights earlier, when those two Spaniards had started after him—for what purpose, he did not know. It had taken him since then to work up the courage to present himself here. He said, "Why are they always digging?"

Aguilar laughed. "They are looking for gold. It is all they

think about. They think it is buried everywhere. So far, they have been bitterly disappointed."

"Why are you not digging?"

"Ah, so now it is you who are asking the questions?" He shrugged. "I have no interest in gold."

Maxtla remembered something. He looked up. "They say that the Spaniards suffer from a disease. Without gold, they will die. They must eat it to live."

"I have heard it said."

"You do not also suffer from this disease?"

Again, Aguilar laughed. "I have benefited from unusual experiences. I have, you might say, been cured of this affliction. Now I am an instrument in the hands of my God. Neither more nor less."

"You are not a god yourself?" The question leapt from Maxtla's lips, as easy as breathing. He was astounded he had not asked it before. "That's what people say, that you are gods."

"So I have been informed. But no, I am not a god."

"And Cortés? And the others?"

"The same. Men, like you and me."

"Why have you come to this land?"

"For my own part, I do not know. I am still waiting to be enlightened in this regard."

Maxtla looked at him. "Like my father. He, too, waits to be enlightened. He seeks after signs."

"We have much in common, your father and I. I have remarked upon it before. But these others"—Aguilar waved about him at the Spaniards dotted here and there, overseeing the work of digging—"they have come for one reason alone. For gold. It truly is a sickness with them, although, in fact, they do not eat the stuff. They want to hoard it, to enrich themselves. This is why they have come."

"Do they mean to harm us?" Maxtla asked.

Aguilar looked up at the sky, pondered. After a time, he lowered his gaze. "How can you ask that? You must have been present in Cholula. You saw what was done."

"No, I was away. Is it true then, what my father said? People were killed?"

"Hundreds. Tens of hundreds."

"By the Spaniards?"

"I regret to say so."

"Not by the Aztecs?"

"No."

"I see." Maxtla felt his heart sink. He'd been afraid of this.

Aguilar crossed one leg over the other. "Now, what is it you were going to tell me?"

Maxtla was about to reply—to reveal this secret he knew—when a commotion erupted just up the street. Two men—native men, dressed as Totonac warriors—darted through the maze of trenches and rubble. Both carried spears, and one held something else aloft, something rolled up, like a scroll.

The pair hurried over to Aguilar and fell to their knees. Both of them poured with sweat, their chests heaving like bellows.

"Cortés . . ." one of them managed to gasp. "We bear a message for Cortés."

Aguilar was about to make a jest—it seemed that everyone had a message for his captain this morning—but he had a sudden instinct that this might be a poor time. "Come, then," he said. "Follow me." He rose to his fret and led the two Totonac men into the palace of Axayácatl.

Maxtla remained where he was near the entrance. His secret burned in his throat. It tickled the base of his tongue. But now he had no one to tell.

"What's this?" shouted Pedro de Alvarado. "What hellish brand of duplicity is this?" He leapt to his fret and stormed about the room, waving his arms and ranting at the top of his lungs. "Damn the lying swine!"

With pleasure, Hernán Cortés watched the man run off at the mouth. He had handed Alvarado the message written by Alonso Puertocarrero, and at once the blond lummox was on his feet, rushing around the room. He could always count on Alvarado to raise an outcry. Out on the eastern coast, at Cempoala, there were now five dead Spaniards—including Juan de Escalante—the result of a cowardly massacre committed by Aztecs. Although Cortés had been as surprised and angered as Alvarado, he'd quickly decided to mute his response. Here was a chance for decisive action, but it would be better if he played his cards close to his chest. Better to let others react first and see where their reactions led. In the future, he might have to answer for his actions today. In any ease, with Alvarado about, a boisterous response was guaranteed.

Cortés glanced at Doña Marina, who sat across the table from him in the small banquet hall where the Spanish officers took their meals. They had just been finishing their luncheon when the Totonac messengers arrived. Cortés had summoned her to join him, thinking her services might be required. Now he smiled. In a low voice, he said, "Do you remember your idea about imprisoning the emperor?"

She nodded. Of course, she did.

"Until this day, I have lacked only a cause for action, a justification. Watch what happens now."

"As you wish, my master. You know I desire only to obey."

Cortés frowned. What did she mean by that? That was the problem with this girl. He could never tell for certain when she was being serious. There was a crookedness to her that he could not quite follow.

More commotion broke out. All the men were now on their feet, shouting angrily.

"Can this be true?" one man cried.

"Was it the little Aztec king who ordered this treachery?" shouted another. "Has he been intending all along to kill us in our sleep?"

"Does he plan to slit our throats?"

"Or slice open our chests and rip out our hearts?"

"Ha! Slather our flesh with chilis and feed us to his miserable gods?"

"Or to his wives, more likely!"

Following Alvarado's lead, they kicked at clay pots, smashed their fists on tables, and paced around the hall. It was time to take action, time to fight back. Either that or be slaughtered like sheep. They demanded that Cortés hear them out.

Cortés stroked his whiskered chin. "What would you suggest then?" he said. "What action should we take?"

Alvarado spoke for the rest. "We should seize Moctezuma himself as our prisoner. We can hold the little vermin as our hostage, here in our quarters. That way, we'll be safe from attack."

The others bellowed in agreement.

"That's it."

"Hear! Hear!"

"Seize the little emperor!"

Once again, they all began shaking their fists and banging on the tables. Dishes rattled, and spittle flew from more than a dozen pairs of lips.

Cortés listened in silence. He rubbed his neck and finally shook his head. "No," he said. "I oppose this plan. It seems too unpredictable. It holds too many risks."

He kept rubbing his neck and gave an inward smile. Well done, Puertocarrero. Now the Spaniards had the finest pretext imaginable to seize Moctezuma—Spanish blood, shed by Aztecs. It was perfect. But Cortés was a calculating man. He saw that the arrest of the emperor was still a risky course. After all, he would have to answer for every step he took, not only to Velázquez in Cuba, but also to the King. As well, that overzealous operation in Cholula might yet return to haunt him. It would be better if he appeared to resist the men's idea. That way, if all went well, he might still claim credit. But if the scheme went wrong, he could defend his own part by saying that he'd been encouraged by his men, that they had all been in it together. He let the clamor continue for a while longer, and then he raised his hands.

"So be it," he said. "Since you insist, I will go along. But, remember—no harm must come to the man. Alive, he may be our salvation. Dead, he is no use at all." Cortés gazed about the hall. Where was Aguilar? "Get me Aguilar!"

"I am here, mi capitán." Aguilar stepped forward. He looked utterly wretched, like a man in despair. "I have been here all along."

"You have?" Cortés looked surprised. Lately, Aguilar had never seemed to be around when he was needed. "I will need you during this mission."

"Sí, mi capitán."

The Spaniards began making their preparations, overjoyed to be taking action. This very afternoon, they would seize Moctezuma II, emperor of the Aztecs, as their hostage. This was more the kind of excitement they'd had in mind when they had come to this bloody place. Maybe they could force the little king to reveal the location of all the Aztec gold.

Now that would be a deed worth doing.

Out on the eastern coast, Puertocarrero had a brilliant idea. First, he would sort matters out at the garrison at Veracruz. Then he would make for Tenochtitlán himself, taking a small party of Spaniards with him, and some of these Totonac warriors, and the Aztec prisoners—the one called Qualpopoca and the rest. His arrival in Tenochtitlán would cause a great stir. *All hail the hero of Cempoala! Look, he brings prisoners!* Moreover, he had the name of that Ah-zaw-tul fellow, the one who had masterminded the Aztec infamy. Cortés would regard that information as a splendid service. He would reward it with riches and honors that would make Pedro de Alvarado sick with envy. Puertocarrero couldn't help but smile at the prospect. He'd be made a lieutenant again. He'd dine in company with Cortés and the other officers. No one would laugh at him then. Why, he had even killed a man. At this thought, he suddenly hunched his shoulders and shuddered. It was true, he *had* killed a man—or, in any case, a native. The horror of it returned to him in a wave of nausea. He fought the sourness down and drew in a draft of air through his nostrils. There. That was better. He reached up and arranged his hair across the top of his head, patted the strands into place.

The Hero of Cempoala!

He decided he could not wait. Rather than return now to Veracruz, he would make directly for Tenochtitlán. He appointed a likely young fellow called Muñoz to lead the bulk of the Spaniards back to the coastal garrison. For the expedition to the capital, he named El Gordito Bustamante as his second-in-command.

"Come, gentlemen," he said. He had to pause because his throat was so dry. He found it difficult to swallow. He could barely believe that he was taking these steps, that he was leading a company of men. But so he was. He willed himself to speak. "Follow me, men. We have great adventures ahead."

He waved his arm to the west, or what he thought was the west—the sea being at his back—and urged his mount on. As he rode, he occupied himself by composing in his mind the little speech he would give when Cortés heaped upon him all the honors that were now his due. He wondered if, just possibly, those honors might include the return of Doña Marina to his bed. God, that would be a prize indeed. He imagined the two of them together, alone. He would do better this time. It would not be like before.

Under arms and accompanied by thirty guards and several lieutenants, Cortés marched into the open air and across a broad plaza to the House of the Eagle Knights. Aguilar and Doña Marina hurried behind him, their services urgently required now. The Spaniards quickly subdued the Aztec sentries posted at the entrance to the great hall, and Cortés ordered that the perimeter of the building be secured.

Then they would force their way inside.

The Palanquin of the Emperor

Pitoque crossed his legs and adjusted his cloak—a particularly handsome robe, made of the finest cotton and striped with cochineal dye. All his life, he had been forced to go about in clothing of rough maguey fiber in order to seem less prosperous than he was. He'd got used to it, more or less.

But that crude fabric caused a constant itch. How pleasant it was now to garb himself in such fine textiles as these. A small pleasure, perhaps, but one that had helped to transform his days at the royal court of Moctezuma into a time of unusual physical comfort. What a relief it was not to be scratching all of the time!

In most other respects, these weeks had been very difficult. He spent long hours of every day and most evenings cooped up, just as he was now, in the House of the Eagle Knights, while the lords of the Triple Alliance prattled on and on. The subject of their discourse almost never varied. It was the Spaniards this, the Spaniards that. Were they gods? Or were they men? Why had they come? How should they be dealt with? Priests were consulted. Oracles were studied. Scientists were commissioned to conduct elaborate experiments on the entrails of prairie dogs.

Occasionally, Pitoque was called upon to offer his considered opinion. As the only man here who had actually boarded one of the floating palaces or who had spent any substantial amount of time in the Spaniards' presence, his views had to be given a certain weight. That was the theory. In practice, he discovered that no one cared in the least what he thought. The entire purpose behind these endless discussions was to discuss endlessly. No one said anything specific, categorical, or concrete—because to do so might force a decision, which in turn would necessitate taking action of some kind. And no one wanted to take action. Everyone just wanted to talk.

The talking went on day after day after day.

The only relief from this aimless debate was provided by Cacama, the king of Texcoco, who had little patience for discussion and speculation. In his view, the Spaniards might be gods or they might be men—it did not matter. They had invaded Tenochtitlán, and no one had raised a hand to stop them. Now they were digging the city up from below and tearing it down from above. They were erecting strange wooden crosses everywhere. They were behaving, not as guests, but as conquerors. It was time to send them away, either politely or by force of arms. Cacama repeated this forthright message over and over again, but each time the other lords promptly countered it with a barrage of doubts and misgivings. The priests and scientists took the floor.

Finally, Cacama gave up. He slumped in his throne, glowering out at the room, refusing to say anything at all. Although he was not an old man, he now looked like some ancient sage, furious with all he sees and convinced that everyone else is a fool.

Pitoque heaved a long sigh. Unfortunately, he believed that Cacama was right.

Just now, the subject under discussion was Spanish excrement. Lately, investigations had been undertaken with respect to the Spaniards' feces. These appeared to differ in no material respect from those of humans, apart from being nearly one-third bigger. Was this a significant factor or not? And no, not a trace of gold had been found. The scientists concluded that either the gold had dissolved entirely during the process of digestion—which would support the argument that these creatures were gods—or it had never been ingested in the first place.

"Never ingested?" Moctezuma interrupted the chief scientist's report. He was evidently dismayed by this idea. "What would you conclude from that?"

The chief scientist paused. "It is difficult to say, my lord. The matter could be argued from various perspectives."

The emperor nodded gravely, as though he found this response particularly trenchant. In fact, Pitoque could see that the chief scientist was simply equivocating. It was obvious the emperor favored the idea that the Spaniards might be gods, and so it was safer not to contradict him, even when the evidence clearly suggested the contrary. Moctezuma's affection for these strangers had wavered only once, during that episode at the Temple of Huitzilopochtli, when Cortés had offended the hummingbird god. But by now, it seemed that the emperor was disposed to forgive even that.

And so the debate rambled on. Pitoque crossed and uncrossed his legs as the lords of the Triple Alliance continued their discussions, conducted their investigations, commissioned their inquiries, and received their reports. Would it never end? He rubbed his forehead and reflected that, at least, one thing was clear. It was not the lords of the Triple Alliance who kept the empire running. If they had been in charge, the entire civilization would have collapsed long ago under the weight of their pointless blather. It was thanks to men such as Azotl that the empire continued to function—practical men making practical decisions about practical matters.

He raised his arms to stretch and sought to stifle a yawn. The air was still. The voices droned on. He felt his neck muscles go slack, and knew he was in danger of letting his head collapse upon his chest, of falling sound asleep, when suddenly the great wooden entrance doors crashed open, and the world turned upside down.

At the din of the doors flying open, Moctezuma's head snapped up, and he practically toppled from his throne in shock. He struggled to collect himself. On shaking legs, he rose from his place of honor and tottered forward to greet his guests, the Spanish commander Hernán Cortés and his company of men, all armed and, to judge by appearances, extremely angry.

The emperor tried his best. He put out his arms and beamed his broadest smile, as if delighted at this intrusion, although everyone in the room could see that some terrible event now hung on the charged and crackling air. "Welcome," he said. "You are all most welcome. I trust that you are in good health. Your quarters, they are satisfactory? The food is to your taste?"

As usual, his words were translated by Doña Marina and Aguilar.

When he understood what Moctezuma had asked, Cortés put back his head and howled. His eyes watered. He shook with laughter. Finally, he calmed himself and stared at the emperor in disbelief. "Food? You speak of food?"

Moctezuma shifted uneasily. This was not the reaction he had expected. He was merely being polite.

"If you wish to know the truth," said Cortés, "I am not partial to picking salamanders from my soup. But otherwise, we are satisfied with the cuisine. Our accommodations are acceptable as well." He made a little bow. "You have my thanks, on behalf of my men. Today, however, I have another matter to discuss."

Moctezuma blanched. "Yes?" he said. "Another matter? To what do you refer?"

"To this." Cortés waved an arm and barked out a series of commands. At once, his men fanned out to take control of the chamber. They placed sentries in every corner and held their swords at the ready. Several carried harquebuses. Cortés turned back to the emperor.

"It seems that Your Highness has been plotting against us all along." He sighed and shook his head, partly in anger, partly in sorrow. "You have been treating us as dupes while you prepared a most cowardly act." Cortés gave his version of the events that had taken place on the coast—first, the fat chieftain, a Spanish ally, made prisoner. Next, an unprovoked attack on his men by Moctezuma's representatives. Spanish blood was shed. He took a step closer to the emperor. "We are not the fools you take us for. Now, as a consequence of this betrayal, it is you who will be made a prisoner. You will either surrender at once or be killed by my men, who are very, very angry. I wonder if I can restrain them."

While these words were being translated, Cortés paced around the hall. Once his meaning was clear, the gathered lords of the Triple Alliance flopped into their seats. They began to mutter in protest. None of the Aztecs had ever imagined such an insult before. To hear such thoughts spoken aloud, so brazenly—it was impossible to grasp. The emperor himself seemed bewildered, like a child after an unexpected scolding. His face was flushed, his mouth hung open, and his breath came in great, audible heaves.

Cortés strutted back and forth across the floor, but now his manner became less threatening. He dropped his voice. He said that he himself was on Moctezuma's side. He was trying to act in the emperor's best interests. It was these others, these hot-tempered ones, who were the problem. He halted and put his arms akimbo. "Please believe that I do not wish to harm you. On the contrary, I hold you in the highest personal esteem, and I hope that we can remain friends, you and I. But I cannot take responsibility for my officers. They are extremely vexed with you just now. What, therefore, will be your choice? Submit to me without protest—or die at the hands of these brutes? You decide."

Aguilar listened to these shocking words and quailed where he stood. He was horrified at what he heard, but he knew that refusing to translate for Cortés would hardly help matters. There was no telling what these soldiers would do. They clearly lusted for blood. Some of their own had been killed. If he failed to cooperate now, he would simply make a terrible situation worse. So he struggled to calm himself, to steady his voice. He turned and explained in Maya what Cortés had just said, and he waited as Doña Marina reported his words in Nahuatl.

As always, the translation was a laborious process, and it was a while longer before Moctezuma could summon the will to reply, but at last he did so. "Do not do this," he implored, barely able to get the words out. "This is unnecessary. There is no cause for anger." He denied that he had ever contemplated any attack on his guests. If any of his officers or servants had offended Cortés in any way, they would be punished. All would be put right. He tried to reason with the Spanish commander. "There is no cause for hostility between us. We have been friends, have we not? We can still be friends." He said it was unthinkable for him to do as Cortés demanded. "The tlatoani cannot be made a hostage like this. It is beyond the realm of possibility. Besides, the people of Tenochtitlán would never accept such an outrage, even if the tlatoani himself agreed to it."

The arguments went back and forth in the three different languages. Again and again, Cortés reiterated his demands, always taking care to dissociate himself from their more extreme consequences. Of course—he kept saying—he had no wish to harm Moctezuma, but he could not say the same for his men. As the time dragged by, some of Cortés's lieutenants began to lose patience. Finally, one of them could stand it no longer.

Juan Velázquez de León let out a roar. "Agh!" he cried, and strode to the center of the room. He had a foaming black beard and a deep, guttural voice, and he made a terrifying sight. "What the bloody hell is this!"

Moctezuma shrank back.

Velázquez turned to face Cortés. "What is the use of all these words?" He waved at the emperor as he might gesture at a dog. "There is nothing to discuss. Either we take him or we knife him. Plain and simple." The man yanked out his dagger, turned, and aimed it at the emperor's chest. "Here. Like this."

Cortés reached out to hold the man back. "Steady," he said. "Calm down."

Moctezuma stood his ground, but he was shaking. A muscle under his left eye had started to twitch, and it wouldn't stop. His throat seemed to seize and release, seize and release, as though he were gagging on something too large to swallow.

Doña Marina saw all this, too. She sensed that the moment had come, the decisive moment. Had not this very maneuver been her idea? Not the timing, perhaps—but the form. The idea had been hers, and she would see it home. Now, without any prompting from Cortés or anyone, she walked up to the emperor and put her nose nearly in his face.

"You should do as my master tells you," she said. "You should give yourself up without a fight, without any more of this nonsense." She assured him that the Spaniards were men of their word. "They will allow you to rule as before, to govern the empire, to enjoy whatever comforts you require. You will lose nothing, but you will gain your life." She stepped back and shook her head, as if this sorry episode pained her greatly, more than she could say. Then she looked Moctezuma squarely in the face. She informed him that, if he did not comply, he would surely be killed. "I have knowledge of these beings," she reminded him. "And you have not. You should heed my advice."

Pitoque tried to make sense of what he heard. But what sense could there be? Here was the emperor of the Aztecs— the *tlatoani*, He Who Speaks—being counseled on the most important decision of his life by a woman, a mere girl. Pitoque could imagine what the emperor was thinking. *This child should be holed up in a smoke-soiled kitchen or relegated to a small courtyard to attend to her weaving, accompanied by the chirping of birds. She should be strolling about the market, bartering for lizards or corn. She should be down on all fours, on a mat of maguey fiber, with her legs parted, ready for a man. That was a woman's place.* Yet here she was instead, shoulders back, eyebrows raised, as she presumed to tell the emperor of the Aztecs, the warrior king, that he must place himself at the mercy of this bearded captain called Hernán Cortés. Had all that was good and right in the universe suddenly been stolen away?

Like the rest, Pitoque watched and waited. What would the emperor do? Would he submit or not? It was impossible to imagine that he would humiliate himself to such an extent. Instead, he would refuse and likely be killed along with all his advisers in this room. Then the war would begin, although Pitoque himself would not be present to witness it. He felt his life slipping away, like water running through his hands.

Moctezuma remained where he was, standing just a few feet from Cortés, and now some sort of shaking fit had taken him. His eyes began to quiver, his hands trembled, and he struggled to find his voice. Finally, he brought himself under a degree of control. He turned and motioned to Pitoque, not seeming to recognize who he was. "Summon the royal palanquin," he said. "We have decided to accept the invitation of our guests."

A gasp went up among the courtiers and nobles in the House of the Eagle Knights, but no one made any move to intervene. No one dared. The lords, princes, and priests of the empire stood about, shaking their heads. None of them had ever contemplated such an impossibility. It was beyond meaning or words. The emperor seized! Pitoque drew his robe about him and hurried out to do Moctezuma's bidding. The Spanish guards first tried to stop him, but Cortés called out to let the man go, and they stood aside. The mission was accomplished quickly, and the empty palanquin soon sailed into the royal chamber, supported by a dozen royal eunuchs.

Moctezuma turned to his courtiers. "Trust my judgment," he told them. "I have been speaking with our gods, and they have decided that it would be well for my health to spend some little time in the company of our guests, to learn their ways, to know them better." The emperor drew up his robes and climbed into the litter. In an instant, he was raised aloft.

Cortés nodded to those who remained in the royal chamber. "Good day to you," he said. "May the Lord Jesus Christ protect you all." He turned and left, and the rest of the Spaniards followed.

Like the others, Pitoque waited for several moments and then hurried out onto the shimmering plaza to watch. With their swords still drawn, the Spaniards guided the palanquin of the emperor across the plaza through the dazzling midday light. The litter tottered down a series of canopied archways that led in the direction of the palace of Axayácatl. No one made an attempt to stop it, and no one said a word.

BOOK FIVE

The Hummingbird Bride

Men of a Different Sort

"Well, well," said Jerónimo de Aguilar. "We meet again."

"So it seems." Pitoque grimaced. "Although our circumstances have somewhat altered."

The Spanish translator agreed that this was so. After exchanging a few pleasantries, the two men found themselves strolling together along a cool stone corridor that gave onto a verdant courtyard sheltered by a broad canopy of cotton. Here, they settled themselves upon a stone bench and stretched out their legs. Several green parrots fussed and darted among the branches of the poinsettias, and butterflies fluttered in the muted light.

Several days earlier, Pitoque had been summoned to attend to the emperor in his new state of captivity. Since then, he had organized a substantial party of retainers and factotums, cooks and slop-waiters, tumblers and musicians, serving girls and concubines. Now they had all taken up residence here in the palace of Axayácatl, in a separate wing, where Moctezuma was to dwell in state. It seemed that Cortés meant to abide by his word, such as it was. The emperor was a prisoner, yes, and so he would remain. Nonetheless, he might enjoy what comforts he wished. He might even continue to go through the motions of ruling the empire—to receive supplicants and emissaries, to issue proclamations, to confer with priests. In fact, there would be just one constraint upon the emperor, albeit an onerous one. Except under Spanish guard, he would not be permitted to leave his prison.

"Unimaginable," said Aguilar. "An unimaginable state of affairs. What do you think?"

"The same."

The Spaniard shifted closer. He lowered his voice. "Just between the two of us, I deeply regret my part in what has been done."

"You had no choice."

"I disagree. A man always has choices. Whether he deigns to exercise them . . . that is another matter."

Pitoque realized the truth of these words. He remembered that night, so many years earlier, in the lands of the Maya, when he, too, faced choices but did not exercise them. In his robes, he still carried a necklace of shells.

The two men lounged side by side, basking in the soft glow of the translucent canopy overhead, observing the frolic of parrots. They spoke of many affairs and found that much united them—more, perhaps, than held them apart.

"I take it," said Pitoque, for this was the conclusion he had finally reached, "that you Spaniards are men. Not gods." He'd finally said it. "I have been in doubt on the question for quite some time."

Aguilar chuckled. "I know it. I believe you have interrogated me on this subject before." He crossed his legs at the ankles. "You know, your son asked me the same question."

"He did? When?"

"Just the other day. He had something he wanted to tell Cortés. All very important. He insisted on seeing the man in person."

"Did he see Cortés?"

"No. Other events intervened."

"A common pattern."

"Indeed."

"So," said Pitoque, "*are* you?"

"Are we what?"

"Men."

Aguilar smiled. "You may take my word for it. Men, we are. Men, we shall remain. Just men of a different sort."

Pitoque sighed. "And these marvels you have," he said, "these smoking spears and giant deer—they are the instruments of men?"

"Of some men. God has granted them to some men and not to others. He favors His own, I suppose."

"We in the Aztec empire—we are without such marvels."

Aguilar crossed his arms at his chest. "You may rest assured," he said, "that this has not gone unobserved."

Pitoque found that he could venture out onto the streets of Tenochtitlán, and no one made any attempt to detain him. Unlike Moctezuma, he was free to come and go as he pleased. On such occasions, he sought out Azotl in his chambers and reported on all he had heard and seen. By this time, the master functionary had arranged employment for Maxtla in the royal aviary, where the boy now spent his days cataloguing the traits and habits of birds.

"Youth," said Azotl. "A tempest of surprises. Surely, you recall."

Pitoque conceded that he did, if vaguely. He was silent for a few moments, but then remembered something he had forgotten. "Speaking of surprises, I have another one to report. The emperor's frame of mind is not what one would expect."

"Not sullen and morose?" said Azotl.

"No."

"Not bitter? Not angry?"

"On the contrary. Indeed, he seems positively happy. I do not understand it. It's the oddest thing."

Azotl clasped his hands in front of him, interlocking his great, slablike fingers. "You know," he said, "it may not be so strange, after all. We encountered something of the sort a few years ago, down at Chimaluaca. There was some dispute— over the payment of tribute, as I recall—and the locals took several of our people hostage, kept them prisoner for a matter of weeks. In the end, a similar surprise occurred."

Pitoque waited for the master functionary to go on.

"Our people went over to the side of their captors. They took up the cause of the Chimaluacans. They even fought alongside them when a party of Aztec warriors went down there to free the poor souls. It turned out that they didn't want to be freed." Azotl shook his head in wonder. Suddenly, he frowned and put his face in his hands.

Pitoque leaned forward. "Is something wrong?"

Slowly, Azotl looked up. His expression, usually inscrutable, was clearly agitated now. He released a long, laden sigh. "Wrong?" he repeated. He lifted his shoulders and let them fall. "I am just somewhat preoccupied. That is all."

"Preoccupied with what?"

Azotl was silent for a time. He let out a long breath. "I may as well tell you."

A disease. A new kind of disease. Or a curse. Something terrible. Something never seen before. Azotl said that reports had been trickling into Tenochtitlán from outlying regions—all of them to the east, all located along the path taken by the Spaniards. They described a new kind of malady, a pox of some kind, lumps that formed upon the flesh of the victims. They sprang open, and life spilled away. No remedy so far attempted seemed to have any effect whatsoever.

"Many have died already," Azotl said. "Dozens. Hundreds."

Pitoque pressed his lips together. He remembered that he had seen someone afflicted in this way—Melchior, the Totonac who had gone away with the Spaniards more than a year before. He swallowed. "And you say that no remedy is effective against this, this . . . ?"

"This curse?"

Pitoque nodded. It was what he had meant, but he had balked at the word. Curses were called down by gods.

Azotl shook his head. "None that have been attempted. But perhaps remedies remain that have not yet been tried. We have yet to encounter this malady here in Tenochtitlán. Perhaps some of our cures will prove more potent."

Pitoque turned and gazed out the window at the interior courtyard, where parrots muttered in their bamboo cages and the afternoon light slanted across the green shrubs and wooden porticos. There was something else he wanted to say. Finally, he remembered what it was. "I have other news to tell you about Moctezuma."

"Yes?"

"No matter what I say—no matter what anyone says—the emperor remains convinced that these Spaniards are gods. He positively worships them. Nothing will persuade him that they are merely humans, like us."

Azotl furrowed his brow, and a darkness seemed to settle over his features. "Hmm. I don't like the sound of that. I don't like the sound of that at all." The master functionary leaned back and folded his arms at his chest. "No. That sounds bad. I want you to keep me informed about that."

Puertocarrero peered up at the night sky, which was muddied, as usual, by a dense layer of clouds. Damn. He kicked at the dirt. Damn. Damn. Damn. For three nights now, they'd not had a decent look at the stars, and it seemed they were going to draw a blank again. Four nights in a row. Yet even when the sky was clear, he wasn't sure how much good it did.

That fool Escalante—it was all his fault. In his haste to march to Cempoala, the late Spanish captain had neglected to include a navigator in his party. True, he had thought to bring an astrolabe, which was a wonderfully useful device—if only someone knew how to use it. Maybe the old goat had known how to employ the damn thing, but unfortunately, no one else did. Each clear night, Puertocarrero had hauled the contraption out and tried to make head or tail of it, but had to give up. He had no idea how the machine worked, and so it did no good at all. On the last clear night, he had finally put the astrolabe aside and had stared up at the constellations cartwheeling overhead, trying to discern some direction or shape. Wasn't that the Big Dipper? And surely that was Ursa Minor. Wasn't it?

The truth was, he didn't know. They were just names he remembered from his youth. He wasn't a sailor or even a soldier, after all. He'd come out to Cuba in order to become a man of property, an owner of land, and he wasn't particularly well versed even in enterprise. What did he know of the stars?

Puertocarrero stomped back to the campfire, where the other Spaniards—all equally ignorant of celestial navigation— were huddled by the flames, shivering. This blasted cold was another unexpected misery. Dear God in heaven, it was freezing up here. "Coño," he swore, as he had lately taken to doing. "Coño y recoño."

He slumped down by the fire and held his hands out to the flames. He had good reason to swear. He and his men were hungry, they were cold, and they were lost. Completely and irrevocably lost. A shadow darted across the ground, and he peered up. It was El Gordito Bustamante, trudging back. He'd been gone just a few minutes to check on the prisoners, who were being kept under guard by a handful of those young Totonac warriors.

El Gordito crouched down. "By the Virgin's sacred tit," he growled. "Down on the coast, all we did was complain about the heat." He shook his head and spat into the fire. "What wouldn't I give now for a little bit of sweat? An arm? A leg? A goddamned testicle?"

Puertocarrero asked if the prisoners were safe.

El Gordito laughed. "Happy as goats," he said. "They don't seem to mind the cold one bit."

Puertocarrero had noticed it before. The Totonacs seemed impervious to the weather. They could go for days without food or water. They seemed ready to march to hell and back without complaint. But thick! Dear God, you couldn't scare a single sentient idea out of the lot, not to save your life. Ah, well. He looked at El Gordito.

"You'll check on them again a little later?"

The Little Fat One, as they called him, spat into the fire. "Why not? I can't imagine I'm going to be able to sleep," he said. "I swear by the virgin cunt of the Mother Mary, I have never been half this cold in my life."

All the others seemed to agree. They shifted closer to the fire. One of the men belched. Another passed wind. God knew where that came from—they hadn't eaten in more than a day. But hunger was not the problem now.

Puertocarrero cursed himself. God, he was a half-wit— merely suspected it before, but now he knew it was true. Somehow, he'd led his men most of the way up a goddamned mountain, hoping they would find a pass somewhere along the way. But they hadn't, and then it had got dark. So here they were, camped out for the night near the top of the godforsaken world, lost in an inkpot of darkness with a keening wind.

Not that their predicament was entirely his fault. Surely, one of those Totonac warriors should have known his way around in these benighted lands. They were native to the place, for God's sake. But when he asked them any questions, did a single ghostly flicker of intelligence illuminate the black pupils of their eyes? No, it did not. They couldn't understand what he was saying. They just stared straight back, waiting for further instructions, which always had to be issued by hand signals. They did whatever he told them and then milled about, waiting to be told to do something else. Nothing seemed to faze them in the least. The only thing he had to watch was that they didn't start torturing the prisoners when he was looking the other way. They seemed to take a giddy pleasure in that. It was some sort of a game.

Puertocarrero slapped at his legs to get the blood flowing again. He let out a whimper and quickly tried to make it sound like a yawn. Damn. This mission had seemed so simple, a straightforward journey west through the hinterlands to Tenochtitlán. How long could it take? A week? That was what he had thought. But it wasn't turning out that way. Already they'd been wandering for a fortnight. Still, he refused to turn back. He had to deliver the prisoners alive to Hernán Cortés, along with a complete description of the heroic events leading up to their capture, including Puertocarrero's valiant attempts to resuscitate the fallen Juan de Escalante, so tragically cut down.

"Ah, Christ," someone moaned. "I can't stand this bloody cold!"

The other men began to grumble and whine, as well they might, and Puertocarrero concentrated on the most pressing issue facing him just now—surviving this abysmal cold. It was nonsense. They were in the tropics. How could they all be in danger of freezing to death? But so it was.

Tomorrow—if they lived that long—he and his men would begin the search for Tenochtitlán once more. Meanwhile, he sent three of the men off to forage in the darkness for any twigs and bark they could find. If this fire went out, they could all kiss the Blessed Virgin's holy ass. That way, when they died from the cold, at least their lips would be warm.

As this thought passed through his mind, he could not help smiling to himself. Spoken like a man—spoken exactly like a man.

Just not spoken aloud.

The Afterlife of Warriors

"Ha!" Moctezuma tilted his head and laughed. "Once again, I win." He swept the gold pellets over to his side of the playing surface. "Now it is your turn to have the first throw."

"Stand back, then. Make way." Hernán Cortés took up his position, several paces from the mud-glazed wall of this large chamber. He tossed a pellet of gold through the air, trying to make it die against the surface of the wall and dribble to the stone floor. Instead, it collided too hard and skittered back out, a good distance from the wall. "Goddamnit." Cortés kicked the floor in frustration and stepped aside so that the emperor could take his turn. "What do you call this game again?"

"*Totoloque*," said Moctezuma.

He set up for his toss, and it was clear at once that he had much more playing experience than his Spanish opponent had. That wasn't surprising. He'd been playing since a child. As usual, his toss landed true, and his pellet came to a stop only a handsbreadth from the wall. Now it was the Spaniard's turn again, and once again Cortés's throw went wrong.

"Damn," he said. "Damn it to hell."

Fortunately for Cortés, his scorekeeper was Pedro de Alvarado, who was an accomplished cheat. No matter how badly he played, the Spanish commander nearly always came out slightly ahead of Moctezuma. Pitoque, who kept score on behalf of the emperor, considered this behavior outrageous, but it was not his place to protest. Moctezuma was certainly aware of the cheating, but seemed not to mind it. He behaved as though it were all a part of the game or, at worst, a source of wicked amusement among friends.

"I'm not sure I approve of the way the Golden One keeps track of the score," he said on one occasion when the score-keeping was especially distorted. "I wonder sometimes if he is operating on the straight and narrow."

"Straight?" said Cortés. "Narrow? But what is my good friend Alvarado if not straight and narrow? You can see for yourself how tall he is and how slim."

This response was translated by Aguilar and Doña Marina, but explaining the idiom took some time. Also, there was the problem of accuracy—although tall, Alvarado was not especially slim. Still, once the translation was done, Moctezuma nearly doubled over. He laughed and laughed, as if he'd never heard such excellent wit.

"Ah, very droll!" he said. "I congratulate you. Such a clever jest."

Pitoque closed his eyes. This praise was embarrassing. The emperor behaved like a child in the presence of Hernán Cortés. He simpered and sighed. He giggled. He preened. Nothing pleased him more than to engage the Spanish captain-general in conversation. He never tired of asking questions about that place beyond the sea, the land called Spain, or about its capital Madrid, or about Charles I, the king of that wondrous domain.

As it happened, Cortés had limited patience for these interviews. To placate the emperor, he generally delegated Aguilar to deal with Moctezuma and his incessant questions. He preferred to go off with Doña Marina or to attend to his other affairs—the search for gold, the task of closing down Aztec temples and rooting out all other signs of idolatry. The Spaniards were also greatly preoccupied with a project of theirs to erect great wooden crosses all over the city. They were hard at it during every daylit hour.

"Very troubling." Azotl shook his head. He meant the wooden crosses that were sprouting up all over Tenochtitlán.

They were causing outrage in every part of the city. "This is extremely worrisome."

The master functionary pushed aside his plate of iguana stew, which he had barely touched. He told Pitoque that the Spaniards now assembled large groups of Aztecs before these crosses and made them bow down. The Aztecs were instructed to abandon their own gods and replace them with this piteous absurdity—what was obviously nothing but two lengths of wood lashed together to represent a sort of stick figure, something a child might draw. He said the people were not responding well.

"Unlike our priests, I do not claim to predict the future," he said. "But I see great trouble ahead. The ditches and trenches are one problem, but the crosses are infinitely worse. And the Spaniards have started to interfere with our temples. You must inform Moctezuma of these matters. He must take some kind of action. He must make his feelings known. Already, you know, we have had reports of ill will brewing—ill will against the emperor himself. Tell him of these matters. Let me know how he reacts."

Pitoque agreed, and Azotl rose from his desk to see his visitor out. The master functionary was definitely losing weight. As well, he was clearly in an agitated state, one that was quite out of character. Normally, nothing upset him. Now he seemed nervous, brittle.

Pitoque could not help asking. "Azotl, are you well?"

The man slowed down and then stopped altogether. In the oblique light, Pitoque could make out some irregularities in

Azotl's complexion, something he hadn't noticed before—a faint constellation of lumps.

He frowned. "What are those marks on your face?"

"Eh? Oh, nothing. Overwork. That's all."

"I see." Pitoque was uncertain what to say or do. No matter what the master functionary said, he did not look in good health. Pitoque hesitated, but could think of nothing else to say except the normal pleasantries. "Take care of yourself. I will visit again soon."

"Do that—and very soon. I want you to report back as quickly as possible."

They bowed quickly to each other and parted.

On his route to the royal aviary, Pitoque again observed the Spaniards at work constructing wooden crosses. As usual, they had gangs of native laborers digging holes in the ground with shovels or hacking with picks at the walls of sundry buildings. Bit by bit, they were tearing the city down.

Gold. Gold. Gold.

Except that the Spaniards were not going to find much of it, or not as far as Pitoque knew. These territories contained little in the way of gold. True, the Aztecs possessed a certain amount, but only because they had been stealing it for years. Now, silver was another matter. The empire certainly possessed silver.

Pitoque skirted another of these countless excavation sites—great mounds of earth heaped up willy-nilly—and continued on his way to the royal aviary, to seek out his son.

‡

"It's true." Maxtla turned his attention away from the maroon-fronted parrot he had been studying from a distance. "Azotl rarely eats a proper meal these days. Some salad. The occasional bit of corn cake. That is all." He pointed back at the parrot, where it perched in the branches of a ceiba tree. "Have you seen such a bird before?"

Pitoque said he had. "Far in the south, the odd time. They are common enough down there. You don't find them much around here. If you do, it means you will come into some good fortune."

"Hmm." Maxtla flopped down on a boulder set by the edge of a narrow stream. "That's something I don't understand."

"What is?"

"That birds are omens." He waved at the sky. "There are hundreds of birds here. They can't all be omens. Some mean peace. Some mean war. So many contradictory portents. They can't all be true."

Pitoque settled himself on a rock not far from his son. "I understand what you mean, but I—"

"Here's an example. Owls. You know the old saying, 'When the owl sings, a man will die'?"

Pitoque knew it well. He also knew it was true. More than once, events had played themselves out just that way. "It is so," he said. "When the owl sings, a man will die."

Maxtla snorted. "But there are all sorts of owls here, as you know. Sometimes they sing. Of course they do. They're owls.

Each time I hear an owl sing, does someone die? If that were so, everyone in Tenochtitlán would be dead by now."

Here was a provocative thought. Pitoque weighed it in his mind. Finally, he thought he saw an answer. "Their song does not mean death, because they are captive here," he said. "An owl's singing only means something in the wild."

The boy seemed less than convinced. He let out a breath and shook his head, clearly changing the subject. "We were speaking of Azotl. I think he worries about the Spaniards. It seems to be affecting his appetite."

"Just as I thought. And you? What do you think of the Spaniards now?"

Maxtla was silent for a time, and Pitoque thought he was not going to reply at all. Finally, the boy spoke up. "I don't know. It's very confusing. I don't know what to think."

"You have seen all these crosses they are putting up, these structures of wood?"

"Yes."

"They make everyone bow down to them."

"I know."

"And the holes they are digging everywhere? All they think of is gold. They think they may do as they please throughout the city. They do not behave as guests should. And this affair of the emperor. I don't know how to describe it." Pitoque remembered the words that Azotl had used. "Troubling," he said. "Worrisome."

Maxtla could not disagree. There were many causes for disquiet just now. For a time, he and his father remained by the banks of the lagoon, both brooding on the troubles that beset the capital of the Aztecs. Finally, they climbed to their feet and ambled down the stone walkway that wound along the stream bank through vine-enshrouded trees. From its roost on the highest branch of a madrecacao, a solitary owl blinked several times, watching them go. In a low and melancholy voice, it began to croon.

"Savage? In what way, savage?" Moctezuma raised his eyebrows and gazed in surprise at Aguilar. The tattoo lines on his face broadened. "Of what do you speak?"

"I think," said Pitoque, "that he is referring to the practice of human sacrifice. I understand it is a matter of some concern among the Spaniards."

"Is it, indeed? And what is the reason for this concern?"

Aguilar leapt in. "It's evil," he said. "It's wrong."

Moctezuma laughed out loud and put his hand to his mouth. "Evil? Wrong? How absurd. I am astonished by your concern. How can you see our practices as being disagreeable in any way?"

Aguilar was about to reply, but the emperor pressed on. He explained that human sacrifices were vital to his people, for how else could the sun be made to shine, or forests to grow, or rain to fall from the sky, or waters to spring from the earth? How else could infants be caused to emerge from the loins of women? How else could men themselves be nourished? How else could there be life? Moctezuma shook his head. No, nothing in all creation was more exquisite than the sacrifice of humans, whose lives were offered up for the greater glory of the sun. The emperor closed his eyes and spoke as if from some inner coil of the spirit.

"It is a joy to stretch a man out upon the sacrificing stone," he said. "Four priests are required to hold him down. Then the incision is made with an obsidian knife. At once, his back arches toward the sky—oh, how divine! The blood begins to flow out over the sacrificing stone. It spills onto the tiles. Next, the ribs must be wrenched apart." Moctezuma put back his head, shivered. He mimed the act of driving his fist into an imaginary chest cavity. "Ah, it is miraculous to wrest a pumping heart from a body that is still alive. To raise that heart toward the sky. To offer it to the sun. Nothing in life compares with this pleasure."

Aguilar stared at Moctezuma with his mouth dangling open. Finally, he spoke. "But they are human beings. And you tear them open as if they were nothing more than . . . than *dogs.*"

"Dogs?" Moctezuma reacted with horror. "Dogs? Oh no, dear fellow. Not dogs. Hardly dogs. It would be better to describe them as our kin, as our brothers. How close to them we feel when their bodies tremble beneath our touch, when we whisper to them and hear their voices murmur back, when we caress their hair and stroke their arms, when we comfort them. It is as if we were lovers, as if we were one."

"Until you kill them."

"You speak as though it were a terrible thing to die."

"To be put to death. It is terrible to be put to death."

"It is nothing of the kind. To be offered in sacrifice is an affair of honor. Think what pleasures await a warrior who is captured in battle—to be given as a gift to Huitzilopochtli! Ah, that is a marvelous fate." Moctezuma closed his eyes again, and his eyelids fluttered as he described the afterlife of warriors, how their spirits return to earth in the shape of hummingbirds or butterflies, how they dart about in endless sunshine, shimmering in the light. "They feast upon the sweetest nectar of flowers, drunk with life. They dance upon the air. They are forever afloat, free at last from the torments of humanity, the agonies of the flesh."

"Agonies," said Aguilar. "You said it yourself. The agonies of the flesh. How can you inflict such—?"

"Agony and joy," said Moctezuma. "Pain and pleasure. When the circle closes, they are one and the same." He frowned at Aguilar, like a teacher being pestered by a backward pupil. "There is no pleasure without suffering and no suffering that is not a kind of joy."

Aguilar seemed about to say more but then changed his mind. He merely pursed his lips. "Thank you," he said, "for your most patient explanation."

The emperor of the Aztecs smiled and settled back into his seat. He tilted his head toward Aguilar. "Your Nahuatl," he remarked, "is much improved."

The Hummingbird Bride

"Come," said the emperor. He rose from his throne and stretched out his arms. "I have decided that we shall venture outdoors today. There is something I wish to show you."

Pitoque and Aguilar exchanged glances. What was this about? A day had passed since their debate on the subject of human sacrifice. Was the memory of that conversation still on the emperor's mind?

"Please," Moctezuma said. "Let us go."

The process wasn't quite that simple. First, Pitoque had to secure permission from Cortés. Then a Spanish guard had to be detailed to accompany them "in order to ensure the emperor's safety," as Cortés put it. The royal palanquin had to be summoned, along with its complement of eunuch slaves. Eventually, all was arranged. Moctezuma rode in his litter, while Pitoque and Aguilar followed on foot. The Spanish soldiers were deployed around them.

The procession wound through the city, dodging the gangs of native laborers, who were still digging up the streets under the orders of their Spanish overlords. As the imperial cortege wound past them, ordinary Aztecs stood back and watched, but they did not fall to their knees. They did not press their foreheads to the ground. Pitoque, in particular, was struck by this. *Ignore the emperor?* It was unthinkable, and yet he saw it with his own eyes. Eventually, the procession reached a small palace that stood by the shores of Lake Texcoco. This was the palace of the hummingbird god.

Moctezuma rose from his litter and led Pitoque and Aguilar inside. Three of the Spanish soldiers followed, with their harquebuses at the ready.

"Each year," said the emperor as he walked ahead, "many great nobles are captured during our raids against enemy tribes. Like other lesser prisoners, they are brought back to Tenochtitlán. One of them—one of the noblewomen taken this way—is chosen by Huitzilopochtli to serve as his favorite, as his bride."

"Chosen?" said Aguilar. "How?"

The emperor flicked at the air with one hand, as if such details were beneath him. "An affair," he said, "of priests." He gestured at their surroundings, the interior of the palace, a haven of cotton canopies and sweet-smelling cedar. "For an entire year, the hummingbird bride is housed in this place and granted every imaginable pleasure. Nothing she desires is denied her. Come. You will see."

Moctezuma led his companions along a hallway and into a bright, airy room flooded by the afternoon light. To the east, the room was open to the outdoors and overlooked a rock garden that ran to a cliff and then tumbled down to the lake. Inside, the floor was spread with mats and cushions of dazzling patterns and colors. Pitoque's gaze was drawn to the right, toward a vast bed overhung by a canopy of cotton. A young woman reclined upon the bed. Dressed in loose robes of cotton, she gazed dreamily out upon the splendid view. She was slender and lithe and seemed to be of more than average height. Her skin was bronze-colored, and her long, dark hair meandered down over her shoulders and across the sheets. She looked to be about eighteen years of age.

Meanwhile, two children knelt upon the floor nearby, wearing only loincloths. They were servant girls, it seemed, waiting to be ordered about. On a table by a wooden railing stood several ceramic jugs containing drink and various bowls brimming with every kind of fruit. Other bowls were filled with what looked like mushrooms.

"This," said the emperor, "is the hummingbird bride." He stood back and raised his arms.

To Pitoque, the scene unfolded in a kind of slow motion. He had the feeling that he and Aguilar had been standing here for several minutes already, silently observing the room and its occupants, before the young woman on the bed took any notice of them. When she did so—when she seemed at last to realize that others had entered her boudoir—she acknowledged them not as they expected, with a start of surprise and some show of embarrassment. Not at all. Instead, she simply rose and sauntered away toward the wooden railing that ran along the edge of the room, overlooking the lake. In the distance, canoes plied the blue and sparkling water like dragonflies skittering in the sun's midday glow. The hummingbird bride turned to face her visitors. She said nothing. She wore a robe of plain blue cotton, and around her head a halo slowly formed, a disk of numinous light. Pitoque saw it and wondered whether his eyes were playing tricks upon him, but at his side he heard Aguilar let out a gasp of shock or amazement. The bride pressed the palms of her hands together in an attitude of prayer. She lowered her head, still surrounded by its ethereal and sparkling crown.

Moctezuma smiled. Pitoque pondered the source of the strange, unearthly light. A reflection from the lake? But Aguilar was overcome. He fell to his knees and began to babble in a tongue that was neither Spanish nor Maya nor Nahuatl nor any other language that Pitoque knew.

Here, the emperor said, stood the most fortunate woman in the world. She had been captured far to the south, near a place called Bochil, and had been brought back to Tenochtitlán, where the god Huitzilopochtli had selected her as the favored one. Several months hence, on the fourth night of the feast of the hummingbird god—at the very height of the festivities— the bride would perform her sacred obligation. The priests of Huitzilopochtli would wait upon her. On her head, they would place a floral crown. They would spread a mantle of flowers over her shoulders. Bells would ring at her ankles. They would decorate her sandals with the ears of ocelots. They would paint her face the blue of cobalt. Then she would be taken down to the edge of the lake and helped into a small yacht. Slaves would row her out onto the water. Despite the glory to come, she would be calm and resolute—owing, in some measure, to the ingestion of mushrooms. It was vital that she betray no sign of distress. She must be calm and resolute as she approached her fate, her union with the hummingbird god.

The rowers would deposit the girl at the little island of Tepepolco, along with her priests and attendants. The party would proceed inland and then climb the steps of a sacred pyr- amid dedicated to Huitzilopochtli. At the summit, the bride would stand alone for a time, peering out through the darkness that swooned around her, glittering with torches and the flickering lights of Tenochtitlán. She would raise a flute to her lips and play several notes. Then she would break the instrument with her own hands upon her knee.

"So fragile is greatness," Moctezuma whispered. "So fleeting is love."

The priests would take the woman then and lay her out upon the sacrificing stone, and already the people of Tenochtitlán would be celebrating. From the moment they heard the last notes of Huitzilopochtli's song wavering across the lake waters and through the darkness, they would begin a serenade of their own on flutes that had been newly fashioned just for this moment—the most exquisite moment, the instant when life becomes death, and death becomes life. Plucked from her chest, the still-pumping heart of the hummingbird bride would seem to throb through the night, like the shimmering pulses of the moon.

Moctezuma turned to Aguilar and Pitoque. "Can you imagine an event more splendid, more wonderful, than the offering up of the hummingbird bride? You have called us evil. But now you see us as we are."

The emperor turned and departed that room with its flood of light, its haloed virgin. Pitoque helped Aguilar to his feet and guided him as he stumbled away. The poor man could barely support himself, so shaky was his balance.

"A sign," Aguilar whispered. "A sign from God. I have seen it at last."

✝

All that afternoon, Aguilar stalked the streets of Tenochtitlán, a man possessed. He had witnessed a sign from God—the sign that God had meant him to see. The instant he had first laid eyes on the young woman chosen by the Aztecs to die, he had known. He felt in his bones that his future was linked to the woman's fate. But how? This question he could not yet answer. He could not yet say how their destinies were intertwined, only that they were. Some act was required of him—he knew that much, sensed it in his veins, in the coursing of his blood. But what was it?

He did not know. Instead, he stormed through the streets, waving his hands in the air like a madman and trying to make sense of the vision he had witnessed that day, the voices he had heard. What had the emperor said? At the time, the words had barely registered in Aguilar's mind, but he must have retained their meaning somehow, for now he remembered. The feast of Huitzilopochtli. The island of Tepepolco. And then . . . the hummingbird bride would die.

Ah! He collapsed to his knees, horrified at the thought, terrified by the grotesque images that swarmed now in his mind. But he soon felt an invisible weight upon his shoulder, gentle as the hand of God, and he pulled himself to his feet. All that afternoon, he wandered the streets of Tenochtitlán aimlessly, until he found himself at the base of the pyramid dedicated to Huitzilopochtli. He had no idea what had brought him here, but here he now was. And what he found in this place—apart from somber priests shuffling back and forth, their hair matted with dried blood—was a vast assembly of wooden cages, each containing a human being, a living, breathing human being. They were cooped up like animals with barely enough room to move their arms or shift their legs. Aguilar realized at once that they were the miserable ones—the ordinary victims of sacrifice. They squatted in their wretched, rickety prisons, staring stupidly at the ground.

Aguilar began to count the cages, but he gave up when he reached one hundred and thirty-two, when he realized that the counting had barely begun. Several slaves wandered up and down the rows of cages, ladling out gruel from large earthenware jugs. They dribbled the stuff through the wooden bars, and the prisoners scooped it up with their hands wherever it had landed, whether slopped in the dirt or splattered on their legs. With immense difficulty, because they could barely move, they ate. They awaited death, and still they ate.

Aguilar wandered back and forth along the rows of cages until it began to grow dark. He knew he was witnessing an immense and appalling crime. He was astonished that no one challenged him or bothered him, neither the slaves nor the priests, but then he realized that no one in Tenochtitlán felt ashamed at human sacrifice. These endless lines of cages might have been a source of pride. He shook his head. It was impossible to understand such evil. It was possible only to weep.

He looked up at the sky and saw the stars beating down like all the eyes in heaven, and the words welled up in him again, but this time they did not speak in strange tongues that he could not comprehend. This time, he understood what the words were saying and what they meant. *For behold, the Lord will come with fire and with His chariots, like a whirlwind, to render His anger with fury, and His rebuke with flames of fire. For by fire and by His sword the Lord will judge all flesh; and the slain of the Lord shall be many.*

He fell to his knees and pressed his hands to his head. *I will set a sign among them; and those among them who escape I will send to the nations: to Tarshish and Pul and Lud, who draw the bow, and Tubal and Javan, to the coastlands afar off who have not heard My fame nor seen My glory. And they shall declare My glory.*

Aguilar gazed up toward the high precipice of Chapultepec that loomed above the city, and he saw a wooden cross in flames and men running in all directions. He heard a wailing of women, a snapping of bones. He turned and offered a sign of the cross and whispered a blessing to the multitude of cages and to the captured men. He beat his fists against his forehead. He fondled the tattered prayer book that was tucked into the pocket of his doublet. He riffled its pages, mouthing their contents into the darkness without being able to see the words. At last, a crescent moon sailed over the horizon, orange as fire, and he climbed slowly to his feet and left that evil place.

And Because He Loves You

Kalatzin clutched her daughter by the hand and stared at the priest, the old one with the hooked nose and the pointed teeth.

He tossed a collection of seashells, contemplated the patterns they made upon a bolt of cotton, and then tossed them again. This went on for a very long time. To her, it felt like several days.

Finally, the priest declared that he had finished.

"I fear," he said, "that the indications are quite clear." He looked up from the chaos of seashells scattered before him. "The girl's eyes will have to come out."

"Out!" Kalatzin put a hand to her mouth. "What on earth are you saying?" She quickly realized her place—a woman addressing an elderly priest—and tried to assume a more appropriate tone. "I mean, surely, you can't be serious. Doesn't this seem rather . . . *dramatic?*"

"Dramatic?" The old priest smiled. Like all the priests, his hair was matted with blood, and he was missing an ear. He reached out and patted Zaachila on the knee. "But life without a husband—does not that seem dramatic as well?"

"I suppose." Kalatzin struggled to maintain her composure. The priest's suggestion had been so shocking, so unexpected. Remove Zaachila's eyes? "But who would want to marry a blind girl?"

"An, you would be surprised." The priest gazed away, as if addressing the wall. "Many men would be quite pleased to do so, particularly men of a—how shall I put it? Men whose outward cast is not all that it might be." He smiled, pleased by this clever locution. "And another advantage—a blind girl would not stray from the hearth, as it were. She would be much less likely to be attracted by another. For many men, this would count as a blessing."

In her confusion, Kalatzin did not at first register the absurdity of the priest's last remark. For Zaachila, the problem was finding one suitor, not fending off a second. She tried to think of some reply she could make. There had to be some way out of this torment.

"Mother . . ." Zaachila implored Kalatzin with her static eyes. "Mother, I don't need a husband that badly. I can live with you and father. I—"

"Hush, child." The priest raised a hand. "This is a matter between your mother and me. You will remain silent."

"But—"

"Silence."

"But they're my—"

The priest brought his hand down hard against Zaachila's cheek. The girl lurched to one side at the impact. Kalatzin shuddered and wished she could do something—but she could not. The man was a priest. Zaachila reached up with one hand to cover the tender place where she'd been hit. Tears welled in her eyes, but she did not cry. She simply rocked in silence, nursing the pain.

The priest looked back at Kalatzin. "I can see that my tidings have caught you rather by surprise. But all the signs are quite definite. If the gods meant for this affliction to remove itself by any other means, then surely it would have done so by now. Obviously, it has not. The way ahead, therefore, is clear. Remove the girl's eyes, and all will be resolved." The holy man smiled and patted Zaachila on the knee again, as if they were confederates once more. "But you may wish to take some time to reflect upon the matter. No doubt you will want to speak with your husband."

Kalatzin closed her eyes. That was certainly so. She had another thought and looked at the priest. "Assuming—just for argument's sake—that we proceed as you suggest."

"Yes?" said the priest. He gave an encouraging nod.

"How would . . . the removal . . . take place? How, in practical terms?"

"Ah." The priest raised his eyebrows. "Ah, well. That, as you might expect, is a matter of some delicacy, a subject better left between the priests and the gods. Suffice it to say that the entire procedure can be accomplished quite quickly. A single morning."

"Mother . . ."

"Silence, child."

"Would it involve pain?"

"Pain?" The priest scoffed. "We have medicines to control such trifles. But what is a little pain compared to a lifetime of marital bliss?" He rose and collected his robes about him. "You will now excuse me. There are others awaiting my attention. Think about what I have said. Take your time." He made a perfunctory bow and withdrew.

For a while, Kalatzin and Zaachila remained where they were without saying a word, both huddled in misery. Finally, the girl spoke.

"Mother," she said. "I would much rather be husbandless than blind."

Kalatzin squeezed her daughter's hand. "I know. I know,

my dear. But perhaps that is only because you can see." She climbed to her feet. "Come, daughter. Let's go home. We'll have to speak to your father about this."

The two women departed the temple and made their way back to the house of Pitoque. Along the way, Kalatzin realized that she had forgotten to ask the price of this procedure. But perhaps she did not need to know the exact sum. In rough terms, she knew the answer already—a great deal. It wasn't likely the priests would remove her daughter's eyes for free.

"You can see that he is cheating." Pitoque dropped into a chair, no longer in the least bit reluctant to seat himself in front of the emperor. "I think you should say something. It isn't right."

"It is not important." Moctezuma smiled. He waved his hand, as if swatting a fly. "A trifle. I pay it no mind."

"But how can they take you seriously if you let them get away with cheating?"

Pitoque and the emperor were both in Moctezuma's private chambers, in the palace of Axayácatl. Another round of *totoloque* had just been played with Cortés and, once again, the blond one, Pedro de Alvarado, had cheated—outrageously. Dozens of gold pellets had poured into the Spanish commander's pockets, pellets that by rights should have gone to the emperor.

"You are making yourself a laughingstock."

"A what?"

Pitoque knew he had gone too far. But it was too late now. The words had been spoken.

Moctezuma drew up his shoulders. "A *laughingstock?* Is that what you think? How very interesting. We shall see, my friend. We shall see about that."

The following day, Moctezuma played another game of *totoloque* against Cortés, and the result was the same—more egregious cheating by Alvarado.

"We are not greatly impressed with the Golden One's scorekeeping," the emperor said, but he spoke in a diffident, playful tone. "It seems he has some trouble with arithmetic. Perhaps he neglected his lessons as a youth?"

The emperor's words were translated, and everyone laughed. But Alvarado went right back to cheating. He didn't care. To him, the emperor's words had no more significance than the babbling of some child. Alvarado could rob Moctezuma when the emperor wasn't looking, or he could rob the little man right before his eyes. It made no difference. Quite a woman Moctezuma had become.

Saved! By the Virgin's left tit, they were saved! Alonso Puertocarrero put back his head and gave thanks to God on high. This was the best news he'd had in ages. He had sent out a scouting party of Totonac warriors, telling them not to bother showing themselves back here until they'd found Tenochtitlán—and now they'd done it! Or, as near as he could make out they had. Problems with language again, as usual.

But judging by their hand gestures and their demeanor, it seemed that they had found the city at last. All Puertocarrero's men had to do was scale this great col that towered ahead of them, and they'd be close enough to the Aztec capital to see it. Tenochtitlán was on the other side.

Excellent. He called his men together and gave them the news. But if he had hoped for an outbreak of cheers and huzzahs, he was disappointed. By now, the men had pretty much lost faith in their commanding officer. Hell, he was the one who'd got them into this mess. Why should they trust him to get them out of it? Still, they might as well climb. They might as well freeze to death up there as perish from hunger down here. There were no cheers, but there was compliance. With their prisoners and their Totonac companions, the Spaniards gathered themselves together for one more mountainous ascent.

As they worked their way up the col, and as the air grew steadily cooler, Puertocarrero wracked his brains for the name of that Aztec who had masterminded the scurrilous attack on them at Cempoala. Oh, he knew it wasn't an attack. In truth, of course, the Spaniards had launched an offensive against the Aztecs. But he had decided that, for once, he would sacrifice the truth to serve his interests rather than the other way around.

Now, what was that fellow's name? True, he'd written it down. Unfortunately, he'd been obliged to put every last scrap of parchment to the flame that bitter night more than a fortnight earlier up on the frigid mountainside. They'd had to burn everything flammable or die of the cold. He'd decided he would simply have to go by memory. He'd repeated the name often enough. But it seemed to have escaped him. What was that bloody name? Goddamnit, he couldn't remember. It had slipped his memory altogether.

He trudged ahead, railing at himself under his breath. Then he had a thought. Maybe if he didn't think about the name, it would return. He plodded upward and tried to think of other things. Doña Marina. Her plump round breasts. He thought of her. He thought of those.

On impulse, Cortés had ordered his two master carpenters to oversee a building project on his behalf. He clasped his hands behind his head and lay back on the eiderdown in the chamber he shared with Doña Marina in the palace of Axayácatl. He told her what he planned—a pair of sloops.

She frowned. "A pair of . . . ?"

"Sloops. Sailing boats." Under the direction of the carpenters, a gang of his men would fetch sufficient lumber—a dense thicket of oak trees stood not far from the lake—and build a pair of sailing sloops. He had already ascertained that the provisions they had brought from Veracruz included a supply of lines and canvas. What hardware they needed, they could fashion here, of copper. He did not expect that the challenges would prove insurmountable.

Doña Marina could not understand what he was talking about. "Sailing," she repeated. "What is that?"

He explained the concept. Sailing—to ride upon the wind. "You did it yourself," he said. "On the voyage along the coast."

She moaned. That had been utterly miserable. She and the other girls had been kept in a stuffy room below. Most of them had been ill. Not she. The others. But she had suffered as well. If that was sailing, then she did not count herself a sailor.

Cortés laughed. "This will be different," he said. "You'll see. You will love it." In fact, he longed to be sailing again. He wished he understood more about it. In another life, he'd have loved to come back as a sea captain, to sail wherever his heart desired, far beyond the reach of governors or kings. "You will see," he said. "You will be delighted."

Doña Marina had an idea. "You must promise me something," she said.

"Yes, my love."

"You must ask the emperor along on the first voyage."

"Why?"

"Because he is sad. And because he loves you."

Cortés rolled over onto his side and peered at this girl who shared his bed—perhaps the one person he had ever met who was less given to sentiment than he was himself. He frowned. Why did she care how the emperor felt? "Are you serious?" he said.

She pouted, and one of her hands worked its way down between his legs. "Yes, my master. And I have a further request."

"You do?"

"I wish to come on that voyage as well, the first voyage."

"But I thought you weren't a sailor."

"Nor am I. But . . ." She faltered.

"But what?"

What she wanted to say was exactly what she could not say. *Because I am sad. And because I love you.* Instead, she made an effort to smile. "I like novel experiences."

"Ah," said Cortés. He lay back and let the blood rise at his groin. "Novel experiences," he repeated. "Yes. I am partial to novel experiences myself."

Doña Marina pursed her lips but said nothing. Something stung at her eyes, but she blinked it away. She would not show weakness. Not now. Not ever.

Voices in the Darkness

Maxtla was passing by the lakeside terrace in the house of Azotl when he heard voices speaking in the darkness. He recognized them at once as the voices of Azotl and Ometzin. He was going to step out to join them, but something made him stop—the word *Cacama*. He shifted closer and listened. Azotl was saying he had lately had a meeting with Cacama.

Maxtla knew the name, of course—the king of Texcoco. He leaned against the door frame, held his breath, and what he heard put a new anger in his chest. It began to pound there against his ribs. He soon felt a burning at his temples.

"I was thinking," said Azotl, "that I might speak to Maxtla about this."

"Why on earth?" This was Ometzin.

"Because I need to get word to Moctezuma. Cacama is

reluctant to proceed further without some sign from the emperor—whether he is for or against. The boy could carry a message to his father, who could speak to Moctezuma. Maxtla would return with the emperor's decision, which I would then take to Cacama. It's the surest way."

"What is sure about it? Why not just announce the rebellion directly to the Spaniards instead? Telling Maxtla would have the same result. Maxtla is still besotted with his precious heroes. He'll tell them. He would betray us all as soon as spit."

At these words, Maxtla bridled. Beads of sweat prickled under his arms. It wasn't true. None of her words were true. In fact, the recent outrages by these forces of Cortés—the imprisonment of the emperor, the digging of the pits, the construction of wooden crosses everywhere, the massacre in Cholula—they had all raised dark questions in his mind about the Spaniards, about what they did and what their presence meant. Once he had thought that any offence against the Aztecs would give him pleasure, but he knew now it wasn't so.

He shifted his weight, and the wall creaked, like the squawking of some small animal, a sound that scrabbled against the hush of the night. He clenched his fists, held his breath, and waited for some response from the terrace outside, but none came. They had not heard the sound, or if they had, they had decided to pay it no mind. Their conversation went on as before.

"I'm not so sure you are right," Azotl was saying. "I believe he would keep our confidence, just as he has done with the secret of the House of Birds. He has not, as you know, mentioned a word about that to anyone. If he had done, we would certainly have seen the result by now."

Here, the master functionary was suddenly overcome by a fit of coughing. It sounded as if his lungs were filled with pebbles and he was emptying them out.

"Are you sure you are well?" Ometzin said. "That cough sounds terrible. Here. Sit down. You look so weak these days."

There was silence for a time, broken only by the sound of Azotl's breathing. He seemed to be struggling just to take in air. Then Ometzin spoke again, but in a low voice, almost a whisper, that Maxtla had to strain to catch.

"The House of Birds is one matter. But this is different. Lives depend upon secrecy. Why, Cacama himself would be put to death if the Spaniards knew he was plotting a war against them."

"It's true," said Azotl. "They would kill the plotters instantly. Think of Cholula."

"I do. I think of it all the time. That's why I'm astonished you would think of telling the boy. His father? Of course. That's a different matter. It shocks me that the two came to be related."

Azotl let out a long sigh, more like a gasp. "All right, then. I'll leave the boy out of it. I'll think of some other way." He began to cough again.

"Here. Wait here. I'll get you something to drink."

At the sound of her approaching feet, Maxtla turned and started to hurry away. Almost immediately, he realized that he wouldn't have time. So he stopped, turned around, clasped his hands behind his back, and began to whistle a tune he remembered from his childhood. When Ometzin entered the room, he looked up as if he had been taken by surprise. "Ah," he said. "It's you."

"Hello, Maxtla. Where have you been all day? At the House of Birds?"

"Yes. I . . . I just got back."

"You did? Why didn't you come out to join us? Azotl and I were on the terrace, looking at the stars. Surely you heard us?"

No. I . . . I was whistling. I can hear very little when I am whistling.

"Is that so? It sounds like a useful skill. There are times when I would be pleased to hear nothing at all. You must teach me."

"There's not much to teach. Whistling's easy. Anyone can do it."

"You underestimate yourself. I've long dreamt of one day being able to purse my lips and have a song emerge. But if you are unwilling to instruct me, I will strive to bear the disappointment somehow. Are you thirsty?"

"Not really. Or . . . yes. Yes, to tell the truth, quite thirsty. This time of year, the air is so dry. In fact, I was just going to get myself something to drink."

"You were? That's strange. You were walking in exactly the wrong direction. I think you know the location of the kitchen by now?"

"Of course, I do. I know exactly where it is. I was just trying to decide what to drink. I was thinking."

"Ah. And walking in circles serves as an aid to cogitation. Of course. How foolish of me not to have understood. In any case, we share a common destination. I want to get something for poor Azotl. His cough is very bad."

They walked out to the kitchen together, Maxtla following the girl. He wondered whether he had sounded guilty to her, but on the whole he thought not. No, he was sure he had pulled the discussion off very well. And now he knew something else. A rebellion was being plotted against the Spaniards, and Cacama was to lead it. That, alone, was an immense piece of information, but there was more. He also knew that neither Ometzin nor Azotl trusted him. How considerate of them. How generous. Typical Aztec behavior. Well, they would see. Fortunately, he knew how to repay this sort of kindness. He knew exactly how to do that.

"A canoe that rides upon the wind!" The emperor Moctezuma turned to Pitoque and held up a large sapota fruit, half-eaten. He rolled his eyes, overcome with excitement. "Can you imagine it?"

Pitoque said that he could not.

And yet it was true. It seemed that Cortés had instructed his two master carpenters to busy themselves with a construction project. While their compatriots rooted about for gold, the carpenters and a gang of Spanish workers had built a pair of sloops. They were ready now to be launched upon the waters of Lake Texcoco.

Just that morning, Cortés had sent Doña Marina to seek out the emperor and to issue an invitation. The Spaniard requested the pleasure of Moctezuma's company for the inaugural voyage of the two sailing craft. It was to take place the following morning. Would His Royal Highness, Emperor of the Aztecs, deign to accept?

How could he not? Moctezuma was instantly enchanted by the prospect, although it was difficult to know which delighted him more—the thought that he would ride upon the lake waters, propelled by the ether, or that his intimate friend, the Spanish captain-general, had singled him out for the maiden voyage. Either way, he was all but overwhelmed. He would be a consort of the gods. He would ride upon the wind.

"A signal adventure," said the emperor. He tossed away the core of his sapota fruit. "I have much to discuss with Cortés. We shall speak of wind and waves and other such themes—matters of mutual interest."

"Yes, yes, my lord," said Pitoque, who deeply wished to speak to Moctezuma about other, more pressing issues—the troubles brewing beyond the walls of the palace of Axayácatl, the digging of trenches, the construction of wooden crosses, the anger festering in the air. All these troubles were apparent to everyone—except the emperor. "It is all very exciting. But I think that you—"

"Clothes. Oh, dear. I have forgotten to inform myself with regard to clothing." Moctezuma glared at Pitoque. He obviously had ears for nothing that did not touch upon this exhilarating prospect—the voyage upon Lake Texcoco. "You must undertake a mission on my behalf, Pitoque. You must go now and inquire of the Spaniards about what sort of dress would be most appropriate for the *tlatoani* to wear while engaged in a voyage upon the lake. I would not wish to make an error in this respect. I wish everything to be perfect."

"Yes, my lord. It will be done at once. But first—"

"But first I wish to know what to wear. You will inquire on my behalf."

"Of course. As you wish. But, just now, there is another matter that—"

"That I will address and dispose of in good time. Right now, I am concerned about clothes. Please oblige me."

Pitoque set off to determine in what manner of dress the emperor of the Aztecs might most suitably garb himself for riding in a Spanish sailing boat. It seemed an absurd order, but he had to obey. Pitoque hiked his robes a little and hurried beneath a long portico that led to a courtyard where the Spanish deer stood about, craning their great necks and whispering to each other. *Caballos*, they were called. He rushed past them and continued on toward the section of the palace where the Spaniards dwelled.

The Last Good Day

Hernán Cortés led the way down toward the lake's edge, followed by Doña Marina and by Jerónimo de Aguilar. The Spanish translator was in a bitter mood, the way he often was now. He seemed haunted by some private fury. He rarely spoke to anyone unless he was first addressed, and even then he answered roughly, with the fewest words possible. Now he hunched his head low upon his shoulders and glowered out at his surroundings like an animal threatened in its lair. Below, the two Spanish sloops were rigged with sheets and halyards and canvas sails, and outfitted with a splendid regalia of ensigns and streamers. The vessels jostled against the makeshift dock that jutted out from the shore of Lake Texcoco.

When they reached the shore, the members of the Spanish party milled about, stretching their arms and legs in the morning sunshine. They were waiting for Moctezuma to appear. Nearby, against the backdrop of a cut-stone wall, a congregation of Aztecs had assembled, perhaps fifty in all—all fascinated by the sight of the Spanish sailing vessels. They shifted their weight from side to side, murmured to each other in low voices, and pointed at the boats each time a trick of the waves caused them to bob upon the water.

Cortés gazed around at the scene and put back his shoulders. He was feeling quite excited about this expedition. He had not been on the water for a long while. He longed to smell the canvas again, to hear the creak of a vessel's hull, to feel the movement of the waves beneath him. All in all, he was extremely glad he'd had this idea.

Something moved at the brow of the low hill above the lake, and Aguilar gazed up. He saw a lone figure appear, marching slowly down toward the dock. This, it turned out, was Maxtla, son of the merchant from Cholula. The boy ventured up to the Spanish party, squinting in the sunshine. It struck Aguilar as odd that the boy was here, alone. What on earth did he want?

Aguilar approached him. "Good morning."

Maxtla made a shallow bow. "Good morning," he replied. He seemed agitated. He kept glancing around and looking back up the hill. He rocked from foot to foot.

"What brings you here?" Aguilar asked.

Maxtla swallowed and started to speak, but a dryness of the throat stopped him. He shook his head and started again. He seemed out of breath, had to gasp between words. "I have brought a message for the Spanish captain, Hernán Cortés."

"Have you indeed?" Aguilar raised his eyebrows. The boy was a little champion when it came to messages. "Well, you have come to the right place. As you can see, Cortés is here." Aguilar inclined his head to the side, where Cortés stood a short distance away, conferring privately with that blond oaf, Alvarado.

The boy bit his lip. "That is why I have come. My message—"

"Yes?"

"Is very important."

"I would expect no less. What is it?"

"I wish to deliver it directly to the commander."

Aguilar shook his head. Had they not had this identical conversation once before? "All right, then. Come. Let us see if my captain is in a mood to receive messages this morning."

He began to guide the boy toward the Spanish captain-general, but just then the Spaniards and Aztecs turned to look back at the rise of land behind them. Aguilar followed their gaze. The emperor's palanquin was approaching, borne by a crew of slaves.

The litter tottered down toward the lake, and everyone stopped whatever they were doing in order to watch. Maxtla did the same. He felt the breath go out of him utterly. He didn't know whether to be dismayed or relieved. He had come out to the palace of Axayácatl this morning intending to tell Cortés everything—the secret of the House of Birds, the plan for a rebellion led by Cacama, the king of Texcoco. But his thoughts still ricocheted in his head like stones skipping upon an endless sea. He knew what he meant to do, yet he had no idea why. He felt a terrible anger, that was all—an anger he couldn't properly name. Against Azotl. Against Ometzin. Against his own father. Against everyone. He was angry even at the Spaniards, whose cause he intended to aid by telling what he knew. All these feelings scattered, regrouped, and scattered again in his mind.

But now it was too late. He stood back and watched as the litter that carried Moctezuma reached the spit of land by the makeshift dock. He saw that his father was among the entourage that marched behind the palanquin. That, however, was not what most commanded his attention. What caught and held his gaze—what held the gaze of everyone gathered by the shore of Lake Texcoco on that sun-splashed morning—was the emperor himself. The curtains of the litter were drawn back, and Moctezuma emerged into the light. The *tlatoani* stood up. He thrust back his shoulders, turned, and offered everyone there the most outlandish sight any of them had ever observed. He was clad like a Spaniard in white cotton tights, dark breeches that reached to his knees, and a red brocade jacket that was buttoned to his neck. Upon his head, he wore a powdered wig and a scarlet hat of felt.

Maxtla felt his knees buckle beneath him, for this image was beyond belief. He had a sudden urge to laugh out loud—the emperor looked absolutely ridiculous. In fact, he did begin to laugh, to his horror. Men had been put to death for less. He struggled to get control of himself as his father approached.

"Hush," whispered Pitoque. "Be quiet. Are you out of your mind?"

"Not quite," said Maxtla, when he had calmed down. "I don't think that I am quite insane yet." In truth, there had been times in recent days when he had wondered whether he was going mad. He looked at the emperor. In a low voice, he said, "What is the man wearing? He looks like a fool."

Pitoque sighed. "I know. I tried to tell him not to do it. But Hernán Cortés was of the opinion that this costume would be ideal, and once Moctezuma heard that—there was no dissuading him. He insisted on wearing what Cortés wished him to wear."

"They're making fun of him."

"So I see."

In fact, the Spaniards that morning were not dressed in any way like the emperor. They wore rough, unbuckled breeches and loose cotton blouses, unbuttoned at the neck. They had kerchiefs wrapped about their heads and knotted at the back. Still, Moctezuma seemed pleased with himself. He did a little turn on the shore to show off the cut of his clothes. The Aztecs who had turned out for the event peered at their emperor with a detached and curious air, one that defied precise defini-tion—partly intrigued, partly aghast. Maxtla could imagine what people would be saying all over Tenochtitlán by this time tomorrow. Not only did the emperor dwell in the same house as the Spaniards; now he dressed like them, too.

Pitoque shifted closer to his son. "Would you like to join us on the boats? I'm sure I could arrange it."

Maxtla did not have to think about the question. He was immediately certain that he wanted nothing more in the entire world than to ride upon the wind, to ride upon the waves. His anger with everyone—with his father, with Azotl, with Ometzin—seemed to vanish, along with his reason for com-ing down to the lake this morning. Secrets? What secrets? He forgot everything but the prospect of racing across the pale blue water, propelled by the wind.

"Yes," he said. "Yes, please."

Soon, the two boats were skidding across the lake in a blus-tering swell. The experience exhilarated everyone, and no one more than Moctezuma. The emperor put out his hands to collect the spray and laughed to feel the wind upon his face. Maxtla was almost as excited, and the two of them were like a pair of children united in wonder at a barely imaginable toy.

Suddenly, the sloop carrying the emperor reared against the wind and plunged into the trough of a wave. At once, a great burst of spray pounced over the hull and took Moctezuma and Maxtla square in the face. They both cried out in a mixture of delight and shock. Drenched, with his wig draped over his forehead like a crown of sopping weeds, the emperor turned and congratulated Cortés on this divine creation, this magical canoe that flew upon the water without paddles or oars. The Spaniard merely stroked his beard and declared himself to be honored that the emperor was impressed. He added that he had not conjured up this idea of harnessing the wind himself, but his tone and manner suggested that, in fact, he had.

Eventually, by a roundabout route, the party neared a rocky little island called Tepepolco, where—at the emperor's insistence—they landed and paraded ashore. Pitoque recognized the island's name—it was here that the hummingbird bride would be conveyed during the feast of Huitzilopochtli in order to be sacrificed to the gods. He glanced over at Aguilar and saw from the man's bearing that he, too, realized where they were—in a place of death. Aguilar's complexion had turned to the color of mud. He looked as if he might be ill. Nonetheless, he seemed to pull himself together and tagged along with the rest.

On their way inland, the landing party passed a stone pyramid—perhaps the same structure that the hummingbird bride would scale on the fourth night of the feast, the final night of her life. Again, Pitoque glanced over at Aguilar, wondering what he must be thinking now, but the Spaniard said nothing.

He merely plodded along behind the others, a grim scowl on his dark face, buried in his own thoughts.

As well as a place of sacrifice, the small island was also a royal hunting domain, stocked with diverse quantities of wild-life. The party passed the day in splendid sport, and they sailed home that evening well supplied with venison and rarebit. As the two Spanish sloops careened across the water, Cortés held a kind of water-borne court. He was in a rare expansive mood and told tales of his youth—unusual for a man who seldom spoke about himself. Doña Marina lounged at his side, barefoot, her hair disheveled and long. She rubbed her master's back and translated his words. To Moctezuma, each sentence she uttered was a new source of wonder. He gazed at Cortés, and then at this native princess, his eyes wide, as the Spaniard recounted a succession of remarkable and baffling tales. His father, Martin Cortés. The hard days of his youth in a place called Extremadura, which was a wild and impoverished region of the land called Spain. How sickly he had been as a boy. His time as a young acolyte in one of the countless churches of Medellín. His studies in Salamanca. His youthful interest in arms and gambling. His decision as a young man to abandon Spain in favor of what he called the Indies. He related the many adventures that followed and spoke even of his disputes with that son of a whore, Diego de Velázquez, governor of a place called Cuba.

Still dressed in his strange Spanish costume, Moctezuma clucked his tongue at almost every word and shook his head in amazement.

Later, the Spanish captain lapsed into silence, his head in

Doña Marina's lap. His breath came in whistles and grunts and he was soon fast asleep. As the two boats creaked across the lake in a light wind, the sun's reflection drained from the waters of Texcoco and the sky dangled like a purple cloak beyond the western mountains above the coppery lights of Tenochtitlán and Tlatelolco.

That day on the lake was the last good day.

When the royal party sailed up to the makeshift dock at Tenochtitlán in the evening darkness, an aide to Cortés was waiting for them with urgent news. A group of Spaniards under Alonso Puertocarrero had trekked into the city that afternoon, hungry and footsore. They had brought some native prisoners with them, and a tale of great treachery against the honor of the Spanish king.

"I see." Still dopey from sleep, Cortés scratched his jaw. "I will enjoy my supper first, and then I will hear what Puertocarrero has to say." He hesitated and then spoke again. "No, wait. I am tired now and I wish to go to bed after I have eaten. Nothing can be done tonight in any case. Tell Puertocarrero to come to me tomorrow. Sometime in the morning. Please inform him of this."

With Doña Marina at his side, the Spanish captain-general set off toward the palace of Axayácatl. He left the emperor of the Aztecs behind, still decked out in his strange nautical garb, now a little the worse for the wind and spray. In his hurry to be off, Cortés did not even wish Moctezuma goodbye.

A Lone Hero, Haggard and Scarred

In the morning, Puertocarrero was summoned to appear before Cortés. He felt he was ready. He had deliberately avoided bathing and had not changed his clothes—the same clothes he'd been wearing ever since his departure from the coast. He knew he looked a mess and likely smelled worse, but this was roughly the effect he wished to have. He was a man who had fought battles, uncovered secrets, and traveled long and hard in the service of his commander. Now here he was, worn and exhausted from his travails, but still eager to serve.

The moment was perfect—except for one difficulty. He still could not remember the name of the Aztec who was behind the whole nefarious business out on the coast. If only he hadn't burned that slip of parchment . . . His only hope now was that, in the presence of Cortés, in the high drama of that meeting, something would shake loose in his head and the name would spring free, like a lucky coin landing in his palm. It was a weak hope, but it was all he had. Goddamn his miserable excuse for a brain.

He patted his hair into place and acknowledged the aide who had come for him. He was ready. He followed the man through a network of corridors. It was certainly a confusing place, Tenochtitlán—and much larger than he'd expected. More civilized, as well. He'd had in mind a collection of mud huts squatting by a murky little pond somewhere. But this was actually a city, as impressive in its way as Madrid. He imagined it would be diverting to wander around the place, to get to know it better. But not now. Now, he had a job to do. He had to win his way back into his commander's favor. If only he could remember that blasted name.

Soon, he was ushered into a large and cavernous hall. Several dozen Spaniards stood about, attended by a smaller number of native servants. A milky light spilled down through a trio of high, narrow windows, equipped with wooden blinds.

"Ah, Puertocarrero," said Cortés. The Spanish captain-general had his hands clasped behind his back. He turned around. "I hear you have endured quite a journey." He smirked. "I also hear you are less than expert in the uses of the astrolabe."

Puertocarrero acknowledged the gibe. "Sí, mi capitán." He took several deep breaths. "I have news, sir, from the coast."

"So I hear. Please. Sit down."

"If you please, I prefer to stand." It was part of the image he wished to project—a lone hero, haggard and scarred, but still standing tall for commander, king, and God.

"As you wish. I myself will sit." Cortés settled himself onto a bench covered with many-colored cushions. He crossed his legs. "Go on. Your news, I take it, concerns Escalante, may he rest in peace."

"In part." Puertocarrero cleared his throat and launched into his chronicle, which bristled with dramatic detail. The duplicitous attack by the Aztecs at Cempoala. The tragic death of that champion of Castile, Juan de Escalante. The great victory subsequently won for Spain under the command of Puertocarrero himself, albeit at the cost of five Spanish souls. And, finally, the information he'd wrested from the Aztec messenger named Salchan—that the attack had been plotted in advance, in cold blood, under the direction of an Aztec lord by the name of . . . of . . .

"Yes?" said Cortés. He leaned forward. "By the name of . . . ?"

Puertocarrero shook his head. Dear Mother Mary, what *was* it? If he didn't remember it now, he might as well turn around and head straight back to Veracruz. Hell, he might as well roll up his breeches and swim all the way back to Spain. *What was that name?* He smacked a hand against his brow. "Forgive me," he said. "I—"

"He's making it up, I'll bet." This was Alvarado. The blond lieutenant marched into a narrow band of pale sunlight and gave a hollow, artificial laugh. He addressed Cortés, ignoring Puertocarrero altogether. "His entire tale has a sound of fabrication to it. I believe . . ." Alvarado stopped, frowned.

"Yes?" said Cortés, who seemed more amused than anything. What was happening to his officers? "You were saying?"

Alvarado raised a hand, begging his commander's indulgence. His upper lip began to quiver, as did his nose. Some dust in the air, or perhaps Puertocarrero's reek, had tickled his nostrils, and Alvarado now looked exactly like a man about to sneeze. And so he was. His head went back and then flung itself forward in a fierce and deafening spasm of air and spray. After an instant of silence, he sneezed again and then again.

That was it! Puertocarrero needed to hear the sound only once, and he was immediately reminded of the name that had escaped him. Ah-zaw-tul! Ah-zaw-tul! He turned to Cortés and beat the fist of one hand into the palm of the other. "Ah-zaw-tul!" he shouted.

Cortés put a hand to his brow. "Has everybody suddenly caught a cold? Or gone mad?"

"No," said Puertocarrero. "I'm not sneezing. That is the name I was trying to remember. It was he who ordered the capture of the fat chieftain. It was he who organized the cowardly attack against us at Cempoala. Ah-zaw-tul."

"Hmm." Cortés looked around. He called out for Aguilar, but the translator was nowhere to be found. He'd been rather scarce now for days. The Spanish captain-general frowned and shook his head in irritation. "Get me Doña Marina, then."

When the young princess arrived before him, Cortés had Puertocarrero repeat the name. He asked Marina if she knew of any such man.

"I do."

"An Aztec lord, I take it?"

"Not exactly. A functionary. In fact, the master functionary. He is a very powerful man, but his actions are largely invisible. He labors in the shadows. Among his people, he is known as tlillancalqui."

"What does that mean?"

"The Keeper of the House of Darkness."

Cortés raised his eyebrows. "You don't say?" He turned to Puertocarrero and his face broke into a grin. "Sounds like the devil himself. I congratulate you. I really do. This is splendid." He climbed to his feet. "I gather as well that you have brought prisoners."

Puertocarrero rocked on his heels. He had hardly dared to hope that everything would work out this well. "Prisoners?" he said. "Why, yes. We have fifteen. We brought them all the way from Cempoala."

"No doubt at immense risk to your own safety and welfare. I congratulate you again."

Cortés walked straight past Alvarado, whose expression had turned to one of exquisite despair. Puertocarrero closed his eyes as Cortés wrapped him in a grand and manly *abrazo*, clapping him on the back at least a dozen times.

This was almost too much to bear. Puertocarrero struggled to keep from crying out loud with joy. He opened his eyes again and stared in front of him at the wall, but the blocks of stone seemed to wobble and bend. His vision swam. Finally, Cortés let him go, and it was a wonder he didn't collapse to the floor, a heap of filthy rags and shivering bones.

"Prisoners!" said Cortés. "Now, isn't that a fine present?" He glanced over at Alvarado and laughed when he saw the baleful look on the man's face. "He brings prisoners, Pedrito. What do you think of that?"

Alvarado said nothing. It seemed he could not speak.

Cortés strode back to the bench and settled himself onto it. He pulled Doña Marina down beside him. "We shall have to reward our friend Puertocarrero," he told her. "We shall have to think of something appropriate, something very, very . . . nice. Meanwhile . . ." He looked up at Alvarado again. For no good reason, except that he was feeling malicious today, he decided to rub some salt in the man's wounds. "You," he said, "Pedrito. I put you in charge of dealing with this diabolical agent of destruction, this Azotl. Put him under arrest. See to it now."

"Sí, mi capitán."

Alvarado did his best to summon a shred of dignity. He clicked his boots against the stone floor, turned, and marched from the chamber. But there was an uncustomary stiffness to the arch of his back, and he did not trade as much as a glance with Puertocarrero. This was a shame. Puertocarrero was more than willing to exchange glances with him.

This Dark-Eyed Princess

Azotl was gone.

Ometzin dropped onto a bench in a green courtyard in the palace of Axayácatl. She struggled to regain her composure, and then she told Pitoque what had happened. That morning, she'd returned from some errands to find the door to Azotl's house partly wrenched from its frame. It hung loose, shifting and creaking in a fitful breeze. She'd crept inside and seen at once the place had been ransacked. She'd called out for Azotl, but no one had answered. He wasn't there, and the servants had all fled. Now here she was, at the palace of Axayácatl, dressed in the disguise of a vendor woman, one of the many who came to the palace each day with goods to trade. She was still out of breath, and her brow was speckled with beads of perspiration.

"We have to get word to Moctezuma," she said. "Right away. Maybe something can be done."

"Why?" Pitoque asked. "What do you suspect?"

"That's why I came to you." She lowered her voice. "I am sorry to say, but I think this has something to do with your son."

"With Maxtla? What do you mean?"

As calmly as she could, she explained to the merchant what she feared. "You must know how he reveres the Spaniards and reviles the Aztecs."

"Yes, of course. But his ideas have been changing. Why, only yesterday, he was part of a sailing party out on the lake. He was like a close companion to the emperor. I saw it myself."

"Wait," she said. "There is another reason." Here she leaned close and spoke in a whisper. She told the merchant about the spirit of rebellion festering outside the palace walls. She said Cacama himself was determined to lead an uprising against the Spaniards, but had so far hesitated to act, not knowing how Moctezuma would respond, whether he would side with the Spaniards or with his own people.

Pitoque took in this information, cursing himself for not knowing already of these matters. But the news did not surprise him. What he failed to understand was how Cacama's plans related to Azotl's disappearance—or to Maxtla. "I am grateful for this information," he said, speaking in a whisper himself. "But you said it involves my son."

"I think he knows about Cacama's plans." She told him about the evening not long before when she had come upon Maxtla at

Azotl's house, and his behavior had seemed strange, even guilty. "I think he overhead us speaking about these matters."

Pitoque swallowed. He felt something like anger rising in his throat, where he could taste it. But it did not taste of anger. It tasted of fear. "And you think he took this information to the Spaniards?"

"I'm sorry. I don't know what else to think."

"Well, I do. My son may be hot-tempered. He is hot-tempered. But he is not a traitor. He would not . . ." Pitoque closed his eyes. In fact, he did not know what Maxtla might or might not do. After all, the boy had helped to desecrate a temple in Cholula. He admired the Spaniards. He certainly hated the Aztecs—or he used to hate them. Besides, Maxtla had never explained his presence yesterday down by the lake, just before the voyage aboard the Spanish sailing boats. Pitoque felt a dampness spread across the palms of his hands. Perspiration began to prickle at his brow. Betray Azotl? His own son? He glanced up at Ometzin. "Wait here," he said. He got to his feet. "I will speak to the emperor now, at once. He may know something of this."

Without waiting for the girl to reply, he turned and hurried away, his slippers padding softly on the cold stone floor.

While she waited for Pitoque to return, Ometzin fussed with her maguey robes, which were rough and uncomfortable. These clothes—the garb of a vendor woman—were part of a ruse that she and Azotl had contrived so that she might make her way into the palace and seek out Pitoque to tell him about the rebellion plotted by Cacama. Now here she was, following the same plan but for a very different purpose. Now she had to report that Azotl himself had disappeared.

She looked out at a stand of jacaranda trees that presided over the courtyard. Butterflies darted among the branches. She thought of Maxtla. Curse that boy. To think that he might divulge the secret of the House of Birds—that was bad enough. But it was almost impossible to conceive that he would betray Azotl and Cacama as well. And how many others? She supposed that a great many people must have been taken prisoner by now—all the conspirators. It was probably only a stroke of luck that she had not been captured herself, an idea that hadn't occurred to her till now. She'd been too upset to think of anything apart from Azotl's disappearance. At the thought of her uncle, she closed her eyes and tried to block the frightening images that careened through her mind. She tried not to imagine where he might be now or in what condition, but she could not stop herself. Had he been tortured? Was he being tortured now? Was he even alive? He had been so ill already, with some sort of fever, a terrible cough, the strange nubbles that had formed upon his face.

These worries spun in her mind until she believed they would drive her mad. Finally, she heard the soft pad of footsteps. She opened her eyes and looked up. It was Pitoque. He hurried over and settled himself onto the bench beside her.

"I don't think it was Maxtla," he said. He told her what he had found out from the emperor—that Moctezuma had been summoned to appear before Cortés just that morning, an hour or so earlier. The Spanish captain-general had been in a high fury. Apparently, this group of Spaniards—the ones who had shown up in the city the previous day—had brought charges that the attack out on the eastern coast, in which several of their kind had been killed, was the result of a direct order from Tenochtitlán. Pitoque lowered his voice. "They specified one Aztec official in particular."

"Azotl?"

"Just so."

"But it's a lie." Ometzin pushed back several loose strands of her hair. "Azotl ordered no such attack. He spoke to me about it. He issued the opposite instructions—that no hostilities be contemplated. This is a complete falsehood."

"I believe you. Still, it is what Cortés told Moctezuma just this morning. I suspect that this is the explanation for Azotl's arrest. I think it has nothing to do with Cacama—or my son."

"If that is so, I owe you an apology."

"Not me. Maxtla."

She lowered her eyes, conceding the point. After several moments, she looked back up. "Did you find out where Azotl is?"

Pitoque shook his head. "But one of the Spaniards may be able to tell me." He meant Aguilar, the one who spoke Maya. "I will find out what I can. What I want you to do is to find Maxtla. I want you both to leave Tenochtitlán." This idea had come to Pitoque as he had hurried back from his meeting with the emperor. He sensed that terrible events were in store now, that the storm clouds building over the city of the Aztecs were about to burst open. He felt a sickening premonition about his wife and daughter and needed to know that they were safe. It had been weeks since they had been in contact. He told Ometzin about the small house by the lake at Amozoc. "I want you and Maxtla to go there," he said. "When matters have calmed down here, I will send for you."

"What about Azotl?"

"There is nothing you can do. Leave this to me. I will do everything possible, I promise."

"You know that he is ill?"

Pitoque grimaced. He had seen the eerie pebbling of flesh on the man's face. He had heard Azotl himself speak of some terrible new malady that had broken out between Tenochtitlán and the coast. But he understood nothing of this disease. It was best to deal with whatever matters lay within his power. "I want you to leave," he said. "You and Maxtla."

Finally, she pushed back her hair and rose from the bench. "All right," she said. "I will tell Maxtla."

"He is probably at the House of Birds."

The instant she heard these words, Ometzin started. Of course. The House of Birds! A wave of relief washed over her. Here was the answer. Why hadn't she thought of it before? Azotl knew the secret of the House of Birds, and now it would save his life. She felt sure of it. The master functionary would never permit himself to come to harm—he was far too intelligent, too crafty. He knew too much. Although she did not understand the details of the secret, she knew that it was of immense importance, a source of incomparable power. Now was the time. Azotl would divulge the secret to the Spaniards, and all would be well. In exchange, he would be spared and freed. For the first time that morning, she felt her heart beat freely.

"The House of Birds," she repeated. "Yes. I will look for Maxtla there."

She turned and was about to start away when someone else hurried into the courtyard—another young woman, not much older than herself. The woman was wearing a beautiful cotton robe, white and trimmed with geometric patterns of cobalt dye. She was extraordinarily lovely—slender and graceful, with a shining bronze complexion. The woman came to a sudden stop, as if astonished to find that she was not alone. She glanced first at Ometzin, then at Pitoque, then back at the girl.

"Ah, the merchant of Cholula," she said. "And who, may I ask, is this?" She smiled at Ometzin.

Pitoque stood. He introduced Ometzin to the consort of Hernán Cortés, the native princess named Marina.

"Doña Marina," the woman corrected him.

"I beg your pardon. *Doña* Marina."

The woman laughed and turned back to Ometzin. She reached out with both her hands. "I'm so pleased to meet you. Why have I not seen you before?"

"I live elsewhere."

"Such a pity. We are starved for feminine beauty in this place. You must promise me that you will return to the palace soon and often. I know you will find much to divert you here."

Ometzin had no idea what to make of this invitation. But, to be polite, she accepted. She said she would be pleased to return whenever it might be convenient.

Doña Marina smiled. "It will always be convenient. How may I contact you?"

Pitoque broke in. "Through me. I will know where Ometzin can be found. She is a friend of my son's."

Doña Marina thrust back her head, apparently impressed. "What good taste your son has in friends." She turned back to Ometzin. "But perhaps you are not doing anything just now."

"I'm very sorry. I have an engagement in another part of the city."

"Oh? What a shame." The woman seemed genuinely disappointed. But she gave a little laugh. "Well, it can't be helped. Soon, then? It would be a great pleasure for me to see you very soon."

"Thank you. Yes, I would be delighted."

Doña Marina let go of Ometzin's hands—she had been clutching them both all this time—and stood back. "Until very soon."

"Until very soon." Ometzin pulled her hood up over her head. She bowed to Pitoque and turned away. She left as quickly as she could, more than a little confused about the meaning of this last encounter. But the important thing was that Azotl was surely safe. He would undoubtedly manage to secure his release.

After all, he knew the secret of the House of Birds.

✝

Doña Marina watched the girl depart and then turned her gaze on Pitoque. "I come to inquire after the emperor," she said, her voice suddenly cold, curt. All the charm she had exuded in the presence of Ometzin had suddenly turned to dust. "My master Cortés wishes to speak to the emperor again. He is severely annoyed about this affair. Please arrange to have the emperor present himself before my captain at once."

Pitoque said it would be done. He turned and retraced his steps back toward the imperial quarters.

Doña Marina remained in the courtyard for a short while, oblivious to the jacaranda trees, or the sparkle of butterflies, or the sunshine slanting down through the shifting leaves. She smiled to herself. Clever machinations were all very well, but nothing made her happier than plain blind luck. Or maybe she could attribute this stroke of good fortune to the god of the Spaniards, whose name was Jesus Christ and who had died for men's sins on a rough wooden cross. Whatever the explanation, she was highly pleased to have met this girl named Ometzin.

Only that morning, she and Cortés had debated the question of how to reward that bony simpleton Puertocarrero for his delivery of prisoners and his denunciation of the Aztec master functionary. Cortés believed that something substantial had to be done. The man's services warranted a generous response, and besides, a large reward for Puertocarrero would light a fire under Alvarado. It would put the blond one in a fighting mood. Cortés liked to shift his lieutenants back and forth in his favor like counters in a game of chance. It kept both men off their balance and eager to impress. It gave Cortés a firmer grip on power.

Doña Marina understood this strategy very well. She had watched Cortés at close range for too long not to have learned a good deal about his ways and his whims, which largely agreed with her own. Just now, she had been trying to think of an appropriate reward for Puertocarrero because it was an issue of some urgency for her. She feared that Cortés, in an ill-judged moment, might decide that she herself might very well serve that purpose. This was a prospect she was determined to avoid, and now she believed she had found a way—thanks to this girl she had just met. Ometzin would be the perfect prize for Puertocarrero. For the girl, the arrangement was apt to be rather unfortunate, a dreary fate. But that couldn't be helped.

Doña Marina swung around on her heels and began to march back toward the Spanish quarters. Her spirits had lifted altogether. How very splendid. Like a bird nesting in the palm of her hand, she now possessed her answer. Reward Puertocarrero by giving him this lovely young girl, this dark-eyed princess, this Ometzin. Perfect. Of course, she'd have to find the girl something more comely to wear. That maguey sack was appalling. Why on earth was she wearing such horrible clothes? Any fool could see the child was high-born and cultivated. Marina put a little skip in her stride. Well, she'd soon see to the girl's wardrobe. It would be fun.

She quickened her pace, almost trotting through the alternating bars of light and shade that criss-crossed the walkway in the early afternoon sunshine. She couldn't wait to tell Cortés what she had found.

Corn Cakes and Star Apples

When Maxtla and Ometzin arrived at Amozoc, the afternoon sun was beating down, and the blue lake waters glittered like countless panes of obsidian in the light. They found four Aztec sentries guarding the cottage—and no one inside. The guards said that Maxtla's mother and sister had departed some weeks earlier, bound for Cholula. The sentries had remained behind to keep watch over the place, as they had been ordered.

Maxtla turned to Ometzin. "It's too late to travel to Cholula now. I guess we'll have to spend the night here."

She nodded, relieved that he had not suggested pressing on. "I, for one, could use a rest." She looked around, taking in her surroundings—the waving fields of gorse, the stone cottage set upon a small promontory, overlooking the sparkling lake and the topsy-turvy hills beyond. She let out a long, low sigh. "Besides, this is divine. I feel I could stay here forever."

Maxtla followed her gaze and found himself looking at the scenery as if through her eyes, the eyes of a stranger to this place. He'd never really noticed before how beautiful the lake was, how remarkable the setting. But he saw it now. "Come on," he said. "I'll show you the cottage."

She followed him down toward the low stone building. They had been traveling now for the better part of two days, mostly in silence. Of course, they were both worried about Azotl, but they believed that the master functionary would know how to ensure his salvation with the secret of the House of Birds.

They were also a little uneasy in each other's presence. Maxtla was still smarting from the conversation he had overheard almost a week earlier—the sting of Ometzin's criticism. For her part. Ometzin felt she owed her companion an apology, but she couldn't quite find the words to express it. So they'd made the journey without conversation, each immersed in private thoughts. They were together now because they had to be, instructed by Pitoque to leave Tenochtitlán. It was for their own good, he'd said. Maybe he was right.

Now Maxtla led the way. He pushed open the cottage's wooden door on its rope hinges. Inside, the place was dark and a little musty from having been boarded up for several weeks, but they soon aired it out. With the light shining in, and a breeze drifting through the cool rooms, the cottage was once again as fine and inviting a place as it had ever been. They had not brought much food with them, just a small sack of corn cakes and some fruit. Maxtla said there was a small village around the lake a little way. He knew a woman there—Youala was her name—from whom he could obtain more provisions.

"I might as well go now," he said. "Do you wish to come?"

Ometzin shook her head. "No. I will stay here, if you don't mind. I want to do nothing except exult for a time in this magnificent view."

She strolled out with him and stood at the edge of the promontory, while he struck off along the serpentine path that wound down to the edge of the lake. The village wasn't far off, although it was invisible from here, hidden by the next outcropping of the shore. He made his way down the trail, grasping at roots and small branches to keep his balance. Several times, he glanced back up and saw Ometzin silhouetted against the blue, cloud-streaked sky. The breeze off the lake played with her hair so that her tresses danced behind her. She arched her back and spread her arms, and he imagined that she was a kind of bird, graceful as a heron. At any moment, she would take flight.

He turned around and slithered down another switchback. It was tricky going. Now his left foot slipped on a loose stone and he nearly fell, but he clutched at the trunk of a sapling and managed to right himself. He looked back up behind him, but Ometzin had vanished from view, obscured by the rising folds of the land. Strange—for no reason he could think of, he had a lump in his throat and felt a thudding in his chest. He shrugged and continued down toward the shore.

Butterflies darted and swerved around him. He thought once again of Azotl and the secret of the House of Birds. He felt sure the man would use that secret now, transform that knowledge into power, and save himself. The secret was simple in one sense, but it was also a matter of immense importance. In the House of Birds, in an obsidian-lined vault hidden beneath the basin of the large lagoon, the greatest treasures of the Aztecs were stored—vast treasures, accumulated over the many generations of their rule. No one knew of the vault except Azotl—and now Maxtla as well. In a time long past, the masons who had sealed the vault had all been put to death, to ensure their silence. Azotl had only to offer up this secret, and his life would surely be spared. The Spaniards would trade anything for gold.

Maxtla clambered down the last few yards of the slope by the lake, and here the path flattened out and skirted the edge of the water. He felt another surge of relief. Only when he'd learned of Azotl's capture had he realized how much the man meant to him—his massive appetites, his lumbering gait, his unexpected outbursts of comedy. He had come to this realization a little late, but that no longer mattered. The important thing was that the master functionary would be spared. If they wanted their treasure, the Spaniards would have no choice.

The path ahead wound up another rise of land. Maxtla scrambled to the top and now, below him, lay the lakeside village, where several curls of wood smoke drifted above the small mud houses. Children scampered in the dirt, and men huddled by the shore, repairing the twine of their fishing nets. Fierce and terrible events were playing themselves out in Tenochtitlán, but here by the lake at Amozoc, life seemed the same now as it had been for a thousand years. Maxtla stood for a time, gazing at the view below. It struck him now as incredible that he had once thought of betraying Azotl's secret to the Spaniards. Imagine if he had! It pained him to think how badly he had behaved, to Azotl, to his father, and most of all to Ometzin. At the thought of her, an unfamiliar bewilderment again washed over him, and he felt as if he had fallen overboard from a sailing ship and had to fend for himself in the surging waves.

He didn't know what he was feeling. He knew only that it had to do with the sound of her name, with the shape of her body, outlined against the blue sky on the promontory above the lake. It was all too ridiculous. But at once he felt a determination swell inside him. He would make it up to them all—to Azotl, to his father, and especially to Ometzin, the one who had trusted him the least. He would make it up somehow.

The decision was made. Immediately, he felt better than he had in weeks, months, maybe years. Through a golden light, a swirl of shimmering dust motes, he hurried down to the village by the lake.

"You say she's pretty. How pretty? What does she look like?"

Puertocarrero felt nervous. He had been summoned once again to appear before Cortés, and in the captain-general's private chambers, no less. Now here he was, and here was Cortés, and here was Doña Marina, too. God, how lovely she looked, graceful as a little seabird. Puertocarrero slumped in his chair for, on this occasion, he had agreed to be seated. He had even bathed and changed his clothes—a most invigorating procedure, he couldn't deny it. But the discussion was not going well.

The main item on the agenda was the reward he should receive for his recent exploits in the service of Spain. He knew what he wanted. He wanted gold, he wanted to be an officer again, and most of all, he wanted Marina. Now here she was, just a few feet away, and yet far beyond his reach. ¡Ay Diós! At the thought of her, the sweat began to prick at his brow, and he worried that he might faint. But the thought was all he had, for the girl was offering, not herself, but a *different* native bride. He grimaced.

"Her looks," he repeated. "You say she is pretty. How pretty?"

By now, Doña Marina understood enough of the Spanish tongue not to require Aguilar's assistance—fortunately, because no one seemed to know where Aguilar was. "Extremely pretty," she said. "Lovely. Divine. A nymph."

"How old?"

"Fourteen, I would say. Fifteen, perhaps."

Puertocarrero grinned. Now they were getting somewhere. A nice young girl to share his bed and his nights. This reward might be all right, after all. "What's her name?"

"Ometzin."

"What kind of a name is that? How am I supposed to pronounce it?"

"Anyway you like. You can change it, if you wish. She'll be *your* wife. You may call her what you please."

"Where is she? When can I see her?"

"Soon."

"Now. I want to see her now."

Doña Marina arched her eyebrows and laughed. "Oh my. You are an eager man, aren't you?"

Puertocarrero was about to make some tart rejoinder, but thought better of it. It was a quick remark that had got him into trouble before, and he didn't plan to make the same mistake again. Besides, he couldn't think of anything clever to say. "Eager?" he said. "That is certainly so. I am eager to serve mi capitán in any way I can." He gazed over at Cortés and did his best to put on a winning smile. "Sir."

Cortés nodded. "You will have your girl," he said. "If you deem her unsatisfactory, we'll find you another. You have done excellent work, and I will ensure that you are rewarded." He touched several fingers to his brow to indicate the meeting had ended. "Marina," he said. "Come. Come here."

He held out his hand, and Marina rose to take it. He pulled her to him, and she fluttered onto his lap like a sleek little bird settling onto its nest. She giggled. She felt like water flowing into a lake. It was increasingly rare that Cortés paid her such favors. She wondered what she ought to do, but could think of nothing—nothing except to revel in such moments when they came.

Puertocarrero scowled. He could see that Marina was now beyond his grasp. Cortés clearly had the girl's heart—and she, his. Damn. He rose, kicked his heels against the floor, and turned to leave. Damn it to hell. How it galled him, the thought of their . . . ah, he couldn't bear it. He shook his head. This other girl had better be pretty as well. He would tolerate nothing less. He hawked his phlegm and marched out of the room. As always, alone.

When he returned to the stone cottage, Maxtla was carrying a dozen pigeon's eggs, a clay pot of salamanders, two armadillo legs, a quantity of squash flowers, a passel of chilis, and a bunch of root vegetables. He found Ometzin strolling down to the cottage herself with an apron full of star apples.

"Look what I found," she said. "Treasure. Treasure plucked from the trees."

Maxtla stopped and stared at her, didn't say a word.

"What is it? What's the matter?"

It was incredible. In his mind, he saw an image of himself some five years hence—as a husband, a father. He was living here by the lake, and Ometzin was his wife. The illusion was extraordinarily vivid. He took a step back, tripped, and nearly fell down. He struggled to keep his burden of provisions from toppling to the ground.

She walked toward him, her apron full of fruit. "Are you not well?"

"It's nothing," he said. "I felt dizzy for a moment."

"Hungry, probably." She glanced at the sack he was carrying. "Come. Let's see what spoils the great warrior has managed to bring back from his campaigns."

That night, they dined outdoors by the wavering glow of a wood fire. The stars sparkled down from an ebony sky and showered the lake with a rain of thin, silvery light. The jagged glow from a pair of torches flickered across the table between them. Ometzin had managed to transform Maxtla's supplies into a small feast, and now they were completing the meal with a dessert of star apples. She bit into the succulent flesh and sighed. She couldn't remember when she had felt so peaceful. It was as if Tenochtitlán and all its troubles existed in some other life, a life that she remembered but that could not trouble her now, not in this tranquil place of starlight and silence. She peered across the table at Maxtla, his features illuminated by the play of the torchlight. She thought how unfair she'd been to think that he had betrayed Azotl.

Across the table, Maxtla was also lost in his thoughts. Try as he might, he could no longer recall why he had felt such anger in the city of the Aztecs. Why had it seemed so urgent to betray them? In his heart he knew the answer. He'd been behaving like a spoilt child. But something had changed, seemingly in an instant. This very afternoon, when he had climbed back up to the stone cottage and suddenly been seized by an image of himself and Ometzin as being married—in that moment, something had changed. In a way, he now felt like an adult, and he saw that adults did not act impulsively, as children did. They behaved methodically, to a purpose.

That was what Azotl had been trying to teach him by telling him the secret of the House of Birds. It was a secret to be preserved, husbanded, kept for a time when it might be needed. If Maxtla had squandered the secret by telling the Spaniards, what would be the result now? Azotl would be helpless to save himself. That was where reckless, childish behavior led—to disaster. He saw now that he had been stupid and unfair.

He looked up, just as Ometzin did, and their eyes met. They both started to speak, and both stopped to let the other go ahead. Finally, it was Ometzin who began. She apologized for thinking that Maxtla had betrayed Azotl.

"That was very wrong," she said. "I am sorry."

"You do not need to be," he told her. He explained that he had nearly done what she had suspected, that he had very nearly gone to the Spaniards with news of Cacama and the planned rebellion. Only luck had prevented him from doing so. "Instead, I spent the day on a sailing boat with Moctezuma."

She laughed. "You have led a life of unusual adventures."

He couldn't deny it. That was definitely so. Now it was his turn to apologize to her, and he did so. He begged her forgiveness for a hundred acts of idiocy, not least among them his tantrum in the House of Birds.

"Ah, well," she said. "We are human. We do not always behave as we ought." She swallowed the last of her star apple. "Apologies accepted."

Maxtla smiled. "Friends?" he said.

She smiled, too. "Friends."

That night—because there seemed no reason to do otherwise and because they both now realized that this was what they had long wanted—they slept in the same room and in the same bed. They explored each other's bodies in ways they had only imagined till now. In whispers, they told each other secrets they had never dared to tell anyone else.

When the sun's light slanted through the wooden blinds on the cottage's eastern face, the two were still asleep on sheets of cotton, sprawled in each other's arms.

The Gods of Malaise

Azotl and the other prisoners—the fifteen Aztecs captured by
Puertocarrero during the battle at Cempoala—were hauled in
irons before the Spanish captain-general and made to stand in
the House of the Eagle Knights. They were barely up to it. They
slumped against the far wall, dirty, bedraggled, their bodies
luridly marbled with scrapes and bruises. They wore soiled
and bloodied loincloths, nothing more. They gazed about
with hollow, baffled eyes. Azotl looked like some mangy carcass draped upon a frame of sticks. His flesh was pocked with
open, running sores.

Pitoque felt the wind go out of him to see the man like this.
He tried to catch Azotl's gaze, but it was no use. The master
functionary hardly seemed conscious. He moved his head this
way and that, but more from habit, perhaps, than from any
clear desire, or ability, to absorb or comprehend his surroundings. His eyes seemed to register nothing at all.

Cortés climbed to his feet and smiled at the emperor,
whom he had ordered to be in attendance this morning to witness the trial of the Aztec prisoners. Slumped upon his throne,
Moctezuma made an attempt to smile back, but only managed
a sort of grimace. He shifted his weight and then swallowed,
with what seemed like an enormous effort. This spectacle was
appalling. Even he could see that.

Pitoque thought he understood what was contemplated here.
What the Spaniard envisioned was not so much a trial as an act of
humiliation. He wished to see the Aztec lords brought low.

The trial, if you could call it that, did not last long. Cortés had one of his officers read out a list of the crimes against the Spanish Crown that the accused had committed. Next, the list was rendered into Maya by a grim-faced Aguilar, who looked as if he had been forced into this duty to judge by his slouching posture, his gloomy cast. He mumbled so often that Doña Marina had to admonish him several times.

"Speak up, why don't you? Do you think I can make sense out of the faintest stutters of the air? Raise your voice. Speak out loud."

But Aguilar barely complied, as if by muffling the words he could somehow dull the edges of their intent.

Exasperated, Doña Marina nonetheless bore on. She translated the Maya into Nahuatl so that the assembled lords and elders of the empire might understand the infamies that had been committed against the honor of the Spanish king, who dwelled in a place called Europe far across the eastern sea. She informed them that the king's honor would be avenged.

She turned to Cortés, and he gazed at her. Obviously, they had planned this speech beforehand. The trial, it seemed, had come to an end. Now—the verdict.

"All the prisoners are to be executed," she declared.

She sat down. Cortés leaned sideways and whispered something to her. Immediately, she grimaced.

"No," she whispered.

"I say yes."

Marina shook her head and closed her eyes. This order was beyond her. Once, she would have done anything to earn her master's favor, but this? Again, she shook her head. It was beyond imagining. "No."

"Yes." Cortés gripped her by the arm. "I mean to make a point, one that no one will ever forget. Now get up. Tell them."

She took a deep breath and climbed back to her feet. She looked up at the ceiling as if seeking some guidance there. Finally, she gritted her teeth and spoke. "Execution by burning," she said. "The prisoners are to be burned at the stake. Let this be a lesson to you all." She dropped back into her seat. Her shoulders sagged, and she stared at the floor.

Burned at the stake? Pitoque felt the blood drain from his face, and his legs went weak. The idea was so shocking that he could not think how to respond. Instead, he peered about himself to see how others were reacting. Aguilar had his head lowered and gazed at the floor. The various Aztec lords, who had spent countless hours in this chamber wasting time with their endless prattling, now silently traded bewildered glances. *Burned at the stake.* Among them, only Cacama appeared unchanged by what he had heard, for perhaps he had anticipated this grisly outcome. He continued to glare straight ahead, his jaw set, his eyes smoldering.

The prisoners—Azotl, Qualpopoca, the rest—did not react at all. Perhaps they hadn't been paying attention, their thoughts caught up with other, more pressing concerns. They were herded out of the great hall, silent as an assembly of ghosts. Only at the last moment did Azotl look up. His one-eyed gaze wandered for a time and then bore straight at Pitoque. In that gaze, if only for a moment, Pitoque saw the

Azotl of old, the master functionary. Azotl lifted his eyebrows, and Pitoque understood what he must do. He must seek out the master functionary where he was imprisoned.

When the prisoners were gone, Pitoque remained where he was, standing behind the emperor. He felt the blood pounding in his skull, and his hands and feet were numb. It had been a shock beyond imagining to see Azotl in such a state. If the master functionary could be so reduced, what hope was there for anyone else? The words of the verdict echoed in his mind. *Burned at the stake.* What kind of death was that? What species of monster had dreamt up such a hideous fate?

The same afternoon, Pitoque sought out Aguilar. He told him he wanted to visit the prisoners, especially the one named Azotl. Could it be arranged?

Aguilar said that he would see what he could do.

In the evening, he came to Pitoque and told him that he had found out where the prisoners were being held. "Come," he said. "Let us go."

They ventured out into the night, to a mansion not far from the palace of Axayácatl. With Aguilar as his companion, Pitoque had no difficulty making his way past the Spanish guards.

"Go inside, if you can stand it in there," one said. "Talk all you want." He started to laugh, as if he'd made a clever jest.

Aguilar waited outside, and Pitoque ventured in alone. He soon found himself creeping through the bowels of the building, a sort of dungeon. He carried a burning torch to light his way. Before long, he found the prisoners. Like the others, Azotl lay slumped on the floor, shackled in chains, caked in filth. He peered up at Pitoque, and his one good eye gleamed with something like recognition.

"Flee," he said, his voice a low growl. "Run for your life. Take only what you can carry. Do not come back."

Pitoque started. What was the man saying? These were the same words, almost exactly the same words, as the omen he had heard—the voices of women moaning in the night. He dropped to his knees. "Azotl," he said. "What are you saying?"

The master functionary shook his head. "Flee," he repeated. "Run. Now."

"Why? I do not understand. What do you—?"

"Look. Look at my face." He turned his head to the side.

Even in the gloomy half-light, Pitoque could see what he meant. The side of Azotl's face was pebbled with small protrusions. There must have been a dozen of them. He remembered the native man he had collided with many months earlier, on the track that ran from Tenochtitlán down to the eastern coast. That fellow's skin had been covered with these same strange nodules, and he had collapsed into a heap and died on the sloping ground. Pitoque and Azotl had spoken of this affliction before.

The master functionary groaned. "It is the new malady I told you of. It appears to follow the path of the Spaniards. Wherever they go, the people become ill—and yet the Spaniards themselves do not suffer at all."

"Are there no remedies?"

The master functionary slumped against the wall. "Nothing works. This affliction is beyond the reach of our herbalists. It comes with the Spaniards, yet I do not know how they spread it around. Some of our people say they carry it about in pouches, releasing it when no one is looking. Others say they are able to shoot it somehow, through the barrels of their harquebuses." Azotl emitted a low rumble, something between a grunt and a laugh. "Out on the coast, where many have died, the people maintain that their own deities are responsible. They say the gods of malaise—Ekpetz, Uzankak, and Sojakak, they call them—go about at night distributing this curse. But I think they are wrong. I think it is the work of these Spaniards."

"Do you believe they are gods, after all?"

"No." Azotl reached up with one hand to probe the hard nubbles that had formed upon his face. "No, I do not think so. But I confess I do not understand why they should remain unaffected." His shoulders sagged. "Flee," he said, or perhaps it was a voice speaking through him. "Run for your life. Take only what you can carry. Do not come back." The master functionary let out a long, heavy sigh. "Take the boy with you and Ometzin. Give them both my love. Now go."

Pitoque shuddered. He thought he should say something important, something a man might remember during what remained of his life. But he could think of nothing. "Goodbye," he muttered instead. "I will remember you to the boy."

He turned and hurried away.

☦

Maxtla stood in the main room of his father's house in Cholula and crossed his arms. He shook his head. "No," he repeated. "My father will not approve it. It's inconceivable."

"What do you suggest then?" said his mother. "You would prefer that your sister remain husbandless for the rest of her life?"

"Of course not. But there must be another way."

"Must there? I would be happy to know what it is."

Maxtla glanced over at Ometzin, who was comforting his sister. The two girls were seated side by side upon a bench covered with pillows stuffed with duck down. Ometzin returned his look and shrugged. She agreed that the idea of removing Zaachila's eyes was madness, but she did not like to speak out on the subject. A guest was obliged to be respectful. She and Maxtla had arrived the previous evening after a half-day's journey from Amozoc. Since then, the family had talked of very little beyond the dilemma of what to do about Zaachila's sight. It was a serious question—of course it was—and yet it was strange that here in Cholula, so short a distance from Tenochtitlán, the topic of discussion could have altered so completely. Spaniards? The fate of the empire? The whereabouts of the master functionary? Of these matters, not a word was spoken. Instead, one girl's eyesight was all.

His mother was adamant—the priests must be respected. Meanwhile, Maxtla repeated over and over again what they all knew to be true—the final decision remained with his father. Maxtla had no doubt what that decision would be. His father would say no. He would never accept the disfigurement of his daughter.

Maxtla repeated this conviction yet again. He got up and walked over to his mother. He took one of her hands in both of his. He said he would speak to his father in Tenochtitlán about the dilemma and return with Pitoque's judgment.

Kalatzin sighed and withdrew her hand. "He should be here," she said. "A man's place is with his family. There should be no carrying of messages back and forth from city to city. He should be here with his daughter and his wife at a time like this."

"You are right." Maxtla remembered that barely two years had passed since his mother had exhorted her husband to do precisely the opposite, to travel widely and to take their son with him. How was one ever to know which choice was right or wrong? "But these are difficult times. They——"

"Difficult? What do you know about difficult times? Your sister and I must live in this city, where there are no suitors because most young men are dead. Graves are everywhere. You have no idea what the Spaniards did. They . . ."

And she was off once more, ranting on about the absence of suitable husbands or of any husbands at all. The horrors committed by the Spaniards during their passage through Cholula were not solely to blame, but they had certainly contributed to the problem. How she railed against the Spaniards, not because they were evil in themselves, nor because they represented an unimaginable threat to the known world, but because they had deprived her daughter of a husband.

Maxtla listened and did what he could to console his mother. In fact, he could hardly blame her. She was certainly right, at least about what the Spaniards had done in Cholula.

He saw that now. He'd been horrified to witness the terrible damage. Even now, months later, parts of the city were still little more than ruins. Dozens of people—people he had known as friends—were dead. Thousands of other Cholulans had been killed as well.

"I know," he said when his mother had finished her tirade. "I have seen it, too. The Spaniards have committed terrible crimes."

Ometzin sat up. "You admit it now? At last?"

Maxtla looked at her and nodded. "I do."

Doña Marina adjusted her robe and tilted her head. She smiled. "I have come to inquire after our little friend."

Pitoque frowned. Lovely she might be, but he had learned to distrust this woman. "Whom do you mean?"

"You know. The girl. Ometzin."

"Ah."

"Do you know how I might send a message to her?"

"May I ask for what purpose?"

Doña Marina pressed her lips together and eased forward in her seat. All around her, the green light of morning cascaded down and splashed about this small interior court of the palace of Axayácatl. Birds chirped in the jacaranda trees. "I have a proposal in mind that will benefit us all. It concerns Ometzin most particularly."

"In what way?" Pitoque took a deep breath. Extracting information from this woman was like obtaining gold from a Spaniard. He had little patience for the task, not now. His thoughts were with Azotl and with their encounter the previous evening. "In what way does your proposal concern Ometzin?"

The conversation meandered on, but eventually it became clear what Doña Marina had in mind. She smiled. "This will be a fine reward for Puertocarrero, who has fought a great battle on behalf of the Spaniards in Cempoala. And it will be an excellent arrangement for the girl, allying her with the most powerful men in the land." Here, she smiled again. "Of course, it will serve my interests, too, for I will be pleased to have her as my friend and companion."

"I see."

"And insofar as your interests are concerned, they will be well served also."

"In what way?"

"You will have my gratitude for your assistance." She leaned closer. "In these uncertain times, you might find such a sentiment of use. I am not without influence, you know. Cortés takes few measures without first seeking my advice."

"Such measures, I take it, include burning men at the stake."

"I had nothing to do with that decision." She shuddered and turned away.

Pitoque considered pressing the point but decided it was no use. What he really wanted to do was leap to his feet, box the woman's ears, and inform her in the firmest terms possible that Ometzin's name must never again, under any circumstances, emerge from her lips. But that was not what he did. Instead, he cleared his throat. He said, "You don't seem to be aware that Ometzin is the niece of a man you are currently holding in chains in a prison not far from here."

"What man?"

"Azotl."

"The master functionary?"

Pitoque nodded.

"She is his niece?"

"His ward. He has raised her almost from infancy."

"That is a very unlikely coincidence."

"Perhaps. But it happens to be true."

Doña Marina said nothing for a while, evidently deep in thought. This information certainly complicated matters. The truth was that she was desperate to find a girl for Puertocarrero. She was terrified that Cortés was beginning to tire of her. Lately, he had taken to staying away all night long, and she knew why. There were other native girls, as young as she, as pretty, as compliant. She looked up at Pitoque. "I have an idea. The girl will marry Puertocarrero, and in return we will spare the prisoner's life. What could be more perfect?"

"You can arrange such a thing?"

She put back her head and laughed, as if he had made a joke. "Oh, I can arrange a great many things, my friend." At least, this was what she said. Lately, she had begun to wonder about her power. She leveled her gaze at Pitoque. "So, where may I find the girl?"

"Not here. She is not in Tenochtitlán at the moment."

"You can get word to her?"

"Yes."

"Please do so right away. Summon her here. There is very little time. Do I have your agreement?"

Pitoque gazed straight ahead, wondering what he should do. If he failed to agree to this request, Azotl would be put to death. And yet how could he agree? How, for the shadow of an instant, could he even consider acceding to this monstrous proposal? He closed his eyes and made a quick calculation. Two days to send a message to Amozoc. Two days to hear back. Four days in all. Who knew what might happen in the space of four days? He decided that he would play for time. He opened his eyes and looked at Doña Marina. "I agree to your bargain," he said. "I will send a messenger right away."

"Good. I will wait."

"You will?"

"Yes. I wish to hear what you say to this messenger."

There was no choice, so Pitoque sent for Toc, who had been minding his master's quarters in Tenochtitlán.

Only a little time passed before the old man shuffled into their presence. Pitoque greeted him with a show of warmth that he did not quite feel, considering the commission he was about to impart. He told Toc to travel as quickly as possible to the cottage at Amozoc. He was to inform Maxtla and the girl that they must return at once. He looked up at Doña Marina, who had raised her eyebrows, obviously waiting for something else to be said. Pitoque took a breath and explained to the old man that the girl was to be offered as a wife to one of the Spaniards, in exchange for Azotl's life.

Toc nodded, turned, and trudged away.

Doña Marina climbed to her feet. "Very good," she said. "I couldn't have put it better myself. We will make excellent confederates in the future, you and I. I can see it already."

Pitoque fought back the urge to reply. Quite simply, the woman horrified him. He was appalled beyond words at her ability to trade in lives as if they were so many pellets of gold, so many quetzal feathers.

Doña Marina gave Pitoque a last smile and hurried on her way.

Alone, he gazed without seeing at the stone pillars around him, the jacaranda trees, the swelling light. He raised himself to his feet and wandered away along the long corridor that led to the emperor's quarters.

Toc did as he was instructed. He journeyed to the lake at Amozoc, but he found no one there except the four Aztec guards, all idle and bored. They told him the two young people had gone on to Cholula. Toc told the guards they might as well return to Tenochtitlán, as surely they ought to have done many days before this. He shouldered his maguey sack and began the trek toward Cholula, the city of his birth.

In a Time of Madness

"I have an idea." Doña Marina ran her fingers across her master's chest, still amazed at the quantity of hair that tufted from every fold and expanse, so unlike the bronze and barren bodies of native men. "A wonderful idea."

"I would expect no less." Cortés lay back upon a plush of eiderdown and clasped his hands behind his head. "All of your ideas are wonderful."

"But this one is the best."

"Tell me."

She crossed her arms on his chest and rested her chin upon the bridge they formed. "I have made arrangements to bring the girl Ometzin here to the palace."

Cortés frowned. "What girl?"

"You know. The one we have promised to Puertocarrero."

"Ah, yes. I remember. But this is not a new idea."

"No. Here is the new part. In return, we shall spare the life of one of the prisoners."

"In return for what?"

"The girl."

"I thought we already had the girl. I thought this was already arranged. Am I not right?"

Doña Marina stroked his chest. "You know, I still cannot believe how handsome you are. It takes my breathe away."

"Don't change the subject."

"I was merely—"

"I know what you were doing. I know you. Now tell me—I thought you had already arranged this affair of the girl and Puertocarrero. Isn't that so?"

"Yes, my splendid one. And no."

"What do you mean, no?"

She explained about the master functionary and his relationship to Ometzin. She said the girl had been sent away from Tenochtitlán precisely because the one named Azotl was in prison. Putting the prisoner to death would hardly lure her back. Doña Marina smiled. "And that is why we should spare him."

"We can't do that. He has betrayed us. There is Spanish blood on his hands and he has been sentenced to death."

"I don't mean forever. I only mean for a time. Until the girl returns. After that . . ." She nuzzled the whiskers on Cortés's chin. She let one hand slide down his chest, and then she ventured lower. "After that," she murmured, "who can say?" She went to work with her lips and tongue.

Cortés nodded slowly. Yes, yes. This plan seemed possible. Strike a bargain, then break it. Why not? "All right," he said. "We shall do as you suggest." He let the girl apply herself at his genitals for a time—to no particular effect—then eased her away. Frankly, he wasn't in the mood.

Toc appeared at the entrance of the house in Cholula. His lean, spare frame slouched against the edge of the doorway, and his melancholy face seemed even sadder than usual. He made his greetings and then announced his business. He had come to summon Maxtla and Ometzin back to Tenochtitlán.

"It is a matter of great urgency," he said, although his tone seemed to suggest otherwise. He looked deeply tired from his trek. "A man's life depends upon it."

Maxtla took his father's servant by the arm and guided him to a bench near the entrance. "Toc, you must first come in and sit down. Rest a while. Then we will hear what you have to say."

Only after Toc had been served some chocolate to drink did Maxtla ask the man to speak. "What is this urgent matter you speak of? Whose life is at stake?"

Toc set down the clay jar. "Azotl's life. He—"

"What do you mean?" Ometzin took a step closer. "He can't still be a prisoner, surely. We thought he would be free by now." She was thinking of the secret of the House of Birds.

"Still a prisoner, I'm afraid," said Toc. He explained what had been proposed. Ometzin would be given as a reward to the Spaniard named Puertocarrero, and in return the life of Azotl would be spared.

"No." This was Maxtla. He was the man in the household and he would not permit it. "That is impossible. I won't allow it."

"Shhh," she said. "It isn't your decision to make." She turned to Toc. "Of course, I'll come."

"No, Ometzin. You and I both know that Azotl has the means to save himself. He doesn't need your help. It must be some kind of trick." To Toc, he said, "Are you sure that Azotl is still imprisoned?"

Toc shook his head. "I know nothing but what I have been told, master. This is the message your father asked me to bring. And I have taken a long while in bringing it. I thought you were at Amozoc. I lost a day's travel there."

Maxtla nodded. "That wasn't your fault. We made the same mistake ourselves. But I still do not understand."

"It doesn't matter whether we understand," said Ometzin. "What matters is that we obey your father's command."

But Maxtla would not agree. The instructions made no sense. Besides, it horrified him to think of someone handing Ometzin over to one of the Spaniards in this way, like an animal or a piece of furniture. It was unthinkable. He refused to agree to any plan but this—he would return to Tenochtitlán himself to find out what was going on. After that, he would send a message back to Cholula.

"But we haven't got time," she said. "Azotl may die."

He took her hand. "And you, too, if you go back there."

The following morning, Maxtla set out for Tenochtitlán with Toc at his side.

"An honor," said the hummingbird bride, whose real name was Bakil. She reclined upon her bed in a pale blue robe. "It will be the crowning moment of my life."

"But you will be dead." Aguilar edged forward. "Your chest will be cut open. Your heart ripped out. Do you understand me? You will be dead."

Bakil took a bite of sapota fruit and spat several seeds into her hand. She flung them to the floor, where the two servant girls scurried to pick them up. "This is not our view. I will have eternal life."

Aguilar snorted. "Because you will return as a dragonfly?"

"Or a hummingbird. To be honest, I would prefer a hummingbird."

"You consider hummingbirds eternal?"

"Of course."

Aguilar fell silent for a time. Outside, beyond a garden of rocks, gulls hovered and swerved above the shallows of the lake. A tart salt smell tickled his nostrils. He took a deep breath and shook his head. "I just don't understand it. The Aztecs captured you. They dragged you back here in bondage. And now you want nothing more than to die in order to assure them of life. It makes no sense to me."

Bakil laughed, a sound like water plashing over rocks. "Nor should it. You are not me. You do not find yourself in my position. How could you understand?"

She rose to her feet and padded across the room. On a trestle table by the wooden railing, several large ceramic bowls had been arranged, all brimming with mushrooms of different kinds, in various combinations. Bakil chose several and nibbled a little from each. She frowned out at the view of the lake, apparently considering the different flavors. Then she popped two mushrooms into her mouth, chewed a while, and swallowed them down. She turned back to Aguilar and smiled.

"You wish some mushrooms?"

But Aguilar shook his head. He did not require the aid of mushrooms to see visions that distressed or confounded him. Bakil turned away. In silence, she surveyed the blue panorama of Lake Texcoco, the island of Tepepolco and, in the distance, a mauve barrier of mountains. After a time, her shoulders slumped and she collapsed into a chair. She had fallen into a kind of stupor, her face bathed in an angelic glow.

Aguilar couldn't take his eyes from her. He heard a chorus of women's voices swelling around him. "Behold," they sang, "a virgin shall be with child, and bear a Son, and they shall call His name Immanuel." He raised his eyes and saw before him an image of the Blessed Virgin, the vessel of the Second Coming of the Lord, except that she was dark—as dark as any native woman of these lands. He fell to his knees and remained there in an attitude of prayer.

The two servant girls traded almost imperceptible glances and stayed where they were, both squatting on their haunches, on either side of the bed. From outside, a trilling of flutes—sweet as the voices of women—drifted across the darkening waters of the purple lake.

"Where is the girl?" Doña Marina had a little dog perched on her lap and was feeding it crumbs of corn cake. She looked up at Pitoque. "I asked you a question. Where is Ometzin?"

Pitoque shook his head. Maxtla and Toc had returned from Cholula only that morning, without Ometzin—exactly the response Pitoque had expected. He turned to Doña Marina. "I'm sorry. There seems to have been a misunderstanding. My son has returned without her."

"Has he? How unfortunate. I thought you sent a messenger to summon them both."

"You understood correctly. That is what I did. But it seems the message was misunderstood."

"A man's life hangs in the balance. As you know."

Pitoque replied that he did.

"May I ask where the girl is now?"

"It is not important."

"Maybe not, because I already possess this information. The cottage at Amozoc. You seem to have forgotten that I was present when you issued instructions to your messenger." She scowled. "Because you have crossed me, I will have to take matters into my own hands. I will have to send messengers of my own."

Pitoque closed his eyes. Would these torments never end? He opened his eyes again, looked at her, and shrugged. There was nothing he could say.

"Very well," she said. She tickled her little dog under its chin. "I will have to proceed on my own terms. It seems we are not such excellent confederates, after all. I shall have to inform my master Hernán Cortés about all that has taken place. I regret to say he will not be very pleased with my news."

Pitoque nodded, then said nothing. He turned and left. He could feel the girl's eyes burning into his back. How he kept from strangling her, he did not know.

"Enough," said Cortés. "I have waited long enough. We will find Puertocarrero another girl. I think we should be able to manage that. Don't you?"

"No." Doña Marina crossed her arms at her breast.

"Why not? What difference does it make? One girl or another—it will be all the same to Puertocarrero."

"It will not be the same to me. I particularly chose this one. I dislike being crossed. I will have this girl and no other. She will become the wife of Puertocarrero. It is what the man expects. He has been promised this girl especially. Why should he accept another?" She kicked at the floor. "That merchant thinks he can get the better of me, but he is mistaken."

"I believe you are right." Cortés raised himself up on the bed. He had decided he would not spend the night here, after all. He would find Alvarado, and the two of them would try their luck among the emperor's concubines—Moctezuma was a generous man. He climbed to his feet and scratched his belly. He peered down at Marina and laughed. "Anyone is mistaken who tangles with you."

She reached out for him, then stopped herself. "Where are you going?"

"Ah? Oh, I must meet with Alvarado, to discuss the executions."

"Now? But it is dark. It's the dead of night."

"True. True. But there are a great many preparations to attend to. You stay here. You go to sleep." Cortés dressed himself as quickly as he could and left in a rush.

Marina watched him go. She was under few illusions. She knew, in a general way, where he was bound. She flopped back down on the bed and pressed her fists to her eyes. Oh, a man would have his adventures—she understood that. But she was determined not to lose her position, no matter what. It was her position that she valued above all. Indeed it was. She kept repeating this idea to herself until she recoiled at the words.

Oh, what was the use?

She closed her eyes and sighed. Why? Because she was sad. And because she loved him.

"She says they're going ahead with the executions." Pitoque settled himself beside his son on a bench in an antechamber of the emperor's quarters. Beyond an open portal, he could see various minions and factotums hurrying to and fro. He had just come from a meeting with Doña Marina. "She says she has waited long enough. She says I have broken my word to her."

"You didn't break your word. I did."

"The consequences are the same. The Spaniards are going ahead with the executions, no matter what. Azotl is to die. Already, Doña Marina has sent men to Amozoc to fetch Ometzin."

"Ometzin isn't there."

"I know." Maxtla had already told him that the girl was in Cholula with Kalatzin and Zaachila. "That's the only good news we've had."

Maxtla let out a long, slow breath and shook his head. He could not understand this. Azotl could save himself so easily— a few words, nothing more. But for some reason, the man had said nothing. Why? He turned to his father. "Is it possible to speak to Azotl again? You did it once."

"True. But I have tried again, and it is not permitted. I was lucky the first time."

Maxtla grimaced. "Then we will have to deal with this ourselves."

"What do you mean?"

In a whisper, Maxtla revealed to his father the secret of the House of Birds. When he had finished, he waited a few moments to let the significance of the secret sink in. Then he went on. "We must go to Cortés now. We must tell him ourselves. We must trade this secret for Azotl's life. And we must demand that Ometzin not be given to this Spaniard, this Puertocarrero. In exchange for these terms, we will tell them the whereabouts of the Aztec gold." The boy stood up. "Come. We must go quickly."

"No," said Pitoque. He sat still, numb with the shock of an idea that had just entered his mind. It had appeared in an instant, the instant that Maxtla had spoken of the secret hidden in the House of Birds. The secret was extraordinary in itself. But in Pitoque's mind, that secret had immediately joined itself with another idea, a terrible idea—terrible but utterly necessary. First, however, he had to ensure that Maxtla was out of the way. The boy would never stand for it.

"Come," repeated Maxtla. "We must hurry."

Pitoque shook his head. "No. I will go to Cortés and tell him this secret. But you must return to Cholula without delay to tell Ometzin what we have decided, and to make certain that she and the others are safe. You should never have come back here. Go now. At once."

Maxtla hesitated. He could see the sense of this plan, and yet he could not bring himself to leave. He wanted to remain here with his father—and yet he also wanted desperately to be in Cholula with Ometzin. How could he choose?

"Go," said Pitoque, who had an idea of his son's dilemma. "Don't think. Just do as I say. Go."

At last, Maxtla nodded. He felt as if all his blood had pooled at the bottom of his legs. He felt tired, hollow, powerless. "All right," he said. "I will go." He turned to his father. Something possessed him, some memory of his younger days, and he leaned forward and planted a kiss on his father's cheek. He spoke in a whisper. He said, "May good fortune go with you."

Pitoque let out a sigh. "Yes," he said. "And with you, my son."

Maxtla turned and hurried from the room.

Pitoque remained seated upon the wooden bench. He listened to the shuffle of footsteps passing back and forth outside the room. Somewhere, in the distance, he heard a chirping of birds. He let the moments pass, one at a time. He had already made his decision, but he wanted to wait a while, to let its meaning sink in. Already, he could feel the awful weight of it pressing upon his flesh, his bones. He would not do as Maxtla had asked him. He would not go to Cortés and offer up the secret of the House of Birds. He understood something that his son did not. He understood why the master functionary had chosen not to save himself. Azotl was beyond saving. Even if the Spaniards did not execute him along with the other prisoners, he was bound to die soon.

Flee. Run for your lives. Take only what you can carry. Do not come back.

Now, at last, Pitoque understood the meaning of those words. They had to do with this evil force, this affliction, that got inside the body somehow and pushed its way out through the skin. This was the evil that the omens had foretold. Pitoque was certain now. He also knew why Azotl had chosen to say nothing about the Aztecs' hidden treasure. He was withholding that secret so that others might use it at some other time— Pitoque himself, perhaps. Maxtla. Ometzin.

He rose and began to stride down a long corridor in the graying light, past the imperial servants. He himself should flee. They all should. They should do as Azotl said—take only what they could carry, run for their lives, never come back. And yet, how could they? How could they flee while Tenochtitlán remained, while this palace stood, while the lake waters sparkled, and the emperor lived? They dwelled in a time of madness. Flee how? Flee where?

Pitoque reached an intersection of corridors and hesitated only briefly before he turned to the right, away from the quarters of the Spaniards. He would tell them nothing. He would do as Azotl no doubt wished. He would preserve the secret of the House of Birds. He would save that power for another dark moment on another trembling day, for he knew that there would be more such moments, and more such days.

Fifteen Stakes, Fifteen Prisoners

At noon, a squadron of Spaniards led the convicted men out into the great plaza, sixteen of them in all. They were each to be lashed to a separate stake, but it seemed that someone had miscounted. Only fifteen stakes had been erected in the square that morning. Alvarado reported the problem to Cortés, who spat, and swore under his breath.

"Mi capitán," said Alvarado. "It wasn't my fault. I am responsible for the prisoners, not for the construction of these devices. I am merely bringing the matter to your attention."

Cortés gazed around the square. He wondered whether Alvarado had been too long in the sun. Initially, he'd chosen Puertocarrero to oversee the execution of the prisoners, but the fellow had unaccountably declined, leaving the distinct impression he didn't approve of the idea. That had been a shock. Cortés wondered whether both lieutenants had gone mad. He hoped not. He clasped his hands behind his back.

He wanted this to be a grand occasion and had ordered all the nobles of the city to attend. They were gathered now on wooden risers that had been erected for the purpose. Here, on a raised viewing platform, he had gathered his senior officers, along with the emperor Moctezuma, who had been brought out for the occasion—bound in chains, just in case anyone was tempted to cause mischief. Several of the emperor's aides had been ordered up onto the platform as well and were being kept there under guard. Cortés himself had a seat waiting for him at the front. Doña Marina was already there, sitting erect and wearing a stiff-looking smile. He wondered where that rascal Aguilar had got to. He had seen very little of the man lately. What in God's name was he doing? Cortés was surprised the translator would choose to miss such a spectacular event. It wasn't every day the Spaniards burned sixteen Aztecs at the stake.

Fifteen. Damn. Couldn't any of his officers count?

"What I wish to know, sir," said Alvarado, "is whether you wish to delay the proceedings while we put up another stake. Or is there some other way of dealing with this lamentable situation?"

Cortés scratched his jaw. "Another stake? How much time would you need?"

Alvarado considered. "Half an hour, perhaps? It depends on how quickly we can lay our hands on additional lumber. Once we do that, it won't take long."

"Oh, hell." Cortés didn't want any more delays. What did it matter whether they executed fifteen or sixteen? He scratched his jaw again—and had a sudden thought. Maybe they could turn this setback into some sort of game, a source of entertainment for the crowd.

On the captain-general's instructions, the sixteen prisoners were lined up at one end of the plaza. Cortés called out for Doña Marina. She walked over with a tentative gait and kept her eyes fixed straight ahead. She was feeling confused this day. In her heart, she recoiled at what was about to be done. She had supported many kinds of killing in the past, but this was different—this making a spectacle of death. And for what purpose? Didn't the Aztecs already fear the Spaniards? As well, she could hardly contemplate so terrible a means of killing. Burning at the stake? Her flesh crawled at the thought. She had made her feelings known to Cortés, but could not sway him, and now she had decided to make the best of the situation, to keep her horror to herself.

"Ah, Marina." Cortés greeted her with a grin.

He had her explain to the prisoners that, at the sound of a harquebus being fired, they were to run across the plaza in a foot race—the most important foot race of their lives. The man who won would reap a glorious award. He would be spared a death by burning at the stake.

She did as he told her. "Do you understand?" she asked the prisoners. She doubted whether any of them realized the futility of this exercise. She wondered if she ought to tell them, but decided against it. Let them live a while in hope. "The finish line is over there," she said.

Alvarado sifted a quantity of powder into the barrel of his harquebus and tamped it into place. He fed a ball into the chamber and checked the flint. All set. He nodded at Cortés.

The Spanish captain-general raised a hand and then let it drop, as if he oversaw foot races every day. Alvarado fired the harquebus into the air, and at once the race was on. With their hands still bound behind their backs, the sixteen prisoners stumbled across the plaza. They lurched from side to side and frequently fell to their knees or flopped down onto their faces. Cortés winced as another prisoner went down— the old one, the one with those great pouches of surplus skin sagging from his crooked frame. He struggled back to his feet and staggered on—but too late. A youngster had already won. Still, the others kept clambering and lumbering toward the finish line. Could they not count, either? Or did they simply feel the need of a little exercise before being put to the flame?

All Cortés knew was that the race had been run and the winner determined. He swaggered across the plaza to congratulate the young fellow, who stood in his loincloth, his chest heaving, a look of euphoria transforming his long, dark face.

"Well done, my friend," said Cortés. He clapped the youth on the shoulder, took a step back, drew his sword, and—with one expert swipe—lopped off the boy's head. He turned to Alvarado. "As you can see, the numbers have been adjusted. Fifteen prisoners, fifteen stakes. You may now proceed."

To Pitoque, it was impossible to see what it was impossible to imagine. To roast a human being as you would roast a pigeon? It made no sense. He huddled in his seat upon the viewing platform, behind Moctezuma and a little to the left. He gazed straight ahead, straight at the unfolding spectacle. He knew what he was supposed to be seeing—fifteen men, including Azotl, being burned at the stake. But the images either did not reach his eyes or did not find a way into his mind. He knew they were happening, but he did not see them. It was he who had caused Azotl this horrendous death. It was he who had held the power to prevent it, but he had not done so. Now look at the result. He looked, but he did not see.

Aguilar saw. He had arrived at the plaza just as the fires roared up. He stood now, transfixed, unable to believe what was taking place. The smoke swirled above the plaza, and he peered up to watch it fade, tatter, drift away. But it did not fade or tatter. It did not drift away. Instead, a great light shone down, and the smoke formed itself into the shape of a woman—the Virgin Mary, Mother of God. He knew her instantly, only now her skin was dark. She had the complexion of a native woman, and yet he knew her. The blue of the sky was the blue of her robes, and the smoke of the fires that rose above the plaza was the dark color of her skin. In her right hand, she held a great metate stone. She turned and flung it into the waters of Lake Texcoco, causing a great tumult of waves and foam and spray to shower the earth.

Aguilar ran a hand over his face and felt the water there, water that burned. Above him, he saw the Virgin turn again, turn back. She gazed directly down at him, at Jerónimo de Aguilar. She spoke in a voice that seemed to sigh, like a wind through the mountains.

Thus will the city be thrown down and shall not be found anymore. The sound of harpists, musicians, flutists, and trumpeters shall not be heard here anymore. And no craftsmen of any craft shall be found here anymore. And the scrape of the metate stone shall not be heard here anymore. And the light of a lamp shall not shine here anymore. And the voice of bridegroom and bride shall not be heard here anymore.

Aguilar fell to his knees. The Virgin was silent now, but above her the clouds broke, and an even greater brightness appeared, a blinding light. An immense white horse rode down from the sky, mounted by a man—a dark man, a native man. Upon his head, he wore many crowns. His eyes flamed, even in the dazzling light. A sword shot from his mouth. And

Aguilar recognized him, too. He was the Son of God, riding on a great white horse that pranced upon the light of the sun. In his hand, he carried a scroll, and now it unfurled—names, names, countless names. The scroll he carried was the Book of Life, a catalogue of the condemned and the saved. In a thundering voice, a trumpet of a voice, the Son of God told Aguilar that the time of judgment had come, that all sinners must die.

It is done! I am the Alpha and the Omega, the Beginning and the End. I will give of the fountain of the water of life freely to him who thirsts. He who overcomes shall inherit all things, and I will be his God and he shall be My son. But the cowardly, unbelieving, abominable, murderers, sexually immoral, sorcerers, idolaters, and all liars shall have their part in the lake which burns with fire and brimstone, which is the second death.

Aguilar covered his face, unable to bear the fierceness of the light. When he removed his hands, he saw that the glow had begun to fade. The horse that bore the Son of God now cantered away upon a meadow of clouds. The smoke in which the Virgin had been revealed now swirled and tattered in the breeze. He knew what he had seen, but not what the images meant. He knew he had been brought here for a purpose, but he failed to understand what that purpose was. Now a sharp, bitter stench stung his nostrils, nearly made him weep. He realized its source at once—the rank scent of human flesh as it burns.

Doña Marina tried to look but found that she could not. Instead, she kept her gaze fixed on Moctezuma. Already, in these last weeks, she had seen the man be pathetically reduced from the mightiest lord in all creation to a miserable sycophant who crawled hither and yon in pursuit of a kind look or a word of praise from her master, Hernán Cortés—the way a blind puppy roots for a vacant tit.

Now he stood quivering in his chains as fifteen of his subjects were put to the torch and as a gallery of Aztec nobles looked on, stony-faced, from a distance. But the emperor did not cry out. He did not protest. He merely trembled. When the main part of the roasting was done, and the fires were burning down, he began to cry.

Cortés was watching Moctezuma as well. Now he had a sudden inspiration. He smiled at the weeping emperor and ordered that he be released. "Free the emperor," he shouted to his men. "Let his chains be removed." He turned to Moctezuma. "Go," he said. "Go among your people. I have inflicted my punishment. You are free now. I no longer require you as my prisoner. Go."

Doña Marina translated these words.

But the emperor did not go. Instead, he staggered about the platform. Twice, he fell down. Bubbles of sweat jeweled upon his forehead and began to run down his cheeks, where they mixed with his tears. He was sobbing like a child. Finally, unable to stand, he sank onto his knees. He pressed his hands together and begged Cortés to reconsider his words.

"It would be better if I continued in your company a while longer. Please—" Here, his voice broke and he could no longer speak.

The Spanish captain-general shook his head and clucked his tongue. Ah, the poor little man. Cortés took pity on Moctezuma. He allowed the emperor of the Aztecs to stay.

Alvarado dispersed the assembly of Aztec nobles and oversaw the disposition of the fires. Once they had burned themselves down, he sent men out with palm branches to collect the bones and to spread out the ashes. To make the work interesting, he offered three pellets of gold to the first man who stumbled upon anything that resembled a human soul. That put a flame beneath their feet.

Alvarado watched the competition proceed and let out a contented sigh. He was happy today, and so he should be. He was happy because he had carried out this latest commission without a hitch, apart from that mix-up over the number of stakes. He was happy because that fool Puertocarrero was nowhere to be seen, off stalking alone somewhere, no doubt, disgruntled because no one had bestowed a native wench upon him yet and ashamed because he hadn't the mustard to seize one of his own, which was what all the other Spaniards did. Pathetic lout.

While the workmen scurried back and forth, he dampened a finger and held it up to test the wind. Sure enough, he felt a light breeze. If it picked up a little overnight, by tomorrow morning no one would be able to tell that fifteen natives had gone up in smoke here this afternoon. In all likelihood, no one would ever know that anything had happened here at all.

✝

Maxtla was striding across the long blond grass of the highlands, returning to Tenochtitlán. He had done what he had said he would do. He had ensured that everyone was safe in Cholula. But now he needed to know that his father was safe as well. He needed to find out what had become of Azotl.

"If you don't go, then I will," Ometzin had told him.

And he had believed her. She was willing to risk being taken by force and thrust into the clutches of that rickety Spaniard, the one named Puertocarrero. She was willing to risk everything, to ensure that Azotl was safe.

Maxtla had believed her, and so he'd had no choice but to return himself. He was confident that affairs had sorted themselves out in Tenochtitlán by now. The secret of the House of Birds—what Spaniard could resist? He began to hum a plaintive melody that he remembered from his childhood—a song his mother had sung to him many times when he was young. He remembered the words and began to sing. He thought of Ometzin and smiled to himself, pleased that he could protect her, pleased at everything. Before leaving Cholula, he'd promised her that he would tell Azotl how much she missed him, that she hoped to see him very soon.

With disaster averted on so many sides, he gave in to a rare urge to sing out as loudly as he could as he marched across the high plain. His only concern was that his father would likely be angry at his decision to come back, but that couldn't be helped. Maxtla was a man now. Terrible events were unfolding, and he was determined to play a part. Besides, if he hadn't come, Ometzin surely would have.

He was still singing when he crossed paths with a messenger sent by Pitoque, bearing news from Tenochtitlán. When he heard what the messenger had to say, he bid the man to continue to Cholula, to carry the same news there. He resumed his trek to the capital of the Aztecs, but at a much faster pace. He no longer sang.

A Language Spoken by Infidels

Pitoque and Maxtla walked through the great plaza of Tenochtitlán, in the direction of the House of Birds. The merchant was trying to explain to his son why he had failed to divulge the secret of the treasure. And now Azotl was dead.

Maxtla glared at the ground. "It wasn't your decision to make," he said. "You decided to end a man's life. You had no right."

"Perhaps that is so." Pitoque lowered his head. "But the decision was already made. Azotl made it. He could have saved himself, but he chose not to. That was his decision, not mine." Pitoque told his son about this new disease—a kind of pox—that had ravaged the master functionary. It was a curse, brought by the Spaniards. It followed them wherever they went, yet they were unaffected by it. It killed only the people of these lands, and it killed them from the inside out, erupting in pustules and lesions. "The truth is, Azotl would have died anyway, and soon. That is why he said nothing. I think he deliberately sacrificed himself to save us."

"Us? Who is us?"

"You. Me. Ometzin. Your mother. Your sister. Perhaps others. Now we alone know where the treasure is hidden. There may come a time when this knowledge will be essential to us, when it will save our lives. I believe Azotl was thinking of our safety. I think he chose to die."

"No, he did not." Maxtla pushed back his hair and took a deep breath. In his heart, he knew his father was right, but the knowledge burned inside him. "It was the Spaniards who killed him. They brought this pox. They put up those stakes. They lit those fires. Azotl didn't choose to die. They killed him."

Pitoque would have acknowledged the truth of his son's words but the two rounded a corner and began to pick their way through a miserable scene. Crosses tottered here and there. The street was strewn with rubble of all kinds, mounds of broken clay, and garbage. Many of the stone walls had been battered down, in case they hid some secret cache of gold. Holes had been excavated almost everywhere. Since the executions, the Spaniards seemed to have gone mad. They had hurled themselves into a whirlwind of activity. Every day, they erected crosses, dug pits. And, when they weren't exhorting their native workers to greater feats of physical labor, they drank pulque and stumbled about. Some relieved themselves in corners or in the full view of each other, as if such behavior was appropriate for public display, as if voiding one's bowels was a demonstration of penetrating wit. They wiped their hands on their pants, tucked in their blouses, and staggered forth to torment the local women or to conduct boxing matches among themselves, with promises of gold to the victor.

"Watch out!" Pitoque grabbed his son's shoulder just in time to avoid another Spaniard staggering past.

The man was obviously drunk. He carried a portrait of the blue-robed woman they all seemed to love so much. "¡María!" he shouted and promptly fell down.

The picture toppled to the ground at his side, and the man slumped back against a pile of broken bricks. Spittle ran down his beard, his eyes roiled up in his head, and he seemed to be unconscious. Just then, an Aztec couple—a woman and a man—hurried by. At once, the Spaniard revived himself. He climbed onto his hands and knees and crawled after them. He pawed at the woman's robe, barked like a dog. All around him, the other Spaniards doubled over in laughter. Then, sensing the opportunity for more sport, they raced to block the couple's exit from the square. Now they would torment the pair, an entertainment that would continue until they grew tired of the game or until someone went too far and one of the victims—perhaps the woman, perhaps the man— was injured or worse. The Spaniards would stop playing after that.

Pitoque had seen this game before. He sensed Maxtla bridling at his side and realized they had better leave. The boy had a hot temper and might try to interfere. They would end up by getting hurt themselves. Or worse.

"Quick. Come with me."

Pitoque took his son's arm and hurried him out of the plaza. When they reached the House of Birds, they found the place deserted but otherwise intact. In their search for gold, the Spaniards had not yet ventured this far. Here was certain proof that Azotl had not divulged the secret.

They made their way inside. When they reached the main lagoon, Pitoque crouched down and gazed out across the expanse of dark water, the surface fretted here and there by the skittering of dragonflies. For a time, neither he nor his son said anything. Finally, it was Maxtla who spoke.

"I hate them," he said.

"The Spaniards?"

"Yes. I didn't before. But now I do."

After a time, Pitoque said, "So, what course shall we take now? Shall we sit idly by while these atrocities mount, while they kill more of our people?"

Maxtla thought about the news he had overheard that night almost two weeks earlier—Ometzin and Azotl discussing the rebellion being planned by Cacama. They'd been debating how to get word to Moctezuma, how to determine where the emperor would stand if such a rebellion were launched. He decided now to tell his father what he knew.

Pitoque inclined his head and frowned. "You mean to join this rebellion?"

Maxtla said that on his way back to Tenochtitlán, the instant he'd heard about what had happened to Azotl, he had reached a decision. He was going to present himself before the king of Texcoco. He was determined to join the Aztec rebellion. His mind was made up. He turned to his father. "Until this moment," he said, "I thought I would do so alone. But now . . ."

Pitoque smiled. "Now you shall have a comrade. It seems, in the end, we will fight together. Is it agreed?"

It was.

The conversation between them did not end there. During the course of that afternoon, they spoke of many affairs, but the rebellion was foremost among them—the fight to turn the Spaniards out of Tenochtitlán and to ensure that they would never return. They decided that Maxtla would cross the lake that same night, make his way to Texcoco and the palace of Cacama. He would volunteer his own services and those of his father. They discussed how they might best contribute to the rebels' cause and what Maxtla would say to the lord of Texcoco. Meanwhile, all around them, a miracle of birds chattered and cawed, swooped through the branches overhead, waded through the shallows of the still lagoon.

Moctezuma arose from his bath grinning, more pleased than apprehensive. He had just received a summons from Cortés. The Spanish captain-general wished the emperor to appear before him—at once. Moctezuma called for a servant to attend to the dressing of his hair. When that was done, and after he had put on a fine cotton robe and a pair of ocelot-fur sandals, he instructed several aides to accompany him. In their company, he hurried from the imperial quarters. His heart pounded out an irregular beat, a combination of hope and dread—the way he always felt in the presence of Cortés.

This time, luck was against him. He found the Spaniard in a foul mood. As always, he had that little wench at his side, that Doña Marina. When Moctezuma arrived, Cortés looked up and glared at the emperor. He did not even bother to utter a proper greeting. Instead, he plunged straight in. He wanted to know whether Moctezuma was familiar with the concept of tribute.

The emperor tilted his head. "Yes, I am. Of course."

Cortés snorted. "A likely story. A few pellets of gold in our dinner—that is all we have received so far." He informed Moctezuma that, henceforth, the Spaniards would require the payment of a regular tithe, and that this payment must be made in gold. He gave a dismissive wave. "These quetzal feathers, these little stones, these bolts of cotton—they are all very pretty. But gold is what we demand. Do I make myself clear?"

Moctezuma blinked several times. "Very clear," he said. "You require gold. Unfortunately—"

"*Unfortunately*, it seems that I must repeat my demand. *Unfortunately*, we have received precious little gold to date." Cortés took a step closer to the emperor and stared at the cowering man. It was as if he was peering directly into Moctezuma's skull, as if he had the power to inspect the contents of the emperor's mind. "Tell me," he said, "are you familiar with the situation in Italy?"

"The situation in Italy?" Moctezuma had no idea what the question meant.

"Italy," said Cortés. "A country in Europe. Are you familiar with what is happening there?"

Moctezuma had to confess that he had no inkling of what his good friend Hernán Cortés was talking about. It pained him to admit his pathetic ignorance, but—

"Just as I thought. You have no comprehension of the pressures I must contend with. Very well, then. I will explain." Cortés began to pace about the room. He pounded the fist of one hand into the palm of the other, intent on making a ferocious impression. It was all a show, of course. He had invented the tale to impress the emperor. "I have lately received reports," he announced, "of grave difficulties in Italy. My king, Charles I, finds himself burdened by many onerous expenses of state and now faces a serious shortfall in his current account. It is not clear whether he will be able to cover the cost of his present military campaign in Italy." Cortés stopped, glared at the emperor. "I need hardly inform you—a great leader yourself—how dire this situation is. Why, the future of Italy rides upon the successful outcome of my monarch's present operations." Cortés approached the emperor, stopped a foot away. He waggled a finger in Moctezuma's face. "The *future*," he repeated, "of *Italy!*"

Moctezuma swallowed, took a step back. What was Italy? Why did its future concern Cortés? What effect could a supply of Aztec gold have on this situation? It was all a blur, and yet it seemed he was now expected to speak. He cleared his throat. "I assure you," he began. "I assure you that—"

"You will assure me of one thing—gold. That is all I ask. Now go."

Cortés waved his hand, and a party of Spanish soldiers hustled the emperor out of the great hall and left him, stunned and panting, in the corridor outside. His aides followed, like turkeys bundled from one yard into another. Moctezuma glanced around and caught sight of one aide in particular— the Cholulan named Pitoque. He shook his head. "Gold," he said. He let out a long, sad sigh. "Gold, gold, gold. It is a grave problem."

Pitoque agreed. A grave problem. Yes, that was so.

The emperor sighed. "I have no idea where the gold is kept. Azotl assured me that it would be better if I did not know." He sighed again. "I wish, now, that I did."

"Indeed," said Pitoque. He crossed his arms and furrowed his brow. In fact, he was relieved by the emperor's ignorance.

Doña Marina squeezed out the cotton cloth, and a wash of water and suds ran down the back and chest and shoulders of Hernán Cortés, forming dozens of foaming rivulets through the dense jungle of hairs that sprouted and curled upon his strange white skin.

"You see?" she said. "Doesn't that feel divine?"

"What did you say?" said Cortés. He'd been lost in his thoughts, and he wasn't happy to be wrested from them—or bathed every other day, as Marina insisted. "Soon, my skin will be turning brown, and I'll be jabbering in Arabic."

"In what?"

"Arabic," he said. "It is a language. Spoken by infidels."

"May they burn in hell." Doña Marina squeezed out another plume of water over Cortés. He looked like an albino monkey hunched in the clay bathing basin. The *padre*, Father Olmedo, had been schooling her in Christian theology, and she displayed some of her scriptural learning now. "May fire and brimstone consume their mortal coils."

"Precisely. Or bathwater fill up their lungs."

"Now, now. There's nothing wrong with a little bathwater. Mmm. How sweet you smell."

"Like a bloody woman."

"No. Like a prince. A royal prince." She reached down and enfolded his penis and scrotum in her hand. "*Son míos*," she whispered. These are mine. In truth, she meant it. She wanted them for herself alone.

Cortés snorted. "Wait till I get out of this basin. I'll show you whose they are—and what they can do."

"Ah, is that a promise?"

"If you're not careful, a threat."

"All the better, my master."

"But, first, use the cloth again."

Surprised, she wrung the drenched cloth over his shoulders and the water streamed down. "Do you actually enjoy this?"

"I am starting to." Cortés settled back in the basin. "*Salaam elaikam*," he said.

"I do not understand."

"Arabic."

"Ah."

"A language of infidels." He scratched his chest and sighed

with pleasure. He closed his eyes and began to think. His reference to infidels had reminded him of what he now proposed to do. He had a mission here, and it was not restricted to the search for gold. There was a higher purpose to be served in these parts—the holy cause of the Lord.

That same afternoon, Cortés decided to dispatch a gang of his soldiers to a region north of the Aztec capital, north of Lake Texcoco, to the Great Temple of Tonantzin—goddess of the earth—where they knocked over the palm-mat shrines and rolled them down the steps of the pyramid. They broke everything into a rubble. Next, they raised one of their wooden crosses at the very center of the ruined pyramid. At the base of the cross, they placed an image of the *Virgen de Los Remedios*, and Padre Olmedo performed a mass on that very spot.

"*¡Viva!*" cried the men. "*¡Viva María! ¡ Madre nuestra! ¡ Viva!*"

The following day, perhaps inspired by a surfeit of religious fervor, a number of the Spaniards ran amok. In hopes of acquiring gold, a group of them took several Aztec nobles captive, bound them in chains, and marched them out along the causeway to the ruined temple. There, the Spaniards pressed burning torches against the soles of their prisoners' feet as an aid to memory. Surely the Aztecs would remember where their treasure was hidden now. But the nobles just gaped and hollered and babbled in that bewildering tongue of theirs. They made no sense whatever.

Finally, the Spaniards had mercy upon them. They set aside their torches, and demanded that the nobles kneel down and declare their fealty to Spain and to the glorious rule of Charles I. They commanded the nobles to kiss the portrait of the *Virgen de Los Remedios*. But the idiots were so lacking in intelligence that they couldn't understand even that. They just lay on the ground, amid the rubble of their idolatrous pyramid, moaning and weeping. The Spaniards left them there. They spat on the ground, shook their heads, and sauntered back toward Tenochtitlán.

Roses in Winter

When he heard of the damage done to the temple of Tonantzin, Pitoque decided to make his way out there. He wanted to see for himself the results of this latest Spanish outrage. In the pantheon of his gods, Tonantzin was the mother of the earth, the giver of life, and the consort of his own patron deity, Quetzalcoatl. By striking at Tonantzin, the Spaniards had struck at Pitoque himself, at his own flesh and blood.

It was a chilly winter's morning when he set out. Beneath a sky of vivid sunlight and clouds like balls of cotton, he trekked through Tlatelolco and then along the causeway that ran across the lake to the north of the city. A light breeze ruffled the folds of his long white robe. As the sun darted in and out among the clouds, he continued north until he reached a rounded peninsula of the mainland. Soon he stood at the foot of the hill known as Tepeyac, site of the temple dedicated to the mother goddess, to Tonantzin.

He started to climb the hill's southern flank. At the summit, he stopped to catch his breath. He looked around and was stunned at the destruction he saw. The pyramid itself had been battered and smashed, reduced to heaps of broken stone blocks. Of the shrine, nothing remained at all. The ground was gashed with pits and trenches—more fruitless excavation work, the endless quest for hidden gold. Nothing was left intact apart from a meager growth of nopal cactus and scrub trees. Pitoque gazed about for several minutes and felt his heart sink in his chest. Surely the goddess Tonantzin must be dead. This lifeless hill, once sacred and lush, was now her grave. He wandered about, prodding at jagged stones with his feet, peering into the cursed holes dug into the barren earth, as if the land itself had been raped by the Spaniards.

Something shifted in the air, and he looked up in sudden surprise. Had he just heard something—a voice? He thought he had heard a woman's voice. He took several steps forward, and now he did hear it, impossible to mistake. It was the voice of a woman, a voice as low and as lilting as that of his own mother when she had comforted him as a child.

"Pitoque," the voice called out. It seemed no louder than a whisper, and yet its force was as piercing as a shout. "Pitoque."

He turned to his left, in the direction of the voice, and his knees went weak. At once, he felt a pounding in his chest and he struggled to breathe. Floating in the air, suspended a small distance from the ground, was the figure of a woman. Over a flowing blue robe she wore a dark blue cloak trimmed with gold, the same finery that he recognized from images that Aguilar had shown him. Her palms were pressed together at her breast in an attitude of prayer. A golden glow pulsed above her head. She was exactly as she had appeared in the pictures he had seen, except for one quality—her coloring. In the likenesses that Aguilar possessed, she had always been white of skin, like the Spaniards, with a golden sheen to her wavy hair and clear, almost transparent eyes. But the woman he saw before him now was dark in color, like a native woman, and her hair was straight and black. It framed her face and fanned out over her shoulders in the cool morning breeze.

Pitoque dropped to his knees and rubbed his eyes. He looked up, and she was still there, as real, as palpable, as the beating of his heart, hovering before him not more than five paces away. She was as vivid a sight as any he had ever known. He could count the folds of her robe, distinguish the separate lashes of her eyes, discern the play of sunlight upon the dark brown skin of her arms. She was the Virgin worshiped by these Spaniards, and yet she was not. She was a native woman. Pitoque raised his hands, as he had observed the Spaniards doing, and clasped them together. He tried to utter some greeting, but his mouth was impossibly dry. He could not even move his lips. It did not seem to matter. It was she who did the speaking.

"Pitoque."

He tried to swallow.

"I am who you think. I am the Mother of God."

He tried to speak. He wanted to ask her, *Which god?*

"The one true God," she said. "The God of all men."

He squeezed his eyes shut and opened them again, amazed. She had understood him even though he had not spoken.

"I have come to enlist your service. Will you help me?"

Still, he could not bring himself to utter a word.

She smiled and informed him that she desired a shrine to be erected in this place of destruction, atop this hill—a temple dedicated to her. Pitoque must return to the center of the city at once and seek out the chaplain of the Spaniards, Father Pedro de Olmedo. He must recount what he had seen and relay her wishes, so that they might be fulfilled.

"Will you do this for me?"

Pitoque cleared his throat. He made a desperate effort and managed to squeeze out a single word. "Yes."

"Good." Her image seemed to ripple in the wind, as though she were made of cloth. She inclined her head. "There is another service I require."

Pitoque inched closer, on his knees. "Yes," he whispered.

"The Aztecs are my children, whom I love," she told him. "But, like all children, they are prone to error. These sacrifices they perform—I find them deeply repugnant. They must cease. Only in this way can great bloodshed and torment be avoided. Here is what I wish you to do. On the fourth feast night of Huitzilopochtli, a woman is to be put to death. You must prevent it. Do you agree?"

"But how? I am only one man. I—"

"You must seek allies. You must find others to help you. It is little that I ask, the saving of a single life. From this one deed, much good will follow. Do you agree?"

"I agree," said Pitoque. Then he frowned. "But no one will believe me. How can I persuade them to listen to what I say?"

She smiled again and pointed at a mound of earth not far from her feet. At once, a bouquet of roses sprang from the soil, as red as blood, even though it was winter now in the high mountain valley and no such flowers would grow.

"Here," said the woman. "Take these roses with you. Present them to the chaplain as a gift from me. They will prove the truth of your words—for how could you have come by such flowers at this time of year, had I not caused them to bloom?"

Pitoque crept forward and reached out to pluck the stems from the ground, but at once they seemed to gather themselves into his arms. He held them against the fabric of his robe, as one might cradle a child. He looked up again and watched as the woman smiled even more broadly than before. He blinked, and her image seemed to fade slightly, but she did not disappear. She seemed translucent now, like an image in glass. She was still there, but he could see through to the other side.

"Go," she said. "Hurry."

He rose to his feet, clutched the flowers tightly in his arms, and hurried back toward the center of Tenochtitlán.

"Yes? What do you want?" Clemente José Hernández, secretary to the Spanish chaplain, peered up at this astonishing little native who stood before him, barefoot and trembling. "What do you want?"

"I have brought roses."

"Where are they then? Why do you bring roses here? I don't see any roses. Who let you into this office?"

"Here they are." Pitoque held the roses up. Was the man blind? "I bring you roses in winter."

"Are you mad? I see no roses. What are you doing here?"

"I wish to speak to the chaplain."

Hernández started to speak, then stopped himself. He'd suddenly realized something extraordinary. This native was speaking Spanish. He had never heard such a marvel before, if he didn't count the dark-skinned slut who had wormed her way into the captain-general's bed. He crossed his arms on the desk and leaned forward. "Who gave you permission to speak Spanish?"

Pitoque stared straight ahead, suddenly unnerved. He hadn't understood this last outburst. The words had flown past him. He repeated what he had already said. "I wish to speak to the chaplain. Please."

"I'm sure you do. Wouldn't everybody?" Hernández shook his bald dome, fringed by a curtain of sparse brown hair. "Alas, the chaplain does not wish to speak to you."

"Please. It is important."

Hernández climbed to his feet. "Who are you? Who let you in here? Where are these roses you speak of? It's the middle of winter, man. Roses do not bloom at this time of year. You should know that."

"Yes. I know. I—"

"Go away. The chaplain is an extremely busy man."

"But—"

"I thought you spoke Spanish. Don't you understand me? I said go."

"The Mother of God—"

"Watch your tongue! I will not have profanity here." The secretary looked around. "Brother Ernesto! Brother Ernesto! Hurry! Come here!"

A large young man hurried to the secretary's assistance. They bundled Pitoque along a corridor. Several of the rose petals fell from his grasp, but the two Spaniards ignored them, as if they did not exist or as if they were invisible. They hauled him outside and gave him a shove. He sprawled to his knees and fell forward into the dirt, the blossoms tumbling around him. He lay there for several moments, gasping for breath. Finally, he pulled himself to his feet and collected the roses. With his arms full, he stumbled down the street.

When a flock of children danced past him, he called out, "Roses? Do you want roses?"

They all laughed and shouted yes, and he distributed the stems one by one. They promptly broke the flowers off and twisted them into their hair. They pointed at each other, giggled, made coy poses, and then scampered away.

The following morning, Pitoque set out very early, when the sun was just rising. He had promised the goddess that he would return. When he reached the foot of the hill at Tepeyac, he briefly considered turning back, afraid of what he had to say and afraid of her response. But would she even appear? Would he see her again? Or had he simply imagined her? Then he remembered the roses, and he knew that he had not been mistaken. She had been real. He began to climb.

When he reached the summit, he gazed around and at once, a vision of blue swelled before him. She was just as he remembered, except that this time she was perched atop the branches of a nopal cactus. Once again, she called to him by name. She wanted to know the result of his conversation with the chaplain. He fell to his knees and crept forward. He had to confess that no such conversation had taken place. On hearing this news, she seemed neither distressed nor angry. She said she understood that simple tasks are sometimes rendered difficult. She reminded him of his promise to help her.

"You do wish to help me, don't you?"

Pitoque clasped his hands together. "Yes," he said. "I wish nothing mere."

"Good. I am deeply grateful." She gestured at the ground near his feet, and again a vivid cluster of red roses sprang from the earth. "Take these to the chaplain as a gift from me. Surely he will see you now."

Again, Pitoque gathered the flowers into his arms. He half-ran, half-stumbled all the way back to the chaplain's quarters. When he arrived, he was panting from the exertion. He tightened his grip on the roses and ventured inside. Brother

Hernández peered up with a look of surprise that quickly turned to anger. He slammed down his writing quill, almost overturning a pot of ink.

"Dear God," he said. "What's this? You again? With your nonsense about roses?"

Pitoque held up the flowers again. "Look," he said. "Here they are. Take them. Please, I wish to see the chaplain."

"Get out."

Pitoque tried to explain. But it was no use. The secretary cried out for assistance, and this time two men appeared.

"Take this lunatic away." The secretary glared at Pitoque. "And if I ever lay eyes on you again, little sir, I will have your head. Mark my words."

Pitoque found himself out on the street again. As he had done the day before, he walked slowly away with the flowers heaped in his arms. He passed a young woman—a girl, really—and offered her the roses.

"They are from the Mother of God," he told her.

She smiled and accepted the flowers from him without a word. She seemed to float away, cradling the roses in her arms as though she held a newborn baby. Pitoque watched her go, then took a deep breath. He would have to return to the hill at Tepeyac and report that he had failed a second time.

But first he decided to seek out the Spaniard named Aguilar. He thought that if anyone could help him to fulfill the offices he had assumed on behalf of the dark-skinned Virgin, then Aguilar would be that man. Pitoque wandered about asking after Aguilar, looking for him everywhere, and the sun had traveled a good distance in the sky before he gave up. The translator was nowhere to be found.

With a sinking heart, Pitoque set out for the hill at Tepeyac to report that he had failed yet again. He shuffled through the gouged and rubble-strewn streets of the city, wondering why the Mother of God had chosen him for this mission. He chased the question around and around in his mind, examined it a dozen different ways, and finally came up with the only answer that made any sense. This must be an act of atonement for that dreadful night in the lands of the Maya. A dozen years ago, he had failed to prevent the deaths of those young girls, all of whom had doubtless been virgins. Now he was required to preserve the life of another virgin, the hummingbird bride, who also came from the lands of the Maya. The circle was closing.

Another reason struck him. The Mother of God had appeared to him upon the ruins of the shrine dedicated to Tonantzin, who was the consort of Quetzalcoatl. Here was another circle closed, for it had been Quetzalcoatl whom he had offended that long-ago night and whose temple had been desecrated in Cholula by his son. The Mother of God had chosen him to atone for the sins he had committed, to put right the misdeeds of the past. Perhaps much suffering could be averted now, if he did as he was told.

But so far he had failed. With a trembling heart, he increased his pace, bound for the hill at Tepeyac.

It was dark by the time he reached the site of the ruined shrine. He climbed to the summit of the hill and looked around in the darkness. Below him to the south, the jumbled lights of Tenochtitlán flickered through the night. Stars stared down from a jet black sky. A night wind streamed through his hair. But the Virgin goddess did not appear. He waited almost until morning, but she was evidently gone. At last, he pulled his robe around him to ward off the cold and climbed back down the southern slope.

The Virgin's Likeness

The moonlight stained the lake with pools and rivulets of molten silver, and Maxtla settled himself alone into a dugout canoe. He took his time, trying to get his balance and recover his familiarity with the paddle. As a young boy, he had spent long hours exploring the lake at Amozoc by canoe, and he sensed his childhood skill returning to him now. He dipped his paddle into the cool water and felt the pressure of the lake in the muscles of his arms and shoulders. Soon, he was knifing through the pale glint of its surface.

In less than an hour, he had crossed the lake and the canoe was snaking through the marshy shallows by the eastern shore. The bow nudged against the bank. He scrambled out into the knee-deep water and beached the craft on the damp, grassy shore.

He took a deep breath and then reminded himself of why he had come. He had come to seek an audience with the king of Texcoco, Cacama. If he repeated his purpose often enough in his mind, perhaps he would cease to find it so daunting.

Now he turned and slid the paddle into the hull of the canoe. He straightened up, patted down the folds of his robe, and began to trudge up the shore and into the city.

At the entrance to Cacama's palace, Maxtla announced that he had come from the court of Moctezuma. In a way, he had.

One of the two guards laughed. "Yes," he said, "and I am the reincarnation of Quetzalcoatl. Go away."

"I have important information to convey to the king."

"I said, go away."

The other guard raised his spear and started toward Maxtla, who realized that he was going to have to enter the palace the hard way. He took a breath and threw himself to the ground, then scrambled between the guard's legs. Instantly, he yanked himself to his feet and took off at a run, racing into the palace. A cry of alarm went up, and he soon realized he was being chased by, not one, but perhaps a dozen guards. He didn't dare look around to count. A succession of torchlit corridors and patios spun past him, and then he saw a brighter glow ahead. He quickened his pace and was just about to dart into a large, illuminated hall when he felt his neck jerk back and he crashed to the ground. One of the guards had him by the collar of his robe.

"Ha! Got you!"

Maxtla let out a piercing, heartfelt howl. When he was done, he swallowed, took a breath, and shrieked again. He did not stop screaming until an elderly man hurried out to see what on earth was going on. Were the guards roasting someone alive upon a spit?

This was Tepehuatl, senior aide to the king. When he saw Maxtla, he stopped and frowned. Oh. It was just a boy. He said, "Who are you?"

Maxtla introduced himself. "I have come on a mission of the greatest importance," he said. "The future of the empire depends upon it."

"The future of the empire?"

"Yes."

"I see. Well, the future of the empire is much on our minds these days. Tell me what you have to say."

But Maxtla would not be put off. Ignoring the pounding in his chest, he said, "I wish to speak to the king. Myself."

Tepehuatl rubbed his jaw. "Well, you are obviously a determined fellow. Perhaps you do have something to tell us, after all. Normally, you know, I would have you beaten, beheaded, and then drowned. But these are unusual times. I will make an exception. Come with me." He waved the guards off, turned, and marched back into the blazing hall, an antechamber leading to the even larger and brighter throne room of the king.

Maxtla crept after him, craning his neck this way and that as he marveled at his surroundings and struggled to compose the words that he would use to win the confidence of Cacama, king of Texcoco, leader of the rebellion against the Spaniards.

Cacama stood in the center of the hall, clad in a dark blue robe, his back to the entrance. Several dozen courtiers stood about in small groups. They all fell silent and looked up as Maxtla entered.

At first, the king did not move, and it seemed to Maxtla that perhaps he never would. But then Cacama turned and revealed his long face, with its riddle of tattoo lines and its somber countenance. Maxtla felt his legs wobble beneath him as he grew suddenly afraid. What if Cacama knew that, not so long ago, he had worshiped the Spaniards almost as gods? In any case, why would the king of Texcoco care about the services of a fourteen-year-old boy who spoke with the accent of Cholula?

"Yes?" said Cacama. He raised his eyebrows.

Tepehuatl cleared his throat. "He says he wishes to speak to you, my lord. He told the guards he comes from Moctezuma himself."

Cacama looked again at Maxtla. "Well, then. What do you wish to say?"

Maxtla swallowed and rubbed his damp palms against the folds of his robe. He announced that he had come to offer his services to the forces of revolt.

"Your services? But you are merely a boy." The monarch settled back onto his throne and crossed his legs. "In what possible respect could you be of use? I have plenty of warriors already."

Maxtla shook his head. "I am not a warrior."

"What are you, then?"

"The son of a *pochteca*."

"A trader's son?" Cacama arched his eyebrows. "Oh, I see. Do you propose a barter of some kind? So many ocelot skins in exchange for the defeat of these cursed foreigners? Is that it?"

Cacama looked up, and several of his courtiers tittered at his jest. He peered back at Maxtla.

"No, my lord. But my father is an aide to Moctezuma. He lives in the palace occupied by the Spaniards."

"I thought you said he was a *pochteca*, your father."

"He is, or was, but his circumstances have changed."

"To a remarkable degree."

Maxtla lowered his gaze in assent. "These are remarkable times."

Cacama gestured to a servant, who brought him his pipe. When the pipe was lit, and after the king had taken several soothing puffs of the smoke, he released a long gray plume and turned back to the boy. "What do you propose?"

The proposal was easily explained. Maxtla would keep Cacama informed about conditions inside the palace, the comings and goings of the Spaniards, the state of their defences, their weaknesses, their strengths. "I imagine this information would be of value to you."

Cacama agreed that it would be. Indeed, it would be of incalculable value—assuming the information was accurate and reliable. He puffed on his pipe and blew out another cloud of smoke. He tilted his head. "But will it be? Why should I trust you? Perhaps you are another of these traitors, like that appalling woman. What do they call her?"

"Doña Marina," said Maxtla.

"Exactly." The king gestured with his pipe. "For all I know, you could be just like her. This proposal of yours could be a trick. Can you persuade me otherwise?"

Maxtla took a breath. He had expected suspicion and had prepared an answer. "I am a native of Cholula," he said. "Perhaps you can tell it from my accent."

The king agreed that he could.

"You have been informed, no doubt, of what took place there?"

"I have."

"Is it any surprise, then, that I should be an enemy of these Spaniards?"

"No. But it remains possible that you are not. Cholulans, in my experience, are no great friends of the Aztecs, either."

Maxtla took another breath. "For the past several months, I have dwelt in the house of Azotl. I—"

"The master functionary?"

"Yes."

"He was a friend of yours?"

"He was. A friend of my father's as well."

Cacama leaned forward. "Describe to me the interior of Azotl's house. Room by room. Spare no detail."

Maxtla did as he was asked. As he spoke, he had to struggle to keep his voice steady. Several times, his lower lip began to tremble, and tears welled in his eyes. He wiped them away and carried on. When he was done, Cacama did not move, immersed in thought. At last, the king set down his pipe, and a servant whisked it away.

"Enough," Cacama said. "I am persuaded. Let us now speak seriously of how you might help us and what you might do."

Later that night, when he departed the palace of Cacama,

Maxtla was a member of the rebellion against the Spaniards. He hurried through the darkness until he found the dugout canoe where he had left it, sprawled upon the sponge grass on the shore. He eased the craft back into the shallows of the lake, climbed aboard, and slipped the paddle into the dark water. The moon had gone down now, and the frail light cast by a flock of stars trickled across the lake. The fires of Tenochtitlán burned to the west, and he paddled toward them.

Pitoque returned to the hill at Tepeyac. A pale light was creeping over the eastern mountains and down through the Valley of Anáhuac. He trudged up the southern flank of the hill. He was all but certain this time that he would find nothing at the summit. He had failed the Mother of God, and so she would therefore refuse to appear before him again. He'd had his chance, and he had lost it. But it turned out that he was wrong.

No sooner had he reached the crest of the hill than he saw her glimmering before him, almost as bright as the sun. He had to squint when he looked at her.

"Good morning, my child."

He fell to his knees. "Good morning."

She asked about the outcome of his second meeting with the chaplain, and he was obliged to tell her once again that he had been unable to speak to the man. She did not seem surprised or angry. Instead, she caused yet another shock of roses to appear at his feet and told him not to lose heart, to be persistent. Soon enough, he would prevail.

"Go," she said. "Explain to the chaplain that I require a shrine to be erected here, in my name. And do not forget my other commission. The girl who is to be sacrificed—she must be saved. Go now. I know you will not fail me."

Pitoque wanted to tell her that it wasn't the chaplain who was the problem—it was his foul-tempered secretary. But he decided not to trouble the goddess with so much detail. She had declared her wishes, and it was his duty to comply. He gathered up the roses as before and set out for the chaplain's quarters.

This time, the secretary was not merely angry. He was livid with rage. When Pitoque appeared before him, Hernández leapt to his feet, shaking with fury. Once again, he called out for assistance, but this time he did not wait for its arrival before taking action. He stormed around his table and made straight for Pitoque, who closed his eyes and turned his face. He kept his arms squeezed tightly to his chest to keep the roses safe, and he waited for the first blow to land.

It nearly knocked him down, that first blow. But he did not fight back. Soon, he was on his knees and pinned to the floor. Punches and kicks hammered down on every part of his body, and then he felt himself seized by both shoulders. He was being hauled out of the room. He tried to resist, but soon several more Spaniards ran up and half-dragged, half-carried him out to the street. They tossed him upon a pile of earth, near another of the countless pits that scarred the surface of Tenochtitlán.

He waited until the Spaniards left. Then he sat up and tried to get his bearings. The earth spun around him, and every part of his body shouted with pain. By some good fortune, he had managed to hang onto the roses. They lay in a muddle at his side.

Pitoque gathered them up and climbed to his feet. Blood drooled from his nose, and he could not see out of one eye. The pain from his wounds was so intense that he thought he could hear it—a bitter, keening wail. He turned and stumbled through the streets toward the palace of Axayácatl. He would try to seek out Aguilar again. There was no one else he could think of who would help him. This time, he did not give away the flowers but kept them clutched to his chest.

After several minutes of staggering through the rubble and litter, Pitoque remembered that he was unlikely to find Aguilar at the Spaniards' palace. The translator was almost never there nowadays. He wracked his brain. Where would Aguilar be? Where would he go? A sudden instinct told him what he should have realized before. He recalled the afternoon, weeks earlier, when he had accompanied Aguilar and Moctezuma to the palace of Huitzilopochtli, where they had met the hummingbird bride. He remembered the Spaniard's response, the way he had dropped at once to his knees in an attitude of prayer. Since that afternoon, Aguilar had almost disappeared. It was suddenly obvious why.

Pitoque wiped his nose with his arm, leaving a long streak of blood on his robe. He was bleeding more heavily than he had realized—the blood was dribbling down onto the roses that he still held pressed against his chest. He changed his direction and made his way slowly to the palace of Huitzilopochtli.

When he arrived, the two Aztec sentries at the entrance stepped forward and crossed their spears to bar his way. In desperation, he started to scream and howl, calling out Aguilar's name over and over again. Finally, Aguilar himself appeared at the door.

"My God," he said. He waved the sentries off and ushered Pitoque inside. "In the name of God, what has happened to you?"

"An altercation."

"So I see. An altercation with whom? The entire army of Spain?"

Before Pitoque could answer, Aguilar guided him into a large salon that was open to the lake. A sudden movement in the room told him that someone else was present, but in his confusion, and with the pain and the blurring of his eye, he could not make out who it was.

"Never mind my questions," said Aguilar. "Let me take a look at that eye of yours. Dear God, what a quantity of blood."

But at least it had stopped flowing now and had started to crust upon his face.

"What are these flowers?" said Aguilar. "Where did you get these? Roses blooming at this time of year? How very odd."

He started to remove the roses from Pitoque's arms, and instantly they sprang from his grasp, transformed themselves into birds of scarlet plumage. They took wing, swerved out over the wooden railing, veered sharply to the right against the blue backdrop of the lake, and vanished from sight. For a time, both Aguilar and Pitoque gazed after them—Pitoque squinting through his one good eye. Neither could say a word. Had the vision been real or had they both imagined it?

Aguilar let out a low whistle and turned back to attend to Pitoque. At once, he let out a cry.

"Holy Mother of God." He fell to his knees on the floor and stared at Pitoque's chest. "Dear Mother Mary."

Pitoque peered down. Even with his blurred sight, he could see what it was—where the roses had been pressed against his robe, where the blood from his face had run, there was now an astonishing sight. The blood had dried into the likeness of a woman's profile.

Aguilar let out a moan. "Sweet Name of Mary."

Later—after he had cleaned himself up a little and changed into spare clothing stored in one of the palace's closets—Pitoque was able to inspect his robe more closely.

Aguilar had laid the fabric out upon a trestle table, and there was no denying what the Spaniard had seen and what Pitoque now saw. After coagulating among the roses that had been pressed against his chest, his dried blood had formed itself into the exact likeness of the goddess he had encountered at the summit of the hill at Tepeyac, the dark Virgin. It was uncanny but unmistakable. The image seemed almost to breathe. It looked almost alive. This was the Mother of God, just like the pictures Aguilar had shown him, but now her hair was straight and black, her skin dark, her features those of a native woman.

"Hallelujah," whispered Aguilar, his eyes closed in prayer. "It is a sign."

Pitoque heard footsteps, an intake of breath. He looked around and saw a woman appear—Bakil, the hummingbird bride. She was twisting a rose blossom into her hair and walked toward them both, shoulders back, head held high, with the bearing of a princess. She gazed down at the image encrusted upon the fabric of Pitoque's robe and briefly smiled before slowly turning away. Pitoque saw now what Aguilar had already seen. He saw that Bakil and the image on his robe were one and the same. Now he, too, fell to his knees.

"It is surely a sign," whispered Aguilar. "But what does it mean? Tell me. What?"

Pitoque swallowed, for his throat was very dry. He closed his eyes and heard the Virgin's voice singing in his mind. He opened his eyes, turned to the Spaniard, and in a low voice began to explain.

The Silence of the Stars

Puertocarrero stalked the streets of Tenochtitlán, enraged at the injustice—the intolerable injustice—of it all. If he had failed Cortés in some way, it would have been different. But he had not. On the contrary, he had performed the most valuable of services. He had excelled in every respect. He had routed his rival, Alvarado. He had captured prisoners. He had unmasked enemies. True, he hadn't expected that they would be burned at the stake. The memory of the executions left a bitter taste in his mouth and a confusion in his mind. How could all his good works have produced such a hideous outcome? It rattled him, more than a little. He had truly not anticipated that death would result from his actions. Now he closed his eyes, shuddered. To calm himself, he tried to think of other matters—his reward, for example. He still had not received his reward.

Granted, he had been reinstated as one of Cortés's lieutenants. That was something. Indeed, it was a lot. But it wasn't everything. He longed for a little native woman to put in his bed, a very pretty one. Was that asking too much? And gold. Had anyone thought to mention gold? Had he received any treasure? None. Perhaps there was no treasure to give? Ha! Cortés had said there would be. He had even written out another of his ridiculous promissory notes, as if they counted for anything. Puertocarrero didn't put much stock in promissory notes. He wanted something solid to the touch. He wanted precious metals, fine jewels. He wanted gold. And a girl. Most of all, a girl.

He turned a corner and suddenly got himself tangled up with one of these Aztecs. Why did they all walk about with their eyes cast down, never looking where they were going? Both of them had tripped and ended up in the dirt. Puertocarrero was first to climb back to his feet, and he peered down at the creature, who was cowering on his knees, eyes as large as plates, hands trembling—the very picture of servility.

"Come on," he said. "Get up."

But the native refused to budge, obviously terrified of suffering a beating.

"I'm not going to hurt you. Get up."

It was no use. The fellow remained where he was in an attitude of supplication, quivering in the grime. Puertocarrero turned away, disgusted with himself. Any other Spaniard would have given the creature a good hiding for the crime of being in the way. But he hadn't the stomach for it. That was his problem. He was too soft. That was why others took advantage of him, why he'd received no decent reward for all he'd done, why he spent his nights alone. If he had any *cojones*, he would march right back and give that cringing native a couple of good kicks. But he knew he wasn't going to. No *cojones*. Too soft.

Another image of Doña Marina wafted through his mind, the outline of her breasts visible against a pale blue cotton blouse. He raised his hands and stared at the sky. Oh, Lord, he wanted a woman in the worst way. At least, he thought he did. He thought a slim little one would do the trick, get the blood flowing to his groin, bring his manhood to the fore. He let out a groan. He lowered his head and suddenly found himself staring straight at another Spaniard, who was walking toward him. Aguilar. The swarthy one. Puertocarrero did his best to turn his wail into a kind of song, a jaunty little stroller's air.

"Are you all right?" said Aguilar. "Are you hurt?"

"No. I am just out for a walk. Why do you ask?"

"It sounded as if you were injured."

"Not at all. I admit that I am a poor singer. But otherwise I'm in a passable state."

"I am glad to hear it."

"And you? I trust you are well?" In fact, to Puertocarrero, it seemed that Aguilar positively brimmed with well-being. His eyes glowed, and his normally somber features had an almost euphoric cast, as if he'd lately walked among angels. What was the explanation for this?

"I am quite well. Extremely well. Thank you."

Puertocarrero sighed, suddenly filled with envy. Seeing the translator in such obvious high spirits merely served to remind him of his own grievances and to sharpen their sting. He flopped down upon a large block of stone that squatted in the middle of the street, another product of the Spaniards' continuing excavations. He planted his elbows on his knees and shook his head. "I have told a lie," he said.

"You have?" The man seemed eager to continue on his way but hung back, evidently out of concern for Puertocarrero. "What do you mean?"

"I told you that I was in a passable state. It isn't so. Indeed, it is far from the truth. I am as far from being in a passable state as this godforsaken city is from Spain, if not farther." He knew he had no right to presume upon Aguilar's patience and goodwill, but he did so anyway. He could not help it. It seemed so unfair that one man should seem so happy, while he—a cousin of the Count of Medellín—found himself in such a dreary pit. He unburdened himself, told Aguilar about all the injustices that Cortés had done him, and the words gushed out as if of their own will.

"If there was some way I could make Cortés pay for what he's done to me, I'd do it. In an instant. I've been promised rewards, and he has not paid them. I'm not sure if you're aware, but my cousin is the Count of Medellín. I do not deserve to be treated this way. It isn't right."

Aguilar made some vague, sympathetic remarks, then bid Puertocarrero farewell and hurried on his way to the palace of the hummingbird god. He shook his head, thinking of the lieutenant's accusations, and knew they were merely the blatherings of a weak, insecure man reeling from a slight. A matter of no importance. But as he picked his way through the shambles of Tenochtitlán's streets, he began to think again. The man was obviously at a low ebb—the sort of fellow who might be in a reckless mood. He might turn out to be just the accomplice Aguilar now needed, even though he seemed fragile and unstable. Maybe those weaknesses could be turned to advantage, as well. They might be useful.

Aguilar rounded another turn and found himself within sight of the palace of Huitzilopochtli. He quickened his pace. He was suddenly quite intrigued by the possibilities presented by Puertocarrero. In fact, the man might be very helpful indeed.

Moctezuma was in the habit of climbing up onto the roof of the palace of Axayácatl by night, in order to observe the stars. From the patterns of the constellations that swam overhead in the endless dark, he hoped to divine the will of the gods. On this particular night, Pitoque decided to approach the emperor where he wandered alone on that rooftop bathed in the pale glow of the heavens. He had two purposes in mind—first, to inform the emperor of Cacama's insurrection and to find out whether or not he supported it, and second, to tell him of the Mother of God and of her demands.

The emperor stood by a railing with his hands clasped behind his back, his neck craned upward. He wore a heavy cloak lined with ocelot fur, for it was cool enough outside that a man could see his breath. Pitoque could make out thin clouds of vapor pluming from the emperor's lips. He stepped forward, and his foot scraped upon a loose piece of slate. Moctezuma started, then peered back.

"Aha. My Cholulan friend. I am glad that you have come. Look."

He pointed toward the sky and Pitoque gazed up. The stars glittered like tiny counters in a celestial game of chance—except that it wasn't a game of chance. All was foreordained, and the stars were oracles, or so it was said. Pitoque tilted his head back even farther and watched as the constellations turned slow somersaults over the earth—the Royal Star, the Great Ballcourt, the Turtle, the Smoking Hearth, the Scorpion, the Lone Maiden. For a time, the two men stood side by side, staring in silence at the mystery of these countless silvery beings, these dragon-flies of light that existed only in the absence of the sun. A breeze ruffled the night, carrying a faint air of salt from the shallows of Texcoco. In the distance, Pitoque heard the barking of dogs.

"Behold," said Moctezuma. "The handwriting of the gods."

After a time, Pitoque asked, "And what do the gods say?"

Moctezuma heaved a long sigh and put a hand up to cover his eyes. At first, he said nothing. Then he said, "They do not speak to me." He lowered his head, and his shoulders began to quake.

Pitoque took another step forward. He cleared his throat and addressed the emperor of the Aztecs. He spoke quickly and firmly. He described Cacama's planned revolt and his own involvement and Maxtla's. He explained everything, as clearly as possible. When he had finished, he waited for Moctezuma to speak. But the emperor said nothing for a long, slow time. The cool wind sailed inland from the lake. Again, dogs bickered in the distance. Finally, Moctezuma tilted back his head and peered up.

"I can make no decision at present," he said. "I must wait for the counsel of the gods. I must wait for a sign."

Pitoque let out a long breath. He did not relish what he was about to do, but what choice did he have? "My lord," he said. "I myself have witnessed a sign."

Moctezuma frowned, but said nothing.

Pitoque continued. He described the shimmering woman he had seen atop a nopal cactus on the hill at Tepeyac—just like the Virgin Mother so revered by these Spaniards, but dark of skin—and he explained what the woman had told him. She wished a shrine to be erected in her honor on that hill, now covered by the jumbled ruins of the pyramid.

"Replace the pyramid of Tonantzin?" said the emperor.

Pitoque swallowed. "Yes, my lord." He understood how

blasphemous this idea was. "That is what she said. In any case, the pyramid is ruined."

"So I understand." Moctezuma looked back up at the darkness overhead. "What else did she say, this woman you claim to have seen?"

Pitoque wondered whether to correct the emperor. The woman he *saw*. He decided against it. Instead, he answered Moctezuma's question. The glowing woman in robes of blue had demanded that the feast of Huitzilopochtli not proceed as planned—that the hummingbird bride not be sacrificed.

Moctezuma said nothing. He continued to stare up at the slow churning of the stars. Finally, he let out a high-pitched sound, more like a whimper than anything else. "You would have us all die?"

"No, my lord. I am only—"

"Do you realize that is what would happen if I were to do as you say? The sun would fall from the sky. The lakes would explode. Fires would burn. A great darkness would fall. The earth would succumb to a deadly cold, colder than the summit of Popocatépetl. This is what you wish?"

"No, of course not," said Pitoque. "But what I'm trying to say is—"

"You're saying the survival of your people is not important?" Moctezuma lowered his head. He turned toward Pitoque. "You may take my word for it that your people, and mine, would certainly be destroyed if I were to do as you say."

Pitoque folded his arms to shield himself from the cold, and told the emperor of the Aztecs what he had told no one else before—about the deaths of those girls years earlier in the lands of the Maya, about the insult offered Quetzalcoatl that long-ago night, about the sins committed later by his own son. "And now," he said, "I have the chance to offer atonement, to put matters right."

The emperor shook his head. He sighed. Now he looked up again at the whirl of lights arching overhead. For the longest time, he remained silent.

"Pitoque," the emperor finally said, "it would be a service to me if you were to refrain from broaching this subject in my presence ever again. I seek clarity, and you bring only confusion. You will speak of this no more. Do I have your agreement?"

Pitoque saw that it was useless to disagree. "Yes, my lord."

"And as to the other matter you raise, this affair involving Cacama, I . . ." The emperor's voice trailed off.

"Yes, my lord?" He could see that the man was crying.

The emperor spoke now amid low, furtive sobs. "I can make no decision at present. I must wait for a sign."

Pitoque let out a long breath. He said what the emperor already knew—that, in this case, events would proceed according to the designs of others. It no longer mattered whether the stars spoke or were silent. He waited for a reply, but there was none. Moctezuma was lost again in contemplation of the heavens.

Pitoque waited several moments. Then he turned and withdrew. He approached the ladder that descended into the palace, and for an instant he saw something—a human figure. One moment, it was there, watching him. The next moment, it was gone. Whatever it was—*whoever* it was—it disappeared down the ladder like some nocturnal creature scuttling out of view. At once, Pitoque's heart began to pound, and he hurried to the ladder, but he was too late. The person was gone. Still, there was something about the figure's shape, movement, flowing hair, that made him think of Doña Marina. Had she been lurking on the roof? Had she been spying on him? On the emperor? He felt a sudden blade of fear knife into his chest, and he turned back to look at Moctezuma again.

The emperor had not moved. His face was still turned away, lifted toward the sky. The pale silver light fell upon his features and ran down his robes, forming a pool at his feet. His shoulders quivered. He was weeping again, overcome by this inscrutable radiance, this silence of the stars.

The Word of a Spanish Gentleman

Doña Marina went directly to Cortés and told him all she had learned—a rebellion was in the offing, led by Cacama. She knew the names of several others involved. Pitoque. Maxtla.

Cortés stretched back on his bed and chuckled. "You are not only lovely. You are a genius."

"Thank you," she said. "How do you mean to respond?"

"I'll have to think."

"Aren't you going to do anything?"

"Yes, but not yet. You know, I find espionage remarkably arousing. Come here."

"But . . ."

"I said, come here. I will deal with those matters in the morning. Right now, I have other thoughts on my mind."

She smiled. "You do?"

"Yes. But you had better hurry. I'm in no mood to wait."

She did as he said. After all, he was her master, and she, his little wife. Besides, they hadn't done anything of this sort in a great many days.

The next morning, Cortés dealt with the rebellion.

Maxtla was riding in a canoe paddled by a pair of Aztec boatmen when he was apprehended. He had been intent on crossing the lake, bound for the city of Texcoco, where Cacama and his army were preparing for war. He had meant to inform them of Moctezuma's decision—or, rather, his indecision—but he did not arrive at his destination. Aboard one of their elegant sloops, a party of Spaniards first fired several warning shots with their harquebuses and then forced the paddlers to reverse course. On shore, Maxtla and his boatmen were put in chains and marched back to the palace of Axayácatl.

Later, the Spaniards surprised Cacama at his palace. They'd received orders to take the king prisoner, along with anyone in his presence who appeared the least bit suspicious. They interpreted this command to mean everyone. They seized two dozen men and marched them around the lake along the northern route. They stationed a substantial guard of Tlaxcalan warriors at Texcoco to keep watch on the city.

Pitoque was arrested in the palace of Axayácatl, in the quarters reserved for the use of Moctezuma and his entourage. At the time of his capture, he was bathing, which was additional bad luck for him. His captors did not permit him an opportunity to dress. Later, a loincloth was tossed at him so that he could at least cover his manhood.

They threw him into a dungeon beneath a minor palace, along with twenty or so others. Water dripped down the walls, covering the mud floor up to their ankles. It was impossible to lie down, for fear of drowning. Day and night, Pitoque and the others huddled in darkness as impenetrable as the center of a clenched fist. They were forced to relieve themselves where they stood. They had nothing to eat and were obliged to drink the only water they had, the water they had already fouled. Half of them were afraid they would die in this place, and the other half welcomed the prospect. It seemed preferable to some unknown but possibly even more horrible fate.

Pitoque did not think that he would die in the dungeon. He didn't believe that Cortés would be able to resist making some kind of spectacle of his prisoners. And so he did not dwell upon the specter of death. Instead, he wondered what had become of Maxtla and prayed that the boy was all right. He also devoted himself to perfecting a strategy for ensuring his own life—and Maxtla's and the lives of as many others as he could manage. He rehearsed countless times what he would say when he was brought into the presence of Hernán Cortés. Over and over again, he repeated the precise words he would use, relying on the Spanish words he had picked up, mostly from Jerónimo de Aguilar.

Finally, after an uncertain length of time, a miserable length of time—he thought it might have been three or four days—he got his wish. With his fellow prisoners, he was hauled out of the stinking hole and herded into the House of the Eagle Knights.

It was struggle to walk. Pitoque had his hands chained behind his back. Shackles dragged at his ankles. After so many days in darkness, he found it almost impossible now to readjust to the light. He squinted at his surroundings—the familiar thrones and canopies of the great council hall, now filled with a gathering of Spanish guards and officers, who stood about chatting and chortling as if these trials of Aztec miscreants had become so commonplace as barely to merit attention.

Pitoque gazed around and saw Cortés, with Doña Marina at his side. The Spanish commander looked a little disgruntled and was muttering something to Pedro de Alvarado. Pitoque shifted his gaze, and then saw Moctezuma himself, slouching upon his throne, miserable and helpless. Pitoque peered around at the assembled prisoners, desperate to see if Maxtla was among them.

And he was. Yes, he was.

It was difficult to tell, but the boy seemed all right, or as close to it as was possible for a prisoner of these Spaniards. He was filthy, clad only in a loincloth, and he bore several crusted gashes on his leg and arms, as well as a bruise or two upon his face. But at least he was alive. Pitoque sought to catch his son's gaze, and finally their eyes met. They both swallowed and nodded at each other, and Pitoque thought he recognized a look of acknowledgment and acceptance. He believed that Maxtla understood as well as he did himself what must happen next.

Pitoque gritted his teeth. He put back his shoulders, rattling his chains. Now was the time. It did not matter that he was in a pitiable state, covered in filth and bruised from much rough handling. Nothing could be gained by waiting. He would have no better chance than this. He summoned every particle of dignity that he could muster, stood up tall and straight, and then turned to Hernán Cortés, who stood near the emperor's throne, with Doña Marina not far away.

"Honored sir," he said as loudly as he could. "Allow me to introduce myself. I am a merchant of Cholula, an aide to the emperor Moctezuma, and I possess knowledge that may be of interest to you."

Immediately, the entire room fell silent, and a hundred Spaniards craned their necks to see who was speaking. They seemed astonished. What on earth was this? A native speaking in the Castilian tongue? They had accustomed themselves to Doña Marina's increasing command of their language—but, after all, she was the courtesan of their commander. Who was this miserable-looking fellow? Wait. Wasn't he the one they had all dubbed the Little King of Plates? And here he was, speaking in the language of the king of Spain! Would wonders never cease? Their surprise was so great that no one bothered to interrupt when Pitoque launched into the speech that constituted his last chance to save his own life and the life of his son.

He took a step forward. "I understand that you wish to obtain gold. Is that true?"

"Gold?" Cortés tilted his head. "You speak of gold?"

"I do."

"And what do you wish to say about gold?"

For a moment, the realization of what he was about to do welled up in Pitoque's chest and almost silenced him. The treasure of the Aztecs, surrendered forever. It seemed unthinkable to take this step, beyond the power of any one man. Was that, in the end, what had sealed Azotl's own lips? Pitoque clenched his shackled fists. He took a step forward, and his chains rattled at his feet. "It so happens," he said, "that I know where gold may be found."

Cortés raised his eyebrows, ran a hand through his beard. "You do?"

"Yes."

"Well, then, speak up. Tell me what you know."

Pitoque said he would be only too happy to do so, but first Cortés would have to agree to certain terms.

At this, the Spaniard laughed. "Terms?" he said. "My prisoner speaks to me of terms? That is an excellent joke. But go on, then. Enlighten me. What are your terms?"

Pitoque spoke as slowly and carefully as he could. He declared that, in exchange for freedom and a pardon—one that would apply to himself, to his son, and to all those who had been taken in the company of Cacama—he would provide Hernán Cortés with the information he most desired. He would reveal the location of the treasure of the Aztecs. "Do you agree to this bargain?"

Cortés leaned to the side to confer in whispers with

Alvarado. After a while, he turned back to Pitoque. "I agree," he said.

"May I have your word?"

Cortés laughed. "You dare to ask for my word?"

"Yes. Your word as a Spanish gentleman and as a representative of the king of Spain."

Cortés shook his head. It was so strange to hear these grand-sounding phrases tripping from the tongue of a native, especially such a frail-looking fellow as this, a man in such a wretched state, dressed only in a loincloth—a prisoner in shackles, with his hands chained behind his back. "You require my word as a gentleman?"

"If you would be willing to offer it."

"Oh, well, then. I see no obstacle. You may have it." He laughed again, astonished by the novelty of this exchange. He took a turn about the floor. "I really must congratulate you on your command of our language. How did this come about?"

Pitoque shrugged. "I simply listened. I have a certain affinity for languages."

"So it would seem. You are clearly an intelligent sort of fellow."

Pitoque said nothing. He waited for the Spaniard to continue.

"Since you are so quick, I wonder that it has not occurred to you that your offer to me is deeply flawed."

Pitoque had expected this response. Still, he frowned, playing along. "Flawed?" he said. "In what respect?"

"In this respect—that I have merely to put a pot of *grasa*

de puerco on the boil and I will learn your secrets very quickly. Then I may do with you as I wish."

"*Grasa de puerco?* What is that?"

With the aid of her master, Doña Marina explained. "The fat," she said, "of a pig—a swine, a hog."

Pitoque thought he understood now. He had seen these portly creatures once or twice while he was on the coast, groveling animals with flat snouts and cloven hooves, like the hooves of deer. The Spaniards kept them in enclosures at their coastal garrison. He did not think they had brought any inland with them. Still, he saw the direction in which Cortés was headed. He understood the reference to boiling. He also knew what to say—and now was the time to say it.

"But you have given your word." He paused for emphasis. "Surely the word of a Spanish gentleman can be relied upon."

Cortés stood still, an astonished look on his face. For a time, he said nothing. Then he put back his head and bellowed. He laughed until his eyes began to water. Dear God, he had just been outwitted, before all and sundry, by a half-naked native in chains. It was galling, but it was true. He had to admit it. He had given his word, and he had failed to anticipate that he would be reminded of it. Now he turned to address this surprising fellow, this Pitoque. He held out his hands in a kind of surrender. "You have asked for my word, and I have given it. There will be no more talk of pig fat. Come. Let us speak instead of gold."

✝

The Spaniards drained the larger of the two lagoons in the House of Birds and set a gang of workers to digging up the bottom. In short order, they broke through the ceiling of the vault that was hidden beneath the basin of the lagoon. They shone torches inside and at once began to roar. Never had they seen anything so glorious.

Several of the Spaniards leapt straight in, and more than one broke a leg or ankle in the fall. Others were more sensible and lowered themselves on ropes. Whether crippled or whole, they burrowed into the cache and began to toss up the treasures that they found—bracelets of jadeite, ingots of silver, disks of gold. They couldn't believe the treasures that they found.

Pedro de Alvarado stomped about, calling for order, for discipline. "A fifth for the king!" he shouted. "A fifth for Cortés! The rest to be distributed according to a plan that will be devised with recommendations from all! No one will be left out! Order! Order!"

But no one paid the least attention to him. Everyone was drunk with riches. The treasures of Moctezuma! In an attempt to impose restraint, Alvarado laid his hands upon an harquebus, tamped in a fistful of powder, and slid a ball into the chamber. He lit the matchlock and held the weapon up. He shot into the air, and was greeted by a cacophony of panicked bird cries.

The blast had nothing like its desired effect. Crazed already with the sight of gold, the Spaniards peered up at the tangle of foliage and realized they were surrounded by a remarkable quantity of birds. Why hadn't anyone noticed it before? At once, the treasure hunt turned into a shooting party. The men lumbered about, drunk with greed, and discharged their firearms at anything that rustled or flew.

Countless species of wildfowl screeched and whistled, darted and swerved. Parrots and quetzals, eagles and egrets, kestrels and kites—all shrieked in terror, raced through the trees, swung high, beat their pinions against the maguey webbing overhead. Their wings split apart, their chests burst open, they erupted in blood, and then they plummeted backwards, down through the branches, thumping upon the ground. The Spaniards clambered through the trees, gathering up fallen birds by the dozen, bunching them together by their twitching claws, and knotting them into braces. They laughed and clapped each other on the back and swore by the Virgin's rump that they had never known such excellent sport. Already they were rich, richer than they had ever imagined—and tonight they would feast on a stew of fowl!

The Dust of His Feet

Doña Marina knew three things about *pochtecas*. She knew that they often spied on behalf of the Aztecs. She knew as well that they were generally rich men, despite surface appearances. She also understood that they would rather die than be separated from their wealth. In the case of the *pochteca* named Pitoque, she knew—or thought she knew—something more. She was convinced that the man was harboring that girl she had grown so fond of.

Ometzin.

She'd already sent a party of men to find the wench at a place called Amozoc, beside a lake, but they had returned empty-handed. The place was deserted. Now she told Cortés what she suspected. The *pochteca* must be hiding the girl in the city of his birth, in Cholula. Where else could she be? They should look for her there.

Cortés was lounging amid pillows piled atop a bench in the chambers that he and the girl shared. He dispatched an aide to fetch Puertocarrero. "What is the place called again?"

"Cholula," she repeated.

"Of course. Cholula. Charming spot."

Puertocarrero arrived. "You called for me, sir?"

"Ah, yes." Cortés looked up and smiled. "Good news. That girl I promised you? I believe you'll find her in Cholula."

"Where is that?"

"Southeast of here. Not far. That merchant, the one who speaks Spanish—get him to take you there. The girl's hiding at his house, apparently. Doña Marina is convinced of it."

"Do you think so?" Puertocarrero ran his tongue over his upper lip. Beads of perspiration sprouted on his forehead, and he reached up to wipe them away. "She's pretty, is she? You're sure she's as pretty as you say?"

"Oh, yes." Doña Marina broke in. "Prettier. The prettiest girl in the world."

Cortés grunted. "If that's so, I'll want her for myself."

Marina suddenly bridled. "Why would you wish another? I do everything for you. I—"

"Now, now. I was speaking in jest."

Doña Marina shifted away from him on the bench. She looked at the floor and pouted. Last night had been another of those nights. Where had he been? She thought she knew. The emperor's concubines again.

Cortés waved at her, as if this dispute were a harmless little game between them. He looked at Puertocarrero. "As I say, I'm only joking. The girl is yours. I give you my word as a Spanish gentleman." He began to laugh.

"Thank you, sir. Thank you very much." Puertocarrero started to leave. Suddenly, he halted. He turned back.

"Yes?" said Cortés. "What is it?"

"What if the merchant refuses to accompany me to this place. Cholula. What if he says no?"

Cortés rolled his eyes. Dear God, this man was a weakling. What did he use for guts? Tapioca? The captain-general stretched out his legs. "What if he says no? Why, then, you threaten to kill him. Isn't that obvious?"

Puertocarrero swallowed. In truth, it wasn't. Not to him. He gazed down at his boots, afraid to reply, trying to think. True, he didn't have to kill the merchant. He merely had to threaten to do so. But he knew the man would never believe him. Yes, he had killed once—that Aztec messenger near Cempoala. But that had been forced upon him and, even now, the memory practically made him ill. Besides, his exploits had already resulted in enough death. He shook his head. He said, "I can't."

Cortés shifted forward on his bench, his eyes wide with amazement. "What can't you do?"

"Kill the merchant. I just wouldn't be able to bring myself to do it."

Cortés ran a hand through his beard. "Dear God," he said. "You don't have to. You just have to make him think it. Besides, what's one death?"

Puertocarrero stared at the floor, overcome with shame. He lacked a killer's temperament—that was the truth—and people could see this. He was not the killing sort. The shame of it welled up in him, and he feared he might do something appalling—weep. But instead, he kept his eyes on the floor and stood there. A laughingstock.

And Cortés did laugh. He put back his head and chortled. Then he began to bellow. What a lost cause he was, this Puertocarrero. You gave him a girl on a platter, and still he couldn't bring himself to take her. Worried about this. Worried about that. Cortés wiped the tears from his eyes. In all his days, he'd never seen such weakness.

Finally, it was Marina who decided what to do. She'd had enough of this aimless chat. That merchant had crossed her. She had decided that the girl would be Puertocarrero's, and she would not be prevented from having her way. Besides, she was furious at Cortés for leaving her alone at night, but there was nothing she could do about that. This comedy with Puertocarrero, however—this, she could see her way through. She rose to her feet now and informed the two Spaniards what she had in mind.

She would seek out the merchant and the boy. She would tell them in no uncertain terms what she required. The merchant would guide Puertocarrero out to Cholula. Once there, he would hand over the girl. If not, she would see to the killing—not of Pitoque, but of his son.

"What do you think of this plan?" she said to Puertocarrero.

"I . . . I don't know," he said. He had no idea what to think. In truth, he had hoped that the girl would come to him voluntarily. All this talk of death—it lacked a certain element of romance. He fussed nervously with his hair. For a moment, he considered accepting the woman's offer, but then he saw it was impossible. No, he would refuse. He was a man, damn it, and he would behave as one. He decided he would handle this affair on his own, after all. He would go to the merchant. He would make his request. Now he cleared his throat and spoke up. He informed Doña Marina of his decision, bowed, and thanked them both. "With your permission," he said. He turned and took his leave.

When Puertocarrero had withdrawn, Doña Marina settled herself on the bench beside Cortés. She gave her master a tentative kiss on the cheek and let her hand slide lightly across his groin.

But he didn't seem interested. He climbed to his feet. "Come," he said. "Let's see how Alvarado is managing the counting of our gold."

"A week, you say? One miserable week?" Aguilar put his head in his hands. "Dear God. Only a week?"

"That's right." As usual, Bakil was subdued in manner, dreamy. "I thought I told you."

"You told me, yes, that the day was coming. But in a week? Dear God, I had no idea there was so little time."

"Time is a bird always in flight."

As always, he and Bakil spoke to each other in Maya, their common tongue. He took several steps toward her. "Don't you understand? If we let this happen, you will be dead in only a few days."

"A few days? A few months? A few years? What is the difference?"

Aguilar put a hand to his brow to still the pounding he felt. He understood the reason for Bakil's unearthly calm. It was those mushrooms. The Aztec priests had put her on a diet of mushrooms precisely calculated to make her submissive. She was going to die—and die for some unspeakable, blasphemous folly—and yet she welcomed her fate. It was unspeakable.

She turned away from him, and he lowered himself to his knees, with his head clutched in his hands. A week from now, the feast of Huitzilopochtli would unfold just as Moctezuma had said. The Aztecs would dress Bakil in bangles and ocelot fur and row her out onto the lake, to the island of Tepepolco. There they would . . . they would . . .

Ah, it was more than he could bear. Somehow, he had to prevent her sacrifice. He was absolutely certain that this was the reason he had survived his years of enslavement, the reason he had been transported here to this strange world. To serve the Lord! To prevent this evil! The room began to swim around him, and the voices rose in his head. *The Lord has His way in the whirlwind and in the storm, and the clouds are the dust of His feet. He rebukes the sea and makes it dry, and dries up all the rivers. Bahan and Carmel wither, and the flower of Lebanon wilts. The mountains quake before Him, the hills melt, and the earth heaves at His presence, yes, the world and all who dwell in it. Who can stand before His indignation? And who can endure the fierceness of His anger? His fury is poured out like fire, and the rocks are thrown down by Him.*

Aguilar's shoulders began to tremble, and his breath came in slow, labored heaves. He began to sob. A week. Only one week.

Hernán Cortés decided it would be a fine gesture on his part to send Cacama and his entourage back across the lake aboard the Spanish sailing sloops. The craft were a source of such fascination for these people. But there were a great many prisoners—two dozen in all—and so it would be necessary to conduct the voyage in shifts, six passengers at a time. He gave the appropriate orders to his men.

Unfortunately, the first group encountered an outbreak of rough weather. Before the sloop was halfway across the lake, it reared up in the wind. The prisoners went overboard, all of them; and soon they were drowned.

Cortés stood on the shore and watched this distressing spectacle. Such an odd trick of the wind. He prodded at the pebbles beneath his feet. Accidents were unavoidable. He could not be too critical of his sailors.

It was difficult to be quite as understanding when an identical mishap befell the second group of passengers, and then—this was plain incompetence—the third.

"Really, now," said Cortés, when the sloop had returned, and its pilot had reported to him, "this begins to look like carelessness, man. I insist on a much greater degree of diligence with this last group."

The pilot saluted and promised that he would exercise more care on this, the final crossing. But the fates were in a dark mood that day. No sooner had the sloop sailed properly out onto the water than the last group of natives went tumbling over the gunwales, just like those before them.

"Went down like stones, sir," reported the pilot. He climbed back up on shore. "On account of the chains, I suppose. We could not save them. I'm extremely sorry."

"I'm sure you are," said Cortés. He decided not to be too strict with the fellow. "Try not to let the day's events put you off your dinner. There's more of that roast fowl, I hear."

Cortés turned and walked back into the city, surrounded by his personal guard.

BOOK SIX

The Sorrowful Night

His Most Esteemed Bloody Highness

"Honored sir." Moctezuma took a step forward. "Sir. I wonder if I might . . ."

"Yes? What do you want?" Cortés glanced up from a long trestle table, where he had gathered his officers for an emergency council. It was late at night, and a half-dozen tallow candles were guttering on the surface of the table, among a clutter of plates and jars and the remnants of food. He had no time for an interruption by the little emperor now. He had all the worries that he could handle at present. His enemy, that swine Velázquez, the governor of Cuba, had finally done his worst, sent a fleet of vessels to these shores with orders to capture Cortés, clamp him in irons, and ship him back to Santiago. Word of the fleet's appearance had just arrived by messenger from the garrison at Veracruz. Cortés raised a fist to his forehead, struggled to calm himself in the face of this emergency. He glared at Moctezuma. "I have very little time," he said. "If you have something to tell me, then for God's sake, speak."

As usual, Doña Marina was present, and she translated his words.

"Yes. Of course." Moctezuma said he would be as brief as possible. He pressed his hands together and dipped on his knees. He edged forward. He had arrived unannounced here at the great hall in the palace of Axayácatl, a place where he had formerly presided at sumptuous banquets of state. Now he was obliged to adopt the attitude of a supplicant. This humiliation grated upon him, of course, and yet he thought he would do anything at all to retain the Spanish commander's favor. On this occasion, he had hoped to find Cortés alone, but instead the Spaniard was surrounded by his officers, and they all seemed to be in an agitated condition, immersed in discussions he could not comprehend. He cleared his throat. "Sir. My honored sir. I have a request to make. It concerns a feast that we are planning in honor of Huitzilopochtli."

"I see." Cortés glowered at the emperor. "Go on."

Moctezuma resumed his presentation. "I wish to ask if you might grant permission for my people to celebrate the festival this year. It is very important to them. To us all, in fact. Your permission would be much appreciated." He swallowed and tried to speak again, but his nerve faltered. He had hoped to find the Spaniard in a better temper. "You . . . you . . . you . . ."

Doña Marina laughed and imitated the emperor's stutter. "He . . . he . . . he . . ."

"Yes," said Cortés, warming to the joke. "I . . . I . . . I . . . That part I understand. But *what* are you asking of me?"

Moctezuma frowned, unsure how to proceed. His courtiers had been reminding him for days, even weeks, to approach the Spaniard on this subject. It was vitally important. But he had kept putting the discussion off. Now there was no choice, time was running out. He swallowed and clenched his fists. "You said before that if I had any requests of this sort, I should approach you. I am here to ask your permission to let the feast go ahead."

Doña Marina translated these words.

"Look." Cortés straightened up and disengaged himself from the other Spaniards, all gathered at the long table amid the wavering light. As he approached the emperor, his shadow swelled on the wall behind him. Cortés emitted a torrent of incomprehensible barks.

"My master says he is very busy just now," Doña Marina said. "You do not seem to realize what has happened."

The emperor looked dismayed. "I hope I am not interrupting anything important."

"*Important!*" Cortés pounded a fist on the table. "It may interest the emperor to know that a scoundrel without equal, by the name of Diego Velázquez, has sent an army to these shores with orders to capture me and to take me back to Cuba in chains. He has sent nineteen vessels. They are on the coast now, near Veracruz. As for the emperor's question, therefore—as to whether or not he is interrupting anything important—you may tell his most esteemed bloody highness that he most certainly is."

Doña Marina did so, making no effort to soften the words or their tone.

"Now," said Cortés. He closed his eyes and clutched his brow, as if in the grip of some barely supportable pain. "Explain it to me again. What is it that he wants?"

Half-terrified now, Moctezuma struggled to articulate his request for the third time. The feast of Huitzilopochtli. Could it please go ahead?

In the end, Cortés gave his assent. "Yes, yes. Have your *fiesta*. Permission granted. Now, let me get back to work."

Moctezuma bowed and took his leave of the Spanish captain-general. He left the great hall with a pair of courtiers in tow and strolled back to his quarters, the hem of his robe playing against the stone tiles beneath his feet. Now that the audience with Cortés was over, he felt enormously relieved. It had gone rather well, he thought. He reflected on how skillfully he had handled a most delicate subject, a question of life or death. It was during the feast of Huitzilopochtli that the hummingbird bride would be offered to the greatest of the Aztec gods. On that night, all of creation would be reborn. The gift of life would be granted all over again. It was essential that the celebration go ahead. If it didn't, everyone would die.

Moctezuma let out a breath. Ah, he felt better now. The feast of Huitzilopochtli could proceed—thanks to him, the *tlatoani*. He had got the measure of Hernán Cortés at last. For the first time in an encounter with the Spaniard, he felt he had got the upper hand. That was a pleasant feeling. A *very* pleasant feeling.

In the great hall in the palace of Axayácatl, Cortés slammed his fist down upon the table, rattling the plates and ceramic jars still scattered there. The candles flickered and sent jagged shards of light and shadow flying across the high stone walls. Cortés had finally got rid of Moctezuma, and he had made up his mind about what to do. He was ready to act.

"Here is my plan," he told his assembly of officers. "I'll march out to the coast myself. I'll take a hundred men—no, a hundred and fifty—and I'll meet these scoundrels head on. You"—he turned to Pedro de Alvarado—"you will be in charge here in my absence."

Alvarado stepped forward, his chest swelling with the honor of it. He snapped to attention. "Sí, *mi capitán*. As you wish."

"Good. I don't expect that you will have much to worry about at this end, assuming you do not rile Moctezuma with your scorekeeping at games. Just keep everything under control."

Alvarado started to make a light-hearted remark but caught himself just in time. He had seen where frivolous comments had got Puertocarrero.

"No sense in delay," said Cortés. He arched his back and stretched his arms. "I'll depart tomorrow, just as soon as we can muster a force." He nodded at Alvarado. "Put out a call for volunteers now. I'll need a hundred and fifty men."

"Sí, *mi capitán*."

"Very well." Cortés turned and motioned to Doña Marina. The two started to leave the room.

Then Alvarado remembered something. "Oh, sir." He started after them. "One more question. Will Doña Marina be accompanying you?"

Cortés briefly considered the query. Of course, she would. He'd need a translator, naturally. Besides, he'd grown accustomed to her company. "She will," he said and immediately realized the problem. The bulk of his men, those who remained behind, would be without an interpreter. He had an idea. "Find Aguilar." In his hurry, he forgot that the translator only spoke Maya, not Nahuatl, the language of the Aztecs. He frowned. "Where the hell has that man got to." He shook his head. "A dour fellow."

"Positively morose," said Alvarado. "But don't worry. I'll take care of everything." As far as he was concerned, one native language was much the same as any other. "You can count on me."

"Good. I leave you in command then." He turned to Doña Marina. "Come, my dear."

She took his proffered arm. She felt suffused with pleasure. Veracruz. Her master was taking her with him to Veracruz. She leaned against him and closed her eyes—and remembered that she had one pressing duty to perform before she left. Never mind what Puertocarrero had done or failed to do. She would discover the whereabouts of the merchant, Pitoque, and she would seek him out. She would state her case to him in the plainest possible terms. Either he produced the girl or she would see to the killing of his son. That, at least, was what she would say. She knew that he would believe her, too. She had no doubt of that—none whatsoever—even though it was not true. The truth was, as she grew older, she found herself becoming less and less enamored of death.

But she would attend to that affair tomorrow. Now she basked in the warmth of Cortés and the thrill of his arm gripped around hers. She wafted through the room as if borne on air.

The Highway of Holiness

Pitoque groaned, put a hand to his jaw. He felt an aching in his mouth, hot as a burning coal. A tooth was on fire, flaming in his head. It had flared up the night before, not long after the sacking of the House of Birds, but now it was worse, incomparably worse.

He raised himself onto his elbows and peered around. Where on earth was he? Gradually, his memory cleared. He was in an attic in the palace of Axayácatl. He and Maxtla had been put here on the orders of Puertocarrero. Something to do with Ometzin. With this fire in his jaw, he found he couldn't quite remember, couldn't concentrate.

The pain spiked again, deep in his mouth. It was so severe that it nearly blinded him. He struggled to make out his surroundings. A tangle of shadows and cobwebs glimmered in the faint play of sunshine trickling down from chinks in the wall. Where was Maxtla? It took him several moments to work out that the pool of darkness a short distance away from him was actually his son. Now the dark shape moved, and Maxtla's head appeared in a ray of pale light.

"Father?"

Pitoque nodded and started to say something, but it came out sounding more like a groan. His jaw practically screeched with the pain. He had felt little more than a vague ache when he'd fallen asleep the night before, but now the pain stabbed through his mouth like the obsidian blade of a *tlacochtli*. It was all he could do to keep from crying out.

"Father," said Maxtla. "Are you not well?"

"Just a toothache," he whispered, remembering the last time he'd felt such pain—in the lands of the Maya, twelve years ago. "Nothing serious."

Maxtla drew himself up and wrapped his arms around his knees. Both of them were still in a miserable state, bruised and filthy from their previous imprisonment, and they'd had little to eat or drink since. But at least they were alive.

Now all they could do was huddle here in this dusty wooden attic and wait for someone to come for them. Pitoque remembered now what had happened. Last night, the Spaniard Puertocarrero had informed them both—Pitoque and Maxtla—that he required the merchant's assistance in locating this girl named Ometzin. He had reason to believe she was staying in the merchant's house in a place called Cholula.

"We leave tomorrow morning," he'd said. "Please be prepared for the journey."

Pitoque had shaken his head. "I will not guide you to Cholula. Not for the purpose you have in mind. Not for any purpose."

The two had debated the question a while, but neither gave ground. In the end, Puertocarrero had thrown up his arms. He had ordered the merchant and his son confined somewhere, and several of his men had shoved them into this abandoned attic.

And here they were, battered, hungry, and thirsty. The pain in Pitoque's jaw suddenly flashed again, and he shut his eyes against the shock of it. It hurt so much that he did not hear the sound of the trapdoor nearby sliding open. But then he heard voices, and the silhouette of a woman appeared before him as if floating in the darkness. He thought at once of the Mother of God. It was the Mother of God come before him again to demand an explanation. Why had he not carried out her commissions? Why was a shrine not being built in her honor upon the hill at Tepeyac? Why was the hummingbird bride still a prisoner, condemned to die?

Pitoque shrank back against the wall. Owing to all that had happened in these last days, he had nearly forgotten that he was under an obligation to the dark goddess. He was terrified now to hear the woman speak.

"Pitoque," the shadow said.

It was not the voice of the Virgin. He drew himself up and squinted through the darkness. The shadow approached and a woman's body entered a faint stream of light. Doña Marina. It was Doña Marina, and he saw now that she was flanked by a pair of Spanish guards. He did not know whether to be relieved or disappointed.

The girl did not linger over niceties. She greeted Pitoque tersely, Maxtla as well, and at once explained why she had come. That fool Puertocarrero was incapable of handling matters for himself, and so she felt obliged to take matters into her own hands—and she had very little time. Even now Cortés was waiting for her to join him. They were setting out for the eastern coast to confront this new enemy that had come. She had very little patience. She informed Pitoque that he *would* guide Puertocarrero to Cholula and hand over the girl, Ometzin.

There was to be no further discussion of the subject. Her will would be done. Did he understand?

Pitoque struggled to stifle the pain in his mouth. He sat upright. "I have already told Puertocarrero that I will not do it."

"I think you will."

"I won't." Pitoque hauled himself to his feet and stood before the girl, oblivious now to her loveliness. He listed from side to side, for he was weak from hunger and his balance was poor. The fire blazed in his mouth. "I tell you, I won't."

"Then it's simple," she told him. "I will kill your son." Here, she turned and smiled at Maxtla. "It would not please me to do so. But I take solace in knowing that I will not have to. For you will do as I request." She shrugged. "Just to be certain, however, I will keep the boy here under guard."

Pitoque tried to think what to do. Should he take the woman at her word or not? He remembered the punishment in Cholula—her coolness as she supped upon a sapota fruit and warned him to leave, while thousands were about to die. He recalled many other instances of her cruelty—the death of Azotl and others. It was true what she said. She would kill the boy.

Doña Marina took a step forward. "Do you understand?"

Now he agreed. He could see no other way.

"Good," she said. "Then I wish you a pleasant journey." Again, she smiled at Maxtla. She turned, nodded at her two guards, and left the way she had come.

The trapdoor slid back into place, and Pitoque heard the sound of something being wedged up against it from below.

Maxtla slumped down onto the floor. "She's lying," he said, although he wasn't sure. "Do not believe her."

Pitoque said nothing. He knew the girl was serious.

"Father, please. Listen to me. Do not do this."

Pitoque peered though the dim light at his son. "You would rather die," he said, "than give up Ometzin?"

"No, that isn't it. I am sure Doña Marina is lying. She will not harm you or me. I'm telling you. Do not believe her."

But Pitoque understood that his son was speaking out of bravado rather than conviction. He knew what he had to do. It would be difficult for the girl—and difficult as well for his son—but there was no other course he could take. He would go to Cholula.

Maxtla pleaded with his father for a time, but eventually fell silent. Pitoque sank back down onto the floor not far from his son. He wondered whether this was a punishment, sent by the Mother of God. He had failed to carry out her demands—and here was the result. Or was the agony in his mouth a portent, like the pain he'd endured twelve years earlier? He reached for the necklace of shells he had carried with him since then, but it was gone, lost during the rigors of these recent days. Tears sprang to his eyes, and he was amazed at his sudden grief. It was as if the loss of those shells meant that those poor young girls were now truly dead.

But there was nothing he could do. And so he waited, huddled in the shadows not far from his son. Both of them watched the dull blades of sunlight as they crept across the attic floor.

☥

"Are you going somewhere?" said Aguilar. He approached Puertocarrero, who was seated upon the edge of his bed, pulling on a pair of leather boots. "Where are you going?"

"Somewhere," said Puertocarrero. He set one booted foot down on the floor and gave it a stamp. God, he was annoyed. He was finally departing for Cholula, but now the journey felt like an encumbrance. First, he had been forced to endure the open scorn of Cortés. The commander had laughed at him, right in his face. The sting of Cortés's contempt still prickled at the base of his neck. Even worse, a woman had taken it upon herself to do what he hadn't had the grit to do. He'd intended to threaten Pitoque with death, but hadn't managed it. And so, before leaving with Cortés for Veracruz, Doña Marina had forced the merchant to do her bidding by threatening the fellow's son with death. She'd come to Puertocarrero's quarters just now to inform him of what she'd arranged. It was her master's wish, she told him, that he begin his journey to Cholula at once. A burning sensation ran up and down his spine, and he glared at Aguilar, who seemed unaccountably curious today. "I'm going *somewhere*," he repeated. "Why do you ask?"

"Mere curiosity."

"I see." Puertocarrero stared down at his stockinged foot. *Adiós*, she'd said in her slurry Spanish. She'd kissed her fingers and fluttered them in the air. *Que vaya con Dios, mi muy estimado señor.* He scowled at the memory. My very esteemed sir, she'd called him—she, who had once shared his bed. No doubt she'd told Cortés every miserable little detail about his performance in bed. No doubt they'd enjoyed a little laugh about that. Or several laughs. The shame swelled in his head, threatened to make his skull explode. He hauled on the other boot, gave its heel a good clump against the floor, and stood up. "You have something you wish to say?"

Aguilar rubbed his hands against his sides, trying to decide how to put his request into words. Someone had to help him carry out the will of the Virgin, help him prevent the execution of Bakil. He required an ally, and it seemed that Puertocarrero might be that man. He cleared his throat and began to speak. He explained that he had been eight years a slave to a native *cacique* out on the coast and had endured many privations, but he had been saved by the grace of God in order to perform some great service. For many months, he had been in a torment over what that service might be, but now at last he understood. He knew what God required him to do.

Puertocarrero reached up and patted his hair. "And what might that be?"

Aguilar took a step forward. He realized he must look and sound like a madman, but he could not help it. "I have seen a sign," he said.

"A what?"

"A sign."

"Really? Where?"

"Here. In the great plaza. I saw the Holy Virgin. Alive. She was everything I ever imagined. Except that her skin was dark."

Puertocarrero frowned. "Dark? How dark?"

"A sort of bronze color. Dark as a native's."

"Dear God, you must have taken a blow to the head."

"No. I am well. I tell you, I saw her."

Puertocarrero snorted. He couldn't help it. The Holy Virgin? Dark as a native? He began to laugh. "If I were you, I would mention nothing of this to Rome. They would not like to learn that the Mother of God is a barbarian. Do not speak of this vision to the pope."

Aguilar realized he was being mocked, but he bore on anyway. He explained to Puertocarrero what the Lord required him to do. The day of judgment was at hand. The sinners would be cast down in eternal damnation. Only the chosen, the pure, would be preserved, for glory everlasting in the new world to come. There would be a test.

"I see. And of what shall it consist, this test?"

Aguilar explained. A native woman—a princess, the most splendid creature ever seen—was to be sacrificed.

"So?" said Puertocarrero with little interest. He was thinking again about his own predicament—off to Cholula, while Cortés marched to the coast to fight a war and Alvarado commanded the Spaniards here. Those were men's duties. What was he—a rodent of some kind, scuttling among the furniture? Even the promised girl didn't feel like a reward anymore. He felt a tumult of fury in his chest.

"Are you listening to me?"

Puertocarrero started. "I beg your pardon?"

"You act as if you're in some kind of daze." Aguilar told him again about the native princess, whose loveliness was impossible to describe, and how she was to be sacrificed—an abomination beyond imagining.

"I see," said Puertocarrero. "When?"

"Very soon. But it must not occur. These are the instructions I have received from the Virgin. The dark Virgin. In truth, she did not tell me directly. But I have been informed."

Puertocarrero slapped at his boots. "You have been informed."

"Exactly. The sacrifice must not occur. The good, the chosen few—they will reveal themselves by intervening to prevent it. And the world will be born anew." Aguilar put back his head, closed his eyes, and began to recite. "Its streams shall be turned into pitch, and its dust into brimstone; its land shall become burning pitch. It shall not be quenched night or day; its smoke shall ascend forever. From generation to generation it shall lie waste; no one shall pass through it forever and ever. But the pelican and the porcupine shall possess it, also the owl and the raven shall dwell in it. And He shall stretch out over it the line of confusion and the stones of emptiness."

Puertocarrero ran a hand through his hair. Dear God, this man was bleak. He reached for his helmet and plume, but Aguilar stood his ground.

"Better times shall come. The earth shall be reborn." He closed his eyes. "Waters shall burst forth in the wilderness, and streams in the desert. The parched ground shall become a pool, and the thirsty land springs of water; in the habitation of jackals, where each lay, there shall be grass with reeds and rushes. A highway shall be there, and a road, and it shall be called the Highway of Holiness. The unclean shall not pass over it, but it shall be for others. Whoever walks the road, although a fool, shall not go astray."

Puertocarrero made to leave the room. He had heard enough. Didn't he have enough worries of his own?

Aguilar stepped in front of him. "You must help me."

"How? How on earth could I help you?"

Aguilar tried to explain. On the fourth night of the feast of Huitzilopochtli, the girl named Bakil would be sacrificed to the idolatrous hummingbird god on the little island of Tepepolco. But first she would raise a wooden flute to her lips and play a trill of notes, a melody that would be heard here in Tenochtitlán, so still would the city have become. Next, she would break the flute upon her knee. And then, right then, the priests would take her. They would lay her down upon the sacrificing stone and cut out her still-beating heart. They would . . . they would . . .

Aguilar realized he was sobbing, overcome by horror. "It must not take place," he cried. "This sacrifice must not occur. The Virgin herself has spoken. Please. I beg you." He fell to his knees at the feet of Puertocarrero. "Do you not see? You must help me. Please."

"Not now," said Puertocarrero. "This is your affair. Your instructions—they have nothing to do with me. Out of my way."

"Wait. I beg you." Aguilar was almost screaming now. "You must—"

But Puertocarrero pushed his way past. He strode toward the door, eager to be quit of this madman, and he would have been—except that he suddenly had a strange, unexpected thought. An intriguing thought, in truth. He stood still, weighing the idea in his mind. The more he thought about it, the better he found himself liking it.

Not only—he now realized—was it the most extraordinary notion he had ever entertained, it was also a plan he could quite realistically carry out. He was not powerless, after all. Al *contrario*. He was the most powerful soul in Tenochtitlán. Perhaps, by helping this lunatic, he could show everyone— Cortés, Alvarado, the lot—what folly it was to trifle with a relation of the Count of Medellín. They would damned well have to take him seriously. He stopped and turned around. He swept a hand across his hair. He said, "The trilling of a flute, you say?"

You Will Have Your Diversion

Four Spanish guards came for Pitoque. They dragged him from the attic, but left his son behind to serve as a kind of hostage, a guarantee that his father would carry out his mission and lead the Spaniards to Ometzin.

Maxtla tried to stop his father from leaving, but all he got in return was a cuff to the head and some rough handling that sent him sprawling across the floor. "Do not believe her!" he kept shouting. "She's lying! Do not do what they say!"

The Spaniards hauled Pitoque down from the attic and wedged the trapdoor back into place. Maxtla's voice, now muffled, still resounded beyond the barrier of wood.

"She's lying, I tell you! Lying!"

Pitoque understood his son's distress—he shared it—but he knew that it served no purpose. He knew what he had to do.

He followed his wardens outside, the pain still raging in his jaw. When he emerged from the palace of Axayácatl, he was almost blinded by the late-morning light, but he soon recognized the tall, lanky figure of old Toc standing across the way. It turned out that the porter had been lurking there for days, hoping to learn of his master's fate.

Pitoque addressed his Spanish guards in their language. He asked them if Toc could accompany him on his way to Cholula. "He is an old acquaintance and friend, and it would be a comfort to have him at my side."

Perhaps the Spaniards were too astounded to object. It was extraordinary to hear Castilian Spanish tumble from the lips of this little infidel. Or perhaps they didn't care. The final decision, after all, would be up to their officer, Puertocarrero. So Toc fell in beside Pitoque, and they set out. The guards herded them off along the streets of Tenochtitlán until they reached the causeway that ran across the lake to Iztapalapa and the southern shore. There, they were under orders to wait.

"Alvarado?" Puertocarrero found his rival lounging on a little terrace that overlooked the city. He was oiling his sword. "Ah, there you are. They told me you were out here. How goes it, my friend?"

Alvarado looked up. *Friend?* "Puertocarrero," he said. "I thought you had gone to that city . . . I forget what it is called. Where we had that battle on the way here."

"Cholula."

"That's right." Alvarado set his sword upon the little table at his side. "Cholula. Can't keep these damn names straight. In any case, I thought you were off to Cholula to collect your just reward."

"All in good time." Puertocarrero pulled another chair out. "May I?"

"Of course. Sit down. What news do you bring?"

Puertocarrero managed a thin smile and shifted forward in his chair. He proceeded to tell Alvarado a tale of treason, of heinous betrayal, of duplicity so foul it could curdle a Christian's stomach. It so happened, he said, that several of the Totonac warriors— the ones he had traveled with from the coast—had come to him just now to warn him that another Aztec uprising was planned. It was to take place on the fourth day of this feast, the feast of Huitzilopochtli, just a few days away. These Aztec devils, they knew that the Spaniards' ranks were greatly reduced in number now that Cortés had led a force away to Veracruz. So they planned to mount an attack. They intended to do so at the very height of the celebrations, when a sacrifice would take place out on an island in the lake. There would be a trilling of notes upon a flute. At that signal, the Aztecs would race from the great plaza, storm the palace of Axayácatl, and put all the Spaniards to death.

"No!" Alvarado slapped his brow. "This is an outrage!"

"It is. But that is not all." Puertocarrero explained to the blond lieutenant that the Aztecs planned to boil the captured Spaniards—alive, where possible—and then to sup upon them, accompanied by sprigs of thistle and dollops of pumpkin-seed sauce.

"Mother Mary's tit!" Alvarado roared. "That's what they told you? You have this on reliable authority?"

"The very finest," Puertocarrero said. He explained that the merchant they called the Little King of Plates had been on hand to interpret the Totonacs' words. "I can assure you, the rumor is true." He sat back in his chair and tapped a hand nervously against the side of his leg. Would Alvarado take the bait?

Already, the blond one was on his feet. "God in heaven!" he shouted. "What a monstrous scheme!" He kicked at the table, knocking it over and sending his sword clanging across the wooden floor. "Damn the traitors! I'll have their balls!" He hurried to retrieve his sword. "I'll . . . I'll . . ."

But Puertocarrero had a better plan. Would it not be better to wait a little, a matter of several days only, until the trilling of the flute? Would not patience, on the whole, make more sense? He explained what he meant.

"Hmm." Alvarado sank back into his chair. "I see what you mean." He nodded, picked up a rag, and resumed the oiling of his sword. "Yes, I think I see what you mean."

When Puertocarrero left the blond lieutenant, he was still attending to his sword, still gazing out at the slow spreading of the light, still nodding his handsome but vacant head.

Next, Puertocarrero sought out Aguilar and luckily found him just as he was leaving the palace of Axayácatl, bound somewhere in a dreadful rush.

"Aguilar!" he called out.

The man stopped and turned. He waited. "Yes?" he said.

Puertocarrero trotted over to him. "I'm glad I found you. Good news."

"Yes?" Aguilar seemed completely distraught.

"I just wanted to tell you—about that woman you mentioned, the virgin to be sacrificed, the one you wish to save."

"Yes?"

"I think I can help you. In fact, I already have."

"You have?" Suddenly, the man's spirits seemed to lift. "What do you mean?"

Puertocarrero began to explain, but then decided that he didn't have time. His men had already begun their journey to Cholula with the merchant under guard. He had to hurry to join them. He told Aguilar simply that all was arranged. He would have his diversion.

"Diversion?"

"Yes—the trilling of the flute. You remember."

"Yes. The trilling of the flute."

"That's right," Puertocarrero said. "That's exactly right. I have arranged a diversion. You may rescue your woman and no one will interfere. I think I can guarantee it."

"How? What do you mean?"

But there wasn't time. Puertocarrero clapped Aguilar on the back and turned to leave. An aide was awaiting him even now, with a pair of horses already under saddle. "Just remember what I said. You will have your diversion. Now I must go."

He took the reins to one of the mounts and swung himself up into the saddle. He squeezed his calves into the horse's flanks. They left Aguilar behind and rode out of the city at a brisk trot, then cantered along the causeway that led to the southern shore. There, they joined a half-dozen of their men who were on foot, with the merchant under guard along with a stooped old coot, who seemed harmless enough.

"Come on," said Puertocarrero. "We have our mission. Let us go."

Soon they were ascending the long, windblown slope that climbed out of the Valley of Anáhuac and into the mountains beyond.

With Toc at his side, Pitoque scaled the rising grasslands, the fire still burning in his mouth. He put one plodding foot in front of the other, wracked by the thought of where he was going and what he must do. In the distance ahead, the pale white pinnacles of Popocatépetl and Iztaccíhuatl reared up through the afternoon haze, and the first faint stirrings of a plan began to murmur in his head.

Let Us Talk of Gold

In the great plaza of Tenochtitlán, native women were fashioning a likeness of the hummingbird god. Upon a frame of sticks, they molded his body with a dough made of crushed amaranth

seeds mixed with human blood. They gave him turquoise ear-
rings and a nose of gold, then draped him with a cloak made of
skulls and bones strung together with maguey fiber. In his left
hand, they placed a brace of arrows. Meanwhile, workers constructed canopies of finest cotton and raised them to provide
shade for the plaza. Human victims had been assembled nearby,
stored in wooden pens and fattened up. Men and women of the
city began to paint themselves in lurid colors and designs. They
put the final touches on their headdresses and robes.

The preparations for the feast of Huitzilopochtli went
ahead, just as they had done for years without number.
Occasionally, someone paused in his labors and reflected that
this year, the celebrations would proceed in the absence of the
emperor, who remained a prisoner in the palace of Axayácatl.
The celebrant would look around at all the trenches that had
been dug, all the crosses that had been built. He would wonder
at the presence of these mysterious Spaniards with their raucous voices, stringy beards, and unearthly stink.

Then he would go back to work.

Puertocarrero clutched the girl Ometzin by one of her arms.
Kalatzin grasped the other. They tugged and pulled and
shouted back and forth at each other in languages neither of
them could understand. The other Spaniards stood about,
laughing, amazed. Two of them held Pitoque and occasionally batted him across the head. Two others had Toc flat out
upon the floor. They were enjoying this spectacle. They'd never

expected Puertocarrero—the butt of countless jokes among them because of his prissy, indecisive ways—to put on such a good show.

"She's mine!" shouted Puertocarrero. "She was given to me!"

"Fiend!" cried Kalatzin. "Bastard! Let her go!"

The woman was making a heroic effort, but it was no use. She wasn't nearly strong enough. With one arm, Puertocarrero yanked Ometzin away from the woman. With the other, he cuffed Kalatzin across the face so that she stumbled back, tripped over her own feet, and tumbled down. Puertocarrero watched her fall. What had come over him? He felt half-crazed. Was this the way a man with *cojones* behaved? He didn't know. All he knew was that his cock was finally hard and quivering in his breeches, and he felt as if he could conquer the world. He felt as if some strange and potent liquor was coursing through his veins, and yet he'd had nothing to drink in days.

"Witch!" he shouted. "Whore!"

Pitoque lurched forward and somehow managed to break free. He lunged at Puertocarrero, but something caught his foot—the leg of one of the other Spaniards—and he, too, hit the floor. Laughter roared all around him, along with women's screams.

"Let me see what I have won!" Puertocarrero pulled Ometzin toward him, grasped the folds of her robe in his hand, and gave a mighty tear. He stripped the girl naked, as though he did such things every day. At once, he felt a stab of regret—but here she was, nude for all to see, and he couldn't help looking.

In a glance, he took note of her melon breasts, her rounded belly, the sparse pelt of fur between her bronze and splendid legs. She was lovelier than anything he'd dreamed of. She was . . . she was . . .

He suddenly put his free hand to his forehead. He was feeling dizzy, queasy. He thought he might faint. In his breeches, something began to recede.

Zaachila threw herself at Puertocarrero, but two of the Spanish soldiers grabbed her first and held her back. It looked to Pitoque as if they might strip her, too. He staggered to his feet, ready to fight. He'd fight to the death now. He flung himself at the Spaniards, but they boxed him about the head, swung him around, and gave him a kick to the buttocks that turned him end over end. He found himself on his chest on the flagstone floor. When he looked up, he saw that the Spaniards were marching away. They had Ometzin and Zaachila both.

Kalatzin stumbled to his side. "Stop them! You must stop them! They'll rape them both. They'll—"

"I know." His jaw pulsed, and the small courtyard seemed to spin around him. He hauled himself to his knees. Everything had happened so quickly. He'd had no time to take the step he'd decided on while traveling south from Tenochtitlán. Now he climbed to his feet, stupid from the blows he'd taken and from the burning in his mouth.

His wife was frantic. "You must stop them. You must do it now. Don't let them go."

He took a deep breath, reached out to brush a disheveled lock of hair from his wife's brow. Something in her gaze told him that they both realized what had to be done. She knew it as well as he did. "You understand," he whispered, "that there is no other way?"

She nodded. "I know."

"You accept this?"

"There is no choice."

Pitoque gazed at her, as if seeing his wife for the very first time, how lovely she was.

"Just go. Save your daughter. Save Ometzin."

Pitoque clambered to his feet and staggered out after the Spaniards. He heard men's voices shouting, and girls' voices screaming. His mouth throbbed, as if flames of blood were shooting through his head. He stumbled out into the street, where Puertocarrero was already mounted upon his horse and was trying to wrestle Ometzin up onto the animal's back, while Zaachila shrieked and fought with the other Spaniards.

Pitoque raised his arms. "*¡Parense!*" he roared in Spanish as loudly as he could. "*¡Parense!* I order you to stop!" His words had no effect, but he knew what would. "*¡Oro!*" he shouted. "*¿Quieren oro?* Gold, I have."

That did the trick. Still clutching Ometzin by the arm, Puertocarrero turned back to peer at Pitoque. He raised his eyebrows and inclined his head. "Gold?" he repeated. "Where is there gold?"

"Release the girl," said Pitoque, "and I will tell you."

Puertocarrero did not go that far. But he did dismount. He handed the reins to one of his men. Holding Ometzin by the arm, he turned to Pitoque. "Tell me about this gold."

"Come back inside my house, then," said Pitoque. "Let us make ourselves comfortable. Let us enjoy drinks of chocolate. Let us speak as gentlemen."

Puertocarrero laughed. "You will not catch me with that old ruse," he said. "You will not get me to swear on my honor as a Spanish gentleman. I saw you play that game on Cortés."

Pitoque gritted his teeth. This was bad news. He had indeed been meaning to try that appeal again.

"Still," said Puertocarrero, "I will accept your invitation. I will enter your house again. Yes. Let us talk of gold."

Pitoque ushered the Spaniard back into his house. He ordered his servants to straighten up the furniture in the court-yard—everything was in chaos after the uproar just ended—and soon he and his guest were seated across from one another, both drinking chocolate. Ometzin and Zaachila were still being held outside by the other Spaniards, and Pitoque demanded that they be brought inside, where he could see them.

Puertocarrero hesitated, then agreed. He called out to his men to bring the girls into the house. Kalatzin hurried over with a robe for Ometzin, who pulled it on. The three women fell to their knees at the feet of the Spanish guards and all now turned their eyes on Pitoque.

Pitoque proposed his terms. He would provide all his wealth to Puertocarrero, his entire cache of gold and other treasures. In exchange, he made just one demand. "You must release the girls."

Puertocarrero nearly choked on his drink. The chocolate spluttered from his mouth. He had not expected this. He had expected something . . . *more.* "That is your one demand?" he said. "That is all?"

Pitoque nodded.

"I see." Puertocarrero wiped his mouth and sparse beard with the back of one hand. An instinct told him to accept the bargain and be done with it. In fact, he was beginning to sicken of this whole affair. That moment, when he'd stripped the girl, something inside him had recoiled. And yet he was supposed to be a man. What would a man do? Most men, he thought, would wish to have a look at the gold. "I shall first have to inspect this treasure you speak of," he said. "I cannot make a decision until I've seen what you are offering."

Pitoque pursed his lips. Yes, he could see the logic of this demand. "All right," he said. "Let's get started."

All Pitoque's worldly treasures were hidden in a vault buried underground beneath the bedroom he shared with Kalatzin. He ordered his servants to bring everything out. Soon the bedroom was filled to overflowing. Golden hoops and necklaces of silver. The finest textiles and painted bowls, all heaped with jewels. Quetzal feathers. And more objects of gold—gold bars and gold discs, gold rings and gold bracelets, even sandals fashioned entirely of gold.

Puertocarrero made a show of uncertainty. He frowned at this, sniffed at that. In fact, he was ecstatic. To think—all this treasure for him. There were only two problems. First, how was he to misrepresent the immensity of this treasure in order to avoid paying the full royal fifth and the fifth to Cortés? Second, how was he to transport all this plunder back to Tenochtitlán?

On the second question at least, Pitoque had an answer ready. He would summon his head porter. The man would assemble a crew of bearers. It would take no time at all.

"In that case," said Puertocarrero, "I accept your bargain."

"Excellent," said Pitoque, whose heart now pained him almost as much as his mouth. His whole life's accumulation of treasure—gone. True, the transaction had saved Ometzin and Zaachila from the Spaniards. But everything gone . . . He sighed and shook his head and asked that Toc be summoned, to see about the porters. Meanwhile, he gathered the women together—his wife, his daughter, Ometzin—and took them to Zaachila's sleeping quarters, where he hoped they would be safe.

While he was waiting for his new wealth to be packed and loaded, Puertocarrero huddled in the interior garden, his head in his hands. The thoughts were spinning in his head. Had he behaved stupidly? What would everyone say when he marched back into Tenochtitlán with some baubles of gold but without the girl? They'd think him mad or, worse, a weakling. He asked himself what Alvarado would do in his place—or Cortés, for that matter—and it was not difficult to imagine. Go back on his word. Take the gold. Keep the girl. That was what a proper man would do.

He gritted his teeth. If they could do it, then by the Virgin's sacred tit, so could he. He sat up and put back his shoulders. Now he felt like a man—not an entirely pleasant sensation, unfortunately. In fact, the feeling had a good deal in common with seasickness. His shoulders slumped. He thought he might throw up.

Aguilar was praying again.

In the palace of Huitzilopochtli, he was settled upon the floor on his knees, his hands clasped before him. Several feet away, Bakil sprawled upon the bed, drugged with mushrooms, oblivious to her surroundings. Earlier that evening, however, she had clung to him for an hour, whimpering like a child. There was a desperation in her now that was aching to reach the surface, but it was buried beneath deep layers of delirium. Only occasionally did it reveal itself on her face and in her voice, before receding beneath another onset of stupor. She was almost constantly drugged these final days, owing to the ministrations of the Aztec priests.

It was the third day of the feast of the hummingbird god, and Aguilar still did not know how he was going to save the girl. In the end, he had almost dared to hope that Puertocarrero might help him. It had seemed that way for a time. What had the man said when he had spoken of the trilling of the flute? *You will have your diversion.* What on earth did that mean? Puertocarrero had not deigned to explain. In any case, he had departed Tenochtitlán, and Aguilar could expect no assistance from him.

Nor was there any question of engineering some kind of escape from this little palace. First of all, Bakil was delirious and would have to be carried. Second, the Aztecs had mounted a guard all around. He had checked, many times. He could discover no way out that was not under constant watch.

On his knees in the palace of Huitzilopochtli, Aguilar prayed for wisdom, prayed for strength, prayed for an answer. But no answer came. He let out a long, heavy sigh. Once again, he had received nothing in the way of divine counsel. His prayers had gone unheeded. The voices he had heard before, the voices of angels that had so recently sung to him—they were silent now. He felt abandoned, utterly alone. Even Pitoque had disappeared.

He climbed to his feet and padded across the floor, stood by the railing that overlooked the rock garden and beyond it to the lake. There was a low table here, laden with the materials for smoking, a habit he had grown fond of during his years on these shores. He fought off the urge to smoke now. He wondered if he had been mistaken about all that had happened. If he truly was the chosen instrument of the Mother of the Lord, would she not have provided him with more in the way of guidance? He peered out at the dark abyss of the lake, streaked with jets of silver.

Puertocarrero clenched his fists. It was time to show he was every inch a man. He stood up and called for his soldiers to join him. It was time to return to Tenochtitlán. "And bring me the girl!" he shouted. "Bring me my gold and bring me the girl!"

He squared his shoulders and marched out into the withering sun. He felt a sudden spasm in his gut, and the bile shot to his throat. Damn. Damn it all. He staggered over to a tree, put out his hands for support, and emptied his stomach into a bed of flowers.

A Lone Boatman

Aguilar fumbled for a pipe and filled it with a plug of tobacco mixed with resin of amber. Using a set of tongs, he raised a burning coal from the brazier and lit the tobacco. When the pipe was ready, he took a long draft and then another. He felt a settling in his brain, a renewed ability to think. Maybe now the ideas would come. He could feel something in his head, a churning of thoughts. But he could not make them out. He turned and gazed out at the lake.

It was dark now, and the waters of Texcoco shimmered dully in the pale moonlight. He peered across the lake's surface, as if somewhere in the distance an answer might be found. But all he saw was the dark silhouette of a lone boatman in a dugout canoe. The little craft slipped through the flickering waters. He watched the boat as it dwindled into the darkness, in the direction of Tepepolco, and suddenly his eyesight became strangely acute. Through the intervening darkness, he watched the boatman lift and lower his paddle, drive forward, pause, lift it again. He watched the distant drops of lake water drain from the blade like beads of molten ore, watched the craft as it cut like a silver knife through the silent lake, dwindling, dwindling, until it was swallowed by the night.

The confused ideas in his head suddenly stopped spinning and settled now into a precise, certain pattern. Aguilar puffed at his pipe. He realized that, at last, he'd had his revelation. There, out on Lake Texcoco, he had seen a lone boatman in a dugout canoe.

He had seen his answer.

"¡*Mátame!*" Pitoque fell to his knees in the dusty lane in front of his house. With both hands, he tore open the fabric of his robe. The folds slid back, exposing his chest. "Leave the girl alone. I beg you. *Mátame.*"

"Kill you? Why would I kill you?" Puertocarrero adjusted his grip around the girl's waist. The treasure was all sorted now, and porters had been assembled to carry it to Tenochtitlán. They had only to load themselves up. He planned to bury some of it along the way, perhaps as much as half. His horse stood nearby, tended by one of his soldiers. He looked down at the merchant. "I have no desire to kill you. I like you. You have done me a kindness."

Pitoque edged closer, still on his knees. His jaw still burned, but he barely noticed it now. Some other force had overcome him. The instant he realized that Puertocarrero meant to cross him—to seize his wealth and to keep Ometzin as well—a chorus of voices had begun to sing in his head. He had heard women's voices. They had sung a melody that soared and swooned, that caused him to fall to his knees, to rip open his robes. Some power flowed through him. It throbbed in his chest, raced through his arms, quivered at his temples. Now it burst from his lips. "I am offering you my life," he cried.

Kalatzin and Zaachila stood off to the side, both of them sobbing. Now they, too, fell to their knees.

"Kill me," wailed Kalatzin in Nahuatl. "Kill me."

"Me," moaned Zaachila. "Kill me."

Puertocarrero frowned. "What are they saying?"

"Don't listen to them." Pitoque beat his chest. "Listen to me. Kill me."

Puertocarrero shook his head. In his confusion, he loosened his grip on the girl, who wrenched herself free. He started after her, thinking that she would run away, but she didn't. She, too, fell to her knees in the dirt.

"Don't listen to them," Ometzin pleaded. "Kill me."

Puertocarrero glared at Pitoque. "What is she saying?"

"She is asking you to kill her."

"To spare you, I take it?"

"Yes."

"And them?" He waved toward Kalatzin and Zaachila, both still on their knees. "To spare them as well?"

Pitoque winced at a spasm of pain. "Yes."

Puertocarrero emptied his lungs in a long sigh. What was happening? He shrugged. "I do not know why I shouldn't kill you all," he said. "You seem to be in such a hurry to die." But he knew it wasn't true, and he didn't want to kill anybody. He didn't want to hurt anybody. And yet, look what he had been about to do! He glanced over at the girl. She was within arm's reach. All he had to do was reach out for her, seize her by the arm, and she would be his. But he didn't do it. He didn't do anything.

Pitoque stayed where he was, in an attitude of supplication on his knees. He said nothing, for it seemed to him that something in the Spaniard's manner had changed. Some transformation had come over him. The voices moaned in his head.

Puertocarrero reached over and ran the back of his hand down the girl's arm, just once. His skin tingled at the touch. He closed his hand around her forearm, and she did not pull away. He glanced at Pitoque. "You mean that you would let yourself be killed to save this girl?"

Pitoque nodded. It was true. He hadn't known it till now. If he had more to give, he would offer that, too. But his life was all that remained. "Do not listen to my wife and daughter," he said. "Listen only to me. You may kill me, in any way you choose. Just let the girl be."

"I have killed a man, you know." Puertocarrero shifted his weight. He was thinking of the Aztec messenger near Cempoala. "I have done it before."

Pitoque waited for the Spaniard to continue.

"With a knife. I slit his throat. There was blood everywhere."

"Yes."

"It wasn't my choice. It was forced on me. But I did kill him."

"I believe you."

"Killing . . . ? Do you think it is something a man gets used to? With practice, perhaps it becomes easier. Do you think so?"

Pitoque shrugged. It might be true. He did not know.

For a time, Puertocarrero said nothing. He remained where he was, slumped on the bench, clutching Ometzin by the arm. Finally, he released his grip. At first, the girl did not move, unsure what to do, wondering whether this was a trick. After a time, she rose to her feet and took a step away. Nothing happened. She took another step. She turned back to look at Puertocarrero, but he merely sighed again. He made no effort to stop her. She settled herself again upon her knees. For the longest time, no one moved or spoke. Then Puertocarrero glanced back at Pitoque.

"Stand up," he said.

Pitoque stared at him.

"Up. Up. Stand up. Get up. On your feet. All of you. Now."

Pitoque did as instructed. He looked at Kalatzin, Zaachila, and Ometzin, so that they would do the same. Now all four of them stood outside the entrance of the house in Cholula, waiting to see what this Spaniard meant to do.

Pedro de Alvarado was having second thoughts.

He'd gone over the situation in his mind again and again, and it just didn't feel right. He knew he had a tendency to behave precipitately at times—it was a problem. What if he were making the same mistake now? Acting without due deliberation? Striking in the heat of the moment? Cortés would not like that. Alvarado had already been upbraided, even punished, on more than one occasion precisely because of his penchant for impulsive action.

Maybe it would be better, just this once, to proceed with more care. He sank back into his seat on the little terrace that looked out over a rather drab view of the dug-up Aztec city. He had to think—not a task that came easily to him. He would consider the situation slowly once more. To begin with, the source.

Puertocarrero.

Now that was clearly a warning sign. Why would Puertocarrero have done him this good turn? He'd have thought Puertocarrero would have engineered events to promote his own career. Instead, he had absconded at once for that place called . . . whatever it was called. A strange action in itself. He'd told his tale—his tale of treason—and then he'd left.

Alvarado struggled to order Puertocarrero's account in his mind—a chronicle of heinous infamy, he had called it. Another Aztec uprising was planned. It was to take place on the fourth day of this feast of . . . whatever it was called. That would be tomorrow. There was to be a trilling of notes upon a flute—and that was to be the signal. The Aztecs would then storm the palace here and put all the Spaniards to death by boiling them alive and then consuming their remains with chilis and sauce.

Alvarado had been appalled. He had been in favor of heading out at once to knock off a few Aztec heads. But Puertocarrero had advised him to wait.

"Wait?" Alvarado had cried. "Wait for what? Wait until when?"

"Until the flute trills across the lake on the fourth night of the feast. Station your troops at the main plaza. When the woodwind trills, send them in."

And Alvarado had liked the sound of that plan. Turn the tables on those Aztec bastards. Just when they thought to launch an attack, take them by surprise, when they were all assembled. Seize the moment. Launch an attack on them!

Excellent. Magnificent. Wonderful.

At least, Alvarado had thought so at the time. But now he wasn't so sure. What if Puertocarrero had been mistaken in some way? Or worse, what if he was lying? It wasn't beyond imagining. And the consequences could be grave. Cortés might be severely annoyed if he found, on his return from the eastern coast, that a war had been waged unnecessarily or by mistake.

No. No. This situation called for a cautious response. Alvarado stretched out his long legs and aligned his boots side by side. He clasped his hands behind his head. He would not commit the same error he had committed so often in the past, blundering off with his sword on high before taking a good, critical look. He decided to verify Puertocarrero's story first. Only then would he proceed.

To find out whether the story was true, he would need that odd fellow by the name of Aguilar. He stood up and called for his orderly. When the man appeared, he asked him if he had seen Aguilar about.

"No, sir," said the man. "Not in quite a while."

"Do you know where he might be found?"

"I can make inquiries. I can look."

Alvarado nodded. "Do that," he said. "And be quick about it."

The orderly saluted and withdrew. Alvarado turned and looked out to his left at a little blotch of blue, all of the lake that was visible from his window. Not much of a view. He wondered if Puertocarrero had got better. Oh, well. There'd be time to worry about that later. Now he had work to do. It occurred to him that his verification plan could begin at once, even in the absence of a translator. He decided to put the order out now—he'd be needing three Aztecs. Three Aztec men. They should be picked up at once. He turned and strode back inside, intending to get this business underway immediately.

Puertocarrero peered up at the sky. Something in the universe had shifted. He felt dizzy now, as if the world had been turned on its head. It was this idea of sacrifice—the idea that a person would offer himself up for another. Somehow, it changed everything. He suddenly wanted to be quit of this whole miserable business. He didn't want to kill anyone or capture anyone or hurt anyone. He realized now that he didn't have to. The choice lay within his grasp. Others might laugh at him, might think him a fool. But if that was the price, he was willing to pay it. He looked back at Pitoque. He said, "The girl may stay."

"I do not understand." Pitoque frowned.

"She may stay. There are plenty of others in Tenochtitlán. Besides, I have your gold now." He waved his hand. "I renounce her. She may stay."

Pitoque put a hand to his jaw to ease another burst of pain. He found he could not speak.

Puertocarrero rubbed his eyes, let out a long, tired moan. A darker thought had occurred to him. He looked at Pitoque. "Do you know what day this is—in Tenochtitlán?"

Pitoque considered the question, trying to think clearly despite the burning in his mouth. Finally, he remembered that it was the third day of the feast of Huitzilopochtli. He said so.

"And do you know what happens tomorrow?"

He nodded, in despair. Now he remembered. He thought of Aguilar. He thought of the dark Virgin who had appeared to him. He realized that there was little chance the Virgin's instructions to him would be followed. No shrine would be built. The hummingbird bride would die. "The great sacrifice," he said. "On the island of Tepepolco."

Puertocarrero swallowed. "Yes. But I think that the sacrifice will not go ahead."

"Why not?"

"Instead, there will be a war between the Aztecs and ourselves. I fear I have made a terrible mistake." He explained what had happened. He recounted his visit to Alvarado in Tenochtitlán. On that occasion, he had invented a complete lie, about a supposed Aztec rebellion. That lie would lead to war. He was sure of it, for he knew Alvarado and how Alvarado would respond. Suddenly, the whole affair made him sick. The war would be his fault. All he had wanted was a girl of his own and to behave like a man—and look what he had caused.

"It's very late," he said. He now realized that what he wanted more than anything else—more than almost anything else—was to make amends. "Maybe it is too late. But there may be a chance that we can prevent this killing. Maybe, if we get back in time, we can find Alvarado, put a stop to his plan. We have the rest of today, tonight, most of tomorrow. Do you think there is time?"

Pitoque struggled to express his thoughts through the circle of pain. "Maybe," he said. "It is possible. If we leave the treasure behind."

Puertocarrero considered this idea but not for very long. "That is out of the question, I'm afraid. We will take the gold with us. Come. Let's get these men loaded up."

He pointed to the gang of porters, who had been assembled by Toc and who now waited in silence outside the house.

Before it was time for Pitoque to depart, Ometzin approached him.

"I'm coming, too," she said. "To Tenochtitlán. I'm coming with you."

"No," said Pitoque. "You must stay here. Terrible things are about to take place in Tenochtitlán. It isn't safe."

"Then why are you going?"

He shrugged. "Maxtla."

"I can help. I'm coming, too."

He shook his head.

"I'm coming with you," she repeated. "I want to be with Maxtla. I don't care what you say."

He looked at her. Before, he would have ordered her to do as he said. He would have brooked no objection, for it is the man who decides, while women and children obey. But the old times seemed to have withered like dead flowers, and he understood from her voice that nothing he told her would change her mind. She would come, no matter what he said or did.

"Come if you will," he said. He took in a deep breath, winced at another spasm of pain in his jaw. "Now I must say goodbye to my wife and my daughter."

He turned away and gritted his teeth. Saying goodbye to his wife and his daughter—this would be the hardest of all.

An Answer to Every Conceivable Pain

Puertocarrero told Pitoque he had once been plagued by the same problem. "Agony," he said. "Damn near drove me crazy."

Pitoque nodded. The pain was so great that he could barely see. It was a struggle just to speak. "What did you do for it?"

"Only one thing you can do." The Spaniard gave a wide smile, revealing a dark gap in his mouth, at the top and to the left, where there had once been a tooth. "It had to come out."

"What did you use? What sort of device?"

"A knife."

"That was all?"

"A knife was all there was. They had to cut it out. I was blind drunk, of course."

Pitoque shut his eyes against another jolt of pain. Cut the tooth out with a knife? It sounded grotesque. In his experience, such maladies were dealt with by gentler means, with herbs and mushrooms. Problematic teeth were coaxed from their sockets, not ripped out with knives. But now, what choice did he have?

"Well, keep it in mind," said Puertocarrero. "If the time comes, I'll be ready to give you a hand. Two, if you wish."

They began to climb the col between the two great volcanoes. All night, they had marched. A parade of porters streamed behind them, bearing all of Pitoque's wealth. Somewhere among them was Ometzin, under the care of Toc. If it weren't for the pounding in his mouth, Pitoque would have felt the loss of his treasure even more keenly than he did. But he couldn't get past the agony of this tooth. What hideous calamity was being foretold by this pain? It felt like the worst omen ever imagined. It felt like the end of the world.

Already, he had lost almost everything. Now the misery of that loss assaulted him again. All his treasure, gone. He could think of only one compensation—his material ruin meant there would be no question of submitting to those infernal priests and their demented plan to remove his daughter's eyes. Even Kalatzin had conceded as much.

"I simply cannot pay for it," he had told her—and who could argue with that?

Puertocarrero pulled a long-bladed knife from the leather sheath that dangled at his waist. He held it up for Pitoque's inspection. "This would do the trick, you know."

The gang of porters waited, and Pitoque practically gagged—another spasm. He took a deep breath and muttered to the Spaniard that he was undoubtedly right. That knife blade looked like an answer to every conceivable pain.

It was the fourth day of the feast of Huitzilopochtli. Aguilar reached the palace of the hummingbird god. At once, he realized that something was very wrong. Various Aztec sentinels were posted at the entrance. He managed to push past them, but he was blocked outside the bedchamber. The guards would not allow him to proceed. He craned his neck, desperate to catch a glimpse of Bakil—and finally he did. She stood in a dull glow of torchlight, attended by various priests, and she had been transformed. Upon her head she wore a floral crown. A cloak of flowers was spread over her shoulders. Bells had been attached to her wrists and ankles. Her sandals were decorated with the ears of ocelots. Her face was painted black and showed no expression. She had probably been drugged with mushrooms again. She likely had little idea of what was being done to her now—or what would soon be done.

But Aguilar knew. And the sight of Bakil in this diabolical costume, surrounded by these morose and ghostly priests with their blood-matted hair—ah, God, it was too much to bear. He made no attempt to call out to her. He knew it would be useless. She was beyond the sound of his voice now, floating away. Instead, he turned and hurried from the building. He began to tear at his hair, he wailed out loud, pointed at the sky. He kicked at rocks and clods of earth. He fell to his knees, sobbing like a child.

If only he were not all alone! He had a plan—or part of a plan. It had come to him that night with Bakil, when he had seen a solitary canoe knife through the moonlit lake in the direction of the island of Tepepolco. He proposed to do the same, to paddle himself out to the island of Tepepolco so that he would be waiting in the darkness when Bakil arrived, with her encirclement of priests and acolytes. He would have to disable the lot—not impossible. He would, after all, have the advantage of surprise, not to mention the even greater advantage of Spanish iron. Besides, the priests were mostly elderly and frail. Perhaps they themselves would be doped on mushrooms.

Beyond that moment, he had no clear idea. He would have to escape somehow with Bakil. But where would they go? How would they elude detection? They required some sort of disguise, some kind of defense, but he had managed to arrange nothing. Dear God, he needed help. He needed an accomplice. He had hoped Pitoque might help him. After all, it was Pitoque who had received the instructions of the Virgin. The Virgin's likeness had appeared upon his robe, a miraculous sight, as wondrous as stigmata. That same afternoon, he and the merchant had made a pact to carry out the Virgin's wishes, to save Bakil, to prevent this murderous rite. But where was Pitoque now? He had simply vanished, and Aguilar was alone. At one point, he had even dared to think that Puertocarrero might come to his aid. But that fond hope had been dashed as well.

And now, inside, the priests were preparing Bakil for her sacrifice. He couldn't bear it. He simply could not. He knelt in the dirt, beating with both fists at his head.

It was in this condition that Aguilar was found by a pair of aides to Pedro de Alvarado, who informed him that his services were required at once.

He stopped beating himself. "My services?"

"Yes," said one. "As a translator. Come. It is urgent. We have been looking for you everywhere. What were you doing just now?"

Aguilar shrugged. He said it wasn't important.

"All right, then. Get up. Come."

They carried harquebuses and they pointed them in his direction.

He wasn't a complete fool. He realized that these men had likely been given orders to shoot and that they would obey. He stood up, slapped the grime from his knees and elbows, rubbed his eyes with the heels of his palms. His heart cried out and every fiber of his body resisted, but he followed these two men, who now led him in the direction of the palace of Axayácatl. His head swam with images of Bakil—of Bakil and of blood.

The fire roared in Pitoque's head. He felt as if a single great flame had exploded in his jaw and was shooting into every extremity of his body. The flame burst through his skin and ignited the air around him. He felt as if his body were flying apart. He slammed back against the hard ground and fought to free himself, but it was impossible. Four Spaniards were holding him down. The one named Puertocarrero let out a roar of triumph and raised a hand that streamed with blood. In it, he clutched Pitoque's tooth. In his other hand, he held his long-bladed knife.

"¡Éxito!" he shouted.

It was some time before the searing pain in Pitoque's mouth had subsided enough for him to make out the truth. The old pain still raged, even worse than before, and his heart quaked in his chest. It was the wrong tooth! The idiot Spaniard had cut out the wrong tooth!

Kalatzin slumped to the floor in this house where she had lived for so very many years. But all was unfamiliar to her. The floor had been dug up. Debris was piled everywhere. Before, there had been order. Now, everywhere she looked, she saw only chaos. She began to cry.

She did not look up when Zaachila came to her. She merely buried her face in her arms and continued to sob. She had lost everything today. Her husband's wealth, and her husband himself. He had gone, no doubt to his death.

Zaachila lowered herself onto the floor beside her mother and put her arms around her, and both women remained that way for a very long time, rocking from side to side and saying nothing.

Finally, it was Zaachila who spoke. "There's one happy result, at least," she said.

"One happy result? What is that?"

The girl laughed. It wasn't much of a laugh, more a rippling little sigh. "This way, I will keep my eyes."

Kalatzin nodded.

"And it means that I can stay with you."

"You would wish that, after all I've done? I wanted you blinded."

"That is in the past."

And Kalatzin smiled, because it surely was.

"The wrong tooth?" Puertocarrero shook his head when he understood the problem. Damn. He could imagine how much the first extraction must have hurt—and now he would have to do another. He reached for his knife, which he had cleaned and oiled by now, and called to his men. "Hold him still." He looked down at Pitoque, shook his head, and grimaced. "Sorry, my friend. But we'll get it right this time."

It wasn't that easy. Puertocarrero managed to remove two more healthy teeth before he finally extracted the bad one. He handed the tooth to its owner as a sort of trophy. By this time, Pitoque was barely conscious, he had lost so much blood.

Puertocarrero hauled himself to his feet and wandered a short distance away. He flopped down beside a jumble of rocks and a prickly pear cactus. Damn. He felt miserable. So this was what it was like to inflict pain. It had given him no pleasure at all. It had made him wretched. Here was further proof, if more proof were needed, that he was not well suited to the soldiering life. He might as well face the truth. He shook his head and attended to the cleaning of his knife blade. He wondered whether another sort of life would suit him better. Just now, he could not think what it might be. In any case, now was not the time to be thinking. There was a massacre being planned in Tenochtitlán. Dear God, they'd better hurry. He put away his knife and climbed to his feet. "All right, men. It's time to go."

He asked a couple of the porters to take charge of the merchant, who was moaning now, delirious, no longer in a condition to walk by himself. Poor soul. He was in a deplorable state. Puertocarrero sighed. As usual, he hadn't been much help. As usual, he'd simply made matters worse. Now, perhaps, they could get to Tenochtitlán in time. Perhaps they could stop a war.

They Do Have Lungs

As prisons went, this one wasn't so bad. By now, Maxtla had explored his attic cell thoroughly and had discovered that it wasn't a cell at all. In different nooks and crannies, he found ways of climbing or burrowing into adjoining rooms and passages. He discovered that he had the run of a fair portion of the palace of Axayácatl—an array of large rooms and corridors and courtyards. All were in a miserable condition, for the Spaniards had been through them by now with their Aztec laborers, digging up the floors and smashing down the walls in their incessant hunt for gold.

Still, as a jail, it truly wasn't so bad. He was able to forage for food, and he found ample water. He could even have escaped, except that he had nowhere to go. He had thought about following his father to Cholula, but he realized that he would have arrived there too late to accomplish anything. Besides, if worst came to worst and Ometzin fell into the hands of that Spaniard, they would have to return here. Maxtla could take matters into his own hands then. Kill the man, probably. It wouldn't be too difficult. Or unpleasant. In fact, he relished the idea—if worst came to worst.

Now, on the fourth night of his imprisonment, he huddled on a sheltered wooden deck, bordered by a wooden railing, that overlooked a small interior courtyard. He had made for himself a kind of bed amid a jumble of musty, discarded bolts of cotton that he had collected over the days. He lowered himself onto these, and suddenly, his arms gave way and he collapsed onto the floor—the way a child might collapse. In truth, he had been feeling a little faint lately, a little dizzy, and there was a constant burning in his head. Here was another reason he had not escaped the palace and trekked south to Cholula. To be honest—and he would never have admitted this to anyone but himself—he wasn't sure he could undertake the journey. Something was definitely wrong.

He felt weak nearly all the time. And he had discovered something else—something that alarmed him, made his heart race, his throat turn dry and raspy whenever he thought of it.

Hard nubbles of flesh had begun to appear on his chest and face, like pebbles beneath the skin. At least, they seemed like pebbles, and yet, when he pressed them, they suddenly turned soft and seemed to collapse beneath his touch. But they did not go away. The first one had appeared out of nowhere, and now there were more of them every time he checked. So far, they were concentrated upon a small area of his body—just his face, his chest, nowhere else. But what were they?

He tried to console himself with more pleasant thoughts. He pulled the sheets of cotton around him and curled up into a ball and thought of his father, his mother, and Zaachila with her strange, steady gaze. He thought of Ometzin and of the brief time—not even a day—that they had spent together at Amozoc. He had barely seen her since then. He thought of her shining black hair, her throaty voice, her haughty ways, the hidden mysteries of her soft brown skin. Like a river, these images bore him toward sleep, when suddenly the nighttime silence was splintered by the bark of men's voices and the clump of heavy Spanish boots.

Maxtla jerked upright and rolled over onto his knees. He crept through the darkness until his head bumped against a wooden railing that ran along the edge of the gallery. Now, the courtyard below seemed to swim with the amber light of torches. Monstrous shadows swelled and shrank and swelled again, like terrible giants rearing across the stone walls that lined the court. About half a dozen of the Spaniards swaggered into view just beneath Maxtla's perch. He recognized one of them—Pedro de Alvarado, the blond one, the favorite of Cortés—and then another. The second familiar face belonged to Jerónimo de Aguilar, the Spaniard whom he and his father had first encountered that long-ago day out on the eastern coast, the one who spoke Maya and had taken up the role of translator, along with Doña Marina. The others, he did not know.

The Spaniards, he saw now, had several prisoners with them—three native men. Aztecs. The Spaniards dragged their captives into the center of the courtyard and shoved them to the ground. The three went down like bales of cotton, for their hands were bound behind their backs and they had no way of balancing themselves.

"Build a fire," said the one named Alvarado. He pointed to some broken-up furniture jumbled in a corner of the yard. "Look. You can use that."

A couple of the Spaniards immediately set about the task. After a time, when the fire was burning well, they stood back and awaited further orders.

"This one first," said Alvarado. With his boot, he prodded a prisoner in the leg. "Strip him."

Ometzin noticed that there was something wrong with one of the porters. He was stricken by some infirmity. Suddenly, he stumbled to the ground, his cargo scattering about him. He remained on his knees, seemingly unable to rise. Spittle drooled from his mouth, and his eyes had a crazed look.

Ometzin knelt by his side. "What's wrong?" She turned the man's face so that she could gaze directly into his eyes, and she felt beneath her fingers some strange texture, tiny lumps of flesh that resisted at first and then gave way. "Can you hear me?"

But the man seemed to hear nothing. He merely gazed back at her dumbly, saliva still dripping from his chin. She looked up and called out for Toc. By now, almost the entire procession had halted.

Soon the chief porter was at her side. He seemed to understand at once. He hunched down and stared at the fallen porter, who by now had collapsed onto his side. A dark, foul-smelling liquid began to stream from the man's mouth.

Maxtla peered down from the gallery. He crouched on his knees and pinned himself against a wooden pillar, taking care to keep in the shadows. His heart pounded in his chest, and he scrunched his brow in an effort to concentrate. He had picked up some Spanish in his encounters with these people—not nearly as much as his father, but some. Now he found he could make out many of the words, although he had to infer the meanings of others. Still, it was no great task to understand the general shape of events. The Spaniards were seeking information of some kind, and they clearly did not care how they got it.

The first of the native prisoners was stripped down to a loincloth, and Alvarado took up a stick of wood. He held it to the blaze until it flashed orange. Then he brought it out and began to nurse it against the captive's chest. It took four of the

Spaniards to hold the man still. He jerked about, arched his back, screamed. Nobody had asked him anything yet.

"There," said Alvarado. "That was simply to get his attention." He turned to Aguilar, the translator. "Now ask him about this infernal plot."

Aguilar knelt by the man. He began to speak to him, but in Maya mixed with a smattering of Nahuatl. He asked whether it was true that the Aztecs meant to attack the Spaniards during the feast of Huitzilopochtli. The prisoner said nothing, just gaped at his surroundings with eyes as large as plates. It was obvious to Maxtla that he understood little of what was being said.

It was obvious to Aguilar as well. He looked up at Alvarado. "The poor man doesn't understand what I am saying. He doesn't speak Maya."

"Speak to him, then, in a language he does understand."

"I cannot. I can barely speak his language. This interrogation is fruitless. It must stop. I told you. I—"

"No matter," said Alvarado. "Here." He turned to one of his men. "Maybe this will improve his conversational skills. Hold his head."

The towering blond Spaniard strode forward and pressed the end of the burning stick into one of the captive's eyes. The flame sizzled, and the yard leapt with an unearthly shriek. Maxtla had to clamp a hand to his mouth to keep from screaming out. He himself felt a gouging of pain that seemed to burrow from his head to his groin. He rocked from side to side on his knees but managed to hold his tongue. Below him, the grisly drama continued. Aguilar translated the blond one's questions as best he could, but the prisoner clearly did not understand. Was an attack planned? Was it scheduled to coincide with the trilling of a flute on the fourth night of the feast of Huitzilopochtli? Did the Aztecs propose to sup upon the Spaniards, in a stew of chilis and pumpkin-seed sauce? Had a special stock of coriander already been set aside precisely for this purpose? The man answered none of these questions, for they were meaningless to him.

Aguilar looked up. "You must stop this torture," he said. "It is pointless. The man has no idea what I'm saying. This interrogation serves no purpose. Please. Let him go."

Alvarado would have none of that. He pushed the translator aside and fondled the Aztec captive with his burning stick. The poor man writhed, thrashed, screamed, and, in the end, died.

"Damn it," said Alvarado. "Damn it to hell. That was a complete waste of time. He told us nothing whatever." He threw his stick into the fire and reached for another. "We will try again."

Aguilar stood up. He said he refused to participate any longer in this atrocity. "You may kill me if you wish. I will not translate your words, because I cannot."

"Do as you please," said Alvarado. "We will proceed without you. I think I know how to pose questions. I think I know how to elicit sense. I will ask the questions myself."

He approached the second prisoner on his own.

This man had evidently used his friend's ordeal to good advantage. He understood that the Spaniards were looking for something and that a lot of inarticulate screaming would not serve. As a result, he replied to each of Alvarado's incomprehensible questions with a bellowed yes. He even answered in Spanish—Sí—which showed additional quickness on his part.

"Now we are getting somewhere," said Alvarado. "Well done. I told you this method would work."

When all of the Spaniards' questions had been answered, fully confirming every detail of the alleged plot, Alvarado was deeply pleased—so much so that he squatted down and gave his prisoner a pat on the check and ran his hand through the poor man's hair. Then he set about torturing him to death with the burning stick. After that, he inflicted the same treatment on the final captive. For a time, the entire courtyard was like a great sloop, tossed from side to side on the swell and ebb of Aztec screams.

Aguilar huddled off to the side. At intervals, he climbed to his feet, and it looked as if he meant to intervene. But something always stopped him. He stepped back, sank onto his haunches again. He could do nothing, for he was badly outnumbered.

When the killing had ended, Alvarado tossed his stick on the fire. "Say what you will about these damn Aztecs," he said, "they do have lungs. I'll grant them that." He turned to Aguilar. "I told you we would get these wretches to talk." He slapped his hands together, pleased at a job well done. "There is nothing left for us to do now but have a little chat with our friend Moctezuma. Then we will make these infidels pay." He gestured at Aguilar. "We shall proceed with the plan we discussed earlier. This very night in the great plaza, at the sound of the flute, we shall attack."

The other Spaniards kicked out the fire with their boots. Meanwhile, at the edge of the gallery, Maxtla pushed his head against the railing's bars. The wooden edges bit into his brow so hard, he thought they would drive right through his skull. Still, he did not cry out.

When Pitoque heard a man calling out to him, he thought at first he must be imagining Toc's voice. He was still almost mad from pain, and everything around him seemed like a kind of dream. Finally, he realized that the voice he heard did belong to Toc and that it truly was calling to him.

They were now more than halfway to Tenochtitlán, but Toc informed him that one of the porters had fallen ill. Pitoque found the porter and crouched down to have a look. He worried that the Spaniards would kill the fellow if he simply lay here, if he did not keep moving.

"How are you feeling?" he asked. A stupid question. It was clear the man was in a miserable condition. "Can you stand?"

The man just stared up at Pitoque without any acknowledgment at all. He seemed to be delirious. Pitoque squinted in the afternoon light and noticed something about the porter's face—it was nubbled all over by little upraised knots, like stones rising through the flesh, pushing against the skin. He was almost certain that he had seen these same protuberances on Azotl's face in the master functionary's final days. But now

Pitoque saw that they were not limited to the porter's face. They were everywhere. They seemed to cover the expanse of his skin, and some of them had burst. A yellow pus flowed from them, mixed with blood.

"I've seen this affliction before," said Toc. "It's some kind of curse, I think. Poor fellow. He can't hear a word we're saying."

Somehow, they managed to get the man back on his feet, and he stumbled forward a few steps and then collapsed. He tried to get up again, but it was no use. He hadn't the strength. One of his legs seemed to jerk to the side in a kind of spasm. He made a terrible, rattling sound, and then he did not move at all. Fluids oozed into small dark pools arrayed on the ground around him. He was clearly dead.

Before long, one of the Spaniards—not Puertocarrero, another one—hurried back to demand why the porters had stopped.

"Man dead," said Pitoque. He stood up and pointed.

The Spaniard looked down and blanched at what he saw. "Good God. What is that?" He stepped back. "Looks like the pox." He called out for Puertocarrero. "Man dead with the pox, sir."

Puertocarrero trotted over on his horse. He took one look and directed that the man be buried. He rubbed his forehead. But there wasn't time for a burial. Then he had a thought. Maybe this was also a good place to hide some of the treasure he'd received from the merchant. He gave directions to Pitoque, who mumbled them to Toc, who instructed the porters. In the end, they buried all the treasure. Puertocarrero told himself it wasn't greed. It meant that they could proceed more quickly now. They'd make better time, and perhaps reach Tenochtitlán before it was too late.

It was near dusk by the time the procession was back on its way, climbing up the southern side of the mountain ridge that bordered the Valley of Anáhuac.

Pitoque trudged upward with the rest. His head ached unmercifully now, but he barely thought of the pain anymore. Instead, he thought of the man who had just died, and he thought of Azotl's words. *Flee. Flee. Take only what you can carry. Run for your lives. Never come back.*

They reached the height of the col that sprawled between the great mountains, Popocatépetl and Iztaccíhuatl. Against a brooding sky, the two summits sailed overhead. They were like floating mansions—greater palaces than the Spaniards had ever seen, palaces that floated not upon the sea but upon the air. Pitoque stood alone for a time and gazed down upon the Valley of Anáhuac and the cities of Texcoco, Iztapalapa, and finally Tenochtitlán, now traced by the shadows of evening. A fleet of clouds scudded between the earth and the low gold orb of the sun, and he had a sudden vision of those great cities in ruins, a rubble of smashed buildings sprawling beneath scattered pillars of smoke, littered with corpses and prowled by scavengers. The temples were all sacked, not even the pyramids remained, and a thin wail of mourners pierced the air.

Flee. Flee. Take only what you can carry. Run for your lives. Never come back.

A cold mountain wind spiraled downward from the sky, and he drew his robes around him. Ahead, the Spaniards were already clambering down the north side of the col with the porters behind. Ometzin came to him, and he put his arm around her. Old Toc looked back.

"Coming, master?"

Pitoque nodded. He and Ometzin waded down through the darkening air, air already rank, air that seemed to rise from the earth as bitter as the festering dead.

In the Aztec Night

"Conspiracy?" said Moctezuma. "What conspiracy? I know of no conspiracy." The emperor sat up in his bed. He was naked, red-eyed, and pale. Several dark strands of hair spilled down his forehead. A group of Spaniards had just burst into his bedchamber and roused him from the enjoyment of coitus. No one had ever done that before—interrupted the emperor in the privacy of his bed. He pulled his eiderdown cover up over his chest. "Why do you speak of a conspiracy? From what I gather, you have killed all the conspirators already."

"They drowned," said Alvarado. "A lamentable accident. Was it our fault so few of them could swim?" His gaze kept wandering over to the girl who shared the emperor's bed. She couldn't have been more than twelve. Pretty child, too. Some of these natives were quite comely—at least when they were young. He waved a fist at the emperor. "But now we have incontrovertible evidence of another conspiracy against us. I merely require you to acknowledge the truth of it."

Aguilar did what he could to interpret between the two men, but it was a miserable business. His Nahuatl was meager to begin with and had all but deserted him now. Besides, his hands were shaking, and his brow still sprouted droplets of perspiration. Never in his life had he witnessed such horrors as those he had seen this night—as those he had participated in this night. Dear God. Dear heavenly God. He realized now what Puertocarrero had done—he had convinced Alvarado that a new Aztec rebellion was brewing. He understood finally what Puertocarrero had meant by those last words. *You will have your diversion.* So, this was to be the diversion—a massacre of Aztecs.

"I said," repeated Alvarado, glaring at Aguilar, "that I merely require you to acknowledge the truth of this conspiracy. Nothing more."

Aguilar did his best to translate these words.

Moctezuma put back his head. "The truth? What do I know of your truth? And even if there was a conspiracy, how could I know about it, imprisoned as I am?"

Aguilar nodded at these words. A good answer. A good answer at last. He turned to Alvarado and conveyed Moctezuma's words in Spanish.

The blond man snorted. He took another look at the girl who hunched on the bed, naked as a little round egg. She had the eiderdown cover wrapped around her hips but made no attempt to cover her breasts. They caught his eye. Unfortunately, he had work to do. He scowled at the emperor of the Aztecs. "You deny the existence of a conspiracy," he said. "What else would you do? I take your denial as further confirmation that the insurrection exists. I bid you goodnight."

He turned and left the room, followed by his retinue. He smiled to himself. That was a job well done. He'd accomplished what he had intended to do. He'd confronted the emperor. Now, when Cortés questioned him on all these matters, he would be able to answer that—*sí, mi capitán*—he had taken all the correct preliminary steps.

He strode out into the darkened corridor and swung to the left, intent on action. But he couldn't get that girl out of his mind. Her little breasts, like a pair of fruit. Sweet little child— sweet as a succulent little bite of melon, something a man could pop into his mouth and swallow right down and feel none the worse. Alvarado resolved to keep an eye on her, for afterwards. Presumably, she had a name. How could he find out what it was? With his men in tow, the acting commander of the Royal Spanish forces in Tenochtitlán marched down a corridor of the palace of Axayácatl, smacking the fist of one hand against the palm of the other. *Aguilar.* Of course. He'd order Aguilar to ask. Why not right now?

He turned and looked behind him, trying to locate the translator. Ah, there he was. What a depressing manner he had. He looked for all the world as if, given the chance and a sharp knife, he'd slit his own throat. Ah, but here was a mis-

sion to put a little color back in his gray complexion. Alvarado
ordered the man to go straight back to the emperor's chambers and get that little wench's name.

"But be quick about it. There's much to do and very little
time. We'll have to organize our native warriors, and I'll need
your help. Hurry."

Aguilar did as he was told and headed back to the chambers
of the emperor. He ran a hand across his brow, and it came
away wet and hot. He was burning up with worry. He'd been
hoping to slip away from Alvarado's entourage as soon as the
group left the emperor's chambers. If he was going to make
his way out across the lake to the island of Tepepolco, he had
very little time left. This latest delay left him almost frantic.
Get the wench's name? What sort of nonsense was that? It was
proof of what an idiot Alvarado was, thinking of women at a
time like this.

Not women. Girls. *Children.*

He blundered back along the passage. In fact, he had a few
words he wanted to say to the emperor himself. That episode
in the courtyard—dear God, dear God. He hadn't expected
acts of such unimaginable brutality. An interrogation, yes, but
not atrocities committed for the sheer pleasure of inflicting
pain. He knew the Aztecs were murdering brutes, but they did
not deserve such torture. None of them did. Now, finally, he
saw a difference between the crimes committed by the Aztecs
and those committed by his own people. However misguided
they were, at least the Aztecs believed their sacrifices served
some higher cause. But the Spaniards killed and maimed for

the sheer pleasure of it, with no thought whatever about what it all meant.

Now Alvarado was bent on even greater carnage. Aguilar rubbed his forehead. Could he stop this massacre that was being planned? Could he rescue Bakil from death and also prevent this other terrible event? He knew what Alvarado was capable of. The butchery in Cholula—that had been mainly his handiwork. Now this attack would be even worse. The deaths would number not in the thousands, but in the tens of thousands. Still, there was a chance. Maybe if he got word to Moctezuma, a warning could be sounded. He quickened his pace. Mother Mary, he was short of time. An image of Bakil flared in his mind, her dark form being laid out upon an executioner's stone. All around him, he saw a city in flames. He heard hyenas cackling with laughter, saw jackals cavorting among the corpses of men. The sky rained blood, and a chorus of voices began to howl, the voices of women wailing in lamentation. *Dead!* they sang. *Dead! All dead!*

Ah, God! He began to run.

One didn't need to be a genius to realize what was afoot, and Maxtla understood exactly what he must do. He must seek out Moctezuma at once, and warn him of what the Spaniards proposed to unleash, the horrors they meant to inflict this very night. At the sound of a flute trilling over the waters of the lake, their warriors would fall upon the unarmed Aztecs in the great plaza of the city.

Maybe this massacre could be prevented. With any luck, with a little courage, maybe it could.

He climbed onto the railing that lined the gallery, then swung himself up onto the roof. By now, he knew the palace's layout, vast though the building was. He scrambled across the roof, skirting two more interior courtyards, until he reached a third. Here, he stopped to rest. He felt the same shortness of breath that had been plaguing him now for days, and his legs were as weak as the stems of frail plants. But he couldn't think of illness now. He flopped onto his belly, let his legs slide out over the edge of the roof, and clung to the gutters. His legs closed around a wooden post and he shimmied down until his feet made contact with a railing below. He balanced himself there and then jumped down to the gallery floor.

Now, where was he? It took him a while to get his bearings, but when he did, he realized he'd been exactly right. He had found the emperor's quarters. He hesitated outside the door to what he thought was Moctezuma's boudoir. Then he clenched his teeth, shoved the door open, and rushed in. Immediately, he found himself blinking in an illumination of torches, in the presence of the emperor and the Spaniard, Jerónimo de Aguilar.

The Spaniard stepped back in surprise, then recognized the boy. "You are the son of Pitoque, are you not?"

But Maxtla was in no mood for niceties. "I see that you are not averse to torturing men to death."

"The interrogation was not my idea. How did you know about it?"

"I was in the gallery overhead."

Aguilar sat down on a bench and buried his face in his hands. For a time, he seemed overcome by spasms, as if he might be weeping. Finally, he looked up, his face drawn and wretched. In a whisper, he said. "I had no part in instigating that business. When it happened, I found myself helpless to prevent it."

Maxtla said nothing. He understood now that men invariably have choices. Sometimes they exercise them, sometimes not—that is all. But on this night of blood, he decided to let the matter pass in silence. Who was he to judge—he who had almost betrayed his own people, not once but twice?

Moctezuma raised his hand like a schoolboy trying to attract his master's gaze. "Torture? Where has there been torture? I myself heard screams. What is going on?"

Aguilar and Maxtla turned to the emperor. Both started to speak, then stopped.

"You begin," said Aguilar. "I was just about to tell him, anyway." His panic was mounting. He had to get out of the palace, commandeer a canoe, carve a wake through the darkness, arrive at Tepepolco. There was still a chance.

Maxtla explained to the emperor what he had just learned. The Spaniards were about to launch an attack in the great plaza. Thousands—many, many thousands—would be killed. He took a step forward. "You must put a stop to it."

"I?" Moctezuma pulled a pillow to his chest, as if it might serve as his shield. "What can I do?"

"You are the *tlatoani*. He Who Speaks." Maxtla approached the emperor of the Aztecs, unalarmed and unafraid. "Now is the time to be heard."

Moctezuma started at the sound of these words. It was as if he had forgotten. For a moment, his eyes seemed to glow with some remembered glory, as if Maxtla's words, the mere reminder, might be enough to restore him to his former magnificence. But the glow faded. Soon his shoulders fell. His jaw sagged, and he nodded sadly. "The *tlatoani*. Yes. That is true. But as you can see, I am now a prisoner here."

"You are the *emperor*. You could get dressed and come with me. I know various routes out of the palace. We could find our way to the plaza and sound a warning. Maybe we could launch a surprise attack. But we must act quickly. There is little time."

Aguilar nodded just managing to follow the gist of this discussion. "There is very little time."

Moctezuma's jaw began to tremble. Finally, he spoke. "But my dear friend Hernán Cortés—I fear he would be angry with me. I fear he would take it ill if I were to cross him in this way."

"Cross him in *what* way? These Spaniards are about to . . ." Maxtla took another step forward and then stopped. He saw that arguments were no use. The man was clearly incapable of any sort of action. It was as if he were under some sort of a spell. The Spaniards had bewitched him, had worked some dark magic upon him. It was as if he'd been drained of blood. "I'll go myself," Maxtla said. "I'll try to—"

"Aguilar!" A Spanish voice roared from the corridor outside. "Aguilar! Where the hell is Aguilar?"

It was Alvarado. A pair of Spanish boots clacked against the stone tiles outside the emperor's chambers. The sound grew closer.

"Aguilar!"

Aguilar turned to Maxtla. His eyes watered with tears, and his voice fell to a whisper, not much louder and yet vastly more urgent than the sound of a man breathing. "I am honestly sorry for the part I have played in the events of this night. I had my reasons, which I will explain to you on some happier day than this, if we both survive to see it. In the meantime, I wish you good fortune."

Without a glance at Moctezuma or at the girl who shared the emperor's bed, he turned and hurried from the room.

Just outside the emperor's chambers, Aguilar ran straight into Alvarado.

"Ah, Aguilar," he boomed. "There you are. Just the man I have been looking for. What on earth has taken you so long? Come, come. We have much to do." He reversed direction and suddenly stopped. "Oh—the name. The girl's name. Did you get it?"

Aguilar realized that he had completely forgotten to ask. But what did it matter?

"Tonatiuh," he said without thinking, speaking too quickly. It was the first idea that came into his head. "Her name is Tonatiuh."

"Ah, Tonatiuh. How pretty." Alvarado grinned. He suddenly checked himself. "But wait. Tonatiuh . . . ? Isn't that the name the natives call me?"

"Oh," said Aguilar. He realized his error. The man was

right. Tonatiuh meant the Golden One, a gibe at Alvarado's blond curls and his strutting manner. "I understand that . . . that she . . . that she was named in honor of you. They gave her a new name, in your honor. To bring you glory."

"In honor of me, eh?" Alvarado laughed. "I like that. Oh, I do like that." He thrust back his shoulders and strode down the hall. "Tonatiuh!" He glanced back at Aguilar. "Come on, man. Keep up. We have much to do this night!"

Aguilar followed, shaking his head. Dear God, the man was thick. He had to get away from Alvarado, find a canoe, and disappear into the darkness on the lake. How he would accomplish these tasks, however, he did not know.

As soon as they had reached Iztapalapa, Puertocarrero decided to race ahead on his horse, intending to find Alvarado and put a stop to his plans. He dug his heels into his horse's flanks and galloped off.

Meanwhile, supported by Ometzin and Toc, Pitoque staggered along the causeway that led across the lake and into Tenochtitlán. The fury in his mouth had partly subsided now, replaced by a dull foreboding. Ahead of them, as the feast of Huitzilopochtli neared its climax, the island-city had become a carnival of lights. Faint snatches of music drifted across the water, interspersed with the beating of drums, the flight of woodwinds, a wavering chorus of human voices.

Pitoque no longer entertained any doubt that something dreadful would happen tonight. The agony of his tooth, combined with the horror of its extraction, had persuaded him of that. For a moment, he thought he heard the trilling of a single flute, but then he realized that it was merely another sharp edge of pain rising up inside his jaw—like an omen of death. He thought of Maxtla. What had happened to Maxtla? When they reached the entrance to the city, he turned to Ometzin and told her she must hurry to the palace of Axayácatl to find the boy. He himself would proceed to the main plaza, along with Toc.

She nodded. "I will do as you say." She frowned. "Will you be all right?"

"Do not concern yourself about me. I am feeling better already. But I am worried about Maxtla. I will look for you later, at the palace of Axayácatl. Good fortune to you both. Now go."

For several moments, they stood face to face, both of them silent. Then they fell into an embrace, each aware that this might be the last time they saw each other. Ometzin finally drew away. She turned to Toc and embraced him as well. Without a word, she turned and hurried off.

Pitoque watched her go. For a moment, his legs buckled beneath him, and he nearly fell down before he recovered himself.

"Are you in pain, master?"

Pitoque grit his teeth. "Less so than before."

"Ah, then," said Toc. "Let us give thanks for that."

"Yes. Let us give thanks while we can."

The two men joined arms and walked into the city of lights, giving thanks with every stride.

✝

Aguilar eased the dugout canoe into the shallows of the lake. He pushed forward—one step, another—and vaulted into the craft. He balanced himself, then reached ahead for the paddle that rested against the gunwale. Beside it, encased in a leather scabbard, rested his sword. Thank God, he'd finally managed to escape that buffoon, Pedro de Alvarado. Thank the Sweet Mother Mary. Now, with any luck, he would have time to reach the island of Tepepolco in advance of Bakil, time to find a likely hiding place, time to prepare his attack. He hoped he would, and hope was the best he could manage now—hope that he would be in time, hope that the boy Maxtla would somehow prevent the horrors that now threatened to break out in the plaza and engulf the city.

A lone boatman in the Aztec night, he dipped the blade of his paddle into the water and began to propel himself toward the island of Tepepolco. It loomed ahead in the darkness, a silver outline against an ebony drape. Silent, solitary, his craft sliced through the still surface of the moon-glazed lake.

Let Them Die

Maxtla slithered down the clay tiles of the palace roof until he reached the drainage gutter. He knew that just below this spot a huge mound of grass had been piled—twice the height of a man—to serve as nourishment for the Spaniards' horses. That would be his landing. Without stopping to think about the consequences, he leapt and soon felt himself being swallowed by an ocean of drying grass. He flopped and thrashed like an inexpert swimmer until he was toppling out of the mound onto a dirt lane that ran behind the palace. All around him, he heard the low crooning and snorting of horses.

Here in the lane were a dozen of the beasts, each of them tethered to a separate stake. They peered at him through the darkness as they might at an old friend come to call in the middle of the night. They tossed their heads as if in welcome. It was the first time he had found himself so close to these strange, deerlike creatures, and he longed to stay, to know them better. But he had another mission now, and he could not wait.

He picked himself up and ran a hand through his hair to brush away the grass, and he felt something that made his blood stop—yet another stonelike protuberance on his forehead. He traced the contours of his face and found several more, both near his left cheekbone. They were spreading. His heart lurched in his chest, and he tried to calm himself, to steady his pounding heart. He could not afford to concern himself with these nubbles now. He would worry about them later. He turned to leave and suddenly felt his legs give way. He found himself on his knees, the palms of his hands pressed against the dirt. He could not afford such weakness. He willed himself back to his feet and slapped the grass from his cloak. He felt a little better. At least the dizziness had gone. He began to hurry in the direction of the great plaza.

Who knew if he had enough time left to arrive before the signal was sounded and the bloodshed began? All he could do was hope. All he could do was try. He stepped up his pace bit by bit, and the dizziness didn't return. He began to run.

A team of boatmen deposited the hummingbird bride by a jumble of rocks on the shore of Tepepolco. The girl stumbled out of the canoe, aided by a trio of priests and accompanied by four young attendants, all girls, all carrying torches. These ones led the way, tiptoeing ahead of Bakil. The small ceremonial party picked its way through the swaying light and the shifting shadows, aiming for the sacred pyramid that stood a short distance from the shore.

Several times, Bakil lost her footing and nearly fell, for she was deeply drugged—by various mushrooms and peyote cactus. The priests clutched her by the arms, guided her steps. They whispered low, comforting words to her and promised her an eternity of happiness, of endless sunshine, sweet nectar, and song. But it was doubtful that she could hear or, if she did hear, that she understood. The procession wound its way inland through the clipped grass and past the whispering stalks of bougainvillea, past the hulking shadows of boulders, dark as ghosts.

Pitoque staggered ahead amid the crush and bustle of revelers, all pushing against one another, all hoping to arrive at the great plaza in time for the moment of rebirth, when a flute's song would float across the darkened waters from Tepepolco and the world would begin again.

Jostled on all sides, he stumbled once and then again, and worried that he might fall and be trampled by the throngs of people swarming through the city. He looked around and realized he had been separated from Toc. A moment later, he found himself shoved up against a stone wall, to be pushed and pummeled there. In his weakened state, he couldn't keep up with the thrash and surge of the crowd, and people kept elbowing past. He realized he was in danger now of suffering a serious injury.

After a time, he crept into the shelter of a small alcove and crouched down in order to rest and catch his breath. He considered what he ought to do. Where would Maxtla be now? No sooner did he ask himself the question than he knew the answer. He felt it in the aching of his gums. Maybe it was just as well that he had sent Ometzin away. But she would not find Maxtla at the palace of Axayácatl. A terrible misfortune would be unleashed by the trilling of the flute from Tepepolco, and it would begin in the great plaza. He knew his son. He knew where his son would go. He knew now to look for Maxtla there, in the plaza. If he could only arrive there in time, to shout out a warning, he might be able to prevent or at least blunt the massacre that Alvarado was planning.

It was time to go.

He straightened up but immediately felt his knees go weak beneath him and he collapsed to the ground. He wondered whether he could move. As long as he had kept himself going, it had been possible to walk. Now that he had stopped to rest, it seemed as if his muscles had seized up and his strength had dwindled away to nothing. He had lost a great quantity of blood. He looked up and noticed that the laneway in front of him was now almost deserted. All of the people had passed him by and now were likely assembled in the great plaza. How on earth would he find one person in all that throng? Still, he had no choice but to try.

With his last reserves of will, he forced himself out into the lane, where he was promptly knocked sprawling by some young idiot on the run. For several seconds, the darkness swam around him. He sat up. Only then did he hear a voice.

"Father!"

By all the gods of Cholula, it was Maxtla, his son.

The hummingbird bride began to scale the stone steps of the sacred pyramid on the island of Tepepolco. Her four female attendants lit the way with flaming torches, and the three priests stayed very close. This was the woman they would kill, and yet now they took immense care that she did not trip or fall or otherwise come to harm. At the summit of the pyramid, Bakil turned and stood alone in the rippling light. She looked out across the lake and the darkness toward the great glittering ornament of Tenochtitlán. In her hands, she clutched the wooden flute that soon she would play, the flute whose notes would drift across the night to herald her death—her death and the beginning of life. With her own hands, she would break the instrument upon her knee. So fragile is greatness. So fleeting is love. She wondered briefly whether she had ever been born, whether she had ever played amid the long grass of the southern lands, ever been dandled upon her mother's lap, ever dreamt of the future, ever sighed at the setting of the sun. She wondered whether a Spaniard named Jerónimo de Aguilar had ever truly existed. Or had she only imagined him?

Had she only imagined everything?

She balanced herself at the summit of the pyramid, allowed the highland breeze to whisper through her hair, let the darkness embrace her. She waited for the world to fall silent. Then she would pray.

Aguilar's canoe ran up against the shore of Tepepolco, wobbled, nearly capsized. He fumbled for his sword, encased in its scabbard, and leapt into the shallows. He lost his footing on the slippery rocks beneath the surface and nearly fell. He scrambled onto dry land and struggled to buckle his scabbard at his waist, while he stumbled and darted through the darkness, desperate to reach the pyramid in time. But it was impossible—he couldn't run with this bloody scabbard. He drew his sword, tossed its leather casing away, and hurried through the shadows and the rocks with his weapon raised high, its blade glinting in the pale moonlight. Dear God, let there be time.

✝

"Excellent," whispered Pedro de Alvarado. "Very well done."

His men had taken up positions all around the great plaza and now would be able to block off every exit. Bands of native fighters were stationed here and there along outlying lanes. Soon the cry would go up—he himself would deliver it—and the Spaniards would fall upon the Aztecs in the square. The Totonacs and Tlaxcalans would rush in behind them. Their tattooed faces would be easy to make out for they had not painted themselves in lurid, unearthly designs, the way the Aztecs had. They had not put on monstrous, unearthly head-dresses or covered themselves in elaborate robes made of animal fur or bird feathers. All he and his men had to do now was kill the painted faces, the costumed bodies—and Tenochtitlán would be theirs. He allowed himself a deep, anticipatory sigh, a sigh of satisfaction. How pleased Cortés would be. In one magnificent maneuver, he—Pedro de Alvarado—would bring an empire to its knees. He would be paid gold for this, vast quantities of gold. That weakling Puertocarrero would fry in his own sweat, overcome with envy.

Alvarado briefly wondered how the commander was doing out on the coast. What battles were being waged there? But he couldn't dwell on such questions now. He had a battle of his own to fight. All he needed to do now was wait for the sound of that bloody flute—and then have at it. Lord of mercy, he felt halfway like a girl, needing music in order to make war. This thought caused him to remember that lovely brown mouthful, Tonatiuh. To think—a native princess named for him. By the Virgin of Seville, some fine sport awaited him once this game was done.

‡

Puertocarrero hauled back on the reins, pulled his horse to a halt. He slumped in the saddle. Not until this moment had it occurred to him that he would have to admit to Alvarado that his story about an Aztec plot was a lie. He would look like a complete fool. How could he explain why he had told such a tale? The truth was ridiculous, and he could invent no other explanation that made him appear less a fool. Alvarado would laugh at him, report the whole affair to Cortés. Puertocarrero would be stripped of his officer's rank, made a laughing-stock—even more so than he already was.

His horse shifted beneath him, and he wondered what to do. Back and forth, he debated the question in his mind. Of its own will, the horse began to walk and then broke into a loping gait. Puertocarrero paid no attention to where he was going, up what streets he traveled or down which lanes. Even if he did confront Alvarado and explain the lies he had told, there was little chance that the blond one would believe him. Why should he? His reason for creating a "diversion" was all such nonsense. He had to determine a way to present his case so that it would receive a fair hearing. ¡Coño! He ducked just in time to avoid banging his head against a beam of wood thrusting out from a building.

He pulled back again on the reins, applied pressure with his thighs, and slowed his horse to a walk. Now they were in the open. He looked around. Where in God's name was he? He halted and stood up in the stirrups, balancing himself with his right hand on the cantle of the saddle. All was darkness. Nothing seemed familiar. That was not surprising—he did not know his way around this city. But now everything was strange. Somewhere in the distance, he thought he heard a hubbub of voices. But he could not tell from which direction. The sounds echoed against the stone walls of pyramids and palaces.

He sank back into the saddle, squeezed his calves, and his horse lurched ahead. He rode on for some distance—five minutes? ten? more?—until he came to another causeway. It stretched away into the darkness, disappearing amid a tangle of silver, moonlit fibers that shifted across the lake. Was he facing north? South? He had no idea at all.

At any moment, the notes of a flute would trill across the waters, coming from Tepepolco. Hundreds, perhaps thousands, would die—because of something idiotic that he had done. And here he was, determined to put matters right.

Here he was—*where?*

On the deep coastal flats, midway between the shore and the mountains of the interior, Hernán Cortés settled himself onto his knees and peered up at the night sky, embossed with clouds. Almost directly overhead, a pale glow of moonlight drained through the dark mantle, and he decided that this illumination was the very eye of God. Cortés was on his return journey now and gave thanks to the Lord of Christendom that beneficence could there possibly be than what had just taken place at Cempoala?

There, on a dark night that shuddered with rain, Cortés and his men had fallen upon the newly arrived Spaniards, who were commanded by a hook-nosed miscreant by the name of Pánfilo de Narváez.

Although badly outnumbered, Cortés and his men enjoyed the advantage of surprise, not to mention the blessing of the Lord, whose bounty is without limit. The battle had been brief and had involved few casualties on either side. It was almost absurdly easy. Deploy his troops on all sides. Wait for darkness. Attack. To avoid any needless loss of Spanish wood, the offensive was executed with more noise than metal, but its purpose was soon accomplished. Once he had realized that he was surrounded, that simpering rodent Narváez had promptly ordered his men to give themselves up, which they did at once. They dropped their swords to the ground, raised their hands, cringed, and cowered. Some fell to their knees. Cortés sent his own troops among them, collecting weaponry but otherwise inflicting no abuse, not even taunts or spittle. He had no desire to further embitter men whose services he would soon require. In the case of Narváez, however, he made an exception. The fellow had already suffered the loss of an eye, and was in a cowed and whimpering state when Cortés ordered him clamped in irons.

"Tomorrow," he instructed an officer, "see that he is transported under guard to Veracruz. He will be dealt with there."

Toward the remainder of his captives, Cortés behaved with true Christian mercy, not to mention his customary tactical genius. Rather than abuse them or lop off their heads—as another leader might well have done—he showered them with honest praise and promised them great adventure and unlimited fortune if they abandoned their perfidy and allied themselves with his holy cause. With few exceptions, this was precisely what they did.

Cortés turned his army—now swollen by the addition of nearly a thousand of Narváez's men—and marched back across the broad flats beneath a withering sun. The green orbs of ceiba trees flashed in the dazzling light. More than ever, he felt ready now to complete his grand mission: to subdue these lands on behalf of his monarch, Charles I of Spain, and in the glorious name of the Lord. God willing, the entire project could be completed without the shedding of blood.

Now, at night, on the moonlit coastal marshes of this strange new world, Hernán Cortés lowered his head and closed his eyes. "Amen," he muttered. Then he raised himself from his knees and strode back to his camp, where Doña Marina awaited him in his tent. At this supreme moment, more than ever before, the glory of the Lord seemed to surge through his veins and to swell, most particularly, at his groin.

All Tenochtitlán fell silent.

all were still. The dancers stood in a rapture of expectation. Nobles and warriors all remained motionless, side by side. The women, looking like tropical birds in their feathers of scarlet and emerald, ceased moving. Only their heads still spun, intoxicated as they were by their dancing and by the mushrooms and the long draughts of pulque they had consumed. Their hearts pounded, but they kept silent. They waited.

Several blocks from the plaza, Pitoque and his son stumbled to a halt.

On the island of Tepepolco, Aguilar caught his foot in the crevice between two stones and sprawled to the ground, nearly impaling himself on his sword. He picked himself up and continued through the darkness. Just ahead, he could discern the shadowy outline of the pyramid. He could see the figures of humans at the summit, their forms seeming to dance in the glow of torches.

From his position overlooking the great plaza, Alvarado raised his right hand. Already, he had decided what his battle cry would be. At the sound of the flute, he would let his hand drop and roar it out.

The Dark Virgin

In the shadow of the pyramid of Huitzilopochtli in the great plaza of Tenochtitlán, a noblewoman named Xela felt a sudden discomfort beneath her headdress. She reached up without thinking, and her fingers met a strange hardness beneath the skin at her brow. At first, the lump seemed as firm as a small stone and then, like a rotted fruit, it suddenly burst beneath the pressure of her fingers, and she cried out, nearly fainting from the pain. She buried her face in her hands, and she realized the nubbles were everywhere.

On the roof of the palace of Axayácatl, the emperor Moctezuma gazed up at the stars, desperate to divine some shape there, some pattern, some sign meant for him. But all he read in the constellations was a gibberish of light traced upon a vast scroll of darkness.

At the foot of the Tepeyac causeway, which ran from Tlatelolco to the north shore of the lake, Puertocarrero dismounted from his horse and stood with the reins in his hands, peering out at the slow play of moonlight on the darkened waters. Without knowing it, he had ridden all the way through Tenochtitlán and its sister city, Tlatelolco, and come out at the other side. He was nowhere near where he had meant to be.

He could think of only one thing to do.

Father, the Son, and the Holy Spirit for forgiveness. He beseeched the Virgin Mary to cleanse his rotting soul. He lowered his head, closed his eyes, and waited.

Far away, in that city known as Madrid, the monarch—Charles I of Spain—slept in his palace. As usual, he dreamt, and as usual, he dreamt in German, which was his native tongue. In fact, he spoke Spanish poorly and understood it hardly at all. He did not dream of a place called Tenochtitlán or of a people known as Aztecs or of an adventurer by the name of Hernán Cortés. He had never heard these names. Even later, when he would indeed hear them, he would never be able to sort them out. They would never seem real. Now, instead of distant lands—populated by brown-skinned homunculi who might or might not have souls—he dreamt of a lithe blonde woman he had once encountered in Bavaria. In his dream, they both were naked, and she was sponge-bathing him with beer. He snorted in pleasure and rolled over in his bed. He did not hear the trilling of a flute as it wavered over the still, dark waters between Tepepolco and Tenochtitlán.

The last notes of a distant melody faded into the darkness, and Pedro de Alvarado yanked his right hand down to his side. "¡Qué se mueran!" he cried out at the top of his lungs. "¡Qué se

The Voice of Stone

Once they heard the sound of the flute lilting across the lake from Tepepolco, Pitoque and Maxtla realized they were too late. They turned back at once. Weak as he was himself, the boy managed to shoulder much of his father's weight, and both staggered back toward the palace of Axayácatl in search of Ometzin. Already, a clamor was rising from the great plaza, a din of shouting voices, the sharp reports of harquebuses. Pitoque understood that he had failed. The commission he had received from the Mother of God had ended in blood and shame. And there would be more blood now, and corpses beyond counting.

The same haunting words echoed again in his mind. *Flee. Run for your lives. Take only what you can carry. Do not come back.* But how could he run? Where could they go? He could barely walk. He leaned on his son and they staggered through the roaring darkness, through the deserted streets of Tenochtitlán.

Jerónimo de Aguilar lurched down the lower steps of the pyramid and collapsed onto his knees. He let his sword fall at his side. Its blade drooled with blood. Everything was awash with blood, it seemed—his hands, the stone steps, his clothes. He had been too late, of course. He remembered seeing Bakil raise the wooden flute to her lips. He even remembered the strange melody of the notes as they sang down a handful of instants earlier, he might have been on time. Instead, even as he had clambered up the steps of the pyramid, his sword raised above his head, he had known it was useless. He was too late. He was still several strides short of the temple's flame-lit summit when two of those monstrous priests appeared in the dancing light. One of them was holding something aloft with both hands, a devil's smile on his blood-smeared lips. Aguilar had known it then—Bakil was dead. Only her heart still lived, and not for long.

After that, everything had begun to blur, to spin around him, to shriek across the night air. He had little idea what he did, only that he heard cries and ignored them, only that flesh is a poor match for iron. Now he lifted himself a little and gazed around. The darkness was tarnished by moonlight, and several torches still burned where they had fallen. There was enough light for him to make out what he had done. They were all dead, the priests, the female attendants. Their corpses sprawled on all sides, and his sword ran with their blood. Call it vengeance, madness, murder, war. He could not remember inflicting this bloodshed, but the evidence lay around him on all sides.

He climbed to his feet and trudged back to the summit of the pyramid. At the top, he turned and looked out through the darkness, over the lake waters streaked with moonlight, to Tenochtitlán. Suddenly, he heard the roaring that tore at the air from the direction of the island-city, saw the jagged flames the base of the pyramid. Longer than he had thought. Already, across the lake, the war had begun. He heard the shrieks and shouts of men and the sobs of women. He heard the reports of harquebuses, like the cracking together of stones.

All for nothing. He had failed. In the only purpose for which God had kept him alive and transported him to this high country, to these strange lands—in that purpose he had failed. In his mind and in the air around him, he heard nothing now but the bark and howl of war vibrating across the water. The angels' voices were silent. He put back his head and gazed at the heavens, saw the constellations tumble across the sky. The night spun around him with the fury of the apocalypse. He began to weep, to tear at his hair.

But he stopped, for he thought he heard a voice. It was not the voice of any angel he had ever heard before. It sounded like rock, like the voice of stone. *Behold, they shall be as stubble; the fires shall burn them; they shall not deliver themselves from the power of the flame; it shall not be a coal to be warmed by, nor a fire to sit before! Thus shall they be to you with whom you have laboured, your merchants from your youth; they shall wander each one to his quarter. No one shall save you.*

Bakil was dead.

The Virgin Mother was dead.

No one shall save you.

Aguilar peered down at his hands. The blood was everywhere.

He climbed to his feet, ran a bloody hand through his hair. He began attending to the last duties he had in this place.

That night, he interred the body of Bakil beneath a pyre of stones. He recited a prayer over the grave and then considered whether he ought to kill himself. Unsure, he began to pray. He hoped that the dark Virgin he had seen shimmering in the clouds over Tenochtitlán might reappear before him or answer him in some way. But he saw nothing, heard no woman's voice. He heard only the voice of stone.

No one shall save you.

They shall wander each one to his quarter.

He made his way down to the lake, where he found his canoe still nudging against the shore. First, he bathed himself in the water, washing and rinsing away the blood. Then he steadied the canoe, pushed off, and swung himself into the shallow hull. The paddle rested against the gunwale. He picked it up and began to propel himself away toward what he believed was the east, away from Tepepolco, away from Tenochtitlán.

When at last he reached the lake's far shore, he climbed out of the canoe and waded through a bed of reeds to the marsh bank. At once, he began to walk. He was thinking—either he would die on this journey or he would one day find himself again in the Yucatán. Maybe he would seek out Gonzalo Guerrero, his old mate from that shipwreck so many years before. This time, Aguilar, too, would have his face painted with tattoos, dangle coils from his ears, wear a plug of jadeite in his lip. This time, he would disappear.

The Pleasure of Eagles and Snakes

Pitoque and Maxtla found Ometzin in the company of the emperor, both of them standing upon the palace roof, watching the flames that now lapped across the night consuming the buildings around the great plaza. The cool breeze off the lake carried the reek of burning flesh, a long wail of fear and hate. The four of them clung to the railing in silence, listening and watching.

Two hours later, the Spaniards lumbered back to the palace in full retreat to barricade themselves within. Several Spanish soldiers found the emperor and his companions on the roof and dragged them down into the bowels of the palace. Pitoque, Maxtla, and Ometzin huddled together against a hard stone wall. Moctezuma held himself a little apart, surrounded by an assembly of aides, servants, and concubines, who had been roused from their quarters.

Meanwhile, filthy with sweat and blood, gasping for breath, more soldiers staggered inside. Clanking in their armor, they reached up with their swords and struck at the air, growled like dogs. They kicked at objects that stood in their way, tables, chairs. Some were badly wounded and clutched their sides to hold in their vitals. Others moaned, twitched, collapsed to the ground. They gave off the foulest stench, pungent as sulfur. They glared at each other, spat, and swore. This battle was supposed to have been a quick and brilliant victory. Instead, unprepared for the furious response of the Aztecs, they had been forced farther and farther back, suffering more casualties and further indignities each step of their retreat. What had been the purpose of this battle?

Alvarado himself had been wounded in the head, apparently by a hard-flung stone. Now he held his hands to his once-golden hair, newly matted with his own blood. He approached Moctezuma, where the emperor stood by a wall.

"Look," he cried, uncovering his wound. "Look at what you creatures have done."

"My dear sir—" began the emperor.

But Alvarado would not listen. He groaned and clasped his head and tottered away, as if this inglorious retreat had been the Aztecs' fault, as if he himself had been taken unawares. An innocent betrayed.

Outside the palace, the city ran wild with rage. The people of Tenochtitlán waved their fists and shouted, pocked the palace walls with stones. The air was shot with the stench of war, sharp as the stink of blood. But still Moctezuma sought to restore peace. He urged his aides to go out among the people, to try to calm them down. Let there be no more bloodshed. Let the killing stop.

It was no use. Even those aides and officers who had been captured along with him ignored him now. In all of Tenochtitlán, Moctezuma must have been the only Aztec who did not want war. But no one heard what he said. No one listened to the *tlatoani* anymore.

‡

Hernán Cortés arrived at Tenochtitlán with his regular troops and with the Spanish fighters he had lately won over to his side. He saw at once that matters had taken a bad turn. The evidence was everywhere—rubble and smoldering fires, the din of war. He kicked at a stone and cursed Alvarado. Was the idea of peace beyond the man's comprehension? He halted his march and waited at Iztapalapa until darkness, when a lull in the fighting allowed him to make a quick foray across the causeway into the city, and to the palace of Axayácatl itself. The Aztecs were caught off their guard, and so Cortés managed the dangerous trek in good time, with only light casualties suffered.

But almost immediately, the fighting resumed with even greater fury. The Aztecs flung rocks and hurled spears, shouted taunts, insults, threats. Across the rooftops of neighboring buildings, they paraded back and forth with the corpses of fallen Spaniards held high above their heads. They sawed off Spanish limbs and threw them onto the barricades atop the palace of Axayácatl. They laughed and roared out that Spanish flesh was too foul for civilized men to eat—no, not with all the chilis in the world!

Inside the palace of Axayácatl, Cortés swore and slammed a fist against the wall. He turned and shouted at the blond lieutenant, his great favorite. He had just learned how this disastrous situation—the Spaniards besieged in their own palace—had come about.

"*What?* Are you mad? Have you taken leave of your useless, inconsequential senses?"

Cortés swept his arm around him, a gesture meant to encompass all of Tenochtitlán. He put a hand to his brow and shook his head. This absurd attack was no way to conquer a foreign state, one that enjoyed a massive advantage in numbers. Would it not have been better to take control of Tenochtitlán and the whole Aztec empire by guile, without a war? Was that not what he had been intent on doing—until now? But now, there was no other choice but to fight—and he was poorly equipped for the task. Even with the men he had recruited on his journey to the coast, Cortés still had fewer than fifteen hundred Spaniards under his command. His Tlaxcalan allies came to perhaps two thousand more. How could they hope to prevail in a war?

"Are you crazy?" he shouted at Alvarado. "I swear you must be the stupidest oaf that ever drew breath. Get out of my sight."

Alvarado drew back his shoulders, still clutching a rag to his blood-matted hair. He began to mumble some ridiculous tale about an uprising that had been brewing among the Aztecs, the need for decisive action. "I had no choice. Circumstances forced my—"

"¡Silencio! I don't want to hear your excuses." Cortés waved the man away. He had to think. He frowned and did not acknowledge the presence of Doña Marina, who wordlessly massaged his shoulders.

It soon became clear what the Aztecs intended. They meant to starve the Spaniards out and then attack them when they were near death. With their superior numbers and with the Spaniards in a weakened state, it would not take long to defeat them—a matter of days, weeks at most. And yet, even now, Moctezuma continued to ramble on about peace, addressing anyone he thought might listen. But no one did.

Cortés was more interested in food, for there was none at all. He stood before the emperor and cast aside every pretense of respect. He spat on the stone floor, his phlegm splattering not far from Moctezuma's scuffed slippers.

"Why doesn't the dog keep even a market open for us?" he demanded. He glared at Moctezuma. "Why don't you see to it that the Aztecs send us some little morsel to eat?"

He spat again, ignored the *tlatoani*'s attempt at a reply, and turned away. The truth was clear to everyone by now. The emperor had no power to see to anything at all. Hunched on the floor amid turkey bones and filth—ridiculed by his captor, ignored by his own people—the great lord Moctezuma II, Emperor of the Aztecs, began to cry.

Pitoque watched, aghast at what he saw. Moctezuma did not weep for the loss of a throne. He sobbed because Cortés had abused him, had called him a dog. He would relinquish his empire and all it contained, but he could not bear the scorn of his fine Spanish god.

Maxtla shook his head. "We must escape," he whispered.

Pitoque gripped his son's shoulder. The boy was wise beyond his years. Escape was exactly what they had to do. But how?

☩

The battles roared. In wave after wave, the Aztec warriors descended upon the palace, while the Spaniards fought from behind barricades on the roof, desperate to hold their attackers off.

The food was gone. No drinkable water remained. Many Spaniards lay dead, while those who survived were haggard and hollowed-eyed from hunger and thirst. The nights were a horror, for then the Aztecs played fiendish tricks. They darted back and forth upon the roofs of neighboring buildings, carrying poles mounted with human heads or human feet, which they waved about. They threw corpses, headless and flayed, into the palace of Axayácatl where they hit the hard stones of the courtyard floor and burst like bloated fruit, splattering blood and tripe against the walls. The Aztec warriors shrieked out terrible, ghoulish threats, which Doña Marina translated without comment.

"They are demanding our surrender," she said.

Cortés held up his hands before his face like a shield. "What else?"

"If we fail to surrender, then we shall be taken prisoner. Our flesh will be boiled and prepared for feasting."

"Holy God!" said Cortés. "What barbarians!"

Marina put up her hand. "But no," she repeated, still translating, "the flesh of Spaniards has proved too foul for civilized men to enjoy. They intend to cut up your flesh and lay it out for the pleasure of eagles and snakes."

"Snakes!" Cortés glared at the sky. "Snakes, they say!"

Marina continued. "On the other hand, they say, a little chocolate sauce can improve the flavor of even the most unpleasant . . ."

On and on it went—the infernal screeching, the bobbing of heads on sticks, the plummeting corpses, the lurid threats. All these, combined with the lack of food and water and the nearly constant fighting, nearly drove the Spaniards mad. They moaned and swore, especially the new recruits who had come with Pánfilo de Narváez and had crossed over to join Cortés. They deeply regretted that decision now. They wished they had remained on the coast—imprisoned, in irons. That fate would be better than this.

A Shroud of Mud and Gold

It was no use. The Spaniards could not possibly hold out. Cortés saw it himself and declared that only one hope remained. With Doña Marina at his side, he approached Moctezuma and made his proposal. Would the emperor himself ascend to the rooftop of the palace and there make an address to his people?

Moctezuma managed a thin smile. "And tell them what?"

"That we wish to leave," answered Cortés. "That we will depart your city in peace and not return. If you consent to give us safe passage, we will go."

Pitoque listened to this exchange in disbelief. He waited for Cortés to continue, but evidently this was all the man had to say. The proposal was laughable. After an unprovoked massacre of the most savage kind, after long days and nights of brutal fighting, after the royal treasury had been plundered, the holiest temples ransacked, the people tormented, after hundreds of men, women, and children lay dead, this was the bargain Cortés offered? That he and his men would leave?

Pitoque knew how he would have replied. He would have spoken in a cold, forbidding voice. "But, my dear sir," he would have said to Cortés, "many days have passed since we ourselves counseled you to take precisely this course. Surely you recall. Have you not left your compliance a trifle late?"

He would then have turned and walked away.

But he was not Moctezuma II, emperor of the Aztecs, who instead agreed to do precisely as Cortés requested. Even now, gaunt and humiliated, smeared with filth, he could not bring himself to disappoint the Spanish commander. Cortés ordered a young officer named Cristóbal de Olid to take Moctezuma up onto the roof of the palace so that the emperor might address the mob below, appeal to them to allow the Spaniards to leave their city in peace.

At the last moment, Moctezuma looked at Pitoque. "Come," said the emperor. "I would have you accompany me."

What should he do? The mission was madness, but Pitoque bowed and accepted his emperor's command. The habits of a lifetime cannot be broken easily.

"Stay here," he told Maxtla, who was in a miserable state, his skin riddled with pox, some of them running with pus. The boy was feverish at times.

"Don't worry," said Ometzin. "I will take care of him."

"I know," Pitoque said, and turned to follow his emperor.

Olid led the way. They scaled a series of ladders through a musty darkness until they emerged into the cool air. The roiling night was beaded with stars. Spanish soldiers huddled against the wooden railings, and a glow of torches surged beyond the palace walls. Aztec voices shrieked and roared from below, punctuated by the clatter of rocks scattering against the slate tiles of the roof.

"Be careful," said Olid.

He was already too late. Pitoque felt something thud against the side of his head, and he flew back, almost losing his footing. But someone stopped him from falling. It was the emperor—the emperor reaching out to save a fellow man. The stone dazed Pitoque, but he felt he could stand. "It's all right," he said. "I am not hurt. I can walk."

From the square in front of the palace of Axayácatl, a young warrior's son by the name of Centeotl peered up at the shapes moving atop the roof. His chest heaved with rage, for his father and mother had both been struck down in the plaza when the Spaniards had attacked. He'd been with them at the time, but he had managed to escape.

His mother and father were dead.

Since then, Centeotl had kept himself in the very heat of the battle, almost without a pause. If he had slept at all, it had been for no more than a few moments—snatches of slumber seized during occasional lulls in the fighting. He had heaved stones and bricks until his right arm burned like fire, until he half-thought it might fall off. But he didn't stop. He meant to kill someone. He was a warrior's son, destined to become a warrior himself—and he had two deaths to avenge.

Now he peered up at these strange shadows creeping atop the palace. Occasionally, they were caught in the glow of torches, and he saw that they were not Spaniards, for they did not dress as Spaniards did. No, wait. There were three of them—and one *was* a Spaniard, accompanied by two others. As he watched, one of the figures stumbled back as if hit by something, a rock perhaps, flung from below. In that moment, Centeotl saw another of the figures go to the aid of the one who had been hit. A blaze of torchlight flashed in a sudden trick of the wind, illuminating the three figures, and Centeotl recognized one of the men. He had been present that day when fifteen Aztecs had been burned at the stake, and he had seen the emperor then, in the company of Cortés.

He saw the emperor now, on the roof of the palace of Axayácatl.

"It's Moctezuma!" he shouted. "Look! It's Moctezuma!"

Almost at once, the roaring stopped, and thousands of Aztec eyes turned up to watch the tlatoani rise above them like a ghost, silhouetted against a swirl of stars.

The emperor began to speak. With his arms outstretched at his side, he beseeched his people to withdraw, to allow these Spaniards to depart their city. The war was over. No more blood must flow.

Centeotl felt flames burning in his chest. He was a warrior's son. His father and mother were dead. Who now could talk of peace? He crouched down and began to cast about for a stone. There were hundreds scattered everywhere, those that had cracked against the palace walls and clattered back to the ground. His right hand closed upon something hard and cold, a rock that fit into his palm as if it had been created for that purpose. He straightened up.

"No!" he shouted and reached back.

He ran three steps forward and flung the stone as high and as hard as he could. Glinting in the light of torchlights, it arched through the air.

Was it his stone that caught the emperor on the forehead? It was difficult to say, for a hundred other stones flew through the darkness at almost the same instant. One of them must have found its mark, for Moctezuma's arms flew up and he reeled back, vanished from Centeotl's sight.

Pitoque wasn't sure what he had seen. Still dazed by the rock that had struck him, he saw the emperor go down—but whether Moctezuma had been hit by a stone or bludgeoned by Olid in a fit of temper, Pitoque couldn't say. It was dark, and his head pulsed with blood, and it all happened quickly. But when he ducked down below the barricade, he saw the emperor crumpled upon the slate tiles, with Olid on top of him.

Maxtla heard a sudden roar. Outside the palace, the din of the battle had redoubled. Voices surged and stormed. A tumult of rocks sprayed against the palace walls. Just then, a wooden ladder began to shake. A pair of Spanish boots appeared and Olid clambered down.

"Dead! Dead!" he shouted. He careened against the walls and stumbled over the remnants of furniture. His sword was drawn. "They've killed him!"

"Who?" someone cried. "What are you talking about? Who is dead?"

"Moctezuma," he gasped. He collapsed against a wall and slid to the floor. He was half-covered in blood. He shivered and shook his head. "They've killed him."

Before long, the emperor's body was carried down from the roof by Pitoque and several others—bewildered Aztec courtiers who had climbed up to rescue the *tlatoani*. Now they laid him out on the cold stone floor. In fact, he was not quite dead, but he was barely conscious and uttered nothing more than low moans. Ometzin hurried over to join Pitoque, and Maxtla followed.

"You're hurt," the boy said to his father.

It was true. A gash had been opened on Pitoque's forehead where the first stone had hit. But Pitoque barely noticed it now. "Do not concern yourselves," he said. "It is nothing."

They did what they could to attend to the emperor's wounds, but their efforts were little use. They could only daub at Moctezuma's head with torn pieces of maguey fiber. There was no water to offer him, no priests to gather around him in prayer, no healers to shake bones or burn incense. Moctezuma was delirious now. He groaned and shivered and coughed.

"What happened?" said Maxtla. "Who did this?"

Pitoque could only speak the truth. He did not know.

In a short time, the emperor's body shook in a final spasm and a dark liquid dribbled from his lips. The tlatoani, Moctezuma II, was dead. Pitoque found a cotton blanket, soiled and torn, and they covered the body with that.

A hundred memories flickered through Pitoque's mind—drinks of chocolate, palaces upon the sea, an emperor's sobs, quetzal feathers and hoops of gold, a royal palanquin tottering through the streets, Spanish sloops that splashed upon Lake Texcoco like fish that flew. All was a bewilderment to him. Nothing made sense. Here before him lay the most powerful man in all creation, the favorite of the gods—a pathetic heap stretched out upon the floor of the palace of Axayácatl.

Cortés happened by a little later and glanced down at the emperor's body beneath its filthy shroud. He shook his head and spat. He called for an orderly. "Get this corpse out of here. It's starting to stink already. Hurry. Be quick about it."

Pitoque led Doña Marina to the body of the emperor, where it now lay on the stone floor in an empty corridor, amid a muddle of broken chairs and empty sacks. He had an idea how he could escape from the palace, along with Maxtla and Ometzin. But he did not express his plan this way to Doña Marina. He said that he had thought of another way to seek peace.

"And what is that?" she asked.

"Return the emperor's body to the Aztecs. They would take it as a kindness."

"A kindness?" She shook her head. "How can you speak of kindness? Besides, look at him." With one foot, she prodded the cadaver. "He's useless now. Useless to anyone."

Pitoque remained silent, unsure how to convince her. Suddenly, someone else spoke.

"What is happening here?"

Pitoque looked up. It was Puertocarrero, who now walked over to join them.

He had reached the palace of Axayácatl only a short time before Cortés. He'd stumbled up to the gates and been admitted. Somehow, he had managed to make his way through the throngs of raging Aztecs outside, taking only a few blows from hurled rocks—enough to draw blood, inflict bruises, but not to bring him down. Now he stood above the emperor's corpse. The commotion outside had faded, and a strange silence hovered on the air.

He looked at Pitoque, and there was a strange radiance in his eyes. He said, "What do you wish?"

Pitoque explained. He thought it would be helpful if the Spaniards offered to return the body of Moctezuma.

Puertocarrero pondered for a moment. "I consider this a very good idea. I shall take it up with Cortés."

In the end, the plan was approved. Even Doña Marina had to admit the sense of it, now that her master had done so himself. Return the emperor's corpse? Why not? Such a gesture could not harm the Spaniards further. It might even prove helpful. It might, as the merchant had said, be taken as a kindness.

That night, the three of them—Maxtla, Ometzin, and Pitoque—slipped out of the palace by way of a makeshift stable at the rear. They lugged Moctezuma's body after them, wrapped now in a shroud of stout maguey cloth. They dragged the corpse up one street, turned a corner, and were almost out of earshot of the Spaniards' palace before a pair of Aztec sentries challenged them.

Pitoque spoke up at once. He explained who he and his companions were and what they had done. He was cut short by Maxtla, who let out a low moan and sank to his knees.

The nubbles had spread all over the boy's body, and many had broken into running pustules. In his saliva, there was blood. The sentries called out for help—men were needed to shoulder the emperor's corpse and to offer support to this young lad, afflicted in a distressing way. Two of the Aztecs clucked their tongues and shook their heads. They held Maxtla up between them. It was not the first they had seen of this disease, and they knew, as their manner suggested, that it would not be the last.

The following morning, Pitoque was summoned before the new tlatoani, Cuitláhuac—a brother of Moctezuma's and former prince of Iztapalapa. It seemed that Cuitláhuac wished to hear the merchant's tale from his own lips, and Pitoque was eager to tell it. He hoped that a new emperor, a man of hardier substance than Moctezuma, would mark a change in the fortunes of his people. But one look at the man was enough to make Pitoque despair. Cuitláhuac was in a worse state than Maxtla, his body riddled with pustules and sores. His eyes shone with a desperate glaze. He had barely the strength to speak.

Pitoque bowed before the new emperor, and his heart sank. This was what the aching in his mouth and all the other omens had foretold—a curse was being spread by these Spaniards, a curse that ravaged only the people of these lands.

A curse that had attacked his only son.

After seven days and seven nights of siege and precious little food or water, Cortés realized that his position was hopeless. The Spaniards could not remain here. There was no choice— they would have to risk an all-out retreat. That night, when a cold drizzle splattered down upon the city like spittle from the sky, the Spaniards and their native allies broke out of the palace of Axayácatl and fled Tenochtitlán.

By a lucky coincidence, their flight coincided with a lapse in Aztec vigilance. The Spaniards had already reached the causeway leading to the southern mainland before their presence was detected by Aztec patrols afloat upon the lake in dugout canoes. Immediately, the Aztecs raised their conch shells and sounded an alarm.

The Spaniards quickened their pace, jostled each other and shoved their way ahead. They were desperate to escape, but the retreat soon bogged down. As a precaution, the Aztecs had dug dikes through the causeway, and this tactic proved disastrous for the fleeing Spaniards, who had to wade across each sudden canal through a deep ooze of mud. The Aztec warriors pressed their advantage, rushing along the causeway from the rear. Dozens of war canoes were launched onto the lake to attack the Spaniards from the water. The result was a massacre. The Aztecs butchered hundreds of their fleeing enemies, who floundered in the water and the mud. Other Spaniards drowned, dragged down by the weight of the Aztec treasure they had stuffed into their pockets or stitched into their clothes.

Hour after hour, Cortés's dwindling army struggled to escape. They forded dikes, sloshed through mud, straggled onto the mainland and hurried through the darkness, stumbling through swamp, staggering over rocks. The din of war bellowed all around them, and their path was always strewn with corpses, trampled into the earth. Day followed night, and still they ran. They fled westward, then north from Tacuba, on a route that took them past Tepotzotlan and Citlaltepec, then east past Otumba to Apan. At every turn, marauding parties of Aztecs attacked them from higher ground with arrows and stones. They turned south at Apan and made for Hueyotiplan, and from there they made toward Tlaxcala. At last, the Aztecs let them go—believing that, surely now, the war was over. The Spaniards were dead, and Tenochtitlán was saved.

The Children of the Sun had triumphed.

✝

Cortés thought himself a beaten man. Of the thirteen hundred Spaniards who had retreated from Tenochtitlán that night, only four hundred and forty men survived. Among the Tlaxcalans, the number of the dead was even higher—more than twelve hundred gone. Countless harquebuses had been abandoned, along with crossbows and cannons. Almost all of the horses lay dead. And the treasures of Moctezuma, plundered by the Spaniards, were now lost forever—cast with broken bodies across marsh and bog or sunk in mud beds at the bottom of the lakes.

On his arrival in Tlaxcala, Hernán Cortés took full account of this catastrophe and at once drew himself apart. He slumped down at the base of an oak tree, its trunk blasted by lightning, and he began to weep at the fate of his men. They had sailed over the eastern sea with their armor and crossbows, their dying Savior on a wooden cross, their images of the *Virgen de los Remedios*, their snorting horses and yelping dogs. Now the commander's dreams of conquest lay in a heap at the bottom of Lake Texcoco, tangled among the corpses of men beneath a shroud of mud and gold.

Never Come Back

Pitoque laid a hand on Toc's shoulder. They stood outside Azotl's house by the lake in Tenochtitlán. Pitoque realized this might well be the last time he would see his friend and fellow wanderer. "Go to Cholula," he said. "Go to my wife and my daughter. Tell them you bring a message from me."

Toc shifted his weight. His eyes watered. "And that message is?"

"Flee," said Pitoque. "Run for your lives. Take what you can carry. Never come back."

"Where should they go?"

Pitoque had only one idea. Kalatzin and Zaachila must flee to the south, toward the lands of the Maya. Maybe there, they would survive. Maybe there, they could embark upon a new life. Here, there was only death.

He had seen what was happening to his son—the same affliction that had struck Azotl and that had now seized the new emperor, Cuitláhuac. And there were many others. He had watched them on the streets of Tenochtitlán. Their stricken faces were burned into his mind. They were the fulfillment of the plague of omens that had besieged the empire for ten years or more—the streaming comets and monstrous dreams, the women howling in the night, the cry of owls. He understood why the stars no longer spoke to men, for the gods had lost the power of speech. It was just as Azotl had told him. A deathly curse had been set loose. It rode upon the backs of Spaniards but did not seem to strike them. It attacked only the people of this land.

Flee. Run for your lives. Take only what you can carry. Never come back.

Pitoque told Toc about a small cache of treasure hidden beneath the cottage near Amozoc. Kalatzin and Zaachila should take as much of the gold as they could manage, hide it well about their persons, and flee. Toc should go with them.

Toc said that he understood.

Pitoque stepped closer. "I know I can rely on you to protect them." In truth, he could not, but he said it anyway. No one could be relied on any longer. All the old rules, the old strictures, had dissolved in the air, leaving everyone helpless. But Pitoque summoned false hopes and spoke pleasant lies. What choice did he have? When truth fails, men deal in fictions. Pitoque told Toc that he himself would follow as soon as he could. He would trace their route and find them. They would all be together then.

"You and the boy?"

"Yes," said Pitoque. "Maxtla and I."

"And the girl?" He meant Ometzin.

"That's right. And the girl."

"Good. That's good." Toc inclined his long, sad head. "What about the boy's health? What shall I say about that?"

Pitoque frowned. Should he lie or tell the truth? Once again, he felt the truth giving way beneath him like a lake bed of mud. He looked at Toc's watery eyes through a misted blur of his own. He said, "Maxtla seems to be recovering already. You must have noticed. Tell my wife he will return to health, but it may take some time."

Toc pressed his lips together. "I understand. The boy will return to health. It may take some time. Yes, I'll tell her." He put a hand to his forehead in a sort of salute. "Farewell, sir." Without another word, he turned and left.

Pitoque stood outside the old house that had belonged to Azotl, lost in his thoughts. Finally, he reached up, as he often did nowadays, and ran his hands over his face, his shoulders, his arms. He was probing for the hardened knots that he dreaded to find. But, once again, his fingers came upon nothing. Azotl had said the malady would be passed from one man to another by some invisible means, some phantom of the air. So far, at least, it seemed that Pitoque had been spared. He turned and went inside the house, where his son now lay in bed, dwindling by the day, already lacking the strength even to raise himself onto his elbows.

Pitoque climbed the ladder to the sleeping chambers.

Hernán Cortés laughed out loud and thanked God for not abandoning him, after all.

He had just received the most bracing news. More Spanish galleons had lately arrived at Veracruz en route from Cuba. They brought soldiers, harquebuses, and cannons. He immediately decided what he meant to do. That afternoon, he informed Doña Marina of his plans. He proposed to win these newly arrived Spaniards to his side, just as he had done before with the soldiers who had arrived with Pánfilo de Narváez. Then he would return to Tenochtitlán, this time to take the city by force.

The dark-skinned princess arose and began bundling up the few articles of clothing she had managed to bring with her during the flight from Tenochtitlán. She was in a strange mood. Only that morning, she had discovered a deeply troubling circumstance. Among the survivors of the flight from Tenochtitlán were three of Moctezuma's concubines and one of his daughters. It was said that two other daughters of the emperor had died during the escape. Apparently, all these girls had been carried from the city on Cortés's especial orders, and that the four who had survived were being housed in another part of Tlaxcala. Four Aztec girls. She understood that a man would have his adventures. And yet . . .

Cortés lay back on his cot in this wretched, fetid building and watched her. "What are you doing?"

"Packing."

"Now?"

"Of course. I cannot wait any longer. I wish to have dinner in Tenochtitlán." She turned to him and smiled. "For there, I shall be a queen."

He did not reply.

She repeated the words. "For there, I shall be a queen."

He reached up, stroked his beard.

"A queen," she said. "In Tenochtitlán, I shall be a queen."

Finally, he smiled. "Of course, my dear. A queen is precisely what you shall be. A most delightful, most splendid queen." He lay back on the cot, closed his eyes.

She watched him, her heart pounding so hard she could hear it drumming in her ears. She held a blouse of cotton, a lovely garment, dyed indigo and trimmed with scarlet thread. She gazed down at it for several moments, thinking how beautiful it was and how happily she used to wear it. But now she gripped it with both her hands and, slowly, silently, she began to tear it in two.

Cortés dispatched a party of his men to the coast. He had initially instructed that they proceed under the command of Alonso Puertocarrero, but the man had unaccountably declined this commission. He'd said he no longer wished to partake of war. So instead, Cortés sent Cristóbal de Olid, and instructed the young officer to proceed by means of blandishments and bribes rather than violence.

Meanwhile, the Spaniards' Tlaxcalan allies busied them-selves with raising companies of warriors in all the vassal cit-ies between Tlaxcala and the coast. Almost every tribe was eager to join in the war against the Aztecs, so fierce was the hatred they felt for the people who had ruled them so cru-elly and so long. Even the Cholulans supported the new cam-paign. Young boys darted about like idiots, almost delirious with excitement. They would be warriors now! They would kill Aztecs! They could think of nothing more thrilling or more noble.

Toc rubbed his forehead and watched a muddle of Cholulan lads assemble and scatter and assemble again. They cried out in voices that cracked, for they were close to being children, not yet fully men.

"War!" they shouted. "War! We are going to war!"

The old porter shook his head and continued on his way until he reached the house of his master, and there he asked to see his mistress Kalatzin. He delivered to her the message from her husband. *Flee. Run for your lives. Take only what you can carry. Never come back.*

Kalatzin frowned. "And my husband?" she said. "What of my husband? And of my son?"

"They will join us when they can."

"And when will that be?"

Toc shrugged. "Soon, with luck." He told her that Maxtla was suffering from this strange ailment, but that, from all appearances, he would soon recover.

"If he will recover," said Kalatzin, "then why must we flee? What are we fleeing from?"

Toc inclined his head to acknowledge the contradiction. He knew there was no point in replying.

Kalatzin straightened her shoulders. "I will go to Tenochtitlán myself, to see about my son."

"No, mistress," said Toc. "I don't think you should do that. Your husband has given his instructions." He told her about the treasure at the lake. "He has told us to go south."

The woman let her shoulders slump. For a time, she said nothing, as the truth sank in. She understood now. She understood her husband's message perfectly. "Then we will go south," she said. She gritted her teeth and looked again at Toc. "You must be hungry. Off you go to the kitchen. I have to think what to tell Zaachila. Must we leave today, or can we wait until tomorrow?"

"Tomorrow would be fine, mistress. I'm sure a day will not make much difference."

She pressed her lips together and nodded. He could tell that she was struggling not to cry. "Tomorrow, then," she said, and walked away.

The following morning, they were up at daybreak, and soon they were marching out of Cholula—an old man, a woman nearing middle age, and a young girl, remarkable for her eerily fixed gaze. They took only what they could carry, and they did not look back. All around them, young boys danced in the dirt and skirmished with sticks.

War! War! They were going to war!

Kill Me Now

On the day after Christmas, in the year 1520—as time would come to be calculated—the Spaniards under Hernán Cortés began their march on the Valley of Anáhuac and upon the cities of the Triple Alliance. One by one, the cities fell—first Texcoco, then Iztapalapa, and then Chalco. Some of the people fought bravely and to the death. But most surrendered with little or no struggle and immediately pledged their support to the white-skinned invaders. Almost every tribe had deep-seated grievances against the Aztecs.

Soon Tacuba was taken and then Tlatelolco. Now all that remained was Tenochtitlán itself. The Spaniards and their allies laid siege to the capital. By degrees, day after day, they throttled the Aztecs. They blocked the causeways that led to the city and used a small flotilla of newly constructed brigantines to control the lake waters that surrounded the Aztec capital. In this way, they prevented supplies from coming in, while thwarting any attempt at flight.

The siege of Tenochtitlán lasted eighty days, and each day was more desperate than the one before. The blockade of the city coincided with the ravages of the new disease, a plague that the people of these parts would come to know as *la viruela* or smallpox. No one was safe from its horrors. It killed slaves and noblemen alike, but it wreaked particular harm among the wealthy, for they had mixed most freely with the Spaniards. Great pustules formed upon every part of their bodies and hardened like stones, then softened. Blood ran from their mouths and noses and every passage, as if they were melting. The afflicted wandered about, moaned, dribbled away. Every day, more were taken ill and more died. Before long, Cuitláhuac himself succumbed to the disease and was replaced by a new emperor, known as Cuauhtémoc, a man of immense physical strength and moral courage.

But he, too, was helpless before this staggering plague. No remedy worked against it. The Aztecs made use of twelve hundred different plants as cures, and yet none had the slightest effect on this disease. Whatever the people could think of, they tried. Pilgrims carried burning braziers upon their heads and offered up sacrifices of opossums at holy sites. Fortunetellers tossed handfuls of beans upon cloaks of white cotton, but failed to discern any signs of a cure. Healers tried every physic in their possession. They used resin to remove the hardened nubs of pustules, and they squashed black beetles into the wounds—useless, like every other method. And so the people died. Women perished, and no one was left to grind the corn. Corpses were carried outside and burned. Or, when an entire household lay dead, workers collapsed a house on top of them. In some neighborhoods, half the people died. Often, those struck by the disease simply lost the will to live and succumbed to lack of hope.

Countless others died from lack of food. For a time the inhabitants of Tenochtitlán survived on lizards and swallows. To make a salad, they combed the lake shallows for salt grass and water lilies. But these delicacies were soon exhausted. Eventually, people were reduced to clawing at the ground for anything that might yield nourishment. Worms, insects, roots, the bark of trees—these they boiled into a kind of soup. They ate straw. They carved up sections of deer hide, boiled them in water, and made a meal of those. They gnawed at bits of wood. They broke up mud bricks and tried to swallow down the dirt. To drink, they had only brine from the lakes, for all the aqueducts had been stopped up.

Memory was a kind of torture. The people could not forget the great market of Tlatelolco, its endless rows of food, delights of every description, more than anyone could eat. To think of the food they had enjoyed! Or, worse, to remember the food they had thrown away! Sometimes, people would speak of such meals. Someone might recall a succulent flank of dog lightly singed on a brazier and covered with chili peppers, served with tortillas and a sauce of tomatoes and sesame seeds—and everyone within earshot would groan.

"Be quiet," someone would say, someone speaking in a low and angry voice. "Shut your mouth. We do not wish to hear."

In the end, they had to make an ordinance. There was to be no mention of food. Men came to blows—men were killed—in disputes over violations of this rule.

Now—when the Aztecs were wilting with hunger, when they were wracked by smallpox—the Spaniards and their allies saw their chance and fell upon the city. They unleashed assault after assault with their horses and harquebuses, their cannons and crossbows, their dogs. The Aztecs had little left to throw in their own defence. First, they hurled spears, then they threw stones, and finally they fought with their bare hands. Not only the men fought. The women fought and the children fought, too. Everyone did. The killing was beyond anything ever imagined. The cadavers clogged the streets.

The emperor Cuauhtémoc resolved at last to anoint a quetzal-owl warrior—a great hero who by his valor would spur his people on to victory. The chosen fighter was outfitted in an elaborate dress of emerald plumage so that he no longer resembled a man—indeed, he looked like some great avian warrior. The sight of him would be enough to make whole armies tremble, so fierce and glorious was he. Much heart-

ened, the people cheered and danced, and the quetzal-owl
warrior waded out to do battle. Almost at once, with three
swings of his sword, he slew a trio of Tlaxcalan soldiers as
if they were nothing but annoying dogs. At once, the roars
swelled upon the rooftops of Tenochtitlán. But then a blur of
smoke erupted from one of the Spanish sailing vessels on the
lake, followed by a thudding reverberation. A blaze of feathers erupted around the quetzal-owl warrior. Dust flew up,
and a shock of debris arched through the air, and the warrior
himself seemed to vanish.

An expectant silence descended on the Aztecs gathered to
watch. Surely the warrior would rise up again. Surely he would
reappear. But the moments tripped by, and the hero did not
climb to his feet. The dust descended, and all the Aztecs could
see was a flurry of Tlaxcalans converging upon the place where
the quetzal-owl warrior had been.

At the heart of Tenochtitlán, no one uttered a word. It was
as if the entire city had seen its soul destroyed. Never before
had a quetzal-owl warrior perished in battle.

Still, there was no thought of surrender. Each time Cortés
offered a truce, the offer was refused. The streets of the city
were piled high with corpses, and the canals no longer flowed,
so clogged were they by the bodies of the dead. The reek was
so thick, it stung men's eyes and stopped up their throats. All
sorts of diseases struck the city, in addition to this new plague
brought by the Spaniards, this smallpox. No one dreamt of

victory anymore. The word was never uttered. If the Aztecs thought of anything, they thought of food—food and a good death.

Maxtla had a good death. Stricken as he was by this merciless disease, he went out into battle. Pitoque would have stopped him, and Ometzin tried to, but they both saw it was what Maxtla wanted. He would die, anyway. He limped out in the morning, carrying a spear with a broken tip, and he did not return. Ometzin herself was infected by the Spanish curse now, and Pitoque cared for her as well as he could. Meanwhile, he scoured his own body for evidence of the disease, for nodules, nubbles, knots, lumps, lesions, any of the small horrors that presaged the final horror, but he found none. For some reason, the gods had so far chosen to spare him. If there *were* gods. If they had not fled. If they still made choices. Two weeks after Maxtla vanished in battle, the girl Ometzin was dead. She died in robes of green, mumbling something about frogs.

Pitoque hobbled about from rooftop to rooftop, crept through alleys, scrambled over pyramids. He was watching, always watching. His stomach had wizened to the size of a hollowed-out gourd, and his legs buckled at nearly every stride. But he meant to witness all that he could, so that the end of the world would be remembered in the new world to come.

The Spaniards laid waste to the city, smashed houses that were empty, hauled down temples bereft of gods, razed granaries that contained not a seed of grain. With their cannons, they blew holes in everything. They set palaces on fire. They destroyed even the pyramids on which the temples had been built, for not once did the Aztecs willingly surrender any portion of the earth, let alone any structure that stood upon it. In time, the city was reduced to a flattened rubble of smoke and debris.

But the fighting did not end there. Half-dead from hunger and disease, the Aztecs fought on. For weeks and weeks, they resisted with their bare hands. But their resistance could not go on forever. On a dark winter night of driving rain, a flame of jasper lit the sky—a comet, like none that had ever been seen before. It spun through the darkness, spiraled over the lake, and circled above the city itself. Around and around it flew until at last it exploded in a fireball among the mountains— an impact that seemed to shake the earth. Pitoque fell back, stunned by what he had seen. He would never be sure if the comet was real, or if the hunger and exhaustion and horror had swelled up within him to create a vision in the air, on that last night before the empire fell.

That night, he was tormented by terrifying images. He saw a sun extinguished by darkness, saw giants stumbling over the blasted land, heard the cries of his wife, his daughter, his son. He saw Ometzin impaled upon stars. He saw jaguars prowling the smoking ruins of the city, jaguars that had fire in their eyes, that tossed the people into the air and swallowed them whole.

✢

Defeat was certain.

Rather than give himself up, the emperor Cuauhtémoc sought to escape the city by fleeing over the lake. But early on the morning of February thirteenth, 1521—as time would come to be calculated—his canoe was intercepted by a Spanish brigantine under the command of one García Holguín, and the emperor was taken prisoner.

That might well have been the most solemn moment in this long and terrible enterprise. But the Spaniards were not much given to solemnity. Immediately on learning of Cuauhtémoc's capture, Pedro de Alvarado, he of the booming voice and the golden hair, boarded another brigantine that raced to intercept the first, the one that bore the emperor. Alvarado demanded that the prisoner be turned over to him. Holguín refused. They traded insults and threats, and the quarrel between the two Spanish sailors came almost to a battle of cannons. Both of these men wished to be the hero who offered up the last emperor of the Aztecs to the greater glory of Hernán Cortés, in the name of Charles I of Spain. At last, Holguín prevailed, and Alvarado settled into a miserable sulk that would last for several years.

The captured emperor was brought before Cortés. This meeting took place high upon the roof of the palace of Atzauatzin, one of the few great buildings still left standing in Tenochtitlán. Pitoque hurried to be there. He scrambled over corpses and dodged heaps of rubble, clutching a rag to his nostrils to ward off the reek of death that snaked through the city. He pushed his way through a throng of Spaniards and climbed to the roof of the palace.

No one recognized him. If the Spaniards noticed him at all, they saw him as some crazed old man, as perhaps he was. His hair had fallen out, his mouth was riddled with cankers, his vision had faded to a blur. He had to struggle merely to stand, and he could barely swallow, so dry was his throat. Still, he managed to hear what was said when the last lord of the Aztecs was hauled in irons before Hernán Cortés. Doña Marina hovered not far from her master's side, still lovely to gaze upon, still loyal to the Spanish captain-general in her every word and deed. Even she failed to recognize Pitoque in his miserable state. He might as well have been a specter, a ghost.

In shackles, Cuauhtémoc stood against a backdrop of the ruined city, framed by lake waters of silver, mountains of blue. He was still clad in the regalia of war—a headdress of quetzal feathers, a cotton bodice to protect his chest, a loincloth, and a richly embroidered cape. He said nothing and looked at no one. He had not meant to be captured. He had not intended to concede defeat. Behind him, coils of smoke twisted above the wreckage of Tenochtitlán, and a glare of light dashed upon the water. A flock of kestrels raced overhead in a great arrowhead, fleeing toward the sun.

Cortés tried to be friendly, as if all that had happened—the destruction of the world—were an unfortunate misunderstanding, a game gone awry, something that could soon be put to rights by reasonable, good-hearted men.

"I assure you that you may continue to rule your kingdom, just as before."

Cortés spread out his arms to encompass the ruins of Tenochtitlán, once the greatest city in all creation. He chuckled, embarrassed, as if all this destruction had been an accident in which the Spaniard had played no more than an incidental part. He was a bystander, nothing more. He shook his head. "I do wish, for your own sake, that you had surrendered earlier, in order to avoid the damage that has, regrettably, occurred."

Cuauhtémoc did not encourage the discussion. He seemed to have little interest in words. He turned to Cortés. "I have done all that I was required to do in the defence of my people. There is nothing left. I did not choose to be made a prisoner, and I do not choose to remain one. I do not surrender. Please, take that dagger you have at your waist. Kill me now."

Pitoque stood stiff and upright, as though all pain, all infirmity, had passed from his body. His vision was suddenly clear. Now he would witness with his own eyes the death of the last of the Aztec emperors, a line that reached back more than three eras, back to the founding of Tenochtitlán and the reign of Acamapichtli, back even to the ancient sway of the Toltec kings. Now all would end.

And yet Cuauhtémoc was not executed on that day. He was permitted to live and to be called by his title of *tlatoani*, He Who Speaks, although his empire had collapsed, his capital was destroyed, his nobles and elders were murdered, and almost all the Aztecs were dead. Even after Cuauhtémoc's defeat, the

Tlaxcalans and Totonacs continued to rampage through the city, seizing people at will, hurling them down, slashing them open, ripping out their hearts. The Spaniards were genuinely revolted by this practice, but they couldn't make their native allies stop.

The Spaniards no longer had the inclination to kill. They wanted gold. They ransacked the ruins of Tenochtitlán, desperate to lay their hands on the plunder they still believed to be hidden in the city, but found little. They lined people up and yanked off their clothes, certain that every native was a thief, a hoarder of gold. They spit, swore, roared. Where was the treasure? Where had it gone? Where? *Where?* The only valuables they found were women, and they kept the pretty ones, if they were free of sores.

The rest of the people—the few who managed to outlive the sack of their city—now fled. Scrawny and gaunt, flecked with mud, riddled with running pustules, they staggered out across the broken causeways, hoping to escape from their enemies, from the rotting corpses, from the stench of death. Who knew where or how they ended their lives? So little was ever recorded. It was as if they had never been born, as if they had never strolled among the flowering trees on the streets of Tenochtitlán or browsed through the market at Tlatelolco or memorized a poem. They might as well have been motes of dust, scattered by the same winds that once blew eleven floating palaces across the eastern sea.

An Image in Blood

Maxtla was dead. And Azotl, too. And Ometzin. But what of Pitoque's wife and daughter—Kalatzin and Zaachila? What of Toc?

They fled, they vanished.

That is all he ever learned. If they left any further mark upon this earth, he did not manage to find it, although he would search long and hard. He folded his few remaining possessions into a sack of maguey fiber—these included the robe he had worn that distant afternoon in the presence of the dark Virgin, the robe with her likeness etched into its fabric in blood—and he trekked south to the lands of the Maya, just as he had promised he would do. But no one he spoke to there had ever heard of a woman traveling with an old man and a young girl, a girl who had a strangely fixed gaze. They had no knowledge of Spaniards, either, or of palaces that floated upon the sea, or of cannons or harquebuses. They could not conceive of creatures called horses, upon which men might ride. They were unacquainted with the principle of the wheel.

When Pitoque tried to explain these mysteries to them, they stared back as if he were mad. In time, he came to believe that possibly it was true. He was still haunted by ghostly memories but—who could say?—perhaps they were dreams. By day, he squatted near the shores of a river called the Mezcalapa, beneath a grove of tulip trees. He mourned the loss of his family and called out to passersby. To them, in exchange for alms, he told his otherworldly tales.

This he continued to do, day after day, as the years rolled past—first five years, and then another five, and then, one hot summer morning, as the sun breached the eastern sky and scattered spidery filaments of light across the slow green river, Pitoque awoke to the sound of a woman's voice. He looked up, and there she was—the Mother of God, the dark Virgin. He recognized her at once. She rode upon the river in a dugout canoe that somehow remained motionless in the moving water. Her long, iridescent hair fluttered about her, even in the absence of any wind.

"Pitoque," she said. "I have looked for you everywhere, and only now have I found you. Have you forgotten your promise to me?"

He pulled himself up onto his knees in an attitude of prayer. Promise? What promise?

"The promise you made to me ten long years ago, upon the hill at Tepeyac." As before, she seemed to understand him, even though he hadn't spoken out loud. "Surely you remember."

And now, as if drenched by a sun shower of recollected images, he did recall. He had promised that a shrine would be built in the virgin's honor, atop the hill at Tepeyac. He had also promised to rescue the hummingbird bride from death. He bowed his head. "I have failed you," he said.

"Yes," she replied. "You have. The girl Bakil is dead, and there have been terrible consequences, and further suffering will come. But there is still time to make amends. I am still waiting for a shrine. It needn't be an elaborate affair. Almost anything would do."

Pitoque told the goddess that he was deeply sorry. In all the commotion of those dreadful times, he had forgotten this second promise. "In fact, it has not returned to my mind until now."

"But will you build it for me? I have waited a very long time."

"Yes, my mother. I will. This time, I promise not to fail."

She tilted her fine bronze head and smiled. "I knew I could put my trust in you."

She raised a paddle and dipped it into the waters of the emerald river. A glow of light encircled her head like a veil, and she guided her craft until it disappeared around a bend, beyond a tangle and froth of greenery.

That same morning, Pitoque prepared himself for the long journey north. He had led a simple life and retained few possessions, apart from some bits of clothing and the robe with the virgin's image, traced in blood. Before the sun had climbed far into the sky, he was on his way.

It was hard going. It had been years since he had walked any distance at all. But he was a *pochteca* by inheritance and conviction. He soon reaccustomed himself to the rigors of the road. As he journeyed north, he thought of all he had lost—his son, his daughter, his wife, his friends. Toc. Azotl. They reappeared in his mind. He heard their voices. They seemed to accompany him on his way. Here and there, he stopped at little shanty villages, where he told stories in exchange for food.

✝

In the fall of 1531—as time would come to be calculated—
Pitoque finally stood once again upon the high col that runs
between the volcanoes Popocatépetl and Iztaccíhuatl. Below
him sprawled the Valley of Anáhuac, much changed now. He
saw that Tenochtitlán had been rebuilt, but not as it had been
in former times. The Spaniards had constructed it in a style of
their own. The lake seemed smaller than before.

Pitoque had no desire to enter the city. Instead, he skirted
the shimmering waters of Texcoco and wandered through the
towns scattered upon the western shore, where white-skinned
men went about in strange wheeled devices drawn by horses.
Brown-skinned men—men like himself—trudged about on
foot, their eyes cast down.

It was dark by the time Pitoque reached the hill of Tepeyac
on the north shore of Lake Texcoco. He began to climb.
When he reached the summit, he found it was unchanged,
still barren save for the odd nopal cactus and a rubble of
broken stones. He slept on the ground that night, and in the
morning, he began the work he had promised to undertake,
on behalf of the dark Virgin, the Mother of God. Using sticks
and mud, he constructed a rickety shrine. He collected pine
needles and spread them out on the floor as a kind of carpet.
He made an altar of sorts, and upon it, he laid out the blood-
stained robe.

For six days, he huddled alone outside his little temple,
waiting for something to happen, but nothing did. On the
seventh day, however, an elderly couple happened by, both of
them with tattoo lines on their faces. They told him that this

had once been the site of the pyramid of Tonantzin, the earth mother.

The man said, "What are you doing here? What is this little shelter you have built?"

Pitoque bowed and then recounted the tale of the dark Virgin. He waved his hand. "This," he said, "is the Virgin's shrine." He invited the couple inside. "Here, drawn in blood upon this cotton robe, is her image."

The couple both let out moans of surprise when they saw. They seemed deeply impressed. They went away a little later, murmuring to one another. They promised they would return.

In time, the word spread. A dark Virgin—*la madre indigena*—had appeared to a native man at Tepeyac hill. She was the savior of the *indios*, it was said, and her likeness had appeared upon a cotton robe, drawn in blood. More people came. They straggled up the hill at Tepeyac to listen to Pitoque's tale and to see for themselves the evidence of its truth—an image in blood.

In greater and greater numbers they came. Some of them were ill, pocked and weakened by these new maladies that had come. Others were in mourning for husbands or wives or children who had been wrested from them and killed. Still others had been evicted from their lands. They came from all around—in time, some came from as far north as the frontiers of the old Aztec empire, from the lands of the Nahuas, the Huaxtecs, the Otomi.

Pitoque tended the dark Virgin's shrine, greeted its visitors, and tried to comfort them with tales of the woman who had floated upon the air, and whom he had once seen, upon this very hill. The Mother of God. Savior of the *indios*. *La Virgen de Guadalupe*, she came to be called.

Humbly and without complaint—indeed, with some degree of pleasure—he carried out these simple duties, day after day, year after year, for seventeen years, until, on a bright winter's morning in 1548, he awoke to a melody of women's voices. He walked out onto the brow of the hill at Tepeyac. In the distance, he thought he saw Tenochtitlán as it had once been— the capital of the world, where tall stone pyramids strained against the sky, reaching toward the sun. He felt a cool breeze in his gray hair and was dazzled by a vision of roses, lovely red roses blossoming at his feet, roses in winter. He gave thanks to the Virgin and bent down to collect them. He felt something give way in his chest, and he understood, an instant before it was so, that he was dead.

Epilogue

Cuauhtémoc, the last emperor of the Aztecs, survived the crushing defeat of his people. For four years, he dwelt in a kind of captivity at the pleasure of Hernán Cortés. On at least one occasion, he was badly tortured by several overzealous *conquistadores*, who were seeking information about gold. Cortés severely reprimanded them, but in the end, the Spanish commander had a falling out with the emperor as well. In 1525, acting on trumped-up charges, Cortés convicted Cuauhtémoc of treason and ordered his execution. According to one version of these events, Cortés later ordered that the emperor's head be lodged in a tree, somewhere near the present-day border between Mexico and Guatemala.

By some estimates, the population of the Aztec empire was reduced from approximately ten million at the time of Cortés's arrival in 1519 to fewer than one million just a century later. Even the most conservative scholars agree that the region's population was reduced by at least half.

By any standard, these are the statistics of genocide. And yet the genocide was not for the most part deliberate. The greatest killer of Mexico's indigenous people was an unintended byproduct of the conquest. The Spaniards brought with them diseases to which the people of Mexico had never been exposed and against which they had no defences.

Smallpox was the most virulent of the new infections, but measles also claimed millions of lives, as did a strain of the bubonic plague that had earlier ravaged Europe. In wave after wave of infection, whole towns were wiped out, every last man, woman, and child.

In the end, the Spaniards probably could have subdued these lands merely by coughing, spitting, defecating, and enjoying sexual congress. They needn't have raised a hand in anger or imposed a single cruel or arbitrary law. But they did those things, too.

After the fall of Tenochtitlán, Pedro de Alvarado remained in what came to be known as New Spain, as did most of the *conquistadores*. He won many victories and caused much bloodshed in continuing wars of subjugation against different Mexican tribes. He died in 1541, not yet fifty years old, while putting down a native rebellion near Guadalaraja. His horse rolled over on him and he was killed.

Diego de Velázquez, the governor of Cuba and Cortés's great foe, died in impoverished circumstances in 1524.

Pánfilo de Narváez, who led the expedition to capture Cortés and return him in shackles to Cuba, was eventually released from imprisonment in New Spain. He died some years later during an expedition to Florida in search of the proverbial Fountain of Youth.

Doña Marina bore Cortés a son. But the captain-general eventually tired of his native princess and handed her over to another *conquistador*, a drunken ne'er-do-well by the name of Juan Jaramillo. She largely disappears from the historical record until her death in 1551. But she lives on to this day in Mexican folk culture as *la malinche*—the archetype of the treacherous woman.

Alonso Puertocarrero renounced the military life even before the fall of Tenochtitlán, which he observed with mounting horror. Later, he turned all of Pitoque's wealth over to the church and entered the Franciscan order of missionaries, the first to establish a presence in New Spain. He journeyed far to the north and founded a mission near the Pacific coast in Alta California. There, he ministered to the Indians until his death in 1542.

Following the sack of Tenochtitlán in 1521, Hernán Cortés ordered that the city be rebuilt—a massive undertaking that was almost certainly the most ambitious and complicated engineering project attempted anywhere in the world during the sixteenth century. It required immense supplies of human labor, and so the Spaniards' former native allies—the Tlaxcalans and the Totonacs—were recruited as forced laborers to rebuild the city they had so lately conspired to destroy.

For himself, Hernán Cortés ordered that a massive residence be erected—on the site of the old palace of Axayácatl. At any one time, more than three hundred workers were employed on its construction. Twenty-seven years would pass before it was completed. By then, it would be a vast, boxy structure, two stories high, with thick stone walls, stout wooden doors, and many of the features of a fortress—turrets and battlements on the roof and slit windows for archers. None of these defences proved necessary, for the building was never attacked.

As the work on his house was getting underway, Cortés found himself beset by nagging domestic problems. A year after the fall of Tenochtitlán, his Spanish wife, Catalina Suárez, traveled from Cuba to be at her husband's side. She was not warmly received, for Cortés had grown accustomed to the company of many native mistresses. These included a girl named Tecuichpo, a daughter of Moctezuma, with whom he had a child. Mainly on account of his philandering, Cortés and his wife quarreled almost constantly until All Saints' Day in 1522. That night, after an evening of revelry—and in circumstances that remain unclear—Catalina died. For the rest of his life, Cortés was to be hounded by suspicions that he had killed her.

There were other marks against him. Jealous of the conqueror's success, various courtiers and *letrados*—or "lettered ones"—in Cuba and at the royal court in Madrid held him accountable for the great massacre that had taken place in Cholula, in which thousands of people had been slain. Here was a second blot on Cortés's record, another that he was unable to live down.

Although he was made a marquis and later married a Spanish noblewoman, the greatest *conquistador* of them all was never to receive the honor he most craved—to be named viceroy of New Spain. Eventually, he was undermined by his enemies at the court of Charles I and rendered powerless. In the mid-1540s, he abandoned the vast territories he had conquered and returned to Spain, where he died just outside Seville in 1547 at the age of sixty-two, a bitter and disillusioned man.

Cortés was survived by Charles I, the King of Spain, in whose name a distant civilization had been overthrown, a culture destroyed, and a colony won. But the king—who, as Charles V, was also the Holy Roman Emperor—was far more German than Spanish and spent his life embroiled in the Byzantine complexity of European politics. He died in 1558, just short of his sixtieth year. Researchers going through his voluminous memoirs would discover not a single reference to Hernán Cortés or Moctezuma or Tenochtitlán or the conquest of Mexico—as if the men who bore those names had never existed, or as if that faraway place had never been.

The Mexican cult of the Dark Virgin—or the Virgin of Guadalupe, named for a monastery located in the province of Extremadura in Spain—quickly took root and began to flourish. Initially, when they learned of the cult's growing power among the native population, the Roman Catholic clergy in New Spain were hostile, sensing something pagan in this Indian fascination with a Virgin who had appeared, after all, on the site of an old native temple, dedicated to the Aztec earth goddess, Tonantzin. Gradually, however, the clerical attitude softened as it became clear how powerful this force had become.

The cult continued to prosper, spreading all over Mexico and beyond. Progressively larger and more elaborate temples were built atop the hill at Tepeyac. Sometime around 1660, a broad boulevard was constructed, leading from the heart of Mexico City to the Virgin's shrine. By this time, thousands of Indian pilgrims were flocking there every day.

In 1757, the Virgin of Guadalupe was declared by papal decree to be the patroness and protectress of New Spain. The Mexican wars of independence in the early nineteenth century were fought in her name. When the first railway line in Mexico was built, it ran from the center of Mexico City to the Basilica de Nuestra Señora de Guadalupe. In 1895, Pope Leo XIII conferred upon her the official title of Queen of Mexico.

Even today, above the high altar within the basilica, there is a glass case that contains an ancient robe, with a likeness of the Dark Virgin still clearly visible, etched into its folds. And still the people come, just as they have done for centuries. Sad-eyed, bronze-skinned, they shuffle forward on their knees, inching closer and closer to the shrine of the Dark Virgin, mother of the Indians, *la Virgen de Guadalupe.* On any day they number in the thousands. They grimace in exaltation. They clasp gifts of flowers. They whisper aloud their dreams.

AUTHOR'S NOTE

This book is based on historical events, but it is a work of fiction. I have tried to keep the recorded incidents and figures of history intact—if *intact* is the word, for much of the history of sixteenth-century Mexico is disputed or conjectural. In any case, I have deliberately tampered with the historical consensus only when I felt there was a compelling reason to do so.

With the exception of Pitoque and his family, who are invented, almost all of the main characters in *The Dark Virgin* are based on actual people who truly existed. Azotl is another invention, but his role and character reflect those of verifiable historical figures—especially Tlacaélel, a counselor to the emperor Itzcoatl, who preceded Moctezuma by nearly a hundred years. The title "master functionary" is an invention, but Keeper of the House of Darkness is not. I have imagined the behavior and personalities of many of the other main characters, but my imagination has been shaped by the many historical documents and chronicles that pertain to them—to Moctezuma II, Hernán Cortés, Pedro de Alvarado, and Doña Marina, among others.

In places, I have somewhat simplified the unwieldy course of history or combined several historical figures into one character (for example, Cacama, the king of Texcoco, who also serves in these pages as an ambassador for the Aztecs). There are many such adjustments, too many to describe here. They are, for the most part, minor. On the whole, I have tried to present an accurate picture of Aztec daily life, based on scholarly sources, but occasionally I have added a prop or a detail of my own creation.

I have also included several, let us say, hybrid characters. The translator Jerónimo de Aguilar, for example, is based on a man of the same name who truly existed. Aguilar's tumultuous experiences—his shipwreck off the coast of Mexico eight years before the arrival of Cortés, his years of enslavement, his liberation once Cortés arrived—are entirely real. Later, he did become Cortés's translator, sharing that duty with Doña Marina. But the historical Aguilar went on to be a diligent servant of the conqueror. I have imagined him otherwise.

Alonso Puertocarrero is a similar case. He did exist (although his full name was Alonso Hernández Puertocarrero, sometimes rendered as Portocarrero), and he did enjoy the company of Doña Marina in his bed—until Cortés decided to take the girl for himself. From that point onward, the real Puertocarrero became little more than a footnote to the historical record. I have devised for him a more prominent role.

The main events of the novel are historically accurate. Against the orders of the Spanish governor, Cortés did set sail from Cuba. His was the third such expedition to the coast of Mexico. He actually did sink all his ships (on his own orders, however, and not those of Alvarado). He formed an alliance with the fat chieftain in Cempoala, marched inland, made war with the Tlaxcalans, and then became their ally. The massacre in

Cholula did take place, but it has never been properly explained. We know only that thousands of Cholulans were killed and that Cortés bore the blame. Why the massacre happened remains a mystery. One account of these times suggests that Cholula was not a vassal city of the Aztecs but a hold-out, like Tlaxcala. Every other version I have read contradicts this theory.

The Spaniards were indeed welcomed into Tenochtitlán as gods. Moctezuma did become besotted with them. He was taken captive (considerably sooner than I have suggested here). Cacama did mount a rebellion, and he was executed, albeit not by drowning. Alvarado did launch a massacre in Cortés's absence, and the Spaniards were driven out of Tenochtitlán. They did regroup. They did return. They did conquer.

The death of Moctezuma, however, remains a murky affair. Was he bludgeoned to death by the Spaniards? Or was he stoned to death by his own people? Even now—almost five centuries later—we do not know. And so I have left an element of doubt.

Smallpox plays a villainous role in this book, as it did in Mexican history. Contemporary scholars generally agree that the contagion arrived in Mexico, not with Cortés in 1519, but aboard the fleet commanded by Pánfilo de Narváez in 1520, after which it spread very quickly. I have antedated its arrival and somewhat slowed its initial advance. Estimates of its true predations vary considerably. But it may safely be said that, along with other European diseases such as measles, mumps, and the plague, smallpox reduced Mexico's population by at least half and perhaps by as much as nine-tenths during the course of the sixteenth century.

Regarding Alvarado's surprise attack in Tenochtitlán, which precipitated the war against the Aztecs, I have made a few changes. The occasion that was being celebrated that night was properly known as the feast of Toxcatl, although it was closely associated with the hummingbird god. The massacre was timed to coincide with a sacrifice on the island of Tepepolco, but the victim was to be a man—a captured warrior—rather than a woman. Apart from Aguilar's attempted intervention, these are the only important elements I have changed.

Finally—the Dark Virgin. There are many different accounts of her appearance on the hill at Tepeyac, near the ruins of the shrine of the Aztec earth goddess, Tonantzin. I have based my version on several of these tales (all of which vary one from another, and all of which are, let's face it, apocryphal). The recorded accounts do agree upon a few particulars. The Dark Virgin appeared to a baptized Indian by the Christian name of Juan Diego on the hill at Tepeyac in the year 1531, ten years after the fall of Tenochtitlán. I have modified the chronology and a few other details in this book.

Everything contained in the epilogue is as accurate as possible, apart from the entry for Puertocarrero, which I created. However, the life I have imagined for him roughly parallels the actual fate of several *conquistadores*.

The rest, *mas o menos*, is history.

OAKLAND ROSS
TORONTO, SEPTEMBER, 2000

Selected Bibliography

Baudot, Georges, and Tzvetan Todorov. *Relatos Aztecas de la Conquista*. México, D. F.: Editorial Grijalbo, S. A., 1990.

Bray, Warwick. *Everyday Life of the Aztecs*. New York: G. P. Putnam and Sons, 1968.

Clendinnen, Inga. *Aztecs*. New York: Cambridge University Press, 1991.

Cypess, Sandra Messinger. *La Malinche in Mexican Literature: From History to Myth*. Austin: University of Texas Press, 1991.

De las Casas, Bartolomé. *A Short Account of the Destruction of the Indies*. Translated by Nigel Griffin. Toronto: Penguin Books, 1992.

Díaz del Castillo, Bernal. *The Conquest of New Spain*. Translated by J. M. Cohen. Toronto: Penguin Books, 1963.

Figueroa Torres, J. Jésus. *Doña Marina: Una India Ejemplar*. México, D. F.: B. Costa-Amic, 1975.

Gruzinski, Serge. *The Aztecs: Rise and Fall of an Empire*. New York: Harry N. Abrams, Inc., 1992.

Johnson, William Weber. *Mexico*. New York: Time Inc., 1964.

Kandell, Jonathan. *La Capital: The Biography of Mexico City*. New York: Henry Holt, 1990.

Katz, Freidrich. *Situación Social y Económica de los Aztecas Durante los Siglos XV y XVI*. México, D. F.: Dirección General de Publicaciones del Consejo Nacional para la Cultura y las Artes, 1994.

McCaa, Robert. "Spanish and Nahuatl Views on Smallpox and Demographic Catastrophe in the Conquest of Mexico." *Journal of Interdisciplinary History*, Winter, 1995.

Ruiz, Ramón Eduardo. *Triumphs and Tragedy: A History of the Mexican People*. New York: W. W. Norton and Company, 1992.

Smith, Bradley. *Mexico: A History in Art*. New York: Doubleday & Co., 1968.

Thomas, Hugh. *The Conquest of Mexico*. London: Random House, 1993.

Wright, Ronald. *Stolen Continents: The "New World" Through Indian Eyes Since 1492*. Toronto: Penguin Books, 1993.

ACKNOWLEDGMENTS

It's often said that writing is a solitary activity, and in many ways that is so. But it's also a communal enterprise. I've been lucky to find myself in a great neighborhood.

Alison MacGregor was a rock of support at the beginning of this project and continued to encourage me all the way through.

Jan Whitford, my agent, handled the logistics and much more.

Thanks to Lorissa Sengara for her perfect pitch and to Becky Vogan for an exceptionally attentive and helpful reading of the manuscript.

I could not have written this book had it not been for Jennifer Glossop, who taught me her trick with index cards and also kept prodding me with the magic words, "I don't know why you don't do more with this idea." Every time she said it, she got my imagination going, and every time it seemed to work.

I am indebted to my employers at *The Toronto Star* for granting me the time and the peace of mind to finish this book. Thanks to John Honderich, publisher; to Mary Deanne Shears, managing editor; and to Colin MacKenzie, Saturday editor.

I especially want to offer my gratitude to Iris Tupholme, whose original vision gave birth to this book, and who backed that vision with her unwavering support and trust. She stuck by this project from start to finish. She made sure that it got done. And somehow, she never stopped smiling.

But I am the one who wrote the book, and whatever errors or oversights or blunders it contains—they are mine.